THE HUMAN-BORN CHRONICLES

by

SUSAN L MARKLOFF

RECOMMENDED READING ORDER

THE RISE OF THE RAIDIN
THE TIES THAT BIND
THE HUMAN-BORN CHRONICLES
THE REFLECTION OF THE RAIDIN

ISBN 978-1-956542-28-8

Printed in the United States of America

First Paperback Omnibus Edition 2025

Book Cover Art by Alice Maria Power
Meeting Sketches by Merdikai
Character & Bestiary Designs by Michaella T. Barnum

Niveus Press
www.susanlmarkloff.com

10 9 8 7 6 5 4 3 2 1

THE HUMAN-BORN
CHRONICLES

by

SUSAN L MARKLOFF

NIVEUS PRESS

CONTENTS

Agerian Sayings & Things

A blow too many – 1. worse for wear. "He took a blow too many, but he'll be all right."

A scale ripped off – 1. being bluntly honest. "it was better to rip a scale off than try to circle the issue."

2. When someone learns a secret and feels betrayed. "I feel I've had a scale ripped off. Why didn't you tell me sooner?"

Barricading – Dodging the question or keeping information from someone. "Quit barricading and tell me."

Bristled – Angry or annoyed. "He stole my sandwich. I have a right to be bristled about it."

By the Elders – 1. An oath taken in the Elders name. "By the Elders, I'll do it."

2. Indicating to someone else that you're serious about whatever you say. "By the Elders, I'm telling you; this happens and you're done."

3. Awe or surprise (usually shortened to just 'Elders').

Downed – Beaten, lost, or unable to continue. Taken from the concept of a "downed dragon" being unable to fight or fly anymore. "Let's face it, if we lose Krelien, we're downed."

Elders burn it all – Similar to "dammit." Usually said in anger and is considered a sort of swear.

Get him/her set – the equivalent of "get them up to speed"

Heseda – The experience a man has where he discovers who his wife is. Usually an "aha" kind of moment.

Keep it under stone – to keep something quiet or secret. "If you want to keep it under stone, you should probably stop screaming about it."

Night chaser – equivalent to "night owl"

Stretched thin – tired. "I'm just stretched thin. Some tea'll help."

Throw [person's name] into the flames – the equivalent of "throwing someone under the bus."

Tossed between a few bratak'ra – indicating that someone looks rough, as though they've been in a scuffle. Or, used to explain how sore or aching someone feels. "I feel like I've been tossed between a few bratak'ra."

Pronunciation Guide

Agerius: ah – jeer – ee – us
Akeno: ah – kay – no
Avemod: ah – vah – mod
Bratak'ra: brah – tak – ra
Caedex: cay – decks
Caliga: kal – eh – ga
Cregorous: kreg – or – os
Drogar: drow – garr
Eccio: ee – see – oh
Erador: air – ah – door
Ferveos: fer – vay – os
Gaeor: gay – ee – or
Grovix: grah – vix
Ira: eye – ra
Izel: eye – zel
Kedar: kay – dar
Kelek: kay – lick
Neri: ner – ee
Preliator: prey – lee – a – tor
Salan: sah – lahn
Sariel: sahr – eye – el
Streya: stray – ah
Taesir: tay – ee – seer
Teneo: ten – ay – oh
Tilion: till – ee – on
Vorex: voor – ex
Zaheri: za – heer – eye
Zelek: zay – lick

A Note from the Author

The Human-Born Era series is a young adult fantasy series that evolves into the new adult category. Books 1 and 2, *The Rise of the Raidin* and *The Ties That Bind,* are both young adult, as are all of *The Human-Born Chronicles* novellas. They were written with sixteen to nineteen-year-olds in mind and can be considered a PG-13 rating for violence, scary situations, and language. If your child has watched a Marvel movie, they can expect the same level of action and the same level of stakes for the characters. Across the HBE series, topics of warfare, domestic abuse, emotional and mental manipulation, violence, and death are all touched on at some point.

The Protector's Pressure has a few instances of emotional abuse, as well as a torture-like situation. *The Shifter's Shadow* deals with an attempted rape. It doesn't go beyond an attempt and suggestive dialogue, but the tension in the moment may be a trigger to some readers. *The Scholar's Scars* deals with an "on screen" death. *The Requisite's Rise* deals with witnessing someone else losing a limb. If your young adult is not able to handle these subjects or these levels of violence in a story, it's strongly suggested that you consider passing on *The Human-Born Chronicles* until they're emotionally ready. If you would like to read the scenes in question before deciding whether to purchase this book, please contact the author via her website: www.susanlmarkloff.com. Be sure to state the book title in your request so that she can provide you with a PDF of the scene.

Forward

The Human-Born Chronicles were never originally planned to be published. In my initial plans for the series, back in 2008, I had little idea who these other Human-Borns were, and how they were going to fit into the story. In 2012 when I drafted the first timeline of the World of Tilion, I had a slightly better idea who they were. By 2017, however, I knew their stories were varied, deep, and not at all what I had expected. And I knew that sharing their origin stories would be helpful to readers who really connected with *The Human-Born Era* series.

To say I was terrified to pen these stories would be putting it lightly. I felt the burden of presenting these characters and their cultures, and wanted to do so respectfully. Because though my stories hold dragons and teleporters and portals to other worlds, I've always striven to ground them firmly in reality. For "the science to check out." For characters to react and respond like real people in real situations.

Compiling all of these stories into one, massive volume sparked in my mind early in 2023, and I'm excited to offer them all in one giant paperback. It makes me feel, as an indie author, as though I'm just one step further on my author journey by doing something of this magnitude.

It is strongly recommended that you read this collection of novellas after reading books 1 and 2 of *The Human-Born Era.* These side-stories serve as backstory or origin stories for six characters that become the focal point of *The Human-Born Era,* and readers will get the most out of them if they read in the intended order.

Five first will fall victim to darkness' finding.
Their falling will not mean defeat.

Instead to another strength flows from the fallen.
Their power becoming complete.

Till Sixth rises loud, and echoes the rest
Causing darkness to sound the retreat.

The duty of First, the Title of Raidin,
The strongest part of the whole.

Then there's the Second, Protector of all.
One noble, a shield for his role.

Third comes the Warrior with fury unbridled,
One call will bring armies to march.

The Fourth is a Healer, with talents unrivaled.
Restoring what darkness would parch.

Fifth is the Shifter, tho' a discordant note,
Their value revealed by time.

Sixth brings the Scholar, seeker of wisdom,
Whose gifts allow truth to chime.

Then Seventh and last, the Requisite true.
Without whom all would be lost

The PROTECTOR'S PRESSURE

Then there's
the Second,
Protector of all.
One noble,
a shield
for his role.

ROUTINES AND WORN PATHS

Oxford University was a campus filled with wise educators, exhausted students, and roaming tourists. Squabbling over who got to stay in the infamous rooms where the likes of Tolkien and Lewis stayed were common. Lecture halls became floors of debates for a myriad of topics. The nearby pub and its famous "Inklings" table was a hotspot for crowds. And while those were all points of interest, and things that he liked about the culture of the campus, Oxford's bustle wasn't what drew Skylar Mitchell to the university.

Obligation did that.

Walking across the quad toward the New Library, Skylar's gaze inadvertently swept toward the New Building dorms. There was the smallest gap between buildings where he could glimpse his most desired home. He figured most students across the globe that commuted to their campus would feel the same as him—longing for the chance to live apart from what he'd always known.

He tugged his jacket a little tighter as a chill swept through the open Longwall Quad.

Despite his best efforts, he still slowed his pace slightly to better linger at the long, elegant dorm building before it disappeared from view.

What he would give to be permitted to stay on campus.

On autopilot, he pulled his phone out and quickly set it to silent mode. Then he ducked into the library and gently shook off a few wayward leaves that had hitchhiked on his jacket. Stuffing his phone back into his pocket, he made his way through the room, seeking out his normal hiding spot toward the windows overlooking the quad.

He preferred the quiet greens with occasional passersby to the windows that faced the road. High Street was usually filled with tourists and caravans of gawkers. Though he'd grown somewhat blind to such people, he never could quite rid his mind of the glances and gazes of unknown people from unknown lands.

Perhaps that was why he didn't like fish. He could feel pity for them, because he understood how it felt to be poked and prodded to see what interaction might be awarded. As if tapping on glass could do anything other than startle and potentially terrify the creatures encased in their prison.

Depositing his leather satchel, he went on the hunt for the stack of boring books he needed for his politics and ethics class. It took a moment to track them down. To the outside observer, his path was unnecessarily winding.

The detours were wholly necessary.

There were areas more frequently used in the library, and Skylar aimed to avoid other people at all costs.

Upon returning to his table, he found his efforts fruitless.

One of the girls from the dull class he had to write his paper for sat there, fingering his satchel as though, if she could just get inside, she might coax a creature within to trust her. For the briefest moment, he considered ignoring her and going about his work. However, she'd managed to take up the bulk of the table with her own bag and had draped her jacket across it, as well. Like she was laying claim or something.

It took everything in him not to roll his eyes and groan.

She whipped her head up to him and plastered a smile on her face. "Skylar! Hi!"

"Hello," he offered dryly.

Giving him a look of embarrassed surprise—an actor's attempt at genuine in her eyes—she placed her hand on her chest and said, "I'm Clara, from Politics and Ethics."

He knew the class. He didn't know her name.

He was likely to forget it once he got her to leave.

Skylar nodded a few times. "Yes, I knew that."

She smiled at him. "Are you working on the term paper?"

"No, I carry these tomes for exercise."

With a giggle, she said, "I heard you had a great sense of humor."

In an attempt to not be outright rude, he let out a small sigh and looked to the wall, letting his shoulders droop slightly.

"Do you want a writing partner? We can test read one another's papers."

"I'm fine, thank you."

"Are you sure?" she asked with a small scrunch of her brow. "I know how harshly the professor grades. Having someone read my paper would help a lot."

"Well, from what I understand of it, there are many people in the lecture. I'm sure you can find someone else to help you out."

A pout formed on her lips. "Oh, well, I was kind of hoping—"

"Look, I'm really not interested in the game, all right?"

Flinching, Clara's eyes widened.

"Just come out and ask whatever it is you want."

She gave him a look of confusion, obviously surprised he saw through her disguise. Then a clumsy smile came to her face. "What do you mean? I'm just looking for a partner for the term paper."

He flopped the books on the desk, almost grateful for the noise they created. It might startle the other attendees and make them choose to stay away.

"No, you aren't." He gave her a bored look. "If you're after political advancement or an invite to the next social gathering at my parents' estate, you would have better luck with my brother."

"Is Charles single?"

"No," Skylar lied.

Her gaze flicked across him, taking in his features.

While Charles was more handsome than him, part of that was

due to his age. Charles had fully outgrown all of his childish features. But that didn't mean Skylar was a slouch in comparison. His black hair contrasted his blue eyes and pale skin well and was always styled simply. And, as to be expected by his parents, his clothes were tailored to fit.

"Are you gay?" she asked with a quirk of her brow.

"No."

"Then what's—"

"Clara, was it?"

She nodded.

"I don't like people who claw at royalty as though that'll earn them favor." He flung his arm outward. "Please leave me alone."

For a long second, she just stared at him with a slacked jaw. Then a scoff escaped her, and she snatched her things before marching off.

Oh, had he offended her? What a shocker. She was allowed to be offended for being found out, but golly, he was supposed to be perfectly fine with being used?

Not on his life.

Never again.

Finally, Skylar thought as he deposited himself into the chair. A moment later, he had his headphones in and began paging through one of the books. Yanking his laptop out of his satchel, he pulled up his notes from the last time he'd been in the library and picked up where he'd left off.

Braham's symphony number four played in his ears, lulling him into his own world, free from people trying to wine and dine him for access to his father. He was only awarded another few moments of total solitude.

Someone sat across from him. He could tell from the way she flopped into the seat that it was his Zaheri, Streya.

"Don't tell me you disprove," he muttered.

She reached across the table and gently removed one of his earbuds.

He continued trying to understand the text in front of him. When she said nothing, he let out a sigh and lifted his gaze to hers.

For someone who was a seasoned fighter, Streya didn't look the part. With her long, golden blonde hair falling in gentle curls, and her subtle makeup, the Agerian looked more suited to be a stunning business woman than a warrior. But he knew that once her hair was put up into a bun and she had an adversary to face, that beautiful woman transformed into a fierce fighter.

"You could have been nicer," Streya said with a knowing look.

"You're right; I could have." Skylar eased back a little. "And we both know where that would've landed me." He waved his hand vaguely. "I'd have her following me about, squawking constantly like that's how friendships are built. And then, in two weeks, when Father hosts the Duke of Wales, she'd clutch and cling at my arm as though affixed there until I invited her to something she already envisions herself attending."

A sad look ghosted Streya's features. "You don't have to guard yourself so harshly."

With a small roll of his eyes, he said, "You weren't there the last time I didn't guard myself."

She nodded. "All right, that's fair."

"Anyway, I'll have you there. I don't need some girl trying to pretend she's my girlfriend to muck it all up." He raised his brow. "It's already a night I wish would pass."

Streya read the spine on one of the books in front of him. "What're you reading, anyway?"

He let out a beleaguered sigh. "That one is *The Ethics of Parliament*, and this one—" he gently lifted the book he had open "—is *A Study of Ethics in Government*." Letting the book flop back down ungracefully, he rolled his eyes. "In other words, lots of lengthy babble riddled with college verbiage to justify why most governments veer toward selfish ambition rather than proper ethical morality."

"Are you trying to fail your lecture?"

"Perhaps."

Smiling wryly, she nodded once. "Want me to hang around?"

"Would you mind terribly?" He winced. "Your presence will help other grapplers stay away."

"Okay. But I'm not reading either of these." She rose to her feet. "I'll be right back with something more interesting to read."

Skylar smiled to her. "I'll save your seat."

As she walked off, he glanced after her before putting his earbud back in.

Streya did have a point, of course. Kindness was a fair shake of it. Even those who acted out of their own goals and desires were due a modicum of his care. Maybe. But were they? He had a hard time truly believing that.

Should you remain kind and smile and laugh even when it's all falsely based? Masks served no one, least of all friendships. He had learned a long time ago to guard himself, and his feelings, well. It wasn't his fault other people could be read easily.

Because he was quiet and kept his head down—literally —first impressions were that he was a loner and shy. But the moment anyone came to the realization that he was the second son of the Duke of Derbyshire, all eyes were on him no matter how hard he tried to be unseen.

They swarmed him, ravenous for his favor. Because, eventually, a social event would happen. And perhaps, if Skylar liked you, an invitation would be offered.

That was the trick of it, though. Skylar didn't like anyone. Not really.

It had been nearly three months since University had started, and still girls were stalking after him as if he were a prized prey.

When would they learn?

To be fair, it had taken his classmates in primary nearly three years to realize he wasn't having any of the games. The whole thing felt ridiculous to Skylar. For so many reasons. The biggest of which was pretty apparent to anyone who could google the family.

Skylar wasn't even in line to succeed their father. Not that he wanted it.

Lately, he'd begun to consider monastery and a vow of chastity in the church. Perhaps there he would find peace. Because no one would hound or bother him, or consider him for great things if he were bound to the church rather than to the crown.

As Streya returned, he spared a quick glance, curious about her reading choice this time.

A smirk played on his face. She'd been on a Jane Austen kick lately, but it seemed she'd devoured Austen's works and had traded them in for a modern-day romance novel. Surely, she hadn't found it in the University's library. She must've brought it from her flat.

The concept of an Agerian nose-deep into a chick-flick romance book made Skylar chuckle.

In the brief time he'd been awarded to know his Zaheri, Skylar had found himself becoming ever more grateful for them. Streya's routine of sitting with him in these moments, her presence warding off would-be frienemies, was probably his favorite thing he did with his Zaheri.

Though his trainings with them had been few and brief, Skylar had enjoyed them. He'd learned from Erador the bare minimum of combat, and Ira had provided a ton of information regarding the enemies he would one day face. But he'd only had one instance where he'd made a shield larger than his palm, and the team's resident grovix, Ryder, had bounced off of the indigo protection. All of his other training had been small and contained within his bedroom, usually in the dead of night. He'd grown to appreciate each of the team members for various reasons in all of those short interactions, and he wished to the highest heaven that he could spend more time with them.

Of them all, though, Streya seemed content to sit and be present rather than sit and speak for speaking's sake. Erador was a man of few words, but he had a booming voice that made him seem a spectacle no matter how little he said. Ira liked solitude and quiet, as well, but her more timid nature was too alike to Skylar's own personality. Whether he meant it or not, he saw more of Ira's flaws than her benefits, all because they were things he didn't like about himself.

And, well, Ira was a romanticist to the core, filled with whimsy and fairytale-like thoughts and feelings. Especially toward people. Ira saw the best in everyone, and Skylar wanted to appreciate that. But, truthfully, he thought she was rather naïve to believe people were naturally good.

Sure, Streya clearly gobbled up romantic stories, but she was grounded and rooted in reality. She was tough and seasoned in her own right, all the while maintaining compassion and showering it upon him when he needed it the most.

Even so, Skylar could tell she refrained from hugging him or offering gentle pats on his shoulder. Her encouragements were always quickly replaced with a stern warning or pointing out an area he could grow, as if she had to remind herself who she spoke to.

A real part of him wished she wouldn't do that.

Streya's phone buzzed on the table, startling them both out of their concentrations. With a quick glance to his watch, Skylar sighed.

Time here, in this quiet respite, always seemed to move faster than the rest of the world.

He hated it.

She eased herself to face him and asked, "You're sure there's no way for you to get out of tonight's dinner?"

"I've already missed too many this month," he grumbled as he stuffed his laptop into his bag. "Father has been cross about it, and Mother keeps reminding me that it's uncouth to travel so late at night alone."

Fidgeting with the book in her grasp, she tentatively started, "Maybe if I could try again to—"

"No, we can't do that," he said quickly, whipping his gaze to hers. Sputtering out his thoughts, he added, "Father already watches my time away from home closely. And he doesn't trust you, no matter what you say of it. And I can't—" He shrank back. "I don't wish to lose what time I get with you all."

A sigh escaped her, and her shoulders slumped. "Okay. But... I'll walk you to the train. I need to talk to you."

Warily nodding, he went about packing up.

A few moments later, they left the library and made their way to the train station just outside of Oxford.

"What's going on?" he asked quietly as they went.

"I'd like to figure out how we can get you on a patrol soon."

"I don't know how we could manage it," he grumbled as his grip tightened on the bag's strap. "It's impossible to sneak out at night. The butlers and maids notice everything."

"I know, but there has to be a way to do it." Streya shook her head angrily. "You're already behind where I'd like you to be. Your shield strength is growing, and that's good, but you have yet to see a single enemy fighter. And ..." Her gaze fell to the ground.

He looked over and studied her carefully. "And ...?"

"Activity has picked up in the last two days," she whispered. "It worries Erador. Ryder, too."

"But not you and Ira?"

"It's nothing we can't handle."

"I don't doubt that."

Squaring her shoulders, she glared a little. "I just wish you could be part of it. This is a prime opportunity for you to encounter bratak'ra and Caligan forces." A frustrated groan left her. "If only we could convince your father."

"I'll talk to Charles."

She blinked a few times and gave him a puzzled look. "What would that do?"

"He trusts you. And Father trusts Charles. Maybe he can help Father understand that I'm in good hands."

Streya opened her mouth and sucked in a breath. Slowly, she let out a long breath and settled on, "All right, I agree. Let me know if Charles will help, and if we can meet up to discuss your training further."

He had a thought as to what she had wanted to say but refrained from pressing her on it. It wasn't something he wanted to hear, anyway.

No matter how true her unsaid statement might be.

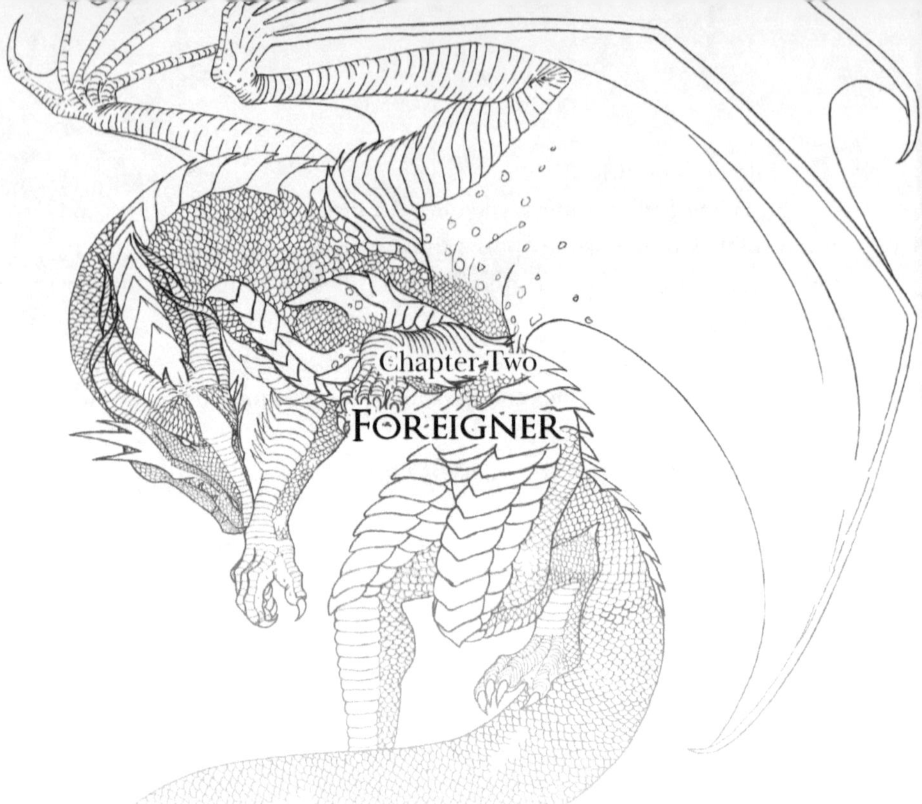

Chapter Two

FOREIGNER

Mr. Brown, one of the Mitchell house staff, opened the door for Skylar as he entered the estate, as per usual.

"Thank you, Mr. Brown," Skylar said with a small smile.

"Welcome home, sir," the butler said with a bow. The older man was a little rotund, with baggy cheeks and a practiced regal tone to his voice. He straightened and said in a slightly quieter tone, "The Lady Mitchell wishes to speak with you before supper."

"Of course she does," Skylar whispered mostly to himself. He gave Mr. Brown a less than thrilled look. "Where is she?"

"In the east drawing room."

Skylar glanced into the building and fought the sigh that wanted to rumble from him.

He began to pull his bag from his shoulder. The butler quickly moved to help him with his jacket. Handing the butler his satchel, Skylar said, "Thank you, Mr. Brown. Sorry to ask you to see to something so trivial."

"It's no bother, sir. I'll have Mr. Carson take your things to your room," Mr. Brown said with an easy smile and small bow.

Skylar made for the hall to the right of the large staircase at the center of the foyer.

There was a memory that sparked every time he gripped the wooden banister on the stairs. Of the one and only time he playfully stomped his feet on the marble stairs, marveling at the echoing in the grand, empty hall. They'd recently moved into the estate. He was maybe four or five at the time. He'd been so enthralled at the place, so captivated by it. It seemed like something out of a storybook, with its grand nature, long halls, and the sweeping banisters.

It was a horribly bittersweet memory, riddled with the joy he'd felt as a boy and replaced almost instantly by his mother's strict reprimand and rough grip on his arm, shaking him harshly.

A tangible part of him wished to stomp again. This time out of a buried fury.

Coming to the east drawing room, one of the butlers nodded to him and opened the door. He stepped into the room before Skylar did and announced, "Master Skylar is home, my lady."

"Thanks, Rip," Skylar said with a small nod as he passed the man only a few years older than him.

Rising to her feet, the Lady Mitchell said, "Ah, about time you returned home." She glanced to the grand clock on the wall. "Cutting it close, I see."

"The train was delayed and could not be helped. Apologies all the same, Mother." His spine hurt every time he tightened it to remain at attention with his shoulders back. It was different than a confident stance. He could manage that without stress pains. This was a binding, whipped-into-submission rigidity. Clasping his hands behind his back to keep from tightening them to fists, Skylar asked, "You wished to see me?"

"Yes, dear," his mother said as she snapped her book shut and set it on the table nearby. She folded her hands together as she straightened, gaining a sort of disappointed look. "There are only two weeks until the Duke of Wales visits."

Where was she going with this?

Skylar's gaze flicked to the wall, and a look of confusion ghosted his features. He wanted to ask, "*And?*" but kept his tongue silent.

A pleased look flickered in her eyes at his silence, only making him wish to deflate all the more. Silence and submission; that was all she wanted from him.

He hated that his heart hurt. Here he thought he'd managed to harden it enough that her dismissal wouldn't sting anymore.

She rolled her manicured hand and said, "You have yet to say who will be your guest for the evening."

Skylar's mouth fell open, and he tried to quickly find an excuse.

"After all, it's about time you became serious about finding someone whom you can court. There are many eligible ladies with good standing, with titles in need of a male heir."

It took every ounce of his self-control to not outright groan and scream about how asinine the whole concept of her conversation was. He wasn't some pedigree dog to find a prized bitch to elevate his status and hers.

He wished he could have been alive to have seen his mother actually act like a normal person. Assuming that had ever been the case. Or had she always been so narrowly focused on securing something as temporary as earthly possessions and stature?

Skylar didn't know. He wondered if anyone, save God, knew.

"Mother ..." he started, deflating a little.

"I can dismiss away Charles's tarrying on the subject—he has important things to focus his attention on presently—but there is no excuse for your ambling," she said cuttingly. That cold look was in her eyes, and Skylar wondered if she'd ever looked at him with warmth. Or was that emotion reserved solely for her princess?

Her fingers flicked in a sharp motion, and Skylar shot to attention again.

"There are bound to be young women with their attention on you. We haven't devoted so much time to your grooming for you to fail in securing some other title alongside your brother. We expect you to have a lady of proper standing when the Duke of Wales visits." Her gaze narrowed and, bitingly, she said, "Is that clear?"

Allowing himself to let out a short breath but keep his expression even, he answered, "Yes, Mother."

A sharp smile quickly affixed to her face. "Quite good. Now go clean up. Supper will be on any moment now."

Turning on his heel, Skylar marched out of the room and made for his bedroom as quickly as possible.

Carson was there, setting his supper clothes on the rack for Skylar to change into.

"Thank you, Carson. If I could have the room please," Skylar hastily said.

"Are you all right, m'lord?" Carson asked. The middle-aged man might have been considered a friend, given how long the man had been seeing to Skylar's personal care.

As Skylar looked to him, he realized his heart had hardened.

Just not to his mother.

Yet.

"I'm fine. I just need a few moments before supper."

With a slow nod, Carson said, "Very well, m'lord."

Once the older man was gone, Skylar slumped and let out a long, slow breath as a frown came to his face. He made for the window and stared at the twilight unfolding across the estate. A pained expression filled his face, and he closed his eyes.

If he had wings, he'd fly away from here. Fly as far and as fast as he could. Change his name. Find some other country to welcome him as a refugee from his loveless prison of a house.

With a roll of his eyes, he admonished himself. How childish of him. So typical of a teenage mentality, to see home as a prison and the world as freedom. But a child was exactly what he was, wasn't he? Was it so wrong for him to wish to be rid of the life he wanted nothing to do with? And it wasn't like he thought himself a pitiable soul. He knew fortune and favor surrounded his every second. He knew he was among the elites of society. He knew there were many thousands, if not tens or hundreds of thousands, of people who envied his life.

Well, they could have it.

What he would give for a small home, a loving family, hugs, and home-cooked meals. A messy floor and a shedding pet, dings in the walls where furniture was moved a little too harshly to fit the too-small spaces, uneven carpets and mismatched silverware. Family heirlooms of almost useless nature, but shared from generation to generation.

For someone to—

A knock sounded at the door, and he pulled himself from his depressing thoughts.

"Carson?"

The butler opened the door and said, "Master Charles is here, sir."

Whipping around, Skylar said, "Of course, let him in."

Charles walked into the room, offering Carson a smile and a nod. His suit jacket was unbuttoned, as was his norm when in the presence of his younger brother. A more casual stance graced his frame as the door closed, awarding the brothers some privacy.

His brother was a handsome bloke. Sporting their mother's dirty blond hair and their grandfather's gray eyes, he had a jovial sense about him. If Skylar had to attribute one word to his brother, it would be "loyal," second only to "joyful." After all, Charles had a lot to be joyful about. The favored son, the heir to the title, the good boy who could do no wrong. The one who got an actual childhood in their little flat that Skylar couldn't remember but Charles would mention. The one that swore that their mother could laugh genuinely, but she hadn't for some time. That swore their father was loving and sacrificed greatly for the family.

But even Charles knew that things were not so simple anymore. Nor had they been for almost all of Skylar's life.

Giving Skylar a worried smile, Charles said, "Mother caught you, I imagine."

"Unfortunately, yes."

Shifting his weight slightly, the elder brother asked, "What will you do?"

Rolling his eyes, Skylar answered, "I could find a date for the stupid event tomorrow. But Mother has required that it be a 'lady of good standing.'" He gave his brother an enviable stare. "Count yourself blessed. They're pardoning you."

"Well, about that," Charles said as he put his hands in his pockets and eased back. "I could alleviate your struggles."

Skylar raised his brow in surprise. "Did you find some girl you actually like?"

"I was considering asking Streya if she would do me the honor of being my guest," Charles answered with a lingering smile.

The younger brother shook back a little. "Wait, what? Why?"

"Oh, come off, Sky; you can't honestly say she isn't gorgeous."

"I ..." Skylar shook his head harshly. "So, maybe she is, but that doesn't mean I fancy her."

"Well, that's grand news. Because I do."

Crossing his arms, Skylar said, "Something tells me that Pa and Ma aren't going to accept her as a 'lady of good standing.'"

"Bollocks on them," Charles said with a roll of his eyes. "Whether they approve or not is of little consequence."

"For you perhaps."

Charles let out a small sigh. "That seems fair, I suppose." He looked to his brother. "Do you approve, or no?"

"It's ... simply that I don't see her that way."

"Truly?" Charles raised his brow and let out a chuckle. "I would have a hard time *not* seeing her in a light of feminine beauty."

Skylar would have to be blind to say Streya was ordinary or plain looking. There simply wasn't any desire within him to view her as anything other than a teacher or—perhaps if he were lucky—as something more familial.

Perhaps because the concept of romance was so lost to him, so buried under most young women's hidden agendas of fame or fortune, he *couldn't* see women as anything but vultures circling a poor chap.

Coupled with her clear age over his, Skylar had secretly hoped she would fill a different void in his life, one that should have been relegated to only one person.

Shaking his head again to clear his thoughts, Skylar said, "It's not objectionable on my part, Charles. She might enjoy it." He offered his brother a smile. "She took quite quickly to your suggestions for Jane Austen novels."

Charles brightened. "Did she?"

With a quick glance to the clock, Skylar took stock of how long they had until supper was announced. He turned his attention to his brother. "We spoke of you today."

The elder brother straightened, and a hopeful smile played on his features.

"I was hoping you might be able to help us."

"With what?"

Treading carefully, Skylar said, "With Pa."

As if he already knew the request, Charles sighed and sunk.

"We were hoping you might be able to convince him that he's hindering my growth, and that I'm safe with my Zaheri."

"Sky," Charles whispered in dismay, "I don't know how you expect me to convey that in a way he'd understand."

"Please, Charles. There must be a way."

They shared a long stare before Charles nodded slowly. He offered a feeble smile. "Of course I'll give it a go."

Skylar smiled back at his brother, grateful once again for someone who seemed to care for him.

Changing the subject, Charles asked, "Did you hear what Ma said of Martha today?"

"No, what?" Skylar asked, eager to hear the absurd praise their younger sister was bound to have been showered with for no adequate reason.

They shared a bit of laughter as Skylar readied for supper. Charles grew somber from time to time, causing Skylar to wonder if his brother would rescind his offer.

The concept was foreign, and Skylar banished it. If there was one person on Earth whom he could rely on, it was his older brother.

Thinking over the concept of Charles pursuing Streya in a romantic sort of way, Skylar figured there were worse things for his brother to do. After all, in such a scenario, perhaps it would award Skylar an excuse to leave the manor and instead live with Charles and Streya. It gave him pause, though, knowing how greatly his Zaheri were disliked by their parents.

No matter how favored Charles was, the chances of their parents overlooking his choice of potential wives was ridiculously slim.

Chapter Three

TWO MEN BEARING TWO OMENS

Polite knocking tapped against the door to the flat. Erador gave a swift glance to the door then back to Streya. "Expecting someone?" the dark-skinned man asked, his light eyes attentive as ever.

"Nope," Streya said, warily looking at the entrance.

Without another word, she and Erador snatched the rifles nearby and went to the door.

Erador lifted his rifle, ready to fire at whomever might be on the other side, as Streya checked the peephole. She looked back at Erador and waved her hand before opening the door.

Charles stood in the hallway, a determined look on his face.

"Charles, what are you doing here? How did you—"

"Skylar told me where you all lived. I need to speak with you," the British man said in a hushed tone.

Streya nodded and stepped aside, allowing him to enter.

As she closed the door, Charles took in Erador's rifle and awkwardly smirked. "Expecting someone else?"

To say Charles wasn't intimated by Erador would be an egregious error.

—— ∙∙∙ 17 ∙∙∙ ——

Charles wasn't tiny, standing a few inches under six feet, and Erador towered over him like a minotaur. With his short dreadlocks and hulking mass, the man brought to mind ancient warrior classes that hung the heads of their kills as trophies. Skylar insisted that Erador was a nice enough fellow, and Charles wanted to believe that. But he couldn't deny that a large part of him was convinced that Erador had a blood-stained blade hanging on his wall. It just felt like something he'd do, given his appearance.

"We're preparing for patrol," Erador answered in his gravely tone. He looked to Streya. "Want us to still head out?"

"Check with Ira that all the sensors are active. I have a feeling I'll need some help with this," Streya said with an uneasy glance at Charles.

Erador nodded then walked farther into the large flat. The thumping of heavy paws could be heard. A moment later, the grumbling growl from Ryder filtered from around the corner.

While Streya moved across the room to put her rifle away, Charles said, "I apologize for muddying it, but I felt this conversation should be had sooner rather than later."

Lifting up on the tabletop to reveal a space for two rifles to be stored, Streya put her gun away and sighed. "This is about your father, I assume."

"This is about Skylar," Charles corrected. "I need to know more about all this before I truly go to war against my father's wishes for you lot."

"I was afraid of that," Streya muttered. She closed the lid and turned, leaning against the table as she surveyed the British man. "So, what're your questions?"

"I thought you wanted help." He gestured toward where Erador had disappeared to. "Shouldn't we wait for the others?"

"There's no reason to keep you. They'll be along in a moment. Ira's just running a test on the sensors."

"Sensors? What sort of sensors?"

"They're modified motion trackers. Specifically tuned and calibrated to alert us to body masses that look like bratak'ra, or werewolves, or dragons."

Charles shifted his weight. "That's what he's up against?"

She crossed her arms, and her gaze fell to the floor. "That's not all he's up against."

"Enlighten me. Give me your history, the backstory. What is this whole mess he's tangled in?" Charles asked with a small scowl.

"The condensed version is this: we're a peaceful nation. We don't want war or bloodshed. But we have an enemy that, for reasons unknown to us, wants to wipe us out."

Gesturing loosely, Charles asked, "And how exactly does Skylar fit into this?"

"He's ... someone who can help end the war."

"How?" Charles shrugged and held his arms out. "I thought he wasn't a fighter, that he makes shields. How does a shield bearer bring peace?"

Ira came around the corner. She always looked delicate and small in comparison to Streya's harder edges and more athletic build. Both women were beautiful in their own right, but Charles had a hard time grasping how Ira was a good fit as a defending warrior. With her small frame, rounded face, and shoulder-length black hair, she seemed better suited for a library. The few conversations he and Ira had, he had found her to be quite intelligent and pleasant.

Erador and Ryder followed. The grovix's monstrous, black-furred build made Charles wish to flee, if only to avoid angering the large creature. Where Ira brought sweet pleasantries, every comment Ryder had ever thrown at Charles was wrapped in a snarl. Ryder was probably exactly what should fight monsters, but that didn't mean there wasn't unease in Charles every time he looked at the golden-eyed grovix.

"Skylar's a shield bearer unlike any in Agerius. With time and practice, he has all the potential to be an impenetrable protector," Ira said as she took her place next to Streya.

Erador leaned against the threshold between the living quarters and the kitchen, crossing his arms. Ryder sat nearby, eyeing Charles suspiciously.

"So, what? He'll trap your enemy in a shield and stop the fighting? That's how you think he'll achieve peace for you?" Charles asked.

Casting a quick sideways glance to Ira, Streya answered, "It's... complicated."

With a roll of his eyes, Charles stepped back a little and let out a sigh. "You're clearly keeping something from me. From Skylar. He may not care, but I do. How do you expect me to be your intermediary with my father if you won't be honest with me?"

"We should tell him," Ira whispered to Streya.

"And if he tells Skylar?" Erador asked in his gruff voice behind the women.

Ryder's bright eyes flicked between Streya and Charles. A small snarl formed on his snout as he grumbled, "We don't need him. We should just take Skylar and train him in secret. Alphas know he wouldn't miss it."

"Don't you dare," Charles commanded as he fisted his hands at his sides.

"We won't do that," Streya said calmly. She gave Ryder a disapproving look. "We'd only create enemies doing something like that."

"I'm just saying it's an option," Ryder mumbled, his brow twitching as he spoke.

"Do we have your word that what we discuss here will stay between us?" Ira asked with a pleading look to Charles. "There are things we've been commanded to keep from Skylar until we're given permission to divulge."

"Permission from whom?" Charles asked.

With a sigh, Erador said, "Our High Council. Think of them as your Parliament."

Nodding a few times, Charles muttered, "Ah, so your governing law then." He lifted his head. "Very well. I can appreciate the rules and commands you're bound to under your Council."

Streya looked to her team before she squared her shoulders. "Skylar isn't the only Human-Born hybrid."

Slowly, Charles narrowed his eyes. "What?"

"We don't know where they are," Ira quickly said. "We only know that there are more. To that end, we won't go into further detail. Only know that Skylar is a piece to ending the war and is not alone in the endeavor."

Letting out a slow breath, Charles eased back slightly, his offensive stance melting. "So he's adept at shields, meaning that these other Human-Borns may be warriors or fighters capable of bringing down this opposing nation."

Ira nodded once. "Yes."

"Do you understand now?" Streya asked as Charles's gaze fell to the floor. "If we aren't given the opportunity to train Skylar appropriately, he'll be unprepared for his part to play. We have to help him hone his skills, or all of these years of the Human-Borns' preparations could be lost."

Raking a hand through his hair, Charles wearily lifted his gaze to the Agerians. "Please know I understand your plight."

Erador rolled his eyes and groaned, "Oh, here we go."

"I need you to understand my father's," Charles said, undeterred by Erador's frustration.

Ira and Streya shared a look before the latter said, "All right. What keeps him from allowing us to fulfill our task?"

"What I'm about to say ... it's speculation. But I believe it's accurate. And I believe it's why my father is so steadfast against Skylar's training."

"Just get on with it," Ryder snapped with a bristling of his fur along his neck.

With a sigh, Charles answered, "If word of Skylar's abilities got out, if people found out what he can do, what he is"—warily, he met Streya's gaze—"it would cause for question in the legitimacy of his ties to my father."

Streya squinted as Ira asked, "You think people would say Skylar isn't your father's son?"

"I think they would question it," Charles reiterated. "And though I'm certain that Skylar is my brother legitimately, and that any tests would verify it, it would require that Martha and myself be tested, as well."

Erador shrugged. "So? What's the problem?"

Uneasily, Charles glanced to Erador before looking again at Streya. "Skylar and I are close enough in age and bare enough physical resemblances to both sides of our family that I'm certain beyond a doubt of his legitimacy. However ..."

A frown came to Streya's face. "Do ...? Do you think that Martha ...?"

"I fear it, yes." Charles gained a sorrowful look. "If, Heaven forbid it, Martha was found to be illegitimate, it would raise many questions. And no matter what a test may say, what doctors may say, there are those who would take the opportunity to have both myself and Skylar removed from the order to succeed our father."

"If the truth is that you're clearly your father's son, how could anyone dispute it?" Erador asked with a scrunched brow.

"Clearly, Agerians don't have such issues," Charles muttered as he gestured loosely to Erador. "The title Duke of Derbyshire is one recovered when my father discovered his ties to a dormant title."

"Dormant title?" Ira asked.

"It's what titles are called when heirs go missing. They move to other countries and get out of the loop, or are cousins fairly removed from the living title holder. The Duke of Derbyshire's title is one that's resurfaced in the last fifteen years. It's not a deep-rooted claim as many other lines may hold. It's tenuous and new. Things like this can break newly revived orders such as his. Unfortunately, everything that my father holds, all that he is, rests on having a legitimate heir take over for him."

Ira nodded a few times. "I see. So, if questions were raised regarding the biological nature of his children—"

"He would stand to lose everything."

A few unsure looks were shared among the Beta Team.

"I will do what I can to convince my father of your intentions, but ... I cannot guarantee that I'll have any success."

Streya offered a small smile. "We appreciate your efforts, Charles."

With a tired look in his eyes, Charles sighed. "I don't want to see Skylar get hurt. And if training is what he needs to prepare himself for what lies ahead, I want to do my part to ensure he's safe."

"You're a good brother," Erador said, as per usual, without a smile or look of warmth in his features.

"Is there anything more we can do to help us gain your father's trust?" Ira asked.

Shaking his head, Charles said, "Unfortunately, no. At this point, all he sees you lot as is a threat to his lineage."

"Why?" Ryder grumbled with a small snarl. "It's not like we want *you*."

Charles ruffled his hair. "That's a fair point. I doubt I'd be much help on a battlefield."

Streya chuckled. "Probably not."

"On that note, though." The human's gaze fell toward the table that concealed the assault rifles. "Is there any chance I might be awarded the opportunity to learn some of your combat skills?"

Offering an apologetic look, Streya said, "Sorry, no."

"Was worth a shot."

Erador gave Streya a bored look. "We done here?"

"Yeah, why don't you two get going. Ira and I will meet up with you in a minute," Streya said.

"Golden. Let's go, pup."

"Don't call me that," Ryder snapped with a clip of his teeth.

Ira glanced between Charles and Streya and quickly said, "You know what? I'm going to head out with them, too."

"What? Why?" Streya asked.

The smaller woman waved her hand dismissively. "No real reason, just a feeling I have that I should go."

Once the three were gone, Charles turned to Streya and offered an awkward smile. "Ira's haste was on my accord."

"Why?" Streya asked with an inquisitive look.

Threading his fingers together a few times, he said, "If I were to ask you to a night out in London, would you accept?"

A blush flamed across Streya's face.

"I take that as a good sign?" he asked with a smile.

She waved her hands frantically. "Sorry, I ... I've never been asked out for a date before."

Bewilderment danced in his eyes. "Truly?" His gaze flicked across her features. "Are the men of Agerius blind?"

Chewing on her lip, Streya drew her hands in and said, "Well ... Agerians do things ... differently."

He was quiet for a moment before he asked, "Are you betrothed or something?"

"No, nothing like that"—she shook her head—"it's more that we ... well ... men get these things called Heseda. Sort of like a pinpoint to let them know when they've met their wife."

A defeated slump of his shoulders had the British man wither before her. "And that's happened to you, I take it," he said, hoping that maybe he was wrong.

She returned to chewing on her lip as she played with her fingers.

With a sad sigh, he said, "Very well. I know when I'm bested." He gave her a warm smile. "He's a lucky man."

The smile that rose unbidden to her face made him all the more envious of whatever man held her heart. "Thank you, Charles."

He nodded then went to the door. Casting a glance over his shoulder, he said, "I'll let you know what comes of the conversation with my father."

"Golden. Thanks again."

Though the look of disappointment ghosted his features, he offered another nod then left.

Once she was alone, Streya let out a long, heavy sigh. That had been unexpected. Not necessarily unwelcome, but unexpected.

As a frown came to her face, she went to her room. It only took her a moment of searching to find what she was after. It was a small box for holding simple trinkets. Tyron had given it to her on her birth day twenty years ago. If she had known they wouldn't be together for her next birth day celebration, she would have asked him to stay longer that night.

Her parents had pulled together a nice bit of decoration and had managed to score her favorite cake from Meesa's bakery on Halios. Several of her friends had come to celebrate the day of her birth, as was customary. A few of them had offered gifts (not as customary). Typically, only family and intimate friends exchanged gifts on such occasions.

She'd fully expected Tyron to show up with a gift. Since she'd grown up with Tyron's youngest sister, the families had become close. If he hadn't arrived with a present, Streya's whole family would have assumed something had caused a rift in the friendship.

Tyron had been late to the gathering for some reason. She'd missed his explanation to her father—her childhood friend Taesir had been busy prattling on about something at the time.

The memory was vivid in her mind. Just as vivid as the last time she'd seen Tyron.

He'd worn the same blue shirt both times. She wondered if he knew it was her favorite. It had this faint stitching in the fabric that Rea had woven in the shape of a dragon. Tyron had owned that shirt for a long time. A gift from his parents when he'd become a Defender.

She'd always thought it was like his own version of a uniform or armor. The dragon stitching was so fine and so fitting for him, as if letting the world know he was special.

Because he was special.

Sinking to the floor, she opened the box, and the memory of it being handed to her sprang through her mind.

"For me?" she asked with a playful smirk. "You shouldn't have."

He rolled his eyes and offered that brilliant grin. "Like you would've let me walk away unscathed if I didn't get you something."

"You're right; I wouldn't've."

She pulled the decorative paper aside—hastily placed on and poorly assembled—and found herself captivated by the box—its beautiful woodgrain, displaying vibrant colors of reds and browns, with the carving of a grovix on it.

A smile wormed its way to her face, and she hushed, "It's beautiful."

"Glad you like it," Tyron said with a smile. When she turned to him, he opened his arms for a hug. "Happy birth day, Streya."

Biting her lip as she fought the resurgence of a wide smile at the memory, Streya blinked away the happy thought, and her mind returned to reality. To her bedroom in the small flat, alone and missing him terribly.

The box was a little worn now, but no less vibrant. She lovingly stroked the side as she rifled through the mementos in the box. Eventually, she found the small note.

Tyron's handwriting had always been terrible and sloppy. Not surprising. Hers wasn't that stellar, either. No one's was, save the Archivists. It wasn't like they had to write a lot. So, practicing their penmanship wasn't high on the priority list for Defenders. Especially Elites.

Despite his crummy handwriting, she still cherished the little note inside with the simple inscription:

Happy birth day

— Tyron.

How many more days would pass before she could see him again?

Her shoulders slumped, and a frown came to her face. She missed him so terribly. There were so many times she found herself wishing to talk with him, to hear his voice, to see his smile. To feel his embrace as he offered a warm, welcoming hug.

A part of her envied Ira tremendously.

Though the woman hadn't voiced it, and only blushed furiously whenever it was mentioned, she clearly had been given the red ribbon that was tied around her neck every day by someone special. And then there was the large ring that sat on the woman's thumb. Ira played with both constantly, a look of far-off wonder glossing her eyes from time to time.

With a small huff, Streya crossed her arms and glared at the floor. It wasn't fair that she should be separated this long from Tyron. Or Ira from whomever she pined for. Or Erador from …

Okay, so Erador probably didn't miss anyone. That gruff, expressionless bulk of a man wasn't likely to be missing from any woman in Agerius. She certainly couldn't imagine anyone finding his demeanor charming. He was a knockout of a fighter, and she was grateful for his presence on the Beta Team, but that didn't mean she found him attractive. There weren't many men she found attractive, and the few whom she did …

A shiver rattled up her spine, and she hastily shoved the note back into the box, tucking the keepsake away.

She'd dallied too long and needed to get back to her mission.

Erador rolled his eyes as they walked through the forest. He let out a scoff as he said, "Please. Charles? He's a nice guy and all, but he's so tiny."

"What do you know?" Ira grumbled with a flick of her hand as though Erador were an unwanted thing.

"I just hope he doesn't distract her," Ryder growled, keeping his head low. His eyes gleamed in the darkness, and the moonlight illuminated the sharper edges of his frame. "She seems to be distracted enough as it is."

"Do you blame her?" the smaller woman asked. "All of this nonsense with Skylar's father is severely impeding his growth." A frown came to her face. "What if, when he meets the other Human-Borns, he's so far behind that they resent him? Or resent us? Streya feels the weight of that burden."

"Not like she's alone in it," Erador said lackadaisically, pulling his hands behind his head and walking leisurely. "We'll bear the brunt, too, y'know."

Ira rolled her eyes. "Of course I know that. And I'm certain that Streya does, as well."

Ryder came to a stop. The two hybrids absently stopped with him.

"But, as Team Leader, I'm certain she feels she holds the bulk of the responsibility for Skylar's training. It's imperative that we do all we can to prepare him for his role."

"As undefined as it is," Erador said with a small smirk.

"Clearly he's meant to be a shield bearer. It's reinforced by his ability."

"Yeah, yeah, I got that. Doesn't mean all the titles for the Human-Borns make any sense."

"You have a gripe with the prophecy? Why are you only now mentioning it?"

"I don't have a gripe with it. Maybe I do. I dunno. It just seems stupid, y'know?"

"Stupid? It's the Elders' Prophecy! You don't get to judge it!"

"I dunno. I think I can. They could've been a little more specific. Like telling us exactly what these kids are supposed to do."

"It states it plainly."

"It states it vaguely."

With a bristling spine, Ryder growled at them, "Would you two shut your blasted traps for longer than a few seconds!" He rolled his eyes and grumbled under his breath, "Alphas, if I didn't know any better, I'd say Zelek has to worry about this rock breather."

"What'd you say?" Erador asked as gold energy sparked around his arms and his jaw clenched.

"Do you sense something, Ryder?" Ira asked quietly as she approached the grovix, completely unfazed by the inaccurate insinuation about her and Erador. Her fingers grazed the ribbon at her neck all the same.

Ryder gave her a teasing smirk. "Nothing *certain*"–he returned his gaze ahead–"but there's something out there."

She ignored his jab at her vocabulary. "Any concept of what it may be?"

Ducking low, Ryder flattened his ears and inched into the thick brush to their left. After a few long seconds of them following him in hunched positions, the grovix whispered, "Bratak'ra."

The shine of horns caught in the moonlight.

Before she could do anything, Ira was shoved aside. Erador and Ryder ran toward the opposition.

Ryder smashed into a mono-horned bratak'ra, dispatching it quickly. Erador was on his heel, his large battle axe in his grasp as he swung it around, unleashing a powerful strike at the pack of bratak'ra.

The golden energy lit up the forest around them briefly, and Ira caught the fact that werewolves surrounded them.

"Watch out!" she cried and swung her arm across her. A golden shield sprang around them in a circled wall that stood only a little taller than Erador. The light from the shield fully showcased where their hidden enemies lurked.

"Nice call," Erador said with a smirk to her from over his shoulder.

The three of them drew in, keeping their backs to each other as they surveyed the enemy. A dozen or so by the look of it.

Ira squinted. What was the purpose of so many? And nearly even numbers of bratak'ra and werewolves. Seemed strange.

They hadn't encountered this many enemies in years. A few stragglers here and there—she was certain they were trying to find Skylar—but nothing in the double digits.

And certainly never this many werewolves.

A sick feeling coiled in her stomach.

"There are a lot of werewolves," she whispered as she surveyed the lanky beasts. Their hunched backs and emaciated frames always made her cringe.

She was grateful none of them looked like Kaldok in the slightest. The thought of her friend made her grasp the ribbon around her neck and send up a prayer for protection.

"I got 'em," Erador said with a smile. The battlefield was the only place he seemed quick to grin.

"You sure?" Ryder asked with a sideways glance. "Can't let 'em bite ya."

"I know that, pup," Erador shot back, his jovial grin gone.

"Don't call me that!"

"Would you two stop bickering?" Streya asked as she landed among them, her nimble wings quickly folding into her back as she got her footing. "What're you stalled for?"

"Waitin' for you," Erador said with another smirk.

She gave him a knowing look and turned to Ira. "Ready for shield maneuvers?"

"Ready and golden," Ira said with a determined smile. She liked fighting with Streya. The other woman's easy confidence in an encounter always lessened Ira's fears. Streya might've been younger than her, but Ira could see the clear reasons why Streya had been chosen as their leader.

"Erador, you get the werewolves on the right. I'll take the ones on the left. Ryder—"

"Yeah, I got it; bratak'ra on me," the grovix growled with a roll of his eyes.

"Ira, make 'em dance," Streya said, wearing a confident smile as she fell into a ready stance. Golden energy surged around her arms like gauntlets, casting a warm glow around her beautiful face.

It wasn't how Ira would usually describe what she did with her shields, but she had come to enjoy Streya's playful description. Cracking her shields into even chunks, Ira made them swirl around the group.

A few shield pieces flitted and flicked around Ryder as he charged his bulk at the bratak'ra. Shields flew around him and protected the large grovix from werewolves intending him harm. Like floating golden walls, her shields were trained and fixed on Ryder's moving form, keeping pace with him easily.

Meanwhile, her shields ducked and swiveled out of the way of Erador and Streya's attacks as they sliced through the air. The two warriors made quick work of the werewolves. The poor beasts did their best to dodge attacks and avoid her shields, but their attempts were fruitless.

In a matter of minutes, the Caligan forces were fully neutralized.

Straightening, Streya surveyed the dead bodies littering their surroundings. "We get them all?"

"Bravo," a smooth voice called from the trees, accompanied by mocking claps.

They spun their heads to the limbs above them, trying to see into the darkness for the source of the voice.

"Quite a spectacular display, ladies," the voice said as it flitted through the trees. He must've been moving from tree to tree. But the branches weren't creaking or swaying with the person's movements.

"Show yourself!" Erador growled, throwing a blast of gold into the air to try to illuminate their surroundings. All they saw were tree branches.

"Aw ... where's the fun in that?"

Pulling her arms up to a ready stance again, Streya called golden energy into her fists. She knew that voice.

"You two are fun to watch," the voice cooed. "I can only imagine what you'd be like in other situations."

Ryder's fur bristled again, and he snarled, "Coward. Lurking in the shadows."

A hum came from around them.

"Where is he?" Ira asked, warily eyeing the darkness.

Erador shoved her into the center of the group, his jaw tight.

"Don't worry about that one. She's not really my type." The voice chuckled. "Well, she could be, given the right stimulation."

"Monster," Erador growled as his grip tightened on his weapon.

A scoff came from too close to be possible if they couldn't see him. "Wrong. I'm destruction." A pulse hit the air as gray dust swirled around them. Their attacker's leather-gauntleted hand snatched Erador's battle axe and, for a fleeting second, they saw the sneering smirk on his face as their attacker snapped, "Get it right."

Streya let out a yell and threw an attack at the man. He disappeared before she could hit him, but the momentum of his shove on Erador sent the larger warrior stumbling to the ground.

With fury, Erador ripped himself to his feet and hollered, "Akeno! You coward! Face me!"

There was a faint glimmer of the gold-orange eyes in the shadows. Akeno ambled backward, wearing a satisfied smirk. "Not today." Another pulse hit the air.

The group continued to grip their weapons tightly as they spun their attention around the small clearing, looking for any sign of the Caligan. After a long, tense moment, they eased a little.

"Akeno?" Ira asked quietly, drawing in on herself. "Here?"

"What does that mean?" Erador asked, his eyes still attentive as he scanned the trees around them.

"Could mean anything," Ryder grumbled.

Streya studied the fallen creatures around them, darting her gaze around the trees surrounding them. "We need to be on guard, extra vigilant. At least for the next few days."

"Something troubling you?" Ira asked.

Gesturing to the dead monsters, the other woman said, "The most resistance we've faced in years, coupled with Akeno showing up? It's not normal. And not normal means there could be trouble."

With a huff, Ryder snarled, "I'll just bite his face off next time."

"Good luck with that," Erador said with a roll of his eyes. "Man's a Jumper. They're tricky and snarky." He crossed his arms. "At least ours is."

Streya let out a sigh and gave a perturbed look. "Don't even mention that brat."

"You've met him?" Ira asked.

As Streya started to walk out of the clearing, she answered, "Tyron told me a little about him before we all left for Earth. Seems like a jerk. Probably has been a real talon in Ty's spine all this time."

"So, you haven't met him," Ira clarified.

"No, I haven't met him."

"Then you can't judge him. Not yet."

"Ira, trust me, nothing good comes from Jumpers. They only cause problems."

Offering a shrug, Ira responded, "I just think we should reserve judgment, that's all."

Slinging his axe over his shoulder, Erador said, "I've heard enough about him to know Streya's not far off."

"Maybe there's a reason for his actions," Ira mused, playing with her fingers.

"I'm not talking about Kaldok, y'know. Just the Jumper."

"What's Kaldok got to do with this?" Ryder asked with narrowed eyes.

Streya let the conversation dip to the background of her attention. Kaldok and the Jumper—both headaches Tyron had to deal with. Sure, Ira talked of Kaldok's virtues and strengths often, but she was biased. She'd known him since she was a child. Streya supposed she could reserve judgment on the werewolf, but she had caught glimpses of him fighting before. He was powerful. And cursed. That had to mean something.

For Ira's sake, she would do her best to keep her comments and wariness about Kaldok to herself. She owed the other woman that.

But she didn't owe anyone anything in regard to the Jumper. He was callous and snarky. Sure, he was handsome enough, and she could sort of understand why so many other women thought his quick, charming smiles were worth fawning over. But being a pretty face accounted for nothing in her opinion.

A man should be strong and dependable. Brave and selfless. Loyal and caring. That Jumper was exactly none of those things.

Streya would sooner trust a bratak'ra to not bite her than put her trust in Agerius' Jumper.

She hoped Tyron was handling it okay. That blasted Jumper was bound to be the death of him. A fixed determination came to her mind. One more person to make sure didn't bring chaos down on Tyron. Not if she could help it.

Chapter Four

The Day the Earth Stood Still

Skylar looked forward to Tuesdays. They were short by all accounts. His classes wrapped by late morning, and he always grabbed the train to London so he could have lunch with Charles in the city. The train's bustle awarded Skylar anonymity for a spell. Between tourists and general passersby, no one paid him any mind.

Well, no one save his Zaheri.

He'd grown accustomed to the ever-present knowledge that someone watched him over the last year and a half. Initially, the concept had been unnerving. Skylar would whip around in a panic, only to be welcomed with the sight of one of his Zaheri shaking their hands dismissively or not-so-subtly trying to not be seen.

Truthfully, that "eyes on your back" feeling was one he'd always attributed to fear at mis-stepping or misspeaking. Now, however, it was a comfort to know someone watched over him and sought to keep him safe.

Safe from what, exactly, he wasn't entirely sure.

There had been a handful of lessons from Ira and notes for him to study that Streya would slip into notebooks and textbooks. He'd seen the sketches and studied the bestiary of Agerius. He'd spoken with Ryder enough times to know that grovix weren't beasts to underestimate or undervalue. The beasts and creatures he might one day encounter were easy, he thought, to wrap his head around.

But this mysterious Caliga, and their shrouded-in-rumor leader, left him puzzled.

What was he to this powerful opposition? Just another shield-bearer in Skylar's mind. Sure, he was told he was incredibly powerful. And yes, he'd made a couple shields that his Zaheri had marveled at.

But he'd never actually protected anything.

Was he truly something powerful enough to withstand this Cregorous or any of his followers? Since he'd never had anything combat his shields, Skylar genuinely worried whether he'd be capable of stepping into the shoes of ... whatever his Zaheri and their people saw for him.

Though, perhaps he was overthinking it. After all, it wasn't as if making indigo shields of raw energy was the norm for people. That had to mean something.

Ambling on his way to the train station, he could hear Erador's heavy footfalls against the pavement not far behind him. The bulky warrior was the funniest to see try to hide himself. On more than one occasion, Erador had stumbled over barrels or boxes, or run smack into other people. Apologizing wasn't exactly Erador's strong suit, and he tended to become a spectacle of chaos in those moments.

The memories made Skylar chuckle a bit as he continued on his way.

He had barely left Oxford's main hub when Ryder suddenly burst through the trees nearby. Skylar nearly leaped a foot off the ground. People nearby shrieked. A handful of phones were whipped out, pointed toward Ryder as they recorded the massive beast.

Erador was there in a flash as he asked angrily, "What are you doing?"

"We have a problem," the dark-furred grovix shot out.

Before he could continue, Streya and Ira joined them. Streya began to shove at Ryder, as though that would make his appearance null to the world around them. "Are you trying to get us all noticed? Why are you out here?" Streya demanded as she continued to push in vain.

Ryder shoved her off and barked, "There are bratak'ra and werewolves nearby! Not a hundred feet away. We have to act!"

"Wait—what?" Streya asked.

"Why didn't any of the sensors go off?" Erador shot to Ira.

The smaller woman shrank further back and fumbled for her phone. "I—"

Their phones all began to blare different alarm sounds, startling everyone nearby. Ira shrieked in startled surprise and dropped her phone.

Skylar gave them wary glances as Streya took hold of his shoulder. "What does this mean?" he asked.

"Erador, you and Ryder will need to eradicate any opposition. They cannot enter Oxford, you hear?" Streya commanded, her gaze steely as it flicked between the two warriors.

Both Erador and Ryder nodded.

"Ira, you and I are going to make sure Skylar doesn't get touched. You got that?"

"Yes, of course," Ira said as she nodded shakily.

Streya's grip on Skylar's shoulder tightened a little as she looked to him pointedly. "Sky, just relax. You can do this. Your ability is made for this."

"Which is what, exactly?" Skylar asked, worry creeping into his voice.

"We're going to need your shields to keep the buildings protected. Those alarms mean we have dragons, werewolves, and bratak'ra coming for us, which means there's going to be Caligans, too."

"Wait ... combat?" Skylar shook despite himself. "But ... but Streya, I don't have any training!"

Her grip loosened, and she placed both her hands on his shoulders. A warm smile filled her features as she said, "Hey, come on; take a breath."

Skylar gave her an unsure look.

"You were made for this."

Was he?

A bellowing, inferno-laden roar hit the sky. He should have anticipated that, given what Streya had said was coming. Skylar ducked and covered his ears all the same.

Screams began to tear around them. People pointed at the sky as a large, gray dragon flew overhead.

He'd read books. He'd studied the bestiary. He'd seen the diagrams.

But actually acknowledging the size and bulk of a real, scale and blood, flesh and bone, flying dragon juxtaposed against a normal late-fall day in Oxford made Skylar's mind stutter in thought.

They were actually, genuinely real.

Someone bumped into him as they fled for the train station. He hit the ground, catching himself and staring at the worn pavement beneath him for a few long seconds.

His Zaheri all went to action. Streya and Ira directed people which way to get to safety. Erador and Ryder were on alert, their attention sweeping to where their opposition would arrive.

A breath rattled from Skylar, and he gripped the walkway.

Streya was right. He could do this. He had the ability to protect people.

He hoped.

Fixing a look of determination on his face, Skylar got back to his feet and whipped his satchel off his shoulder. With a quick glance to Erador and Ryder, he turned to the buildings around them. His eyes flicked here and there, taking a moment to properly gauge how tall each building was, where they would be most likely to crumble if an errant attack hit the structure.

The handful of shields he'd made, and the several tiny ones he would make as practice in his bedroom, required him to be aware of exactly what the shape and dimensions of his protected target were. If he was off, the shield would be short, leaving a portion of whatever he aimed to keep safe exposed.

It never occurred to him that he might not have the strength to make that large of a shield.

He simply made it.

Taking in a long, steadying breath, he slowly exhaled and called on a large shield to rise around the buildings. And before his eyes, indigo shields crept across the structures. Over walls and doors and windows. A massive shield wall formed in a moment's time, making a barrier for the bulk of Oxford's buildings.

Assuming that where Erador and Ryder stared was where their enemies were coming from, Skylar had effectively managed to make a massive wall that would keep any creatures or Caligans from getting through.

A self-satisfied smile came to his face, and he let out a small laugh.

He turned to Streya, his mouth open to ask a question, but he could do nothing beyond smile at her.

Because she wore a proud look on her face and that warm smile was still there.

"That's golden—"

A pulse hit the air, and she shot her attention toward the noise. All of that warmth she had was gone in an instant, replaced with gritted teeth and a glare.

Skylar's heart lurched into his throat at the sight of her change.

"Given how inexperienced you are, that could be called impressive," a smooth male voice said.

Stuttering his eyes to the speaker, Skylar was met with the sight of a man who looked every bit a problem. From his crooked grin, orange-gold eyes, tilted head, assured stance, and blood-stained leather boots, to his deep V-neck shirt and branded scar on his collarbone, this unknown man held no fraction of concern or fear.

He smirked to Streya.

Erador charged without warning, a surging mass of gold around his form as he moved to slam a blow into the unknown man.

And in the blink of an eye, the man disappeared into gray dust.

Skylar's gut clenched, and he could feel his lungs go tight.

Erador stumbled into the fading dust and, before he could whip around, the unknown man appeared in another pulse of noise and flash of gray dust, landing a harsh kick against Erador.

The hit was so hard, it sent Erador sailing, crashing through a stone wall across the street at alarming speed.

Skylar had never witnessed his Zaheri in combat. There had been one training session where he had seen Streya and Erador spar. But beyond that, he'd always assumed they were untouchable.

They were his protectors, weren't they?

And less than two minutes into the engagement with their enemy, Erador had been sent sailing by a brutal kick.

It wasn't simply that Erador had been hit. It was the strength behind their attacker's kick, and the fact that he hadn't used his energy to land the blow. He'd simply kicked Erador.

Just how strong was their attacker?

"Get back!" Streya yelled as she yanked Skylar behind her.

As Skylar fumbled over his stiff legs and started to fall, a furious growl from Ryder was cut short by another pulse of noise.

What was this guy?

And why hadn't Skylar been told that hybrids could *teleport?*

A gold shield flashed across Streya and Skylar.

"Aw ... aren't you trying be clever, little girl," the man said with another sly smirk as he landed on top of her shield. The pressure from his boots made a more vibrant gold, skittering away like one of those pressure electro-magnetic toy things you could buy in novelty shops.

The mysterious man disappeared in a pulse and landed behind Streya. Inside her shield.

On impulse, Skylar flung his hand out toward her, and an indigo shield flashed against her side as she turned to the intruder.

The Caligan's intended blow of gray energy met Skylar's shield.

As it impacted and the man bounced back from the recoil, Skylar felt his brain scream, *Pain!*

Faintly, he heard a cracking and, half a second later, Streya's golden shield broke into shards that surged on their attacker.

Skylar fell to his knees and trembled a little as his senses swayed.

Ira leaped over their attacker and pushed a domed shield around his bemused form, gracefully pushing off the top of the egg-shaped shield and fleeing before the shield smashed and imploded.

But their attacker was nowhere to be found as the shards of broken shield dove inward. Just gray dust.

Erador was a dozen feet or so away from them, on his feet. He furiously punched the air, swiping at gray dust. Laughter bounced around him.

"Gotta try harder than that," the Caligan teased as he continued to dodge by basically evaporating into the air.

Shaking his head, Skylar struggled to his feet. His shield still stood, though Streya was nowhere near it by now.

Ira stood next to him, her hands up and golden energy concentrated in her fists.

Ryder and Streya were focusing on new enemies appearing. Not a large number of opposition, Skylar felt, given what this one guy was capable of. He saw a couple mono-horned bratak'ra, a handful of werewolves, and a bunch of gray energy wielding people—Caligans.

The beasts were larger than he had imagined. *Which is stupid*, he thought. *Ryder's about the same height.*

Streya spiraled into the air, propelled by her abruptly appearing wings. Golden energy swirled out from her form, slashing at their enemies. Ryder took out werewolves and bratak'ra with tenacity and alarming speed for his bulk.

Focusing on the still-standing shield he'd used to protect Streya, Skylar noticed a spiderwebbed impact mark, he presumed from the hit that the teleporting man had landed. The shield swirled indigo, more translucent in some areas than others. He'd managed to, it seemed, fortify the shield most heavily where the man had punched.

Maybe his instincts were really good.

Whipping his gaze over to Erador's growling fury, Skylar glared.

The teleporting man was playing with Erador. Every glimpse of him that Skylar got, the guy had his hands in his pockets and wore a self-assured smirk. Meanwhile, Erador now held his energy-infused battle axe, the blade glowing with increasing intensity the longer it was in Erador's grasp, as if it were showcasing Erador's frustration.

Skylar didn't have much time. He'd have to be fast.

Blink-of-an-eye fast.

He glanced to his cracked shield. His instinct had worked there. Perhaps it would come through for him here, too.

Snapping to Ira, he yelled, "How do I make a shield do the shard thing?"

Ira flinched at the tenacity in Skylar's voice. "W-what?"

"Streya made her shield crack or something. How did she do it? How did you do it?"

"Don't even think about it, boy," a dark voice spat right next to him. A crackling accompanied it.

A sharp shiver rattled up Skylar's back, and his skin grew goosebumps.

Ira's eyes widened in fear for a split-second before she threw her arms down at her sides.

There was a flash of gold, a blast of noise, and a rush of air, the force of which blew Skylar and Ira a few feet away, scraping against the ground harshly.

Stumbling upright hastily, Skylar threw his hands about to try to clear the dust around them. Every swipe of his right arm sent a jarring pain along his side. A stinging pain shook his left leg, but he ignored it even as he continued to falter on his footing. This guy was hard to see with full visibility. This wouldn't help them at all. And Skylar felt his visibility was absolutely terrible.

He couldn't seem to stop tilting here and there. It was as though a chunk of his eyesight was blocked. He couldn't feel the cracked shield anymore. It must've broken. Did that have something to do with his impaired vision?

Panic hit his chest, and he swung his arm across himself and Ira, intending to make a curved shield around them.

A pulse hit the air nearby, and the mysterious attacker slammed into Ira. She let out a small cry of pain, cowering on the ground underneath a straining golden shield that pulsed gold from her chest, into her arm and, seemingly, into her shield.

Their attacker's arms were coated in gray energy as he pushed his fist into her shield, pressing her tighter against the hard ground.

"C'mon; don't shut me out, sweetheart." He chuckled.

A second later, Ira's shield broke, and she let out a yelp of pain.

In an instant, the man's energy was gone from his arms as he snatched the ribbon from her neck, twining it in his fingers. "Seems this flimsy thing means something to you."

"Leave her alone!" Skylar spat with a glare.

There had to be a way to make his shield into a weapon! He'd seen Streya do it!

He flung his hands, but all that happened was his shield completed the circle around them.

Their attacker laughed as Skylar whipped his gaze around at the shield angrily. "Don't know what you're doing, huh?"

"Bloody shut it!" Skylar yelled and raised his fist.

What was he going to do? Punch this guy? Erador couldn't do that!

In a flash, their attacker snatched him by the throat and slammed him against his shield. "Oh, are you gonna protect her, boy?" he crooned with a condescending smirk.

Furiously swiping at the teleporter's arm, Skylar grimaced and kicked. The bottom of his shoes barely scraped the man's chest.

The teleporter ducked just before a golden attack sliced his shoulder. Without hesitating, he tightened his grip on Skylar's throat and threw him at Streya. The British teen sailed through his shield, and he felt it break around him, creating a hole for his body.

"Skylar!" Streya screamed in an unbidden way. Her wings pushed, and she caught him in her grasp before he smashed into the ground.

Another pulse hit the air, and Skylar looked up in time to see a gray energy attack, formed like a scythe blade, bearing down on them. The teleporter was above it, his hands swirling in motion as though directing the sharp attack.

Erador let out a yell of wrath as he leaped over them and smashed his energy-trailing battle axe into the teleporter.

Their enemy gritted his teeth as he was sent crashing into the trees so quickly he couldn't teleport before hitting them.

Landing in a protective stance in front of his teammates, Erador seethed, "You want some? Come and get it, Akeno!" He pointed his battle axe at the felled trees in a tight grip. "Stop bounding around like a cursed leaf and face me!"

"Erador, stop!" Streya commanded.

Skylar gagged as he held his bruising neck. He winced and let out a whine of pain as Streya gently took hold of his side to help him up.

Fear ghosted her features as she asked, "That hurts?"

"Yeah," Skylar wheezed out as he grazed his fingers across his side. A sharp breath escaped him as his body screamed in flinching pain that radiated up his torso. "How ...? How'd I ...?"

Ira ran to them and said, "Take it easy. You should sit down." There was a wide tear along her jacket sleeve where her forearm had braced her shield earlier. The red ribbon she usually had around her neck was clutched in her small fist.

"Sit down?" Ryder growled. "This is no place to rest!"

Clenching his jaw as he glared at the trees, Erador griped, "He's right. We need to get out of here. Get to a less populated area."

Skylar had never seen Ira glare. She'd always been smiles and calm. Seeing her glare at Erador made him stutter back a bit.

"Skylar has fractured some of his ribs, at the very least! He needs time to heal!"

The British teen paled. He had fractured ribs?

How? It wasn't like he'd been hit!

Letting out a sigh, Streya said, "No, they're right. He'll have to heal as we go."

"Heal?" Skylar sputtered. "How'd I fracture my ribs!" He hopped to his feet and had to stagger himself to solid footing.

"I told you you should've taught him about what happens when shields break," Erador shot to Ira.

"It was next in his training! It isn't my fault he hasn't been permitted to enhance his skills!" Ira snapped.

Streya took hold of Skylar's arm and began to pull him toward the train station. "C'mon; we have to go."

"Go where?" Skylar asked. "Stop. Stop!" He ripped his arm free and shot accusing looks to his Zaheri. "How did I fracture my ribs?"

"Your body will reflect the damage your shields take when they break," Ira said quietly, drawing her hands in as she shrank.

"What?" Skylar hushed as his head went a little fuzzy.

Wearing a look of worry, Streya started to say, "Skylar, we have to—"

"What's going on!" Skylar yelled louder than he'd intended. He didn't mean to glare. He didn't mean to sound so angry. But in that moment, he was getting an awful feeling. One he'd felt before.

Had they ...

His chest went tight, and his ribs ached their damaged state.

"We're under attack, that's what's going on," Erador said plainly, sounding a little annoyed.

"I bloody see that," Skylar said darkly, still wearing a glare.

"We'll explain everything—"

Ira whipped her wide eyes to her Team Leader. "Everything?"

"—in a bit, but first we have to get to safety," Streya continued without getting caught by Ira's surprise.

Skylar's mouth was screwed shut as fear prickled his heart. His hands fisted at his sides. He wanted to do as she said, because a part of him acknowledged that it was the wise thing to do, but questions were mounting rapidly in his mind.

He'd trusted them ...

Pushing a pang of sorrow down with a gulp, he conceded a little cuttingly, "Fine."

Ira gently reached out to him, and he flinched away from her usually comforting touch.

When he turned to her, she said, "You have to lower your shields before we leave."

Doing his best to rein in his frustration at his lack of understanding, he let out a huff. "How do I do that?"

Ryder's ears flattened as he growled, "We're wasting time."

"He should lower them before we leave. Elders know what would happen if we left and these were still standing," Streya commanded to the grovix.

His ears still flat against his head, Ryder snarled, "There are sirens approaching."

"What?" Skylar asked as he whipped his attention to Ryder.

Erador looked around, his gaze distant. After a second, he looked to Streya. "He's right. Coming from the south."

Before anyone could say anything else, Ira took hold of Skylar's hand to get his attention. "You have to imagine them disappearing. It'll cut the connection between your energy and their creation. It's just like with the smaller shields you've made before."

Skylar's stomach shook, creating enough of a tremble that it reminded him of his sore ribs. He looked to his side in concern.

"It won't hurt you."

The sharp way he looked back to Ira made the smaller woman step back. "You said disappearing," he whispered back. "Like dissolving, or something else?"

"However you need to tell your shields they've done their job."

"There are lots of ways to do it, and none of them are wrong," Streya added.

For a brief moment, Skylar truly despised his father.

He should have known all of this *before* today. Before they had gotten attacked.

Focusing his attention on the large shield barring enemies from the bulk of Oxford's buildings, Skylar found himself glaring a little. Like he was furious with his own shields more than anything else. But no, he wasn't. They'd done their job. He could see small areas where the shield had been impacted by attacks and cracks were left behind.

Imagining the shield becoming a vapor, it slowly disappeared and evaporated into the air. Indigo mist flitted in the breeze.

The screech of sirens broke around them, and they all spun to attention. Cars boxed them in. A larger van stopped in front of them. The royal guard's emblem was emblazoned on the vehicle, flags to designate them as official royal-duty cars sat near the sideview mirrors.

Erador raised his battle axe, and Ryder bristled with a growl.

He wasn't thrilled with them at that moment, but he couldn't let any of his Zaheri do anything stupid.

Skylar darted to them and said, "Wait, no."

"What do you mean no?" Erador asked angrily.

A clicking tone sounded before a man's voice called over a speaker, "Put your weapons down and put your hands in the air! We have orders to take you into custody for endangering a member of the royal family."

"What?" Streya asked with an indignant scrunch of her face.

"That's not true!" Ira squeaked, fidgeting with her hands.

Skylar's gaze clicked unblinkingly at various points.

Great. Bloody fantastic.

Someone had alerted the royal guard that he was in danger, and they now assumed his Zaheri were the cause of it all.

This day was buggered.

"We've gotta go along with it, guys," Skylar whispered.

"Why?" Streya asked as Ryder let out a furious rumble.

"They'll take us to London. Charles is there. He'll be able to help us clear the misunderstanding."

"What misunderstanding?" Erador asked with a glare.

"Put the weapons down *now*," the intercom-voice said again.

Skylar spoke quickly, "Look, some wanker called them and said I was in danger. All they see is you guys armed and a little ragged, and, well, Ryder—"

"What's that mean?" Ryder asked with an angry snarl.

"—and a bunch of dead things lying about, and here I am with you. To the best of their knowledge, you're the ones who mean to hurt me."

"But that's not true," Ira reiterated.

"We know that," Skylar said as he gestured to them, "but they don't. If we retaliate, it'll just make it all worse."

Her shoulders falling a bit, Streya let out a sigh. "We should do as he says."

"Streya, you sure?" Erador asked with a wary glance to the vehicles surrounding them.

"I think we can make a run for it," Ryder muttered.

"Charles can help us, and then we can get things sorted and"—a frown came to Streya's face as she looked to Skylar—"and prepare for the next attack."

Skylar's eyes widened.

"This was too few for a full-scale attack," she whispered to the teen. "They'll be back, with greater numbers."

Looking over his shoulder at the royal guard, Skylar let out a sigh. "Then we better get to London now so this can all get settled."

Erador clenched his jaw as he set his battle axe on the ground. "I get why we're doing it, but I still think this is a bad idea."

"There's no good options right now, Erador," Ira said as she slowly raised her hands.

The humans surged forward and ripped Skylar away from his Zaheri. "Wait—you don't understand!" he called as cuffs were slapped onto Streya's, Ira's, and Erador's wrists. Someone moved to try to muzzle Ryder, only for him to lash out and snap his large maw in warning.

"Don't touch me!" Ryder growled.

Several people shot back.

Erador broke the cuffs easily and snatched Ryder's scruff, keeping him from attacking any of the humans.

A few of the guardsmen trembled at Erador's nonchalant nature to breaking free.

"We won't hurt you, but it would be best to not bother with Ryder," Streya said calmly.

She was met with blank stares.

Ryder glared and snarled, "That's me, you blasted humans."

Despite the irregular nature of the Zaheri, the commanding officer said, "Load them up. They'll be London's problem soon."

Before Skylar could try to go with his Zaheri, someone snatched his shoulder and shoved him into a car. In a few seconds, he was squished between two armed, burly guardsmen. He managed to get his phone out of his pocket before he sank into the seat and the car began to rumble quickly along the road.

He swallowed hard as he opened his phone and tried to figure out how to word what had happened to Charles in a text.

This day was completely buggered.

Chapter Five

THE MONSTER'S NEPHEW

Akeno leaned against the trunk of the tree, completely unfazed by the hit he'd taken from Erador. His shirt was torn up a little from the attack, yet he appeared otherwise unscathed. From his vantage point, he could easily see what was transpiring for his targets.

Rounded up by humans. How pathetic, he thought with a small scoff.

This was the best these Zaheri could muster? His master wasn't going to be pleased if the First Human-Born proved to be as useless.

He was already disappointed for the rest of his task. This group was going to be so easy to squash. It left him little enjoyment. Toying with Berserkers like Erador was only fun for a short while. Seeing them break into furious attacks, kicks, and punches that didn't land did entertain, but became boring too quickly.

At least there were two women for him to play with. That would be fun. And that dumb beast of a grovix was made for a muzzle. It would be kind of fun to watch it writhe in pitiful attempts to break free from his tethers as Akeno laid the group to waste.

He caught the expression on the Second Human-Born's face as the boy was shoved into a car and smirked to himself. *Interesting.*

Not only was the boy woefully untrained, but he appeared completely in the dark, based on the snippets of the argument Akeno had caught. And now he looked toward his Zaheri as though he didn't trust them.

That was enticing.

A young woman stumbled out of a nearby building, her eyes wide with fear as she surveyed the carnage. While the Zaheri had been no match for him, they'd done a fair job of wiping out the meager group that had accompanied Akeno for distraction's sake. It left quite the display of battlefield horror for this young woman to behold.

He stepped onto the walkway. "You okay, little lady?" he asked with a smirk.

She sucked in a surprised gasp and tore her attention away from the death littering the area, looking to him.

A glint filled Akeno's orange-gold eyes.

"Wh-who are you?" She trembled.

With a shrug, he said, "Consider me the calvary."

"Oh, thank God!" she cried as she ran to him for comfort.

Akeno gained a devilish grin as he offered mock sympathy. "There, there. Don't cry, pretty thing." His arms wrapped around her, and he whispered darkly, "I'll take good care of you."

It would only take a minute for her to regret the decision to run to him.

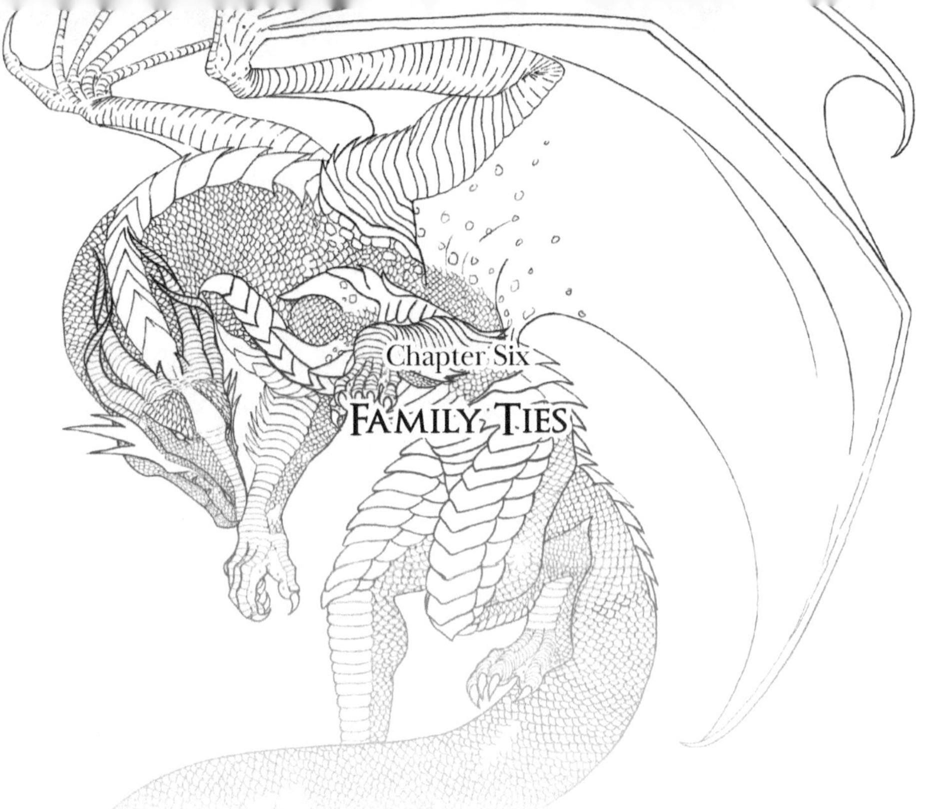

Chapter Six

FAMILY TIES

What do you mean you were attacked??
What happened??
Where are you? Where are your Zaheri?
Are you alright?

Rapid fire questions pinged Skylar's phone, and he ignored the little typing bubble as he did his best to explain what was going on to Charles. He tried to type as quickly as his brother, but his thoughts kept jumbling, and he needed to delete out sections a few times. He didn't do a great job condensing things, and his rambling probably made it harder to decipher on his brother's end.

They were arrested???

Skylar shrank in his seat, trying to guard his phone screen from the men crowding him in the back of the sleek sedan. It seemed neither of the men cared about Skylar's texting, which felt odd to him.

If he'd been attacked and almost taken hostage, why wasn't he being calmed down and told everything was going to be okay? Why did they seem to be apathetic about his communication with others? Why was he being treated almost as though he were the guilty party?

Taking a short breath, he steadied himself and typed out a response to Charles's question.

That's what the captain said. That they're under arrest for intending harm to a member of the royal family.

He was grateful he'd silenced his phone for classes. There were no alert sounds letting anyone know that he was in the middle of a discussion. On the flip side, it made for an awfully quiet car ride, which wouldn't have been a problem if Skylar wasn't alone.

If Streya were here, he could ask her all the questions that kept rolling in his mind.

What the bloody hell was going on?

Sure. Yes. Okay. They were attacked. Obviously by Caliga. Obviously Streya expected this to only be the beginning of their combat troubles.

But that didn't answer anything of importance. At least of importance for Skylar.

Why hadn't they told him that his shields could cause damage to his body when they were hit? Why hadn't they insisted he have one break so he could know what it felt like and how to handle the physical toll it took? Why hadn't they realized that this whole "he needs time to heal" thing might be a bit much to bloody spring on him out of the blue? Why hadn't they explained that shields could break and be used as weapons? Why hadn't they told him that some Caligans were way stronger than others? Why hadn't they said anything about how bloody terrifying dragons were the first time you saw them? Why hadn't they said anything about other bloody abilities that hybrids could have, like bloody teleporting? Why didn't anyone from Agerius come to their aid?

Why did they keep it all from him?

And what in buggery were they going to do now?

Did they just not trust him? Did they think he wasn't smart enough to grasp the concepts of things? Did they think he wasn't strong enough to take on whatever bloody mantel they expected of him? Did they think that somehow keeping him out of the loop was best? Were they embarrassed by him and his lackluster efforts today?

What weren't they telling him?

His phone buzzed, and he glanced at the notification.

Don't worry, Sky. We'll get it sorted. It'll be alright.

Would it?

Skylar gripped his phone and cleared the notification, a frown stuck on his face.

Streya had seemed so proud of him when he had made the large shield, so ... maybe it wasn't that she was disappointed in his skills.

But it still begged the nagging questions of why.

Why hadn't she told him more?

All those days, sitting across from him in the library—bloody hell, even the few times he'd been able to sneak lessons in without his parents knowing—how bloody hard would it have been to say, "By the way Skylar, you should be aware that when shields get hit, the caster suffers injuries in direct correlation to the damage taken by the shield; and if they break by impact, it'll cause more damage?"

Seemed pretty bloody simple.

Why had they been such wankers about it all? Couldn't they have been more transparent? Why hadn't they been? What made them be so tight-lipped?

Was it all because his father had been so adamant about Skylar not training? For the love of God, it wasn't like Skylar objected! So, what was the deal with them keeping things from him?

And why did it feel like there was a whole lot more they weren't saying?

Stewing on it wasn't going to help—he knew that—but the crushing silence gave him little alternative for his thoughts to focus on.

That was until he realized that going to London didn't just mean he'd see Charles. His father would be there, too.

Skylar was gruffly escorted down one of the hallways of the Parliament building, the Palace of Westminster. He was surrounded on all sides by guardsmen who refused to answer any questions he asked.

When they'd arrived, he had noticed that the large, blocky police bus was absent, and he'd snapped, "Where did you take them?" only to be met with chilling silence.

These older men all gave him angry looks, like somehow Skylar was responsible for their predicament.

A part of him felt maybe they were right to believe that.

He was led into one of the large, ornately decorated rooms. When he spun to look at the guard that had not-so-subtly shoved him farther into the room, the older man sternly said, "You're to wait here."

Skylar responded with a small huff of frustration.

And then he was alone. Silence seemed his best companion this past hour or so. It was the last thing he wanted.

Where had they taken his Zaheri? Why wouldn't they bring him to the same location? God help him, hopefully, they weren't at Scotland Yard. Being in a separate building would prove difficult. He couldn't imagine where else they'd be detained.

They had to get out of here! Streya had said another attack would come. That meant that being stuck in London was a terrible idea.

The door opened, and he whipped his attention to it, finding his father and brother stepping into the room. Charles followed their father, giving him a wary look. Meanwhile, their father looked cross and stern.

Forcing the fear of his father's disapproval back with a gulp, Skylar asked, "What's going on? Where are my Zaheri?"

A scowl appeared on his father's face. "That's none of your concern."

"What?" he whispered with a downcast expression.

"You aren't to entangle yourself with this problem any further. Is that clear?" his father commanded.

Despite his faltering courage, Skylar fisted his hands. "Father, you have to listen to me. This isn't the end—"

"That's *enough*, Skylar."

"No, it isn't! You have to listen! They'll come ba—"

"I said, *enough*!"

"Innocent people could get hurt!"

Their father clenched a pocket watch in his grasp and seethed, "Skylar Andrew Mitchell, you will cease speaking immediately."

Charles poked forward tentatively. "Father, Sky has a poi—"

"Silence, both of you!" he thundered, slamming the pocket watch onto the floor, sending it clattering into pieces upon impact. He pointed an accusing finger at Skylar. "This is precisely why I told you to leave those God-forsaken aliens behind! We cannot afford to be caught up in this mess!"

"I didn't have a choice. It's not like I asked for this," Skylar shot back with a faltering glare.

"Then you will leave it immediately! Those bloody beasts will be kept under lock and key for the rest of time, or so help me I will dispose of them myself."

"You can't do that," Skylar said with a scoff and a roll of his eyes—a brazen action for him in his father's presence. "They'd tear you apart."

His father growled over his second comment, his face tight with fury, "You, *boy*, cannot dictate anything upon anyone else."

Even though his father stared at him with utter annoyance and anger, Skylar spoke like he didn't want to shake. "You have to let us go *now*."

Their father might have been a man in his fifties who spent all day sitting at desks and talking politics with people, but that didn't deter him from marching the distance between him and his son. He snatched Skylar by the shirt and threw him roughly into a nearby chair.

Skylar couldn't help but tremble a little as he clutched the arms for stability as his father towered over him.

Behind them, Charles shot forward and held a hand out toward their father's back. "Father, wai—"

"You will stay here until *I* say you can leave," their father spat darkly at his son. "You will *not* see those monsters. You *will* deny any involvement. And you *will* stay out of it. Scotland Yard and the British National Army will see to handling this mess."

Clenching his jaw, Skylar swallowed back his shaking. *Don't cry. Don't cry, you idiot. Don't. Cry.*

This was his father, for the love of God. He shouldn't look at his son with such condemnation.

Though the words shook out of him through gritted teeth, Skylar whispered, "You can't stop me."

Every edge to his father was hard as he sneered at his son, "Yes. I can."

Charles stared at their father in thinly veiled horror.

Skylar's mouth contorted around his fear. "They won't be able to stop it."

Their father scoffed and curled his lip. "So says a child." He turned and walked to the door easily, as if he hadn't just caused terror in his own son. "You are confined to this room under guard. I will get you when this is over."

He snapped his attention to Charles, meeting his eldest son's barely hidden scowl. "Charles, with me."

For a second, Charles stayed put, his expression signaling that he wished daggers could manifest in his grasp.

"*Now.*"

The elder brother's jaw was tight as he said, "Yes, *sir.*"

The Duke of Derbyshire's eyes narrowed before he marched out the door with his shoulders back and his eyes fixed ahead.

Charles strode to his younger brother's side and gave Skylar a squeeze on the shoulder. "I'll be back as soon as possible," Charles quickly hushed to his brother.

A frown had etched into Skylar's face as he looked to his only confidant.

"Charles!" was snapped from the hallway.

Despite himself, Skylar flinched.

With a look of sorrow in his features, Charles whispered, "Stay strong, Sky." He retreated out the door hastily, but his fists were still clenched as he went.

When the door closed with a tomb-like *boom*, Skylar sank into the chair.

Not even a few hours into his first real test of this mess, and he'd already failed. What good was he, if all he'd ever be was trapped by people who had no concept of the severity of things?

Separated from his Zaheri. Closed off from his brother. Trapped in some miserable room.

If he was meant to be a hero, someone had chosen wrong.

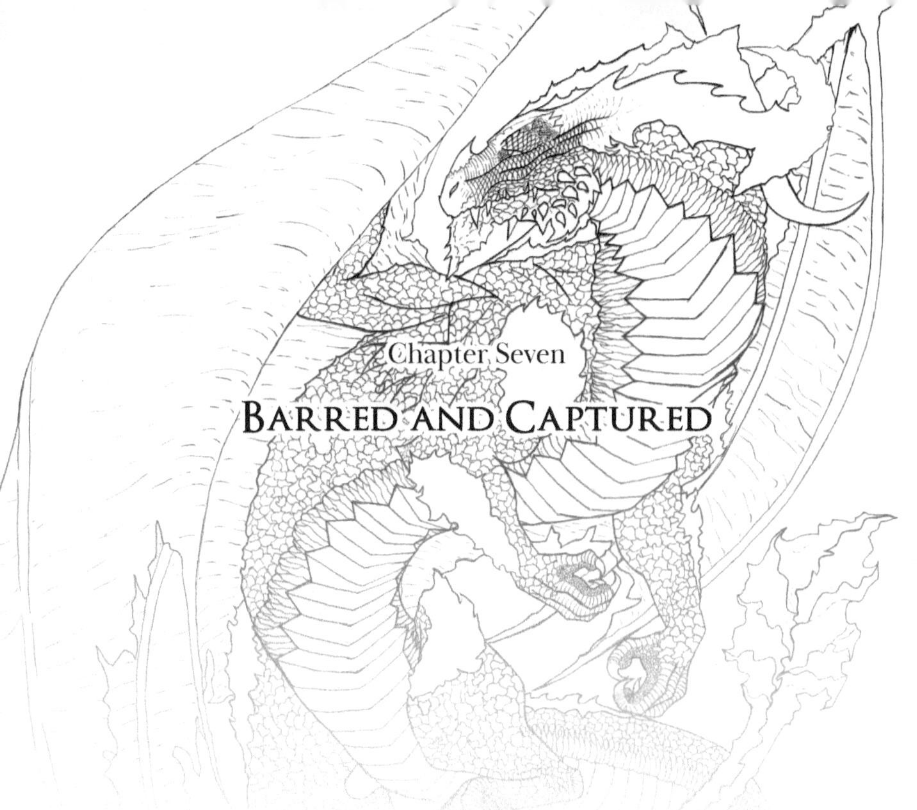

Chapter Seven

BARRED AND CAPTURED

Erador paced the cell, his jaw tight and fists clenched. He kept crossing and uncrossing his arms, glaring at the floor, the wall, back to the floor again.

Ryder's bulk made the space too tight, forcing the large grovix to restrict his pacing to one or two steps before he had to stomp back again. He kept stamping his feet like a horse, angrily growling and bristling, his muscles tensing all along his massive frame.

Meanwhile, Ira was a small, unassuming ball in the corner, clutching her red thread in her trembling fingers. She sat on the bench in their cell, her shoulders drawn in and features awash in confusion.

Streya wanted to say she was unshaken, that she was confident and steady, ready for whatever was about to happen. That she knew exactly what to do and how to get themselves out of the predicament they were in.

But she'd be lying.

Yes, she understood that, at the time, Skylar's suggestion to go to London was the best course of action. She could see why the boy had insisted on going along with the police. At the time, it would have only caused further panic if they had stolen Skylar away somewhere. And highly likely, Erador might have killed someone in his protectiveness over the boy.

Here and now, however, she regretted listening to Skylar.

How foolish could she be? Letting Skylar dictate things was beyond insane. She should have listened to her instincts and had Erador snatch Skylar then had them all flee. They could have holed up someplace, talked over things in private, and planned for the next wave.

Because there would be a next wave. And now they were *stuck*.

Sucking in a breath, she tried not to shake. She stepped up to the bars and gripped them tightly before closing her eyes slowly.

What would Tyron do?

Probably bash through the walls, find his Human-Born, and protect them with his life.

Elders, Streya wanted to do that. She wanted to just have Erador rip a hole in the wall behind her, and then tear through the city to find Skylar.

But she had no concrete idea where he was.

Okay, just think, she told herself.

This was London. Skylar had been taken in a different car. He was the son of a duke. They wouldn't throw him in a prison cell, especially if, as she thought, he was being seen as a victim of some terror attack. So, he was probably with Charles, at Parliament.

But if they were seen as terrorists, why had no one come to question them? Why were they simply being detained?

And what if Akeno followed them?

Fear twisted her stomach, and she felt like she might be sick. The impulse to rip a hole in the wall returned.

She couldn't protect Skylar while she was stuck here. And Akeno was a Jumper—walls didn't prohibit him.

What if he stole into Parliament, tore through the building, and killed Skylar while they were stuck here trying to play by the rules?

No, no, no, she told herself. She had to trust that the Elders would protect Skylar right now. *This is daylight incursion. Humans are at stake here. Skylar is safe. I have to trust Skylar is safe.*

Please let Skylar be safe.

"What're we gonna do?" Erador snapped.

Streya clenched her jaw and tried to keep herself calm.

"We can't stay here! Skylar is—"

"Skylar is safe," she said, keeping her back to the fuming warrior so as to give herself the time to gather a stern expression on her face.

A grumble rolled from Ryder as he chuckled darkly. "Sure he is. Nothing says safety like a bunch of politicians."

Streya turned to them as Erador pointed his rigid arm toward the hallway and burst, "He's anything but safe, Streya! Akeno could jump in there—"

"No, he can't," Ira said in her quiet voice.

Everyone snapped their attention to her. She'd been silent the whole way here, and it'd been nearly twenty minutes since they'd been shoved into this cage.

"What do you mean, he can't?" Streya asked then opened her mouth again to continue.

Shaking her head, Ira sucked in a trembling breath. "No, you don't understand. Jumpers have to know where they're going. They have to know the layout of a building if they're going to jump into it. They have to know the route to take to travel to a destination. It's why he and Vorex don't just appear inside Mount Ara or inside people's homes. They only ever appear on the streets, and the larger ones at that. They have to know where they're going, or they risk ending up inside of something, like a wall, or a person even."

Squinting at her, Erador grumbled, "That doesn't make sense."

Ira let out a huff and rolled her eyes, losing some of her fragility. "It makes perfect sense, you loon."

"So, you're saying he'd need to know that Skylar is in Parliament," Streya clarified.

"No, I'm saying he'd need to know that Skylar—or us, for that matter—are in London. Sure, he might have followed us, but I'm certain he couldn't have followed so closely as to remain undetected. And remaining in another dimension to follow us is incredibly difficult." She shrank back. "Or so I've read."

Closing her eyes and shaking her head to wrap her mind around the concept of jumping, Streya waved her hands a bit. "So, the chances of him being a threat to Skylar right now?"

"Likely slim," Ira said, starting to sound a little more like herself. The tremble was gone from her voice, and she'd stopped shaking. However, the red fabric was still tight in her grasp.

Angrily crossing his arms over his chest, Erador slouched.

A growl rippled through Ryder. "So, what are we gonna do? We can't stay here."

"Obviously," Streya said with a nod. "But we can't just break a hole in the wall and go hunting for Skylar. We're in London—it's crowded and a lot of people could get hurt if we just started tearing through the city. We'd only cause more harm than good if we went outside of things to find Skylar."

"He needs to know what's going on," Ira said. "It's obvious that he feels a scale's been ripped off."

"'Cause it has," Erador grumbled, still tense and glaring.

Streya had been thinking about that. While she'd briefly mentioned that she intended to tell Skylar everything, they as a team hadn't discussed it. She wasn't prone to making a decision without their input, but in this situation, she felt they needed to divulge everything they could to Skylar.

With how human communication worked, the chances of the teen remaining in the dark about the fact that there were more Human-Borns were insanely small. And she couldn't risk him finding out some other way. They had to be honest with him. They had to ensure he still trusted them.

Elders, she hoped he still trusted them.

What if he didn't? What if he felt betrayed and abandoned?

She wanted to smack herself. She should've been more transparent from the beginning. Given his home life, he'd see any lack of information as betrayal. And given how cold he was to people he didn't know or trust ...

A new fear tangled in her heart.

What if he refused to trust them? What if he felt that they'd become just like his family? Did he resent them now? Would he even come to see them? If she could go back in time ...

Rolling her eyes a little, she nearly hit herself. If she could go back in time, she'd change so many things. And one of them would be the choice to listen to the Council's command regarding keeping the Human-Borns in the dark.

Streya had noticed how mature Skylar was from the instant they'd met. He wasn't some brat who couldn't handle the reality of things. It wasn't like he was emotionally unstable and would have started screaming and throwing a tantrum, or run off to find the others. He was a bright young man with solid reasoning skills.

She should have just ignored the Council's command, trusted her instincts, and told Skylar everything months ago.

But ... that's not what Tyron would have done. He would've followed the Council's command. He might have hated it, but he wouldn't have outright disobeyed the Council.

A small part of her snickered at her, as if saying, *"You stupid girl. Constantly comparing what he'd do rather than just doing what you think is right."*

"Streya?" Ira asked in a small voice, pulling the Team Leader from her winding thoughts.

Before Streya could respond to Ira's concern, Ryder bristled and growled, "That's it! I've had it with this stupid tiny space! And if you're not going to give us direction—"

"No!" Streya hollered, reaching her smaller hands toward the hulking beast as he prepared to launch himself at the bars.

In a flash, a golden dome appeared around the grovix. Ryder bashed his face against it and howled. Against the small confinement of the shield, he threw Ira a murderous glare. "Release me!"

Erador rolled his eyes and grumbled, "The pup has a point."

"No, we listen to Skylar," Streya said with finality. "He said that he and Charles would be able to sort this. It's only been twenty minutes. We can wait."

"We can't wait, Streya!" Erador fumed. "Another wave could fall any second now!"

"I know that!" she threw back. "But we have to consider collateral damage of every action we take! Including sitting still and trusting Skylar!"

"And more importantly," Ira said, forcing them all to look her way, "we have to rebuild Skylar's faith in us. From his perspective, we've lied to him."

"We haven't lied to him," Erador griped with a roll of his eyes.

"From his perspective, we have," Ira reiterated. "The boy has grown up in a world devoid of trust and love. We were his only respite. And now we appear identical to his family."

"We aren't!" Ryder barked. His fur bristled from the crown of his head down to his spine.

Streya sighed. "We know that. But Skylar ..." Her shoulders fell. She wanted to frown but fought against it. "Sky's had a rough go for a family. We didn't reveal everything to him, and that's going to make him feel betrayed. So"—she straightened—"we're going to trust him. Because that's what he asked us to do."

"Streya," Erador said through gritted teeth.

"We trust him, Erador. That's final."

A rumbling breath escaped the dark-skinned warrior as he crossed his arms, gripping his biceps.

Ira gave him a confused stare. "Why are you so agitated?"

Flinging his arms out, Erador burst, "They took my axe!"

"Oh *Elders*," Streya groused. "*That's* what has you so bent?"

"It's *my axe!*"

She wanted to laugh but knew that would only stoke Erador's fury. She gave Ira a small smirk instead, finding the Archivist shaking her head as if saying, "*really?*"

They would get through this. Somehow.

They just had to trust Skylar.

DESTRUCTION WALKING

Throwing a woman's lifeless body into a ditch, Akeno stepped into the Fifth Dimension and traversed back to the portal. Five girls in two hours. That'd been fun.

Only four of them were dead, though. And only one of them he'd thrown into another dimension.

It'd been so long since he'd watched the delicious explosion of a body as it entered a dimension it didn't belong in. He should have let himself enjoy that more. He'd definitely let the passing time stop him from making sure the first one screamed.

Reaching the portal, he took a moment to survey the town at the foot of the hill. He needed a clear layout of the tiny hamlet. It sparked old memories of some of the little pockets of towns from his youth. Which did an excellent job igniting an old fury from the past and why vengeance ran thick in his veins.

Akeno never particularly liked how the red portal felt when it flashed into his grip. It made his fingers twitch and a numbness claw at his forearm. He always shook it off, but that didn't mean he delighted in the unsettling feeling.

Pain wasn't bad. It could be pleasurable, in fact. But irritability? Useless. Annoying.

He jumped to the basement hallway for time's sake. The dalliances he'd allowed himself on Earth had delayed him, and the Master might not take kindly on it. Though, if anyone would understand and dismiss Akeno's actions, it would be the Master.

Another thing that would annoy the other generals. It made him positively thrilled that so many of them were so convinced he got preferential treatment. He didn't, of course. A brainless Backwater could see that. Still, so many of the others would gripe and moan about Akeno's supposed "free pass."

No one got free passes. No one got special treatment. No one got second chances. If Akeno stepped out of line, he'd be struck down swiftly. There would be no chance to beg. No chance to appeal to the Master. They all served at his pleasure, not the other way around.

The other generals were all just that stupid. Kelek especially.

Darkness, if the other man hadn't been such a devout mouthpiece of the Master's deity-like status, Akeno was almost certain the Master would have cut him down a long time ago. Especially after the massive screw up that cost them Morgan.

He would never say it out loud, but Akeno still blamed Kelek for what happened to her.

Truthfully, he felt the Master did, too.

Striding into the war room, he found his uncle's sharp gaze analyzing the map on the table.

Akeno bowed low. "Master."

"What did you find?"

"Streya's a defiant little bitch."

Cregorous' brow rose in mock surprise. "Shocker." He straightened. "The Second?"

"Ill prepared," Akeno answered with a roll of his eyes. "I'm so bored. A brute, a brick of useless information, a pup, and Streya. It's such a dull challenge."

A scowl fixed onto Cregorous' face. "I don't care."

Letting out a small sigh, Akeno shrugged. "The Second will crumble. He's untrusting of his Zaheri and clearly has no training."

Shooting Akeno a glare, Cregorous asked snidely, "Then what in darkness kept you?"

"Sorry, Master," Akeno said, averting his gaze a bit. "I couldn't help myself. The human women were so"—a sick grin twisted his face, and he let out a pleasured sigh—"enticing."

Cregorous scoffed before gaining a smirk.

Pointing to the map on the table, Akeno added, "The portal should be moved. They were gathered by humans and taken to London."

"Gathered by humans?" Cregorous asked incredulously. He shook his head and grumbled, "This had better not be a waste of nineteen years." He leaned over the map, his shoulders tightening as he studied it. "Very well. London, it is. Tear the city apart."

With a bow, Akeno said, "Master," and jumped back to his chambers. If he hadn't taken his fill of the human women, he would seek out a mistress. But, as he'd had his fun, he didn't see the point.

Food sounded good. He was awful hungry after his wickedly delicious stint on Earth.

As he snatched a servant and gave him orders to bring food, Akeno wondered if the humans would ever find the bodies.

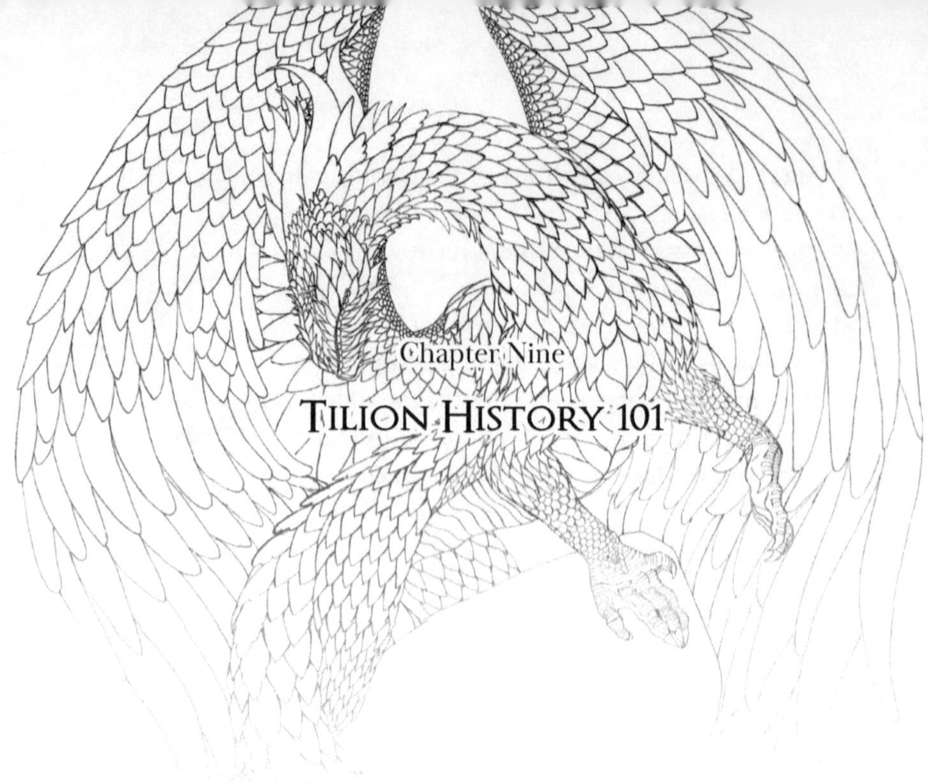

TILION HISTORY 101

An hour later, Charles snuck into the room where Skylar had been left. For a split-second, he wondered if his little brother had simply broken out and fled.

Panic hit the elder Mitchell son. Skylar didn't know where his Zaheri were, and they were the only people who could keep him safe.

"Sky?" he asked a little more frantically than he'd intended.

There was a brief pause before a quiet, defeated voice sounded from the corner, "I'm here."

Charles came around the sofa and found Skylar in the darkest corner of the room, his body tucked into the fetal position. The younger man gripped his arms, keeping them locked around his knees as he stared blankly into space.

Gently, Charles eased to kneel next to him and whispered, "You all right?"

For a second, Charles could see the tears welling in Skylar's eyes. It cut into his chest. He wanted nothing more than to pummel their father.

Skylar pinched his eyes shut and shook his head before he opened his eyes again, glaring at his knees. "No."

Charles would've been gobsmacked if his brother had said, "Oh yeah, I'm fine! Let's go get lunch now."

Patting his arm, Charles said, "C'mon; let's get you some food."

"I'm not hungry," Skylar muttered, resting his head against his legs.

The elder brother gently squeezed Skylar's arm until his younger brother looked to him. A determined look was in Charles's gaze as he said, "Sky, you need to eat something."

Though Skylar frowned, he let out a sigh and stood. Blindly, he followed Charles out of the room.

As they passed the guards stationed there, Charles held up his hand. "Just going out for a bite, chaps. I'll have him back within two hours."

Sharing a look, the guards eyed Charles suspiciously.

"Trust me; I'd sooner die than do something to get my father more irate."

"Fine," one of the guards relented, wearing a perturbed stare. "Two hours, you hear?"

"Cheerio," Charles said with a smile as he gently shoved Skylar down the hall.

Once they were outside, Skylar mumbled, "I'm really not hungry, Charles."

"It'd be a miracle if you were," Charles said as he pulled his brother down the street. "C'mon; we have to hurry."

"Hurry where?" Skylar asked glumly.

"Scotland Yard."

Skylar gave his brother a confused look.

"I found where they're keeping your Zaheri. We only have so much time until the guards change and my friends can't get us through."

Light sparked in Skylar's eyes. "Are we going to break them out?"

Wearing an apologetic look, Charles said, "That'd get us both killed. Or exiled. I can't pull that off."

"Then wh—"

"Something tells me you need to talk to them, and that they need to talk to you."

Skylar stuffed his hands in his pockets. "I doubt that."

"Sky, come off it."

"I promised them we'd be able to get it sorted if we came here." His eyes were glued to the sidewalk as they went.

Charles kept a grip on his arm, guiding him along faster than his tired pace. "We will, I promise. We'll get them out of there."

"Really? How?" Skylar snapped a frustrated look at his brother. "Father's basically going to imprison me for the rest of time. My Zaheri *are* locked up. And meanwhile, there's another looming attack."

Charles swung a panicked expression to him before pulling a determined look in his eyes and facing forward. He readjusted his grip on Skylar's jacket to keep them moving down the sidewalk. "You're sure about that?"

"Streya practically said it was guaranteed."

Clenching his jaw, Charles muttered, "Then we truly have little time."

The knowledge that he was going to see his Zaheri sent dueling emotions in Skylar's chest. Frustration and relief collided, and he felt his lungs stiffen. God knew he wanted to see them, make sure they were okay, hear any sort of affirmation that they thought things would work out all right. But on the opposite side of the coin sat his stewing anger over their silence in regard to his abilities.

By the time they reached Scotland Yard, Skylar felt he might throw up.

As they entered, a woman around Charles's age approached them with a nod before leading them down a hallway. "You're late," she hushed to Charles.

He offered a sideways smile. "Breaking out of Parliament is harder than you think."

She coughed a laugh. "You do it every day at lunch easily enough."

"That's different, and you know it, Taylor."

"Sorry, Lord-in-Training Mitchell," she said with a cheeky grin, and he rolled his eyes at the jab. "Figured you were due some levity."

Skylar's brow pulled together as he took in the display. "You two know each other?"

"Nope. First time meeting the chap," Taylor said.

Despite his misery, Skylar managed a smirk at her upbeat demeanor.

Charles let out a small sigh as Taylor pointed to Skylar victoriously.

"Aha! See, I told you I could make him smile," she said with a small jab of her elbow into Charles's side.

"Yes, you did," Charles replied dryly.

"That's twenty quid."

She actually reminded Skylar a bit of Streya when she was carefree, which wasn't often. Taylor had darker blonde hair and a rounder face than Streya, but her build was similar to the Agerian's.

He wondered if perhaps Charles secretly liked this woman and was only distracted by Streya.

"Taylor, enough fun. We're on borrowed time here."

"You aren't kidding." Taylor raised her brow. "Everyone's talking about it. You know this isn't—"

"Not yet," Charles hissed to her.

She looked to Skylar and nodded once. "Right. Sure. Anyway, you know Interpol's coming, right?"

"What?"

"Just heard the whisper of it. Everyone's gawking."

Charles ruffled his hair and grumbled, "That's ... not great."

"Look, I'll do what I can to help."

A knowing grin sparked to Charles's face. "And this is as much as you can help."

"Admittedly, you're right. But hey, it still was comforting to hear, right?"

"Only marginally."

"Marginally is better than not-at-all."

She had a point. It wasn't much of one, but it was a point.

They took a brief stop by a simple cafeteria where Taylor snagged a handful of protein bars and bottles of water.

When they came to a door guarded by two men, the guys smirked at Charles.

"To what do we owe the pleasure?" one of them asked.

"Graham, now isn't the time," Charles said.

"Cheerio then. We can get you forty-five at most."

"It'll have to do. Thanks, mates."

Skylar gave his brother a confused look as they stepped through the door. "How do you know these people?"

Wearing a giddy grin, Taylor said, "He never told you about the darts incident?"

Charles gave her a scowl.

She patted his cheek. "It's a great story. You should tell him some time, Charles." Taylor continued down the hall, leaving the two brothers alone.

Skylar looked to Charles and asked, "The darts incident?"

"For the love of Saint Peter, can we please discuss this another time?" Charles said quickly, shoving Skylar down the hall.

The surreal levity of the last ten minutes had Skylar's mind reeling as he remembered why they were at Scotland Yard. *Right. The fate of the world stuff. How could I forget?* Skylar thought.

The trio came to a large cell where the Zaheri were being kept.

A golden shield was domed around Ryder, and the grovix appeared to be shedding in droves. Erador gripped his muscled arms tightly, his jaw was clenched as he sat on the hard bench. Streya paced. Ira seemed fine, sitting with her hands drawn in her lap.

Streya spun around to them and ran to the bars, gripping them in desperation. "Skylar! Thank the Elders you're okay. Where did they take you? Are you all right?"

"I ... I'm fine," Skylar whispered.

Taylor held out the protein bars and bottled water. "I brought you guys something to eat. Figured you might need it."

"We need to get out of this blasted hole," Erador growled.

"Release this shield so I can make that happen!" Ryder snapped at Ira.

"That won't help us," Ira chided.

Erador shot to his feet and pointed an accusing finger at Taylor. "Bring me back my battle axe, lady! It's mine, and I want it back!"

With a shake of her head, Taylor asked, "What battle axe?"

Releasing a groan of fury, Erador grumbled, "I swear by the Elders, if those lousy humans don't return my axe—"

"Erador!" Ira hollered as she stood.

He turned to her, his fists clenched.

She pointed at the portion of the bench he had been seated at previously. "Sit. Down."

Like a toddler, Erador stomped back to the bench and plopped down, angrily crossing his arms over his chest.

"Yeah ... I'm gonna leave them to you, Lord-in-Training," Taylor said with a smile as she patted Charles's arm. "Uh, don't break them out."

"Oh, thank you for that direction, Taylor. I fully intended to just ignore the security cameras, and the many police, and help them escape from Scotland Yard. But now that you've given me instruction, by golly, I'll not do that," Charles said bitingly.

"Well, someone's in a mood," Taylor said with a playful grin before walking off.

Once they heard the door close at the end of the hall, Erador grumbled, "Now we break out, right?"

"No," Streya said with a glare at the ceiling.

Erador pointed emphatically at the bars to their cell. "It's—they're—it's simple metal! It's not like they're actually keeping us from getting out of here!"

"And how would you intend to become reunited with your precious battle axe if we broke out of this place now?" Ira asked with a pointed look.

Erador went back to sulking.

Quick glancing at the team, Charles asked, "Are you doing all right?"

"We're physically fine," Streya said with a frown. "But Charles, we have to get out of here. Skylar, too. That first encounter was only the beginning of our troubles."

"Skylar said you thought another attack would come."

"It will come," Ira pressed. "It's already been well over two hours. The fact that we haven't been overrun is a spot of the Elders' favor."

Squinting at them, Charles asked, "The Elders?"

"They're ancient and powerful dragons that have given Agerius its law."

Skylar sank a little and looked to the floor.

"What makes you so sure there'll be another attack on Skylar's life?" Charles asked.

Streya clenched the bars a little before she let out a steadying sigh. "The number of enemy fighters we encountered were far too few for a legitimate strike against him. Or us."

"And you're sure he's the target?"

"Of course he's the target," Erador grumbled.

"There's no reason for Caliga to strike at us. Not when he's around," Ryder growled.

Charles looked thoughtful, staring at the middle distance as he pursed his lips.

Inclining her head a little, Streya asked, "What is it?"

For a brief moment, Charles met Streya's gaze before he looked to Skylar. Quietly, he admitted, "This isn't an isolated event."

Skylar's mouth fell open. "What?" he breathed.

"Elders help us," Ira whispered as she sank onto the bench.

Erador snapped to his feet and demanded, "We have to get out of here now! No more waiting!"

"This is bad. This is really, really bad," Ryder said as he started to pace, only to run into the shield obstructing him. "Release me from this blasted prison!" he commanded Ira.

"What haven't you told me?" Skylar suddenly burst before Streya could make a comment about how bad things were.

Everyone flinched at the anger in his tone.

His face was tight and red, his jaw trembling. He shook out a breath as he added, "Multiple attacks? This isn't isolated ...?" His gaze was fixed on Streya's, and she wore a look of scared sorrow. "What ...? What haven't you told me?"

Pulling herself from her fear, Ira stood and quickly made for Streya's side. "Skylar, it isn't that we wanted to keep things from you. We were told to remain quiet about certain things."

"What things?" Skylar bit out.

"Skylar ..." Streya said quietly, and he looked to her with distrust. "You aren't the only Human-Born."

Skylar's stomach fell to his feet.

Okay. *Now* he was going to throw up.

"What?" he hushed as his anger flattened to worry. "Wh ... where are they? Who are they? Are they being attacked, too?"

Streya shook her head. "We don't know where they are, or who they are. We just know that there are seven in total."

"And I doubt you know anything about the multiple incidents," Charles muttered. "Given your reactions."

Spinning his attention to his brother, Skylar asked, "How many other incidents are there?"

Charles held a hand up and gently placed it on Skylar's shoulder. "Take a deep breath, Sky. Okay? I don't know a lot. Just what little I could read before I found out where they were keeping your Zaheri."

"What do you know?" Ira asked, clutching the red ribbon from her neck. It appeared to have been ripped by the teleporter.

Streya's fingers clutched the bars tight.

With a shake of his head, Charles said, "Not much. There are scattered reports of 'pillars of light' across the globe."

"*Pillars of light?*" Skylar asked with a twinge of annoyance at his own lack of understanding.

"The portal," Ira said with a nod.

"Makes sense that humans would struggle with what to call it," Streya agreed. Before Charles could ask for clarification, she added, "It's the gateway to our world. Humans can't see it in its dormant state, and they can't interact with it. We call it the portal."

"It's terribly concerning," Ira hushed. "Multiple attacks at the same time ..."

Erador glared at the floor. "Cregorous must have control of the portal on Tilion."

A low growl rumbled from Ryder.

Silence passed for a few seconds before Charles said, "I can't guarantee they happened at the same time. Timestamps are all over the place, and every article is a 'developing story.' The only countries I know for a fact are confirmed are Japan, England, Australia, and America. There's still a lot of discrepancies for what area of Africa the pillar was seen. Likewise with South America."

"Wait, wait—what?" Skylar asked as he shoved Charles's hand away. "Are you saying this is legitimately global? As in, every continent is affected?"

"Possibly. It's still really unclear."

Sucking in a sharp breath and holding it for a few seconds, Skylar stiltedly turned to his Zaheri. "What ...? What else aren't you telling me?"

Erador flicked his gaze to Ira before he sighed. "We told you about Cregorous."

"Yeah, he's not the one we met earlier. You called that guy Akeno," Skylar accused.

"One thing at a time, Skylar," Streya said carefully. "We'll tell you everything, I promise."

"Streya, are you sure?" Ira whispered.

Streya deflated and closed her eyes. After a few long seconds, she took in a determined breath and said, "He deserves to know. We've kept too much from him as it is. And Elders know we can trust him."

"But the Council—"

"The Council isn't here," Ryder grumbled. "I'm sure that even Alpha Frost and Alpha Blaze would agree. The boy has a right to know whatever we know."

Giving Ira a sympathetic look, Charles nodded. "They're right. He does."

Easing back a little and losing some of his harder edges, Skylar asked, "What more do I need to know about Cregorous? Is he coming after me?"

"That's not likely," Erador said easily as he leaned against the wall.

"Why?"

"Cregorous wouldn't have sent Akeno to do something he intended to do himself," Streya admitted.

Charles shrugged. "Who is this Cregorous guy? You mentioned him earlier."

"The bad guy," Skylar said, "for lack of a better term."

"He's the ruler of Caliga, the nation that wishes us harm," Ira clarified.

"So, like a king?" Charles asked.

"Only one with immense power."

"Something a lot of kings have."

Streya shook her head ardently. "No, Charles, we aren't talking about wealth or power because he owns people or commands armies. This is legitimate power." She held her hand out, and the sparks of gold formed into a spherical orb.

"Cregorous is much stronger," Ryder said.

"Coupled with the terrifying strength he possesses and his abilities ..." Ira started.

Charles looked to Erador. "You said he might be in control of the portal on Tilion. What does that mean? And why's that a problem?"

"Tilion is our world," Ira answered. "As to why it's a problem ... think of our portal as one of your one-way streets. You cannot simply traverse it freely. If it's open from one side, you have to wait for it to close before you can travel from the other side. So, in this instance, if Cregorous holds dominion over the portal now and opens it to Earth, we cannot return to Tilion until he closes it." Charles opened his mouth to ask something, but Ira continued, "And we cannot rest in the hope of reinforcements. Cregorous would certainly use shields to keep Agerians away from the portal and ensure his continued control over the portal's use presently. We will not see additional Agerian Defenders until Cregorous comes to Earth himself."

"Abilities," Skylar whispered, and everyone looked to him. He lifted his head and added, "Why didn't you tell me that some people could teleport?"

Charles's brow shot up, and he threw frantic glances to the Zaheri.

Ira winced and played with the ribbon in her grasp. "I suppose a human might call it teleporting."

"Wait—he isn't making that up?" Charles asked as he pointed at Skylar.

"We call them Jumpers," Streya said calmly.

As Charles's mouth fell open, Ira added, "They possess the ability to phase in and out of dimensions. Little is known of how it works exactly. The ability is rare."

"How rare?" Skylar asked.

"There's only one in Agerius, and ... well ... he's not exactly a shining example of an Agerian," Streya said with a roll of her eyes. "He's a loudmouth and doesn't like people."

"And, to our knowledge, only Cregorous, Akeno, and another of the generals have the ability," Ira said.

Holding his hand out, Charles asked, "Generals?"

"He has six. Akeno is one of them, his most ruthless."

"That doesn't bode well," Charles muttered as Skylar deflated. "What makes him so dangerous?"

"He's strong, and the only ability we're aware that he holds is jumping. But that makes him difficult to fight. And he's known for being truly monstrous to his victims," Streya answered.

"Monstrous how?"

"From what we can tell, he ... likes to ... torture ..." Ira drew in on herself the more she spoke.

Skylar swallowed. Well, this day just kept getting sodding better, now didn't it?

"We can handle fighting him, now that we know he's our opponent," Streya said confidently. "It means someone else is going to have to suffer Cregorous, but that's not our problem."

That only slightly eased Skylar's concerns. Because sure, that meant he didn't have to deal with the ruler of Caliga, but some other person out there in the world did.

It didn't seem fair.

But maybe this other Human-Born was better prepared for an encounter with Cregorous. So, maybe Skylar didn't have to worry.

For some reason, he did, anyway.

"You ... you still haven't explained why you mentioned Cregorous before," Skylar muttered, fleetingly looking to his Zaheri.

"Right," Erador muttered as he sat up a little. "Well, Cregorous sorta has been unchallenged forever."

"How long is forever?"

"Give or take two thousand years."

Charles made a face like he was trying not to gag. "Wai ... wha?"

It was the least articulate that Skylar had ever heard his brother. But admittedly, he wasn't feeling any more eloquent as his mouth just hung open like he hoped to catch fish in it.

"Are you saying this guy has been alive for—"

"Hybrids live longer than humans. Much longer," Ira said quickly, waving her hand dismissively. "That's not important right now. When Cregorous rose to power, he was—and has been—unmatched in strength and abilities. But our Elders delivered a prophecy that we Agerians have clung to ever since. Over the years, for some, I'm sure it became more like a legend. But what you need to know is that the Elders foretold that seven humans would be born with the abilities of hybrids and would be capable of stopping Cregorous' reign."

Shaking his head, Skylar said, "So … okay. Fine. So there's seven of us Human-Borns. Am I the youngest one or something?"

"Not to our knowledge," Streya said with a shake of her head. "The prophecy gave us titles for the Human-Borns, and based on what we know, you all were born in the order the prophecy states your titles. So, you're all the same age." She gave Skylar a pointed look. "You're the Second Human-Born—the Protector."

The title did little to lift Skylar's spirits. If anything, it plummeted a boulder into his gut.

Some Protector he turned out to be.

Fisting his hands, he trembled a little. "So then, why …"

His Zaheri all gave him rapt attention.

"Why didn't you tell me everything that can happen with shields?" A glare fixed to his face as he looked to the Agerians. "Why didn't you tell me about the injuries that can happen? Or about how you break them? Did you think I couldn't handle it? Did you think there'd been a mistake? Wh …"

He hung his head and cursed himself. *Do. Not. Cry.*

Streya looked crestfallen and pinched her eyes shut. "It's my fault, Skylar," she whispered.

He looked to her with wide eyes as a breath rattled from his lungs.

The Team Leader's shoulders were drooped as she said, "When your father reacted so poorly to us, to your role, I was trying to find a way around it all without getting you in further trouble with your parents. Because I didn't want them to punish you or grow to resent you. So, I tried to come up with some way to help you along without getting—"

"They already hate me!" Skylar burst as tears filled his eyes. "What more would this have done, huh? Made them doubly hate me?"

"Sky, wait a minute," Charles started.

"You can't deny it!" Skylar shot at his brother with a trembling jaw. "They do! They … they don't …" The words almost tumbled from his quaking body.

They don't love me.

He felt the tears slip down his cheeks and angrily rubbed them away. *Dammit, no, not here. Not now. Don't cry.*

Charles gripped Skylar's shoulders and shook his brother. "Don't say that, Skylar! It's not you! It's Pa being a blasted fool! It's his damned pride that's the problem, not you!"

A hand gripped Skylar's, and he jolted at the connection, turning to see Streya straining past the bars to hold his hand.

Tears sat in her eyes as she said, "Skylar, please, don't say those things."

Dammit, why wasn't she my mother?

Against his active thought, he gripped her hand.

He couldn't look away from her as he whispered, "What if I fail?"

A steely look was in her eyes as she gave him a pointed stare. "You won't fail, Skylar. You're the Protector. The Elders don't make mistakes. They chose you for a reason."

Sniffling back his tears, he asked, "What do I do?"

She gave him a warm, encouraging smile. "We all need to find a way out of here that won't get you in trouble and won't cause more issues with your family."

She looked to Charles. "How do we do that?"

Gently letting go of his brother, Charles sighed. "I don't know."

"There has to be a way," Erador growled.

"What would happen if we just broke out?" Ryder asked.

Charles shook his head. "No, Streya and Ira are right. If you do that, it'll only cause greater issues. There has to be a peaceful way to make those in power understand the severity of what we're up against."

"We're running out of time," Ira said. "Another strike could come at any moment. And if we're still here in London, countless lives could be affected."

A sick feeling tore into Skylar's stomach.

This was so much worse than he'd originally thought. If they didn't get out of London soon, hundreds of thousands of lives could be lost in an instant.

That Akeno guy was a beast. Even their defending attacks could cause more harm than good in such a tightly packed city. Tourists, officials, and citizens—all jammed into this one area.

The thought of a dragon tearing through the sky and billowing fire onto the streets. Of people screaming and running in a futile attempt to save themselves as it raced by in the air. Of bratak'ra and werewolves tearing into homes and ripping people apart. Of Akeno doing God knew what to how many people, all because it satisfied his sick mind.

And all because Skylar was stuck there.

All because of him.

The door banged open, and Taylor called in a hushed urgency, "We gotta go! Sergeant's coming, and we're outta time!"

"What? Already?" Skylar shook as he clutched Streya's hand tighter.

"Curse it all, she's right," Charles swore as he looked to his watch. "We've gotta go or we're in trouble."

"But we don't know how to get them out of here," Skylar pleaded.

"I know, Sky, but if we stay, then we're all sunk. We'll ..." He looked to the group and, for a few seconds, hopelessness ghosted his features.

Skylar's world spun for a moment. There had to be a way to fix this whole broken mess and get them out of the city before more Caligans showed up! There simply had to be!

Charles gripped Skylar's jacket and started to tug him away. "We'll figure it out, but right now, we gotta move."

"But," Skylar feebly said, feeling his grip on Streya's hand loosen.

"It'll be okay, Skylar," Streya said as she let him go.

He looked to her desperately.

She offered another warm smile. "It'll be okay."

He'd never felt the need to cling to someone until that moment as his brother pulled him down the hall and out the door.

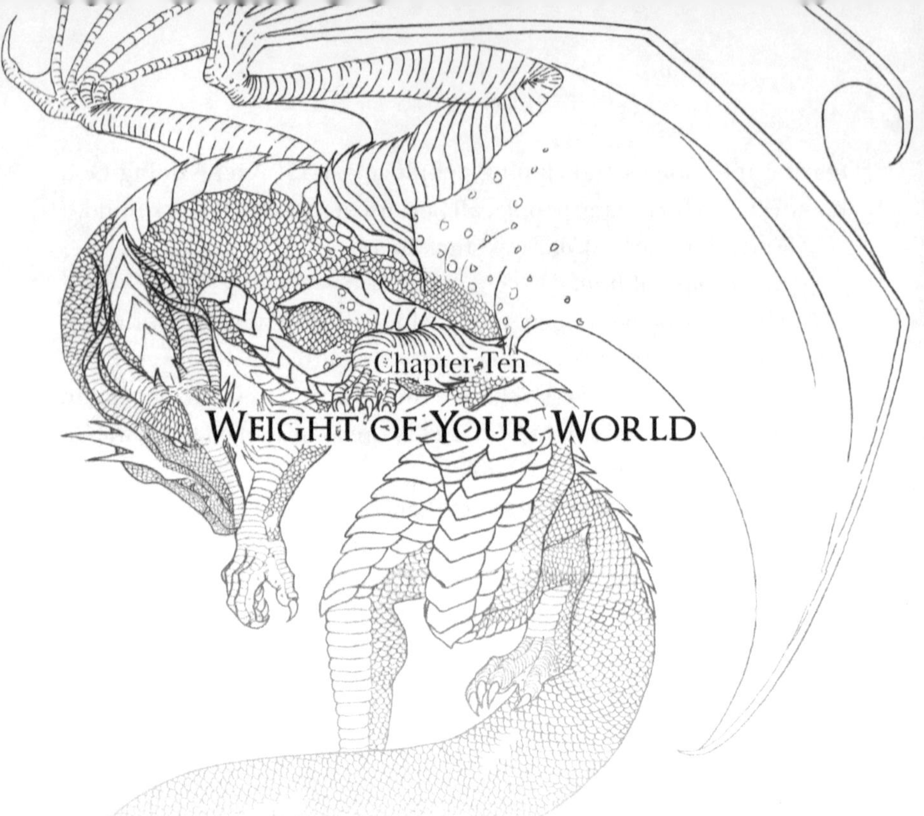

Chapter Ten

WEIGHT OF YOUR WORLD

Despite Skylar's lack of appetite, Charles had insisted they get something to eat. "You have to keep your strength up, Sky. If this mess is only beginning, you can't be running on empty," Charles had said as he'd shoved a sandwich, chips, and a smoothie into Skylar's grasp at the nearby Tesco.

They made it back to Skylar's lavish confinement with a few moments to spare and were relieved to discover their father hadn't come by at all.

Skylar had been quiet since leaving his Zaheri. Once Charles closed the door, he watched Skylar plop onto the couch.

Stuffing his hands into his pockets, Charles let out a heavy breath. "So, as a hybrid, I guess you're sorta immortal now, huh?"

For a moment, Skylar didn't move. When he did, he flopped his head onto the seatback of the couch and stared at his brother with a befuddled expression. "Everything we were told, and *that's* your takeaway?"

"I have lots of takeaways." Charles ambled to the couch opposite his brother's and settled himself slowly. Silence hung for a moment as the elder brother gathered his thoughts. "You're fighting a teleporter?"

Skylar nodded subtly.

Charles let out a scoff and sat back. "And here I kept thinking navigating Parliament was difficult."

"I used to think classes at University were so dull that they'd be impossible to pass," Skylar muttered. "Then I thought it'd be impossible to ever learn anything about what I can do, or who I should be." He shook his head, staring at his hands. "And now both of those seem so easy. A stroll in the park compared to figuring out how to get my Zaheri out of that bloody Yard."

Scratching his forehead, Charles sat forward, resting his arms against his thighs. "Maybe Interpol coming will be good. Maybe there's a way to sneak out during the transfer or something."

"What's the point?" Skylar asked quietly.

A disapproving scowl slowly formed on Charles's face. "What's that supposed to mean?"

"It's pointless." The teen had barely moved since Charles had sat down, his eyes fixed on his open palms. "There's no way to do anything carefully or discreetly. Not with my Zaheri. Even if they did break out, what good would it do? Sure, they could fight back. But Erador barely could get a fix on Akeno, and that was after he got himself thrown through a wall."

Charles's mouth opened a few times as he tried to formulate what to say.

"And so they get out and fight, and maybe that's good and well. But who knows how many more are coming? A couple dragons would lay waste to London. Bratak'ra and werewolves would tear people to shreds. And even if I somehow was there to help, what good would I be?"

His face screwed in self-loathing as he let out an angry scoff. "Protector. What a joke. I couldn't even protect myself earlier. If it hadn't been for my Zaheri, I'd probably be dead right now."

His brows knit together as he fought to not crush himself under the weight of responsibility. "All these people. All these innocent people. They're all completely unaware of the danger that could smash on top of them any second now. It's all my fault. If I'd just never been born, then none of this would be happening."

Charles stood up so fast he shoved the couch back with a squeal against the wood floor. He marched the distance between the seats and roughly yanked Skylar upright by the collar of his jacket.

Letting out a shocked breath, Skylar stared at his brother with wide eyes.

"Stop talking like that!" Charles yelled. Every inch of his features was tight with fury. "Would you listen to yourself? This is happening because some bloody tyrant wants to wipe out his only opposition! He's at fault, not you!"

"Opposition?" Skylar asked as he gritted his teeth, still stuck in a spiral of self-imposed responsibility over the events of the day. "I'm not a threat to him, Charles! I barely constitute a chess piece in this whole thing."

His eyes pinching shut in fury, Charles shook his brother as though that would knock some sense into him. "Shut up!"

Skylar had never heard Charles bellow. His brother was always calm. And while his outburst a few seconds ago had startled him, the command genuinely surprised Skylar. He couldn't even figure out how to form a word in that instant.

Taking advantage of his brother's stunned silence, Charles ripped his eyes open and said forcefully, "Sky, there are only five bloody people in this country who can do anything at all about what's happening. And if you've suddenly lost the faculties to do basic math, I'll remind you that you're bloody one of them!" His grip was tight on Skylar's jacket collar as he spoke without thinking.

In that moment, Charles was so furious at so many things that he couldn't afford to think through his comments. Fury at the world for demanding so much of them both. Fury at their parents for putting their own problems onto Skylar. Fury at the authorities for blatantly ignoring the threat that bore down on them. Fury at a system that he couldn't warp no matter how badly he wanted to make it happen. Fury that his brother felt worthless, when the people who should feel worthless paraded around without a care in the world to those they hurt.

Fury that he couldn't make it all easier for his beloved brother.

"Bollocks on all of this! Bollocks on Pa! Bollocks on the authorities! We're going to get you out of here and get your Zaheri out of the Yard because it's bloody what has to happen to make this all right! And you can't take ownership of bloody other people's cock ups!" He gave Skylar another rough jostle. "Dammit, Skylar, this is what you were made for, for Christ's sake! You can't doubt yourself because other people are being bloody wankers!"

Things went still and quiet for a moment as they just stared at one another; Skylar with wide eyes and a slack jaw, and Charles with a stern look and gritted teeth.

Pinching his eyes shut, Charles gently let go and eased back. He'd gripped Skylar's jacket so tightly that the fabric had wrinkled and bunched despite him no longer holding on.

He let out a beleaguered sigh and said, "Sorry for yelling, but I didn't know how else to sodding say it."

Skylar was stuck, not because he felt scared of his brother or was scared of how angry Charles had been. No, he was stuck because of what Charles had said.

This is what you were made for.

It rang in Skylar's mind, echoing through his consciousness.

Being made for something. He'd always wanted to believe that God didn't make people just for kicks, that there was purpose to every life. But Skylar had often wondered if that'd been some fable—at least for his life.

After all, what goodness could he bring the world, if he couldn't even find love within the confines of his own family? What change for the better could he bring, if disdain seemed his parents only view of him? So, the concept of being made for something had become a scoff-able concept. And the idea of being made for something grand and excellent? Even more so. Here and now, however, Skylar found the phrase oddly comforting.

His brother had raised a fair point. No matter how you looked at it, Skylar wasn't just some average person who had stumbled into this situation and suddenly found themselves front and center. It wasn't as though he were some bystander, completely incapable and incompatible with the events surrounding him. Streya had said he was chosen for a reason, that their Elders didn't make mistakes.

It still felt awkward and impossible.

Yes, he could create indigo shields. Sure, he could heal faster than a normal person. So he could hear better and see better than anyone else he knew.

But did that really make him capable of being someone of value? Someone made for something extraordinary?

The logical side of him—so typically the dominant part—screamed that he was being idiotic. Of *course* he was made for something extraordinary. How many people did he know who could make indigo wisps of sparking energy appear in their grasp? It wasn't like anyone else could suddenly step up and offer to take his place and become whatever being a Human-Born meant.

Looking to his hands again, Skylar felt the phrase resonate again. *This is what you were made for.*

A knock sounded at the door, and the brothers turned as one of the guards stepped into the room. "Sir, there's a gentleman here from Interpol. Says it's urgent."

Charles let out a short sigh. "Yes. I'll be right with him."

Once the door was closed, he turned to his younger brother. "I meant it, Sky. You're not responsible for anything that happens today. You didn't ask to be locked up here, and you didn't tell anyone to lock your Zaheri away. The guilty parties will have to take ownership of the part they played, however this works out. But you haven't done anything wrong. And the world is the better having you in it." His expression softened. "God knows my life is richer for it."

As Charles went to leave, Skylar lifted his head and said, "Thanks, Charles."

A smile came to Charles's face as he met Skylar's gaze. "That's what older brothers are for, right?"

Skylar offered a small smile in return before Charles left the room.

He couldn't deny that there was wisdom in Charles's words. But all that meant for Skylar was he needed to be bold and unafraid of consequences.

Yes, he hadn't asked to be kept in the Parliament building all day, but that didn't acquit him of all responsibility. After all, if he knew another attack was imminent, and that it could be drastically worse than the previous one, that meant he was duty-bound as a morally upstanding individual to do *something*.

But that was so much easier said than done.

Breaking himself out was easy. Breaking his Zaheri out would be infinitely harder. It wasn't like they were easily accessible—they'd been placed in a much deeper part of Scotland Yard's building. And no matter how morally correct breaking them out was, mindlessly destroying buildings and putting people's safety at risk wasn't appropriate either.

And then there was still the issue of whether Skylar was brave enough to take a stand against enemy fighters.

His mind flashed back to Akeno's mocking duel with Erador. To the Caligan's swift movements that seemed impossibly fast. To the strength Akeno had and how easily he'd been able to lift Skylar off the ground and slam him against the shield.

To fight a foe like that ...

Skylar had never been one to go looking for trouble. He didn't like the concept of fighting in general. Wars, violence, even ceremonial swords, they set his teeth on edge.

A small chuckle tumbled from him. Maybe there was some validity to this concept of him being made for this. "Protector" certainly didn't sound so offensive.

Then he'd just have to figure out how to make impenetrable shields.

Could he teach himself something like that before something terrible happened? Ira was right; they were on borrowed time. Any moment could sound the alarm for the next wave of panic and chaotic fighting.

What was the right thing to do? What was feasible and possible to accomplish, given his predicament?

He looked to the door.

Interpol, huh? Maybe he'd just start screaming. Make someone listen to him.

Then he glanced to the ceiling. Well, maybe instead it was a good time to pray for some divine intervention.

Charles stepped into the hallway and found an ordinarily dressed man standing among the guards, holding a sealed parcel. He'd assumed Interpol had a dress code that required suits and ties, not standard street clothes. Though he couldn't deny there was an air of authority around this man.

He looked more like a fighter than a law keeper, with broad shoulders, a stern expression, and hard features. Features that sparked the thought of a soldier in Charles's mind rather than a man from Interpol.

With a nod to the guards, Charles said, "Give us some space, chaps."

The guards offered nods of understanding then stepped down the hall, out of earshot. Good. They knew when they shouldn't try to meddle. It saved Charles a potential headache if he was going to try to plead to this Interpol officer.

Offering a hand, Charles said, "Charles Anthony Mitchell, Duke of Derbyshire's son."

The man took his hand. "Good to know you."

Charles squinted. No introduction?

Bloody hell, these Interpol guys sure loved their secrecy.

"Look, mate, I know you have your orders, but I don't think you understand the whole picture."

"And what might that be?" the Interpol officer asked plainly. No hint of sarcasm or annoyance or ... anything. Just a simple question. His gaze was straightforward, piercing, unblinking.

It was hard for Charles to get a read on this guy. Usually, he could at least feel someone out and determine whether they were quicker with a smile or obstinate, or just blatantly against whatever the conversation's topic surrounded. But this guy? Nothing.

Taking the opportunity to plead his case, Charles said, "My brother isn't a threat to England. He isn't a threat to anyone. Hell, he's the biggest pacifist I know. I think wild rabbits would view him as a trusted ally."

The unnamed man simply stared.

Charles raised his brow. When no response came, he added, "And his protectors—the people locked up at Scotland Yard—they're called his Zaheri. They don't mean anyone on this planet any harm. I know that makes them sound like they're aliens, and maybe they are. But they, y'know, bloody come in peace."

Still, the man said nothing.

"I'm doing a cock up job of this," Charles said with a roll of his eyes. Frustration bubbled in his chest at how little headway he was making.

"But I have it on good authority that the kerfuffle in Oxford earlier was tiny compared to what's coming. It was a scouting party or something. Because they want to hurt my brother. And these sodding enemies can teleport apparently. Not to mention any other number of terrible things that I'm not even aware of. So, we should just let them go so they can do what they do best."

"Which is?"

Okay, interaction. Charles could work with that.

Maybe.

"They're protectors. Skylar—you know, the young man you want to bloody take away in chains—his special title literally is 'Protector.' He only wants to keep people safe. Same with his Zaheri. I'll go before God, King, and country to vouch for them. And if you won't let them go, then"—Charles flopped his hands uselessly at his sides—"then I'm just going to have to go to war against my homeland."

"That will not be necessary."

Brow pinching in confusion, Charles's gaze flicked around a bit before landing on the Interpol officer. "It won't?"

"Master Charles—"

"Charles is fine"—he gave the Interpol officer a look of confusion at the antiquated title—"Master?"

"I hate to be impertinent, but this rambling? It is wasting precious time that dwindles quickly."

Squinting narrowly at the man, Charles asked, "Are you sure you're with Interpol?"

Meeting Charles's skepticism, the man simply said, "I assure you, Master Charles, I have the authority to release both your brother and his Zaheri so that they may fulfill the tasks assigned to them."

"How?" Charles asked. "They're under guard. All of them are."

The strange man didn't flinch, but the way he looked at Charles made him feel that this man could be a powerful enemy. Truthfully, Charles was suddenly grateful this guy seemed to be on their side—authority radiated from him.

"A man may raise actions against, but they cannot stop what must be done," the unknown man said simply.

Though he couldn't be certain, Charles knew that there was enough evidence to lend him faith that this man—whomever he was and wherever he had come from—was on their side. And something told him that, somehow, this mystery man was going to be able to help Skylar and his Zaheri.

Slowly nodding, Charles said, "All right then. What do you need from me?"

Chapter Eleven

PREPARE FOR BATTLE

Skylar was inspecting the window to see if he would set off any alarms if he broke out of the building when a tall, imposing man in simple garb strode into the room. His march was purposeful and with authority, and his presence made Skylar jolt to attention.

"You are Master Skylar?" the man asked plainly.

"Wh-who are you?" Skylar asked as bravely as he could, fighting the impulse to prostrate himself before the man.

"Are you, or are you not, Master Skylar Mitchell, brother to Master Charles Anthony Mitchell?" he asked again, this time a little more urgently.

Nodding a bit, Skylar answered, "I am, but why are you using our full names? And what's with the 'Master' bit?"

"With me," the man said simply as he marched the small distance between them, snatched Skylar by the jacket sleeve, and hauled him out the door.

"Wa-wait! Where are you taking me!" Skylar attempted to break free from the man's iron grip. "Who are you?"

Practically dragging Skylar down the hall, causing the boy's shoes to squeal against the fine marble floor, the man remained silent, as though haste bade him onward.

Just as Skylar was about to hurl another demanding question, the man hushed forcefully, "It would do you well to be silent for the moment."

Fear clutched Skylar's lungs as he whipped his gaze around. Charles was nowhere to be seen, and the guards who had been stationed outside the door seemed apathetic to the display. Was this ...?

Was this man the guy from Interpol? What was going to happen?

What little confidence that had blossomed in Skylar's chest during Charles's absence fled, leaving only worry and concern for what lay ahead.

"Cease struggling and come. We have little time," the man commanded.

The assumed Interpol officer kept a hold of Skylar's shoulder, guiding him out of the building. There was no car waiting for them outside, nor were there any armed guards pointing weapons accusingly at Skylar.

Confusion danced in Skylar's mind. He pulled his brow together and gulped in courage. "You have to let me go, and my Zaheri. People are going to die if you don't."

They came to the street, and the man swept his gaze at the passing vehicles before unflinchingly dragging Skylar along the way.

"Don't you care about innocent lives? You have to release my Zaheri and let us get out of London." Skylar was grateful for the man's silence, because for once it helped him bolster strength in his convictions.

Once they were across the street, the man let go of Skylar's shoulder and said, "Master Skylar, under what other guise would you assume someone may free you and your Zaheri from your current predicament?"

For a long second, Skylar stared blankly at the unnamed man. Then, in a hush, he said, "You aren't with Interpol."

"Those I represent are far more powerful than any man-made institution. And we must stop dallying. Time grows ever shorter." He turned to continue down the sidewalk, heading toward Scotland Yard. His pace was quick and purposeful, but his gait also suggested pristine purpose. Even his back was straight and sure.

Skylar was awed by him.

"You are correct, Master Skylar. You and your Zaheri must be released to fulfill your task."

Skylar had to jog to keep pace with him. "Who are you?"

"My name means nothing. Listen now and closely. In the question of shields and their weaponization, you must be diligent in how you weaponize them. They are not innately offensive creations of your energy."

"Wait, wait—how do you know about—"

"Listen and do not ask questions," the man cut in, his gaze drilled forward as though honed on their destination. "The act of breaking a shield by your action is preferable to having it shattered by outside means. It will not cause your body injury, whereas the latter will bring reflection on your physical being. However, neither will negate the energy required to make the shield initially. Do you understand?"

"I think so, bu—"

"Causing a shield to shatter and weaponizing it is an active thought you must give. Your shield cannot do what you do not ask of it. Shields are extensions of yourself, just as your energy. Therefore, it cannot act on its own. Your instinct may guide you, and may prove your unexpected ally, but you cannot rely solely on that. Do you understand?"

"Sure, fine, but—"

"Shields do not have to be opaque to be effective. Transparent, unbreakable shields are attainable. Do not expect to reach that point in one day."

"Who ar—"

"I will not say it again: be silent and listen well," the man said with a reprimanding look to Skylar. They were nearly to Scotland Yard. "You have more energy within you to accomplish your task than you realize. You will be capable of creating more shields than you think. You are a powerful wielder. Do not think your growth today as some miracle. Your body and mind know the totality of your limits. You must continue to press toward them. Is that clear?"

Skylar's head spun. Now he had even more questions, and they all centered around who the bloody hell marched at his side.

Before Skylar could figure out whether to reply or demand an answer to the question of who this man was, they reached the Yard. The mysterious man snatched his jacket sleeve again and dragged him into the building without a bit of hesitation.

His urgency made Skylar's stomach twist and flop. Whoever he was, wherever he'd come from, he moved so swiftly that it brought the worst possibilities to Skylar's mind.

As he was roughly pulled through the lobby, Skylar caught Taylor's surprised expression as she power-walked to them.

"Um, hi, who are you?" Taylor asked.

"I am here for the prisoners," the mysterious man stated, pulling Skylar to a halt at his side. "You will take me to them."

"Uh, I don't think I have that sorta authority."

"At present, you do. All others are occupied, and you will see to showing me to their holding cell."

Taylor gave Skylar a concerned look before she whispered, "Are you the guy from Interpol?"

He remained stoically silent.

Her phone pinged, and Taylor fished it out of her pocket, still staring at the unknown man suspiciously. She did a double-take at the notification on her phone before sweeping her gaze to the man. Waving to herself, she hushed, "Follow me."

Skylar's heart thudded against his chest as worry tightened his lungs. The air felt near collapsing with tension that plopped upon them unceremoniously.

The moment they were in the hallway that would lead to his Zaheri, the mysterious man released Skylar's jacket sleeve and fell into step behind him and Taylor.

Though he wasn't being dragged along anymore, Skylar found himself practically running to the cell. Taylor kept pace with him at his side.

She felt the need to move quickly, too?

"Skylar," Streya said in a surprised gasp.

"It's only been two hours since you were here," Ira said warily, glancing to Taylor.

"Yep, time for you lot to get outta here," Taylor said as she unlocked the cell.

"Wait, seriously?" Skylar asked her.

Ripping the door open, Taylor answered, "Charles said to trust the big guy."

"How did you get permission to let us go?" Streya asked as she stepped into the hall.

"I don't really know, but this guy must be a friend of yours, 'cause—" Skylar gestured behind him and turned, only to find the hallway completely empty.

Taylor's mouth fell open, and she trembled a little. "Uh ... where'd he go?"

"Don't matter. We're out. We're leaving," Erador said as he and Ryder stalked toward the entrance.

"Wait! No! Not that way!" Taylor shook out. Her eyes kept darting to the empty hall in abject fear, her face going pale.

Skylar didn't blame her. He hadn't illusioned the terrifyingly stoic man, had he?

Another bout of fear charged through Skylar's brain.

Had ...? Had he teleported?

But ... but Streya had said there was only one Agerian who could do that. And their mysterious helper didn't present at all the picture that Streya had painted of the Agerian Jumper. That only left Caligan Jumpers.

Why would one of Cregorous' goons—or Cregorous himself, for that matter—help them?

Again, Skylar felt the walls spin and his stomach went all gurgled. He cursed Charles's insistence on eating.

Taylor blinked a few times and shook herself before pointing to the opposite end of the hall. "There's a back door. You should go out that way."

"Where's my axe?" Erador demanded.

"Look, mate, I told you, I don't know anything about an axe."

A string of grumbling curses tumbled from Erador, and gold energy flitted around his fisting hands.

Taylor shuddered back.

Streya might've been smaller than Erador, but that didn't stop her from grabbing him by the ear and yanking hard as she reprimanded, "Stop scaring the people who are trying to help us, you blasted idiot!"

"Ow, ow, ow, ow, ow, not the ear!" Erador whined, practically folding in half as Streya tugged him down the hall. The other two followed on her heel.

Skylar turned to Taylor. "Thanks for your help."

Letting out a shaky breath, Taylor pulled her phone out and tapped a few commands. She held the screen up to him with a small smile. "What help? I don't see anything out of the ordinary here."

In the brief glimpse Skylar got of her phone screen, he saw that she had a heart emoji next to Charles's name.

So, whether Charles liked it or not, it appeared Taylor did, in fact, like him.

An unbidden smile came to Skylar's face, and he nodded to her. "See you later, Taylor."

"Look forward to it, little Mitchell," she said with a mock salute before she quickly went the opposite direction of their retreat.

"Do *not* call on your axe," Streya commanded once they were outside and a block away from Scotland Yard.

Erador threw his arms out in frustration. "How do you expect me to fight without it?"

Ryder was doing his best to remain hidden, shoved into some shrubbery that mostly obscured him. Skylar figured someone would eventually notice the grovix's maw poking out of the bushes, despite Ira's attempt to block passersby's view of the hulking creature.

Taking a breath, Streya said, "We need to focus on getting out of the city. We can get back to the flat and arm up there."

"I don't have another battle axe, Strey. I'm not leaving it behind."

Ira fidgeted with the ribbon in her grasp as though they were rosary beads. "I actually agree with Erador on this."

"What?" Skylar asked with a look of disbelief.

"We shouldn't leave an Agerian weapon in the hands of humans. The metal is completely different, and Elders only know what humans might try to do with Erador's energy that he's stored in the blade."

Conceding defeat, Streya admitted, "That's actually a good point." She straightened and gave Erador a pointed stare. "You can sense it, can't you?"

The towering warrior lifted his head and glanced around. He pointed to Scotland Yard. "It's in that building. Can't tell you where exactly."

Streya took in a long breath before slowly releasing it, a calmer look coming to her face as she exhaled. "Okay. How long has it been since we were attacked in Oxford?"

With a quick glance to her watch, Ira answered, "Almost five hours."

"Praise the Elders we haven't been hit yet," Streya hushed with a look of wonder. "Then Erador, you have to act quickly. Do a sweep of the building from the outside and call your axe from the area where the least amount of damage will occur, and then get back here."

"Then what?" Skylar asked.

"We run. Well, we'll fly." She gestured to the Zaheri. "And Erador will have to carry you."

A small rumble came from Ryder. "Well ... the boy could ride on my back instead."

"You ... you'd be okay with that?" Skylar asked with a quirk of a smile.

Rolling his eyes, the grovix said, "It's not as if I've been waiting for an opportunity for someone to treat me like a blasted horse. But it makes the most sense, given our problem."

"'Cause it'll free me up if we get attacked," Erador said with a nod. He reached into the bush and condescendingly patted Ryder's head. "Nice thinking, Ryder."

Ryder whipped his head away and nipped toward Erador's fingers. "Don't pet me."

"Erador, get moving. We're already pressing the Elders' favor as it is," Streya commanded.

"Done and done. Be right back," Erador said before he turned back the way they'd come and jogged toward Scotland Yard.

A flash of white hit the sky and screams filled the air.

"Never mind, Erador! We're out of time!" Streya hollered.

There was the sound of crashing cement mixed with the sounds of some cars colliding, followed quickly by a bellowing cry from a Ferveos dragon.

Fear sent Skylar's stomach into a tangled mess. All he could think in that moment was an echoing, *Oh no.*

They were too late.

All these people were going to die.

Ryder snatched Skylar's jacket sleeve, yanking him toward the shrubbery. It jostled Skylar from his morbidly depressing assessment of their situation. He looked up to see Streya in the air, her wings shifting here and there on the breeze.

"Where is it?" Ira asked as she hastily wrapped her broken ribbon around her wrist and tied it into a tight knot.

"Over the water, by a big bridge!" Streya called back.

"The Tower of London?" Skylar asked quietly. "Why there?"

Landing gracefully, Streya said, "Ferveos." She met Skylar's concerned gaze. "We can handle this. They aren't terribly bright, and if they're the first ones through, we can use that to our advantage."

"How?"

"We lead them out of the city," Erador said as he joined them. His battle axe glowed vibrant gold, and cinderblock dust clung to the grooves along the blade. He looked to Streya. "Means they'll probably move the portal though."

"Could be a good thing," Streya mused. "Could buy someone else time before Cregorous moves on them."

"Fair point."

"Okay that's enough chat. We gotta move. Out of the city and head north. We've gotta make noise to get their attention."

A grunting yell came from Erador, and he smiled victoriously. "Finally! A plan I can get behind!"

Ryder ducked low to allow Skylar to climb on his back. "You'll have to hold on. Don't be afraid of hurting me. Grabbing my fur won't be a problem."

"You're sure?" Skylar asked as he shifted a little on Ryder's back. It was much like riding bareback on a horse. Only Ryder was much furrier, and his shoulders and hips were much bigger.

Offering a smirk over his shoulder, the grovix said, "Don't belittle me, kid."

"You keep him safe, Ryder," Streya commanded.

"I will," Ryder said with a nod. "Hold on," he reminded Skylar before taking off.

Despite the fact that Skylar had been bracing himself, he still let out a small yelp and had to fall onto Ryder's neck and grip tight.

"I told you to hold on!" Ryder growled.

"I tried!" Skylar hollered back.

It was going to be a miracle if they survived this mess.

Erador cloaked himself in golden energy and shot into the air. Ferveos were appearing from the unusually bright cylindrical portal.

After nineteen years on Earth, Erador had only recently grown accustomed to London's urban sprawl, and to not constantly flit his gaze skyward for dragon incursions.

He was grateful that his training always took over when he saw a Ferveos in the air. Otherwise, he might've been concerned.

While he wasn't a Skycaptain, and wasn't built for sustained aerial combat, he was the bulkiest of the Beta Team. Well, next to Ryder. But Ryder was leading the charge out of the city. Hopefully the grovix's absurd amount of shedding throughout the day would prove their ally and provide any werewolves and bratak'ra a scent to follow.

They had to get the dragons' attention and draw them out of the city. Right now, the portal rested over the large river, sitting near London Bridge.

He might despise the densely packed city, but that didn't mean Erador wanted it to be laid to rubble.

With the dragons still over the water, Erador tore his energy-cloaked form through the chest of the first Ferveos. That would get the rest of the dragons' attentions.

Streya shot through the air on her nimble wings. Slices of gold energy tore from the edges and ripped into the nearby dragons and Caligan fighters.

Swinging his axe into position, Erador pulled energy from his core and sent it charging down his arm and into the blade. In mere seconds, his weapon was humming and shining a bright gold.

A Ferveos let out a furious bellow and changed its trajectory, heading toward him.

Beating his wings to keep himself elevated, he called at the roaring monsters, "That's right! Come at me!"

"Do you have to antagonize them?" Streya chastised as she joined him.

"You said get their attention!" he snapped, pointing his glowing axe toward the dragons. "I got their attention!"

Streya rolled her eyes and returned her focus to the enemies pouring from the portal. A scowl formed on her face before she beat her wings and charged into the thrall.

"Where are you going?" Erador hollered in annoyance. "I thought you said lead them *away*!"

"Yes, *you* lead them away!" she yelled over her shoulder.

With agile accuracy, she dodged and skimmed past Caligans that shot from the white cylinder, sending bolts of golden energy from her wings to strike and take down anything close enough. The river below plopped and splashed as dragons and Caligans fell into the water.

She didn't know if it would work, but she had to send a message. Get the attention of the man behind the attack and hopefully get him so enraged that he moved the portal after them. If that was even possible. Ira had hastily said she thought it was, given Cregorous' strength. The portal didn't usually move, but it had been speculated that a powerful energy wielder would be capable of doing it while it was active.

All of this was, assuming, that her actions would make Cregorous angry enough to move the portal.

It wasn't highly likely.

But she had to try.

Skylar would take the blame if too many deaths and damages were caused to London. She had no proof that would be the case, but a sinking feeling sat in her heart that the cold attitude Skylar's father sported toward him would only grow more stonelike after today. And she had to do everything in her power to ensure the boy she protected would be free from guilt or blame.

Arching her back as she neared the portal, she concentrated a swell of energy to pool in her arms. Then she thrust her arms at the gateway, sending a stream of gold to collide with the active portal.

Gritting her teeth, she poured as much strength into the action as possible without depleting herself. She just had to get Cregorous' attention. There was still going to be the issue of wiping out opposition and keeping Skylar safe.

A groaning filled the air around the portal, and she frantically beat her wings away from the white cylinder. There was a stuttering in the white glow before it started to surge forward.

Sucking in heavy breaths, Streya folded her wings and let gravity catch her. She flapped her wings open before the water and soared across the river swiftly.

Crackling energy sounded behind her, and the clashing of blasts erupted. A second later, Erador was at her side.

"What'd you do?" he cried, throwing wild blasts into the thrall following closely on their heels. The roaring groan of the portal was just behind it all, rolling after them.

"I'm going to catch up to Skylar! You keep them occupied!" she answered.

A growling grumble came from Erador, and she knew it was him cursing her lack of answer.

Streya fisted her hands, feeling the joints protest. She'd thrown a lot at the portal, and her body was displaying its pain at her overuse. Despite all the years of training, her hands just never seemed to recover as quickly as other Paragons'. Especially Tyron's.

Fear seized her heart again, and she begged the Elders to keep him safe. Then, forcing her worry over Tyron away, she pushed her wings faster, urging every fiber of her being to its maximum. She had to get to Skylar and keep him safe. Above all else, she had to keep Skylar safe.

No matter the cost.

Chapter Twelve

THE DEFENDER STANDS

Ryder moved much faster than Skylar would have anticipated. For how massive the grovix was, he tore through the street with ease. When they approached a car in their way, Skylar almost yelled at his Zaheri to watch out.

The concept of dodging didn't seem to register with Ryder. Because the big black grovix simply shoved the car aside and continued on his way, completely undeterred as he raced on.

"Get aside!" he yelled when people somehow missed his hulking mass charging toward them.

They kept the thundering pace for a few moments, facing little by way of obstacles. It was then that Ryder's ears shot up, and he flashed a glance over his shoulder. The action caused Skylar to do likewise.

He was probably going to have nightmares.

A dual-horned bratak'ra was closing in on them. There were a handful of mono-horned ones on its heel and werewolves nearly keeping pace with the larger beast at the lead. One of the werewolves launched ahead, its gangly form and starved eyes eager to fill its emaciated belly.

Gritting his teeth, Skylar called for a shield to ghost above him, blanketing him and Ryder as they continued their march. The werewolf smashed into the shield and crumpled off with a yelp of pain.

If the beast hadn't been so terrifying, Skylar might've felt pity for it.

Ryder leaped over a small creek and spun around, Skylar nearly falling off, sliding a little on the grovix's back and letting out a struggling vowel while looking pretty ridiculous.

"Hey, you dumb brutes!" Ryder challenged.

Whipping his attention across the creek, Skylar saw what made Ryder call out.

The bratak'ra and werewolves must've thought the chase was too taxing, because they were beginning to break off and look for human targets.

With a scoffing growl, Ryder mocked, "Too stupid and too slow to keep up?"

The dual-horned bratak'ra's irises sliced into a barely noticeable slit. A snarl rippled its wide maw as the beast spat, "You'll regret those words, grovix!"

"Gotta catch me first," Ryder said with a laugh before returning to his racing speed, Skylar frantically snatching at the grovix's fur for stability.

Thundering footfalls echoed behind them, spiraling worry in Skylar's thoughts. He gripped Ryder's fur and asked, "Was that really such a good idea?"

"Oh, you want them to kill humans?" Ryder threw back at him.

"No, thank you."

"You're welcome then."

They had barely continued the chase when a blast of fire struck a nearby building.

Despite the movement, Skylar gripped Ryder's ribcage with his thighs and twisted to make a shield and catch the debris. He had to see where to make the shield, and they had too many bratak'ra or werewolves on top of them to stop.

Other blasts began to smash into the buildings around them, most of them coming from Caligan energy attacks. Gray sparks flashed and people screamed, ducking for cover and fleeing from anywhere the strikes landed.

The sky was chaos.

Streya, Erador, and Ira were all mobile, flying around and engaging their enemy. Occasionally, they bounced off rooftops to get their bearings before throwing themselves into a squall again.

But they were still in the city limits. There were too many people who could get hurt.

"Hey!" Skylar yelled. He waved his hands as best he could, having to fall back and grip Ryder for support a few times. "Hey, down here! I'm down here, you wankers!"

"What're you doing?" Ryder barked.

"Too many buildings are getting hit! People could be inside! Or they could get crushed! We gotta get their attention and get them out of the city!"

A growl rumbled from Ryder, and he sucked in a breath. "You're gonna make me test my limits, kid." He picked up speed, pushing himself faster as he dove out of the way of attacks. There were several near misses.

Skylar kept a shield at the ready in his grasp, practically playing tennis with the gray blasts of energy. If tennis had ever been played while riding bareback on a horse.

Ryder was panting heavily as they broke out of the suburban sprawl of London. Rolling hills speckled with sheep and the occasional house became the terrain.

They passed over an old stone bridge, and once on the other side, Skylar rolled off of Ryder's back and whipped around to see how bad things were.

His breath lodged in his throat.

Things were *really* bad.

A dozen or so Ferveos littered the sky. Caligan fighters flew in droves, diving toward the ground. And from the streets exploded more bratak'ra and werewolves, seemingly all following the pack ahead of them.

Fear over doing nothing spurred Skylar to start waving his hands frantically and scream, "Hey! Hey, down here!"

It didn't work.

Some large gray attack tore at a building, smashing the corner of it and sending the whole structure toppling.

Skylar couldn't scream, no matter how badly he wanted to.

He just ... had to pray ...

Shoving his arms out, a wave of indigo surged from him and smashed into the building. He didn't know what else to do, and he prayed the shield did what he asked.

Grab the people, push them out, keep them safe.

Chunks of the building were tossed into the fields. Sheep scattered in baaing panic. Bratak'ra and werewolves slammed to a stop and, on a dime, ran for the livestock. Meanwhile, a Ferveos whipped its large head toward Skylar.

Skylar pulled an indigo shield along his forearm and raised his arm in the air. "I'm the one you want!"

As if it were a klaxon, the Ferveos let out a deafening roar, its gaze fixed on Skylar.

He knew it was coming, but Skylar couldn't stop himself from cowering back and covering his ears. Pinching his eyes open, past the stinging pain at the volume of the beast, he yelped as Ryder snatched his jacket and ripped him aside just before a Ferveos landed.

Ira landed next to Skylar and pushed him away from the dragon. "Help me with shields over the buildings!" Ira directed, and he nodded in response.

Streya shot past the Ferveos as it reared back to unleash a blast of flame. Her thin, agile wings were cloaked in golden energy. As her body flew by the dragon, slices of gold tore from her and into the beast's neck.

A sputtering, spurting groan came from the dragon as a rush of exploding flame shot skyward. The blast smacked into other airborne enemies, including other dragons.

Erador was a swirling mass of chaos, bounding from one creature to the next with stupid dexterity for someone of his bulk. He swung his axe around, and a tornado of gold swirled through the air, impacting Ferveos and airborne Caligans, sending them falling to the ground in heaps.

Ira and Skylar kept shields around the buildings to ensure any fallen bodies wouldn't cause further damage. Skylar treated his shields like large scrapers for Ira's, literally shoving the bodies that accumulated into the once-empty fields.

Ryder tore through the fields, ripping at the opposition. He took the distraction of the sheep and used it to his advantage. He'd take out a werewolf or a bratak'ra then lead the furious pack into a sheep field and duck out of the way. The dumb beasts kept falling for it, surging after the sheep with salivating maws. It let Ryder then burst into the thick of them and take a few out in one charging mass. He was ruthless as he tore into the enemy creatures.

Though panic was fueling a fair bit of his actions, Skylar found his breathing fairly even. This was working. They were actually managing to quell this army that had descended upon them.

They were going to make it out of this.

A pulse hit the air, and the next thing Skylar knew, a boot connected with his chest, and he was sent flying backward.

Skylar tumbled and bounced, not landing well at all. With a pained, airy groan, he rolled onto his knees and held his aching sides. His jacket was torn up from the tumble, and bruising was going to happen … everywhere.

Frantically, he looked around to find that he wasn't anywhere near where he'd been. Ira, Erador, Streya, Ryder, the enemy fighters—all of it was replaced with rolling hills of lavender and whipping winds. A taller hill sat a little way from where he was, a small stone pedestal signaling the mount. Mam Tor.

They were in Castleton, a tiny town in Derbyshire about thirty minutes north of London. How?

Grimacing as he got to his feet, Skylar held his injured side. He'd gained an abrasion from impacting something in his fall. Probably an errant rock.

Another pulse filled the air, and Skylar spun to it, witnessing Akeno's form sauntering out of gray dust. The Caligan general wore a bemused smirk.

How had they wound up so far away from the others? Could this teleporter make other people teleport, too? They were at least ten minutes away from where they'd been by flight. And that was if they even realized that Skylar had gone missing.

His jaw trembled.

"I expected more," Akeno grumbled with a bored look. "After all, they had all this time to train you. What were they doing? Sleeping?"

Skylar chose to respond with a glare.

"That's dull," Akeno said, rolling his eyes. "At least we could have a chat before I kill you. That might make this last longer."

He'd wanted to remain silent and try to make Akeno feel the unease in that sort of treatment. But Skylar couldn't help himself as he asked, "How can you say that so easily?"

"What? That I'll kill you?" Akeno asked with a scoff.

"Yes. I ... I'm a person. I haven't done anything to you."

Akeno shrugged. "I don't care. About either of those things. After all, it's not like you're the first person I'm gonna make sure bleeds out."

"What broke in you?" Skylar asked with a scrunched face.

A sick grin came to the Caligan's face. "Ever think that maybe you're the one who's broken?"

In a flash, Akeno snapped forward and had an energy cloaked fist in the air.

A surge of indigo sparked across Skylar as he shoved his hand out. The wall of indigo met the smash of gray in an opposing blast.

Akeno easily leaped back and landed on his feet.

Skylar went sailing across the valley, his trajectory aiming him for the crest of another tall hill. He yelped as he went flying, and when he glanced to see how close he was to impact, he frantically called for a shield to catch him and break his fall.

His back hit the shield, and as he tried to scramble up, Akeno landed on top of him, sending an energy-coated fist into Skylar's stomach.

Another flash of indigo managed to appear and bear the brunt of the attack, but Skylar was still sent sailing through his broken shield. Pain radiated across his right arm as though something had just whacked it hard.

The stinging sensation distracted him for half a second before he called for another shield to catch him. He landed on his feet and immediately leaped off it. The Caligan had intended to kick Skylar, narrowly missing the teen.

Flailing his arms for something to grab on to, Skylar worked to get some distance between himself and Akeno.

He spun on his heel and begged the shield to shatter and explode at Akeno's form. Throwing his arm across his body like a sideways pitch in baseball, the shield burst upward.

But Akeno had already jumped out of the way, gray dust littering the air.

"Bugger all," Skylar cursed before a harsh kick landed on his back, sending him falling down the sleek, grassy hill. He managed to snatch a hold of some root and draped a shield over himself just before a gray attack surged over his body.

Akeno didn't quit. He was there in an instant with another attack.

In desperation, Skylar let go of the root and had the shield disappear from beneath his feet, sliding out from under the protective indigo mold. Letting gravity help him, Skylar fled down the hill.

He just had to buy himself time for his Zaheri to show up. Once they did, he'd be okay. *Stay alive. Don't die. Stay alive.*

The crackling of energy made him drop to his knees and roll once the attack passed over him.

Akeno must've anticipated that. How, Skylar didn't know.

What were the chances the Caligan could know that Skylar would roll right rather than left?

Landing on top of Skylar, Akeno snatched his neck and let his energy char at Skylar's skin. He tightened his grip as Skylar cried out in agony.

A wide, demonic grin cracked his face as he cackled. "That's right—scream."

Skylar gritted his teeth and glared at the Caligan before a wall of indigo tore from Skylar's form, propelling Akeno off him.

He begged the shield to pin Akeno and hold him somehow, just give him time to hide or something. Gagging coughs tore at his damaged throat as Skylar hobbled into the town of Castleton. It was a quiet, tiny little place nestled at the foot of all these rolling hills.

Ducking behind a building, Skylar propped against the wall and did everything in his power to not tremble.

Every inch of him ached. He was bleeding from several different injuries, his head throbbed, and his vision felt off. In an attempt to stave off hyperventilating and going into full blown panic, he forced smoother gulps of air into his quaking chest.

Skylar had never been one of those kids who was afraid of the dark. He didn't fear corners or strange shadows in winter. Howling winds didn't send shivers up his spine. Heights didn't faze him. He liked water. Tight spaces were comforting. To the best of his knowledge, he'd never experienced night terrors. Genuine fear had never crippled him before.

But here, hunched against the wall of the restaurant in Castleton, hiding from someone he couldn't pick out of a crowd, feeling his body whimper and whine in echoing pain ...

He had thought death didn't scare him.

He was wrong.

Resting his fractured arm against his chest in an attempt to stabilize it, Skylar fought his short, panicked breaths. But he couldn't get himself to calm.

Whistling caught his attention, and an ambling gait kicked errant stones.

Skylar suddenly hated whistling and hoped he would never hear it again as long as he lived.

He prayed he'd live longer than a few more seconds.

"Come on out, little defender," Akeno sang in a smooth voice. "I'm not done playing with you yet."

Despite his best efforts, Skylar sank against the wall and clenched his jaw to keep from crying. His jaw trembled, and his chest shook.

God. Jesus. Someone.

Save me.

A hand snatched his shoulder, and Skylar was suddenly thrown to the stone street. He immediately huddled into a ball and called a domed shield to protect him. The swirling indigo was his only aid in that moment.

"Don't be like that." Akeno laughed as he lashed out at the shield. Sparks of white, like hot lead, shot off each impact of gray against the vibrantly colored shield. "Just sitting there is boring. You were supposed to be fun to cripple!"

Cracking started to ripple across Skylar's shield, and he screwed his eyes shut as he made the thick indigo protection shatter.

For the briefest of moments, the air held a million shards of sparkling indigo.

And somehow, Akeno had been caught off guard.

At least for a brief pause.

The specks of indigo smashed into Akeno as though they were tiny bolts of bullets aiming to defend Skylar.

"Clever thing you are," Akeno snapped as he swirled his hand and sent a scythe-like swirl of gray through the indigo attack.

As the energy scythe swung around, Akeno caught sight of Skylar trying to flee.

A crooked smirk filled Akeno's face as he said, "More running, huh? That's the best you can do?"

With a pulse, he jumped and cleared the distance between them. His scythed energy sliced the air, intending to cut at Skylar.

It was stupid and reckless, but Skylar didn't know what else to do.

Kicking himself into the air, he pulled an indigo shield from the ground. As he spun, he kicked the shield, sending the wall of indigo colliding into Akeno and obliterating his gray attack.

But, oh right.

The ground.

Skylar slammed into the stone and immediately regretted every action that had led to that point. His arm was definitely broken now. Boy, he was stupid—using his fractured arm to catch himself.

At the sound of crackling energy—the horrid soundtrack to this battle—Skylar whipped his head up and desperately pulled another shield to cloak him.

It was weak. He could feel it.

And it didn't stop Akeno's fist as it slammed through the shield and shattered Skylar's shoulder.

Everything went still and quiet as Skylar lay on the ground, trembling. Akeno towered over him, still wearing that satisfied smile.

Thudding caught Skylar's attention, and he weakly lifted his head to see Caligans landing among them. None of them moved to attack.

"I really did expect better," Akeno mused as he slowly approached Skylar's broken body. "A shield expert. That's what I was told I'd be facing. And look at you." He scoffed. "This is the best that the Elders could muster? This is the fabled Human-Born of the Agerians' wretched prophecy?"

Though he quaked with every miniscule action, Skylar fought to his knees so he could better face Akeno. He couldn't see much out of his right eye, and he didn't know what that meant. Everything hurt, so it wasn't like he could pinpoint which injury was causing his vision loss.

"I can understand my master's desire to let you all live until now. It does get dull, striking at enemies who can't give you any fun. But this was just pathetic. I barely had to try." Akeno laughed in a condescending way. "I suppose you could boast that you scratched me. See?" He pointed to a cut across his cheek and brow.

Skylar faltered and had to use his good arm to catch himself. Even his "good" arm was scratched and aching.

Akeno snatched Skylar by the hair and hoisted him up a little, causing the British teen to let out a whine of pain. The noise seemed to please Akeno, and he jostled Skylar again, smiling fiendishly when the boy involuntarily cried out.

"I do enjoy noises like that," Akeno hushed. Then he gripped Skylar's throat, making the boy gag out a breath.

It was a meager attempt, but Skylar gripped Akeno's arm with his good hand, as though that might somehow make the monster let go.

Quirking his head to the side, the Caligan smirked. "So, what are you anyway? Some palace brat?"

A slice of gray energy tore at Skylar's arm. He dug his fingernails into Akeno's arm, trying to keep fighting.

"Maybe that explains why you're useless. Even so, I thought prophecies were supposed to be absolute." Akeno shrugged. "And maybe once upon a time, they were. But y'know what I think?"

"You talk too much?" Skylar gagged out as his frame quivered.

Another slice of energy cut at Skylar's arm, and his fingers twitched.

Was there any part of him that wasn't bruised or bleeding?

"Don't worry; you're not gonna die yet. After all—" Akeno glanced over his shoulder and smirked "—your Zaheri have to see their failure for their own eyes."

No ...

Please ... no.

Charles. Streya. Erador. Ira. Ryder. Taylor. The few people in this world who seemed to like him. Seemed to care about him. They'd all gone to such lengths to help him.

Was this really how it ended?

Skylar, broken and bruised, unable to fight, and the only people in this whole bloody world who loved him to witness it firsthand?

Akeno looked back to him, wearing a satisfied smile. "Even the Elders supposed chosen ones are still no match for the might of Caliga."

That couldn't be true.

It just ...

It couldn't be true.

Somewhere at the edge of Skylar's hearing, he heard a frantic, furious scream from Streya. A simple scream.

A pleading scream.

"*Skylar!*"

Akeno pulled his energy-cloaked fist back then moved to crush the boy's skull.

Tears fell down Skylar's cheeks as he closed his eyes and thought, *I'm sorry, Streya.*

I ...

I tried ...

A blinding flash hit the air, and a cracking of bones sounded against Skylar's face. The pressure on his throat disappeared and he hit the ground.

Strength seeped into him, and Skylar felt some of the aching in his body lessen.

He opened his eyes to see a solid indigo shield conformed to his entire body, a hairsbreadth from his skin.

A long, steadying breath escaped him, and the shield around him flashed again, gaining a set of imposing looking wings.

Get. Up, a chorus of voices said to him.

Without any pain or hesitation, Skylar slowly rose to his feet. To the Caligans surrounding him, he suddenly looked a warrior, shining in vibrant indigo, bathing Castleton's dusk-filled streets in the warm glow of his energy.

Someone hollered a command to attack.

Skylar didn't know how to fight but, in that moment, he moved as though he did.

Attacks ricocheted off him and struck down the attacker. Bodies flung themselves at him and were crumpled to the ground at impact.

Shards soared off Skylar's body-molded shield and sliced like swords, cutting into attackers in droves.

He dodged attacks as if he'd practiced the movements a million times. His shield-formed wings pushed him into the air, slicing off bullet-like shrapnel at the army intending him harm.

Landing back on the ground, he ran forward without abandon. Snatching enemies in his grasp, he hurtled them into the ground. Shoving them aside when they approached. Catching their attacks in his grasp and pulling their strength into his own.

He was invulnerable.

It was a surreal moment. But that's all it was. A moment.

As quickly as the change had come, so did it flee. In a snap, Skylar felt the molded shield fly off him and disappear into dust, and he collapsed to the ground.

His eyes rolled here and there, and the world swayed under him. His skin trembled and shook. Numbness prickled his hands, making it hard to feel the solid ground beneath him.

Streya caught him before his face hit the stone street. Gently taking his face into her grasp, she begged, "Skylar, c'mon; look at me. Stay with me."

Raising a shaky hand toward her arm, he barely hooked his fingers enough to grasp her forearm as he quaked, "What took you ...?"

Her eyes kept flicking across his battered body, her breaths coming out ragged and quaking. A smile exploded on her face that she sucked back with restraint. Tears spilled from her eyes. "I flew as fast as I could ..."

"Is he gone?" Skylar begged.

Sniffling back her tears, she nodded a bunch. "Yeah, Sky, he's gone. You did it. We're safe now."

His eyes slid shut, and he fell forward. She guided him into a gentle embrace.

Despite the pain and utter exhaustion lacing his whole body, Skylar managed to smile and slur out, "I did it."

Streya let out a grateful laugh as she looked at the stars beginning to fill the twilight sky. "Yeah, you did it, Skylar."

Against all likelihood, somehow, in some miraculous way.

Skylar had managed to not die.

Akeno was blown backward, landing solidly but holding his shattered, bleeding hand. He smirked at the boy's growing shield and whispered, "Well, a bit of fun after all."

Streya flung herself at the Caligan, a look of unadulterated fury in her expression.

He spun and caught her arm, dragging her with him in a jump.

She was thrown against a wall on the far end of the town, and Akeno sneered at her. "Remember your place, Agerian."

Without hesitating, she kicked him off her. He didn't stagger back like she'd wanted, but he did disappear into gray dust with that horrible pulsing sound.

Running as fast as she could, she cut through anything that tried to get between her and Skylar. She had to get to him. She had to save him.

She couldn't lose him.

By the time she got back to Skylar, she saw the last tendrils of a shield pop off his frame. Her eyes must've been playing tricks, because she could've sworn the shield had looked like a mold of Skylar's body.

The boy collapsed to the ground, and she barely made it in time to catch him. He wasn't ...

He couldn't be ...

"Skylar, c'mon; look at me. Stay with me," she shot out in a panic. The words flew from her so quickly that they barely sounded like individual words.

Slowly, his exhaustion-laden eyes met hers, and he meekly offered a smile as he mumbled out, "What took you ...?"

Praise the Elders.

He was alive.

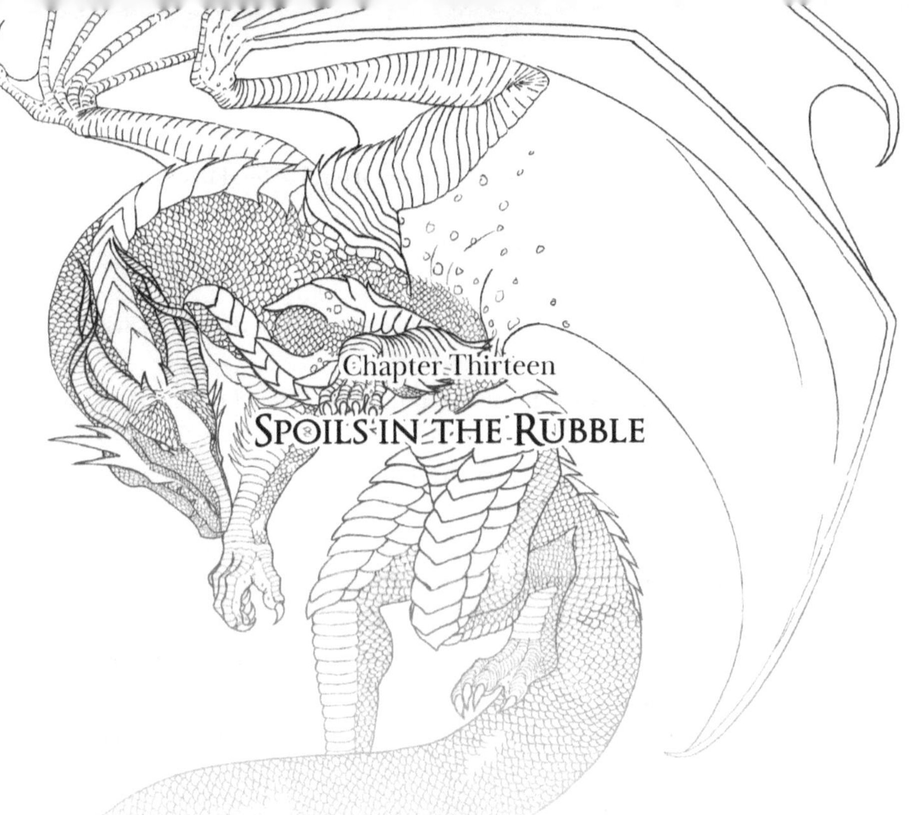

Chapter Thirteen
SPOILS IN THE RUBBLE

It didn't feel real for Charles to be knocking on the same door, to the same flat he'd visited the night prior. So much had happened in twenty-four hours that acknowledging this was the same spot seemed impossible.

When Streya opened the door, he barreled into the flat, asking, "Where's Skylar?"

"In Erador's room. We ... we figured it'd be better if he came here rather than your parents' estate," Streya answered.

"He's okay?"

"He's ... he's alive."

Swallowing hard, the elder brother cuttingly said, "That doesn't assuage my concerns."

"I know—just ... please, sit for a minute," she said as she gestured to the small table adjacent the kitchen.

Charles snuck a glance down the hallway that he assumed led to the bedrooms. Ryder was jammed at the end of the hall, his mass covering the entrances to two doors. He looked every bit a guardian spirit of sorts, his eyes unblinkingly staring, daring anything to harm his charge.

As they sat, Streya fidgeted with her fingers. "It ... wasn't stellar.

Skylar wound up facing Akeno—the teleporter. He held his own, but he got beat up pretty badly."

"But he stopped this Akeno bloke, right?"

"He made him run."

A short huff left Charles. "So that beast is still out there somewhere."

"Unfortunately."

Staring at the table, he chewed his thoughts. "How ...? How bad is he?"

"Skylar's healed up by now. And he showered, so quite honestly, to you, he'll look perfectly fine."

Charles slowly met her gaze and whispered, "Physically."

She nodded.

"Can I see him?"

"Of course." She offered a small smile. "But just so you know... he hasn't really talked much since it happened."

Without another word, Charles rose to his feet and marched down the hall.

The black grovix nodded to his right then went into the opposite room, allowing Charles to enter before stationing himself back in the hall.

Skylar sat on a bed that was a little too big for the size of the room. But, if this was Erador's bedroom, the man would need something longer than a standard twin-sized mattress. There were no wall decorations. Instead, a handful of sketches showcasing the schematics for pistols, and the intricate designs of swords and battle axes were pinned to the plaster.

The only other furniture in the room was a chest of drawers, and it appeared they weren't all capable of closing fully, as some clothes spilled out.

Charles gave Ryder a glance before closing the door. He eased onto the bed, taking stock of Skylar's appearance.

He wore a shirt that was too big—likely borrowed from Erador—and his pants were a light blue fleece—Charles figured Streya had loaned those. Skylar's eyes were distant and drooped. Heavy dark rings sat under his eyes, and his shoulders were hunched. He slowly looked to his elder brother and said in a cracked voice, "Hey."

Unable to stop himself, Charles pulled Skylar into a relieved hug. Skylar barely returned it, weakly offering something of an embrace.

"Thank God you're okay," Charles said before letting out a long sigh. He pulled away, but kept a grip on Skylar's shoulder. "What the bloody hell happened?"

With a weak shrug, Skylar muttered, "Got into my first fight."

"In some households you'd be considered a man now."

"That's not funny," he said with a feeble look of disdain.

"Sorry," Charles whispered as he sat back and frowned. He studied his brother's dulled features. "Sky, what happened?"

Skylar's eyes flitted across his lap. Within a few seconds, tears welled in his eyes.

It cut Charles's heart into pieces to watch his brother crumble so quickly.

"I ..." Skylar choked out, his mouth hanging open uselessly for a beat. "I almost ..." He met his brother's gaze and croaked out, "He almost killed me."

Charles wasn't someone to go looking for a fight. He wasn't a violent person. He didn't leap to anger or fury. But in an instant, he felt white-hot rage flood his body and his mind.

What he would give to be able to drive a sword through this Akeno's heart.

He gripped Skylar's knee and swallowed back his desire to hurt something.

"I got separated from my Zaheri, and he was ... It was a game to him. He enjoyed hurting me. And it wouldn't stop—*he* wouldn't stop. He just kept coming." Skylar pinched his eyes shut and shuddered. "I ... I'm so tired, but ..."

"Hey," Charles offered a gentle squeeze on Skylar's arm. "You're safe now. Your Zaheri won't let anyone get to you."

"But what if they can't?" Skylar burst out, meeting Charles's gaze with wide, fear-filled eyes. Tears slipped down his cheeks in a messy cascade. "They couldn't stop him from pushing me away before. What if he comes back? What if he does it again? Wh—" A sob racked up his chest, and Skylar gripped the fabric of the quilt on the bed.

For no good reason, Charles abruptly asked, "What made him run?"

Sucking in shuddering breaths, Skylar asked, "Wh-what?"

"Streya said he ran. What made him run?" Charles asked.

Skylar sank back a little. "I ... I ..."

"You did something, right?" the elder brother asked softly. "I'm not asking for me. I'm asking for you."

Easing against the headboard, Skylar nodded feebly. "Y-yeah ... I ... I dunno what, but ... I did. I did make him run."

A small smile graced Charles's face. "Then that means he's not coming back."

The fear still flitted in Skylar's eyes as he looked to his brother for confirmation. "You really think so?"

"People usually only run from things that scare them."

The concept made Skylar let out a cough of a laugh. Akeno scared of him. That felt backward.

Charles had a point, though. Whatever had happened, whatever had made Skylar gain all that strength and that super strong shield that had molded to him, Akeno hadn't been able to lay a finger on him. And now that he thought about it, the Caligan general had been nowhere to be found immediately afterward.

Skylar slumped as he felt his heart slow its pounding. Comfort washed over him at the thought that yes, he was safe. And yes, Akeno wouldn't return. Because Skylar had done something in that fight that had made him run away.

Which meant that at least for right now, Skylar could sleep.

As his eyes dropped, Skylar looked to his brother, and a ghost of a smile flickered on his face. "Thanks, Charles."

Gently holding his brother's face, Charles smiled warmly at him. "Anytime, Protector."

"Very funny," Skylar mumbled sleepily with a lopsided grin.

"From what I hear, very accurate." Charles got to his feet. "Get some rest. You deserve it after today."

Fighting past his exhaustion, Skylar asked, "We aren't going home?"

For a second, Charles didn't move. Then he subtly shook his head and answered, "Not tonight."

A long, slow breath soothed out of Skylar, and a look of relief flooded his features.

"You let me worry about that, okay? Right now, all you have to do is rest."

"Y'sure?"

With a nod, Charles smirked back. "Positive."

"'Kay," Skylar muttered, his eyes already closing as he began to fall to his side, blearily grasping at the quilt and haphazardly wrapping himself in it before collapsing onto the pillows.

Staring at his brother with gratefulness in his heart, Charles readjusted the quilt to properly cover Skylar's body. For a few seconds, he just stayed there, grateful to see his brother still alive. Then he ruffled Skylar's hair before he turned to leave.

As Charles walked away, he prayed that this was the worst Skylar would ever have to face.

He knew it wasn't.

Skylar shakily groped the walls as he ambled down the hall in the dead of night.

Ryder snored in the living area, sprawled on the floor. Erador was draped over the too-small-for-him couch.

Charles wasn't there. Or, at least, Skylar couldn't see him in the darkness of the flat. He wasn't sure where else his brother would have been sleeping, if he was there at all.

The concept of Charles not being present sent another wave of heart-thudding panic in Skylar's chest.

He knew Ira was in the room opposite Erador's, which meant Streya's was the smallest one by the bathroom.

Skylar practically ran there.

As he ripped the door open, Streya bolted upright, whipping a pistol from under her pillow and pointing it at the door. A small blue glow came from the magazine slot, vibrant in the dark room. Her arm was rigid and tight as she took stock of the fact that it was Skylar standing in the threshold, not an enemy.

"I ... I ..." he trembled.

He hadn't run to someone in the middle of the night since he was a child. Until just now, he was almost positive he'd never suffered nightmares. But everyone had nightmares. Kids had them all the time. So, Skylar must've run to someone at some point.

Logically, he probably had run to Charles as a child and not his mother, given how apathetic his mother tended to be with him.

Now, in this moment, though, he found himself craving a motherly comfort.

Streya was up in a flash, and before he could voice why he was there, she pulled him into a tight embrace.

"He's gone, right?" Skylar asked through mounting tears.

"Shh ... it's okay, Skylar," Streya said as she gently stroked his hair and rocked him as though he were a baby.

He gripped her tighter. "I know it's stupid ..."

"No, no, it's not stupid," she corrected. Pulling back to look at him, she gave him a gentle look. "Even warriors get nightmares."

"You're just saying that," he muttered as he rubbed his runny nose.

She offered a smirk. "Erador just puts on a good show. He comes running to the door for midnight comfort, crying for 'Mommy' all the time."

It was a lie, but it made Skylar laugh at the image of Erador—towering, intimidating Erador, dreadlocks and all—stomping through the flat screaming, "Mommy."

Gently stroking his cheek, Streya asked, "Why do you think I've got a gun under the pillow tonight?"

"Yeah, sure, you're scared."

"I am," she stressed. "Sky, I ..." A frown came to her face, and tears glassed her eyes. "I can't imagine what I'd do if ..." She shook her head. "Elders, I was so scared I got there too late."

A new wave of tears filled his eyes, but these weren't as painful. His mouth contorted around the simple question of, "Really?"

"Skylar," she said with a smile, "you mean the world to me. To all of us."

She ... she was actually saying it. Someone, other than Charles, cared about him. And not because of a supposed title or supposed wealth or supposed influence.

"We love you, Skylar," she said simply, like it was the easiest thing to say in the world.

When was the last time he'd heard that?

He didn't know.

But it brought a watery smile cracking to his face as he coughed a few choked laughs before hugging her tight.

Someone loved him.

In that instant, he felt he'd found the family he'd been silently praying for.

Chapter Fourteen

THINGS NEVER CHANGE

The days and weeks that followed were some of the worst of Skylar's life.

Reporters stalking the estate, trying to break in to get "exclusive coverage." Screams for Skylar's identity to be made public and his future put out for the world to decide. The government arguing over who got him.

And a deafening silence at home.

His parents had been furious that he'd stayed with his Zaheri. Thankfully, they didn't know where the Agerians lived, so that kept them from a legitimate incident erupting in the quiet suburb of Oxford where the Beta Team called home.

Charles had, it seemed, spent the night with Taylor.

Then there was fury over that mess.

"Nothing happened," Charles had insisted to their parents. But suddenly, he spoke of her more often, and his phone pinged more frequently. After a couple days, Charles divulged to his trusted brother that he and Taylor were "officially" dating and had maybe possibly kissed a few times during his night-long stay at her flat.

By all appearances, the Duke of Derbyshire had lost full control over both his sons in a day's time. Not that he ever had control over them in the first place. But, perhaps he had always assumed he did.

For everyone's safety, the Beta Team was "welcomed" into the Mitchell Estate. Skylar was pretty certain the only one welcomed was Erador, and only by his mother.

He and Charles were quick to insist that Erador was gay, and by the time the Beta Team moved in, their mother seemed convinced ... mostly.

There was then a lot of yelling and reprimanding from his father while his mother sat there looking cross. Skylar tuned it out. Just nodded at proper intervals and muttered apologies occasionally to appear like he was actually worried about their perception of him.

He just wanted to get out of the room and move on. Because, by that point, he couldn't care less what his parents thought of him. There were a total of five—now six, including Taylor—people in the world who genuinely seemed to like and care for him. And they were the only ones he was interested in keeping their approval.

And poor Taylor. She came to the estate to help with the Beta Team's move in and was scrutinized by the duke and his wife the entire time. But, the good sport she was, Taylor seemed to play it off as a joke and might've only served to make the Mitchells more furious with her when she'd respond to jabs with cheeky grins and finger guns.

Charles continuously had to hide grins and cough away fits of laughter at her behavior. Skylar had to leave the room at one point.

Having the Agerians and Skylar at the estate kept them under better security, which meant any reporters trying to get information were effectively locked out. However, on the flip side, it meant the government knew exactly where they all were. And there were many discussions about what to do with the superpowered British boy and his four alien friends.

There were calls for them to be locked up and experimented upon. Thank Jesus, someone had the sense to remind those calls that Skylar and his Zaheri were living, breathing sentient beings. It didn't stop several scientists from leaving slipped notes and letters explaining the "advancements" that could be made by studying someone like Skylar.

With how little his parents seemed to care for his wellbeing, it was a little shocking they didn't ship him and his Zaheri off in the dead of night.

It gave Skylar a glimmer of hope that maybe, just maybe, his parents did love him.

Maybe they just really sucked at showing it.

Then the declaration from the king came down. Skylar would remain a British citizen, and would therefore retain all of his rights in full as a protected member of society. His Zaheri were pardoned alongside him, and it was noted that their bravery helped save many lives, and that the attack could have been far more disastrous without their assistance.

Erador had grumbled, "*Assistance?* Are you serious? Is this blasted king stupid? We didn't assist! We *did*!"

"He can't publicly say that they incarcerated us and might've been the cause for London being targeted at all, now can he?" Ira had scolded.

The king's declaration included one other caveat: Skylar was stripped of any ties to his father's title. He was still clearly the Duke of Derbyshire's son, but would not and could not, as whatever enhanced human he was, ever take on the title of Duke. It seemed a lot of screaming died down after that announcement.

Skylar assumed the screaming had been brought on by other lords and ladies who were concerned that he might one day turn his powers against opposing members of the royal family in order to claim a better station for himself.

Obviously, they didn't know he could only make shields.

But he didn't mind their misunderstanding because it had given him the freedom he so greatly wanted. He was no longer bound to status and grandeur. Not fully, anyway.

His parents still expected him to continue studying at Oxford, still expected him to become an upstanding member of British society, and spread the Mitchell name into another generation. But, at least now, he didn't have to worry as much about disappointing them. And they didn't seem to put quite as much pressure on him anymore, either.

It didn't stop the derisive comments, though.

His father would let out snide jabs at Skylar's expense. His mother would sneer scathing remarks under her breath. Not all the time, but they were still there.

But they didn't sting anymore.

Skylar finished his fall semester from home, which he was grateful for. It awarded him more time at the estate, which meant he finally got to experience training.

His confidence blossomed over the winter holidays. Making shields became second nature to him, to the point that he used one to catch Margaret without actively thinking about it when she tripped in the hall one day. She had thought it was hilarious and squealed in glee. His mother had admonished him and stolen her away.

He'd shrugged and gone on his way. It was a shame that his little sister hadn't been allowed to play some more. He actually had been enjoying seeing her so happy.

The new year came, and with it came a new semester. Skylar insisted on studying from home again and took a lighter course load. His parents made no comment on either.

Meanwhile, his Zaheri occasionally left for hours at a time, returning to Tilion for "routine meetings." Whatever those were. Skylar had learned a little more about their world and how their laws were established during his time at home. Truthfully, he spent more time learning about Tilion and his Zaheri than any of his university studies.

He did a little digging into the other locations that had been impacted by the day they'd been attacked. It wasn't anything concrete, and finding specific locations had proven to be difficult. Reports varied widely, and almost all the reports cited two different areas where the pillars of light had been seen that day.

It meant that either one location was wrong and the other was right, or the portal had opened in two different areas because the Human-Borns in question had moved during the day, just as Skylar had. He couldn't be sure. And what little information Taylor was able to get didn't shed any further light on things.

Skylar hoped that, eventually, he would get the chance to meet the other Human-Borns. He found himself thinking about them fairly often.

What might they be doing? Who might they be? What sort of upbringing might they have come from? What cultures did they live in? During Christmas, he wondered if any of them were celebrating it, too.

He'd toyed with going to social media and blatantly asking for the other six Human-Borns to please announce themselves so they could meet virtually. But, for all he knew, being Human-Born might've launched someone to fame in a different country, and anyone might respond in the hope to gain popularity.

Streya had said they were all the same age, which meant a bunch of other eighteen-year-olds would qualify across the globe. The chances of getting truthful responses weren't likely, and he didn't want to weed through any fake ones to possibly track down the others.

"You should leave it to the Raidin," Ira said one night as Skylar bemoaned his efforts in finding the others.

"The Raidin?" he asked.

She nodded. "You all have titles. The Raidin is the First Human-Born. Then the Protector—that's you."

"What're the other titles?"

"Warrior, Healer, Shifter, Scholar, and Requisite."

Skylar squinted at her. "Why's 'Raidin' the only odd-sounding name?"

"Oh, well, it's an old title in Agerius," Ira said as she settled onto one of the plush couches in the estate. "It means 'The Elders Warrior.'"

Easing back in his seat, he mumbled, "So, only the First Human-Born got a title that means something special."

"What're you talking about?" Streya asked as she walked into the conversation, wearing a proud smile. "Protector means something special, too, y'know."

He cocked a brow at her. "Really? What's it mean?"

Ruffling his hair, she said, "It means 'Brave Man.'"

He was pretty sure she was making that up. He smiled, anyway.

Skylar grimaced as his shield took another blow from Erador's battle axe.

The Zaheri swirled the axe in his grasp and leaned back. "You're going to have to eventually learn to move."

"Yeah, sounds grand. How?" Skylar snipped back, lowering his shield.

It was the first warm day in February, which meant Skylar could finally go outside with his Zaheri for a training session. So far, all of his training had been small, confined to the manor. And, while there was a slight chill in the air, the sun was warm and the ground was devoid of snow or mud.

"Your shield can move," Ira offered, raising a small one in her grasp. The golden slab slid back and forth in the air. "It doesn't have to remain stagnant."

Scratching his head, Skylar said, "Yeah, I know that, but how do you override your brain in the moment?"

"What do you mean?" Streya asked.

"I mean, how do I get my brain to stop thinking I have to hold my hands up to keep the shield standing?" The teen waved his hand toward Erador. "Every time he comes at me, my reflex is to throw my hands up and hold the shield in place, like I have to keep my hands against it for it to stay upright."

"Oh, that's not so complicated to fix," Streya said with a shrug. "You just have to start making a shield move with you."

Squinting at her, Skylar asked, "All right ... how does one accomplish that?"

Ryder threw him a look. "You did that when we were charging out of London, remember?"

Easing back on his heels, Skylar replayed the events in London. A hum left him. "I guess I did."

"So, your body's reflex is interfering with your instincts," Streya said. She gestured to Skylar. "You already have the instincts on how to make solid shields that protect your back. It's now just a matter of training yourself to remember that you don't have to keep a hold of your shield to make it effective."

Nodding a few times, Skylar answered, "All right, fair. How do you suggest I do that?"

"I think you should try the conforming shield," Ira offered.

Streya winced. "That's actually a good idea."

Holding his arms out in an exasperated gesture, Skylar said, "C'mon, guys; I told you. Something made me capable of doing that. I don't think I'll ever be able to manage it on my own."

"Sure you can," Erador said with a shrug. "I've seen Agerians do it."

"He's right." Streya nodded to him. "Bulwarks manage things like that all the time."

Skylar deflated and shuffled his weight.

Gaining a motherly expression, Streya said, "I'm not saying make a shield across your whole body. Start small." She walked up to him and took hold of his arm. "Your hand and arm, start there. Make a shield that conforms to your limb and keep it on for fifteen minutes. Flex your fingers around it and have the shield work with your body, not against it."

"You make it sound easy," Skylar grumbled.

"You're thinking too much." Twirling her hand, she pulled golden energy to flit around her arm. A moment later, a shield appeared across her hand and up to her elbow. "See? Anyone can do it. You just have to let instinct guide you."

Ira squinted at Streya's action, her gaze clicking across the shield the Team Leader had created.

Dropping her hand, Streya said, "Now you give it a try."

The teen let out a sigh. "Okay, fine." He stared at his hand and tried to imagine a gauntlet there.

Nothing happened.

Maybe he had to imagine putting a glove on or something, sliding his fingers into armor.

Shuffling his weight, he flipped his wrist a couple times.

Maybe just looking more intently at his joints would help him figure out how to make a shield move fluidly with his actions. Or maybe he had to pull a shield first and have it wrap around his arm. Maybe that would be how he could get it to work. Or maybe just pull energy into his grasp? That was hard, though. Shields sprang up with ease, but getting his energy to just flit in his palm had always been a task that required effort.

"You're thinking too much," Streya teased.

A groan of frustration escaped Skylar. She was right, of course. But he didn't like that she could tell he was overthinking things so easily.

But he was overthinking it, wasn't he?

After all, when he got dressed in the morning, it wasn't like he had to psych himself up to put his hand through the sleeve of his shirt. He just did it.

His energy was a part of him. Shield creation was what he was made for. That meant he just had to relax and let instinct guide him.

Letting out a slow, even breath, Skylar looked to his hand again.

He began to imagine an indigo shield covering his forearm and hand, and he felt something in his mind click.

In a flash of indigo, the shield appeared on his arm, fully conformed to his limb.

Skylar let out a triumphant laugh as he smiled. "I did it!"

"Good for you," Erador said. He swung his axe around and started toward the teen. "Now move with it."

"Erador, no!" Streya reprimanded as Skylar took a tentative step back.

"Oh, come on!" the hulking Zaheri burst. He waved his hand emphatically at Skylar. "He's got the shield! It would hold against my hit!"

"Why don't we let him get used to having a shield conform to his arm *before* we start trying to break it?" Ira said sternly.

Groaning at the sky, Erador threw his head back and dropped his arms defeatedly at his sides.

Ryder gave the ladies a stare. "You're too soft."

"No, you're too rough!" Ira shot back.

Even though they were arguing over how they treated Skylar differently, the teen chuckled.

He glanced to the shield on his arm and fluidly swirled his wrist, watching the protection move seamlessly with his body.

Taking in his Zaheri's bickering, Skylar let a contented smile fill his features.

Though he still had the occasional nightmare that echoed fears from the day of the attack, he couldn't deny that he was happy with what had been born from that terrible day. Charles and Taylor had become a couple, his gilded cage had been opened, and his Zaheri had become more involved in his life.

It wasn't perfect.

But Skylar was happy.

Chapter Fifteen

AND THEY MEET

A few days later, Streya burst into the drawing room that had been dedicated as the Beta Team's hangout spot. She clutched her phone and spoke quickly, wearing a wide smile, "Guys, Tyron connected with me!"

Skylar's brow furrowed. "Who's Tyron?"

"The Alpha Team Leader. His team protects the First Human-Born," Ira said with a smile as she got to her feet.

Excitement shot through Skylar, and he leaped up. "Really? Wh-what's he say?"

"He wants to come here, with the First Human-Born. He thinks you two should meet," Streya said.

Erador lounged back, propping his hands behind his head. "It'd be good to see Ty. Might be able to convince him to spar." Glancing to the ceiling, he mused, "Wonder if he's gotten any stronger."

Ira rolled her eyes. "He wouldn't be coming here to satiate your desire to see who's stronger."

"It's probably still Ty," Streya said with a smirk as she typed on her phone.

A grumble came from Erador as he shot Streya a glare.

"Would Tyron come alone with his Human-Born?" Ryder asked, his muscles tense.

"It may be good to have them all come," Ira said. "That way, Skylar can meet the whole team."

"You just wanna see Kal again," Erador grumbled. "And we shouldn't have them come here to satiate our own desires."

Skylar gave Ira a confused look. "But ... I thought Kaldok was the werewolf-cursed one. Isn't Zelek the one you talk about all the time?"

Ira flamed red and sputtered out a string of nonsense before squeaking out, "I don't talk about him all the time." She fidgeted with the ring on her thumb.

Staring at her phone screen, Streya smiled fondly. "It'll be so good to see him again."

So, Streya knew Tyron well then. Skylar wondered how. Were they like brother and sister, or something more? He thought about pressing but figured he shouldn't. It wasn't gentlemanly to pry from someone who they fancied.

Erador smacked Ryder and asked, "Why'd you ask about whether the whole team would come? You know someone on the Alpha Team?"

Flashing a sideways glance to Erador, Ryder growled, "Yes."

"Ty agrees that the whole team should come," Streya said with a nod. She straightened and pursed her lips. "How should they get here? It'd be awful expensive to have them fly."

Ira frowned. "And no one would allow Kaldok on a plane, I'm certain of it."

Shrugging, Skylar said, "Then let's have the jet pick them up."

"Would your father be okay with that?" Streya asked warily.

Wearing a sly grin, Skylar answered, "Charles can request it."

"That's true." Ira gained a gleeful look. "And they'd have to allow whomever we asked for on the jet!"

"Great, then we'll ask him! I hope it works out. It would be good to see everyone," Streya said.

"Even the Jumper you don't like?" Skylar asked.

"I never said I don't like him. I just ..." She rolled her eyes. "Okay, I don't like him."

As Erador propped his feet on the coffee table, he said, "Eh, we just don't know him well. If he's still alive, that means he can't be all bad. Ar'on'd have pummeled him otherwise." He gestured to Ira. "And Kal was there to keep him in line. I bet he's fine now."

Streya rolled her eyes. "Sure, fine, maybe. It's not like I'm gonna be spending time talking to him, anyway."

The following day, Charles got permission for a royal jet to be dispatched for the transportation of the First Human-Born and her Zaheri.

And before Skylar knew it, the day arrived.

He paced in his room anxiously. He'd been going through it all over and over again in his head. The First Human-Born was coming, and they were going to meet. Finally, he was going to see what another Human-Born was like! He'd come up with these crazy ideas in his head for what they might be like or what they'd sound like, almost like he'd created a cast in his head based on their titles.

But the First Human-Born had been an enigma. "Elders Warrior" meant little to Skylar. But he assumed they'd be a fighter of some sort, capable of being their de-facto leader.

Just after the attack, he'd been so concerned that the other Human-Borns might resent him for his lack of progress. Now, though, he'd gone through training. He'd progressed in his shield creation and felt so much more confident in who he was and what he was made for. Charles's screaming command those months back kept coming to mind whenever Skylar felt himself veer toward misery or depression.

This is what you were made for.

The impenetrable shield that had appeared for him when he needed it most. His slow but steady growth as a shield maker. Even his blossoming confidence in the past few months all pointed toward this being squarely the path he was meant to walk.

What else could he possibly be made for than this?

Despite his assurances, he still felt anxiety twist his stomach.

Any moment now, the cars would arrive with the First Human-Born and their Zaheri. Not only was he about to meet a fellow Human-Born— someone who could genuinely understand what he felt regarding this whole thing—but he was about to meet a whole team of Agerians. He'd been told a little about them but didn't have a clear picture of what they were like.

The whole thing welled intense excitement within him. Sort of like the night before a long-awaited vacation—the enthusiastic anticipation it created when you were about to do something you'd been dreaming of.

It'd only been a few months since he'd known the Human-Borns existed alongside him, but he'd yearned to meet them so badly that it felt like he'd been waiting for them his whole life.

When he heard the *click-click-clack* of Ryder's nails against the wood floor, Skylar ran to the door.

As Ryder passed, he grumbled with a scowl, "They're here."

Skylar didn't care that Ryder seemed fully peeved about something. He was so thrilled that he had to keep himself from running down the hall and tumbling down the stairs.

Voices flitted from the sitting room just off the foyer.

"I'm just saying, does this have to be done right away? Can't we take in some sights or something first?" a girl asked timidly.

Skylar halted on the stairs.

Oh no ...

They ... they didn't want to be here.

"Hey, calm down. It's gonna be fine," a male replied softly, as though trying to offer comfort.

"Are you sure we should be here?" Skylar could barely hear her and had to stretch his hearing. "We're so out of place."

Oh. So she just didn't like the estate.

Well, they had something in common then.

The ball of worry loosened in Skylar's chest.

He continued down the stairs, ripping his jacket off because he suddenly felt terribly warm and self-conscious.

Deep breaths, idiot. It's fine. They're nervous, too. It's okay, he told himself.

He hit the foyer floor and noticed the imposing bulk of a creature standing just inside the threshold to the sitting room. The man was clearly the werewolf that Ira had talked about. Though he must've been seven feet tall, he had his shoulders drooped and ducked, as if trying to make himself appear smaller.

The werewolf's—Ira said his name was Kaldok—ears pivoted toward him, and he cast Skylar a glance, shrinking back against the threshold in worry.

Skylar offered a smile and a nod, trying to convey that he didn't fear him. Then he stepped into the threshold and took stock of the group.

Two grovix stood among them all; one with brilliant white fur who turned to look at him upon his appearance. Red eyes met his, and the feline features softened slightly. At the window stood a younger, lean man, wearing a jocular grin and an easy stance. Meanwhile, a gruff-looking gentleman, who looked positively exhausted, stood with arms crossed tight across his chest not far from the lean, easy-going one.

And near the fireplace mantle stood a tall, toned man with a soft edge to his features as he gently held the shoulders of a teenage girl. "Jen, we were invited here," he was saying.

"On that nice jet," a man with styled hair by the window said.

The other grovix, the one with tan fur, grumbled, "Nice to you."

Fighting past trembling, Skylar forced himself to be as laid back as the guy at the window and said with a small smile, "I'm glad you liked it."

All eyes turned to him, and Skylar had to actively tell himself to not flinch or shy back. They were Agerians. They wouldn't hurt him or judge him.

They could be his family, too.

The man standing in front of the teenage girl whipped around and immediately eased once he took in Skylar's features. So, that was probably Tyron.

And the girl standing next to him had to be the First Human-Born. Tyron had called her Jen. Skylar couldn't help but smile at her.

She looked so refreshingly normal. And how she stared at him wasn't this look of sizing him up or trying to figure out how to get something out of him. There was an uneasiness there, and he understood it all too well.

Something else they had in common.

Nothing else occurred to him in that moment except to just act in boldness. It was strange, he thought, how confidently he was standing in that moment. Had he really become so comfortable with who he was in such a short amount of time?

Throwing his jacket onto the nearby chair, Skylar crossed the room. Smiling at her, he said, "You must be Jen." He extended his hand to her, and she stared back at him with a look of surprise. "Pleased to meet you. My name is Skylar."

"Hi," she said as she carefully took his hand. Her gaze flitted around the room, and she awkwardly added, "Uh, nice house."

Skylar grimaced a bit. "Ah, noticed it was absurdly grand, did you?" Of course it was making them uncomfortable. Look at the bloody place. It was like they'd stepped into a museum, not someone's home. It wasn't cozy or welcoming. He frowned and muttered, "I knew we should've met somewhere less formal."

Jen flashed her hands out and quickly said, "No! I mean, it's fine. It's just ... We're ..."

A smile quirked on his face. He almost told her to calm down, that he understood. But he appreciated how out of sorts she felt. It was so liberating to know that someone else felt just as unsure of what to do or say in this moment.

She pointed toward the ceiling with a wince. "We're not exactly used to ... y'know."

Nodding, he found himself smiling at her again.

As they continued talking, Skylar wondered if perhaps, just maybe, this was something as cliché as the beginning of a beautiful friendship. He certainly hoped that was the case. Because, for absolutely no good, understandable reason, Skylar found he was comfortable with her. Something told him that they were going to get on grandly. And he couldn't wait to get to know her more.

His first real friend.

The WARRIOR'S WRATH

Third comes
the Warrior,
with talents
unrivaled,
one call will
bring armies to
march

PART I

WHAT COULD HAVE BEEN

Chapter One

A No Good, Very Bad Night

Zelek paced a small path in the team's tiny house, scrubbing his jaw as he looked out the window. Lightning flashed across the sky, illuminating the outline of Tokyo's distant cityscape.

They had been tasked with protecting Takeo.

He'd never anticipated they would need to keep an eye on his parents, too.

Dover sat curled in the corner, as if trying to make his large, bulky frame fit into a small space to avoid causing any issues. The grovix's ears were drooped and low, a barely audible whine escaping his efforts to remain quiet occasionally.

The door opened, and Zelek whipped around as Lorn and Rowan stepped into the small entranceway. Lorn carefully took his shoes off and deposited them neatly with the other outdoor shoes. Rowan kicked his off, flinging each boot with a frustrated spasm and sending them clattering against the wall.

"How bad is it?" Zelek asked, wanting to curl in on himself.

Lorn's red hair was drenched from the rain, his eyes downcast as he shook his head. "I ... It ..."

Giving Lorn a sideways glance, Rowan gently pushed forward and approached Zelek. "The wreck was bad. They probably died on impact."

Zelek's stomach twisted.

With a frown, Lorn asked quietly, "What's this mean, Zelek?"

Shaking his head a little, Zelek stepped back, his gaze distant. "I don't know." He blinked a few times before marching to the computer.

"What're you doing?" Rowan asked.

"Trying to see what happens to orphans on Earth," Zelek muttered. A pang of wounds he thought had healed long ago resurfaced in his mind. It brought sympathies for the now-orphaned three-year-old boy who they were supposed to protect.

Lorn gained a little more vibrancy as he nodded. "That's a good idea. Maybe there's a way to ensure we can track his whereabouts."

"Finding the boy was hard the first time," Rowan said. "You really think we'll be able to track him down again?"

Dover slowly got up and went to Zelek's side. "You okay?" For how imposing Dover looked, his unsure tone conveyed all of the youth he possessed.

"I'll be fine," Zelek answered mindlessly, scanning the article he'd found. It wasn't terribly promising.

Orphanages and low adoption rates. The culture they were in appeared to be concerned with having children of their own, likely to pass on their family names and genes. Which, best Zelek could gather, made sense for the people. They were honor-bound, and family genealogy was important. And lots of kids were left in this sort of holding pattern. Families wouldn't relinquish their right to them out of shame or the stigma of giving up their child.

Zelek swallowed hard. Humans and their pride made his heart hurt sometimes, especially when innocent children were in the crosshairs.

Takeo would become a ward of the state. With no biological parents left to claim him, he would be available for adoption. That was good.

Or was it?

By the looks of things, the boy could wind up adopted by any number of people. He might not even stay in Japan. He could wind up being adopted by a family in another country altogether.

On one hand, Zelek didn't see an issue with Takeo being adopted, regardless of where he ended up. Because if he got adopted, he'd be loved and cared for. That was what mattered at the root of it for a little boy who was suddenly parentless.

But, on the flip side, Zelek had a job to do.

What if Takeo got adopted by some couple living in another country, and what if that family kept moving from time to time for some reason? Humans seemed to love doing that. Not all of them, but more than Zelek would've anticipated. Just picking up and moving clear across oceans for reasons unknown to him.

Could they afford to keep up with that sort of lifestyle? They had to remain nearby to do their job effectively. How else would they protect the Human-Born?

And then there was the issue of allowing Takeo to be removed from his native culture. Sure, it didn't mean much to Zelek, and they had only recently become fluent enough in Japanese to really get by. But human cultures were important, it seemed. There were so many different ones, and Takeo was clearly a Japanese boy. He should be allowed to stay in his own culture.

But what if he got adopted by some big, wealthy family, and that came with human security and personnel who would hinder Zelek's task of protecting and eventually training the boy? What if that sort of family refused Takeo's involvement with Agerius, or even forcibly kept the team from preparing Takeo for what his role was?

There had to be an answer that would allow the boy to be safe and guarded and kept in his own native country, and also allow Zelek the ability to fulfill his role as protector and trainer to the Human-Born.

Pushing off the desk, Zelek straightened. "I'm going to speak with the Council; see what they might say."

Lorn nodded. "Perhaps the Elders will provide answers."

"Perhaps. Keep watch over him best you can. I'll be back as soon as possible." The Team Leader snatched his wallet and jacket and stole into the early morning rain.

The storm should've cleared by now, but it continued in its drudgery, offering a misting, dreary drizzle to welcome a new day.

Zelek hopped onto the nearly empty train and made his way into the center of Tokyo. Though seats were available, he chose to remain standing. The gentle rocking of the train car would likely put him to sleep, and while exhaustion clung to his body from his all-nighter, he couldn't afford to rest now. Not until he knew what to do next.

The train was quiet, save the occasional *click clack* of the wheels against the rail or jarring *thump* of the car when it went over a connection. Silence was typically something Zelek enjoyed. But now, after almost twelve hours of timid, unknown quiet, he found himself yearning for familiar sounds.

He wished he could just fly. Stretching his wings right now, in this bleak, rainy atmosphere, sounded wonderful. He shook his head. No, he'd get to fly once he got to Tilion. And he'd have to fly fast.

Taking in a long, steadying breath, he exhaled slowly, letting his eyes close. Perhaps he should have slept for a little, just to get his strength up.

He'd have to get a stout cup of tea from Hama's in Agerius before he left. That would help keep him awake for the return trip at least.

By the time Zelek arrived at his destination, the car had begun to fill with early risers aiming for the city. So many people just going about their workday, all completely unaware of the lives lost overnight.

As Zelek stepped onto the platform and made his way to the garden, he found himself swept up in the reminder of just how big this world was. So many people were in this one city, and there were even more cities just like it, or at least similar to it, across Earth. An unfathomable number of lives from here to the other side of the world.

He glanced to the slowly dawning sky. Pockets of blue could be seen through the parting gray clouds.

Was Kaldok all right?

Tokyo was a bustling city, practically bursting at the walls because of the number of people who lived there. The whole reason they were settled on the outskirts was because of Dover. Zelek's brother was bound to have been stuck in a crummy situation.

Did he get to wander the streets and explore the world he now lived in? Or was he confined because of what he looked like? Did his team care about him? Did they treat him well?

Zelek knew little about most of the Alpha Team members. Council Member Blaze was, best he could tell, a fine speaker and dignified Alpha for the grovix, but what sort of person was she? Did she treat Kaldok with any respect, or only disdain? And what of the others? Grand Master Ar'on was gruff and quiet. Zelek knew nothing of the Jumper, or the other grovix who had been assigned alongside Kaldok. And though he'd never really gotten to know him, Zelek did trust that Knight Commander Tyron was a steady leader for the group. But no matter how nice someone might seem, no one aside from Zelek and Ira had ever really bothered to see Kaldok as more than a werewolf.

Hastening his steps, Zelek pushed his concern for his brother aside. He had to focus on his Human-Born. That had to take precedence. Kaldok would be fine.

Kaldok was always fine.

Arriving at the portal, Zelek did a quick sweep of the area to ensure no one was around to see his disappearance. He'd have to time his return well; otherwise, he'd arrive and startle some poor passerby. With it being early morning, he figured he had a few solid hours before the park became busy. Even then, it wasn't a popular time of year for people to mill around the garden. Not with most of the trees leafless and the air still a bit chillier than humans seemed to prefer.

Once he was on Tilion, he summoned his wings and tore to Agerius as fast as he could. The city was bustling and bright. It was late morning, by his gauge of the sun's position.

He landed fairly steadily and ran into Mount Ara's entrance, slowing his pace as he entered the High Council Chamber.

Council Leader Ger'in turned to him, his brows knit together in confusion. "Zaheri Zelek. What brings you home?"

"There's been an incident, and I require the Council's advice on how to proceed," Zelek said through smooth, heavy breaths. He wanted to gasp air into his lungs but forced himself to appear more collected and sure for the Council.

Ger'in nodded. The air of regal wisdom in his subtlest movements hadn't changed since Zelek had left for Earth. His silver eyes stuck out sharply against his dark, wrinkled skin. The neatly trimmed beard along his jaw looked longer to Zelek since the last time he'd been in Agerius nearly a year prior.

"Very well." Ger'in turned toward the Council. "We must listen well and advise wisely for our Gamma Team Leader."

All eyes turned to Zelek as he said, "The Third Human-Born's parents were killed."

A rash of surprised gasps and whispers sounded around the chamber.

"Not by Caligan means. Humans have these devices called vehicles. It's a way they travel great distances. The Third Human-Born's parents were in an accident while traveling in their vehicle and died as a result."

Council Member Aros, the only clean-shaven member of the group, and the only one to sport shorter hair, looked thoughtful before he met Zelek's gaze. "What will become of the Third?" Much like Ger'in, Aros was revered as one of the wisest in Agerius, as well as one of the eldest. Both the senior Council Member and Council Leader had witnessed much of Agerius' history, though Zelek didn't know how old either of them were.

"The best we can discern, he's an orphan. The country we live in will put him into an orphanage, and by all accounts, it appears he could become adopted."

"Adopted?" a Council member asked.

"Taken into another family. Given their name."

Ger'in's eyes narrowed. "You stated that he 'could become adopted.' Is there an alternative?"

With a helpless shrug, Zelek answered, "I don't know. The culture points to the value of his life, and he could be taken into another family. But there's evidence that he might remain in this orphanage. Perhaps for his entire youth."

One of the Council members stroked his beard. "Hmm ... that does not seem fitting for a Human-Born."

"I'm unsure what the right course of action is."

A thoughtful expression filled Aros' features. "Is it possible that you, Chief Master, might be capable of adopting this boy?"

Reluctantly, Zelek admitted, "The thought had come to me, but I can't see how the humans would allow me guardianship over a boy I have no ties to. And ... it appears most of these orphanages seek parents. Meaning a husband ... and a wife."

Another Council member frowned and leaned back. "A shame none of the Gamma Team is married. Perhaps then the issue would resolve itself."

"Indeed," Zelek muttered as his gaze hit the floor.

Without missing a beat, Aros suggested, "Perhaps, Chief Master, there is someone who may appear as your wife—"

Zelek's head shot up and shock radiated his features.

"—that you may appear acceptable to the humans as a father for the boy?"

One of the women on the Council raised her brow in surprise. "It would be most irregular to require that a man act the role of husband for some poor woman solely to achieve a goal."

A small discussion broke out as to the morality surrounding Council Member Aros' idea.

Zelek didn't really hear it. He was a little too focused on the fact that someone specific had come to mind when Aros had made the suggestion. Zelek hadn't seen her in over three years.

And never mind that! He'd never actually ever voiced any of his feelings for her! He couldn't ask her to just show up and pretend to be his wife!

His head spun at the concept, images of what could be splashed into his mind with all the warmth and joy of potential.

His wife ...

With a defeated sigh, the female Council member said, "I concede your point. But can we honestly expect a woman to be willing to take on such a commitment for a simple guise?"

Aros rocked on his feet a little, keeping his balance, thanks to his staff. "Perhaps, if she were herself a Zaheri and understood the graveness of the situation."

"So you would ask another Zaheri, from another Human-Born, to move posts?" Ger'in asked as he furrowed his brow.

"No, no, not permanently. Temporarily. Until the boy can be placed under Zaheri Zelek's care."

Ger'in looked to Zelek. "Do you believe such a solution would provide the humans enough trust in you as a fitting father to the boy?"

Zelek swallowed. His mind was still stuck on the concept of it all. Of what it all could mean. Of what could happen because of it. Of what unspoken things would be made blatantly bare to her because of it all.

Then another thought crashed in.

What if the Council chose this placeholder wife for him?

Though he trembled at the thought that uttering her name would only careen them both into a horrible end, Zelek knew beyond a doubt that there was no one he'd ever want to pretend to be his wife aside from her.

And ...

It was the best chance at securing the Third Human-Born as his adoptive son.

Slowly, Zelek nodded. His mouth was a little dry as he managed to say, "I believe so. And" —he met Ger'in's gaze— "I know who would be fitting to aid me."

Ger'in's expression softened toward a bit of surprise. "Oh? Who would that be?"

"Ira. Of the Beta Team."

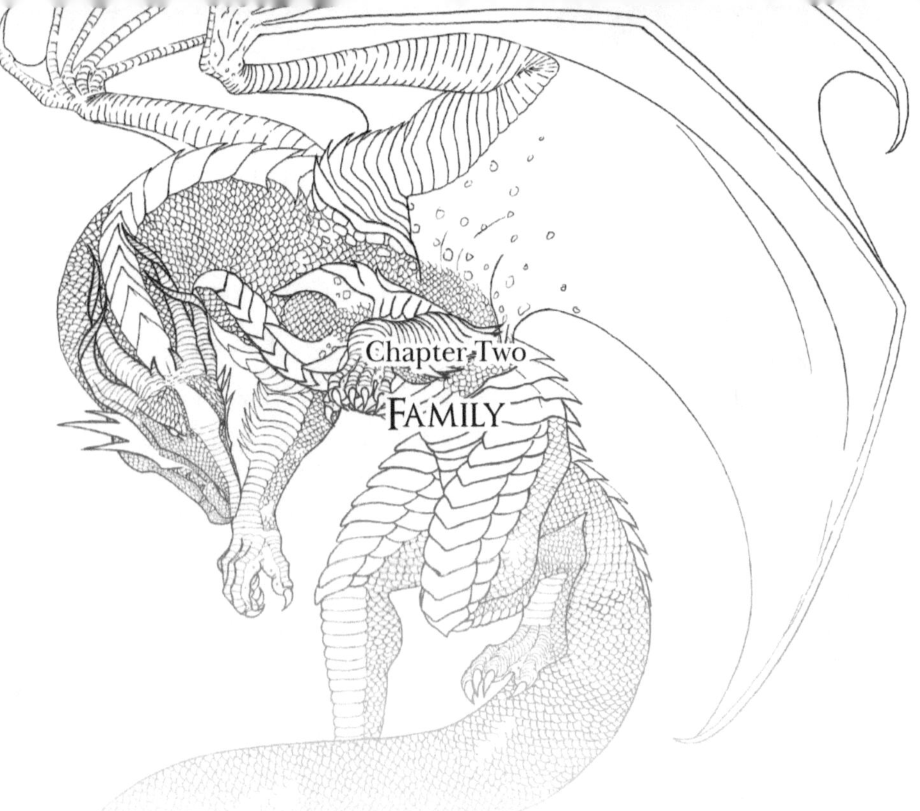

Chapter Two

FAMILY

Zelek sat outside of Hama's, tapping at the brim of his mug with his thumb. This was the stupidest idea he'd ever agreed to, though he'd never say it out loud. Because the idea had come from Council Member Aros, and he didn't have stupid ideas. Normally.

Maybe stupid wasn't a good way to describe it. *Sensitive*, or *clumsy*, or *bad* might've been better words. Granted, Council Member Aros hadn't had any reason to believe Zelek might have someone in mind because of specific things that had happened that Zelek just hadn't acted on.

For good reason, Zelek thought.

After all, Zelek wasn't exactly a pure-pedigree Agerian. There was bad blood in him. In Kal, too. There was a reason people really distrusted Kaldok, even after he'd conquered the curse and shown everyone what could happen if someone was strong enough to push the curse away. But all anyone saw were the remnants of their bloodline. Of whom they were related to.

And in a way, Zelek didn't blame them. It was the thing keeping him from acting on his feelings for Ira.

"Zelek?"

149

He startled and nearly dropped his tea, sloshing some over the brim. Elders, she'd gotten here fast.

In hindsight, he should've showered, or shaved, or something. As it was now, he probably looked horrendous.

Great. Good job, Z. Way to really impress her. Hey, Ira! How're you? I look like a trash heap. Come be my pretend wife.

And when he got a look at her, that's when he really felt like someone who'd rolled in the dragon's den.

Her hair was a little longer but still framed her oval face perfectly. There was a hint of worry in her beautiful dark eyes, her smaller body drawn in as she fidgeted with the hem of her shirt. It took everything in him to not just give her a goofy grin. It cracked through a bit despite his attempt to remain calm, because Elders ... He hadn't grasped how much he missed seeing her until just now.

"Hey, Ira," he hushed.

A concerned look was on her face as she offered a small smile. "You look stretched thin."

Self-consciously, he averted his gaze from her and ran a hand through his hair. "Yeah ... it's ... been a rough day."

She nodded a little. "The Runner that was sent for me didn't say anything beyond you needing help with something."

He gave her a wide-eyed stare.

"So ... is something wrong? How can I help?"

Darting his gaze around, he gently took her arm and started to guide her back toward the entrance of Agerius. "Uh ... mind if we talk as we go?"

"Sure," she said with a nod. "Zelek, really, what's wrong? You look like you've been tossed between a few bratak'ra."

"There's no easy way to say what's going on. So ... I'm just gonna have to say it." He scrubbed his scalp. "The Third Human-Born became an orphan last night. His parents were killed in an accident while they were in their car."

Ira sucked in a surprised breath. "Oh ..." Her gaze fell to the ground as they continued on. "What ...? What does that mean for you?"

"That's kind of the problem. And where I ... could use your help." He looked anywhere but her. His skin itched, and he fought the urge to scratch his arm. "Do ...? Do you know anything about how humans handle orphans?"

She blinked a few times. "Um, no. I haven't had any need to research it. Though now that you mention it, that would be a wise thing to study."

Fondness filled his features as he gave her a soft smile.

"Is there something about how they handle orphans that requires my help?"

Slowly nodding, he admitted, "Yeah."

Chewing on her lip, she waggled her mouth a bit, searching the stones beneath her for an answer to his simple response.

Before she could smack him or demand an answer, he hushed, "Humans, they ... they do this thing called adoption. Where people can take orphans into their homes and make them part of their family."

His heart pounded as he tried to figure out the best way to say why he'd asked for her. It'd been two hours, and he still hadn't really determined how to go about it. Not without just blurting out all sorts of other things, too. Things he didn't want to admit, because if he was anything at all like his uncle, that meant he could really hurt her someday, no matter how he felt now.

She stared at him intently, only flicking her gaze forward briefly to ensure she didn't run into anyone.

"They might be open to allowing a single father to adopt a young boy, but ... it isn't likely. Not when there are lots of other families who might be ... y'know ... whole."

Her eyes widened.

Zelek stopped, and his gaze darted as he tried to work out the right words. He felt like he was going to be sick. "Ira, I ... I stand a better chance of appealing to the humans if ... if I had ..."

"A wife?" she squeaked, barely above a whisper.

Forcing his eyes to meet hers, he quickly said, "It would just be a façade, a pretend sort of thing. It wouldn't be anything legitimate. I mean, it might for humans, I don't know, but—"

"Okay."

Words got caught in Zelek's mouth, and he choked a bit, his fingers going a little numb as he stared dumbly at her.

A smile wormed its way to her face, and a brightness was in her eyes. Oh no. Oh no. He had to get his mouth to work.

"If getting married is what—"

"No, we shouldn't do that," he shook out quietly.

Her smile fell, and she seemed stuck for a moment. A forced sort of compliance came to her face as she tried to smile again. "Oh, okay …"

"Ira, it's … it's not you. I … There's …"

"It's all right. I understand."

Zelek's eyes widened as he looked at her. "You do?"

Despite her words, her eyes were downcast, and a frown was on her face. She gained a sad smile and said, "It's because of Kaldok, right? You don't want to leave him alone."

A crushing sort of weight pulled his heart into his stomach.

"I don't blame you. Or him. I care for you both too much to hold that against either of you." Ira gained a resolved look and squared her shoulders. "So, you just need me to" —the brave look in her eyes faltered as she looked at him, and her words came out quieter— "pretend … to be your wife?"

His head felt a little off kilter again as his mind spiraled into the imaginary world where he and Ira could just be married and be happy and be forever, and there was no bad blood or curses or side-glances or concerned looks.

Nodding shakily, Zelek said, "Yeah, just until we can secure the Third Human-Born as, well …"

"Our son?" she asked with an unsure look that held all the hope of truth.

Despite his best efforts, Zelek couldn't stop himself from smiling fondly at her. "Yeah."

Ira returned his smile and nodded. "All right then. I suppose we should get moving."

Over the course of two days, Zelek and Ira sat through several meetings. There was an inspection of the tiny house (the Gamma Team had hastily moved anything that looked suspicious out of the building, literally dumping it all in a nearby field under a makeshift shelter, and Dover disappearing into the forest) and many questions.

They sat, waiting for an answer, in one of the orphanage's little rooms. Zelek kept playing with the wedding band on his left ring finger, still feeling a bit of the shocking excitement when Ira had slipped it onto the digit.

He remembered far too fondly how her hand had tightened around his when he'd gently slipped the simple gemmed ring onto her ring finger. They'd both been hard-pressed to not smile a lot at each other, and at the people conducting the interviews.

Zelek knew enough Japanese to sound mostly fluent, only stumbling over a few words here and there. By all accounts, they were a happy, young married couple who had recently moved to Tokyo because of a job Zelek was offered. They did background checks, which meant nothing to the Agerians. In hindsight, they marveled at the fact that they had come back accurate to the story.

Several of the interviewers asked after Ira's heritage, to which she aptly responded that she wasn't sure what ethnicity her family line had come from and had stumbled over the question regarding her family's history. Which Zelek explained in Japanese was complicated and that Ira wasn't aware of her family's genealogy, nor was she interested in researching it. The answer seemed to appease those asking the question.

He had to admit that she did look, as a human would say, of Asian descent. With her rounder face, smoother complexion, and her pin-straight dark hair, she certainly could be mistaken for someone with an Asian heritage.

As Zelek glanced toward the door, Ira reached over and gently put her small hand in his. When he looked to her, she smiled and said, "It'll be all right."

Without actively thinking about it, he squeezed her hand before twining their fingers together.

As he sat back, she rested her head against shoulder, letting her eyes dip closed. A contented smile sat on her face.

"Mr. and Mrs. Astley?" an older woman asked as she cracked open the door.

Both of them quickly rose to their feet as Zelek said, "Yes?"

The woman smiled at them. "Please, come with me."

Still holding Ira's hand, Zelek led them down the hall. They were ushered to another room and entered to see a wizened Japanese man with many wrinkles adorning his face and a head full of gray hair sitting at a large table. He stood and gestured to the two seats across from him.

"English?" he asked through his thick accent.

Zelek offered a small smile. "If you don't mind."

The man nodded and held up the small stack of papers in front of him. "Thank you for your patience. We had a rather prominent family that was interested in the boy, as well. We nearly told you that we would set you up with another child, but then we were made aware of this." He handed a single sheet to them.

Tentatively, Zelek reached forward and took hold of the paper. It had both Japanese and English writing on it, and within a few seconds, Zelek realized what it was.

Humans left these things called wills that stated any special wishes or pertinent information regarding what should come of their belongings or estates, or children, should they die. And it didn't seem possible, but Zelek's human name was on this sheet of paper, listed as the guardian for the Yoshi's son: Takeo.

The man let out a small laugh. "You could have just told us you knew Yoshi Yamato and his wife, Sora." He took in the look of surprise on Zelek's face and nodded. "You weren't made aware, were you?"

"No, sir," Zelek answered with a shake of his head. "Though I'm glad for it."

Taking the sheet back, the man said, "Well, seeing as you were listed as the boy's intended guardian, there's no more discussion to be had." He waved toward the glass door.

Zelek and Ira spun around in their seats as the door opened, and a young boy tottered into the room, holding a stuffed animal and looking thoroughly exhausted and terribly guarded.

Quickly getting to his feet, Zelek went to the child and knelt down to his level, offering a small smile. "Hey, Takeo. How're you doing, little man?" he said in Japanese.

Ira came and knelt at his side.

Takeo's eyes were a little red and puffy. He sucked in a breath and mumbled out in fairly clear diction for a three-year-old, "Want Okasan and Otosan."

Ira looked to Zelek, not understanding the Japanese that had been spoken.

He hushed, "He wants his mom and dad."

Returning her attention to Takeo, she gently reached out and rubbed his face, wiping at some tears that hadn't dried fully. "I know, sweetie. Mommy and Daddy can't be here right now."

Zelek gently took hold of Takeo's arm and translated in Japanese. He then added, "I knew your daddy, and he told me to take very good care of you."

A light filled Takeo's eyes as he took in what Zelek said. He reached his stubby, little fingers out and grasped Zelek's free hand.

"Are you hungry?"

Takeo nodded.

"Well, why don't we go home and have some dinner?"

Again, the boy nodded. He still looked exhausted, but not as fearful. And when Zelek opened his arms, Takeo readily held his hands out to be picked up. Half a second later, Takeo flopped his head down onto Zelek's shoulder, holding him as though he felt safe in Zelek's arms.

Turning to the older man, Zelek offered a smile and a bow of his head. "Thank you, sir."

The man bowed back.

Zelek looked to Ira and offered his arm. Without hesitating, she looped her arm around his.

By all appearances, they were a family.

Chapter Three

RED RIBBONS

Takeo had passed out after dinner, sprawled on his bed as Dover lay nearby. The boy had been enthralled with the grovix, and they'd played enthusiastically while dinner was prepared. Squeals of delight and little playful yips had been the soundtrack in the tiny house, and something about it made Zelek smile without active thought.

For being a three-year-old who had been through a veritable battlefield of emotions over the last few days, Takeo was handling things splendidly. He'd taken to Lorn and Rowan quickly, smiling and interacting with them easily. Whatever was going through the boy's head, he seemed comfortable.

And most importantly, he was safe.

Zelek was still confused about how the situation had worked out so well, and how he'd wound up in the Yoshi's will. It didn't make any sense. He'd never interacted with them, not even by accident.

"The Elders must have intervened," Ira had said. Because of course Ira was the one to remind him of faith.

Now that it was finished, and Takeo was legally where he belonged, it meant that Ira had to return to her part of the world. Wherever that was.

He almost asked where she'd been living, but they weren't supposed to know where one another were. They weren't supposed to be aware of any Human-Born's location but their own. It felt stupid, but the Council had been clear about keeping things separate.

The ring on his finger kept grabbing his attention, stealing his thoughts and making him wish for impossible things. Things like happiness, and no war, and forever. Things like family, and peace, and joy. Anything but the reality that Ira had to leave, that they had to be separated.

A part of him piped in with the reminder that they should be separated, that he should let her go and find happiness with someone else. Someone not ... him.

Once the boy was changed and laid to bed, Zelek turned to Lorn and Rowan. "I shouldn't be long. Call if anything comes up."

"Will do," Rowan said as Lorn nodded.

As Zelek and Ira slowly made their way to the train station, he said, "Thank you. For your help, I mean. I know you have other responsibilities."

She smiled at him. "I was happy to do it."

"I just hope he doesn't start asking after you," Zelek whispered. "I hadn't thought about that, and he's already been through a lot."

"Takeo will be golden. I'm certain of it."

Giving her a small grin, he asked, "What makes you so sure?"

Ira stared at him fondly. "Because he has you," she whispered.

They should've walked slower. Zelek couldn't get into what he wanted to say with lots of other people around. They'd arrived at the station much sooner than he'd hoped.

The rest of the journey was quiet for them. Whenever their eyes met, they'd quickly look away, back at the floor or out the window. Anywhere but each other. Zelek figured they must've looked like immature children.

Once they were in the garden, he tried to work up the courage to explain things to her, but they continued walking in silence, ambling along the path to the portal.

When he realized they were halfway there and he was running out of time, he stopped in his tracks and gently pulled on her jacket sleeve to stop her. She opened her mouth to ask what he was doing.

"I would marry you," he hushed, meeting her gaze.

Her mouth fell open, and her face slacked.

"In a heartbeat. I would marry you, and we'd get a house, and have a family, and I'd love you more and more every day, and I'd never leave your side, even if you were angry with me. I'd ..." His eyes searched hers. Then, gently, he cupped her cheek and drew closer. "I'd kiss you and do everything in my power to make you know how much you mean to me."

"Zelek," Ira breathed, her eyes sparkling in the moonlight.

"But I can't," he said with a frown and a deep crease in his brow. "Elders, I want to," he practically begged.

She shook her head ever so slightly. "Why?"

"It's not 'cause of Kal."

"Then wh—"

"It's because of Kelek."

Her face scrunched in confusion.

"He's our uncle. And ..." His shoulders deflated. "Ira ... he killed our father."

Realization dawned on her face, and she shook her head. "Zelek, you aren't him."

"I want to believe that. I want to believe that I could never hurt Kal, that I could never hurt you. But he killed his brother. Elders, Ira, I'm related to him. I'm *named* after him."

"That doesn't mean anything," she begged quietly.

He stroked her cheek with his thumb.

"You are Zelek. My Zelek. You always have been, and you always will be. You are a noble man who fights so ardently for those you care for. You're a strong, brave, caring man who could never hurt the people he lo—" Her voice caught, and she jerked back a little.

Without missing a beat, he hushed, "I love you."

"You do?"

Nodding subtly, he added, "I have for a long time." A wanting sort of look ghosted his features, and his frown deepened. "Ira, I adore you. In every dark moment, you've been the stars that lit the sky and gave me something to follow home. Your voice is the thing that calms me in an instant. You captivate me, stun me, move me to wonder and stand in amazement at who you are and what you know. Your compassion humbles me so much more than I could imagine." He nodded a few times. "I do. I love you." A determined sort of look filled his eyes. "I love you so much."

Before he lost his nerve, he kissed her.

And for a moment, they were lost in each other.

Zelek's brow pinched. He knew he had to let go. He had to step back. He had to stop kissing her. But Elders, he didn't want to.

He wanted to push further. Dive deeper. Never let her go. Stand in front of her and keep her safe. He wanted the rings on their fingers to signify a real marriage, not some false one. He wanted to run away with her, take Takeo into his arms, grab her hand, and flee. Find some place where there was no war, no Caliga, no fear. Just life, and love, and happiness.

But that wasn't real. It couldn't be.

Maybe someday. Maybe in some other time. But right now?

Right now, he had to let her go.

Gently pulling back, he rested his forehead against hers and searched her eyes. "We can't ..."

For a few long seconds, she just stared at him with tears mounting in her eyes. Then she slowly nodded.

Closing his eyes, he whispered, "I'm going to marry you someday, Ira."

She nodded against him. "That's a promise?"

Zelek eased back and fished a small cloth bag from his jacket pocket. "In Japan, they have this thing about red ribbon," he started as he opened the bag. "That in all the stories where soul mates are, they're tied together by a red ribbon. They each wear one, and it lets them know" —he met her gaze, finding her hanging on to every word— "their soul mate is out there, waiting."

She looked down to his palm, finding two simple strands of red ribbon in his grasp.

"Someday, when I know I can keep you safe," he hushed, "I'm going to marry you."

Tentatively, she took one of the strands of ribbon into her hand and, while she looked at him, she tied it around her neck. Before he could do anything with his, she snatched it and wrapped it around his wrist, tying it securely there.

Enveloping her into an embrace, he whispered, "Please stay safe, love."

Ira smiled through her tears. "And you, my Zelek."

He kissed her on the forehead before gently kissing her on the lips. They stayed frozen like that for a few long seconds, cherishing the moment, committing it to memory.

Until they met again.

PART II

WHAT IS

Chapter Four
ALL'S HELL THAT ENDS WELL

The rain wasn't horrendous on the streets. Sometimes heavier, but all in all, it was a fairly calm storm for the citizens of Tokyo's nightlife. Bustling about, undeterred by the thunder and flashing lightning high in the skies. None of the buildings had been struck, so it was assumed to be a sort of heat lightning storm.

But above the clouds, and above the towering skyscrapers of Tokyo, a battle raged in the nighttime air.

Several Ferveos snapped and bellowed, their roars masked by the thunder below them. Bursts of flames, mistaken for bolts of lightning, flickered against the dense cloud cover that blanketed the city, as though protecting the innocent humans below that dodged puddles and the occasional sweep of heavier rain.

Zelek evaded a Ferveos' snapping maw and landed an energy-cloaked blow to the beast's jaw. Rowan soared through the air, slashing outward with his axe and a stream of golden energy, slicing at wing membrane and scales.

Meanwhile, Lorn had the greatest task of all—catching the beasts in large, netted shields as if they were a pod of fish that had been caught.

The golden net shimmered in the storm, flickering brighter with each bolt of lightning that danced across the floor.

"We should try it!" Dover said, hopping in place next to Lorn.

"The last time we tried it, you crashed into a tree," Lorn snapped back, his gaze flicking between the grovix at his side and the dragons in the air. If he missed one, Rowan would never let him live it down.

Dover cast him a perturbed look. "It's not my fault I don't understand how wings work. If you'd just let me try this more often, maybe I could get the hang of it."

Swirling his hand along his side, a golden ramp formed. Lorn gestured toward it and returned his attention to the battle above them. "There, use that to get into the air."

"All right, fine," Dover grumbled as he pounced onto the shield. Charging up the ramp, he called back, "But I wanna learn how to fly sometime!"

"It's not likely!" Lorn hollered back, shifting his laden net to catch a second dead Ferveos.

Takeo paced behind them on the roof, angrily kicking at gravel and swiping at his rain-drenched hair. For a Japanese teenager, he was unusually built. With a narrow waist, broad shoulders, muscles he'd toned specifically for fighting, and thick legs that were like planted boulders when he needed to be immoveable. Twin swords were strapped to his waist along his back. In keeping with proper samurai practice, he only ever wielded one at a time, with both hands. But he insisted on carrying two—just in case one broke. Despite the colder temperatures, he wore a loose-fitting T-shirt that now stuck to his body from the rain.

With a growl, Takeo marched forward and whined, "When do I get to take one out?"

"Takeo, enough," Lorn chastised. "Zelek will let you know when it's your turn, if you get one at all." He tucked in on himself a little and grumbled, "Last time we let you get involved, you made a huge mess."

"Look, it's not my fault a chunk of bratak'ra went sailing. And hey, aren't you guys proud of how strong that last slice was? I cut the thing clean in half."

"Yes, exactly," Lorn snapped, keeping his eyes glued to the sky. "It took us hours to find all the pieces."

As the teen opened his mouth to retort, Lorn cut him off, "No more grumbling! We wait for Zelek's order."

Angrily crossing his arms over his chest, Takeo hunkered down and fumed, tapping his foot in a growing itch to tear the Ferveos above them apart.

Meanwhile, in the air, Zelek and Rowan threw attacks at the remaining three Ferveos. But they were met with minimal damage to the dragons. Dover hurtled himself at one of the beasts and latched on to its head, scratching and biting with fury as he tore scales off and scratched at eyes.

The dragon thrashed beneath the grovix and threw him off.

"Whoa! Catch me! Catch me!" Dover wailed as he sailed through the air.

With a grunt, Rowan snatched the warrior grovix. However, it took a few attempts for him to get a good grip on Dover, the grovix's armor getting in the way of a firm hold.

Pointing at Dover, Zelek yelled, "This is precisely why grovix shouldn't be airborne!"

"It's not my fault!" Dover protested. "If Lorn had just—"

"No!" Zelek and Rowan said.

The tree incident was enough to make Zelek never let Dover try flying again. There was a reason grovix didn't fly. Dover's insistence on trying was wearing his patience thin.

Crazy pup, Zelek thought.

A blast of flame soared toward Zelek, and he pushed a golden burst of energy through it, cutting a sort of channel that deflected the fire alongside him. Redirecting the attack, he let it pierce through the dragon's barely open mouth, slicing gold, like a spear, through the dragon's skull. A rumble of explosions erupted from the dying beast as it began to fall to the ground.

Frantically, Lorn surged over the net in time to catch the dead Ferveos.

"Two more," Zelek muttered before turning his attention back to the remaining foes, just in time to avoid a slashing taloned foot. He looked around to see that Rowan had deposited Dover onto the back of the attacking Ferveos.

Well, the pup shouldn't be airborne, but he was good at ripping apart dragons. For how young he was, Dover was pretty fearless. Zelek couldn't really say how many grovix would literally leap at the opportunity to go toe-to-toe against a Ferveos while in the air. Their grovix pup was certainly brave.

The dragon rolled, hurtling Dover from it.

Pushing himself as quickly as he could, Zelek managed to catch Dover and swing around to ease him onto the rooftop with Lorn and Takeo.

As Zelek landed, Rowan quickly behind him, Takeo grumbled, "*Now* can I take care of this trash?"

Giving Takeo a pointed look, Zelek said, "No."

"Oh, c'mon!" Takeo practically stamped his feet as he hopped in place, pointing at the opposition that flew toward them. "I can take these beasts out, no problem."

"That's not the issue here," Zelek said with a taut jaw.

Rowan leaned forward and whispered, "These are older Ferveos. Their scales are thicker. Our attacks weren't doing much damage."

Holding his hand up as though to silence Rowan, Zelek snapped, "I don't need tactical advice from you right now."

"C'mon, Z, my attacks will cut through them like butter. You want them netted or not?" Takeo challenged.

Zelek glanced at the approaching Ferveos then to his team members. Everyone simply stared back at him.

When he looked back to Takeo, he saw that impatient, reckless look in the teen's eyes. That meant the boy was likely going to just blast into the air and rip everything apart, likely making Lorn have to work extra hard to catch all the pieces.

Raising his index finger, Zelek said, "Don't rip them to pieces."

"How many pieces is okay?" Takeo asked with a smirk.

"Two big ones, per Ferveos."

With a scoff, the teen said, "That's easy."

His shoulders slumping in defeat, Zelek gestured toward the beasts that were nearly upon them and muttered, "Fine, but don't make a mess."

"'Bout time," Takeo grumbled. He crouched down and concentrated. Imagining his energy conforming to his body, he pulled the Mask off his form, letting it spring to his side in an identical pose. Wearing a confident smile, the teen launched himself into the air, his wings bursting from his back the moment he was airborne.

Takeo spiraled into the air, slicing attacks of red energy shooting off his wings as though blades, striking both Ferveos as he soared between them. Each cut nicked and tore at scales, exposing flesh and bone beneath.

He deftly whipped out his first sword, the blade glowing a bright red as he effortlessly slashed down, cleanly cutting the head off the first Ferveos.

His Mask soared toward the second Ferveos, a vibrant light of red in the sky as it hurtled at the beast. It tore into its face on impact and ran across its spine, producing a blade of energy that it used to slice down the monster's back. The red energy cut straight through the dragon, cutting it nearly clean in half, if it hadn't been for its neck and head that were still intact.

Coming to a hovering rest above the dead dragons, Takeo's Mask surged back into his form. As he sheathed his rain-touched blade, he effortlessly glided back to the team below.

"See?" he said with a shrug as he landed. "Told ya it'd be easy."

The door to Takeo's room slid open just before sunrise, and the teen grumbled as he pulled his blanket over his head.

"C'mon; up you get," Zelek called from the hall.

"Don't wanna," Takeo mumbled from under the blanket.

He had a second to respond when he heard Zelek's foot hit the floor.

Takeo shot upright and hurled the blanket off. "Okay, okay! I'm up!"

Ruffling Takeo's unkempt hair, Zelek said with a grin, "Good. You're getting heavy."

Takeo swatted Zelek's hand away. "Right. Don't wanna give the old man a back injury."

"Yeah, you keep that sass up. Just wait till we spar, and I'll show you how old I am," Zelek said without a bit of worry as he left the room.

Hastily getting changed into his workout clothes, Takeo ruffled his messy hair into a semblance of order.

Truth be told, he hadn't been able to win a spar against Zelek... yet. He'd come close a couple times, but his guardian and mentor always got in that last good hit that sent Takeo crumbling to the floor. And sure, he had made fun of Zelek, but he had to admit the fact that the Agerian could pick Takeo up and hurtle him into the koi pond out back without grunting, wheezing, or gasping. And that genuinely impressed the teen.

Zelek was only an inch or so taller than Takeo, and he certainly looked smaller. But that just meant Zelek was a whole lot better at handling weight than Takeo. Just because Takeo was bigger didn't mean he was stronger.

Yet.

As he ran toward the dojo's main hall, he heard Zelek clap a few times and call, "C'mon, Takeo! The sooner we do this, the sooner you get breakfast!"

"You mean the sooner *you* get breakfast," Takeo shot back as he took his place on the mat, immediately falling into a ready stance. He groaned once he realized Rowan stood before him, not Zelek.

Throwing the Team Leader a small glare from over his shoulder, Takeo grumbled, "I thought you said you were gonna show me how old you were."

Rowan chuckled. "He'll throw you about later, Squeak." He fell into a ready stance. "But first, it's time to see what you learned from last week."

Wearing a confident smirk, Takeo mirrored Rowan's stance. "Come at me, Senpai."

The two were still for a few long, quiet seconds.

Lorn leaned toward Zelek and whispered, "Fifty yen says Rowan breaks first."

With a scoff, Zelek cast him a glance and hushed back, "Wow, you really like losing."

A long growl came from Dover's stomach, and the grovix drew in on himself as the two bystanders gave him a look.

Self-consciously, Dover whined, "What? I'm hungry!"

Meanwhile, Takeo's face continued to tighten, his frown deepening the longer he remained still. His arm muscles twitched.

This was a test. He was supposed to show what he'd learned from Rowan last week.

Last week, he'd been charged with learning to be patient and wait out his opponent. Let them strike first.

But this was *so boring.*

Takeo was sure several minutes had passed. That had to be right. There was no way it'd been less than five minutes since he'd fallen into his ready stance against Rowan. It just wasn't possible.

That was long enough, right?

His legs refused to remain still any longer. Subsequently, his head agreed. He charged forward, jabbing his arm out in a furiously swift punch.

Rowan deflected it easily.

The teen refused to not land a hit today. He had to land at least one. It was about time he landed more than a few hits against Rowan in hand-to-hand combat.

All of Takeo's Zaheri were lean and nimble in their own way. Rowan had insanely strong arms, despite how spindly his limbs looked, with hands that never wavered when a weapon was in his grasp. Zelek's core and legs were sharp, both in strength and reflexes, and his reflexes were what always caught Takeo off guard. Lorn had a rounded stamina across his form that allowed his shields to appear with barely a thought. And Dover, despite his massive bulk, was almost all muscle and could keep pace with any of them at full sprint for over thirty minutes.

One of these days, they'd all be bested by him. It was only a matter of time. After all, with a name like "The Warrior," Takeo had to be stronger than them eventually. Maybe not yet, but it would happen. It had to happen.

Takeo moved with all the swiftness he could muster, which was basically on par with the swiftness of a rhino. Every jolting punch or sharp kick was deflected by Rowan.

Screw this! Takeo thought and called on one of his blades leaning against the nearby rack.

Rowan was a weapons expert, so it was only fair Takeo get to beat him with a weapon.

In a fluid movement, Takeo snatched his red energy glowing sword and gripped it with both hands before swinging it at Rowan.

There was a clang and a clash, and Takeo felt the Agerian metal of the blade shiver its reverberation down his arms. He glared at Rowan past the dueling blades. *How'd he summon his sword so fast?*

With a look of disappointment and a sigh, Rowan said, "First, you barely lasted a minute before striking, and then you go and pull a weapon in a hand-to-hand spar? Are you trying to show how little you've learned, Squeak?"

"Hey, it was way longer than a minute!" Takeo spat, pushing against the opposing blade with a grunt.

"Only, it wasn't."

Clenching his jaw, Takeo pushed a burst of red energy through his blade. The force shoved him and Rowan apart.

Rowan slid across the floor, looking wholly unfazed as he settled to a stop and raised his sword above his head, calmly waiting for Takeo's next move.

Takeo kept his sword in his grasp but didn't lift it. Not yet. *Patience. Right. Fine.*

Letting out a breath in a huff of annoyance, Takeo lifted his blade, holding it in a ready stance in front of him. He could feel his fingers itch at the lack of momentum. His red energy sparked from the blade, as though trying to voice his frustration.

This was a fight, not some statue contest.

Ugh. This is the worst.

A small smile came to Rowan's face as he ambled forward, keeping his sword pointed toward Takeo.

Good. Movement. Takeo could work with this.

He mirrored Rowan's slow advancement. Soon, the two were walking in a circle as they sized one another up.

From the front of the room, Zelek said, "Take consideration of your opponent. What're their strengths? What's their weakness?"

"What if they don't have one?" Takeo asked, keeping his eyes trained on Rowan.

"Everyone has one."

Sure, Takeo thought sarcastically. *Everyone but me.*

Takeo was the most rounded of them all. Fine, so his defensive strategies weren't that great, but they were still better than Rowan's. Leagues better than Dover's.

And he was way stronger than any of them. He was sure of it. And he was the only one who could make Masks.

Fine, assess your opponent, he thought.

Rowan. He knew Rowan. The man had strong, steady arms. His legs weren't as powerful.

That meant he needed to take out Rowan's legs.

How?

Flashing his gaze across Rowan's stance, Takeo felt he'd been baited. Rowan held his sword above his head, as though leaving his legs open to attack. Heck, his whole body was exposed.

But Rowan could make shields if he needed to. And Lorn wasn't far, keeping his gaze fixed on the spar.

Ah crud. This wasn't just a simple test. Lorn was probably under instruction to intervene if Takeo struck with an energy attack. Probably to try to teach Takeo something about opponents that fight with allies or something. They'd done that a month or so ago. And Lorn had been the trump card.

But Takeo had squared off against Zelek in that spar. Rowan had been the one to sit out.

Was it Dover he had to worry about?

A quick glance to Dover revealed that wasn't likely. The grovix was shifting his weight and had a whining, pitiable expression on his face. He was probably hungry, distracted by breakfast waiting for them.

Zelek maybe?

Takeo glanced at the Team Leader, finding his expression neutral and placid. *Great. Unreadable. That's helpful.*

Better to try to see who flinches. That'd be his tell for who he needed to worry about on the sidelines.

Just as Takeo was about to step forward and start his attack, Rowan surged forward.

Oh crap!

Takeo stuttered and parried the slashes of Rowan's sword. His feet skittered backward as he successfully evaded every attack Rowan attempted.

Wait a second, he was on the defensive?

That was infuriating.

Shifting his weight slightly, Takeo skimmed his sword against Rowan's advancing blade, letting the Agerian fall forward.

The teen had expected to see a look of surprise on Rowan's face. Instead, he saw Rowan spin on his heel and slash his sword at Takeo.

Takeo was getting hangry. Time to end this and get breakfast.

In an attempt to surprise Rowan, Takeo cloaked his arm in red energy, snatched the blade coming for him, and ripped it from Rowan's grasp. There was a *thump* somewhere toward the end of the room, but Takeo was a little too focused on how flabbergasted Rowan looked now that he was unceremoniously unarmed.

Chucking the sword aside, Takeo resecured his grip on his sword. Then he raised the blade to try to subdue Rowan ... only for another gold energy sparking blade to appear and clash against his.

Gritting his teeth, Takeo grumbled, "I should've known you'd jump in, Z!"

Not justifying Takeo's frustration with an answer, Zelek pushed the teen back as the two traded slashing blows. Clangs of metal and sparks of energy were the soundtrack to the bout.

Both moved with fluidity and trained precision. But Zelek had an advantage that Takeo didn't—he could make shields. The small golden pieces of protection appeared at any opening Takeo tried to take advantage of.

Leaping back a few paces to afford some space, Takeo muttered, "Boss battle it is."

Zelek and Rowan steadied themselves, neither looking concerned. Rowan had regained his sword.

Takeo focused on his stance and again imagined his red energy cloaking his whole body. The Mask pulled from him and mirrored his stance as they faced the Zaheri.

Swinging his sword into a more comfortable grip, Zelek fell into a ready stance. Rowan charged forward.

The Mask tore at Rowan while Takeo ran for Zelek.

Little blasts of gold hurtled at Takeo, who deflected each small attack with his sword. With a yell, he brought his sword up and met his blade with Zelek's. He kept running, making Zelek slide against the floor. The Zaheri hit the wall, but his sword didn't waver against Takeo's.

A confident smirk came to the teen's face. "I almost got you pinned."

"Sure you do," Zelek said with a smirk.

In a deft movement, Zelek kicked off the wall and propelled over Takeo. His back skimmed Takeo's, and the Zaheri snatched the boy's wrist. By the time Zelek landed, he sent Takeo's face into the wall, pinning the teen's arm behind his back. The awkward position had Takeo barely holding on to his blade in his free hand.

Through gritted teeth, Takeo made a last-ditch effort to flick the sword at Zelek.

Flying through the air, Zelek's sword dispatched Takeo's blade.

At the same moment, Takeo felt his Mask disappear. Straining his eyes to look over his shoulder behind Zelek, he saw the remnants of his Mask flitting into the air in two pieces. Rowan had sliced it in half.

Takeo pinched his eyes shut and grunted in annoyance.

"Sorry, Squeak. You'll have to try better than that," Zelek said with an easy grin.

Glaring at the wall, Takeo grumbled, "I can still get out of this," as he tried to worm himself free.

Zelek rolled his eyes and patted Takeo on the head before he let him go. "Sure you could."

As his arm was released, Takeo inadvertently let out a whine and whipped his arm around, holding his wrist tenderly. The way Zelek had been holding his arm behind his back had hurt something fierce.

Ruffling Takeo's hair, Zelek said, "C'mon, Squeak; let's get some breakfast before the humans arrive."

A look of envy ghosted Takeo's features as he saw Zelek turn and grab his sword from where it hung midair. Then the Team Leader knocked his forearm against Rowan's in an X sort of shape—an Agerian celebration.

With a sigh, Takeo snatched his fallen sword from the floor and followed them.

One day.

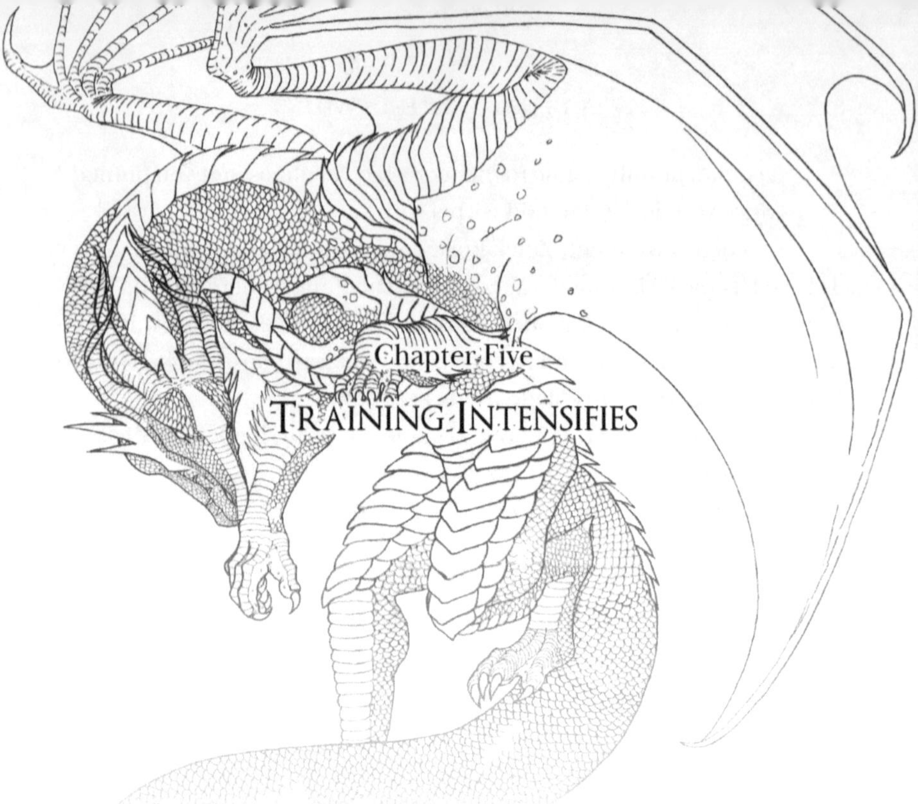

Chapter Five

TRAINING INTENSIFIES

The dojo was alive with activity. The daily lessons carried on, but this afternoon, Takeo wouldn't be partaking in any of the human training.

As Zelek and Rowan ran their classes alongside other martial arts masters, Lorn and Dover stayed with Takeo. The boy sat with several swords sheathed in a rack next to him. He had a blade in his lap, running his hand just above the blade in smooth, even movements.

Takeo had been quiet since they had sat down, mulling over Rowan's comments during their lunch.

"You're still too impulsive," Rowan said.

"My body itches, and my muscles twitch when I'm still. It's not my fault!" Takeo shot back.

Zelek hummed. "That might actually have more to do with your energy than with your body."

"Huh?"

Waving his hand in a general fashion, Zelek answered, "You could have excess energy in your system, too much for you to figure out how to use, so your body translates that as meaning you need to act. You might not need to."

Takeo deflated. "What's all that junk mean?"

Zelek gave him a cross stare while Lorn said, "You may need to focus on pushing that excess energy into a weapon."

"I already do that."

Shaking his head, Rowan said, "Lorn misspoke. Not into only one weapon, but into multiple weapons." He rose to his feet and went to the hallway.

"Multiple weapons?" Takeo questioned, glancing at his sword. "But I thought—"

"That's your primary weapon. And yes, it should be the one with the most energy in it since that's the one you decided you want to use most often," Zelek interjected. "But that doesn't mean it has to be your only weapon."

Before Takeo could ask a question, Rowan returned and said, "Your assignment this afternoon is to take the swords I've laid out for you and push energy into as many of them as you can."

"But that'll drain me, won't it?" Takeo asked.

Snatching his bento box and walking back to the hallway, Rowan said, "If your muscles are twitching after thirty seconds, trust me, Squeak, you need to get rid of a lot of energy."

And now Takeo sat with the first sword, his mind dulled by the boring, simple blade. He was almost positive he'd fall asleep. Dover's steady snoring wasn't helping.

After an hour or so of silence and pushing energy into the blade, he flopped his hands on the floor and threw his head back. "This is *so boring.*"

Dover snorted in his sleep and blearily lifted his head. "Huh?" the grovix sleepily asked.

Flicking his gaze to Takeo, Lorn went back to the book in his hands. "Zelek and Rowan had a point. No matter how boring you might see this, it's something you should do. It'll help you get that twitching in your muscles to stop."

"My legs won't stop twitching now!" Takeo said as he flung his hands out. "How am I supposed to focus on pushing energy into all these boring-looking swords if my feet keep wanting to tap?"

Lorn ruffled his hair. "Weave your energy in a pattern."

"Huh?"

With a flick of his wrist, Lorn pulled a spherical shield above his palm. It was mostly translucent, but there were strands slowly spiraling around the ball and laying into the shield. "See that? I'm trying to do it slowly." He thrummed his finger across the ball-shaped shield, and it started to rotate slowly. "I learned this a long time ago. Making shields stronger means weaving more energy into it. You can do the same with your energy as you push it into the blade. I treat it sort of like fabric being laid across the shield. Right now, I'm trying to show you on a more base level—like threads." The shield fell into dust, dissipating into the air as Lorn sat up straighter. "Pull an orb."

Squaring his shoulders, Takeo fought the urge to grumble. He did as he was instructed.

Lorn pointed to the red energy. "Now you just have to imagine it forming into a flat piece instead and give it a pattern."

"What sort of pattern?"

"Whatever you want."

Through a yawn, Dover said, "Maybe you could choose the pattern from your blade."

Squinting at the grovix, Takeo asked, "What do you mean?"

Dover got up and stretched before he went to Takeo's sword. Nudging it out of the sheath, he tapped the blade with his paw. "See? Your red energy makes a pattern naturally in this sword. Just use that."

"That's a great idea," Lorn said as he raised his brow.

The grovix threw him a perturbed look. "Don't sound so surprised."

"I am surprised. That's solid insight."

A grumbling growl came from Dover.

Chuckling nervously, Lorn looked back to Takeo. "All jokes aside, Dover has made a good observation. You can use your first blade as a template. Envision the same pattern laying into the... boring blade."

Takeo let his energy fall and picked up the simple sword in his lap, inspecting the blade. There was almost no evidence he'd even pushed energy into this sword. He scratched his hand through his hair and glared at the sword.

With a glance to his Agerian designed sword lying nearby, he watched the inlay of his red energy pulse and snake across the black blade. He hadn't put any thought into the pattern when he'd pushed energy into that sword, so why did he have to think so hard for this one?

Probably because this one was so ordinary looking. A generic grip and blade. Nothing special or extraordinary. It didn't have any of the touches he'd designed for his sword.

Letting out a breath, he resigned himself to the task at hand. Maybe if he revisited the memory of designing his sword, that would help him here.

When Zelek had told him that they all thought he was old enough to have his own sword, and get to design it, too, Takeo had barely believed it was true. But then they actually had sat down to help him design the sword. He'd never been one for studying, but he'd found himself researching katanas and ancient samurai swords for inspiration. He must've looked at hundreds of pictures to narrow down his design. It took him a week to finalize it. Even then, he'd still been scribbling and erasing just before he'd handed the sketch to Zelek.

Zelek had nodded and smiled approvingly as he surveyed the design. Then, a few weeks later, Takeo was presented with the sword for his fifteenth birthday.

He'd ripped the sword out of its sheath and went to the practice room to flail it around wildly, pretending to fight off a whole swaths of enemies. He'd called on a feeble Mask to act as his opponent. Dover had pretended to be a bratak'ra as Takeo narrated his make-believe battle.

His life wasn't perfect, but it was happy.

Lots of memories had been made with his Zaheri. From the small house he could barely remember to the dojo, Takeo could say with confidence that most of his memories were happy ones.

The small house. He hadn't thought about that old place for a while.

He was so young when he'd come to live with his Zaheri. And for the bulk of his life, they were the only family he could remember. His parents were faint wisps in his mind now, but he must've known their faces at some point. It was probably to be expected, though, that he couldn't recall their faces. He was only three when they'd died. Not many people remember with clarity anything from their earliest years.

Sometimes he felt guilty that he couldn't remember what his parents looked like. Did that make him a bad son? Was he bringing shame to his family name by not remembering them with picture-perfect memory?

Truth be told, it was one of the reasons he didn't love school and had been so grateful when he'd graduated from PK Academy. He had trouble making friends. Most people were so tied up in their lives, in their families. And so many had families that were uppity and snooty, like they somehow were so much better than anyone else.

Takeo didn't see how one family could be better than another just because they had money. Money didn't mean much. Not really. The way he saw it, even wealthy people got sick. Even wealthy people died. So, in the end, everyone was the same.

And then there were the handful of kids who thought it was funny to joke about how his parents had died. How he was adopted. Like that mattered.

Couple that with his less-than-great grades, and his height and bulk, and he'd often been seen as just some stupid, brawny kid.

His Zaheri had taught him after his first fistfight that violence wasn't the right way to settle those sorts of things. That he had to learn to let those people make their comments and move on. Fistfights landed kids with nicknames like "delinquent." And it wasn't like in manga or anime where everyone found him appealing because of that. No, they had outright avoided him once he'd beaten up a kid in grade school.

That was fine by him. He didn't need any of those stupid kids. He had all the family and friends he needed in his Zaheri.

Though, now that he was thinking about his younger years, and that small house, he found a faint memory flickering to the surface. Of a smaller woman with a sweet face and kind eyes. It was so hazy. He couldn't imagine a name to that fuzzy face.

Was it possible he could faintly remember his mother?

"Uh, Takeo," Lorn said, breaking the teen from his thoughts.

Snapping his attention back to the present, Takeo looked to his Zaheri.

With a wince, Lorn said, "You might want to move to another sword."

Takeo blinked a few times before he looked to the sword in his lap. The blade was glowing a violent, vibrant red.

Just as he opened his mouth to ask what that meant, the door slid open and Zelek stepped in. "How's i—" His eyes went wide at the blade, and he nearly shouted, "What did you do?"

"Is this bad?" Takeo asked, a bit scared to move the sword. The way Lorn and Zelek looked at it made him worried it'd blow up if he moved too suddenly.

"It's fine, I guess. But ... don't put any more energy into that blade, okay?" Zelek said warily.

"Why?"

Gesturing to the sword, Zelek answered, "Agerian metal can only hold so much energy. If you put anymore into that blade, it could explode."

Takeo swallowed. "Uh ... can I move it without it exploding?"

"You ... should be able to."

"That doesn't make me feel better."

"Hey, uh, Lorn?" Zelek gestured to the blade again, still staring at it with caution. "Do me a favor and just ... cover that in a shield for me." He chuckled nervously. "We really can't afford to blow up the dojo."

"And us along with it!" Takeo snapped. "Why didn't you say something about this?"

Gaining a stern look, Zelek set his jaw. "I expected you to pay attention and ask questions!"

"It's not my fault!"

"It kind of is."

Takeo snatched the sheath and covered the vibrantly glowing blade. Red energy illuminated the sheath. "There. Didn't blow up."

Rubbing his forehead, Zelek said tiredly, "Please pay attention to what you're doing."

"Fine," Takeo grumbled as he grabbed another sword.

Zelek's gaze flicked at the action as the boy went to the task of continuing to push energy into another blade. He straightened a little and studied Takeo.

Catching Zelek's stare, Takeo snapped his gaze to the Zaheri. "What?"

"Nothing, just ... be careful."

"I already told you I would," Takeo grumbled as he returned to his task.

Before he left, Zelek stepped over to Lorn and whispered, "Keep an eye on him."

"You got it," Lorn said with a few nods as he set his book down.

Zelek slid the door shut and went back toward the practice rooms at the front of the dojo. He ran a hand through his hair and let out a long, woofing breath.

That boy had way more energy in his system than any of them had realized.

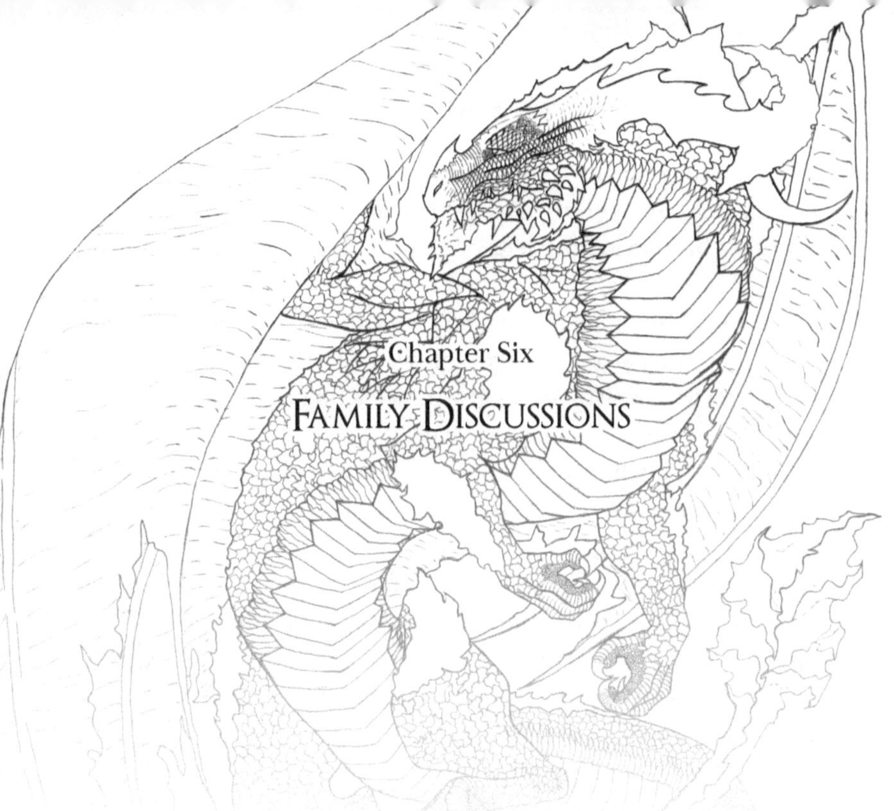

Chapter Six
FAMILY DISCUSSIONS

Takeo fastened the chest piece onto Dover's frame with a final click of the clip. "What's next?" he asked Lorn, who supervised the grovix's preparation.

"The helm," Dover said with a nod toward Lorn. As the Zaheri handed Takeo the helm in question, Dover added, "And you gotta be careful. It fits a certain way."

"Like everything else," Takeo said as he rolled his eyes. "I wasn't gonna force anything on you that didn't fit right."

Dover lifted his head so that Takeo could get the snaps in the right place. With his armor on, the grovix looked every bit a war-ready creature. It was funny to Takeo how much older Dover looked when he wore his armor. Without it, there was this youthful kind of look in Dover's eyes, like how some dogs still have some puppy in their eyes even when they were old.

"All right, everyone ready to go?" Zelek asked as he entered the room.

Getting to his feet, Takeo asked, "Can I please take my sword tonight?"

Zelek slumped a bit. "Takeo, we've talked about this."

"Oh, *come on*," the teen griped in an exaggerated fashion. "I finally don't have twitching legs or arms. I can be smart about using it, I swear!"

"That's not the issue," Zelek responded with an even expression. "You can't just walk around Tokyo with a sword." He gestured to Rowan as he entered with a pistol in his grasp. "This isn't new. Pistols are easy to conceal. Therefore, that's what we use."

His face scrunching in annoyance, Takeo begrudgingly snatched the pistol from Rowan's outstretched hand. "You let me take the sword last night."

"Last night, we were on rooftops, far away from any potential witnesses." As Takeo opened his mouth to retort, Zelek held up his hand and commanded, "No more whining. There's no evidence that there are dragons in the sky. We're doing ground patrol, and that means pistols." He gave Takeo a stern look. "Are we clear?"

"Yes," Takeo barely admitted above a whisper.

"Yes?"

"*Sir.*"

Zelek gave Takeo a long stare before he nodded. "Next time, let's try this without an argument."

Rolling his eyes, Takeo let Rowan push him forward, and the group filed out of the dojo.

As they started their slow trek toward the train station, Takeo asked, "So why are we going into Tokyo again? If there's no dragons there—"

"The garden holds the portal activation. If anything were to happen, it'd happen there."

Takeo looked to Dover. "So, who's babysitting Warhorse?"

"You are," Zelek said with a smirk.

Whipping his gaze to the Team Leader, Takeo started to protest, "Wait, Z, c'mon—"

"Patience is something you've been lacking lately. You're taking the slow path tonight." Zelek's eyes were trained forward as they continued on.

Angrily crossing his arms, Takeo grumbled out nonsense as he fumed. Going the slow path was going to take over an hour. Meanwhile, everyone else would get to sit on the train and relax? That didn't seem fair.

He straightened and smugly looked to Zelek. "Oh yeah? Well, who's gonna keep *me* safe? That's your job, isn't it?"

Zelek scoffed and shook his head.

"Please," Rowan said with a roll of his eyes. "Like you can't keep yourself protected. I thought you were the big, bad Warrior?"

"I am!" Takeo shot, flinging his hands to his sides.

"Oh, are you?" Zelek said with a sideways look. "I thought you just said you needed to be kept safe."

Returning to sulking, Takeo crossed his arms again and resumed his nonsensical muttering.

Lorn looked at Dover. "You think you can keep him in line?"

Dover gave a confident smirk. "Leave it to me."

The shield-bearer looked less than thrilled. He came up to Zelek and whispered, "Are you sure? The pup as Takeo's only defender?"

Zelek waved his hand subtly but continued walking as though he hadn't heard Lorn's concern.

A moment later, they arrived at the path that would lead to their marked trail into Tokyo. Zelek gestured to it. "There ya go. We'll see you in town."

Still sulking, Takeo angrily marched into the brush with Dover right on his heels. The other three Zaheri continued on their way to the train station.

Once Zelek was certain that Takeo hadn't followed them, he looked to Lorn and said, "And now we take the other path."

Lorn halted. "Other path?"

"Yeah," Rowan said with a nod toward the trees. In the dim light, there was the faintest hint of an opening.

Looking thoroughly unimpressed, Lorn muttered, "I think I'm missing something."

"Sure seems that way," Rowan said with a chuckle as he picked through the brush and disappeared into the forested area.

As he deflated a bit, Lorn said, "He doesn't have to make me sound stupid."

Zelek offered a bemused smirk. "Don't worry; he's just trying to pretend like he didn't walk right past it the first time I told him about it."

"See, that makes me feel better."

Takeo waved the branch around, smacking at errant leaves and low-hanging branches. The pathway was just wide enough for him and Dover to walk side by side. "I can't believe he's punishing me," he griped.

"He's trying to train you," Dover corrected with a flicking glance to the teen.

"No, he's definitely punishing. And for what? 'Cause I still can't beat him in a spar?"

Letting out a heavy sigh, Dover answered, "Again, he's not punishing anyone." He dipped his head, flattened his ears, and glared a little. "But I kinda feel like I'm being punished."

"Hey!"

"What? I'm not the one who spent the last twenty minutes complaining! That sure sounds like punishment to me."

"I'm not complaining. I'm ... commenting."

A chuckle rumbled from Dover.

Throwing his head back, Takeo groaned, "I'm not some stupid kid, y'know."

Dover said nothing.

"Hey! You're supposed to agree with me!"

With a shrug, the grovix answered, "You might realize I've never corrected them when they call me a pup."

"So?"

"I'm just saying that being young isn't bad. At least, I don't think it is. Maybe it is. I dunno. I'm still trying to figure that out."

"Warhorse, you're not helping."

"We're both young. That's how it goes. Someday, we'll be old, and we can tell other younger people what to do."

"I'm not—" Takeo threw his head back and growled at the sky. "I don't want to tell other people what to do."

Quirking his head toward the teen, Dover flicked his ears. "What do you want?"

Takeo slumped. "I dunno."

They continued in silence for a moment, and then Dover said, "Then maybe you should just listen to Zelek."

Crossing his arms over his chest, Takeo threw a look at him. "Oh, like if I knew what I wanted, I'd be allowed to complain?"

"It'd at least show that you had a goal."

"I have goals."

"Name one."

"You first."

An annoyed ripple formed on Dover's snout. "I told you first!"

"Yeah, and? So?"

"So that's ... that's not how this works!"

"Too bad. I said so."

"No, *I* said so. I'm older than you!"

"You just said we're both young!"

As the conversation devolved into a lot of name calling and nitpicking, Zelek sighed heavily from the path just above the bickering youth.

"So ... what exactly was your plan here?" Lorn asked with a scrunched brow as he looked to the Team Leader.

Throwing his hand toward the grovix and teen arguing below, Zelek said, "I thought Dover would be able to bring some more maturity to the conversation."

"Ah, like ... giving Takeo someone around his age to talk to."

"Kinda."

Rowan let out a snort. "That worked marvelously."

Zelek gave him a cross stare. "And congratulations." He swept his hand toward the bickering children. "Now you get to go supervise them."

"What? Why me?"

"Well, for starters, let's consider how Takeo addresses you versus me, and then answer that question."

As Rowan's shoulders slumped, Lorn leaned toward him and said with a grin, "He's right, y'know. Takeo calls you Sen—"

"I know what Takeo calls me," Rowan growled.

"After you, Senpai. See you in the city," Zelek said as he walked off at a brisk pace.

Lorn mockingly patted Rowan's shoulder. "Have fun, *Senpai*."

Rowan watched them go and remained still for a long moment. The argument from Dover and Takeo was growing louder, only serving to annoy him more. Slowly closing his eyes, he shook his head and grumbled some foreign curse before descending the slope down to the bickering pair.

Lorn wasn't the youngest of the group, but he wasn't that much older than Dover. Being one hundred and ninety-eight, there was almost a one-hundred-and-fifty-year gap between him and Rowan. And then Zelek was another couple hundred or so years older than him.

In comparison to his teammates, and especially his leader, Lorn felt like a baby.

It was baffling enough that Lorn had managed to become an Elite before the Human-Borns had arrived. He'd felt there were much stronger shield-bearers out there than him. He was grateful for it, no doubt, because he'd been given opportunities to learn from some of the best.

He wasn't the youngest of the Elite—he was pretty sure that title belonged to the Jumper. But the Jumper had a valuable asset in his ability to phase into and out of dimensions. Lorn was just another Bulwark.

Being stationed alongside the likes of Rowan and led by Zelek, Lorn felt blessed beyond measure for his posting. He'd learned a lot from the two of them. Especially Zelek. And being away from Agerius had helped open himself up to things that other Agerians just ...

Well, now it felt like a lot of Agerians were close-minded.

When he'd been assigned to the Gamma Team, he'd told his parents about the posting and about who all was chosen. His parents had gone bristly when the subject of Kaldok and Zelek had come up.

Lorn came from a family of woodcarvers. His parents didn't hold any great energy strength, but his shield-creation had come from his grandfather. Abilities were hereditary, and even dormant ones in family lines could spring back up in later generations.

Back then, before he'd left for Earth, he'd taken his parents' warning to watch his back and be careful about trusting those two. He'd been given no further explanation. Just don't trust Zelek, even though he'd been appointed to Team Leader.

And he'd listened to it.

Wariness had been his default, and silence his automatic response. He watched everything and said little because he trusted his parents and believed them to be good people. And that was the thing of it: they were good people. He knew that. It wasn't like they were unfeeling or uncaring. When someone needed a bed for their child but couldn't raise up a proper barter, his parents were quick to accept whatever was offered. They gave as much as they could and helped people often. So, why would he not trust their advice?

But after a year on the team, Lorn had trouble understanding why they were so distrusting of Zelek. He could almost understand Kaldok's treatment—being a werewolf and all—but he'd heard the story from Zelek's side, because Dover had asked. And from Zelek's perspective, he had every right to hate other Agerians. Yet, he didn't. And that startled Lorn. Kaldok had every right to hate other Agerians, and he didn't. These two brothers were so forgiving that it hurt Lorn's heart.

Now, here, as they entered the garden for patrol, Lorn had a million little questions he wanted to ask.

He didn't usually get one-on-one time with Zelek. Ever since Takeo had been adopted, that had been Zelek's primary focus. He'd been a stellar father, too. Lorn sort of felt like an older brother, helping where he could but offering no assistance when it came to discipline or boundaries.

Zelek, on the other hand, seemed to be a natural. He got angry, sure. But whenever he did, he sent Takeo to his room and walked off to go assess how best to handle the situation. He gave himself time to calm down before bringing down any potential punishment, not without immediately letting Takeo know that whatever he'd done had been wrong.

That kind of gentleness ... That kind of love ...

It humbled Lorn and made him wish he could tell his parents that they were wrong. About everything.

He wasn't Zelek's go-to for discussion and confidence. That was Rowan, who was older. It made Lorn want to roll his eyes sometimes, because Rowan wasn't wiser. At least, he didn't think so. Of them all, Zelek was the wisest and needed no council. But he was always so quick to act as though he did.

More proof to Lorn that Zelek wasn't worthy of the distrust placed upon him.

Lorn wanted to ask why he was met with distrust. Why were he and Kaldok so shunned? And if they were so distrusted by the citizens, why did the Council name them Elites and, ultimately, Zaheri? Wasn't there backlash from other Defenders? Or was it only the citizens who distrusted the brothers?

That felt like prying, though, and Lorn didn't like to overstep his boundaries. He wasn't a trusted confidant of Zelek's. He had to accept that. No matter how much he wanted to know more about his Team Leader. No matter how many questions he had.

Questions like: was he married to Ira? If he was, why didn't he wear a symbol displaying that he was a married Agerian? The ribbon he wore at all times hadn't been on his wrist until after she'd left. Surely they didn't get married in the short time Zelek had returned to Agerius for the Council's advice. And if they hadn't, why not? Zelek wasn't exactly young. Neither was Ira.

Was he protecting her from his stigma? Was she forbidden from accepting? Was there some other thing barring their relationship? They clearly cared for one another.

In the few days that Ira had spent living with them, Lorn had been convinced that they were married, or at least intended. But then, after they'd left, Rowan had made the comment that he wished that Zelek and Ira could just be together.

What was stopping them?

So many questions.

And he didn't know how to ask them.

Chancing a glance at Zelek, he took in the small frown on his Team Leader's face.

Setting aside his unease, he asked, "Everything okay?"

Zelek flicked his gaze to him and let out a smooth breath. "I'm just wondering something."

Lorn raised his brow. "What?"

"Well," the Team Leader started, "it's been almost a year since all the Human-Borns were likely made aware of who they are."

"Assuming they were all born a month apart."

"Right." Zelek nodded absently. "And it's nagging at me." He looked to Lorn. "We haven't received any guidance from the Council regarding what to do next."

"What do you mean?"

"When we were assigned as Zaheri, they told us to wait until they were seventeen to tell them who they were and then train them." He shrugged a little uselessly. "For how long? Until when?" He rubbed a hand through his hair. "I kept thinking we'd receive word sometime after they were all told about who they are. Sometime in the last year."

His gaze falling to the pathway, Lorn's brow furrowed. "That's a good point." He looked back to Zelek. "Maybe they're waiting until all the Human-Borns have been training for a year?"

"Maybe." Zelek let out a sigh. "It just seems strange. I'm not saying we're a special case—we don't know what the other Human-Borns have been through and what the other Zaheri have had to overcome—but I had to adopt Takeo. I went to the Council for their advice on the matter." He held his hands up in a vague shrug. "And outside of that initial advice, they haven't given any commands."

"Even when you've gone back for check-ins?"

Zelek nodded. "It's just making me wonder. I know that Ira always talked about how Archivists theorized that the Human-Borns would be adults before they took on their mantles."

Quirking his brow, Lorn shrugged a bit. "Well, eighteen in most human cultures is considered adulthood."

With a scoffing chuckle, Zelek answered, "Yeah, because the ripe old age of your late teens qualifies adulthood."

"Oh good, it's not just me," Lorn said with a nervous smile. "I kept thinking that was awfully young."

"Well, maybe to us it is," the Team Leader said with a reassuring grin. "Just because we don't consider someone an adult until their mid-twenties or thirties doesn't mean humans have to. After all, we do live a lot longer than them."

That was a fair point. Humans had such short lifespans. Maybe eighteen was a good marker. Lorn wasn't sure, though. He still felt twenty made more sense, given how many decisions seemed to rest upon the shoulders of a new adult in most human societies.

Looking back to Zelek, he asked, "Are you going to ask the Council the next time you're in Agerius?"

"I dunno," Zelek answered with a shrug. "I'm probably just overthinking things."

As Lorn opened his mouth to disagree, a blinding flash of white filled the pathway ahead of them.

The portal was never that bright, or that big. It made Lorn flinch back and shield his eyes. Pinching them open, he saw through his whitewashed vision as bratak'ra and werewolves tore from the blinding white.

Zelek sprang into action, spurring Lorn to do likewise. It wasn't good that the team was divided when this happened. They needed Rowan and Takeo here. They were the important ones. Lorn was just a Bulwark.

Even so, he'd do whatever he could to protect innocent lives.

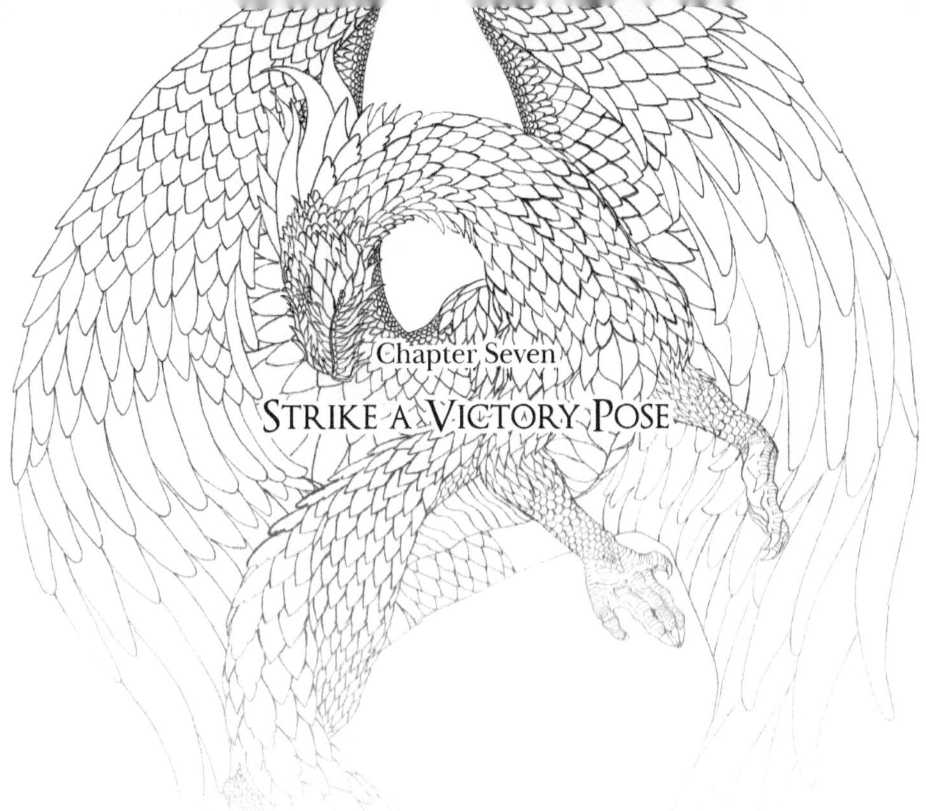

Chapter Seven

STRIKE A VICTORY POSE

"You're stubborn, and that's the problem," Rowan said as he and Takeo walked along the path that would lead them to the garden. Dover stuck to the trees, keeping himself cloaked in shadow as best he could.

"Stubbornness can be a good thing," Takeo shot back.

"Oh so rarely."

"Fine. Then, you'll see. I'll make it a good thing."

"Yeah, good luck with that."

Stuffing his hands in his pockets, Takeo scuffed his shoes against the pavement. The gardens weren't as popular during the winter months. Sure, there were the occasional joggers or strolling couples, but they were few and far between come November. At least it was still a little warm, awarding him his T-shirt and loose-fitting pants.

Rowan seemed content to let the conversation die. And Dover was so hidden in the trees, it wasn't like he could contribute anymore.

It wasn't Takeo's fault that he was hotheaded. It was who he was. His Zaheri just didn't get that. No matter how much they said they understood.

You couldn't change some things about yourself, no matter how hard you might try. He'd never be able to be calm and cool like they wanted him to be.

Sure. Fine. Whatever. So his legs didn't twitch, and his arms didn't itch anymore. But that had nothing to do with Takeo's temperament. Even so ...

"Is Zelek disappointed in me?" the teen asked quietly.

Rowan gave him a confused stare. "Why would you ask that?"

Rolling his eyes, Takeo sarcastically said, "Really? You're surprised I'm asking?"

Even though they were on patrol, Rowan walked in a leisurely, relaxed manner. Takeo had always wondered how. Though, now that his muscles weren't spastic, it was easier to mimic.

"Zelek isn't disappointed in you. Far from it."

Takeo frowned and looked to the pavement. "Yeah, sure."

"If anything, he's incredibly impressed."

Whipping his head toward Rowan, Takeo stared at him in surprise.

"Your strength is remarkable. We always knew you'd be powerful, but Elders, you're off the charts. Way beyond our expectations." Rowan gestured loosely. "And then there's your fighting tactics. You've picked them up so quickly that we have to keep teaching ourselves things so we know them well enough to train you." He ran a hand through his hair. "Why do you think we employed other martial arts masters?"

"That's for me?"

A scoff came from Rowan. "Squeak, everything's always been for you." He jostled Takeo a little roughly. "Are you seeing anything when you open your eyes? Stop thinking like a teenager and look around. *Of course* it's all for you." With a smirk, he added, "It's our job, remember?"

"Right," the teen whispered.

With a sigh, Rowan muttered, "Don't tell me that's back."

Self-consciously, Takeo looked away. "What's back?"

"You being worried you're just an assignment to us. We've talked about that."

Takeo offered an easy smile. "No, I know. I don't doubt that anymore."

"Good. If you did, I'd have to beat it out of you."

Letting out a chuckle, Takeo was about to respond when a burly man stepped onto the path. He made no motion to move out of their way.

There weren't many lights in this area of the garden, and Takeo was dealing with a silhouette more than a good view of the person approaching. But then he realized there were harder edges than normal clothing would allow, and that the man nearing them was a hulking mass, dwarfing them both.

A grating bass voice came from the man as he said, "Now, that's not fair." He lifted his head, and Takeo caught a glint of excitement in the man's eyes. "That's what I get to do to him."

Rowan shoved Takeo aside as the unknown man shot forward. There was a surging, static sound before gold and gray clashed in a low boom.

Takeo skidded to solid footing and fell into a ready stance, pulling red energy into his arms like gauntlets. He wished he had his sword. With a glance to his loose footwear, he tried not to dwell on the fact that Zelek had been right—loose, slightly oversized sneakers *weren't* the right shoes for patrol.

Their attacker surged from the dust created by the initial attack. Rowan moved swiftly to dodge his blows.

Takeo couldn't fully make out their attacker in the darkness and dust, but he was a tower of a man. Armor glinted in flashes here and there, and it appeared their attacker wore a full complement.

Furious blows were traded, and Takeo studied. He knew Rowan would be fine. Should be fine.

He hoped Rowan would be fine.

Despite Rowan's smaller size—both in bulk and in height—he thwarted every attempt by their attacker. Flashes of gold and gray energy sparked between them, occasionally illuminating the square features of their attacker. Takeo caught small glimpses of a marking on the man's breastplate. It looked like the marking was engraved into the armor with blood.

Rowan landed a kick, sending the man skittering back a foot.

That small gap was all Dover needed.

The armored grovix launched from the shadows and slammed into their attacker, sending him soaring off the path and thudding against a stone wall. Dover leaped back and barked, "The portal's open!"

"About time!" the man said victoriously as he charged forward again.

He was stopped abruptly by Takeo's Mask.

The shadowy, energy-built version of Takeo sparked a furious red as it acted like a wall against their attacker, holding him at bay.

"Clever boy." The attacker laughed. "But Masks don't scare me!"

"How about the Warrior?" Takeo yelled as he leaped through his Mask, taking it on as though a second skin, and landed a harsh blow against their attacker's chest.

Their assailant was sent flying through the trees, toppling a few over in his wake.

Takeo spun to his Zaheri as his Mask pulled back into his body. "What do we do?"

"Get to the portal and contain what we can," Rowan said quickly as he snatched Takeo's shoulder, shoving the boy forward.

Dover was already charging down the path ahead of them. His pounding paw-steps rumbled the pavement, cracking the stone beneath him.

Takeo could see a white light through the trees but couldn't discern much from his current vantage point.

"Who was that?" he asked Rowan.

Rowan threw him a look and asked, "What makes you think I know?"

"You fought him like you've fought him before."

Shaking his head, Rowan answered, "I haven't, but I know people who have."

"So?"

"His name's Caedex. He's one of Cregorous' generals."

Takeo nearly tripped. "*One* of his generals? Meaning there's more brutes like him?"

"We'll explain later! Right now, we have to take care of this incursion!"

"What makes you so sure it's an incursion?"

"Cregorous wouldn't send a general at us for nothing. This screams of something bigger." Rowan shook his head angrily. "I should've listened to the warning in my head. Four Ferveos was too many last night. We should've investigated."

"Hey, whoa, what's this mean?"

"Later!" Rowan commanded as he picked up his pace. "Why are you running so slow?" he shot with a perturbed look at Takeo.

Gritting his teeth, Takeo lied, "Uh ... my, uh ... feet are cramping."

"Then drink some water and hurry up!"

The sounds of fighting grew louder. It prickled energy down Takeo's arms in anticipation. He'd been waiting for a chance to really let loose and see what he could do. Sure, he'd been sparring with his Zaheri and had taken out some enemies over the past three years, but this was different. An incursion meant lots of enemies they had to neutralize.

Which meant that Takeo could see what he was really made of.

A dual-horned bratak'ra leaped over the rise in the path ahead of them. Takeo had fought mono-horned ones in the past, but never had he encountered a dual-horned one.

This was going to be good.

He shouldn't have been smiling as he drove his energy-cloaked fist through the bratak'ra and continued running toward the chaos. He shouldn't have felt so excited. He shouldn't have been fighting the urge to laugh.

But something in Takeo felt awakened as he fought through the contingent of enemy fighters that were splayed throughout the garden.

Some were bound to have escaped the garden and were rampaging the streets. Others might've taken to the air. But Takeo could only focus on the enemies in front of him in that moment. And his brain was sending all sorts of happy endorphins through his body as he released attack after attack.

Despite all the energy he'd pushed into the three simple blades this afternoon, he felt his stamina was far from maxed.

An errant attack of gray surged toward Takeo at his side. He almost screamed, "*You dare attack me?*" like some overpowered anime character. Instead, a gold shield appeared and Zelek was at his back.

The Zaheri threw him a wild look. "Why are you smiling?"

"I've never felt so alive!" Takeo screamed with a fully aware, sarcastically maniacal sort of laugh as he continued to barrage his way forward.

Zelek gave him a slightly disturbed stare.

Takeo knew Zelek was keeping pace with him, fighting at his flanks and watching his back. They moved in a synchronization that he wanted to marvel at but just enjoyed the deadly dance they performed. Fighting in tandem with a partner had been one of his recent trainings, and Zelek had been his partner in every session thus far.

That practiced movement played out as they managed to always avoid one another and strike down enemies. There was no clumsiness, or confusion, or bumping into one another as though they hadn't expected the other to be there. That hadn't been the case in Takeo's initial training.

He didn't realize it, but he was playing off of Zelek's momentum. His Zaheri was the one orchestrating their direction, even though Takeo was ahead of him.

Gold and red energy surged and flared, blasted and clanged. Zelek's fluidity was seamless and poised, well-practiced and rehearsed. The nimble leanness of his body was on display, a stark contrast to the bulkiness and rigidity in Takeo's movements.

Takeo was a wrecking ball that could really only barrel forward. Meanwhile, Zelek was able to turn on a dime and land a precision blow or fire a skillful shot with his pistol. Zelek continuously glanced to Takeo, taking note of where the boy was in relation to him.

They'd cleared nearly every enemy in the area, and the portal was closed, returned to its airy, spherical shape, dancing in the air like a will-o'-the-wisp. Rowan and Lorn had disappeared with Dover toward the city, Zelek trusting them to dispose of any Caligans that had made it out of the garden.

With a roundhouse kick, Takeo sent the last couple Caligans crumbling to the ground. His shoe went flying into the brush from the force behind his blow, and when he landed, he had to step back into his other shoe.

Zelek took stock of their surroundings, gauging the bodies strewn about for any signs of life. He sucked in heavy, even breaths, keeping his arms up and ready to attack if necessary. His golden energy illuminated the area around him, casting attention to the sweat that had accumulated on his brow. He'd been hit a handful of times by errant blasts or wayward punches, but they'd amounted to scrapes and minor cuts.

He turned toward Takeo and found the boy's Mask standing at

attention nearby. Takeo punched the air as though in a boxing match and let out a whoop.

"I am so ready for another fight! Let's go!" He hopped around as though doing a variation of a victory dance, continuing to punch at the air. Spurts of red energy crackled from his fists with each jab. "Oh yeah! Who's the king? I'm the king!"

"Takeo," Zelek said.

"Those Caligan fools got nothing on me!"

"Takeo."

"Aw yeah, they met the Warrior tonight!"

"Takeo!"

The boy halted his jubilation and spun to his Zaheri.

Zelek gestured to Takeo's shoeless foot. "Where's your shoe?"

"Uh ... I dunno."

"You don't—" Zelek scrubbed his scalp and fumed, "This is exactly why I told you those were inappropriate shoes to wear for patrols!"

Takeo rolled his eyes and grumbled, "I knew you were gonna fix on that. It's no big deal." His rejoicing shot down, he started to walk off, but Zelek snatched his arm.

"No, excuse you, where are you going?"

Lifting his arm to indicate the direction, the Japanese teen said, "Back to the dojo. I need shoes."

"We didn't spend fourteen thousand yen on those shoes for you to be so flippant about losing one." Zelek used his pistol to point toward the brush where Takeo's shoe had likely gone sailing. "You're going to go find that missing shoe!"

"What? In the dark? How am I supposed to find it?" Takeo shot back with a wild gesture.

"Not my problem! I told you to wear combat boots. You insisted on wearing those loose pieces of ridiculousness." He waggled his pistol at the brush again. "Ergo, your consequence."

With a grumbling noise of frustration, Takeo began stalking off toward the brush. "This is totally unfair!" he hollered over his shoulder.

"This is why good shoes actually lace closed!" Zelek retorted without missing a beat.

Takeo spun around and pulled his still-shoed foot up, hopping a little as he gestured at the sneaker barely fixed to his foot. "These have laces!"

With a scoffing laugh, Zelek said, "And yet, somehow you lost one. So, all that says is *user error.*"

"Well—just—aren't you ..." Takeo's words devolved into grumbling strings of frustration as he stalked into the brush.

Zelek let out a long, slow breath as the others came up to him. He turned to the three and asked, "Did we get them all?"

Rowan shrugged. "Maybe."

"Maybe?"

Lorn shifted his weight and ruffled his messy red hair. "There were a lot of them. And only five of us."

"I don't smell any bratak'ra or werewolves, though. I think we got all of them," Dover offered with a hopeful look.

"I suppose that's comfort," Zelek whispered.

Rowan's expression grew serious. "Caedex was here."

Zelek snapped his head up as Lorn asked, "Wait—what? When? Where?"

Nodding his head down the path where he, Takeo, and Dover had come from, Rowan answered, "That way. He was here before the portal opened, I think. He seemed to be happy it was open. But we were so far away and in the denser area of the garden. We wouldn't have been able to see the portal if it was open by then."

"Did you take care of him?" Zelek asked with a raised brow.

"No," Rowan said with a shake of his head. "Takeo landed a blow that sent him sailing through the trees. It was a hard hit. Bound to have at least knocked him out."

"We should see if Takeo managed to subdue him," Zelek muttered as he rubbed his jaw. He glanced toward the portal.

Dover followed his gaze. "What's wrong?"

His gaze still stuck on the portal, Zelek whispered, "Why haven't we received reinforcements?"

Looking hopeful, Lorn offered, "Maybe they figured we could handle it?"

"A general and at least a fourth of a legion?" Zelek asked as he looked to his team members. "Sure. Maybe."

"You don't sound sure," Rowan said.

Zelek gestured to the portal and stared at the middle distance as though gathering his thoughts. "The portal's closed now. If Caedex's here, that means he either came here on his own or was sent by Cregorous. If he went on his own, he'd still cause a scene in the Expanse. The Scouts and Preliators would've seen that."

"So ... what?" Dover asked.

Zelek's gaze darted around at nothing in particular. "I'm just trying to figure out why we haven't even had a Runner show up to see if we're okay."

Slowly, Rowan nodded. "That's ... a valid concern."

Steeling himself, Zelek squared his shoulders and quickly said, "We should regroup at the dojo, gather our weapons, and prepare for the worst. Just in case."

As they spoke in quieter voices, Takeo emerged from the brush, putting his lost shoe back on. His phone pinged, and he fished it out of his pocket.

"How long do we think that bout lasted?" Zelek asked.

Takeo's brow knit together, and he swiped at his phone, scrolling through something.

Lorn glanced at his watch. "A bit over a half hour from start to now."

Nodding, Zelek said, "Okay, then we should be able to get back to the dojo and collect ourselves."

"Wait," Dover said. "Shouldn't we do a sweep of the city just in case there's more Caligans around?"

"He has a point," Rowan admitted with a wince.

"You're right; that's the prudent thing to do. Okay, we'll sweep the city as a unit—just in case," Zelek said. "Go as quickly and quietly as we can."

Takeo's brow knotted tighter as he slowed his scrolling, looking through photos and posts on his screen.

"You really think no one heard all of this?" Lorn asked.

"I'm sure they did," Zelek answered. "But if the city does have any stragglers, it's safe to say they'll be quieter and try to blend in."

"Really? You think Caligans are that smart?" Rowan asked doubtfully.

"I'm not ruling anything out."

"Guys," Takeo said in a loud voice.

They all turned to him, and he slowly met their gazes.

As he lifted up his phone to show them his screen, they saw the Twitter newsfeed filled with the trending hashtags and popping with more and more photos and videos of portals opening in varying locations.

"How many other Human-Borns haven't you told me about?"

Chapter Eight
THE GENERAL OF RAGE

Caedex lumbered out of the trees, shoving felled trunks aside with ease.

This kid was going to be fun.

While he might not have any flashy abilities, like Akeno or Vorex, Caedex had secured his spot as the strongest physically of Cregorous' generals early on. Izel definitely had tried to claim the position, and occasionally would demand another chance to best him, but Caedex always came out on top.

And he'd be damned before he let that title get ripped away from him.

The only one stronger than him was the Master, and he'd never be stupid enough to try to spar against Cregorous again. He'd done it once when they were younger. He didn't need another rough scar across his chest.

But this kid?

He'd been told these Human-Borns were some sort of stupid prophecy kids. They'd known for years that there was some foolish attempt on the Elders' part to reclaim dominance.

But they all knew dominance belonged to Cregorous. The only reason things had stalled was because of that damned shield over Agerius.

And, well ...

The Master had clearly grown hungry for a challenge.

None of the others grasped it. But Caedex did. The more you easily dispatched enemies, the more mindless it became. How boring it got. Agerian after Agerian would charge at him, flailing their little weapons and holding their energy like it would do something. And Caedex could almost effortlessly destroy them. He wasn't on Cregorous' level—no one was.

But that just meant his Master was that much hungrier for an actual contender.

There'd been no one for Caedex to struggle against and grow from in thousands of years. Sure, he'd begun to take after Akeno and play with his victims, but it just wasn't the same.

Where was some challenger to really have to try for? To break a sweat on? To revel in putting down? Where was the excitement of wildly throwing attacks and trading blows? To feel his energy swell within him and charge against resistance?

If he felt such thirst for challenge, how much more did Cregorous hunger for it?

Surely that was reason enough for their Master to have allowed the last nineteen years to occur. After all, where was the fun in blindly smiting resistance?

In that way, he could understand Akeno's depravity. It would be far more enjoyable to watch these Agerians work hard to raise up "prophesied" fighters. There'd be a challenge then. And when they snuffled out the pathetic little Human-Borns, it would be a delicious victory.

Because they'd crush Agerius' spirit as they crushed the children they'd placed their hope on.

And this kid he'd been assigned to?

Darkness, he was so excited to see him break.

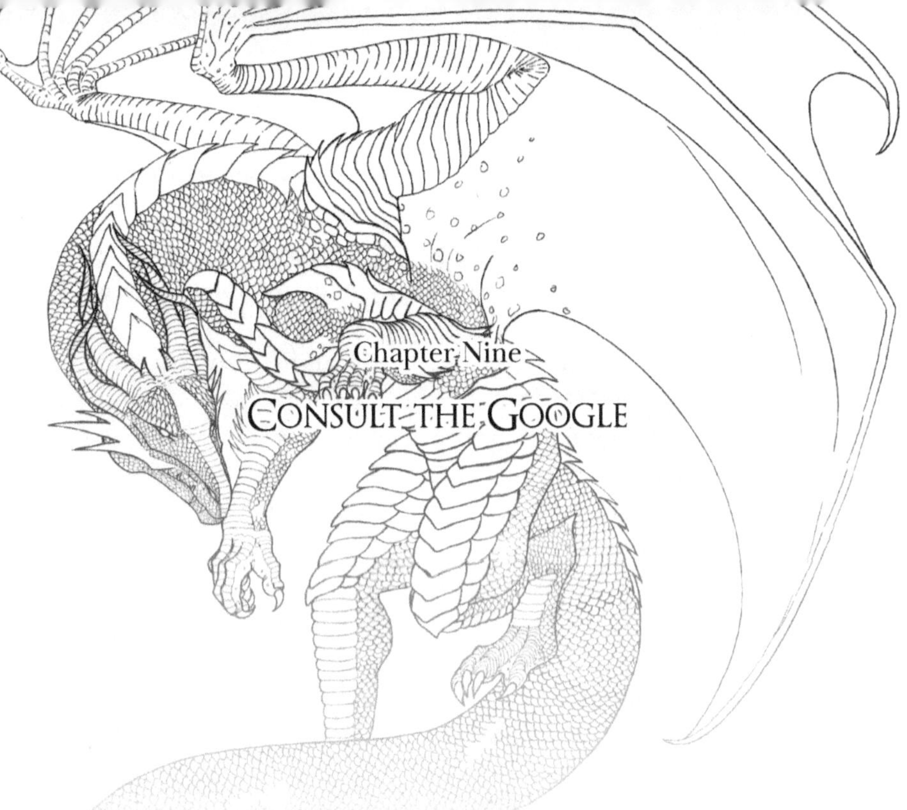

"Aren't you gonna answer me?" Takeo shot as Zelek walked back down the path.

Dover led the way, sniffing at the air wildly.

When no one responded, Takeo gritted his teeth and moved to grab Zelek's shoulder. "Zelek!"

The Team Leader spun and snatched Takeo's arm, waving at the others to keep going as he continued to stare hard at Takeo. "Takeo, you need to be quiet right now."

"What are you keeping from me, Z?" Takeo demanded.

"A lot."

Takeo blanched, rearing back slightly and losing his hard edges.

"Technically, I told you more than you should know. And the things I was allowed to tell you, you found out far sooner than you should've."

Forcing himself to look frustrated again, the teen started, "But why didn't—"

"There are certain things we were told to keep from all of you."

"All of ... Z, how many of us are there?"

"If I answer, will you promise to leave your other questions until we get back to the dojo?"

The two grew silent, simply staring at one another. Takeo could tell by the hard look in Zelek's eyes that there was no negotiating or arguing on this matter.

He could either agree and get the one answer he wanted now or disagree and get nothing. Not the first time such a decision was given. And Takeo had chosen disagreement enough to know that all it got him was more frustrated and Zelek furious from his whining.

But this was huge! They'd kept things from him! How was he supposed to be all chill now? Especially knowing there were others?

Other Human-Borns.

They hadn't denied it when Takeo had asked, and Zelek had just basically acknowledged that there were other Human-Born hybrids out there. All this time, Takeo had thought his only family was the four Agerians guarding over him and training him.

But this!

This meant there could be way more people out there just like him! People he could relate to! Who could relate to him!

He had to know how many there were, which meant he had to be okay not knowing any other answer until they got back to the dojo. That could take a while if they were going to sweep the city for any stragglers.

Though he hated it, Takeo nodded his agreement.

"Seven, including you," Zelek answered swiftly as he dropped Takeo's arm and continued his march after the others.

Takeo was stuck for a minute, left standing on the path as his mind spiraled.

Six other people were out there who were like him?

Absentmindedly, he stumbled after his Zaheri, completely deaf to their conversation as they inspected the damaged trees where Caedex had gone flying. He was too lost in his rampaging thoughts in that moment.

What were the other Human-Borns' titles? He knew he was the Warrior, and that his energy color was probably significant. But his Zaheri didn't know how significant. Did that mean all of the other Human-Borns had red energy, too? Or did they all have red-tinted energy? Where did Takeo fall in the hierarchy? Was there potential that he could be their leader? After all, if he was the Warrior, that had to mean something. Like he was probably the strongest.

But Warrior was vague now. Before, he thought it meant kind of like the ultimate warrior, or ultimate fighter. The tiptop of what a hybrid could be as a warrior. But what if one of the others was the leader?

He was actually okay with that.

He *might* be okay with that.

Maybe not.

It really would depend on whoever that person was.

Oh *crap.*

What if they were all snooty, and arrogant, and stuck up? What if these other Human-Borns were all older than him? Way older than him? What if they only saw him as a kid to talk down to? What if they thought he was stupid or something, just like those rich kids from school who looked down on him and thought he was some brainless muscle?

He'd been told—he used to think—a lot about what his Zaheri knew. He knew the rough layout of Tilion and knew Agerius was a large valley city of sorts. He knew grovix had two specializations. He knew dragons could be small—called Scouts—or large—called Preliators. He knew his Zaheri were chosen among thirty or so Agerian Defenders called Elites, the best of the best in the Defense. He knew there were ranks and that Zelek was a Grand Master, Rowan was a Chief Master, and Lorn was a Knight Commander. He knew there were specializations each Defender could obtain—Zelek was a Spartan, as was Rowan, and Lorn was a Bulwark.

All Takeo had ever been told regarding being a Human-Born was that there was a prophecy, and he was in it.

Well, prophecies could include ... girls ... right?

Oh *double crap.*

He'd have to deal with *girls?*

Or worse! What if he had to deal with girls who thought they were stronger than him? That wasn't possible, right? He was the Warrior! That *had* to mean he was the strongest.

Right?

Right?

Frantically, he whipped his phone out and proceeded to nearly hurl it to the ground as his fingers stuttered and fumbled. He started to manically scroll through the posts. There had to be locations stamped on them. That'd at least give him a clue. Maybe even glimpses of the other Human-Borns. Something.

Australia. Okay, that ... he didn't know anything about Australia. Except that kangaroos were there. And wicked big spiders.

Uh, where else? Where else, where else, where else?

America. Okay, well, that might not be bad. It might be, though. He'd interacted with a few American tourists. Most of them were nice, but some were really annoying.

England. Oh great. Some English person. Great. That'd just be ... great.

He didn't know anything about England, actually. Not outside of the fact that they seemed to think they invented tea. Jerks.

Argentina? Uh ... okay ... Oh! South America. 'Kay.

He knew even less about Argentina.

Some really far away pictures taken in Tanzania by hikers at some mountain there. Where the heck was Tanzania? Africa? Okay, well ... That's where lions were, right? And safaris or whatever.

Nothing else.

Nothing else! Where's the other Human-Born? he thought in a panic.

He double-checked his counting. They were short one. Did that mean something terrible? Did that mean the last Human-Born and their entire community had been wiped out by their attackers?

He angrily shook his head. That couldn't be possible. They were prophecy people, right? So, like, divine intervention or whatever, right?

"Takeo!" Zelek hollered.

Takeo nearly dropped his phone as he startled.

"C'mon; we're heading into the city."

Reluctantly putting his phone back into his pocket, Takeo nodded and answered, "Yeah, 'kay." He continued his zombie-like walk as he followed his Zaheri on autopilot.

What the heck was going on?

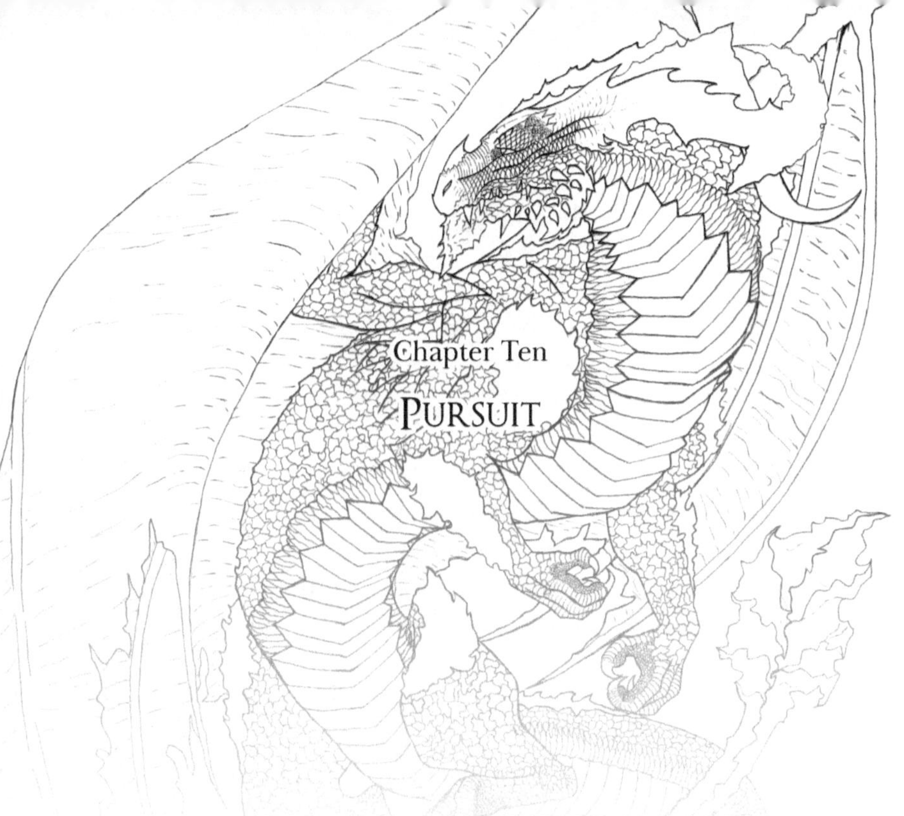

Chapter Ten

PURSUIT

They'd been scouring Downtown Tokyo for almost two hours. Dover stuck to the streets with Rowan while Lorn, Takeo, and Zelek stayed high, hopping from rooftop to rooftop. Staying on the ground let Dover stick to the shadows of alleyways and small pockets as he sniffed out potential stragglers.

Lorn went on ahead of Zelek and Takeo, following the instruction of Rowan from below to see if he could get a better view of a potential Caligan.

Letting out a slow breath, Zelek took quick stock of his team members before gently pulling his earbud out. He turned to Takeo. "You all right, Squeak?"

The teen had been quieter than normal. "Boisterous" was a word Zelek often thought of when he had to describe Takeo. It wasn't that Zelek thought the loud, rambunctious nature of the boy was bad. Given his skills, Zelek felt it was only right that Takeo was a bundle of excitement most of the time. Now, though, Zelek was genuinely concerned he'd somehow broken the air of assurance that Takeo usually held.

Takeo flitted his gaze to Zelek before looking back to the rooftop.

He kicked an errant pebble and stuffed his hands in his pockets. "You said no questions till the dojo. I'm just trying to play by your terms and conditions."

Zelek deflated a little before ruffling the back of his head. "Look, Squeak, I didn't want to keep everything from you. And I had to be hard on you back there. This is serious."

"I get that."

"You're sulking."

Shuffling his weight, Takeo begrudgingly argued, "Am not."

The Zaheri raised his brow and smirked. "Are to."

Takeo rolled his eyes and let out a huff.

Losing the smirk, Zelek said, "I know you think it isn't fair, that somehow we've gone and ripped a scale off you, but the truth of it is that we didn't."

Whipping a perturbed stare to Zelek, Takeo opened his mouth to retort.

Zelek continued, "This is an incursion" —he gestured toward the boy as though to indicate his phone— "and it's not only us who's targeted. From the glance I got of your screen, we're dealing with a much bigger issue."

"Yeah, all seven of us getting hit. Maybe."

When Zelek clenched his jaw and a look of fear ghosted him, Takeo's gaze shifted to a spark of worry.

"You ... you expected that, right?"

"No," Zelek whispered. When he met Takeo's gaze, his stern gaze was replaced with uncertainty. "Takeo, if all of you have been hit simultaneously, then we are *all* in very real danger."

No longer angry with his Zaheri, Takeo frowned as he started, "What would that mean?"

Shaking his head, Zelek said, "I know you want answers, and honestly, so do I." He gave the teen an understanding look. "We have to wait till we get to the dojo to discuss all of this further. Right now, there's too many things unknown. But we can't leave until we know the city is safe."

Slowly, Takeo nodded.

Zelek smiled to the boy and placed a hand on his shoulder. "Thanks, Takeo." He started to put his earbud back in when a screech hit the air.

They both whipped their attention toward Lorn's position as they saw Caedex barreling down on him, a storm of gray energy around his bulky form.

As a puff of air sent a prickling sensation along Zelek's arm, he shoved Takeo aside as a Ferveos shot out of the clouds at them.

Lorn was grateful Rowan had asked for him to provide an aerial view of the street. It awarded Zelek a chance to talk with Takeo. The boy needed a minute to be reassured.

Peering over the side of the rooftop and surveying the slowly emptying streets of Tokyo's nightlife, he sent a few of his shields to flit around the buildings. His eyes glowed gold, and he used the shield pieces to give him an enhanced view of the street below.

Nothing out of the ordinary.

They hadn't seen a single bit of evidence that there were any stray Caligans. Dover hadn't smelled anything, and neither had Rowan or Lorn seen even a hint of the bland Caligan garb. He supposed you could call them uniforms, but he felt that was dishonoring the uniforms he and the other Agerian Defenders wore.

Agerian uniforms were made of fine fabrics and tailored to each Defender, all adorned with their rank and specialization. Caligans wore rags. The fabrics were all a bland light gray, with no distinguishing features. If it weren't for the fact that—just like Agerians—Caligans came in all shapes, colors, and sizes, it'd be impossible to tell one Caligan from another. Truthfully, though, he never looked closely enough at any of their enemy fighters to distinguish any of them.

The only reason he knew what the generals looked like was because their garb was different. And Caedex's was vastly different, with it being entirely made of metal plate. That had to be heavy. It surprised Lorn that the brutish general had survived so long, given that dexterity had to be hard in such a cumbersome set of armor.

But maybe that was the reason—the heavier the armor, the more it protected.

Ruffling his messy red hair, Lorn leaned back and tapped his earbud. As his eyes returned to their normal color, he sighed, "Nope, nothing."

"I guess that's good," Rowan said over the radio.

Lorn crossed his arms. "I'm seriously doubting we missed any."

"You sure about that?"

With a shrug, Lorn responded, "C'mon, Rowan; you really think, after scouring for nearly two hours, we could've missed something?"

"That seems shortsighted."

"Ha-ha, very funny," Lorn said dryly and rolled his eyes.

He hated that Rowan thought that was a genuine joke. Just because Lorn could use his shields for clearer vision from far away didn't mean he was somehow blind to what was right on top of him.

"We're nearly out of Bunkyo. That means we're only about twenty minutes from the dojo. They'd have to have somehow been hiding behind us this whole time."

Rowan sighed. "I guess you're right."

A tremor ran up Lorn's spine, making the hair on the back of his neck stand on end. Tension pooled in his gut, and he spun around as he heard the crackling of energy.

Elders save them.

Somehow, the Caligan *had* been right behind them.

Frantically, Lorn swiped his arm up, and a golden shield appeared.

Caedex broke right through it.

Thank the Elders Lorn was quick.

Leaping backward had meant practically throwing himself off the roof, but he knew how to make his shields work with that sort of situation. A golden landing appeared for him. It'd been a while since he'd had to use a shield as a platform, and it took him a second too long to get his footing.

Whipping his gaze up, Caedex was nearly on top of him.

The platform dipped backward, turning into a long ramp. Lorn shot a glance behind himself. There was a shorter, narrower building below. Solid footing. He needed that to gather his options.

He kicked off the ramp to hurtle at the roof below just before Caedex landed on the tip of the golden ramp. As he spun in the air, Lorn flicked his hand up, and his shield popped, tearing shards upward.

A storm of gray energy swung around Caedex, combatting the attempted attack. His wings shot from his back, and he surged forward.

What Lorn would give for wings at that moment. The shield-bearer called a weak panel of gold in front of him. He used that to kick off, practically sending him like a bullet to the roof below. But it did the job. He got out of Caedex's way in time. His shield got obliterated, though.

Pain skittered across Lorn's arm, but he pushed it to the back of his mind. A golden shield appeared under his feet, letting him surge across the rooftop like a frozen pond.

Caedex was still coming, his rampaging gray energy showing no signs of lessening anytime soon.

If he could get to the ground, Rowan and Dover could help him.

But it begged the question: where were Zelek and Takeo?

He needed to buy himself some time. A few seconds would do. Just to get to the end of the roof.

As he slid across his shield, he fractured it and sent the fragments to stand on either side, creating a hallway of sorts as Caedex landed and followed after him. A few gray attacks unleashed from the beast. Small pieces of golden shield flew about the front of Lorn's retreating form, protecting him.

Throwing his arms from his sides, across his front in a V shape, the golden walls shattered and tore inward, all on a trajectory toward Caedex.

Though there was no great storm of gray to combat the sparkling golden shards, Caedex continued on as though nothing had impacted him. His armor didn't even appear dented.

A throbbing filled Lorn's temple. He gritted his teeth and demanded it be silent as he fell off the edge of the building.

Caedex tore after him, leaping off the roof without a bit of hesitation, his whole arm engulfed in gray energy.

Whipping his arm around, Lorn called on a large, circular shield to surround himself. Gravity had him slap against the bottom of the ball's interior, as if he were a hamster. The difference being, he could ground himself to the wall he had his feet against. Down could still be down as the large ball-like shield continued to roll with momentum as though it were sliding down a ramp.

The blast created from the gray attack meeting resistance sent

Caedex hurtling into the air, needing to use his wings to not fly too far away. He got his bearings then furiously flapped his wings, tearing back at Lorn.

Lorn glanced behind himself and cursed.

His ball-like shield hit the ground with a bouncing *thud*, continuing to roll across the asphalt and skim past cars. Praise the Elders that no one was in the street at that time. Otherwise, they would've been crushed by the golden shield.

Meanwhile, Lorn tumbled about inside the shield, his feet ungrounded from the impact with the earth. He stamped his foot down and connected with a flat enough portion of the shield to ground himself, and the ball righted. Spider cracks appeared across the ball, obscuring his vision of his attacker.

He didn't have time to break the shield as Caedex crashed through the golden sphere and Lorn crashed out the other end, tumbling and rolling until his back slammed against a car. Alarms started to blare.

His vision swayed this way and that as he grappled for the ground's stability before he began to dry heave. Fingers trembling, Lorn tried to force his vision to align and for his stomach to stop convulsing so he could call a shield to protect him.

There was a crackling of energy.

Swallowing back the bile in his throat, Lorn feebly called a golden shield across the front of him. It flickered like a lightbulb about to go out.

Before the gray energy slammed into him, a flash of red tore through the area.

Takeo charged forward, his sword in hand. Red energy surged around his eyes and trailed in his wake as he screamed in fury, a loathing glare etched on his face.

Caedex rebuffed the boy's strong, swiping blows from the energy-flaming sword. They parried back and forth, clangs hitting the air and opposing energies sparking like hot lead.

Gray energy built in Caedex's grasp, taking on the rough shape of a sword. He swung the energy to combat Takeo's opposing slash.

The might behind both attacks collided and erupted, rippling a small explosion on the less populated street at the edge of Bunkyo's sprawl.

Takeo was hurtled back toward Lorn, smacking into the feeble shield and inadvertently breaking his Zaheri's defense.

Dust clung in the night air, and a few of the nearby buildings groaned from the force of the explosion. Most of the windows were cracked or outright broken.

Takeo planted the blade of his sword into the chewed asphalt and pulled himself upright. Red energy continued to spark off him as he glared at the dust, daring Caedex to reappear.

"Lorn!" Zelek cried as he flew near. His wings beat against the ground to slow his descent, pushing the dust away from the immediate area.

Still gritting his teeth, Takeo reluctantly looked away from the street to survey Lorn's condition.

His stomach lurched when he did.

Slumped against a nearly demolished sedan, Lorn's smaller frame was battered. Blood dripped from his brow. There was a chunk of something in his side, staining his shirt. A bone poked out of one of his arms, and the other definitely didn't look okay.

Slowly lifting his head and grimacing, Lorn whimpered, "What took so long?"

Zelek gently held Lorn's shoulder. "Ferveos. Came out of nowhere. We're going to get you back to the dojo so you can heal."

"I like that plan," Lorn whispered as his head dipped.

Thundering paw-steps made Takeo whip around, only to see Dover charging toward them with Rowan on his back.

As the grovix slid to a stop, Rowan hopped off his back and asked, "Is he okay?"

Lorn slurred something that might've been an attempt at, "I'll be fine."

"Help me carry him," Zelek said to Rowan.

"What about Caedex?" Takeo demanded, pointing his sword down the street, a glare back on his face.

Dover quickly shook his head. "We didn't see him."

"Then we go after him!"

"Takeo!" Zelek snapped, his jaw tight.

The boy met Zelek's hard stare.

"Trust me; he'll be back. Right now, we get to the dojo and regroup. Lorn isn't safe here."

Takeo tightened his hold on his sword, his muscles suddenly itching again. "I get to end him next time," he growled.

Zelek flicked his gaze to Lorn before he muttered, "Maybe."

Chapter Eleven
PRECISION ATTACKS

The city sprawl was jarringly similar in many ways to Caliga. A gross difference was the harsh lights everywhere. With the violently bright lights illuminating every corner of buildings and alleyways, Caedex had kept wishing to shield his eyes leading up to his strike against the Agerians. On his return, however, victory had focused his vision, making him ignore everything surrounding him on his march back to the portal.

His fingers twitched, craving to close around a throat or slam a skull into the ground. Gray energy kept sparking down his spine, begging to slice through a heart. Chasing the shield-bearer had spun a storm in Caedex's chest, and he needed some way to outlet the brewing thunder.

It'd been so enthralling hunting the frantic redhead who had done so much to try to save himself. And to ultimately see the Agerian fail, to see the panic in his actions, to see the furious desperation in the Third's eyes ...

Darkness, Caedex was so turned on.

How long had it been since he'd had a chase like that? It felt so good.

He wanted more.

When the portal flashed from white to red in Caedex's grasp, he immediately lumbered for the war room. Time had passed, and the Master would demand an answer for the delay. There was a real chance Caedex might be breathing his last breaths.

But the gamble had paid off. The delay had proven necessary. The Zaheri were fractured, and the second strike would award them not only a dead Human-Born, but four dead Zaheri, as well.

Caedex bowed as he entered the war room and could feel the annoyance in the room. He refused to let it shake him. "My Lord, I know I've delayed."

"Oh, have you now?" Cregorous spat. "How convenient for me that you can tell the passage of time."

"I've struck down a Zaheri."

For a few long seconds, Cregorous stared at the general.

Slowly, Caedex lifted his gaze and gained his typical assured stance. "Their shield-bearer is dead."

An approving hum left Cregorous. "One of you actually accomplished something of merit."

Pride swelled in Caedex's chest.

Darkness, he'd bested both the Right *and* Left Hands?

Today would award him great things.

His energy prickled his skin in desire for carnage. The image of smashing the Third's face in, the pleasure he'd feel as the bones of the child gave way under his force, the thrill he'd get knowing this day would propel him into a new rank among the generals ...

"Your forces?" Cregorous asked, pulling Caedex from his hungry thoughts.

"Decimated. The Ferveos lasted longest. The dull beasts proved an ample distraction while I destroyed the shield-bearer."

"Well played."

"The portal location may need adjustment."

"Where?" Cregorous asked, leaning over the table and surveying the map.

Caedex stepped up and pointed to the location where he'd been sent, the island enlarging for him to better show what he knew. "This proved profitable for the first strike, but they clearly moved in this direction, out of the city limits. I believe they aimed for these mountains."

"Fine," Cregorous said, waving his hand dismissively. "Ten minutes, then reconvene."

Bowing low, Caedex said, "As you wish, Master." He immediately made for the kitchen, craving meat to rebuild his stamina.

The fact that another battle lay moments away brought a resurgence of the gnawing desire to unleash everything he had. Lay everything before him to waste. Carve into the Third's body and tear his Zaheri apart.

He hungered—ached—for that.

Chapter Twelve

A Dark Night

"C'mon, Lorn," Zelek said gently as he held a mug up to the young, battered redhead.

The group sat in the dining area next to the small kitchen. The table gave Lorn something to lean against so he wouldn't have to support his slumping weight. There was a pierced hole in the wall from—they assumed—Takeo's sword. The boy must've called for it without concern over what damage he might cause to the dojo itself.

Wincing, Lorn wrinkled his nose. "Don't wanna."

Rowan rubbed his forehead and grumbled, "For Elders' sake, I know it tastes bad, but it'll help you heal faster."

Takeo sat cross-legged nearby, leaning forward a bit with an inquisitive look on his face. "What sort of tea is that?"

"It's from Agerius," Dover said as he sat next to the boy. "Caretakers came up with it a few years after we came to Earth."

"So, this is a new thing?"

With great distaste, Lorn took a sip and immediately looked like he had to force himself to swallow the drink.

Casting Takeo a glance, Rowan answered, "In Agerius, they'd use other methods. But without a Caretaker here to help us and use the various equipment they have, those methods would be useless."

Zelek continued to give Lorn a scolding look as the younger shield-bearer fought through the medicine. The Team Leader briefly looked to Takeo and added, "Kind of like how humans train doctors and field medics to handle emergencies. We're Defenders, not Healers. So, there was a Caretaker who come up with the idea of a tea made from some Agerian herbs that would heighten our natural healing."

The room grew quiet as Lorn choked down the rest of the steaming drink. He let out a gagging breath. "I hate that stuff."

Takeo squinted. "You've had it before?"

Waving his hand dismissively, Zelek said, "We all did shortly after we got it."

"Why?"

"The Caretakers weren't sure if we'd have any negative side effects, so they wanted us all to try a little," Rowan said with a grimace. "It works, but it doesn't taste good."

Gripping his ankles as he slumped, Takeo asked, "So, what now?"

Zelek let out a small sigh before he stood, helping Lorn up in the process. "First, Lorn goes to bed to rest while he can."

Gently holding his injured side, Lorn slurred, "I can do that."

"I'll help him," Rowan said as he went to take Zelek's place.

"Once you do, call Kusuo and Shun."

Rowan flinched and stared at Zelek with wide eyes. "Zelek, are you—"

"We're going to need help."

A frown came to Rowan's face before he settled a little and nodded. Slowly, he basically dragged Lorn toward the bedrooms.

"Dover, I want you to go rest, too," Zelek said to the grovix.

His ears flattening, Dover said, "Are you sure? Wouldn't it be better if I walked around the dojo, just in case?"

Shaking his head, Zelek said, "Not right now. We have to grab sleep where we can, and for the moment, it's quiet. Take advantage of it. But stay in your armor."

Dover nodded and stood, heading to the entrance of the dojo.

Once they were alone in the room, Zelek sat down next to Takeo. "So, what're your questions."

"How do I kill that guy?" Takeo bit out.

Though a hard look was on his features, Zelek sighed. "Takeo, you need to take a breath."

"He almost killed Lorn."

"I know that."

"So he should die!" Takeo said as he slammed his palm into the table, cracking the wood a bit. Red energy flicked and sparked around his shoulders like fireworks. "Murderers don't get second chances! Death, that's it!"

"I know how you feel, but that isn't the right answer."

"What are you talking about?" The boy shot to his feet and started gesturing wildly. "Of course that's the right answer!"

Zelek moved his head just a bit to be able to give Takeo a stern look. "Sit down."

"I can't."

"Sit. Down."

Fisting his hands, Takeo stomped around the table to sit across from Zelek, crossing his arms as he plopped himself down.

"You're right to be angry, okay? Your feelings are valid and completely understood," Zelek started calmly.

"You don't sound like you understand," Takeo grumbled as he glared at the table.

A sharp breath escaped Zelek, and he clenched his jaw. "I get it, Takeo. Caedex is a murderer. He isn't the only one. There are several that we know the names of, and even more we don't. They're monsters. They kill, rape, and steal. They delight in other's pain. And they don't care who they hurt in the process." He gave the boy a furious look. "You're absolutely right that they deserve to die."

"Then why—"

"How many people did you kill tonight?"

Takeo blanched and stuttered out a broken word. He blinked a few times before giving Zelek a confused look. "What?" he whispered.

The Zaheri still held a stern expression on his face, not even blinking as he asked again, "How many people did you kill tonight?"

The itching in Takeo's limbs picked up again. "That's different," he said through gritted teeth.

"Is it?" Zelek asked, a flicker of compassion and pain beneath the forced somberness.

"They would've hurt people. Could've *killed* people."

"Yes, they could've."

Snapping a glare on his face, he spat, "Why are you making it sound like they wouldn't have? They're Caligans!"

"Yes, they are."

Red energy flicked around Takeo's form for a second as he felt his emotions and thoughts spiral into fury. Fury at the calm questions Zelek was asking. Fury at the insinuations he was making.

Fury that Zelek was in any way comparing *him* to *them*.

"Takeo, take a breath," Zelek said softly.

Slamming his fists into the table and breaking off a few chunks, causing the whole thing to splinter and crack, the boy growled, "How could you compare me to them?" He pinched his eyes shut and angrily shook his head. "We're nothing alike! They're evil! Caedex tried to kill Lorn! And he looked happy about it! I'm not like that!"

A frown came to Zelek's face. "Are you sure?"

Takeo threw a spite-filled look at his Zaheri.

It didn't scare Zelek. He didn't even flinch. "You were smiling earlier."

"That was different." Takeo's voice cracked as tears started to form in his eyes.

Zelek sighed again and leaned back, resting against his palms as he stared at the ceiling. "Y'know. You've always reminded me of my brother."

Takeo sniffled in his emotions, his gaze stuck to the broken table.

"Kal's the calmest person I know. Gentlest, too. Brings peace and serenity with him wherever he goes, like a foundation to whoever's nearby."

Angrily swiping his fisted hand under his nose, still glaring at the nothing in the middle distance, Takeo grumbled, "So?"

"I always hated that he called himself a monster. 'Cause he's my brother, I never see the beast he does. But"—Zelek sat up, a forlorn expression filling his features—"then I see him fight." Gently shaking his head, he continued, "He never looks happy or excited, but ... I can see the beast he talks about." He gave Takeo a soft look.

Takeo had been angrily removing his tears as Zelek spoke. He offered a feeble glare. "I'm not like Caedex."

"But you could be," Zelek cautioned. "Takeo, I'm not saying you're a monster. I'm not saying you're him. But you and Caedex are similar—in how you fight, in how your energy displays itself, even in how you barrel forward toward your target." The Zaheri ran a hand through his hair, ruffling it in the process. "Everyone I know has had to face the reality that we've killed people. We've had that weigh on our hearts and souls. We've had to grapple with it. I'm not saying we don't do it—you saw us all tonight; we struck down ..." He covered his face with his hands, resting his elbows against the table. Shaking his head, he slowly looked at the boy across from him. "I don't ... I don't want to think about how many people I've killed trying to defend what I care about." Slowly lifting his gaze to Takeo, he added, "But I've done it. I'll continue to do it. Because, if I don't, everything I love dies." His expression grew resolute as he sat up. "But I'll never go *looking* for revenge."

Gripping his pants, Takeo defiantly said, "I'm not like him."

"Then don't go into the next fight looking to kill him."

"And what if there's no alternative?" Takeo asked with a glare. "What if the only answer *is* to end his miserable, terrible life?"

"Takeo, I'm asking you to be aware that there are two ways to go about this, and it all starts and ends with you and your choice."

"I won't be a murderer."

"Then don't go into this with the intent to kill Caedex."

Takeo opened his mouth to retort.

"Knock him out, yes. Subdue him, yes. Hurt him enough that he stops, yes. But kill him?" Zelek paused and stared hard at the boy across from him before gently shaking his head. "No."

Slumping back a bit, Takeo loosened his muscles. They still itched a little, but he calmed himself down enough to not want to fist his hands.

This was really annoying.

Maybe some of what Zelek had said made sense. But, right now, it all felt totally hypocritical. Like, somehow killing someone because you're defending something doesn't matter. But killing someone because they deserve it does.

It felt unfair, wrong, and backwards. Killing was killing, right?

Therefore, it didn't matter what the intention was. And Takeo was a Human-Born from some prophecy, which meant he got to choose stuff like this, right? Prophecies were, like, divinely inspired, right? So, that meant Takeo couldn't do the wrong thing, right?

He didn't want to talk about this anymore. Zelek seemed to have this hard line. You didn't cross it.

Maybe Zelek had been alive for too long, or hadn't actually faced death, or hadn't lost someone close enough to him yet to realize that some people just didn't deserve to draw breath anymore. Some people just needed to be taken out so no one else got hurt.

Maybe that was Agerius' problem. All this "only defend" nonsense was getting in the way of the answer. Run Cregorous and all of his lackies down until they're dust.

Poof. Peace.

He managed to not roll his eyes as he muttered, "I hear you."

Zelek let out a sigh of relief before giving Takeo a small smile. "Good."

"So, what else haven't you told me?" Takeo asked. He wanted to change the subject quickly. That way, there wouldn't be any other interrogations. So that Zelek wouldn't see that Takeo had only kind of heard him.

"Right," Zelek said with a small nod. "Like I said, there are seven Human-Borns total. I don't know where the others are—none of us do. But you're all around the same age, I think. The High Council seemed to be of the mind that each of you were born in the same Earth year."

Okay, that was kind of good to hear. That meant they'd all be seventeen or eighteen.

"You're the Third Human-Born," Zelek continued.

"And my title's the Warrior, right?"

"Yeah. The order of them is Raidin, Protector, Warrior, Healer, Shifter, Scholar, and Requisite."

Takeo's face scrunched in annoyance. "Why do the First and last have weird titles?"

"Raidin is an old name in Agerius. It means 'Elders' Warrior.'"

With a shrug, the teen asked, "Okay, so what then? Why didn't you tell me about them before?"

"We weren't supposed to even let you know you were a Human-Born until you were seventeen."

Holding his hand out as if to say "*what the heck*," Takeo asked, "What? So, you're saying the others only have what? A year of experience?"

"Most likely, yes."

"That's stupid!" Takeo shot with a look of judgment. "Why wait so long to tell them? What if they're super unprepared for all this nonsense today?"

"We'll just have to hope they aren't."

"But it's still stupid!"

Zelek pinched the bridge of his nose. "I'm sure the Council decided seventeen was a good age so that all of you would be mature enough to handle things." He gave Takeo a knowing look.

"Don't give me that look."

"What look?" Zelek asked with an exaggerated shrug and a "*who me?*" expression.

Letting out a huff of air, Takeo asked, "What else don't I know?"

"That's basically it. You know the rest."

"How many generals does Cregorous have?"

"Six that we know about."

"*That you know about?*"

"There could always be more. We've never been to Caliga, and we have no intention of going there anytime soon."

Takeo looked to the ceiling and rolled his eyes. Then, looking back to his Zaheri, he asked, "So, what now? I know you asked Rowan to get Kusuo and Shun. What's your plan?"

"Well, to start, I'd like you to see about pushing as much energy into swords as you can."

"I already did that."

Zelek gestured toward the Japanese teen. "You've got energy sparking off of you. That means you've got excess. You'll want to have as much in reserve as possible against Caedex."

A light hit Takeo's eyes. "So, you do want me to fight him?"

Giving the boy an unsure look, the Agerian answered, "If Lorn doesn't recover in time, that means we'll only have so much to work with when it comes to defending the dojo. You and Caedex are at least evenly matched by way of energy strength and stamina. Both of us will see to Caedex."

Not quite the answer Takeo wanted, but he understood why Zelek was being so overprotective. He'd been that way earlier, so of course he'd be like that whenever Caedex returned. It meant he wouldn't have Caedex all to himself like he'd hoped, though.

"That'll leave Rowan and Dover to handle everything else. It's still too few, I think. But if we can get Kusuo and Shun to help us, give them a couple assault rifles, that means Lorn won't have to keep an overly fortified shield around the dojo. At least not forever."

Shuffling his weight, Takeo asked, "So, what's the goal here?"

"Get them off Earth."

"That's it?"

"Yes, that's it. Get them to retreat so that the Council can send reinforcements in case they come back."

Takeo shrugged. "Why can't the Council just send reinforcements now?"

Digging his phone out of his pocket, Zelek started to scroll. He shook his head as his shoulders drooped. "I don't know how he's doing it, but I think it's safe to assume that Cregorous has the power to open the portal to multiple exits simultaneously." He flashed his gaze to the teen before looking back to his screen. "These timestamps are all the same, but they're all over Earth, in different time zones. That means, somehow, Cregorous can manipulate the portal."

"So, the portal doesn't normally let you do this whole multiple exits thing?"

Dismally shaking his head, Zelek answered, "No. The portal is almost like a computer. It can't turn on without power. And it doesn't generate power on its own; it requires an outside source."

"Us?"

"Hybrids," Zelek clarified. "Humans can't see the portal in its dormant state. They don't produce enough raw energy to see it. But hybrids? We can interact with it; give it the energy to open." His gaze fell to the middle distance, and he muttered, "Ira said there was the question of whether the portal could be manipulated by more powerful hybrids. Was this what she meant?"

"So, you can't make the portal do whatever you think Cregorous is doing?"

"No." A pensive look came to his face. "This all screams of a bigger problem, though."

"What sort of problem?"

"I dunno," Zelek muttered. His brow pinched, and he shook his head. "He shouldn't know where any of you are. But somehow, it looks like he's managed to pinpoint exactly where he needs to hit."

"I thought you didn't know where the others were?" Takeo said skeptically.

"I don't," the Zaheri said as he set his phone down then gestured to the device. "But these hits seem precise and intentional. Not like wild guesses." He scratched his chin. "If they were, we probably would have seen other locations tagged. Not to mention the fact that he just *happened* to know which activation you were near? Not likely."

"So ... what then?"

Zelek was quiet as he stared at the table. He said nothing for a fair pause before he quietly muttered, "I don't know."

Something about his silence made Takeo think that Zelek might know more than he was letting on. However, whether it was Takeo's own reluctance to divulge his true feelings surrounding killing Caedex, or just a weariness over everything that had happened in the last four and a half hours, Takeo didn't press him.

Standing with a small groan, Zelek said, "Get to your assignment. I'm going to check on Lorn and Rowan."

Takeo watched him go but remained sitting for a moment.

It all felt so stupid, like the Agerians weren't using their heads.

Monsters like Cregorous—and his lackies—didn't care whether actions were noble or done only because of righteously defending something. They probably found that all laughable. And truthfully, Takeo did, too.

Bad, tyrannical people who used their strength to step on others were bullies. And bullies needed to be stopped. And stopped in this instance meant dead. Because that was the only way to put an end to all the pain and chaos.

How long had Agerius suffered because of these maniacs? And

all because they were too scared of the morality of simply snuffing out the problem?

Getting to his feet, Takeo made his way toward the practice room where his swords would be.

No matter what Zelek thought, he was wrong in this instance.

Caedex wouldn't be allowed to live. Not anymore.

Takeo would see to that personally.

Zelek wearily scrubbed a hand through his hair. Then, as he pulled his hand down, he fixated on the ribbon wrapped around his wrist.

Fear clutched his heart, and he had to tell himself to push it aside. To not fear over Ira. Not fear over Kaldok. They weren't alone on their battlefields. They had skilled fighters at their sides. They were skilled themselves.

Elders please, he begged the silence, *don't take them away from me.*

Footsteps made him straighten and gulp his frown away. Glancing over his shoulder, he saw Takeo stalk off into the training room where the Agerian swords were kept.

A new worry ghosted his thoughts.

"How'd Squeak take the news?" Rowan asked, drawing Zelek's attention away from the boy.

Turning to face Rowan, the Team Leader said, "All right, I think."

Rowan's gaze flicked toward the training room.

"What did you see in him?"

"During the fight?"

Zelek nodded. "Yeah. I don't want to say I'm concerned, but—"

"You're concerned."

"I'm"—Zelek rolled his eyes—"worried."

With a scoff, Rowan said, "Zelek, that's the same thing."

A scowl was his response.

"I think you're 'worrying' over nothing."

Absentmindedly shaking his head, Zelek muttered, "I really don't think so."

Rowan's eyes narrowed. "You're really rattled."

"It's ... something I saw when he was fighting." Shaking his head, Zelek sighed. "Maybe you're right. Maybe it's nothing."

"Maybe you're distracted," Rowan said with an understanding expression.

"Ro, that's not—"

"It'd be understandable. Your brother and—"

"Rowan, stop," Zelek gritted out, holding his hand up to try to silence the comment. He didn't need the reminder. The reminder hung on his wrist, taunting him with its superstition and its hope.

Whether it'd been the action or the cutting way Zelek had said the simple command, Rowan didn't immediately try to say anything. And in that brief pause, Zelek asked, "Kusuo and Shun?"

"They're both coming," Rowan said with a nod.

Zelek straightened. "They picked up? At this hour?"

Chuckling a little, Rowan said, "I know. I was shocked when Kusuo answered—right after the ring."

"I didn't think them for night chasers."

"Me neither. Not with how early they get here in the mornings."

Nodding subtly, Zelek muttered, "Regardless, it's a good sign—the fact that they answered in the dead of night. I feel like most people would've just let it ring."

Rowan shrugged. "Maybe they heard the fighting."

His eyes flicking about the hallway, Zelek asked, "You don't think they've already pieced it together?"

"They're sharp, but c'mon, Zelek. We cover ourselves well."

"I dunno," Zelek said as he raised his brow and rubbed a hand through his hair. "We do keep a grovix in the dojo."

"Yeah, and no one's ever noticed." Rowan held his hands out as though to congratulate himself. "I say that's impressive."

Zelek wasn't so sure. Humans seemed happy to ignore things that were out of the norm, dismiss the strange away, or come up with a logical reason for what trick they were convinced their eyes played on them.

Regardless, he was grateful.

Letting out a sigh, he met Rowan's gaze. "I'm gonna grab my sword before they get here."

"Golden. I'll get my axe."

"Grab a couple assault rifles," Zelek said as he started to his room.

"You think they'll help?"

"I'm going to hope for it."

Once in his room, Zelek paused and collected his thoughts. It was nearly one in the morning. The world around them would likely be asleep. But, at any moment, another strike could come. Caedex's blow to Lorn was well planned.

The brutish general was smarter than he looked. If he had to guess, Caedex would throw himself right at Takeo, leaving the other fighters to worry about the Zaheri. Which meant Zelek needed to be prepared to do battle with Takeo against Caedex. He wasn't going to entrust that to Rowan, and Lorn should stay behind a shield. There was no telling how long the next bout could last and what sort of numbers they might face.

He wanted to be grateful for the fact that Cregorous wasn't the one after them. But all that did was twist anxiety in his gut.

Clutching his sword tight in his grasp, Zelek sucked in a heavy breath and held it for ten seconds before slowly releasing it.

It wouldn't be anyone but the First.

Cregorous wouldn't leave the First Human-Born to any of his generals. He'd go after them himself.

He clenched his jaw and gripped the sword tighter. He had to keep it together. He couldn't fall apart. Not now. Too much needed to be tended to. Lorn was still recovering. Takeo needed stability. Dover needed direction. Rowan needed level-headedness.

Now wasn't the time.

Tears pricked Zelek's eyes, anyway. Sniffling back his fears. Swallowing back his unease. Blinking away his worry.

"Be safe, Kal," he whispered shakily to the quiet room.

As he slid the door open and marched down the hall, he left his fears for his brother and Ira, the people he loved most next to the boy at the other end of the building, behind.

He would cling to faith. Because, in that moment, that was all he had.

Chapter Thirteen
THE MIGHT OF THE WARRIOR

Kusuo and Shun were two humans who had recently been employed by Zelek and Rowan to lead advanced martial arts training at the dojo. Their rapport with both Agerians was solid, which was why Zelek had considered them for assistance.

Both men were upstanding members of Japanese society and had trained and become certified in various martial arts practices. They knew how to be strict on some people and softer on others. In the few months they'd been working at the dojo, Zelek had come to admire them both.

It didn't take as long as he thought to bring them up to speed, and then subsequently convince them to help. Once both men understood the gravity of the situation, they'd quickly volunteered to render their aid.

A short lesson on the use of Agerian assault rifles later, and both humans were insisting that Zelek and Rowan try to get what little rest they could to prepare.

After a fair bit of back and forth over the necessity of staying alert and ready, Zelek and Rowan agreed to each take a small rest while the other was awake. And while they were awake, they, too, pushed energy into swords to have in reserve.

There had been an attempt to convince Takeo to rest, but that had ultimately ended with the boy fuming and stomping off to continue pushing energy into swords.

Somewhere around three in the morning, Lorn awoke. He moved slowly and lifted his arm gingerly but looked far better than he had earlier. There were a few faint bruises here and there, but any cuts had healed, and his eyes weren't sunken or heavy any longer. He went about making a hearty meal for everyone, with Kusuo's help. They all knew they needed to keep their strength up, and a meal with stout tea was exactly what they required.

A few questions were asked over the meal by the humans. Dover was introduced, and he had a grand time going into the details of how best to take down a werewolf or bratak'ra. Takeo joked around and energetically described the fight in the garden from his perspective. Shun was convinced he could teach the boy more about kendo and vowed to become his teacher in the subject.

Come the end of their meal, Lorn insisted on setting up a shield.

"Are you sure you're up for that?" Zelek asked.

With a nod, Lorn answered, "We have to make sure we're ready, right? What better way to do that than to cover the dojo in a shield?"

"All right," Zelek admitted. "But don't push yourself. You've already been through a whole mess."

"Hey, with me doing this, I have every intention to say that earns me the right to stay here while you guys go into the thick of things."

Rowan scoffed. "Wimp."

"Hey!" Lorn said with a scowl. "*You* go against Caedex, and then we'll see who's a wimp!"

The two began to argue about the merits of Lorn's encounter with the general. Meanwhile, Takeo quietly reignited his fury at the Caligan in question and vowed he wouldn't let the monster live if he had the chance.

That had been half an hour ago.

Takeo sat on the steps of the dojo. His sword was sheathed in his lap as he stared into the night. Tokyo's lights cast a colorful array on the horizon, while Lorn's golden shield illuminated the area, bathing the trees and foliage around the dojo in warm light.

Dover lay nearby, his pose attentive and ready, his head held high. He occasionally sniffed the night air or flicked his head or ears toward something that caught his attention. Otherwise, he could have been mistaken for an ornate statue with how still he was.

The door to the dojo opened, and Zelek stepped outside. "Hey, Squeak, how're you doing?"

"I'm fine, Z," Takeo said without looking away from the city.

Leaning against one of the support posts for the porch roof, Zelek gave the boy a skeptical look. "You're allowed to blink, y'know."

"I blink," Takeo fired with a quick, perturbed glance to his Zaheri.

They grew quiet, all of them staring into the night. Wind rustled through the trees. Dover sniffed the air intently before he let out a heavy breath.

Out of the corner of his eye, Takeo looked to Zelek. The Team Leader looked so calm and relaxed, arms crossed over his chest as he leaned against the post. There was barely even a hint that the Agerian was tired, his eyes sharp and determined.

Takeo genuinely did admire Zelek and wanted his approval. He hadn't realized how badly he wanted Zelek to be proud of him until tonight. Until Zelek was sitting across from him, giving him a stern, authoritative look and practically reprimanding Takeo for wanting to enact judgment.

Looking back toward the city, Takeo had to wonder if Zelek was proud of him. Would he be proud of him if he killed Caedex? Probably not.

Takeo wanted to grip his sword but refrained. He didn't want to give himself away.

A flash of white hit the sky, flickering for a moment. Alarms started to sound inside the dojo.

Zelek pushed off the post. His brow twitched.

Slowly, Dover rose to his feet.

The portal continued to flicker in the distance.

Takeo's brows knit, and he asked, "Does it normally look like that?"

"No," Zelek whispered. His arms were loose at his sides, but his fingers slowly moved toward his sheathed sword that hung on his belt.

A moment later, the portal stopped flickering and ...

It looked like it was moving.

Takeo sprang to his feet as Zelek hopped down the steps. Rowan and Lorn appeared at the door.

"Keep the door open," Zelek said, his gaze fixed on the moving portal.

"Is the portal ... moving?" Rowan asked, his jaw slack and concern written on his features.

Gripping his sword, Takeo gritted his teeth and glared. His Zaheri's unease sent worry coiling in his stomach.

A roaring filled the air as the portal continued to surge across the landscape toward them. The bright white cylinder almost sounded like a tornado as it moved but left everything untouched in its wake. It was strange to see something so massive cause no damage.

The closer it got, the tighter Takeo felt his muscles become. He bent his legs and fell into a ready stance, prepared to push himself into the air at a moment's notice.

Zelek mirrored him.

Another tense moment passed, and Takeo glared at the portal. Once the large cylinder hit the trees that would have led them to the walking path to the city, it slapped to a stop.

At the same instant, Caedex leaped from the blinding white cylinder. Gray energy rivaled his bulk as he flung his arms out and a storm of gray tore from him, aiming for the golden-domed dojo.

Takeo didn't see anything else. His gaze was fixed on Caedex's form and his gray energy. So, even though countless other warriors ran from the portal, all beelining for the dojo, he took no notice of them. They were Rowan, Dover, Kusuo, and Shun's problem.

His target was in the sky, hurtling an attack at them.

Without a breath of communication, Takeo and Zelek launched into the air. Gold and red trailed in their wake as though supercharging their leap. They unsheathed their swords at the same time and effortlessly sliced through Caedex's storm of gray.

The armored general didn't seem deterred in the slightest. He spun in the air, a swirl of gray surrounding him, as Takeo and Zelek flanked him.

Both opposing warriors raised their weapons to deflect and were pushed to the ground, landing solidly across from one another.

Caedex landed with a heavy thump, rattling the earth under his bulk. A wicked grin sat on his face as he looked between the two of them. "You better make this fun for me."

Takeo thought his jaw would break with how tightly he clenched it. He charged forward. Zelek was only a second behind on the other side.

Caedex certainly was powerful, and fast. He dodged blows and deflected hits more often than not as the three moved as though they'd practiced a scene. Takeo and Zelek moved in smooth transition, one striking while the other moved to support, and then they traded. Caedex must've survived this long because he knew how to handle multiple enemies at one time. He barely seemed fazed by the strength or number of blows he had to work with.

A few trees fell as the fight wore on. The ground became chewed and uneven under their feet. There were other sounds of battle in the distance, but it was so far behind Takeo's active thought that it only served as background noise, like a strange soundtrack to his fight with Caedex.

Though red energy sparked in his eyes and around his chest, Takeo could acknowledge that adrenaline was his fuel in that moment. He and Zelek began to move faster, dodging and hopping back, and then surging forward with slicing blows.

They began to move so fluidly that Caedex couldn't defend appropriately and took a few hard hits. His armor dented and split.

Then there was a growl of fury, a swirl of gray, and a flash of light reflected off Caedex's armor.

Zelek's sword clamored to the ground, and the air left Takeo's lungs.

Caedex had snatched Zelek's smaller form, twisting his arm to force him to release his grip on his sword. Then he had Zelek's face in his large hand. In a crushing movement, he smashed Zelek into the ground with a blast of gray energy.

All Takeo felt in that moment was blinding fury.

His Mask appeared without any active thought and slammed into Caedex, shoving the Caligan general off of Zelek. Furious instinct guided Takeo as he and his Mask fought Caedex.

The energy in his blade began to wane.

Caedex laughed as he released a large blast of gray and opened his mouth to say something.

Probably something stupid. And stupidly arrogant.

Before the Caligan general could actually say anything, the violently vibrant blade from earlier was in Takeo's grasp and slicing through the large gray attack.

Caedex's eyes were wide in surprise as the blast of red smashed into him and sent him sailing. A large tree broke his trajectory and groaned as it cracked.

A laugh tumbled from Caedex as he lifted his head and spat out blood. "You're a lot of fun, kid."

Heaving breaths growled from Takeo as he stood with a blaze of red energy around him. He was squarely between Zelek and Caedex, his Mask at his side, echoing his rage.

Caedex pushed off the tree and said, "I always thought Akeno's fascination with playing with his victims was weird." A glint filled his eyes as he grinned devilishly at Takeo. "Now I kinda get it."

A sputtering cough came from behind Takeo, and he whipped around to see Zelek's battered face. Fear eclipsed Takeo's reasoning as he took in the extent of the damage.

Blood stained Zelek's teeth as he coughed. A gouge had been torn into his shoulder, revealing bone. The blast of gray from Caedex had torn Zelek's face and must have fractured his cheekbone and jaw with how uneven he looked. An eye was bloodshot as he tremblingly tried to get himself out of the small crater his head had made from impact.

Tears welled in Takeo's eyes as he whispered in a cracked voice, "Otosan."

There was a crackling surge of energy behind him.

With a yell, Takeo brought the sword around and sliced through Caedex's attack like a stone dividing a river. Then Takeo released the sword and sent it sailing at Caedex.

Caedex barely avoided a deadly impalement. The sword still caught his arm and tore his armor.

He whipped a hatred-filled gaze to the boy but stuttered for a second.

Takeo charged forward, and half a dozen blades flew behind him, all glowing red. His Mask leaped over him and snatched a sword, descending on Caedex.

Regaining his crazed excitement, Caedex snatched the sword and dispatched the Mask.

Another Mask appeared above Takeo and went to rip the sword from Caedex's grasp. However, gray energy flashed along the blade and struck the second Mask, obliterating it to red dust that danced in the breeze. He brought the overtaken blade down against one of Takeo's swords, met with a tear-filled glare from the boy.

Takeo's arm trembled as he fought against Caedex's brute strength. Caedex's broken armor rattled as his own arms shook.

With a wild grin and a crazy look in his eyes, Caedex said, "Would ya look at that? We're equally matched, kid!"

Readjusting his footing as he pushed against Caedex's might, Takeo spat, "No, we aren't!"

Another laugh came from the general. "What're you gonna do, kid? Avenge your dead Zaheri?"

It took everything in Takeo to not check on Zelek.

Caedex had to be lying.

Zelek couldn't die.

It was impossible.

"That's cute," Caedex mocked.

A wave of fury spiraled in Takeo's chest, manifesting as a surge of red energy that pulsed and pushed around his core before exploding outward with a deafening blast.

The trees bowed, leaves blasting off the branches. The ground beneath Takeo trembled and shook, chunks of rock hurtling and kicking outward. Glass in the distance broke. More than a few trees crashed to the ground. Shocked yells echoed from near the dojo.

Caedex was thrown back, another large chunk of his armor decimated from the blow.

At the popping blast, all of the red vibrancy in the blades that hung in the air near Takeo flickered then clamored to the ground. Takeo's knees buckled, collapsing him onto the broken ground, his heart feeling strained as it weakly, desperately continued to pound.

Rumbling to his feet, Caedex said dismally, "You're ruining my armor, kid." He lumbered closer. His body had sustained injuries, and blood seeped here and there. A deep cut ran down his brow and across his cheek. "So, I guess there's something those stupid Agerians can say: their little fighter could at least dent my armor." He laughed condescendingly. "But that's the best he could do."

Takeo's body shook as he held his chest. Squinting his eyes open, he tried a feeble glare at Caedex.

"Not sure what's happenin', huh?" Caedex asked mockingly as he flicked his wrist. The sword he'd overtaken flew into his grasp. "That's what happens when you overexert yourself. Shoulda used those handy swords as your reserve rather than deplete what you had in your body, stupid kid."

A flash of gold smacked Caedex's across the face, and he let out a grunt of annoyance, holding his eye.

Tremblingly, Takeo looked back to see Zelek standing unsteadily, his arms up in a defending stance. Gold energy flickered along his forearms, mostly holding form, but not definitive like it normally was. His face was half bruised, an eye swollen shut. Heavy breaths shook his shoulders. Blood dripped down his normally strong jaw.

"What?" Zelek panted. "Surprised I'm still standing?"

"Nah, man, this is great," Caedex said with a devious smile. "Now I can kill the kid knowing you got to watch."

Though he swayed, Zelek growled, "That's not going to happen."

"Well, ain't that noble of you."

"'Course it is," Zelek said with a smirk.

Takeo's brow twitched in confusion. Why was Zelek smiling?

"Nobility runs in my blood," the Zaheri said with a grunt before he lowered his hands.

A clanging slice hit the air, and Takeo whipped his head to Caedex, seeing Zelek's sword impaled into the Caligan's shoulder.

Caedex let out a bellow as gray energy swirled around his form. He threw his hands out, and the attack surged forward. For half a second, Takeo thought it was going to hit him and moved to snatch one of the nearby swords. But then he realized it was too high.

It was going to hit Zelek.

His brain furiously asked, *What do I do? I can't let Zelek die!*

Zelek leaped over Takeo. One arm was clearly broken, but his legs and other arm were still good.

"Takeo, run!" Zelek commanded as he started to trade blows from Caedex with kicks.

The sword impaled in Caedex swung free and landed in Zelek's grasp in time to deflect a crushing blow from the Caligan. Gray and gold sparked and crackled as Zelek used the momentum to skim the blade along Caedex's armor.

Gripping the chewed earth in his fist, Takeo cursed himself. He wouldn't run. Even if he could, he wouldn't do it. He wouldn't leave Zelek.

A crack hit the air as Zelek landed a fist on Caedex's face, sending the Caligan tumbling.

Holding his broken arm against his chest, Zelek panted in breaths. "Leave, Caedex! I won't tell you again!"

The towering general laughed before spitting out in his growling voice, "Or what, Agerian?" Blood stained his brow, and his cheekbone had clearly been broken by Zelek's punch. He'd sustained injuries, but he stood and cackled. "Darkness knows you can't kill me!"

Zelek's stance faltered a little, and Takeo tremblingly worked to get up.

In a flash, Caedex tore forward. For his bulk, he shouldn't have been able to move that fast, especially with his injuries.

What was fueling him?

And how did Takeo get whatever it was?

A golden shield sputtered to life in front of Zelek as he raised his sword. The shield shattered, and Caedex's hit impacted the Zaheri, sending Zelek sailing.

Gritting his teeth, Zelek managed to land on his feet, sliding across the uneven soil.

Takeo whipped his head up in time to see Caedex unleash a furious attack. One straight on course to hit Zelek.

He was spent. Caedex's mocking point had been accurate. Takeo had used too much brashness in his last attack and should've used his head. He'd called the swords, and they'd been right there. But in that instant, he hadn't thought to use them. It was stupid and reckless, and now it was going to ...

"No!" Takeo yelled as he forced himself to his feet.

He refused to let Zelek die. To let any of his Zaheri die.

Not here. Not now.

In that same instant, even though a second prior he'd known there wasn't enough energy left within him, Takeo felt a surge roll through his body, like a wave crashing onto the shore. From his heart and through him, he felt strength stampede out and into his limbs, down to his fingers and toes.

His body flared red energy and effortlessly stopped Caedex's attack.

Takeo didn't know what was happening, but his feet were stuck for a second as his body radiated his red energy.

He glared at Caedex, who stared at him in confusion.

Strike him down, a chorus of voices sang in his head.

Without hesitating, Takeo smacked his fist and palm together. He felt Masks hop off his form and fall in line behind him, at his sides, all around him. In a few seconds, he had a small army of red Masks.

It shouldn't have been possible. He'd only ever been proficient with one Mask as his ally. But in that instant, he knew controlling this whole slew of Masks would take almost no effort.

They surged out. Some ran toward Caedex, but the bulk tore for the dojo.

He could see them all, like he could view the battle above it all and see through his Mask's eyes at the same time. They slammed into Caligans. Crushed werewolves and bratak'ra. Tore monsters off Dover and decimated the enemy. Shoved Lorn aside as they blasted through Caligans that were about to descend on him. Covered Kusuo and Shun on the roof like guardians of immoveable stone. Battled at Rowan's side and made openings for him to strike down their enemies.

A moment of that awesome power passed, and then a snapping hit the air. In that same instant, Takeo felt his world crumble to black.

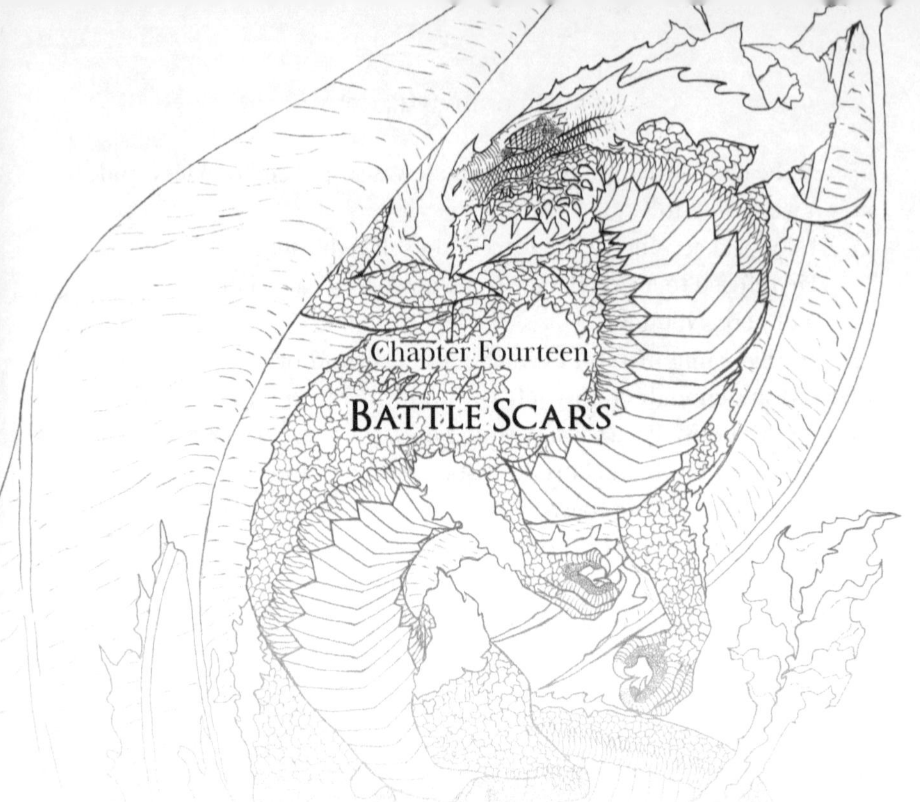

Screams and twisted pain littered his mind as Takeo shook awake, stumblingly ripping the blanket off as he sat up. Before he could even consciously acknowledge he was awake, he let out a cry of, "Zelek!"

The afternoon sun filtered through the eerily quiet dojo as Takeo scrambled out of his room.

Zelek's room was next to his. Upon opening the sliding door, he was met with a neat bed and ordered setting. Untouched by all appearances.

His stomach flipped, and he spun on his heel, tearing through the dojo. He thundered through the hall and felt the floor and walls rattle as he went.

"Zelek!" he cried again, ripping sliding doors open frantically.

Lorn appeared and snatched the boy. "Whoa, Squeak, calm—"

"Where's Zelek?" Takeo hollered, nearly throwing Lorn into the wall.

"What's wrong?" Zelek asked in a panic as he appeared behind the nearby sliding door to the dining room.

Evidence of the battle was still all over Zelek. Purple and green bruising along his face and puffiness near scrapes and cuts. A few small butterfly closures covered the larger injuries. His face wasn't deformed anymore, so the bones must have been set and healed. He was bare-chested, a heavy bandage on his left shoulder and most of his arm, and the left side of his chest was bandaged. A few of his fingers were wrapped.

Takeo flung his arms around Zelek, hugging him fiercely. Tears welled in his eyes.

Zelek smiled fondly at the boy as he returned the embrace. Ruffling his hair, he said, "Good boy."

Gently pushing off his Zaheri, Takeo sheepishly looked away and ignored his grateful tears as he said, "I'm just glad you're ... y'know, so I can prove I can beat you in a spar."

A chuckle came from Zelek before he ruffled Takeo's bedhead again. "Yeah, you keep right on thinking that'll happen."

Lifting his gaze to Zelek, Takeo smiled.

"You did good, Takeo," Zelek whispered, wearing a proud smile.

There were so many questions and so many things he wanted to talk about and figure out but, in that moment, Takeo just wanted to live in the warm, happy knowledge that everyone was alive, safe, and smiling.

Takeo stood in front of his parents' burial site. Fresh flowers laid on the stone marker.

There was a well of confusion in his mind. Confusion over what he was supposed to be feeling when he looked at the stone with his parents' names on it.

He was supposed to be sad, right?

A flash of the memory tore across his vision. Of Zelek's bloodied form, broken and beaten. Of his staggering, swaying stance as he defiantly stood up to Caedex. And how it sparked a deep, sharp pain in Takeo's chest.

He'd called Zelek *Otosan*. A common way to call someone dad. It hadn't even occurred to him in that crushing moment to call him anything else.

But that was dishonoring his actual father, wasn't it?

He wanted it to make sense. He wanted his life to make sense. He wanted to acknowledge freely how he saw his Zaheri and call them by their appropriate names. Not nicknames. Not their given names.

By the family names he didn't realize he yearned to call them by until they were nearly ripped away from him.

If his parents were here, would he see them all differently? He would, wouldn't he? That knowledge hurt his chest more. Because he didn't want to see his Zaheri as anything different.

He was a terrible son.

Zelek walked toward him, rewrapping a worn red ribbon around his wrist.

Takeo sniffled back his tears and looked back to the burial marker.

The Zaheri placed his hand on Takeo's shoulder. "You all right?"

Shoving his hands into his pockets, Takeo tried to figure out the answer to that question. How to verbalize it so it made sense.

Zelek pulled his hand back and eased, turning to look at the stone. "It's okay if you don't want to talk about it."

"I called you Otosan," Takeo sputtered.

A sad smile came to Zelek's face as he gently looked at the boy. "Yeah, you did."

"Was ...? Was that wrong?" Takeo asked as he glared at the tears forming in his eyes.

Soft fondness filled the Zaheri's face. "Not to me."

Chancing a glance at the ribbon on Zelek's wrist, Takeo considered the question that played on his mind. "So ... then ...?" he started quietly.

Zelek gave him an inquisitive look.

"Who does that belong to?" the boy asked as he pointed to the ribbon.

For a second, Zelek looked flustered, a tint of embarrassment playing on his features. Then he smiled softly and looked to his wrist. "Her name is Ira."

"Is she your wife?"

Gently running his thumb along the fabric, Zelek whispered, "Not yet."

"Hey ... uh ..."

A smirk played on Zelek's face before he looked to Takeo.

"Think she'd mind if I called her Okasan?"

Without warning, a brilliant smile erupted on Zelek's face. He had to look at the ground as he rubbed a hand through his hair. "Jeez, Takeo, you're gonna kill me here."

"Sorry, Otosan."

The smile lingered for a soft moment before Zelek looked back at the boy. "I ... never actually thought you'd call me that."

Takeo's eyes widened a little. "Wait, you ... you thought about it?"

Nodding subtly, the Zaheri gained a faraway look, his gaze on the sky. "There was a moment where I seriously considered running away with you and Ira, pretending like Agerius' problems weren't ours."

"Why didn't you?"

Shaking his head with a small sigh, Zelek answered, "Because it wasn't the right thing to do." He looked over at him. "It's what I wanted. Nearly more than anything." A smile cracked his face. Somehow, he looked younger when he smiled like that. "Ira and me together, and you as our son, it ... it felt too fantastic to be possible. Ira is a Zaheri, too, protecting her own Human-Born. We both had a job to do, in different parts of the world." He looked toward the sky again, a frown coming to his face.

"I wish we could've been that," Takeo mumbled as his gaze fell to the ground.

Looking back to him, Zelek pulled him into a side hug, draping his arm across his shoulders. "We will. Someday."

"Soon?"

"Elders, I hope so."

Slowly, Takeo looked back to the burial marker. "Do you think they'd be proud of me?"

Another warm smile graced Zelek's features. "I know they would be."

A satisfied grin came to Takeo's face.

Ruffling the boy's hair, Zelek said, "Now, come on. We wait any longer, and we have to take the late train."

"Could we fly instead?" Takeo asked as he fell into step with Zelek.

"Are you kidding?" Zelek said with an incredulous look. "We do that, and we basically throw a sign over us blaring, 'please come take us away.'"

"No one's come around to ask questions by now. You really think the government's gonna come after us?"

Shaking his head, Zelek answered, "Let's just say I'm not taking it off the table."

"What would that mean?"

"We'd have to run."

"Where?"

"There's another small house we have farther into the country, tucked in a forest. It's nothing great, and we'd be on top of one another, but we'd be safe." His gaze trained forward, Zelek whispered, "Elders, I hope we don't have to resort to that."

Takeo looked around the landscape surrounding them. He had to admit he didn't want to have to leave Tokyo's suburb if it could be helped. He loved it here. And he had everyone he could ever possibly need.

Why should he ever leave? It wasn't like anything better awaited him somewhere else.

"So, what do we do now?" Takeo asked in an upbeat manner.

"We keep training. Especially on your impulse control."

"Hey, I nearly had Caedex," the teen said as he pointed at Zelek, as though trying to get the Zaheri to agree. "If he hadn't run, I would've demolished him."

"Yeah, on that subject," Zelek muttered before he asked louder, "What in the blazes happened?"

With a small scoff, Takeo mumbled, "I wish I knew."

"You don't have any clues?"

Takeo shrugged. "All I know is, suddenly, I was epic powerful." A light sparked in his eyes and lit up his features. "Did you see how many Masks I made? I wish I could've counted them. It had to be at least thirty."

"Did you do anything? Think anything that sparked it?" Zelek asked, ignoring his exuberance.

"Just got up and tried to get between you and Caed—ow!" He winced as Zelek smacked him several times in the arm, a look of annoyance on his face.

"That's what you get for being so stupid!" Zelek reprimanded, continuing to lightly flick his hand in exaggerated smacks. "What were you thinking?"

Meeting Zelek's flailing assault with little whiffling whacks of his own, Takeo griped, "I was thinking I didn't want you to die!"

"That's very nice of you, but next time, worry more about yourself, you numbskull." Zelek dropped his hand and continued walking along, gently shaking his head. "So, nothing happened outside of you standing up and suddenly getting strong for no good reason?"

Scratching his head, Takeo said, "Well, there were voices."

Zelek squinted at him in confusion.

"Dunno where they came from. Just heard a bunch of voices at once."

"Really?"

"Yeah. They told me to strike Caedex down. Which I was gonna do before he bolted like a loser."

The Zaheri hummed.

"What're you thinking?"

"That you shouldn't have telepathy."

"Whoa, seriously? I have telepathy? That's epic!" Takeo asked with way too much excitement.

Barely repressing the urge to roll his eyes, Zelek gave him a bemused smirk. "I don't think you have telepathy."

"But then—"

"I think you might've *experienced* telepathy," Zelek clarified. He gestured vaguely. "There aren't any Telepaths in Agerius. So, we don't know a lot about them. Well, normal people don't. Ira does. She's basically a historian, so she knows a whole lot more about dead abilities than anyone."

"Dead abilities?"

"A slang way to refer to abilities that we don't see often or aren't actively held by anyone in Agerius."

Takeo nodded. "So, what makes you so sure I don't have telepathy?"

"Well, for starters, you would've started experiencing it a long time ago." He rolled his wrist a bit as he glanced to Takeo. "Remember how you started manifesting your energy when you were around eleven? And your Masks started a little while later?"

"Yeah. So?"

"So, if you were also a Telepath, you would've started to experience signs of it back when you started to show signs of the Mask ability."

Begrudgingly, Takeo admitted, "Yeah, I guess that makes sense." He perked up a little and asked, "But then, what happened to me?"

"Like I said, I'm wondering if you experienced telepathy. If one of the other Human-Borns has that ability and ..." Zelek shrugged as he raised his brow. "I don't know."

"What? Like they helped me?"

"Maybe. There's a lot about the Human-Borns we don't know—how you interact, even what your abilities would be. We had guesses based on your titles, but beyond that, it's all speculation and theory. But if you're all meant to take down Cregorous, either one or all of you needs to be powerful enough to stand up to him."

They fell quiet for a moment as Takeo mulled over his thoughts. He chanced a glance to Zelek. "And Cregorous is stronger than Caedex."

"A *lot* stronger."

"Oh," Takeo muttered as he looked toward the ground, his brows pulled together. "But ... wait. You said Cregorous has six generals."

"Yeah."

"And there's seven of us."

Zelek gave him a pointed stare. "Takeo, what's your point?"

"Did one of the other Human-Borns have to face Cregorous?"

As they neared the train station, Zelek whispered, "Yeah, one of them did."

"And they're okay?" Takeo hushed in awe.

Before they joined the crowd entering the station, Zelek offered a smirk and nodded. "Yeah, they're okay."

Takeo blindly followed his Zaheri as they made their way to the train. Okay. Yeah.

Takeo suddenly had an extremely real, extremely tangible goal to shoot for.

This was no longer about beating Zelek in a spar. That would happen someday.

No, one day, he wanted to beat the Human-Born who stood against Cregorous in a spar. That was his new goal.

Excitement filled his bones at the thought of what that Human-Born must be like. Who they were. What they were capable of. How strong they might be.

He couldn't wait to meet them.

Chapter Fourteen

THE TANK JOINS THE PARTY

His training over the last few months had been rigorous. Takeo had insisted on it. Ever since Zelek told him about the fact that a Human-Born fought Cregorous, Takeo had been downright militant in his training, looking for ways to stretch himself and get better at everything he could.

He went into the mountains and ran through the icy air with Dover as his partner, learning how to keep his stamina up in less than ideal conditions. He wasn't great at that. Cold air was his nemesis, it seemed. He could barely stand thirty minutes before he was gasping for air and begging to return to sea level.

Rowan and Lorn sparred with him at the same time, working in tandem as defense and offense. It took Takeo a month to finally beat them. And when he did, he'd whooped and hollered in joy, dancing around the dojo as though he'd just won gold in the Olympics.

But achieving that goal meant he had to push further. Dover was introduced into the fighting to add an element of chaos. The grovix was heavy and brash. Takeo broke a few bones here and there when Dover rammed into him. He'd always healed by day's end, but it meant a whole day of no sparring.

In those instances, Takeo took to learning how to control his itching muscles without having to push energy into swords. That worked, but there were only so many swords on hand. Meditating and breathing exercises became his practice.

At first, he'd been terrible at it. Sitting still for longer than thirty seconds led to him nearly screaming in annoyance at how boring it was. Zelek had demanded he shut up and try again.

It took a week, but Takeo eventually got to a full ten minutes where he could sit quietly, visualizing his energy sparking around him and tempering it to a smoother rhythm that flowed around his body rather than skittered and skipped in a chaotic way. Imagining his energy as more fluid helped Takeo feel less jittery. Something about it helped him see his energy as a pool of water that could be brought to a low point, like a well, that would eventually refill. If he wasn't careful, he could use up everything he had stored in his body and would be left with nothing as he waited for the well to refill.

He assumed that was what had happened when he'd fought Caedex. He'd used up everything he had in his body, which had left him without anything else to draw on during the fight. The energy he'd stored in the blades could've been used, but he'd never been so low before. It had created a reaction in his body to not have his energy at full capacity. A reaction that had brought him to his knees and kept him from fighting back.

And then there was Zelek.

Despite months of practicing, he still couldn't beat Zelek alone in a spar. He'd tried everything he could think of. The only way he could win against Zelek was with someone else's help.

Then, about three months after the attack, he'd nearly had Zelek beat all on his own.

Nearly.

They'd been trading blows. Well, Takeo had been trying to land blows, and Zelek had been hitting him pretty easily. The Zaheri seemed untouchable, always able to deflect Takeo's punches.

With a roll of his eyes, Zelek grabbed hold of Takeo's arm and bent it in such a way that forced the teen to crash to his knees with a yelp of surprise.

"You aren't thinking, Squeak," Zelek said, keeping hold of Takeo's arm.

"Yes, I am!" Takeo shot back, uselessly trying to rip his arm free.

"No, you aren't." He released his hold on Takeo and stepped back. Gesturing vaguely at the boy, he said, "The only reason I keep beating you is because you're not using your head. You're stronger than us, Takeo. If you paid better attention to who your opponent is and what their weaknesses are, you would be able to take all four of us out with relative ease."

Takeo crossed his arms over his chest and sulked. "I am looking for weaknesses. You just don't have any."

A laugh tumbled from Zelek, and he shook his head. "Yeah, don't I wish." He eased back into a ready stance. "Again. And think this time."

Takeo let out a grumble and fell into a mirrored pose.

"Stop seeing Zelek as untouchable," Rowan said from the sidelines. "You know he isn't."

Swallowing back the nightmarish memory, Takeo steadied his breathing. Rowan had a point: somewhere in Takeo's mind, he did see Zelek as unbeatable. And if he stopped to think about it, he might realize that thought was borne out of a wish to never see Zelek that broken again.

If he and Caedex were evenly matched, then Takeo should be able to beat Zelek in a spar. And while he'd said over and over again that he was aiming for that goal, Takeo wondered.

Secretly, did he really want to beat the man he saw as his father?

Could he ever really bring himself to hurt Zelek?

But sparring wasn't battle. He'd never hurt Zelek so badly that his Zaheri wouldn't bounce back. Zelek had bounced back from all of his nasty injuries from Caedex, which meant that he'd be able to heal from any potential injuries from Takeo.

He wasn't untouchable.

Okay, Takeo thought. *Today's the day.*

He'd beat Zelek in a spar.

Pushing himself forward, Takeo launched an attack. And almost immediately, Zelek was there to deflect.

How's he doing it?

Landing off his rebuffed hit, Takeo sprang back again. And again, was pushed aside.

There's something he's doing.

Again, he leaped forward, and again his blow was easily deflected.

Zelek isn't using energy. There's something he's—

As he moved to attack again, he caught it.

Zelek's gaze had flicked ever so subtly to Takeo's right leg.

Dang it, that's it!

Takeo double-backed and launched from his left foot instead of his right.

All this time, he'd had a tell and hadn't even realized it.

He always led his attacks with his right foot. All Zelek had to do was keep a brief glance on that, and it let him know when Takeo was about to leap into action. Which let him keep more attention on Takeo's upper body and what arm he might be leading with, or what kind of punch he might try to land.

Takeo moved to land a punch, doing everything in his power to not rely on his instinct to lead with his right foot. But Zelek dodged it, not deflected. Good sign.

In dodging Takeo's punch, Zelek leaped off the floor and landed a kick to Takeo's shoulder, sending the teen fumbling to the floor.

Stumblingly getting back to his feet, Takeo spun around.

"It's about time you realized your tell," Zelek said with a grin.

Lorn smacked Rowan hard across the arm. "I told you he leads with his right foot!"

"What do you want me to say?" Rowan shot back. "He's left-handed!"

Takeo blinked a few times. No, he wasn't. He was ambidextrous.

Had Zelek really been the only one to notice?

Sure, he favored his left arm in combat, but he clearly led with his right leg. And he wrote with either hand, though his penmanship was best with his right. He could fire a pistol and rifle with either hand and both eyes open. And he did most other mundane tasks with both hands interchangeably.

Was that how Zelek kept beating him?

So, Zelek's secret was simple—he was observant.

Truthfully, something that Takeo wasn't.

Charging forward, Takeo started to try to land rapid-fire punches. Using both hands wasn't Zelek's strength. Yes, he used both, but—

He used his right hand more often than his left.

In a moment of either luck or sudden skill, Takeo managed to block a hit from Zelek's right hand, pushing his forearm aside.

Zelek stumbled a little in his stance, and victory rose in Takeo's chest.

"I've got you now, Z!" he proudly announced, moving to strike a blow to Zelek's chest.

Only for Zelek to land a kick to Takeo's face and send him plummeting to the floor in a heap.

An airy groan stole from Takeo as he grimaced.

He'd been so close.

"Better luck next time, Squeak," Zelek said with a smirk as he ruffled Takeo's hair.

Through his gasping breaths, Takeo pointed weakly at his Zaheri. "I almost had you."

"Almost isn't enough."

As Zelek walked off, Takeo flopped back onto the mat and let out a frustrated breath.

Thumping footfalls made him turn to see Dover come to his side and flop down.

"Good try," the grovix said with a smile.

Takeo chuckled a little before looking back at the ceiling. He absentmindedly patted Dover's head and muttered, "Yeah."

One day, he'd beat Zelek in a spar.

That day wasn't today.

The following morning, Takeo was woken before sunrise to start training. Kusuo and Shun were there with a few other humans who had been brought into the Agerian's confidence. They all trained together in the dawning hours of the day.

Though Takeo hated mornings, he admitted to himself that it was good practice. If there was ever an attack in the early morning hours, he'd at least be slightly used to combat right after waking up.

They'd been practicing for almost an hour when a group of strangers appeared at the sliding doors to the dojo's practice room. Their guests seemed awed by all of them, and Takeo didn't realize they were there until Lorn shouted, "We have company!"

Takeo whipped around toward them, his muscles going tense at the thought of another incursion. But these people were being way too calm.

There were a couple teens with them, two grovix, and—

A werewolf.

Takeo clicked his gaze to Zelek and saw a hint of a smile on his Zaheri's face.

The humans training with them darted to the walls, leaving only the Agerians and their charge standing, surveying their visitors.

Lorn cast Rowan a look and muttered, "What're they doing here?"

"What do you wanna do, Zelek?" Dover asked from behind them all, surveying the two grovix standing among the unknown visitors.

An inquisitive look played on Zelek's face, and he hushed, "Let's see what they're made of."

Lorn groaned and whined, "Really?"

Rowan looked far too happy at the answer.

"But ... that's ..." Dover started, cowering slightly.

"Go for the tan one," Zelek said before he glanced back to the grovix. "He is your brother, right?"

The group of newcomers was whispering among one another, too, suddenly appearing apprehensive.

Takeo wished he knew English so he could better understand what they were saying.

By the sound of it, these were Agerians, which meant ...

Zelek stepped next to him and whispered, "See the guy in the blue shirt?"

"What about him?" Takeo hushed back.

He was a larger man. Looked like he'd be good to fight someday. If he was a Zaheri. He certainly looked like a warrior.

"The girl next to him is a Human-Born."

Takeo met Zelek's gaze for a second before homing in on the girl.

She was tiny compared to him. A solid six inches shorter at least. And her frame was substantially less than his.

Excitement prickled energy along his arms.

"Is that …?"

"She's the one who stood against Cregorous," Zelek said with a smile.

A wide smile came to Takeo's face without any hesitation.

His first spar with the Human-Born who was strong enough to stand against Cregorous. This was going to be good.

The Healer's Heart

THE FOURTH IS A
HEALER, WITH
TALENTS UNRIVALED.
RESTORING WHAT
DARKNESS WOULD
PARCH.

Chapter One

AFRICAN SKIES

Eshe had always liked sleeping with the goats. It was where guests were supposed to sleep, she knew. But the baby goats were always so sweet and cuddly with her, snuggling in the night and stirring just before dawn.

It had earned her a reputation for being odd.

Well, that and her refusal to marry.

No one in the village shunned her, but there was always an underlying confusion from others. It wasn't as though she could blame her being part-dragon on her oddity. Not when she'd always been a bit different from the other girls in the village.

Unlike most of the women in the small village, she kept her hair long and neat in tight, small braids that she wove atop her head and adorned with a headband. It wasn't the style of a Masai woman, but as Eshe wasn't married, she had not yet shaved her head, as was the tradition. Additionally, she'd found her hair was much stronger and healthier than most women's. She used to cut it regularly, as it grew quickly, and she hadn't enjoyed being such a visual outcast. That was, until she met her Zaheri, her protectors.

With the dim light provided by the tiny window of the goat's hut, she expertly wove her hair into place and fastened her headband.

Today was a water fetching day, which provided another reason that kept her grateful for her hair. She didn't have to fuss over having a piece of fabric at the ready to protect her head when she carried a bucket back to the village.

The air was chilly, as per the norm for pre-dawn in November. Spring was ending, and the autumn months would be upon them soon.

As she exited the hut, the small goats rose and followed, hopping and letting out their braying excitement to go explore the village. The rest of the village had started to awaken, too, with the occasional door opening as the women started for the cooking hut and the men made for the fields and the cows.

Eshe was the one typically in charge of preparing the morning meal. She liked mornings best and had been taught by the best cook in the village.

The woman in question was already moving about the cooking hut, seeing to the fire.

Amara, Eshe's aunt, smiled warmly to her. "Early as usual." She laughed.

One could consider Amara the matriarch of the village, as she was the eldest woman. She bore a handful of wrinkles across her face, but they were only really noticeable when she smiled broadly. Which, admittedly, was often. Like everyone in the tribe, she was slender. Years of hard work had kept her strong and trim, as was necessary when every moment of every day was spent aiding the tribe in some way, shape, or form.

Eshe's mother had died shortly after her younger sister had been born. Their father no longer lived with the tribe; instead, he worked the docks for a fishing company in Kilimanjaro. Sometimes little bits of money found their way back to the tribe on his behalf, but those gifts were few. Eshe's sister, meanwhile, lived with another tribe several days journey away, married to a respected man there.

While she missed her family greatly, her tribe had been just as influential in her upbringing as her parents. Her aunt especially.

Eshe returned her aunt's wide smile. "Would you like me to fetch more wood?"

"Please," Amara said with a nod. She indicated an empty bucket. "And water."

No further instructions needed, Eshe left to go procure both items.

Though they were low on water, there would undoubtedly be enough for the morning's ugali. Ugali was the standard fare for the village and was the primary item for every meal. Occasionally, a goat might be bought at market, or a cow might be slain, but those were extremely rare treats. Meat was a valuable commodity and cost a fair amount of money. And money wasn't necessarily something that the tribe had an abundance of.

A dish made from maize, ugali was a filling, doughy bread that satisfied hunger and supplied enough nutrients to accomplish the tasks of the day.

Eshe enjoyed making food. Truthfully, she enjoyed everything about her life. It was peaceful, quiet, and joyful. Laughter was a near constant in the village. She didn't know what it meant to "want." Sometimes, on market days, she might smell the tantalizing scents of the bar-b-q, as the warriors—the men—of the village called it and was grateful for the opportunities to taste some of the well-prepared meat. But even that was something she did not "want" for, or even find herself yearning.

In fact, yearning was an emotion she didn't have.

At least, not often.

She had to admit that over the last year or so, the sensation had showed itself more and more. As a girl, she had never looked beyond the village, or the trees surrounding her beloved home. Lately, though, she found her gaze drifting to the sky, or to the vastness beyond the fields, without any active thought.

This morning was one such time.

It was this strange sensation that would overtake her. She had done nothing special or extraordinary. One minute, she was walking happily to gather the twigs and pail of water, and she would casually glance to the field just past the village border.

And her feet would stall.

Something about the openness of the world was beginning to pull at her, as though beckoning her to step beyond the border. That, in taking one step, she might take another. And another.

But then, where might such a step lead her?

Recollecting herself, she gathered the small twigs and the pail of water then went back to the cooking hut. A moment later, she was pulling the ugali together and preparing it. Dawn had crested by the time she put it into the pot and over the fire to cook.

Amara and she were both quiet as they worked. There was no need to fill the silence or ask how the other was doing. Nothing had changed from the day prior. If they had a visitor—especially a white person—they likely would speak of the foreigner. A man had visited a year ago, and his insistence at helping the women with their daily tasks had set fits of laughter as the soundtrack for his entire visit.

Men didn't help with fetching water, or cooking, or milking the cows, or in the building of houses. Men saw to the cows, their transportation and safety from the grazing fields back to the village. They made shoes for everyone who wanted a pair (or could afford the tires from the market). They saw to the bar-b-q of goats or cows when they were afforded the treat as a village. But most daily tasks, especially those pertaining to food and water, were left to the women.

Amara was just completing putting together the tea for everyone as the ugali finished. They took everything outside, and the village ate their breakfast together.

There were talks of the men visiting the corn farmers on their way to the grazing fields with the cows. One of the men joked that his brother had gotten a spear stuck in a tree the day prior, poking fun at the younger man's poor aim.

The goats sat around Eshe's feet, leaning against her legs. She paid them no mind. Anyone else would have swatted at the small animals to go somewhere else, but she liked having them around. It was why some of the girls jokingly called her a "goat lover."

Once the men were off, herding the cows toward the path that would lead to the grazing field, the women set out to prepare for their trek in the opposite direction.

"Eshe, you see to the donkey," Amara said with a wave of her hand toward the stubborn creature standing in the taller grasses.

"All right," Eshe said with a smile.

A moment later, she had the donkey led to the hut where the water canisters were all located, along with the saddle for the unfortunate beast.

One of the other girls, just two years older than Eshe, named Malaika, laughed as she helped with the saddle. "He is always so calm with you! Is it because he senses the goats love you? Is that what must be done to make him be sweet?"

Lovingly stroking the donkey's snout, Eshe smiled fondly at the creature. "I do not know." She threw her friend a teasing smile. "Perhaps you should not yell at him, and then he will like you."

"If he would not step on my feet, I would not yell at him," Malaika said.

They both laughed as they fixed the saddle in place.

Two other women walked up with Amara, each carrying pails and canisters to fasten to the donkey's saddle.

A moment later, they were off. They reminisced about their last visitor and how funny he had been with his camera and his constant talking to it. How he'd been quick to try to do everything they did, inspiring much laughter from all the women at his insistence. He'd looked utterly ridiculous, and Eshe had found it a truly strange sight to see a man with a water pail upon his head. He'd struggled so greatly to keep it balanced, which had baffled her. All the women barely needed to have one hand upon the pail to keep it steady as they carried it back to the village.

The hour walk to the lake always went by so swiftly, even if they went in relative silence, which was seldom the case. There was always some story to be told or reminisced over.

As they walked on their return journey, Amara went to one of the medicine trees and started to carve at it. There was a small cold that had circulated through the village again. With all of them sharing from the same bowls and cups, it was not uncommon for minor illnesses to sweep through the whole village.

The "medicine tree," as they called it, had lost its luster for Eshe. Only partly because of her advanced healing as a Human-Born. Though she loved the tree for its beauty, she would often find herself feeling sorrow that she could not simply divulge to her family and friends that she could sweep any ailments away with a flick of her hand across theirs.

Amara held a small piece of the tree to her.

"I am well, thank you," Eshe answered with a small shake of her head.

They continued on their way, and Eshe found herself puzzling over the question of whether to let her tribe know of her healing ability.

Sariel, one of her Zaheri, had introduced herself to Eshe just over a year prior when the teen had gone to market in search of some new fabrics. Eshe had to sell a beloved goat to afford the cloth, so her disposition had been sullen when Sariel had approached her.

To this day, Eshe couldn't forget her first impression of Sariel. Her diction was perfect, as was her garb. If it hadn't been for her lighter complexion and long hair, she would have been mistaken for a traveler from a distant village.

She had spent the day with Eshe and her aunt as they'd walked through the market before returning to the village to prepare the evening meal. Upon their leave, Amara had invited Sariel to join them and stay the night, assuming that Sariel had traveled a great distance to attend the market.

It was later that evening, after everyone had eaten and most had retired to bed, that Eshe had gone to check on the goats and ensure their visitor was comfortable. That was when Sariel had told Eshe about who she was and what she was capable of.

Since then, it was a chore for Eshe to not immediately leap to aiding someone who was either injured or ill. But Sariel had given strict instructions that Eshe was to keep her ability a secret. At least, for now.

When they neared the village, they heard the faint sound of a motorbike.

"I suppose Obi decided to allow Papa a trip to town," Malaika said.

"I thought Papa left on foot this morning for town," Eshe said.

Amara laughed. "It would be like him to be impatient. He does know the way to the gongo."

"Papa" was what they called the village elder. He was the oldest man in the village and had to walk with a stick to maintain his balance. Since he could no longer assist with the caring of the cows, his days were typically spent in town with friends, enjoying a healthy amount of gongo—an alcoholic drink that a man in town made in his home.

As the motorbike came into view, however, they quickly realized it was not Obi who was coming to the village.

Over the last year, both Sariel and Eccio had become known as great friends of the tribe. To the tribe's knowledge, they lived in a town a day's walk from the village. Eccio was prone to bringing gifts for them to enjoy. One time, he had gone so far as to purchase a goat for slaughter, providing the exquisite treat.

Since then, he had been viewed as almost royalty to the tribe.

Cutting the engine of the motorbike, Eccio waved to the women and offered a wide smile. "Jambo!" he called. Unlike Sariel, his paler skin and almost Asian build made him a beacon among them. He stood no taller than any warrior in the tribe, but he always stood out whenever he accompanied the men.

The children of the village came running, staring at Eccio with wide smiles.

"Jambo, Eccio!" Amara responded with a smile.

As per usual, Eccio offered to help, resulting in giggles from the younger girls among them. Despite how strange it was for a man to assist, they let him take the donkey's rope and tug the creature along.

"How does the day fare?" Eccio asked, his accent thick as he spoke Masai.

"Well, thank you," Amara answered. "What has brought you to us?"

"I'm returning from town and took the long road. I procured some sugar recently and wanted to offer you some."

By now, the children had gaggled around Eccio, nearly causing him to trip by how closely they packed in. And hearing of sugar sent them into excitement. Another rare treat for them.

Putting on as sweet of a smile as possible, Malaika said, "You are becoming a king among our people, dear Eccio."

Eshe offered a knowing smile to her in-disguise Zaheri. "Yes, indeed, you are."

"You flatter me," he answered with a smirk. He pulled his hat off and turned to the boys who had congregated around him. "Now, who am I trading with today?"

Hands flashed into the air, each holding a different homemade cap. Most of them had been made from old school uniforms or leftover fabrics. Several of the older boys, who were off with the men attending the cows, had traded similar items with Eccio in the past, now proudly sporting their western-styled ball caps almost every day.

This would be the fifth occasion that Eccio would graciously gift a nicer item under the guise of a trade. Eshe wondered what he did with the other caps. She'd noticed that the last time he was with them, he'd traded with the eldest boy there. Previously, he'd traded with the youngest. She studied his actions as he selected the youngest boy today, trading his fine-looking black ballcap for a shirt-sleeve cap.

The boy in question quickly put his new ballcap on his too-small head and gave Eccio a toothy grin.

Offering assurances that he would be back and have another cap to trade for next time, Eccio knocked his forearm against each of the boys', making an X with each bump. It was his way, Eshe assumed, of sharing excitement or saying goodbye.

Now that she thought of it, all the boys knocked their forearms together in an X shape.

Eccio's influence on them had cemented, whether he'd intended it or not. Did he notice?

He spoke with Amara as Eshe and the girls saw to putting the water away and caring for the donkey.

Inside the cooking hut, Malaika hushed to Eshe, "I wish we had met Eccio before I'd been married."

Eshe wanted to admonish her but couldn't bring herself to it. For a few reasons. The greatest of which was that Malaika was older than her; it wouldn't be right for Eshe to correct her, no matter how much she felt it was a bad comment.

Though, she could understand Malaika's position. Eccio was a foreigner and quite obviously wealthy. Purchasing a goat and constantly offering gifts to the tribe was a clear display of his stature. Though none of them had been to the town he and Sariel lived in, Eshe knew it had become almost a fable or legend to the tribe, as if Sariel and Eccio were angels or helpful spirits sent to aid them.

Ultimately, Eshe chose not to answer Malaika's comment and went back outside to grab another water jug.

As she neared the donkey and moved to undo the ties that held the four large water jugs in place on the saddle, Amara called, "Eshe, come here."

Handing the ties to another girl, Eshe walked up to Amara and Eccio. "Yes?"

"Sariel has requested to see you," Amara said.

"She has?" Eshe asked in pretend surprise. She had figured Eccio was there for her under the guise of some wayward delivery.

Eccio nodded. "I was asking Amara if it would be all right for me to take you to our town to see her."

That was fair. Eccio was a man who, while trusted, was not officially part of the tribe. He didn't live with them and didn't hold claim to any of the women as his bride. And while Eshe was of age, she knew Eccio wasn't interested in marrying her.

Though the women would be abuzz with rumor and gossip once they'd left to see Sariel.

"I would be against it," Amara said with a stern look, but her smile betrayed her, "but good Eccio saw Papa in town and spoke with him of it over some gongo."

A smile came to Eshe's face as she gave Eccio a genuinely surprised look. "You had gongo?"

He returned her smile. "After much refusal, yes."

Amara raised her brow and pointed a rigid index finger toward him. "You will have her home before nightfall."

"On my honor," Eccio said with a bow.

"Then you may go. And send with her our wishes to see Sariel again soon." She patted Eshe's shoulder as she gently pushed the teenager toward Eccio. "Be good for Sariel."

"I will," Eshe said with a smile as she fell into step with Eccio.

Once they were a few paces away, she hushed, "You will have started terrible rumors now."

Placing his hand on his chest, Eccio jokingly said, "Madam, I would never."

As she laughed, she asked, "Is all well?"

"We need to go check on Ardent after the rainstorm two nights ago."

"I trust she will be well?" she asked with a small frown of worry.

"Ardent is sure to be fine. However, it's prudent to check on her and ensure she has remained well fed."

With a nod, Eshe answered, "Very well." Her demeanor fell more casual as she smiled. "I am glad to get to see her. I have missed her so."

Eccio got onto the motorbike and steadied it as Eshe climbed onto the back seat. "You are her dear little treasure. She'll be thrilled we brought you."

As the motorbike kicked to life, Eshe laughed.

She loved her village, and her people.

But there was no denying that there was a freedom she only had amongst her Zaheri.

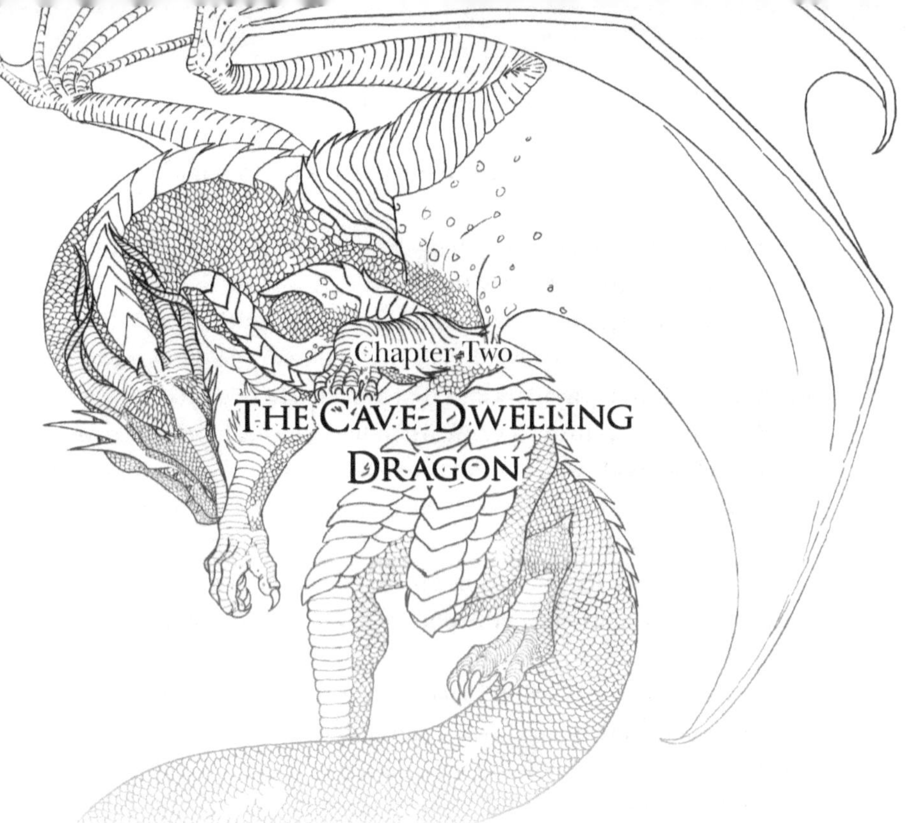

The trip to Sariel was far shorter than Eshe had anticipated. Ten minutes on the motorbike later, they turned down a worn path, blanketed in a thick cover of trees. A moment after that, Eccio slowed the bike as they came up to where the Zaheri lived.

Eshe had never been to their home. She, like the members of her tribe, were under the assumption that Sariel and Eccio lived in a village with their own tribe. Or, at the least, their own families.

Quickly, Eshe realized she'd been mistaken.

A hamlet might have been a better description of the Zaheri's base. There was only one building, but it was wider and longer than the typical brick and mud homes of the Masai. And there were windows. The doors appeared fluid with the building, leaving no cracks, like the plank and latch doors on the huts in Eshe's village. And the windows weren't lopsided or shaped strangely, as was common for everyone— even in town. The roof was metal, which wasn't necessarily impossible, but it was a sign of wealth—you didn't get metal for your house unless you had the funds to afford it. And clearly, there was more wealth in the Zaheri's purse than Eshe could have imagined, given how large the building was and how much it must have cost to put a metal roof on the whole structure.

Several cows, well fed and fat by the look of it, grazed not far from the house. A few goats stood with them.

Warden lay in front of the building, soaking up the sun. Without her armor, the Warrior grovix looked like a dusty red lioness, save the sweeping black and gray markings that speckled her lion-like paws and flitted up her wide, sturdy legs. Warden had a large, blocky face for a creature whose body was so similar to a lion's. Her ears were long but thin, and the slope of her brow exuded an air of nobility. Her tail was long and fairly fluffy.

Pulling to her feet, Warden smiled to Eshe. "It is good to see you again, child," the grovix said, coming to rub her snout against the teenager's frame.

Taking hold of Warden's face and gently resting her forehead against the large creature's brow, Eshe closed her eyes. "I have missed you, beautiful lioness." She stepped back and took in the expanse of the building before her. "Your home is lovely."

Eccio propped the motorbike next to the building and said, "It took us a little time to get it functional." He rubbed a hand through his hair as he opened the door and stepped inside. He gently took his shoes off and deposited them neatly by the door.

Eshe followed, with Warden behind.

"The indoor plumbing took a little while to get situated," he continued as he moved through the building.

The larger windows awarded a fully lit interior—a foreign concept to Eshe. She was accustomed to walking into a building and having to adjust her eyesight or rely on candles or, when they had one, a flashlight. The walls were straight as pins, not a hint of bowing like she was used to.

And then there was the floor.

Eshe liked walking barefoot. Not everyone did; many wore shoes fashioned from old tires. But she had always liked the feeling of the earth beneath the skin of her feet. Every building she'd ever set foot into was built right on top of the dirt of the ground, with no transition or steps up.

The Zaheri's building not only had steps up and a floor, but it felt smooth under her feet. It wasn't slippery, but there was a definite, drastic difference from what she had known her whole life.

She stilled on the foreign floor, her eyes glued to it.

Whatever it was, it was almost as glass, but not clear. A gem maybe? No, gems would have been even more exquisite. Surely her Zaheri were not so wealthy that they could walk across fine stones?

Sariel came around a corner and caught Eshe's straying gaze. Though she had wrinkles and an air of wisdom about her, she was a beautiful older woman. With bright green eyes and darker skin, Sariel must have been truly stunning in her younger years.

The Team Leader was braiding her dark brown hair over her shoulder as she joined them. She smiled and said, "It's called tile."

Eshe looked up in question.

"What the floor is made of. Made of ceramic; the same substance your bowls and cups are sometimes fashioned from."

Fascinating.

Eshe gently scuffed her bare foot against the tile, marveling at the smoothness under her feet. Some dirt fell from her toes, and she whipped her gaze up to Sariel as fear gripped her chest. "I should not stand on it—my feet are dirty!"

Eccio laughed and came up to her with a rag in his grasp. "It's no worry, Eshe. Don't fear."

"Tile is easy to clean. And it stays cool, so it provides relief on the hot days," Sariel said as she finished braiding her hair. She gestured to the house. "Would you like to see the rest?"

Leaning forward and peering into a room to the right, Eshe found herself conflicted. Yes, she wanted to explore all of this. She also wondered what Eccio had meant by saying "indoor plumbing."

What was it? The word "plumbing" meant nothing to her and was as foreign as if he'd spoken another language.

Perhaps he was, and she didn't realize it.

But, between exploring the grand building and visiting Ardent, Eshe knew which she wanted to do more.

"I do not wish to delay our visit to Ardent," she answered.

Sariel nodded. "That's a fair point. Then let us be off."

The group left the building, and Eshe found herself marveling at how sturdily the door shut at Eccio's gentle pull, clicking into its frame with ease.

Warden led the group as they started walking down a path just wide enough for two people to walk side by side. By now, the afternoon sun was warm above them and had soaked into the dry soil under Eshe's feet, wrapping her in the comforting warmth of the earth.

"Is the tribe well?" Sariel asked as they walked.

Eshe nodded. "Yes. I believe Amara yearns for you to visit. She talks of you often." She threw a smile over her shoulder at Eccio. "And several girls pine for Eccio's attention."

Eccio rolled his eyes and shook his head, continuing on without comment.

"I would much like to see Amara again. She is a dear friend."

"Perhaps you can attend the market with us next week. She enjoys your input on fabric choices."

"We haven't been to market in a fair while." Eccio nodded subtly, sliding his hands into his pockets. "We could do with purchasing another bull."

The comment made Eshe almost ask where her beloved Agerians received such finances, but she refrained. Prying into the wealth of her Zaheri was not proper. They were a blessing, both to her and her people. Asking questions about how they afforded such grand items was unnecessary.

"How long will it take to get to Ardent's home?" Eshe asked.

"Around thirty minutes. We dug out a deeper cave for her, so it's well hidden and off any main paths."

Warden let out a low growl. A second later, Eshe heard the slithering of a black mamba as it scurried into the brush. Now she understood why Warden led the group. Even lions would flee from the imposing grovix that looked as though she prowled in her gait.

Absentmindedly, Eshe found herself gazing toward the horizon again, her mind flitting back to the concept of far-off lands. Of the Zaheri's home world. Of what it must look like. Of what part Eshe might play in her destiny as a Human-Born.

She understood she was a prophesied child, and her destiny was to see the end of the tyrannical reign of a man named Cregorous. If she truly thought of it, though, she questioned how such a thing could be made possible. She was, in the basest sense, a poor choice for a prophesied hero. Even by the standards of a normal human.

Yes, she appeared to have a rapid sort of healing in her own body, and could heal others. Beyond that, she saw little she could contribute to a war, especially a war with a monstrous king.

Perhaps, as she grew, that would change. Perhaps there was some hidden talent within her that would prove useful. Regardless of that, Eshe knew that, at the absolute least, she aimed—yearned—to heal in the aftermath. War sounded terrible, and painful. Her tribe knew of violence from wild animals and had heard stories of warring tribes in other areas, but firsthand knowledge of war ...

Her tribe had been blessed that they knew no such level of violence.

She prayed that she would be able to undo the damage that the monstrous king of Caliga had caused.

Even so, she was nearly positive that she would disappoint other Agerians. She was not some war-ready heroine. Nor did she want to be. Yes, she could feel her beautiful violet energy within her and call it into wisps and small spheres of glowing orbs to float alongside her and dance in the breeze. But that was all she seemed capable of with her energy.

On the first occasion where she had spent time with her Zaheri, Sariel and Eccio had worked with her to see if perhaps she could turn her energy into any sort of a weapon. She hadn't liked the concept and had asked for a demonstration of what they might be looking for.

Eccio had taken down a tree with a blast of gold from his palm.

Eshe immediately refused to learn anything like that. Even if she could accomplish such a thing, she could not bring herself to ever use something so beautiful in such a violent action. It had led to a long discussion that Eccio wasn't a violent person, which Eshe could see plainly in how he carried himself and how softly he spoke, and that Agerians who did perform such attacks only did it to protect others.

It sparked a different conversation about shields, which Sariel had demonstrated. Eshe wasn't against the concept of shields. She rather liked the idea of creating a barrier that could keep others safe. But try as she might, she could not accomplish the task.

By all appearances, Eshe could only heal others. Which she thought was a little silly since they had told her that all hybrids had a rapid healing ability. If they got cut or suffered an injury from an enemy, their wounds patched quickly.

"So, then what is the purpose of a Healer to the Agerians?" Eshe had asked.

That question was what had introduced her to the enemy of Agerius: a nation called Caliga, and their king, Cregorous. Sariel and Eccio hadn't gone into detail of what made Cregorous so dangerous, but they'd explained in the simplest terms that he was powerful enough to make it so that anyone who stood up to him didn't live. Most of the time, all it took was one attack from him, and Agerians were dead.

The thought of someone so powerful and so ruthless made Eshe's stomach twist in anguish.

What suffering had Agerius endured while waiting for her? How long had this war gone on? How many lives had already been lost? Why had she not been born sooner?

All questions she never voiced. Because all of them were likely unanswerable.

They had traversed over a hill and followed the path as it dipped lower. Shortly thereafter, it plateaued. Eshe could clearly see the mountains they were aiming for and wondered if, perhaps at the base of one, that was where Ardent's cave rested.

"Are you all right, Eshe?" Sariel asked, giving the girl a look of concern.

Mulling over the question, Eshe frowned, her brows dipping in a little. "I have recently found myself ... wanting to leave the village." She looked to Sariel, confliction in her gaze. "I have never dreamed of traveling beyond the tribe. Or ever leaving it. But in recent days, I sometimes find that I stare at the horizon and become ... lost in it." She flopped her hands at her sides uselessly. "Some strange desire in me to go somewhere else. And I cannot say where it has come from or why it persists."

Sariel rested her hand on Eshe's shoulder. "Your tribe is your family. Your people. It's only natural that you should find yourself wishing to stay with them. And it's only natural, given all that has changed in your life in the last year, that you might find a growing wish to explore the world, or perhaps even ours."

"But which is the better desire?" Eshe asked with a pleading look.

With a small incline of his head, Eccio answered, "Neither is wrong. They're both driven by good, wholesome things in you."

"Eccio is correct," Warden said, keeping her gaze forward. "One does not override the other. Both have their merits."

"Then which is correct for *my* life?" the teenager asked.

"No one can tell you that. It's something you must determine for yourself. What path you wish to follow," Sariel said.

"But, one day, I will need to leave the tribe, yes?" She looked to each of her Zaheri. "In order to fulfill the destiny your people have for me, yes?"

"One day, perhaps." Eccio gently shook his head, glancing toward the sky. "We cannot say where or how your role will be fulfilled. And we can't say when it'll happen either."

"What matters right now is for you to remain safe and happy until that time comes," Sariel said.

Eshe nodded subtly, her gaze drifting to the path ahead of them.

She wished it could be easier, that someone could simply tell her what was right and what was wrong. Though she could understand that staying with her tribe and leaving were both acceptable options for her life, and neither held greater value than the other, she wished that weren't the case. Then her decision would be easy.

While it was true there was nothing actively tying her to the tribe to stay for her whole life, it still rattled discomfort in her at the prospect of leaving. The village was all she'd ever known. Her people were her life.

Glancing at the Zaheri around her, she began to wonder if that thought was false. Yes, the tribe was what she knew, where she'd grown up. They were the people she loved most. But there was a small fact she hadn't allowed herself to dwell on much.

Her Zaheri were becoming just as important to her.

So, maybe it was that the growing desire to leave was rooted in her destiny. That maybe it was time for her to consider that her life, her world, her family, could grow to include many, many others far beyond her village.

She let these thoughts go when the opening of a cave came into view as they continued down the path. They stepped into the dark cavern, and Eshe could feel the mustiness of longstanding moisture that clung to the rocks of the cave walls. The ground beneath her grew hard, and she had to keep her attention so she wouldn't inadvertently cut her foot open on a jagged stone.

A rumble came from a few feet in and, a second later, Ardent's silhouette could be seen.

Eccio tidied up some large branches and assembled them into a pile toward the middle of the space. Once that was done, a small spurt of flame flew from Ardent's mouth, igniting the wood and illuminating the large cavern.

It was a domed cave, easily twenty feet tall, and there appeared to be burrows that led into the rocky hills.

"Eshe dear, it is good to see you," Ardent said with a smile. Though the fire cast a warm glow, it could not hide the cool blues that made up her scale coloring. Flecks of white littered her body, as if little droplets of paint had fallen on her.

Approaching the dragon, Eshe rested her hand on Ardent's snout, feeling the smooth scales and marveling at her beauty. "I am glad to see you well," Eshe said as Ardent bowed her head, letting their brows rest together for a few seconds.

"How are you doing, Ardent?" Sariel asked as she, too, approached the dragon.

A small huff came from the Scout. "I will be glad for nightfall. I have been cramped within this cave for two days too many."

"Are you in need of food?" Eshe asked.

Ardent shook her head. "No, dear child, thank you. Dragons can go weeks without food, especially when so inactive."

Eshe's eyes lit up. "That is amazing."

With a chuckle, the dragon answered, "It is how we are."

"I'm grateful for it," Eccio said. "It would've been hard to procure enough food for you otherwise."

"Will you hunt tonight?" Warden asked.

"If you would have me," Ardent said.

Quirking her head a little, Eshe asked, "You hunt together?"

Warden offered a swift nod of her head. "Often. We can keep one another safe from detection that way."

"And then neither of us have to stay up all night," Sariel said with a gesture to Eccio.

Eccio offered a bow to the dragon and the grovix. "Thank you for that."

Absentmindedly, Eshe ran her hand along Ardent's long neck. She stilled when she reached the dragon's shoulders, her eyes narrowing slightly as she asked, "Ardent, are your wings sore?"

Gently flapping the wings curled at her sides, Ardent nodded. "They are. It comes from days of not being able to extend them fully."

Giving the dragon a soft look, the teenager asked, "May I?"

"I would be grateful for it, thank you."

Eshe placed her hand on Ardent's wing joint. It wasn't that she could actively see past the scales and see the sore, tired muscles, but there was definitely something in her that alerted her mind to the strained muscles and ligaments. And though she didn't fully understand a dragon's anatomy, Eshe could tell exactly where to push small waves of her healing to provide relief for her Zaheri.

As she aided Ardent, Eccio crossed his arms over his chest and asked, "You can tell when muscles are sore, too?"

"Not often, and I have only noticed it recently," Eshe answered, her attention still trained on Ardent's shoulder.

A hum came from the dragon. Something about the sound warmed Eshe's heart.

"Thank you, Eshe. That has brought much relief."

Eshe smiled up at her. "I am happy to offer what I can."

As the group settled around the fire, Eshe took the opportunity to sit in front of Ardent, letting the dragon's folded front legs be her seat. Ardent's graceful, towering presence behind her gave Eshe a foreign but lovely feeling of being wholly protected.

They talked of, it seemed, trivial things. Warden shared with Eshe a story of how she had driven out a pack of lions from their little home. It sparked a bit of laughter from the girl at the concept of imposing lions and their reaction to seeing something as terrifying as Warden appear to chase them.

Eccio shared with the others about how they would attend the market the following week, inciting a conversation about possibly purchasing fabric for Warden to wear under her armor. The Warrior grovix did not appreciate the concept.

Sariel talked a little of their plans for their home, and what they hoped they might be able to grow in the garden in the coming season. Eshe finally asked about what "indoor plumbing" was, which led to a clumsy explanation from Eccio.

It was a quiet, peaceful time. They laughed and shared stories. They asked questions of Eshe. Random ones, the teen thought. Questions like what her favorite color might be, or what season she favored most. If she liked certain meals over others. Things of that nature.

The time passed quickly, and before Eshe knew it, they had to return to the house so Eccio could take her home in time for supper with the tribe.

As she left, Eshe found herself already hoping for another opportunity to spend a day with her Zaheri and learn more about them.

Eshe had been lost in thought for most of the day. Her rest had been mostly solid, but she dreamed of doors and stepping through them, only to not remember what she had witnessed beyond each threshold. But she awoke starving for something totally unknown.

She'd done as usual—made the morning ugali, helped prepare the cows for their trek to the grazing fields, assisted with a few of the younger children who, for some reason, were much more unruly than normal. Lunch came and went.

As they waited for the afternoon tea, one of the younger children started to beg for a story. Stories were common among the tribes, and some of the best ones got passed between them. Infrequently, someone would come up with a new one.

One of the girls tugged on Eshe's arm, begging for something new.

"Something new?" Eshe asked with trepidation.

Stories had never been natural for her, yet she couldn't deny that, since spending time with Ardent yesterday, she found herself thinking of flying and what it must be like. Eshe didn't have wings, but Eccio and Sariel did. She'd seen their wings but had not been able to witness them flying.

To fly must be an interesting feeling. The swell of air and how the muscles must move to propel someone skyward. To see the world from the clouds. Or perhaps not see the world below, as clouds sometimes hid the sky. What might that look like? Would it feel like entering another world? One of weightlessness and never-ending skies?

She could only imagine what it must be like.

Her gaze flitted to a bird in a tree as the child tugged again. "Please, Eshe? Please?"

"All right," Eshe said with a small smile, her attention still fixed on the little bird hopping from branch to branch. When it took off into the sky with chirping calls, she let out a breath and looked to the child at her side. "Something new ..."

The other children gathered around, staring at her with anticipation. Eshe was rarely the one to tell a story, and this would be the first time she told a new story. A few of the other women listened in, intrigued smiles playing on their faces. Amara stood with one of the infants in her grasp, waiting to see what Eshe might say.

"Well," Eshe started, settling on an overturned bucket. She decided to follow her daydream of flying. It had been so prevalent on her mind, anyway. Perhaps she could tell a good story because of that. "Once there was a girl who wanted to fly.

"She watched the birds in the sky, saw how they danced on the breeze. She looked to the sky and saw its openness, wishing to soar into it. But she found herself scared because the ground was her home. It was all she knew.

"As days passed, she found herself looking at the birds more and more, wondering what it must be like to fly alongside them. Then, one day, she looked to the sky"—she looked up at the cloud-speckled blue sky—"and could not deny the wish anymore." She looked back to the children, who were now staring at her in rapt attention. "She told herself, 'Today I will fly.' And—"

As she looked back to the sky, her words caught in her throat.

Ardent was soaring toward them.

For a few long seconds, Eshe lost the ability to think of anything beyond how utterly beautiful the dragon looked. Her scales shining in the sun, sparkling blue points of light like a glorious beacon.

The adults all gave Eshe puzzled looks before they turned their attention to what had captured Eshe's gaze. Screams of surprise flew quickly, and children were scooped into arms as hurried commands to get inside came from several different women.

Amara's screaming shook Eshe from her dazed revere.

"This is not a sign meant for smiles, Eshe!" her aunt said in a commanding voice, snatching her niece's shoulder and shoving her back.

Eshe had to force herself to not smile at Ardent's approaching form. Flying so easily, her wings flapping in fluid movement, keeping her moving steadily in the sky. She had to be at least twenty feet above the ground.

Then the fear hit her chest.

Why would Ardent be flying in the middle of the day toward the village?

There was a rumbling of motorbike engines, and Amara whipped her head toward the entrance of the village. A second later, Eccio and Sariel rolled up, quickly turning off their engines and getting off their vehicles. A second after them, Warden came charging behind, her armor glinting here and there as the sunlight caught the metal.

Another rash of screaming tore from the women, and the children cried, fleeing to the nearest huts for safety.

"Come!" Amara screamed, nearly yanking Eshe back.

Eshe turned and gripped her aunt's arm. "I—" Her mouth fell open, taking in the look of terror that had gripped her aunt's face.

Amara gave her a confused look, her eyes wide and fingers tight against Eshe's skin.

Something truly terrible must have happened for her Zaheri to appear in such a fashion. Sariel and Eccio had been so careful in all of their interactions with the tribe. Ardent and Warden had been so diligent in making sure they were not seen.

"I cannot," Eshe whispered, and in that instant, Eshe felt a chasm tear between them.

Amara's brows pulled together as her mouth gaped open, a look of betrayal filling her features.

Eshe's stomach hurt at that look.

"Eshe!" Sariel cried as she ran toward them.

Amara stumbled back, waving a shaky hand at Sariel and Eccio. "Wh ... what have you brought upon us?" she cried.

"Amara, please, listen to me—"

"Demons! You are not the angels we thought! You are *demons!*" Amara screamed, staggering over her feet as she ran for the nearest hut.

Ardent landed with a *thud* just beyond the village, her great wings sweeping dust to soften her impact.

Doors slammed shut, but the loud accusations filtered through the cracks between the wood planks. The goats and donkeys had fled. The village was suddenly barren of her tribe, leaving Eshe standing alone, her arm still slightly outstretched where Amara had left it.

It seemed the choice was made for her.

Turning to her Zaheri, Eshe fought the tears that were abruptly filling her eyes. "What has happened?"

Sariel gently cupped Eshe's face, swiping away the tears with her thumb. "We are unsure, but the portal to our world has opened. We had to act."

"But nothing is here," Eshe said, a new wave of fear filling her at the fact that her Zaheri had come despite there being no danger.

"Sariel," Warden called.

Eshe, Sariel, and Eccio turned to the Warrior grovix.

Warden shook her head slightly. "It is not enemies coming for us."

Before anyone could ask for clarification, from the trees not far from where Ardent stood, came five grovix. They were all armored and each imposing in their bulk and gait.

Eccio released his grip on one of the swords that hung on his belt and threw Sariel a look of confusion.

Too stunned at her tribe's reaction, too cut at Amara's shove away, Eshe stood holding Sariel's hand, barely focusing on what was transpiring.

The grovix all came forward, Ardent's seven-foot-tall stature lumbering over them, as the group came together.

Steeling herself, Sariel gave the five grovix hard stares. "What are you doing here?"

Eshe didn't understand the words that came out of Sariel's mouth, causing the girl to stare at her Zaheri in fearful confusion. She had always assumed that both Eccio and Sariel could speak another language, as they did look like foreigners, but had never heard anything other than Swahili or Masai from her Zaheri.

One of the grovix bowed, flattening its ears. "Grand Master Sariel, forgive our haste." He straightened, a hard look in his eyes as he stood resolute before the Zaheri. His coloring was an array of browns, blacks, and whites that speckled across his form. He had white patches around his eyes and more canine features, evident against Warden's more feline shape. With larger, light brown eyes and a narrower snout, he, too, held a sort of noble air about him, but it was slightly different from Warden's. "I am Beta Vallis, and those grovix who accompany me are Betas, as well. We come at the order of Council Member Aros."

"What?" Eccio asked as he pulled his brows together. "Council Member Ar—when? When did he send you?"

Eshe flashed another scared look toward Eccio. She didn't understand what was going on, and the lack of comprehension of their words was not assisting in the quaking of her stomach.

"Not an hour ago. We made for the portal as fast as we could." The grovix looked at Sariel. "There's more."

"What is it?"

"We cannot be certain, but ... we sensed bratak'ra and werewolves near the portal."

"What?" Eccio asked, his sharp eyes studying the grovix before them.

Warden shook her head. "That cannot be."

"I can only tell you what we sensed. The Defender that came with us to open the portal brought a Scout along with him as added defense. He said he heard something on the breeze, as well."

"What Scout?" Ardent asked.

"I believe he said his name was Ventus."

Nodding slightly, Ardent muttered, "He is a good Scout." She met Sariel's gaze. "If he heard something amiss, it would be prudent to trust him. Not all Scouts hear the smallest sounds. He is one of them."

"You think there's an incursion coming?" Eccio asked, his jaw tight.

"It would add up," Sariel hushed. When she met Eccio's gaze, she added, "Why else would Council Member Aros act like this?"

"How would he know there's an attack inbound?" he whispered back.

"The Elders," Sariel offered with a small shrug.

Eccio deflated a little and opened his mouth to comment when he caught Eshe's terror-filled expression. He snapped his eyes to Sariel and hushed, "Eshe doesn't know what we've been saying."

"I know," Sariel said, wearing a look of worry. "See to setting a defensible position. I'll see to Eshe and try to ease the tribe's fears."

Nodding a few times, he said, "All right. Sar" —he gently caught her arm as she turned to steer Eshe aside— "everything's going to be okay. He's going to be okay."

For a second, Sariel warred with what to say, her mouth opening and a faint word escaping before she sighed. "Thank you."

As Eccio walked off, the grovix and dragon going with him, Sariel turned to Eshe and said in Masai, "Something is coming, Eshe."

"What did they say?" the teen asked, her gaze flitting after the retreating grovix. "Are they friends?"

"Yes," Sariel answered softly. "I know you will have questions. As do I. But there is danger coming for us. For you."

"For me?"

"They would not be interested in us. We aren't special. You are."

"Wh ... what does this ...? What ...?" Eshe started to have trouble breathing. Her heart hurt, and her stomach hurt, and she could feel the eyes of her tribe on her back while faintly hearing their curses and accusations.

She would take the warring desires over this. She would take the confusion over this pain that she couldn't heal because she knew it wasn't physical. Nothing in her system said it could be fixed. It was emotions gripping at her body and crying out because she wouldn't.

"Eshe, dear, breathe. Everything will be well," Sariel said in a smooth, calm tone, gently stroking Eshe's cheek.

Forcing a few steadier breaths into her body, Eshe bit back tears. "It does not feel that all will be well."

"Then we must have faith that it will." There was no hint of fear or worry in Sariel's eyes. She simply looked at Eshe with a tender sympathy that lay just above a fierce determination.

Shakily nodding, the teenager calmed a bit. "What must we do?"

"Help me try to calm the tribe. We will not let anything happen to them, Eshe, I promise."

Sariel wanted her to help calm the tribe? How was she supposed to do that? They had run and left her. They hadn't tried to pull her with them. Even Amara had ...

The pain spiked in her stomach again.

This girl suddenly did not wish to fly.

Amara huddled by the door, confusion swimming in her mind.

Their trusted friends were not friends at all. They suddenly appeared not even human. And they had brought with them demons; monsters straight from nightmares. Beasts that spoke—and *dragons*.

No matter how beautiful the large reptile might be, and how carefully the large four-legged, lion-like creatures walked and spoke, it only pointed all the more to demons.

Beasts could not speak.

Any moment now, the donkey would likely start screaming in tongues unknown, just as Sariel and Eccio now were speaking.

They had trusted them. Welcomed them into the tribe. Shared meals with them.

Were they wrong? Were Sariel and Eccio *not* their blessed gift from above, and instead harbingers of evil that now would bring death and damnation upon them all?

A spark of shame flitted in her mind. Had she unwittingly given Eshe over to them? Sacrificed her niece because they had been kind to the village? Given them gifts?

Eshe had not been worth whatever little the demons had given them.

But she could not save her niece now. The girl had chosen to stay with them. Perhaps she was lost to the tribe.

Pain crippled Amara's heart at the loss of her beloved niece.

Sariel and Eshe started toward the hut, and everyone ran for the farthest wall, letting out cries of alarm as they scurred. Amara tried to guard them, frantically wondering if she could bar the door somehow.

But Sariel did not come try to wretch the door open. She stopped several paces from the door and called, "Amara?"

Just moments prior, Amara would have leaped at hearing Sariel's voice. Would have come running with a smile and embraced her friend. How quickly that had changed.

She pinched her eyes shut and forced herself to not answer.

"I know you're scared," Sariel continued. "I know you may not trust us anymore. But we are not here to hurt you, or anyone in the tribe. We love your tribe. We are here to protect it."

Amara wanted to believe that. Wanted to take their blessed angels into the tribe and graciously welcome their protection. But angels didn't bring dragons. They didn't bring speaking animals. Demons did that.

"It's all right," Sariel said with a sad smile. "You can stay in there. It will not change our plans to safeguard this village and your people."

She neared the hut, and Amara felt the great conflict of wanting to flee back to the others and stay at the door.

Gently, Sariel placed her hand on the wood plank door, offering an understanding smile as she met Amara's gaze through the cracks in the wood. "All will be well," she hushed as if it were a promise between them.

Amara ripped her gaze from Sariel's, staring at the ground as she tried to make sense of what was happening.

But the dirt beneath her feet held no answers.

Eshe followed behind Sariel as they went to the others. She had to actively fight the urge to turn and look back at her village, because there was always a chance someone would open themselves back up to her.

That chance felt terribly unlikely, but she hoped for it all the same.

"No luck?" Eccio asked them, and Eshe was grateful he spoke Masai.

"Perhaps it's for the best. If they stay in their huts, we'll have more room to move about without them potentially getting hurt," Sariel answered.

Fear slammed into Eshe's mind, and she burst, "The warriors! And the cows!"

"I know," Eccio said with a frown. "We can't go for them now though."

She searched his eyes for a reason.

"Given the timeframe the other grovix have given, we may be facing our enemy within moments," Warden told Eshe, coming up to gently nudge the girl's arm with her snout.

"We'll go for them the moment we have the danger cleared." Eccio offered a small smile. "I promise. I'm not going to leave them defenseless."

Sucking in a long breath, Eshe squared her shoulders. She had to remember who she spoke with. Who she was receiving these promises from. Yes, she had only known her Zaheri for a little over a year. Yes, they were not her family. Yes, she still knew little about them in comparison to others she held dear.

But she trusted them.

She knew they were people of their word. Their actions would back up their assured statements. If they could not be trusted, they would have stolen Eshe away yesterday. Instead, they had simply spoken with her, laughed with her, shared their home with her. Ardent had been her steady comfort just yesterday. Warden had approached her with care and affection.

These people did not intend to hurt her or her people.

Calmness filled her chest, easing the crippled feeling in her body and slowly ebbing the fears away. A small smile came to her face. "I trust you."

Sariel smiled back at her as Eccio cast lopsided grins toward Warden and Ardent.

"What can I do?"

With a shake of her head, Sariel answered, "Leave it to us. We won't let anything happen to you."

She wanted to ask how.

Before she could, Eccio nodded to Sariel. "You better get to it. We'll head out."

"Be on your guard," Sariel said as they took a few steps beyond the village entrance.

"I always am," Eccio said with a smile over his shoulder. A second later, a golden glow filled his body. A second after that, a duplicate of his form made up of his beautifully glowing energy walked at his side.

Eshe's mouth fell open as she took in the almost angelic vision before her.

Gently pushing her back, Sariel said, "You and I will stay in the village."

"But how will we protect it?" Eshe asked, still glancing back at their defenders.

"I will make a shield."

That seemed unlikely. All of the shields Eshe had seen were walls. Could large enough ones be made all around the village to protect them? What about if their enemies could hurdle over the shields?

Sariel didn't answer Eshe's questioning look. She simply eased her stance and gently flared her hands out. A couple feet from where they stood, a golden shield began to rise from the ground. It grew and swept over their heads, and Eshe watched it fly across the whole of the village. A dome was forming, encasing the whole village underneath its radiant, golden umbrella.

Eshe couldn't stop herself from smiling. It was stunningly beautiful. The golden energy swayed and swirled, sparkling as the energy holding it in place danced across its form.

As she brought her gaze back down to the ground, she caught curious eyes poking out of barely cracked-open doors. She could hear the hushed whispers of confusion. Her tribe was as enamored with the beautiful display as Eshe was. But clearly, they were still guarded.

Perhaps, once this was over, the tribe would be able to see that Eshe and her Zaheri were good and did not wish ill upon them. Perhaps it would all be well, just as Sariel had said.

An inferno-like bellow hit the air, and Eshe curled in on herself, slapping her hands over her ears. Then a blast of flames smacked against the shield, radiating a white impact mark that flashed back to gold almost instantly.

"Wh ... what was ...?" Eshe started to ask as she slowly straightened, catching sight of the massive form of a black-scaled dragon as it flew past. Her eyes widened at its bulk. It was so much larger than Ardent.

The beast was so high in the air, and the shield made it hard to see clearly, but the black dragon was clearly not a beautiful creature. Imposing and mean-looking, with sharp features.

Sariel gently held Eshe's arm. "That is a Ferveos."

Ardent's blue-scaled form streaked through the sky, attacking with ferocity against the larger creature. A few other dark-scaled dragons filled the sky. Shouting and flickers of gray energy came from beyond the shield. Roars and howls hit the air.

Eshe drew in on herself, trying to fully grasp what was happening.

A war had just befallen her village.

Chapter Four

THE THINGS UNPLANNED

"With six grovix total, I'm inclined to suggest we break into three units," Eccio said.

Warden nodded. "I will see to two of the Betas. Vallis, you see to the others."

With a sharp nod of agreement, Vallis answered, "We will focus on the werewolves. Your pack should focus on the bratak'ra."

Eccio turned to Ardent. "I'm going to send my Mask with you."

Shuffling her weight and gaining a small scowl, the dragon said, "I do not require assistance."

"Ardent, we don't know what we're up against yet. Even if all the Mask does is act as a guard for your back, it's the only way I can see maintaining eyes on everyone."

Vallis quirked his head to the side and gave Eccio an inquisitive stare. "Will that not divide your attention?"

Gently shaking his head, the hybrid answered, "No, I've learned how to be in two places at once."

Warden gave Ardent a knowing look. "He has a valid concern."

The dragon let out a growling huff. "I understand and appreciate your concern, but if we face no more than six Ferveos, I will be fine on my own."

"Understood," Eccio said with a nod. "If it appears there's less than six, I'll recall my Mask."

A golden dome formed across the village, clicking into place within a moment.

The grovix all turned their attention to the east, their fur standing on end.

Charging paw-steps met their ears as they took in the blurry figures approaching them. Ferveos could be seen in the sky. One flew faster than the others.

Eccio pinched his brow as he studied their approaching opposition. It didn't look as bad as he would have anticipated.

Gently tapping Ardent's shoulder, he said, "Change of plans." As Ardent looked to him, he added, "How do you feel about me riding you?"

"What?" Ardent asked with a wrinkle of her snout.

"I know I'm not a Skycaptain, but this doesn't look right." He gestured toward the nearing Caligans. "I need to get a view from the sky of what we're up against."

Crouching down, Ardent said, "Very well."

Eccio hopped up onto her, standing on her back rather than sitting. She stood, and he gripped a spike along her neck for stability.

"Get ready," he called to Warden. "I'll be back in a moment." His Mask hopped up behind him, weighing nothing to Ardent.

The dragon pushed off the ground, soaring quickly into the air but staying lower so as to avoid early confrontation with the Ferveos. As they got closer and Eccio was able to get a better look, he realized that their opposition was fairly minimal. Less than a quarter of a legion, if he had to guess. Six Ferveos.

In the distance, he caught the portal as a vibrantly glowing pillar as it snapped shut.

He tapped Ardent's neck and called, "You're sure you can take on six by yourself?"

"Do you think I'm incapable?" Ardent snapped with a small glare.

"Not at all," Eccio said with a smile before he leaped off her back. His Mask followed suit.

Falling to the ground, he took swift note of the fact that—as he anticipated—the werewolves and bratak'ra were ahead of the Caligans. He prepared himself for impact with the ground, shooting a blast of gold at the horde beneath him.

Cries of surprise erupted, and then he landed with a dull *thud* that definitely squashed several Caligans. His Mask landed behind him, mirroring his ready stance.

The opposition was only stunned for a second, maybe two, before they sprang into action.

Eccio didn't worry about getting hit. Injuries would happen. So long as he ensured he only got scrapes and cuts, and didn't suffer any major attacks or blows to the head, he'd be fine. If he hadn't been capable of making Masks, he would have likely been named a Berserker, someone who could take multiple hits without succumbing to their injuries.

Brandishing his short swords, he tore into the fighters who would do Eshe harm. His Mask stayed at his back, covering him as they moved in synchronized harmony.

Learning how to use his Mask most effectively had taken him years and lots of concentration. No one could truly teach him how to use them, as he was the only person in all of Agerius who could make them.

The most assistance he'd received came from Council Member Aros. The elderly man had stumbled upon some lessons in the Archives of Agerius and offered them, along with some minor guidance. Council Leader Ger'in was the only other person to provide assistance. They knew people from before the war with Caliga who had been capable of making Masks.

He'd learned that the more he worked with his Masks, the more they could almost gain a constant thrum in his subconscious. With some simple instruction, they now could move with little active thought from him. When he needed to, he could send them to opposite sides of a battle and briefly see through the Mask, much like how some shield-bearers could use their shields to heighten their eyesight.

Right now, he just needed his Mask to keep him guarded from blind spots.

He could hear the roaring and howling of the werewolves, bratak'ra, and grovix colliding. Though he wanted to look toward them and ensure they were okay, he had to trust Warden and Vallis to do what they did best.

Warden was the elder of the two, and she'd proven herself as a sturdy Warrior grovix over the years.

There weren't many Caligans left, maybe a couple dozen. Eccio had taken a few hits, but nothing he couldn't work with. Golden energy swirled around him from his blades, mingling with the deadly dance of his golden Mask behind him.

A pulse hit the air, and Eccio had a second to react before a foot neared him.

Crossing his blades in front of his body, he braced against the hit, sliding across the sun-soaked ground and tearing at some of the spindly grass. Panic gripped his heart as he darted his gaze to the Jumper who had appeared.

Relief flooded him when he took in the ornate, flowing robes.

Still a problem, but at least it wasn't Akeno.

Cregorous' generals were all known by the Agerian Defense. Some were more brutal than others. They each held a strength or abilities that made them formidable foes.

In his time as a Defender, Eccio hadn't encountered any of the generals until he'd become an Elite. And the only one he'd ever faced was Izel, a brutish beast, but not the strongest of the generals.

The one who stood before him was plenty dangerous, because little was known of him. He was clear to pick out, though.

With a robe that had flowing, ornate colors and was made up of fine threads, pristine shoes, and immaculately fine silken pants, Vorex was a brightly ornamented contrast to his fellow generals. Gold rings adorned his slender fingers. He had multiple piercings in his ears, mostly along his cartilage, and all sporting gems that shined and glittered in the sun. His face was long and sported a superior look through lidded lids, as though he were actively looking down on Eccio. Though, if he had to guess, they were nearly the same height.

Sweeping a hand through his styled, orange-tinted hair, Vorex let out a troubled sigh. "I do hate that I got sent to this place. It's so dusty." Holding his hands out in a way to display all of the fineness of his robe, he added, "Men like me don't belong in hovels like this."

Eccio clenched his jaw and held a firm stare on his face.

As he fixed his hair a little, Vorex bemoaned, "And then you were so quick to see me. Not many can do that. It was supposed to be painless so I could finish my task quickly."

"Which is?" Eccio asked, already knowing the answer. They had to be there for Eshe.

"Oh, come now, don't tell me you're just another stupid brute," Vorex groaned with a roll of his eyes. He crossed his arms and shook his head dismally. "I'm wasted on all of you. No one seems to appreciate the things I crave."

So, he was a talker. Okay, Eccio could play that game.

He eased his stance a little and smirked as he waggled one of his swords toward the general. "Impractical garb and too much jewelry?"

"Opulence, Agerian," Vorex corrected with a grand sweep of his arm. "The only other person who ever seems to enjoy it as much as I do is Avemod. Alas, even he wastes all of the finer things."

Boy you love to hear yourself talk, don't you? Eccio thought with a roll of his eyes.

"But we're wasting time," Vorex said with a smooth smile. "And you're clearly not one I'd like to converse with, what with your whole demeanor radiating boorishness."

"You don't want to be here, that's fine. Go home."

With another deep sigh, Vorex glanced toward the sky. "I would love to. But I cannot disappoint my Master."

"Sure you can," Eccio said with a quirk of his brow.

A small scoff left the general. "What little you know, boorish one."

Swirling his swords and falling into a ready stance, Eccio said, "Why don't you try me?"

"You had better not bleed on me. I can't get blood out of these cloths."

"It's your blood you should be worried about."

"That's not likely," Vorex answered with a smirk. Then he flicked his wrist, and Eccio suddenly fell through the ground.

Quite abruptly, he was in the air, falling behind Vorex.

An overly confident smirk was on the general's face as he landed a kick on Eccio, sending him flying.

Eccio caught sight of the hole just before he sailed through it. Ringed in gray energy that swirled and popped, there was a literal hole in the air that looked like it led to the ground, despite being perpendicular to the hard earth.

Bracing himself, Eccio flipped and intended to land on what he assumed would be solid ground. As he sailed through the rift, however, he was met with Vorex's fist cloaked in gray energy.

Swiftly raising his own gold-covered arm, Eccio blocked the hit but still skittered back to the ground, landing nearly where he'd been before. Frantically looking around, he tried to figure out where Vorex might open another one of those Dimensional Paths.

He'd heard they existed, that Jumpers could make them. Like doorways through dimensions, they could shove people into completely different areas without having to actively hold on to them and jump them through the dimension they could navigate.

Now it made sense why so few people could speak to Vorex's abilities and strengths. It wasn't that Vorex was fast on his own two feet. He was fast because of those Paths.

Vorex squinted at him. "You were quick. I'm not used to someone with reflexes like that."

Falling into another ready stance, Eccio prepared himself. He just had to think. Vorex was going to use those Paths and rely on them to keep Eccio off balance. But he hadn't continued to shove him through Paths after he'd punched him.

Quickly glancing back, Eccio caught a Path disintegrating into gray dust. He'd stopped just before falling into the next trap Vorex had laid.

Before he let Vorex fully collect himself, Eccio charged forward.

A scoff left Vorex and, a second later, a Dimensional Path appeared in front of Eccio.

Which he'd figured would happen since Vorex didn't want to get his clothes dirty. Eccio didn't care where it would have sent him, because he pivoted on a dime, stopping just before the Path, and skirting around it.

Shock radiated on Vorex's face as he skittered back.

Golden blades in hand, Eccio swung dual slices of gold energy in a sweeping attack.

A pulse sounded, and Vorex was gone.

Eccio quickly charged forward into the empty space where Vorex had been and felt the brush of air as the general landed behind him. A crackle of energy spurted and littered the ground.

"Hold still!" Vorex growled.

"And give you a chance to trip me up?" Eccio called as his Mask appeared so he could have something to kick off against. He swirled in the air, landing behind Vorex's thundering form.

Ignoring Eccio, Vorex slammed an energy-cloaked fist into the Mask that stood defenseless before him. The Mask broke into golden light on impact, flitting away in the breeze.

Stinging pain shook up Eccio's left arm, making him grunt and flinch back. He'd expected Vorex to go after him.

His robes flowing with his movement, Vorex spun and hurtled a gray attack at Eccio.

Pushing himself into the air, Eccio skimmed across the opposing attack and managed to pivot midair. He hurtled one of his energy-infused blades down at Vorex, a trail of gold in its wake.

The sword flew like an arrow and slashed through Vorex's arm, shredding the long sleeve of the robe, along with his skin, leaving a deep laceration.

A cry tore from the general as he slapped his hand onto the injury.

Eccio landed and had to stagger to regain his footing. His left arm was tingling to numbness. He hadn't had a Mask get hit in a long time and wasn't acclimated at all to the resulting pain it would cause him.

Vorex wasn't all talk. He was strong enough to obliterate a Mask with one hit.

"My sleeve!" Vorex spat with a hatred-filled look at Eccio. "How dare you?"

Narrowing his eyes, Eccio panted out, "Sorry, did you forget this was a war?"

With a growl, the general glared. All of the lackadaisical, grandiose ease he'd held before was gone, replaced with a sinister, furious look. "You'll regret that," he said darkly. A pulse hit the air, and he disappeared in gray dust.

That seemed odd.

Eccio straightened, having expected that Vorex would continue fighting him. Footsteps made him look back.

The grovix and dragon were running toward him. Vorex must've realized he was about to be outnumbered.

"Are you all right?" Warden asked as she came to a stop in front of him.

Nodding a little, Eccio answered, "Yeah. But there's something really wrong."

Ardent landed among them. "What do you mean?"

Thinking through what the general had said and how he'd behaved, Eccio said, "Vorex made it sound like he'd been sent here rather than somewhere else." He glanced back at where Vorex had been a moment prior. "And he said I'd regret tearing his sleeve."

Vallis let out a scoff. "That's what gets him riled?" He shook his head. "Caligans."

"Do you believe he will return?" Ardent asked. There were minor scorch marks across some of her scales, perhaps where she'd skimmed fire from Ferveos' blasts.

"He certainly made it sound like that was the case." He flicked his left arm, trying to shake away the tingling.

Lifting her head toward the village, Ardent said, "We should return to Sariel and Eshe." Before Eccio could say anything further, she turned to him and added, "And perhaps you should ride upon my back again."

"I can fly."

"I'm certain you can, but if Vorex is to return, there is no reason for you to expend more strength than necessary."

Warden gave Eccio a small nod. "She is correct. You are the only one who could properly do battle against him."

Nodding subtly, Eccio relented. "Very well. Let's get back so we can figure out what to do next." As he climbed onto Ardent's back and took hold of one of the spikes on her neck, he found himself glancing at where Vorex had been.

He didn't look forward to fighting the Jumper again.

<h1>Chapter Five</h1>

GREEDY DECEPTIONS

Vorex appeared in the sparce wooded area not far from where he'd been dueling the Agerian. Curses filled his head as he clutched his wounded arm, agonizingly waiting for the cut to heal. He glared through the sporadic coverage at the Agerians as they gathered. Several grovix among them, and a Scout.

And then that stupid Agerian.

For some brute, he was fast. But, more importantly, he'd had the gall to cut him. He hadn't been cut by a blade in centuries.

Throwing a murderous glare at the group while they talked, he felt his vision focus in on the Agerian. He was attentive and had listened to everything Vorex had said.

Curse that Agerian. He wouldn't have spoken so much if he'd thought for even a second that the man would escape his Rifts. No one had been that attuned to how Rifts worked, especially after sailing through only two of them.

The Agerian flicked his arm about, as though trying to expel something. Vorex's gaze narrowed. Perhaps breaking the golden Mask had rendered pain for the Agerian.

None of the Caligans—not even the Master—could produce Masks. Truthfully, Vorex had been a little surprised to find an Agerian who could summon one. If he didn't despise the Agerian so much, he might be impressed. He might even tell the Master about him.

But, as he did despise the Agerian, he wanted him dead.

"I can fly," the Agerian said a bit defensively to the dragon among them.

The Scout nodded solemnly. "I'm certain you can, but if Vorex is to return, there is no reason for you to expend more strength than necessary."

"She is correct. You are the only one who could properly do battle against him," one of the grovix said.

A scoff tipped from Vorex. Yeah, he wasn't going to let a battle against that Agerian last long next time. Their next altercation would be short and brutal for that arrogant, Mask-wielding Agerian.

He watched them go then dipped into the Fifth Dimension, following them from a slight distance. The Agerian had been moderately proficient at reacting to Vorex's movements through dimensions. While he was positive this Agerian wasn't a Jumper, Vorex didn't want to take any chances.

They arrived at a village domed in a golden shield. It splattered a golden array as Vorex walked through it, undeterred, as per usual. Shields only barred enemies from entering the Third Dimension. They weren't so absolute in the Fifth.

Sweeping his gaze across the village, he took note of what was where. Where the livestock was kept so that he could stay opposite the creatures. Where the entrance of the village was, because any defenders would face that direction.

Once he had as near a perfect layout memorized, he returned to the portal, cursing silently the whole way there.

It'd been ages since he'd needed to actually traverse the Fifth Dimension to get to where he was going. Tilion's Fifth Dimension was awash with well-worn paths he'd made, and traversing the landscape was nearly instantaneous for him. But here? Darkness, it took him five minutes to get back to the portal.

Five. Whole. Minutes.

He was even more angry about his cut now. It was barely healing. Again, he blamed it on the Agerian. Not on the fact that his body wasn't used to healing from cuts.

When he arrived at the portal, he angrily snatched the white orb and demanded it take him to Caliga. The white sphere flashed and was instantly replaced with the red orb in Cregorous' mansion.

Moving with all swiftness, he went to the war room. The mistresses he passed were speaking in hushed excitement, but there weren't many other servants around. Hope sat in his chest that he was among the first to return.

That would afford him the chance to change into his jacket and find someone to clean and repair his shirt. He refused to go into the final altercation looking like a messy Backwater. He was that Agerian's better, and he'd sooner die than look like some unkempt thing.

As he reached the basement, the hollow screams from the experimented beasts muffled against the walls. A mistress stumbled out of the War Room, a dazed look on her face and a stuttering in her gait.

So, the Master was starting early today.

Not surprising. Darkness only knew how the Master was feeling. The euphoria surrounding imminent victory was tantalizing. The Master likely felt it tenfold.

The mistresses were probably all getting their fill of the Master today.

Rapping his knuckles against the wall, Cregorous called a second later, "Vorex."

Giving just a second's pause, Vorex slid into the room as Cregorous finished fastening his pants. Vorex bowed, keeping his injured arm behind his back.

"Out," Cregorous commanded, sucking smooth, heavy breaths into his lungs.

A second mistress gave Vorex a slightly peturbed look before she fixed her dress and left the room. Cregorous grabbed a glass of water and took a healthy draught. "Report."

"The Fourth has reinforcements."

Quirking his brow, Cregorous hummed before he eased to the table at the center of the room.

"It seems a pack of grovix was sent to aid in protecting the child."

Red flashed across Cregorous' shoulders, and a Rift ringed in red appeared near the ceiling, producing a man who fell to the floor. A crack hit the air as his legs broke and he cried out in pain. He wore an Agerian uniform—slate blue cloth and silver thread.

In a flash, the man was thrown onto the table, Cregorous' grip tight on his throat.

"You missed something," Cregorous seethed, a neutral expression on his face.

The man clawed at his forearm. Panic filled his features as he gagged, his mouth contorting around soundless words. His thrashing slowed after a second as Cregorous' grip tightened more and more.

In a swift movement, Cregorous hurled him back, sending him flying through another red-ringed Rift.

Flicking his gaze between the table and Cregorous, Vorex asked, "Master?"

"He'll serve as an example for the others," Cregorous said simply as he snatched the water, taking another long swallow. "Continue."

Vorex was grateful he was among the generals. Others didn't get as much of a chance to mess up.

Agerians even less.

Every time an Agerian informant messed up, they were killed almost instantly. Today, it seemed the Master was truly craving carnage, as he'd killed the Agerian face-to-face. He only did that when he hungered for that kind of intimate death.

Shaking his head quickly, Vorex said, "Nothing more. I breached the shield they made around the village. Striking at the Fourth will be simple once I take out their only fighter."

"Good. A fleet of Ferveos will go with you in the next strike."

Strange. But not really his problem.

He nodded. "Yes, My Lord." Then, turning on his heel, he started to march out of the room.

"And Vorex," Cregorous said, making the Jumper freeze in his tracks.

Fear clutched Vorex's chest as he held his breath.

Cregorous' hand slammed onto Vorex's mostly healed wound, and then Cregorous tightened his grip, forcing the Jumper to grit his teeth. Vorex refused to cry out, even as every part of him screamed agony.

He'd noticed. Of course he'd noticed. Vorex shouldn't have even tried to hide it.

"Don't disappoint me again," Cregorous demanded before he harshly shoved the general into the hallway.

A shred of dignity swelled in Vorex when he didn't fall to the floor; he'd managed to stagger to surer footing in front of his Master. So, he bowed low and let out a relieved breath when Cregorous walked back into the war room.

Jumping to his chambers, Vorex ripped the tattered garment off and snatched his jacket instead.

He would not appear injured next time.

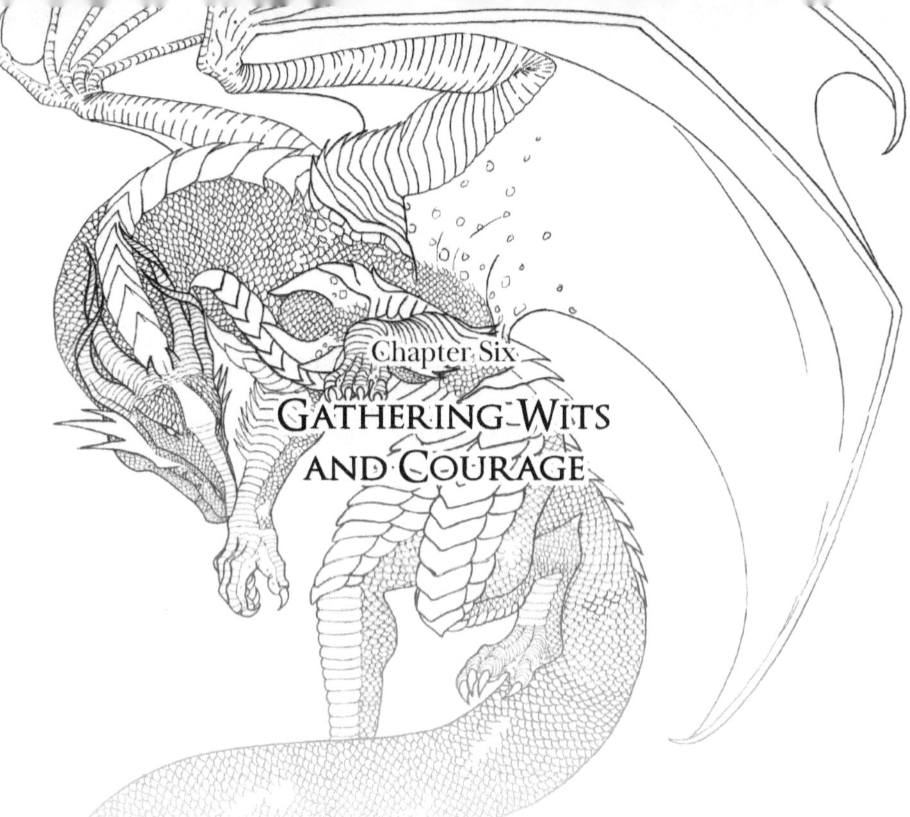

Chapter Six

GATHERING WITS AND COURAGE

Eshe rushed to the group as they landed within the shield Sariel had made. "Are you all right?" Her mouth fell open at Eccio's injuries. "Here, let me help."

Though Eccio let her pull him toward her, he said, "I'll be fine, Eshe. None of my injuries are terrible."

"What happened?" Sariel asked, flicking her gaze across Eccio's many small cuts and abrasions.

"There were six Ferveos. I would say there were around thirty bratak'ra and werewolves combined," Warden said as she sat.

"That's all?" the Team Leader asked in astonishment.

As his injuries patched faster, thanks to Eshe's assistance, Eccio said, "Maybe a hundred Caligans. And Vorex." He quirked his brow. "Most of this is due to him."

"Vorex?"

"He's fast, but it's because he's a Jumper."

Sariel's brow pinched together. "We knew he was a Jumper."

Shaking his head, Eccio clarified, "Sar, he can do something else with it. I've heard a little about them—pathways that Jumpers can make.

— 307 —

He's adept at them. Nearly threw me off balance a couple times. He's adaptable, too; learns quickly where to strike. He took out my Mask shortly before he fled." He let out a sigh. "I think he'll be back."

"What makes you say that?"

Ardent folded her wings at her sides, shifting her weight slightly. "The numbers sent were not those of a genuine attack. More likely a scouting party."

"To assess what they're up against," Sariel hushed.

"I think so," Eccio affirmed with a nod. "Vorex made it sound like he was told to come here as opposed to somewhere else."

Sariel snapped her attention to him.

"I'm worried this is bigger than just us."

Eshe cast wary glances to her Zaheri. "What does that mean?"

Gently placing her hand on Eshe's shoulder, Sariel said, "I will explain in a moment." She looked back to Eccio. "Regarding your Mask: are you going to be hindered because of its loss?"

He shook his head. "No, I can make another one. I can have two at a time, if necessary. But I'll need to rest up a little, and preferably get something to eat."

"What sort of food would be best?" Eshe asked.

"Ideally, meat. Protein helps with replenishing energy."

That would be hard to come by.

Warden rose to her feet. "We will see to a hunt then."

"No, we need to get to the men and the cows; help get them back here where it's safe," Eccio corrected.

"Eccio is right. We can focus on getting a proper meal once we know the tribe is under protection," Sariel said. "Warden, you and the Betas aid Eccio in getting the men and the cattle back here safely. Ardent, I ask that you stay here to provide sharp eyes and attentive ears."

Ardent bowed her head in a regal fashion.

As his wings broke from his back, Eccio gave Eshe a gentle squeeze of her hand. "Thank you. We'll be back as quickly as possible."

"Be safe," Sariel said before he took to the sky and the grovix began their run to the path that would lead to the grazing fields.

Watching them go for a moment, she then turned to Eshe. "Let us go answer your questions."

Eshe wished she could have healed the grovix, too. Though she couldn't understand a word the five others said, that wouldn't limit her healing. They didn't seem terribly injured, but she had noticed several cuts that she would like to heal, if she had the chance.

The sounds of fighting had been so foreign to her. The yelling and growling, the yelps of pain. The large, dark-scaled dragons falling from the sky, landing with reverberated *booms* as they impacted the dry earth.

By the time the noise had died down, Eshe had found herself clutching her hands in front of her chest, her arms drawn in as though to somehow comfort herself.

It pained her to watch them run off outside of the protection of Sariel's shield. Though she was grateful for their efforts to keep everyone from the tribe safe, she wished things had happened when everyone was already in the village. Sending anyone out into an unprotected area set worry in her gut.

She and Sariel walked into the hut where the goats slept. No one would be in there. A swell of comfort came over Eshe's soul as the baby goats brayed at her and hopped around her feet as though nothing terrible had happened. As though she was still the same person they had adored before.

Gratefully scooping one of the smallest ones into her arms, she settled onto the animal skin bedding that she so often slept on. The small goat happily snuggled her, its warmth soothing her fears almost instantly.

Slowly, Sariel joined her, letting out a long breath. She paused, a pensive look filling her features. Then she looked at the teenager and said, "What I'm going to tell you ... I'm not supposed to. I'm not sure when we would have been permitted to divulge such information. But given what's happened—what's happening—I want you to be aware of what could be transpiring."

Eshe swallowed and nodded, studying Sariel's words. She held the goat in her grasp a little tighter.

Turning to face her fully, Sariel said, "Eshe, you aren't the only Human-Born."

The revelation settled into Eshe's mind, taking a moment to sink in. For some reason, it brought a surge of hope in her. "I ... How many others are there?"

"Six," Sariel said, keeping her gaze trained on Eshe and reading every response the girl gave her. "To the best of my knowledge, you're all the same age."

"So ... I am not the one meant to stop Cregorous after all?" She wasn't disappointed. It meant that the weight of her Zaheri's world was not on her shoulders alone. There were others with whom she could bear the burden.

Her brow pulled together. "I am not the First, am I?"

Shaking her head a little, Sariel answered, "No. You're the Fourth Human-Born."

A new fear churned in Eshe's mind, and she tried to figure out how to voice it. It sparked so quickly she had to make sure she could communicate it well. Slowly meeting Sariel's calm gaze, she asked quietly, "Are the others being attacked, as well?"

"I don't know," Sariel said a little desperately, a frown coming to her face. "But what Eccio said of the general who attacked, it leads to the possibility of that."

"Will they be all right?" Eshe asked, trying not to cry at the prospect of other teenagers like her suffering from unbidden attacks. It hurt her heart that there could be people out there, somewhere, potentially getting injured. If only she could somehow go to the wounded ones and heal them.

She just had to pray that they would be well.

Nodding a little and shaking out a small laugh, the Zaheri answered, "I'm sure they will. They have ..." Her assurance faltered, and she had to steady herself.

"Sariel?" Her brow pulled together in concern as she gently reached out for her Zaheri's shoulder. "What is it?"

Lifting her head to meet the teenager's concerned expression, Sariel offered a watery smile. "My husband is somewhere, protecting another Human-Born."

Sorrow caught Eshe's voice, and she let out a gasping breath.

"He will be well; I'm certain of it." Sariel sniffed back her tears and nodded a few times. "But I do miss him. Greatly."

Her frown deepened as Eshe surveyed Sariel's pain. Had ... had they been separated this whole time? That felt terribly cruel. Eshe hoped they might reunite soon.

Collecting herself, Sariel straightened. "Now, we must prepare ourselves."

"You do not think this is over?"

"No. Eccio is wise enough to recognize when things are amiss. If he believes Vorex will return, we must be prepared for that."

The girl nodded a few times in understanding. Then a pensive look filled her features as she asked, "What ...? Why were we not allowed to know of one another?"

"I don't know," Sariel answered with a small shake of her head. "Our governing head—we call them the High Council—they believed you might not be mature enough to handle everything if you were told too much too soon."

"So ... is it possible one of the others is strong enough to stop this war?"

"That's what we believe, yes. You know your title."

"Healer."

Sariel nodded again. "Yes. The others are Raidin, Protector, Warrior, Shifter, Scholar, and Requisite." A reassuring smile came to her face. "It is safe to say that the Warrior will be capable of great strength."

Though she was worried that Sariel might say otherwise, Eshe carefully said, "And you do not believe that Cregorous will be coming for me."

"I cannot say. Though, if his actions in the past are any indication"—worry wrinkled her face as a deep frown returned—"he will likely go for the First Human-Born. They pose the greatest threat to him."

Cocking her head a little, Eshe asked, "Why?"

"The day we were assigned as your Zaheri, it was the day we knew the Human-Borns had risen."

"How?"

Gently shaking her head, Sariel sighed. "Eshe, the reason why Cregorous has held power all these years is not from lack of wish on Agerius' part. He is so much more powerful than anyone living within Tilion. There is no rival to his strength. But then, one morning, he was shoved back through the portal to Tilion. Whoever he was attempting to attack was stronger than him. Strong enough to push him backward through the portal. We were all told by the High Council that the First Human-Born had shown itself."

"He attacked them? When?"

"It was nineteen years ago." Sariel shifted a little, her brow slowly furrowed as she looked to the floor. "Nineteen years ago today."

Eshe blinked a few times, her mind swirling. "But ... would that mean the First Human-Born ...?"

Nodding a little, Sariel answered, "Was an unborn baby."

Astonishment clouded Eshe's thoughts for a moment. She had always been told that Cregorous was cruel and relentless, a monster by every right. But, to attack a child who had not yet even been born ...

It felt more heartless than she could ever imagine.

A pause fell between them. Eshe thought over all that Sariel had told her and wondered if perhaps Sariel's husband was protecting the First Human-Born. She felt even greater sorrow at that concept. No wife should have to fear her husband's death at the hands of a monster.

Gently taking Sariel's hand, Eshe said, "All will be well."

Giving the girl a proud smile, Sariel nodded. "Yes, it will." She squeezed Eshe's hand and asked, "Do you have any other questions?"

"What should I do now?"

"For right now, rest. Ardent and I will keep watch. Once Eccio returns with the men and we know everyone is safe, we will assess what to do next."

Nodding slowly, Eshe chose to say nothing.

Her Zaheri rose and left the hut.

She was grateful that Sariel had left her alone for a little while. Everything had changed so quickly. Her world felt upside down, as though she were standing on her head. Absentmindedly petting the small goat in her lap, her mind wandered.

What was she to do?

It wasn't her fault. She knew it wasn't her fault. All the same, guilt weighed on her heavily.

Her people were huddled in huts, scared and confused. The men were likely yelling at Eccio, maybe even jabbing their spears toward

Warden and the other grovix. Maybe even throwing accusing words at them.

Everyone was under attack. It wasn't just Eshe. Was she the target? It seemed that was so. But in targeting her, it had endangered everyone she loved.

Biting back tears, she looked to the goat falling to slumber.

What should she do?

Maybe it would be better if she left. Once they got out of this horrible day and were free from attacks, she could just leave. Go be with her Zaheri. Move on. She had been wondering if that was her destiny before. It wasn't like it hadn't entered her mind.

But then, why did it hurt her heart so to imagine walking away from the tribe?

Amara's look of betrayal stung her mind in remembrance.

She looked to the small hut she sat in. Her home. Her comfortable resting place. Laughter had been shared here. Joys had been had. Children she'd seen brought into the world. Friends she'd seen get married. Stories told. Prayers shared. Jokes and little playful moments speckled her memory.

To leave would cut her deeper than any wound.

Even if everything beyond her village was wonderful, was glamorous and beautiful, was more than she could imagine...

These were her people.

But that meant if she loved them, she might have to leave them. Because what if something more happened? What if another attack came? What if her Zaheri were not so swift? What if they had not arrived in time today? Who might have suffered on Eshe's behalf? How many might have died?

Sucking in a steadying breath, she tried to resolve to leave in her heart.

Despite her attempts to steady herself to that destiny, she could not stop herself from crying.

Chapter Seven

ANGELS OR DEMONS?

The men had returned with the cows. Immediately, the tribe's elders gathered in a hut, leaving the rest to do as they needed. Some of the men stayed outside the hut, spears raised and distrusting glares on their faces. It seemed they didn't even dare to blink.

Eccio had been able to explain that the men needed to return to the village. Sounds of battle had filtered to the field where the men had been with the livestock, so they'd already begun their return journey, fearing for the village's safety. When they had seen the grovix approaching, they'd thought they were lionesses seeking a hunt and had thrown spears. Eccio had landed before them a moment later, immediately spurring the eldest men into fear at the sight of his wings.

It had taken some calm, reassuring statements from Eccio. Unfortunately, his attempts to appeal to his history with the tribe hadn't garnered any positive results. The men swiftly saw him as a would-be enemy, much like the women and children's reactions. After several moments of back and forth, he'd convinced the men to return to the village, insisting that he and the others would keep their distance.

True to their word, the Agerians stayed at the edge of the shield to ensure they gave the tribe space. There had been a lot of yelling when they had all returned, and many of the men had threateningly jabbed their spears toward the grovix if they got too close to the cows.

The grovix had all gone off for a hunt and had recently returned with a meager amount of food. Much of the wildlife had fled due to the battle, which wasn't terribly surprising considering how attuned animals were to danger.

As the grovix divvied up food, Ardent stood watch, her gaze unblinking at Eshe, who sat a little way off.

Amid all of that, Sariel kept pacing, wringing her hands, and anxiously looking outside the shield.

Eyeing her warily, Eccio took a deep breath before walking toward her, stopping a few paces away to not overwhelm her. No part of him moved except his eyes as he tried to work through how he was going to encourage her. After a moment, he said, "Sar, I think you need to take a breath."

"Multiple strikes are the only thing that makes sense," she said in a rush, keeping her eyes locked on the field beyond her shield.

"I'm aware of that."

"Which means Cregorous has control of the portal."

He nodded again. "Also, yes, aware of that."

The Team Leader whipped a fearful gaze to her friend. "Which means—"

"Which means Ar'on's gonna be fine." He reached out to try to gently take hold of her arm. "Sar, c'mon; it's Ar'on. He's—"

She moved too quickly, out of his grasp. "He's an idiot, and acts rashly, and—"

"And you haven't heard from him."

She flashed a furiously hurt look at Eccio.

"I'm sure he has a good reason," he said softly, trying everything in his power to comfort her.

Her face pinched in annoyance before she crossed her arms. "I'm sure *he* thinks it's a good reason."

Eccio opened his mouth to reply.

"That doesn't mean it's a good reason!" she snapped, not allowing him the chance to defend her husband's actions. Or lack thereof.

Elders, this was harder than he'd thought.

When the first year had gone by and Sariel had no communication from Ar'on, they'd just assumed he had his hands full. After all, he had an irate Council Member, a woefully unprepared pup, and the Jumper to deal with.

Despite the age difference between him and many of the elders among the Elite Defenders of Agerius, Eccio had become a part of their group. He'd trained under many of them early on, eager for any assistance or insight into how to properly control and utilize his Masks.

The memory of Ar'on's rants after the appointments of the Zaheri came to Eccio's mind, and he had to keep himself from smiling. Sariel had been her usual calm self, so assured that everything was fine. That everything would be fine. Kept interjecting in Ar'on's livid grumblings that perhaps he would help the Jumper gain some respectable attitudes and routines.

Eccio had done his best to remind Sariel of those things whenever concern over Ar'on had come up. Because it was entirely possible that maybe he had just been so busy with keeping things together that he hadn't had time to communicate with her.

And for a while, that'd worked to satiate Sariel's fears over Ar'on's lack of contact.

That was ... until she'd heard about how Tyron kept up routine communication with the Caretaker, Janet.

Tyron could find the time and ability to keep in touch with the woman he was courting, all while on another world. Eccio had to be impressed with that.

But it also left him with almost nothing to comfort Sariel with regarding Ar'on's silence.

"Somehow, Tyron can find time to write regular letters to Janet, but Ar'on can't take a moment to let me know he's still alive?" Sariel had fumed.

"Well, we can at least take comfort in knowing that he's still alive, right? The Council would've told us if he was injured or something," Eccio had offered, trying to calm her down.

"That doesn't help!" she'd snapped.

Elders, sometimes he was the worst at diffusing her anger. It sparked so infrequently. Though the cause was almost always something Ar'on related.

He wanted to curse the Alpha Team member. "Don't let Sariel die" had sounded like a simple command when Ar'on had given it to him. Now Eccio almost wanted to ask him, "Oh yeah? And what do I do when she tries to kill *you*?"

This time, it wasn't anger fueling Sariel, though. She was genuinely terrified for him. And he couldn't blame her. If he allowed himself, he'd be terrified about what all of this meant.

The portal was never a large, bright white cylinder. The only time it'd looked like that was the day the First Human-Born arrived, shoving Cregorous back to Tilion. Which meant tons of energy was being pumped into the portal. Which could only mean that Cregorous was striking, and striking hard.

Cregorous wouldn't come for them. He'd go for the First.

Managing to lay his hand on her shoulder, Eccio said, "He's going to be okay, Sariel. He's a strong fighter. You know that."

She slowly met his gaze, her frown deep and sorrow-filled. Carefully taking in a long, steadying breath, she nodded and opened her mouth to reply ...

When Eshe's friend, Malaika, suddenly ripped the Healer upright and started dragging her toward the tribe, screaming, "Eshe is not a demon!"

Eshe sat with the baby goats as they played in the brush near the huts, absentmindedly watching them. She could feel her Zaheri's protective gaze, as though silently letting her know they were near.

She had been drawing mindlessly in the dirt when Malaika came near. Meeting Eshe's gaze, she cautiously approached, acting like Eshe was a wild animal or something to fear.

Eshe eased back a little, picking up the smallest goat as it hopped over to her.

"They still like you," Malaika said with a small laugh.

Nodding a little, Eshe warily met her friend's gaze a few times, trying to do everything in her power to appear harmless, which she was. "I am glad for it."

"So ..." Malaika said carefully, inching closer but still wearing a look of distrust. "You ... are not a demon?"

Eshe shook her head.

Malaika threw a worried look toward the Zaheri, her gaze clearly fixed on Ardent. "Dragons have always been bad."

"I know," Eshe said dismally. "But Ardent is not."

"Ardent?"

"That is her name."

Chewing on her lip, Malaika sat down, but in such a way that she could bolt back to the others if necessary.

The friends sat in silence for a moment or two. Malaika studied Eshe, her eyes unblinking.

Eshe tried not to shrink under her friend's intense stare.

"Eccio made a demon come out of him."

Whipping her gaze to Malaika, Eshe quickly said, "No, it is not a demon. He is not a demon. It ... They call them abilities. Things we can do because of what we are."

Malaika narrowed her eyes, her stance still guarded. "What are you?"

"They ... call themselves hybrids. Part human and part ... dragon."

The comment made Malaika's brows dip into a faint glare, as though challenging Eshe with the look.

"They do not want to hurt us," Eshe hushed desperately.

Tapping her feet against the ground, Malaika continued to eye Eshe suspiciously. After an agonizingly long minute, she asked, "What can you do?"

Her shoulders slumping, Eshe frowned. "Very little."

Malaika's face scrunched in confusion.

"I can only heal," Eshe said as she held her hand out. Violet energy swirled about her palm, dancing into the shape of an orb.

At the sight of the energy in Eshe's grasp, Malaika stuttered back, but she didn't run. Her eyes were locked on the violet energy, watching it with conflicting emotions playing on her features.

"Stronger hybrids can fight with their energy." Eshe looked up at the shield surrounding them. "Make shields to protect others." She shrugged as her violet energy disappeared. "I cannot do either of those things."

"You can heal?" Malaika asked with a stern look.

Shuffling her weight a little, Eshe nodded and met her friend's gaze. "Yes. Any physical ailment."

Malaika lost all of the guarded edges as she scooted a little closer. "Is that why we are being attacked?"

So the tribe did see her as a blight. They did blame her for the circumstances.

They weren't wrong, but that didn't make the reality hurt any less in Eshe's chest.

A frown came to her face. "Yes."

Throwing a wild look to the Zaheri then back to Eshe, Malaika said, "They are protecting you."

"Yes."

Malaika suddenly snatched Eshe's wrist and dragged her upright, yanking her back into the village and toward the tribe. The small goat Eshe had been holding let out a yelp of surprise and hopped away.

"Malaika, what are you doing?" Eshe asked in fear.

If they tried to attack her, or banish her right here, what might happen? What might her Zaheri do?

If her Zaheri intervened, tried to keep her safe, would they be forced to fight her people? What if someone got seriously hurt? So hurt that Eshe couldn't heal them?

Panic over what Malaika was doing, what it might cause, made Eshe feel like she couldn't breathe.

"Eshe is not a demon!" Malaika called as the people of the tribe started to flee her advance.

Eyes wide, Eshe sucked a surprised gulp of air into her lungs.

Malaika ... was on their side?

The tribe all stilled and stared at Malaika with eyes filled with confusion and concern.

Pulling Eshe to a stop at her side, Malaika continued to hold on to her friend and smiled broadly. "She is a Healer! Blessed by God!" She pointed at the Zaheri back at the shield edge. "Eccio and Sariel—and the others—they are angels! They are protecting Eshe from the demons!"

Papa and Amara pushed forward, a few other village elders stepping out with them.

"What are you saying, child?" Papa asked in an accusing way.

"Eshe is a Healer! She is not an enemy of the tribe; she never has been."

Papa seemed unconvinced. "If Eshe were a healer, why would she not show it sooner?"

A fair question.

Shying back, Eshe admitted, "I was fearful of what you would think."

It was the truth. She had always been scared of what the tribe might say, how they might react. Yes, she had been told by Sariel not to tell anyone, but her fear over her people's reaction was really what kept her from saying anything.

Giving the other village elders a look of doubt, Papa said, "I do not trust it. There is no proof Eshe can heal the sick."

Gently reaching her hand toward Papa, Amara still stared at Eshe as she said quietly, "Perhaps there is."

One of the other village elders nodded. "Yes. Tendaji has suffered from a cough for many days. The medicine tree has had no effect."

Everyone looked to Tendaji. He was a few years younger than Eshe, and he clutched one of the traded hats from Eccio in his grasp. He met Eshe's gaze, and there was a hope in his eyes. A few rough coughs racked his body before he asked, "Papa?"

With a sigh, Papa said to the boy, "It is your choice."

Malaika let go of Eshe's wrist as Tendaji slowly walked up to her. He studied Eshe, his gaze searching hers before he nodded.

Eshe gently reached out and cupped his cheek. She could sense the illness in his chest, how it hindered his lungs and caused him to cough. Leaning forward, she rested her forehead against his and closed her eyes, envisioning the illness healing within him and repairing his strained muscles from the coughing.

After a few seconds, she stepped back and smiled at him.

Tendaji smiled wide before he spun around to face the others. "It is gone! My chest does not hurt anymore!"

Gasps of awe and looks of wonder filled the tribe.

Malaika smiled broadly and jumped in celebration. "Eshe is a Healer!"

A few of the men jumped in place—a way of celebrating or expressing excitement—and a moment later, Eshe was swarmed by the people she so dearly loved.

Amara hugged her fiercely, begging her for forgiveness. Eshe cried and assured her that she understood.

As the tribe rejoiced, a few of them waved the Zaheri over, calling to them to join.

The Agerians carefully approached, moving slowly so as to not scare anyone. Chants of praise began to sound from a few of the villagers, praising God for Eshe and for her protectors.

Papa clapped his hands, wearing a joyful smile. "We must make a sacrifice!"

"No, that isn't necessary," Sariel quickly said.

"It is. For blessings and protection. Gather the fattest cow! Men, we must prepare the bar-b-q!"

Eccio was quickly surrounded by a few of the men and boys, urging him to go with them into the grove of trees where they prepared the bar-b-q. It was not the first time he and Sariel would participate in the roasting of an animal and the preparation of the meal, but the whiplash of the village's reactions sent a skittering confusion through them.

Sariel pushed him away and smiled. "Go. We will be fine."

Holding his hands out, Eccio smiled to the men around him and said, "I will meet you there in a moment." He nodded to Papa. "I promise, I will be there. I need a moment."

Papa nodded his understanding then again called for the fattest cow. A few of the men went off to search the herd.

Once they had some space around them, Eccio turned to Sariel. "If I'm back in the thicket, I won't be able to be the first defense."

"Let's ask if Warden might be able to go with you," Sariel said.

Through the tears in her eyes, Amara nodded to them. "Yes, that would be fine. Please, all men may go."

"Warden is actually a female," Eccio said with sideways smile.

Warden looked at Vallis. "Then Vallis should go with you."

Scrunching his brow, the Beta grovix said, "That isn't necessary."

"The people here have specific ways of doing things. Men are the only ones allowed to be present for the slaughter and preparation of animals," Sariel explained.

With a bow of her head, Warden said, "I am not offended, Vallis. It is what must be done."

Though his ears dipped a little, Vallis nodded. "Very well. If you insist."

Before he and Vallis followed the men of the tribe, Eccio looked at Sariel and offered an understanding smile. "He *will* be fine, Sar. Ar'on is a fighter. Nothing will stop him from seeing you again."

Offering a grateful smile, Sariel nodded. "Thank you, Eccio. Truly."

As they walked off, Sariel turned to Amara in time to catch her tight embrace.

"I am sorry for doubting you, Sariel."

"There is no need to apologize, my dear friend," Sariel answered, returning the woman's hug. "I know much has happened."

Stepping back but still holding Sariel's hands, Amara smiled brightly at her. "Come; we must go make chapatis."

Though she allowed Amara to drag her and Eshe after her, Sariel said, "Amara, it truly is not necessary."

"But it is. You are our angels, and we called you demons. We must give you all you need to protect our blessed Eshe."

"Better to go along, I believe," Eshe hushed with a smile to Sariel.

"I believe you are correct," Sariel replied with a small laugh.

Though it had been a short time of separation with the tribe, neither of them could deny that it brought great relief to see the villagers smiling and laughing once more.

TWO WORLDS, ONE FAMILY

A typical bar-b-q could take anywhere from four to six hours from beginning to end. Usually, it would be started in late morning, not midafternoon. But given all that had transpired, and the fact that the tribe wished to slaughter a cow both for the Zaheri's strength and for a sort of offering to the Agerian's deity, it made sense to start the bar-b-q, even if it might not be ready before any additional attacks came.

As the men slaughtered the cow and prepared the meal, Eccio assisted where he could. They cut the meat up into more portions than normal, hastening the process to ensure even the grovix would be able to partake of the meal.

Eccio was asked many questions, and he did a fair bit of translating for Vallis, as there were many questions about the grovix. What were they? Why could they speak? Were they blessed with speech by their deity? What sort of food did they typically eat? Who fashioned their armor? How old were the grovix that protected them, and how long had they been fighting in the war against the demons?

Some of the villagers grasped the concept of another world better than others, but they were few. Most of the tribe believed that the

Agerians were genuine blessings from heaven, sent to protect Eshe from the demons. Though Eccio tried to correct them that the enemies they fought were not demons, that they were men from a nation named Caliga, the tribe seemed to have a better time believing they were witnessing something divine.

In a way, Eccio didn't blame them. To a human, their energy would seem mystical. Their wings would inspire more thoughts of the supernatural. Any human, tribal or otherwise, would have trouble considering the possibility of another world and what could inhabit that other world.

Meanwhile, Ardent was asked questions by the women of the tribe. The children played on her, climbing up onto her back and pretending to ride her, marveling at her wings as she opened them and closed them for their amusement. The fact that she could speak Masai and carry on conversations without assistance marveled the villagers. Her speech being slow, careful, and at times eloquent led the tribe to quickly accept her.

Warden likewise was peppered with questions. Once they learned she and her fellow Zaheri had lived on Earth for nineteen years, she was asked what she thought of Tanzania. Of the Masai people. Of the animals she had encountered and likely eaten. Did she miss her home? What was it she missed most? Could she describe it?

Sariel aided in explaining a little of what Agerius was like. What their homes were like. How the nation cared for one another. How the mountain range acted as their natural defender and protector. What sort of plants lived there, what sort of crops they could grow.

A brief mention was made of Sariel's husband, to which Amara asked quieter questions that only she heard the answers to.

As discussions were had, Eshe saw to healing the grovix of any injuries they had sustained in their first bout against the Caligans. Warden translated the four grovix's questions or comments. All of them thanked Eshe profusely, which eventually led to one of them making a comment about how grateful they were to have a Healer for Agerius' Defenders.

"You do not have Healers in Agerius?" Eshe asked Warden.

With a shake of her head, the Zaheri grovix answered, "None.

And I am not aware of the last time someone was born with the ability. It was well beyond my time."

"Truthfully, we rarely need a Healer. And when those injuries are sustained that would benefit from a Healer's ability ..." Sariel's attention drifted to the ground. She looked to Eshe with sorrow in her eyes. "Unless the Healer was able to get to them almost immediately, it would not help."

Nodding a little, Eshe hushed, "Injuries from Cregorous."

"Yes. Sometimes his generals can be as brutal, but not as effortlessly."

Eshe squared her shoulders. "I will do all I can to erase such moments in Agerius."

Casting a glance to Sariel, Warden said, "You will not have to leave to Agerius anytime soon, dear child. I'm certain that our High Council will not see you removed from your homes and families until you are ready."

Eccio emerged from the brush with what looked like a cow's leg wrapped in leaves. "I come bearing gifts," he said with a grin. As he handed the leg to Amara, he added, "Another leg should be ready in a moment."

The grovix sniffed at the meat, their snouts twitching and their ears erect. Their eyes trained on the cow leg, they watched it intently as it was passed to Amara.

Seeing the food reminded Eshe of the fact that Ardent had mentioned going for a hunt yesterday. She turned to the dragon. "Were you successful in finding a meal last night?"

Ardent nodded. "Indeed. Thank you for asking."

"Will you eat anything now?"

Gently shaking her head, the dragon responded, "I will be fine as I am. The meat here should be offered to others. I will not feel hunger for another day or two."

That concept fascinated Eshe. The fact that Ardent, for all her size and strength, could go so long without food. While she had heard a handful of tales surrounding dragons, and all of them stating the creatures could live for thousands of years, she'd never imagined there could be some truth to those legends and stories.

As more of the meat came cooked to the Masai perfection, and everyone partook of the meal, Eshe sat quietly and surveyed it all. Basking in the joy and peace that her people held so innately and required no effort. Taking in how they laughed with the Agerians.

Warden's comment about Eshe not needing to move to Agerius anytime soon did comfort her. But Eshe had begun to realize something.

Through all of the highs and lows of the day, she realized that, even when her tribe had run and tried to push the Agerians aside, underneath it all was their desire to embrace the foreigners. The only reason they had pushed them away was for fear of demonic things. But now they sat without worry or fear among a dragon and talking beasts. They shared bread and meat with them.

Though some of the grovix could not understand the villagers, they managed to communicate through smiles and facial expressions. The language barrier was not hindering the blossoming friendship between the two groups. It had Eshe wondering if perhaps, just maybe, it was because both Agerians and her tribe shared similar hearts.

Hearts bound to joy, peace, and prosperity.

Whether it was true or not, it left Eshe smiling. Quite without warning, she was unafraid of what might come from this day.

The last portion of any bar-b-q meal was the serving of liquified fat that had been boiled with tree roots and herbs. The tribe called it medicine. Though Eshe could tell that the Agerians didn't need the drink, they still partook of some, leaving the bulk for the tribe to keep for the next day or two.

Eccio handed the bowl to Papa and offered his thanks.

"For you," Papa said, trying to offer it back to Eccio to finish.

"I do not wish to appear ungrateful, but I would much prefer your people have excess." Eccio gently placed his hand on Papa's shoulder. "We are grateful for your hospitality, my friend."

Taking hold of Eccio's arm, Papa smiled a toothy grin. "It is always open to you and your people."

"Thank you," the Zaheri said before he walked over to the group of Agerians. He adjusted his swords strapped to his belt.

"How are you feeling?" he asked Sariel.

"Quite well," Sariel said as she looked at her domed shield. "It has retained its strength, and I trust it will continue to offer protection for us."

Warden and Vallis walked up to them as the former said, "We are ready to leave when you are."

"We can go now," Eccio answered.

Giving him a concerned look, Sariel said, "You needn't go beyond the shield."

He glanced toward the sun's position and gently shook his head. "It's already a small miracle we haven't suffered any further attacks yet. I would much prefer we be prepared and ready for them outside of the village."

"Very well," Sariel said with a sigh. "Be careful."

Patting Eshe's shoulder, Eccio offered an easy smile. "Always am." He ruffled his hair as he fell into step with the grovix, and they made their way out of the shield's protection.

As they watched them go, Eshe turned to Sariel and asked, "If I were a fighter, would you stay here?"

Sariel gave her a knowing look. "You needn't dwell on that."

It was hard not to think how things could be different, how much better protected all of them might be if they could stay together. But Eshe acknowledged she was a poor person to have in the midst of a battle. She could learn more offensive tactics, but even after today, she could not see herself taking up any sort of violent actions.

She would probably only serve as a distraction or get in someone's way.

Yes, it was better that she remained in the village. She just hoped that her stationary nature would not be a detriment or hinder Sariel.

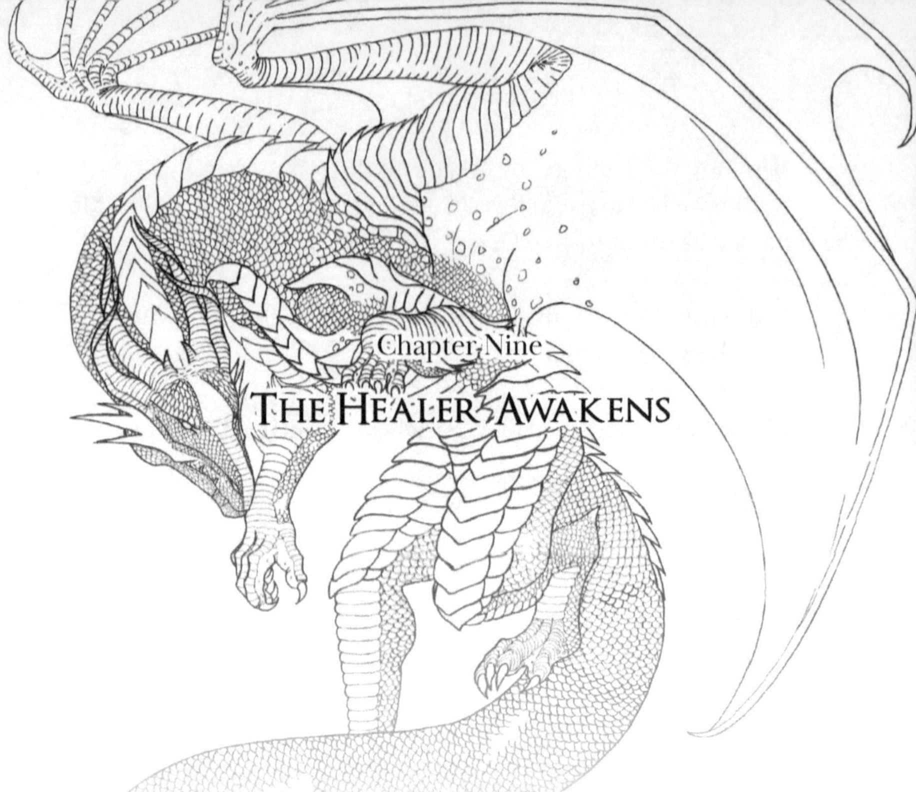

THE HEALER AWAKENS

It felt strange to sit and wait for danger to strike. While raids from Caligans could happen at a moment's notice in Agerius, with no warning, this was wildly different. They knew a strike would come and simply had nothing more to do to prepare than wait for it.

And if another attack didn't come, that just meant that, eventually, Agerian reinforcements would arrive to check on them. Eccio hoped for that outcome but felt that was highly unlikely. If nothing barred the Agerian Defense from getting to the portal, why would they delay in checking on the safety of the Human-Borns?

The Council cared too deeply for the children to let something like this be brushed aside or shrugged off.

You didn't station protectors for nineteen years then just go, "*Ah, well, they're fine*," after they were attacked.

But the waiting was beginning to make Eccio's skin itch.

Warden cast him a glance, her ears flattening against her head as she grumbled, "I have always disliked inaction."

"You and me both," he responded with a scoff.

"It is staunchly against our nature," Vallis offered to her.

He looked to Eccio. "Are you prepared to face Vorex again?"

Nodding a little, Eccio replied, "I think so." He gained a grim look. "I'm concerned; there's no doubt. Fighting a Jumper is ... difficult."

"If only we could understand his habits or patterns," Ardent wished. "That would likely offer you all the support you require."

"I did pick up that he tries to disorient his opponent by throwing them through repeated Paths. I managed to catch him off guard because I stopped myself before I could fall into the next Path he had planned to push me through."

Vallis' ears twitched as he looked to Eccio. "Perhaps therein lies your solution."

His gaze trained on the horizon, Eccio nodded. "You think I should beat him to his first attempt."

"Yes," Vallis said with an assertive nod. "If you strike him first, swiftly, he will not have time to move into any of his actions."

"That's assuming he doesn't jump at me first like he did last time."

"Maybe it would be well if one of us stayed with you," Warden offered.

Eccio winced, rubbing a hand through his hair. "A part of me would wish it, but I think it still stands best to allow you to operate as a pack. I wouldn't want to divide your efforts."

Before anyone could make any other comments, a blast of white hit the air on the horizon, closer than it was before. The portal flickered a few times, as though the connection had not yet solidified, which was odd.

First, the portal was massive, and now it was flickering.

The reality that Cregorous possessed that much power, that much strength ... it made Eccio's stomach twist.

His jaw clenched. He hated that it had come to this. He prayed that they would have more time to prepare the Human-Borns for their task.

Because, at that precise moment, it felt utterly cruel to point at a destructive power like Cregorous and say to children that they had to face it.

A Mask pulled off Eccio's frame, falling into a ready stance next to him.

A skittering hit the air, making the grovix bristle and Ardent letting out a threatening growl. Eccio's muscles tensed, and the hair on his arms stood on end.

He snatched his swords and brought them up in front of him just before Vorex appeared and smashed into him, sending them both hurtling through a Dimensional Path.

Eccio kicked off the Caligan and flipped, landing solidly on the ground, his swords held tight in his grip. His Mask flashed at his side, falling into an identical stance.

Vorex straightened and fixed his jacket. Gone were his flowing robes, replaced instead with an ornate jacket that moved freely but was sleeveless, showcasing the remnants of their last fight. The laceration had mostly healed, but there was a red mark on his arm, a ghost of the injury.

"I have to say, you are impressive," the Caligan said with a sly smile. "Not many non-Jumpers can sense the pulses of someone moving through dimensions."

"Let's just say I learn fast," Eccio said as he charged forward.

"So do I!" Vorex yelled as they collided, trading blows. Sparks of white shot off each impact of Eccio's golden blades and Vorex's energy gauntleted arms. They both moved rapidly, almost in a blurry clash of energies.

Eccio's golden Mask surged off his form, slamming into Vorex and pushing him back.

Gripping the Mask's shoulders, Vorex propelled himself into the air and disappeared into a jump.

Immediately, Eccio turned his back, letting his Mask do likewise against him. Things were horribly still for a moment. Then the skittering feeling surged across Eccio's skin, and he dove forward just before a Dimensional Path opened underneath him. At the same time, Vorex appeared above both him and his Mask.

The Caligan ignored him and slammed an energy-cloaked foot into the Mask, sending it spiraling into the air and disintegrating in the breeze. Then he landed and swept his foot along the ground, the Dimensional Path swirling with the motion.

Better prepared for the stinging pain of losing a Mask, Eccio recalled the dusted fragments and sprang into action. He deftly avoided the moving Dimensional Path while simultaneously trading blows with Vorex.

Abruptly, the Path swung over him like a net and sent him through a vertigo-inducing trip as he flipped upside down then right side up in the span of a second or two. Staggering to get his footing, he barely deflected a punch from Vorex, even as his vision spun and swayed.

He couldn't deflect the second hit, and Vorex managed to snatch one of his swords. A flash of gray charged through the weapon, overpowering the expended gold energy that barely remained in the blade.

Stumbling back from the punch, Eccio blinked a few times to try to get his vision to settle.

Vorex tore at him, swinging his overtaken sword. A laugh was on his lips as he mocked, "Nothing without your little Mask?"

A second Mask surged off Eccio, slashing an energy-bladed sword against Vorex's attempted blow. The overtaken sword flew from Vorex's grasp, and the Mask landed a kick on the general, sending him colliding with the ground. He scurried to his feet and let off a sparking attack that impacted the Mask, taking chunks out of its form.

Eccio leaped over the Mask and unleased a slicing strike of golden energy down on the Caligan. Vorex, however, dove out of the way of the strike, barely escaping the attack as he jumped into the ether.

As Eccio spun to get his bearings, a blast of gray smashed into his Mask, sending it to golden points of light that surged back into Eccio's form. He leaped back in time to avoid Vorex's swift movements, and the two returned to trading blows.

A confident smirk played on Vorex's face as he went to land a punch on Eccio.

It was then that a third Mask tore from Eccio's chest, shoving Vorex back.

Fury radiated from the Caligan's face as he kicked the Mask off and thrust his arms down.

A massive Dimensional Path opened underneath Eccio. One he couldn't dodge. He fell through, landing somewhere back in the midst of the battle. Amid Caligans, and werewolves, and bratak'ra fighting the grovix. The dragons fought overhead.

Warden ripped him aside, and he managed to snatch on to her

barely exposed fur, sliding onto her back for support. Her armor made for a bumpy, uncomfortable ride.

"I lost Vorex!" he hollered as he felt the pain from his broken Masks begin to radiate along his sides.

A growl tumbled from Warden.

Pushing himself up, Eccio said, "I'm heading to the village."

"Go. We will see to things here!"

"Be safe!" he yelled as he called on his wings and hit an upward draft, flying as fast as he could to the village.

The battle raged beyond the golden shield, sounding much fiercer than before. It had been nearly ten minutes since the first dragon had been heard, followed quickly by other sounds of war. And it hadn't let up.

Shaking her head, Eshe hushed, "You should be out there."

"I belong here, protecting you," Sariel said. "They will be fine."

A handful of the men stood with them, holding their spears that they used to chase away lions.

"We can protect Eshe," one of them said.

"No, you cannot," Sariel said with a stern look at them. "Your bravery is admirable, but the foes we face would laugh at your spears."

There was a pulsing sound, and then a flash of gray erupted inside the shield. From the gray mist sauntered Vorex. There were a few scrapes and bumps along his form, and his exquisite attire was rumpled and dirty.

"That's actually accurate," he said with a smooth voice and a smirk to Sariel.

Shoving Eshe behind her, Sariel pulled golden energy into her arms, wrapping gauntlet-like forms up to her biceps.

"This can be painless," the general said with a hard look. "I'm not the one who delights in suffering."

"Because it's dirty?" Sariel quipped.

With a growl, the Caligan muttered, "I'm sick of this." He charged forward in a flash, disappearing midway through his charge. He appeared behind Sariel, a gray energy-cloaked hand reaching for Eshe.

Sariel caught his leg and hurtled him back, slamming him into the ground in the process.

A few of the men shoved Eshe behind them, forming a circle around her.

Flipping to his feet, Vorex immediately dodged an attempt from Sariel. The two fell into what could look like a practiced dance as they parried blows from one another.

Vorex suddenly jumped, throwing Sariel off balance. He appeared behind her and moved to land a blow on her back.

A figure soared toward them and crashed through the shield.

Eccio slammed into Vorex, sending them both hurtling to the ground.

Gripping Vorex's jacket tight in his grasp, Eccio got dragged by the Caligan as he lurched upright. They both disappeared into a pulse of gray then reappeared a moment later, Eccio beneath Vorex. His knuckles were white as he held the fabric fast, refusing to let go.

Vorex began to pummel Eccio in an attempt to get him to release his grip.

Fighting past the Caligan's punches, Eccio shoved his hand against Vorex's face and released a blast of golden energy.

There was a sound of fabric tearing as Vorex ripped himself off Eccio and spun in time to land a harsh kick across Sariel's face. She still managed to land a golden spurt of energy that impacted Vorex's shoulder.

The Caligan disappeared again.

Fumbling to his feet, Eccio snatched Sariel by the waist and shoved them out of the way as Vorex reappeared. The overtaken sword flew through the shield and landed in the general's grasp.

It was all chaos and noise. Blasts and bursts of gold and gray. Frantic movements and attacks on both sides. Punches and kicks. Yells of charged action and grunts of pain.

Such ferocity from Vorex. Such determination from Eccio and Sariel.

Eshe just wanted it to stop.

Her heart thundered in her ears. She didn't know how to help. She didn't know what to do. Helplessly, she watched Eccio and Sariel valiantly fight a foe who could move like the wind.

The men around her gripped their weapons tightly, shuffling their feet as fear gripped them, making their arms and legs tremble.

This wasn't right.

A soft pulse rocketed the air, and Vorex stilled.

At that same instant, Eshe felt something hit her body. A sort of thrum that reverberated from her heart and out to her fingers. There was a whisper in her head. Voices she didn't recognize. Some were pained; others were confused. All felt panic. Almost identical to what Eshe felt.

Then a supernatural calm filled her, and Eshe felt the fullness of what healing could mean. What healing could do.

From the ground, Eccio covered Sariel, trying to catch his breath and figure out what the Caligan could do next.

Vorex whipped his attention over to Eshe. He dropped the sword and grumbled, "Dammit," before he disappeared into a pulse of gray dust.

Staggering to their feet, Sariel and Eccio looked to Eshe.

Violet energy cascaded off her form, flowing around her like she had been clothed in the essence. It billowed and curled from the crown of her head down to her feet. Then it spun up and around her, swirling for a moment as though collecting itself.

Eshe slowly opened her eyes, her normally dark irises shining a vibrant violet.

Without warning, the violet energy pushed out with a gust of wind.

The breeze was enough to just sway over everyone in the village, but it was strong enough that it flew far, far outside of the village, out into the field where the battle raged on.

As if on the air itself, the violet energy swept across the field, gently pushing against everything it touched like a smooth breeze.

Caligans stopped mid-action. Stuttering on their footing, they dropped whatever weapons they had before fleeing. They ran as though they knew no other option, retreating in the direction of the portal.

Back in the village, Eshe let out a heavy breath and staggered, her eyes fluttering closed. One of the men caught her as she held her head.

Sariel and Eccio ran to her.

"Eshe, are you all right?" Sariel asked, gently taking hold of the girl's arm.

"I ..." Eshe started. Her limbs were heavy, and something in her felt strained. "I am very tired."

A small laugh escaped Eccio. "Yeah, I know the feeling." He pushed Sariel closer to Eshe then fumblingly started to walk away. "I'll go check on the others." It took him a few flaps of his wings before he could lift off the ground and fly off.

Searching Eshe's exhausted eyes, Sariel whispered, "Are you truly all right?"

"Yes, I ... believe so," Eshe said through half-lidded eyes. Clarity came to her as she gripped Sariel's arm. "Are you?"

"I am well," Sariel answered with a smile. "All is well."

Relief flooded Eshe, and she hugged Sariel.

Releasing a heavy breath, Sariel held the girl in her arms. Meanwhile, her mind spun in confusion.

What had just happened?

She glanced to the sky. Stars were filling the twilight that fell around them, and silence had replaced the sounds of war.

Cheers erupted from the tribe as they celebrated the victory.

But it all left Sariel wishing she could discern better what Eshe had just done, and why it had made Vorex run from them.

Looking down at Eshe, she pushed her questions back and settled on the grateful knowledge that she was safe.

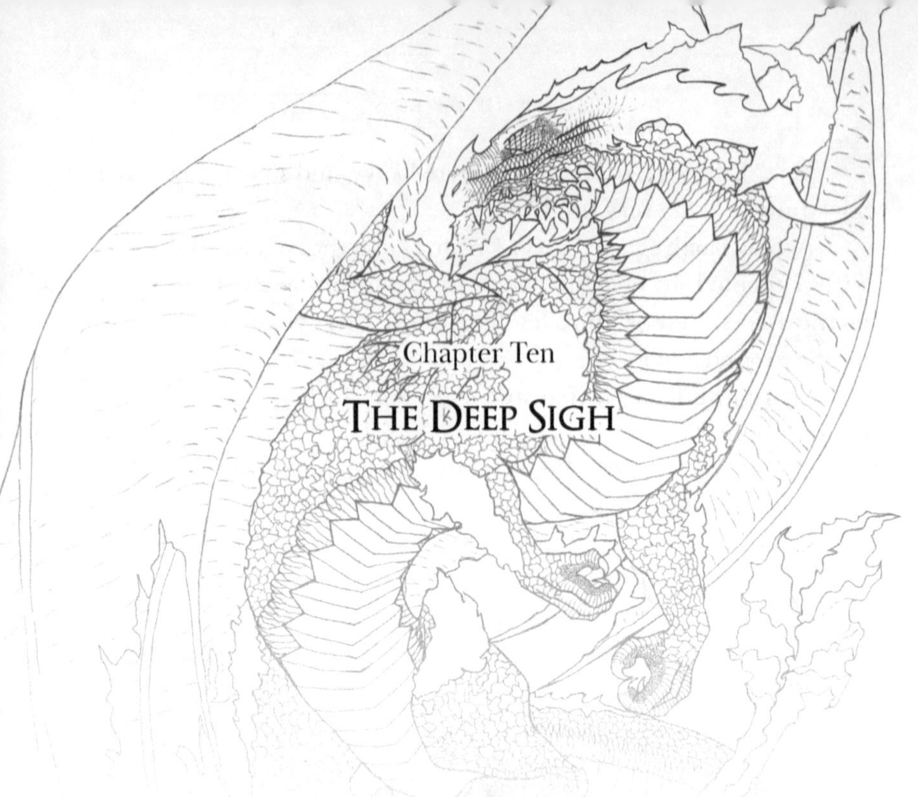

Chapter Ten
THE DEEP SIGH

Eshe's strength returned shortly after Eccio returned with the rest of the Agerian defenders. There were far more injuries from the final confrontation. And though Eshe wanted to heal them, everyone insisted she rest first before she considered helping anyone.

As she rested, the Agerians talked quietly around a small fire while Ardent was out gathering some food for the grovix.

"They just ... ran?" Eccio asked, gently rubbing his forehead. His face was bruised and cut up from the pummeling he'd taken from Vorex.

"It was most strange," Warden said. Her armor had been removed, revealing several cuts and bruises of her own.

Ardent appeared, carrying three dead antelopes. She deposited them, and the grovix began to tear at the fresh meat. The dragon took some for herself this time.

Gently holding a wet cloth to her bruised face, Sariel said, "It's possible that Eshe's wave of energy startled them."

"Enough to make that many Caligans flee?" Eccio asked, rubbing his own wet rag across the back of his neck.

"It was not simply that they ran from the battle," Vallis said around a chunk of meat. He quickly swallowed. "They stopped for a moment, and then they fled."

Sariel and Eccio shared a confused look.

"They left in the end. Should we worry over it?" Ardent asked as she settled. There were a few scales missing along her body, and she walked with a limp.

"Worry? No," Sariel clarified. "But it should be investigated. This is something completely unheard of."

Leaning back a bit, Eccio muttered, "What I would give for Ira or Teneo to be here."

"We will have to consult an Archivist. They would be the only ones with any potential knowledge over what transpired."

Gently shaking his head, Eccio whispered, "It's just so strange. Vorex looked at her and disappeared almost immediately."

"It could have simply been that he didn't know what would happen," Warden offered.

"That is a fair point," Sariel said with a nod. "That much energy surrounding Eshe? It could have just been that he feared a massive attack."

"Okay, that makes sense," Eccio admitted with a small bounce of his head that he immediately regretted, letting out a hiss of pain.

Eshe walked up from behind him and gently laid her hand on his shoulder.

He opened his mouth to tell her not to worry about him, but then he slumped a little, leaning into her touch. "Don't worry too much about me," he mumbled. "The others could use help, too."

With a small smile, Sariel said, "I will be fine."

"As will I," Warden said.

"Me, as well," Ardent added.

Raising his hand, Eccio stuttered out, "For the record, I'm not a wimp. I fought really, really hard."

Little chuckles rumbled from everyone around him.

Sariel patted his arm. "Yes, you did. You should be proud of your efforts." She looked over at the grovix. "I feel indebted to you all. Without you, I'm sure we would have been in danger."

Sitting up, Eccio gently pushed Eshe's hand away, giving her a smile. "Sariel's right. Without you five, I don't know how we would have managed."

"Then it is Council Member Aros who should be thanked," Vallis answered.

"Yes, it is," Sariel said with a small nod of her head. She looked to Eshe and asked, "How are you feeling, dear?"

"Better after my rest," Eshe said as she moved to sit next to her. "Though I wish there was more I could do to help."

Shaking her head, Warden said, "You have done plenty already."

"We are simply grateful that you are safe," Ardent added.

Eshe smiled. "I most certainly am." Casting a glance around at her Zaheri, she asked, "What will happen now?"

"Well, the grovix will return to Agerius," Sariel said. "I will go with them for now."

"You will?" the teenager asked with a look of surprise, a frown coming to her face.

"Only for tonight. I want to ensure that the High Council knows that we are all right, and to thank Council Member Aros for sending the grovix to our aid."

Eccio gave the teen an assured look. "Don't worry; Warden, Ardent, and I are staying right here tonight."

Shuffling her weight a little, Eshe asked with trepidation, "Do you believe they will return?"

"That's not likely. If there was going to be another attack, it would have come by now."

"Eccio is right. Cregorous would not have thrown all of that at us then stopped unless there was something that gave him pause," Sariel affirmed.

Hope welled in Eshe's chest at the prospect of what could have made Cregorous and his generals choose to halt their attacks. Perhaps the other Human-Borns all had managed to scare their opposition away. At least for now.

She quietly mulled over what had happened to her. There was no doubt her Zaheri had likely discussed what they'd seen. She would bring it up, but she had no clue what had happened. And she did not wish to dwell on the confusion of it until she had at least some idea of what she'd done.

A part of her wanted to know what had happened on the battlefield. She knew her energy had gone out into the field but, even in that moment, she didn't know what it had done. Reflecting on what transpired, she knew she'd been motivated by the wish to make the Caligans stop, to make them see what they were doing and how much pain they were causing.

It certainly seemed as though whatever she had done had made their enemy run. As things stood, she was grateful for that outcome, even if she couldn't articulate what she had done or how she had done it. Right now, she wanted to bask in the comforting knowledge that everyone she loved was safe. All was well.

Just as Sariel had promised it would be.

Chapter Eleven

THEY COME BY BUS

In the days following the attack on the village, there was great trepidation throughout the tribe. There was no guarantee there wouldn't be another attack from Caliga. So, every day that passed as if it were any other felt like a false sense of security.

Sariel's visit back to Agerius had awarded her confirmation that all of the Human-Borns had survived, as had all of their Zaheri. The Council then instated a monthly check from each team of Zaheri. It would keep any suspicious activity that happened on Earth within the Council's knowledge.

A week after the attack, things began to return to a much more peaceful and normal routine. The tribe stopped looking to the sky in fear and instead returned to their usual upbeat enthusiasm. The Delta Team became much more frequent visitors, and several of the men begged for training in some of the combat that Eccio knew.

The men who had witnessed Eccio and Sariel's fight with Vorex had been stunned to amazement by the brawl. While it had made them fearful of their attacker, in the aftermath, they yearned to know that level of assured skill and fighting.

Within two weeks, the rumors surrounding the tribe had spiraled out of control, completely without the village's knowledge. The nearby town had witnessed enough of the enemy fighters and their movements toward the village. And with that town being a hub of many of the tribes, and many from the bigger town farther out from Eshe's quiet little tribe, lots of people had now heard of the pillar of light and the monsters that had appeared from it.

It was Papa who made an offhand comment over some free-flowing gongo that Eshe had been targeted and why she had been under attack.

Days later, a woman arrived at the village with her sick daughter. The medicine tree wasn't having any effect, and they could not afford to head into the far away city to possibly see a doctor. She begged to see Eshe, offering up maize in payment for Eshe's time. Eshe would never say no to a pleading parent, payment or otherwise.

By the time the next market day came around, the tribe became flooded with people who had heard of Eshe's healing ability. They all brought payment of some sort, which Eshe handed off to the tribe. Sariel and Eccio acted as gatekeepers, working to ensure that Eshe would not simply say yes to everyone and inadvertently tax herself.

Most of the time, the people who came to her were suffering from minor things—coughs and colds, and minor stomach bugs. She could heal many of those patients without a hint of it draining her energy.

One day, a friend from a neighboring tribe came to them and said a tribal elder from two-days' journey was on his way to see them. To see Eshe.

Papa had raised a fuss, muttering about the village in a jumbled frustration. When the tribal elder arrived, he explained the situation.

Most of his village was sick with an unknown disease. One of their eldest men had traveled a great distance to a doctor and learned that it was something called HIV and AIDS that the tribe was afflicted with. They were a larger tribe, but the illnesses were becoming too much, and their young men were suffering most greatly. It could cripple them and send the whole tribe into extinction unless something could be done to help them. They had many cows, and he was willing to offer many if Eshe could see to the healing of the sick.

The visiting elder stayed the night with them as Eshe discussed it with her Zaheri. It sounded as though close to thirty people would be looking for healing, and Eshe had never healed either disease before. She could not guarantee that it was doable.

After much deliberation, Eshe resolved to be honest with the tribal elder. She told him the truth, that she had never healed HIV or AIDS and didn't know if she could totally heal either of them.

He seemed grateful that she was willing to try. He insisted that even if she could not, he would still bring the agreed upon number of cows (fifteen, the standard number for a good wife).

Almost two weeks later, Eshe's tiny village was filled with visitors.

She'd been terrified as she went to heal the first patient. A young girl who clearly was the sickest among the infected. Within fifteen minutes and careful concentration on Eshe's part, the girl was fully healed.

It took Eshe two days to heal them all, and she found herself physically exhausted afterward.

Her spirits, however, had never been higher. Her actions had brought a completely unknown tribe from the brink of death and raised them to health. She found herself truly grateful for her ability and wished to one day thank the Elders who her Zaheri spoke of for blessing her with this gift.

News spread far and wide of Eshe's healing ability. Soon, prosperity was being showered upon her tiny village. Her people found themselves with the healthiest livestock, because they could afford grain for them. Goats could be purchased for slaughter once a month if they wished. School was available for the first time, if the children wished it.

However, they remained as prudent as possible, looking to save what they could. Because, with every day that passed, her tribe knew that, someday, someone might come to take her away to the destiny that awaited her beyond the village.

They did not fault her for it or try to heap shame upon her for considering embracing her destiny. Her people had come to see her as a blessing, as a divine gift. They knew her gift was much larger than their small tribe could contain, no matter how much they might wish her to stay. Not for her gift—that was a blessing, no doubt—but for who she was. She was part of the tribe, and would be always, no matter where she went.

On the days she was not needed for healing some visitor, Eshe reveled in spending time with her Zaheri. Ardent took her flying, during which Eshe giggled the whole time. Warden had come to sleep with her every night. Even the goats eventually took to snuggling with the large grovix.

Eccio did his best to teach her basic defensive movements, which was the absolute most she was willing to learn regarding combat. All the same, she was grateful for his guidance. Sariel taught her how to make various foods that she had never heard of before. Different types of breads and sweet treats. Different herbs to use for meats.

It was a glorious time for Eshe.

She felt she had truly come into the path that was destined for her and could see no danger upon it. Even with the looming threat of another attack, she held no fear for it. If another attack should come, she had faith that all would be well, just as it had been the last time.

Then, one morning in March, things changed.

The Delta Team was visiting. Eccio was going to aid the men with the cows for the day, and Warden was to accompany them in case of lions. Ardent and Sariel came to help with the fetching of water, as Ardent could carry much more than the poor donkey from the village could.

They had just finished breakfast, and the men were getting themselves ready to leave, when Warden and Ardent both sparked to attention. They had heard the portal activate, and it sent everyone into ready mode.

Ardent took to the sky to get a better look, quickly realizing that only one person had arrived.

She was sent to go see who it was and returned with Lorn from the Gamma Team.

"Lorn, what brings you here?" Sariel asked in surprise.

With a sigh, the redheaded shield-bearer replied, "I'm not bringing good news, unfortunately."

"What is it?" Eccio asked, giving the younger man a questioning stare.

"I don't have much time, so I may wind up leaving you with questions. I'm to collect Ardent, Warden, and Eccio, and they're to return to Tilion with me."

"What?" Sariel asked, her eyes widening in alarm.

"Why?" Ardent demanded, towering above Lorn's smaller frame.

"The Council has decided to disband the Zaheri." He held up his hands to silence what was sure to be outrage. "The First Human-Born decided they want to contest the idea, so they're actively going around and rounding up all of the Human-Borns to be able to appeal to the Council together, in person."

Eccio leaned forward a little and clarified, "Wait. So ... you know all of this, meaning ..."

"The first three Human-Borns have already gathered. They're bound to be behind me by a few minutes, and then they'll have to travel here. Council Member Aros sent the locations for each Human-Born, so they're following that."

A snort of frustration left Warden. "Why would the Council demand such a thing?"

"Tyron said they think we've become emotionally compromised and can no longer objectively train the Human-Borns."

"Tyron was with you? Was Streya still with the Second? Is Zelek?" Sariel asked.

Lorn nodded. "Zelek decided to send us back to see if we can rally citizen, grovix, and dragon support. The Beta Team was recalled at the same time as when Tyron received the information that the Zaheri were to disband." He gave Sariel a sympathetic look. "The Alpha Team has not disbanded."

Sariel's face dropped, a hint of aghast fury in her features. "What?"

"Why doesn't that surprise me?" Eccio muttered.

With a small shrug, Lorn said, "I think they're refusing to go back to Agerius until all of the Human-Borns are together."

Holding a hand out, Eccio pinched his eyes shut as he gathered his thoughts. "Wait. So, why are you here? You said you were going back to Agerius to rally support."

Lorn raised his brow. "I was."

"What happened?" Ardent asked.

"We were intercepted once we got to Tilion. There was a group of Defenders there who were just about to head out to collect the rest of the Zaheri that—" he used air quotes "—'aren't necessary' anymore."

Eccio started to form the question before he deflated. "The Council thinks we're all going to be defiant and not come back because the Alpha Team hasn't."

Sariel sucked in a long, tired breath before slowly releasing it.

As Eccio turned to her to say something, she held her hand up to his face and commanded, "No comments."

Obliging Sariel's fury, Eccio turned back to Lorn. "So, why are you here?"

"Rowan, Dover, and I volunteered to go to the rest of the teams in their stead. It was the only thing we could think to do that might award us some time," Lorn answered. He glanced around and finally recognized all of the villagers staring at him and giggling. "Why are they looking at me?"

"You're very pale," Eccio said simply. He then waved his hand toward Lorn's hair. "And you're a redhead."

Pinching his brow in confusion, Lorn turned his attention to Sariel as she asked, "So. you're supposed to just take the bulk of Eshe's protection with you?"

The younger man's brow dipped, and he pulled his lips in, completely unsure of how to say what was in his head without getting Sariel furious.

A laugh tumbled from Eccio as he pointed at Lorn. "You're thinking what I'm thinking."

"I am not," Lorn defended quickly.

Ignoring Lorn, Eccio turned to Sariel and chuckled. "Unless you want us to be defiant like your husb—"

"No, I do not," Sariel ground out, a glare fixing on her face.

"Okay then."

Warden gave Sariel a befuddled look. "You wish us to simply leave?"

"I don't wish it," Sariel corrected with a frown. "But no good will come from all of the Zaheri brazenly ignoring the Council. Some of them"—she rolled her eyes and angrily shook her head—"some of them being obstinate may not be the end of all things. But if everyone followed their example, only bad things would come of it. We have to be prudent and careful in our choices."

Lorn frowned, a troubled look coming to his face. "I'm sorry to have to bring you this news."

"It's not your fault," Sariel said with a motherly understanding smile. "I appreciate that you've done what you can to keep the rest of us from trouble."

"We should go. Sariel's right. Right now, we have to listen to the Council. We can help the others with rallying support," Eccio said.

A frown residing on her face, Sariel said, "Let's tell Eshe."

The Delta Team pulled the girl aside to inform her of what was going on. Eshe began to ask questions that hurt them all more than they wished. Would she see them again? Was this goodbye? What if something bad happened while they were gone? What if the Council didn't let her see them again? She was assured on every point that things would be fine and all would work out right in the end.

She hugged each of her Zaheri fiercely. Though she had been reassured that this wasn't the last time she would get to see her beloved Agerians, Eshe clutched them all the same. They in turn held her closely, stalling for time because they didn't want to leave her.

Then they had to tell the tribe.

They kept it a little simpler and didn't reveal anything about leaving Eshe for good. It was simply that they had to return to their world, and they weren't sure when they would be back. Urgent business was sending them away.

There were many hugs and clear longings for more time.

And before they knew it, they were gone.

A sullen feeling swept through the village, and the men chose not to take the cows to the grazing field. Instead, they simply fed them grain from the last market. Each of them were scared if they left, they might somehow find Eshe had been stolen away in their absence.

Meanwhile, Eshe's mind swirled in question. She'd retreated to the hut the goats stayed in, cherishing whatever time she was given with her beloved animals.

Three more Human-Borns were on their way to her at that moment. They would arrive within a few hours, at the most.

A mixture of excitement and fear warred within her. She so wanted to meet them and get to know them. Find out what they were like.

Encourage them if she could. Figure out what her place was among them.

The familiar tug hit her heart again. The realization that the time was fast approaching for her to leave her village. It felt wrong to leave now, just as they were gaining such prosperity and wealth thanks to her healing ability. To rip that away from them and return them to the tiny village no one thought twice of; wasn't it cruel for her to abandon them?

But she knew that her destiny laid beyond the village barrier. It was alarmingly apparent that she was not meant to stay in her tribe forever. Soon, others would arrive who would likely ask her to leave with them, and quickly.

She would have to explain to them that she could not leave yet. Another village was traveling to be healed by her, and she could not abandon those weary travelers who had likely already begun their journey.

Though what lay ahead was a little daunting and slightly terrifying, the fact that she wouldn't be alone brought great comfort to Eshe. The other Human-Borns were her age. They could become her foundation through the trials she was bound to face.

All would be well.

There was a commotion and the rumbling of a bus. Eshe scurried to her feet, gently placing the small goat back on the ground before she dashed out of the hut.

The tribe had gone to greet the newcomers, likely hoping for another Healer among them. Eshe had forgotten to tell them that she was the only one with that ability. Hopefully, it wouldn't create an issue with the Human-Borns, or their Zaheri. She didn't see Sariel among them, though.

Quickly going to the cooking hut where Sariel had gone with Amara, she nearly collided with the Zaheri as she stepped outside.

The bubbling excitement sent jitters in Eshe's stomach. "Are you coming?" she asked.

Sariel nodded a few times. "Yes, I'll be along in a moment."

As a few shouts came from near the bus, without thinking, Eshe turned and darted toward the commotion. Obi was shouting something about a demon, and a few of the others were likewise screaming.

There was some shoving and shouting. English words were being thrown around, but Eshe had neglected to learn any English from her Zaheri. She should have, in hindsight. But she hadn't expected them to be taken from her so abruptly.

Everything settled a little, and there was a girl talking in a calmer tone.

Eshe saw Obi jab his spear toward what looked like a werewolf. But the creature made no motions that seemed threatening. In fact, he appeared to be doing all he could to show he was friendly.

"What did you do?" Obi asked accusingly.

Gently nudging past her packed tribe, Eshe called, "Peace, Obi. They are friends."

As she spoke, her tribe parted for her, revealing a small girl around Eshe's height, standing in front of the werewolf. Vibrant grass had sprung up, and Eshe was thrown by it. Grass wasn't uncommon, but what rested beneath her feet was so green and so strong. It wasn't the rainy season. The grass shouldn't have been able to grow like that.

Lifting her gaze to the girl in front of the werewolf, Eshe felt she understood.

Perhaps there was another Healer among them after all. Or, at least someone who brought with them the ability to display peaceful intentions.

A werewolf. The chances of that man being one of the Team Leaders was unlikely, no matter how kind he might be. From what Eshe understood of Agerius, he was likely shunned in their culture.

Which meant that, as Sariel had explained, that man was one of the First Human-Born's Zaheri.

Which meant the girl who defended him was the Raidin, the First.

Offering a smile, Eshe strode forward to the girl with hazel eyes and brown hair that was pulled into a ponytail. The African held her hand out and called on a violet orb as a greeting, hoping that she would somehow be understood, knowing it wasn't likely.

She said it, anyway.

"Welcome, Raidin."

The SHIFTER'S SHADOW

FIFTH IS THE SHIFTER, THO' A DISCORDANT NOTE, THEIR VALUE REVEALED BY TIME.

Prologue

The only reason Lexa liked her birthday was because it was the one day she could ignore her parents and spend quality time with her gram without reprimand.

It was like, for one day, her parents dropped the façade and were honest with everyone. And Lexa was allowed to be just as honest and pretend *they* didn't exist. Unfortunately, her passive-aggressive silence on the day of her birth didn't seem to faze her parents in the slightest.

Whatever. Who needed them?

Hell, Lexa didn't even live with them. The only reason she knew they existed was because her gram insisted they show up from time to time. They'd lavish gifts of monetary value, but never was a single thought put into whether Lexa would like the item in question. And it wasn't that they could just throw any random cheap thing at her. Gram saw everything, and her old but sharp eyes would notice any lesser-valued item.

To Gram, Lexa only got the best. And Lexa knew it.

Which was why Lexa knew she'd get the last laugh.

Gram was leaving everything to her. If she didn't love her grandmother so dearly, she would dream about the look of shock on her parents' faces when they realized they weren't getting any of the family money. But deep down, Lexa knew that, when Gram died, she wouldn't care about the money. She probably wouldn't even care about retribution and the comeuppance of her parents' selfishness.

Whenever the realization dawned on her that her gram would die one day, Lexa pretended like the thought was a balloon she needed to pop then shove the broken pieces aside. She wasn't going to think about that. It hurt too much. And right at that moment, there was nothing but happiness for Lexa.

Her sixteenth birthday. A day spent completely in Sydney; Lexa's favorite place in the world. Gram liked to travel, so she would take Lexa with her almost everywhere she went. There were photos of Lexa sitting in Paris when she was six. She'd toured New Zealand when she was ten. She got to ride a camel in Egypt when she was thirteen. She'd been more places than most people got to travel their entire lifetime. But, for Lexa, she would still say her favorite place was Sydney. She loved the city and all of its bustle, and all of the culture captured within it. Gram, however, did not.

Further proof that Lexa's grandmother truly loved her. She would leave their beachfront, quiet home east of Sydney, all for Lexa, and smile the entire time.

Gram had already taken her out to the fanciest lunch where Lexa had felt like a queen being doted upon. They went shopping at all the best clothing stores (and Gram even let her buy a dress that might've been just a tad too short). Gram listened as Lexa pointed out the architecture of various buildings and what she liked about them, going on to say that she wanted to study architecture at University. They talked about everything.

Lexa was positive she had the coolest grandmother on the planet.

"So, what'll we do now?" the teen asked as she basked in the city life of Sydney. "We've got some time to kill till the show, right?"

The highlight of the night was supposed to be prime seats at the Opera House for their production of *Hamlet*. Lexa and Gram both preferred *Midsummer Night's Dream* of Shakespeare's plays, but she could see the appeal in most of his works.

Lexa took note of which street they were on and realized that her grandmother had been walking purposefully. "Where're we going?" she asked.

Catching Lexa's look, Gram smiled back at her. "I have another present for you."

As she rubbed her hands together, Lexa asked with intrigue, "*Ooo* ... what is it?"

"We're nearly there."

That didn't make a lot of sense. They were in the residential area of Sydney. The high-end residential area. Where all the apartment buildings towered high and were sleek and window-lined.

"Come along," Gram said as she turned into one of the tall, opulent apartment buildings.

Excitement overloaded Lexa's head as she barely contained a squeal. She was almost certain what was about to happen and what her gift was.

Gram waved to a man wearing a suit and tie. He was well-groomed but had a funny sort of shape to his face, Lexa thought.

He came up to them with a smile. "Mrs. Ackart, lovely to see you again."

"I trust you're doing well, James?" Gram asked.

"I am, thank you. And you?"

"It's been a lovely day. We're celebrating my granddaughter's birthday." She gestured to Lexa. "Lexa, this is James, the manager of the building."

He bowed to her, wearing an easy smile. "It's my pleasure to meet you, ma'am."

Doing her best to remember all the polite things she was supposed to do in these situations while feeling all of the euphoria bubble in her body, Lexa nodded. "The pleasure is all mine."

"I trust everything is arranged?" Gram asked in her negotiating tone. It was colder than her usual timbre, and she always held her head higher as though assessing anyone in her line of fire of their worthiness.

"It is. You may head up at your leisure," James answered.

"Thank you, James," Gram said as she walked briskly toward the elevator.

Lexa was too excited to speak. She just smiled and waved at him, following Gram with a jitteriness to her step.

Once at the elevator, Gram entered a code, and then the doors opened. There was only one button in the elevator, and Gram tapped it. Lexa almost fainted.

"There are many apartments I thought might be fitting, but finding the right staff? Now that was a problem." Gram shook her head a little and *tsked.* "It was easier to just buy the building and hire my own people after extensive background checks. No unsightly neighbors, no one accused of any crimes on payroll or as a tenant. That's security, darling. Don't let anyone tell you otherwise."

"Yes, Gram," Lexa said as she nodded so much she thought her head might pop off.

The elevator dinged, and the doors swept open, revealing what Lexa was sure was the most luxurious flat in all of Sydney.

Her mouth fell open as she walked into the flat on autopilot. She drank it all in, convinced if she blinked, it would disappear.

There was a large, opulent sitting room, complete with a fireplace. A grand staircase swept to the second floor on her left. There were a few doors on the wall to her left, but she didn't care what was in there just yet.

She floated through the living room area, basking in the sunlight that came through the floor to ceiling windows directly across from her. More doors on the far-right wall, and a kitchen in the back left corner past the stairs.

"I did promise that if you did well in your exams, you would get your wish," Gram said with a pleased smile.

"Oh, Gram." She smiled with a wide, open mouth as she spun slowly, trying to take it all in. "It's stunning!" She went to the windows and gaped. The city splayed across the landscape. "The view"—she spun back around and grazed her hands across the sofa—"the furniture"—she gestured to the staircase—"you're a legend, Gram!" She flung her arms around her grandmother.

With a laugh, Gram hugged her back. "Happy birthday, Lexa." She pulled back and gently tapped Lexa's nose. "But there's still one more thing to give you."

Letting out a small cough of a laugh, Lexa said, "Gram, I can't even imagine how you could do better."

"This is a selfish gift. Lord knows I won't live here, and though I do trust you to be good, I won't be here to watch over you, so..." She turned toward the kitchen then waved toward herself.

"Gram, what—" Lexa started as she turned to the kitchen.

A woman with long red hair stepped out of the kitchen, wearing a look of assurance that Lexa envied. The red-haired beauty had freckles adorning her face and a fierce look in her eyes.

For half a second, Lexa was going to ask who she was. Then a man stepped around the red-haired woman, and Lexa felt her stomach flop.

He offered a half-smile to her before he came to a stop next to the woman and clasped his hands behind his back. The muscular build of his torso was starkly visible with the tight shirt he wore. His defined jawline and gray eyes. The gently styled hair.

She'd crushed on other boys before but ... *oh my*. This was a man who stood before her, and she felt herself melt a little.

"Oh, Gram, please tell me he's one of my presents," she whispered and felt a blush creep up her neck.

The man and woman shared a quick glance of confusion.

Gram laughed in a chortling sort of way and gently patted Lexa's arm. "Not in that way, dear—you're still far too young for that." She gestured to the man and woman and continued, "This is Ethan Mears and Ashley Carter. They are your new bodyguards."

Lexa cocked an eyebrow, finally looking away from Ethan. "Bodyguards?"

"If you're going to live in the city, I told you that I would want you to have someone keeping an eye on you." Gram waved her hand toward Ethan and Ashley. "And these two come highly recommended."

Darting her gaze around the room, Lexa chewed on the inside of her lip. Well, whatever the reason, this hunk of a treat in front of her was going to be hanging around her, which meant that maybe right now she was deemed too young, but ...

That could change in the next couple years.

And Ashley seemed cool. Like she'd get that Lexa would want her own space and whatever.

Ethan could invade her space anytime.

A thought occurred to her. Would he follow her to school? That would be wonderful. Imagine all the questions and all the rumors, and they'd be so juicy, and Lexa could already think up the many different avenues those rumors could go.

Ashley smiled at her and said, "We just want to keep you safe, not take over your life."

"So ... where will you guys stay?" Lexa asked, unable to stop herself from glancing at Ethan.

"Oh, they'll stay here, dear," Gram said with a gesture around the apartment. "Why else do you think I would have gotten such a large flat?"

"Not all the time, mind you," Ethan said as he held his hand out.

Lexa loved his voice and wondered if she could find a way to record him talking so she could just listen to it whenever she wanted.

He gestured to Ashley. "We get contracted out to the Opera House pretty often."

"That's how I found them," Gram said. "They're some of the best security out there."

Ashley nodded. "We'll be accompanying you tonight."

Doing her best to play it cool, Lexa shrugged and offered a smile to her new bodyguards. "Yeah, okay."

Gram clapped her hands. "Splendid! Oh, I am pleased to see you hit it off with them. I was so glad to have found them. You wouldn't believe the trouble I had finding reputable people ..."

As Gram continued to drone on about how hard it had been for her to keep this all a secret from Lexa, the teenager in question let herself simply smile at her grandmother with all the love she could feel brimming in her heart.

Her life was about to become better than she could have ever imagined.

Chapter One

BRATTY AND THE BEAST

"I could've taken it," Lexa snapped as she stepped into the opulent flat. She pulled off her leather jacket as she walked, whipping it around to convey her annoyance. Asher followed closely behind. "It was just some stupid Caligan dag."

"Surrounded by *other* Caligans and a few bratak'ra!" Asher retorted. Flailing her hand toward the teen, she added, "This is why I've been so against you coming to investigate any alarms! You don't listen!"

An indignant noise left Lexa. "I listen!"

Asher deflated and gave the teen a bored look. "What did I say before you ran off?"

"I dunno. Something boring about bratak'ra horns or something."

The Zaheri's face scrunched in frustration as she clenched her fists in front of her, as though doing that would keep her from strangling Lexa. Her freckled face started to turn red, nearly matching the color of her thick, braided hair. "You don't even hear yourself when you talk, do you!"

"Teneo was droning on! What else was I supposed to do? He's boring!"

"Listen!" Asher scream-begged. "That's what you were supposed to do!"

Rolling her eyes and letting out a scoff, Lexa crossed her arms over her chest and popped her hip.

"We were trying to figure out *why* they were here! We haven't seen that many Caligans in years, and now we have no clue what they were doing because you just ran off!"

Lexa gave her a condescending look. "Uh, fair bet they were here 'cause of me. That's your whole issue, right?" She turned and sauntered into the kitchen. "I can take care of myself, Ash."

Marching after the teen, Asher slammed the refrigerator door shut as Lexa opened it, causing the younger girl to veer back to avoid being hit. "No, you can't. Not if something bad happens. We're trying to keep that from being the case, but you keep making it increasingly more difficult."

Forcing the refrigerator door open, Lexa rolled her eyes. "What could possibly happen?" She snatched a water bottle out of the pristine fridge then closed the door. "Nothing ever happens. And tonight was the only time anything ever *has* happened, and you didn't let me *do* anything!"

Asher's face went red again as she gestured wildly at the teen. "That's because you didn't listen! We could have neutralized the whole situation if you'd just stopped!" She took a deep breath, collecting herself.

Magically, Lexa didn't say anything in the small pocket of silence.

"Don't you remember anything we've told you about who could come for you?"

Swallowing a mouthful of water, Lexa pulled the bottle away in a lackadaisical manner. "Yes, yes, I know. Some big baddie named Cregorous might come on a rampage. I get it. This is *super* serious."

"It is," Asher bit out through gritted teeth. "And every time you run off, we can't protect you if you're attacked."

Lexa scoffed. "What? By the big bad monsters? Please, they can't touch me. Remember? I can do this—"

She disappeared into orange dust, a pulse entering the place where she had been standing.

Asher closed her eyes and let out a beleaguered sigh.

From the little balcony on the second floor that overlooked the living area, Lexa hollered, "I'm the best Jumper there's ever been! They've never seen anything like me!"

Glancing toward the ceiling, Asher walked out into the sitting room to see Lexa's form retreating from the balcony, walking toward her room. A door slammed a few seconds later.

The Team Leader flopped onto one of the couches and let out a long, steady breath.

It was times like these when Asher wondered what in the Elders' names had happened to have it all go so sideways with Lexa. The teenager had been so good at first. She'd listened to what they'd said and hadn't constantly pushed her boundaries. She'd always let one of them go with her wherever she went, just as her grandmother had required. She'd even allowed Teneo to help her with her studies from time to time.

Oh, well, maybe that was it.

If Asher thought about it, maybe the problem was Lexa thinking she truly was untouchable. Because it seemed like perhaps the origin point of all the teenager's unruly behavior started when she was told who she was, what she was, and what she could do.

Maybe they shouldn't have told her what her ability was. Would that have kept the girl from learning how to jump into other dimensions? Or would she have discovered it all on her own, anyway?

Regardless of what could have been, the problem was here and now. And as much as Asher wanted to go check on the guys, she had to stay with Lexa.

That girl could be her own demise if they weren't careful.

There was a *ding* followed by the clear sound of the elevator doors sliding open with a thrum.

Asher rose to her feet and asked, "Everything go okay?"

Drogar looked wholly furious. It seemed to be his state of being, though, as if he was angry with the world for existing. Despite all the time they'd been together as a team, he seldom smirked. And in the few times he had managed to smile a little, it had been at some terrible joke Ethran had made. Drogar was undoubtedly the most unhappy person Asher had ever met.

Contrasted against Drogar's default exhausted expression, Ethran literally seemed like a rainbow of smiles and happiness. Finger guns, wide grins, and tripping over flat surfaces were Ethran's default. The younger man was prone to elbowing Drogar, wearing a cheeky grin as he tried to goad the older warrior into admitting whatever asinine thing he'd said was funny.

Between the three of them, Teneo was unabashedly the odd one out. More round in all of his features—including his girth—he was quick to remind anyone that he belonged in the Archives, not on a battlefield. His knowledge was invaluable, and Asher was quite grateful for it. He was levelheaded and cool, able to assess situations quickly and determine the best course of action at the drop of a needle.

Ethran threw her a confident smile as he said, "Situation's under control."

"Really?" Asher asked with a doubtful look.

He was covered in dirt. Leaves stuck to his shirt and had caught in his gently styled hair. Against the disheveled look, his gray eyes were as bright and lively as ever.

Glancing down at his appearance, he gestured to himself. "Oh, no, this wasn't 'cause of Caligans. I just fell down."

"As per usual, you inspire much confidence," Asher said, fighting a smile.

With a roll of his eyes, Drogar stepped into the living area and made for their surveillance tech, placing his worn sniper rifle on the appropriate rack as he went. "All Caligans accounted for and neutralized."

"And no one saw you?"

Teneo shook his head. "No, we remained undetected." He cast Ethran a wary glance. "Well, mostly."

Glancing around to his fellow team members' unamused looks, Ethran held a finger up to silence their lectures. "Hey, for the record, I only fell down after I took out the bulk of the Caligans."

Drogar crossed his arms and gave Ethran a pointed look. "Yes, that is true."

"And hey, I told you I'm off balance without my axe."

"It's truly baffling," Teneo said, giving Ethran a look of wonder.

"What is?" Ethran asked.

Waving his hand at the warrior, Teneo answered, "You! So sure-footed in battle but ... utterly undone by flat surfaces."

Ethran pursed his lips and teetered his weight between his feet. "That doesn't feel like a compliment."

"It isn't," Drogar said.

Asher pushed the subject of Ethran's clumsiness aside and turned to Drogar. "Did you get any idea at all what they were doing here?"

With a shrug, the elder hybrid answered, "It wasn't gonna happen, Ash. We might've had a chance to snatch some conversation if Lexa hadn't—"

"I know what she did. Please let's not mention it."

Drogar held his hands up defensively but rolled his eyes a little.

"What do you think, Ten?" Asher asked as she looked to the Archivist.

For a few long seconds, Teneo stared absentmindedly at the middle distance. Then he let out a sigh before meeting Asher's gaze. "It screams we should be cautious."

Squinting at the rotund man, Ethran asked, "Why?"

"It's been years since we've seen that many Caligans. It must mean something. Whether small or large, we should be on guard."

Asher rubbed her hands together as she frowned. "That's what I was thinking, too."

"Hey," Ethran said as he walked over to her. "C'mon; we'll be fine."

She managed to only smirk at him as she asked, "You and your two left feet?"

"For your information, they're both right."

The Team Leader let out a small chuckle as Drogar groaned and slumped a bit in annoyance.

Whirling toward Drogar, Ethran said, "Hey, that was funny!"

"No, that was *terrible*," Drogar griped. Ignoring Ethran's attempt at humor, he turned his attention to Asher. "Were you able to get through Lexa's dense skull how dangerous her actions were tonight?"

Asher deflated. "I'm pretty sure she thinks she's untouchable."

Scrunching his face in annoyance, Teneo muttered, "That girl is going to be her greatest foe, I just know it."

Ethran scrubbed a hand through his hair, a few leaves coming loose in the process. "Maybe one of us should talk to her?"

Drogar wore an unenthused look as he relented, "You're the only one left to try to reason with her."

"You are her favorite. Maybe that'll work to our advantage," Teneo offered reluctantly.

Slumping a little, Ethran wrinkled his face and let out a noise of discomfort.

The click of a door came from upstairs, followed by Lexa's purposeful footsteps. "So, you guys got to have all the fun without me, huh?" Lexa grumbled as she gracefully hopped down the steps.

"Yes. Fun. That's exactly what we had," Drogar snarked.

"And what? Did you lose to the ground again?" she asked with a playful smirk to Ethran.

"Again, I'm off balance without my axe," Ethran defended. He gestured toward Asher. "C'mon, Ash; help me out."

Ignoring Ethran, Asher looked at the Australian teen. "Lexa, we need to talk."

"Oh my *God*," Lexa groaned, throwing her head back in exasperation. She started to stalk toward the kitchen. "You aren't my gram; you don't get to tell me what to do!"

"Only, we do," Drogar said.

Stopping in her tracks, the teen spun to face Drogar. "You don't get an opinion, D."

"And you don't get to talk back if you can't address people by their full name!"

Ethran stepped between Lexa and Drogar, holding his hands out to them. "Okay, all right, yeah, let's just ... y'know... breathe."

Lexa swatted Ethran's outstretched hand. "Really? You're gonna try to stop me? Did ya forget I can jump?"

"We're trying to keep you safe, Lexa," Asher said with a stern look at the girl.

"From what?" Lexa flailed her arms about as she spoke. "They can't hurt me if they can't catch me."

"That's arrogance talking," Teneo said in his higher pitched voice.

"No, that's reality, T." She crossed her arms over her chest and gave him a condescending look. "You're just jealous that you aren't a Jumper."

Teneo's face pinched in annoyance. "Of all the things I wish I could do, jumping isn't one of them."

Letting out a scoff, Lexa rolled her eyes. "Yeah, sure, you keep telling yourself that."

"Lexa, please, just listen to us," Asher begged. "What you did tonight could've gotten you hurt."

"If it could, then why didn't I get hurt tonight?" Lex asked pointedly, giving Asher a belittling stare. "If me springing into action and taking out a Caligan is *so* dangerous, then why didn't it get me killed tonight, huh?"

Behind her, Ethran held his hands out and gestured to himself, opening his mouth to reply.

Asher pointed to Ethran and snapped, "Because Ethran took out the dual-horned that was closing in"—she gestured to Drogar—"and Drogar took out the other Caligan that was literally right behind you! Didn't you hear the gunshot and notice the body that just sort of collapsed behind you?"

Wearing a cheeky grin, Lexa snarked, "So, what you're saying is you and Teneo suck."

Asher's face contorted in fury, and she sucked in an angry breath.

Ethran quickly placed a hand on Lexa's shoulder and said, "No, what she's saying is you're lucky we were paying attention."

Turning to Ethran, Lexa lost all of the hard edges of her stance. Her expression softened, and she looked him in the eye.

"You really could've been hurt tonight. It's 'cause Drogar's fast and I listened to Ash that you weren't." He gestured toward Asher. "Ash is right, Lex; you gotta listen to us. To *her*."

Lexa looked away from Ethran for a few seconds, chewing on her lip and shuffling her weight a bit. When she looked back at him, she asked, "So, you're saying I should just ignore my instincts?"

He looked to Asher, trying to get some feel for what she wanted him to do.

Wearing a look of exasperation, Asher gestured to the teen as if to say, "*Go with it; she's talking to you.*"

Searching for what to say, he shrugged awkwardly and choked out a few words before landing on, "I'm saying ... your instincts might be good, but you haven't experienced enough to act on them yet. Not when it comes to battle situations. Maybe after another tag along or two, you'll realize the right way to act on those instincts. 'Cause tonight wasn't it."

The teen deflated and begrudgingly crossed her arms over her chest, practically pouting. "Fine."

Ethran raised his brow and looked at the rest of the team. Drogar stared at Lexa with a look of absolute exhaustion mixed with utter annoyance. Teneo was shaking his head slightly, staring at the ceiling as if he was commenting on Lexa's reaction in his head. And Asher, well, she was frowning, and Ethran hated it.

"Okay ... so ... anything else you wanna say?" he asked.

Lexa met his gaze and smiled. "'Night," she said simply, in an upbeat manner, as she patted him on the cheek then pranced up the stairs.

"That ... that wasn't what I ..." Ethran slapped a hand over his face.

Drogar narrowed his eyes as he looked at the younger warrior. "Were you seriously trying to get her to say *I'm sorry?*"

"It was worth a shot, right?"

"Are you new?" Asher asked with a small chuckle.

"Good, laughter. I like seeing that on you," Ethran said with a wide smile, his whole body lifting.

Teneo let out a sigh and moved toward the surveillance room. "I'll take the first watch tonight."

"Thanks, Ten," Drogar said as he started toward his bedroom.

As they walked off to their respective areas, Asher headed into the kitchen and made for the stove, snatching the kettle off the burner. She glanced over her shoulder and saw Ethran follow her, as if he were a puppy that needed to follow its owner everywhere it went.

"I'm fine, Ethran," she said as she went about filling the kettle.

He leaned against the counter. "She'll warm up to you eventually."

"I doubt that."

"Why?"

"I'm not a handsome man," she said without thinking and almost immediately bit her lip and glared at herself. She was grateful she'd already returned to the stove and was facing away from him.

A smile eclipsed his features as he looked at her. "You think I'm handsome?"

Plastering on a placid expression, she looked over her shoulder at him again. "I implied that *Lexa* found you handsome."

"Well, that's stupid and not at all what I was hoping for."

Asher slumped with a sigh, thrumming her fingers against the counter. Her gaze drilled into the kettle. If she just ignored it, he'd drop it.

Sure. Right.

'Cause Ethran was so prone to letting this go.

He came to stand next to her, staring at her imploringly, still wearing that goofy grin as he said, "C'mon, Ash; one date. That's all I'm asking for."

"And how many times would this make?" she asked, raising her brow and shaking her head.

"Uh ..." He glanced toward the ceiling before finally looking back at her. "I dunno. A lot?"

"Ethran, we've talked about this."

"Yeah, and I still disagree."

If she didn't like him so much, she'd smack him.

"Now isn't the time. I've told you this." She turned toward him, wearing a pitiful attempt at a glare.

"I can ... what's the word ..." he grumbled as he searched the middle distance for assistance. Snapping his attention back to her, he smiled victoriously and continued, "Compartmentalize! I can do that!"

"We have a job to do, Ethran," Asher ground out, pinching her eyes shut. The kettle started to thrum as the water boiled. "And Lexa keeps making it more and more difficult. We can't let ourselves get caught up in—"

"We!" he said in exuberance, pointing at her with both index fingers.

"—any—what?"

"We! You said we! That means—"

Smacking his hands down, she gave him as stern a look as she could muster. "Ethran, enough!"

The smile fell from his face, slowly replaced with a look of worry.

Asher slowly drew in a breath, unable to break eye contact with him. In a small voice, she said, "I can't compartmentalize. I won't."

He darted his gaze between hers and the counter as his brow pinched in concentration. "What if I said—"

"Don't say it."

"But—"

"Maybe ... later ..."

Releasing a laden sigh, Ethran conceded, "Fine. But I'm gonna hold you to it."

She didn't trust herself to respond with anything but a resigned look.

"I'm not giving up."

Oh Elders, she wished he would. Because every time she had to tell him no, it hurt her more than before to see his disappointed expression.

Gently patting his arm, she whispered, "You should go clean up."

The kettle whistled, giving her an excuse to step away from him and concentrate on something else. She could still feel his gaze on her, studying her movements.

With a small nod, he said, "Yeah, probably a good idea." As he started to step away, he added, "Hey, make me a cup, too?"

Nodding at the kettle, Asher said, "Sure."

Once his footsteps retreated, she relaxed a little and let herself frown.

It wasn't like she wanted to turn Ethran down. It wasn't like she reveled in seeing him ask over and over again. It wasn't like she pined for someone else. She knew how it went. She knew why he asked.

But blast it all, this wasn't the right time.

Looking over her shoulder and finding the kitchen empty, she wondered why he hadn't just said something back in Agerius. If he did have a Heseda—the experience men got when they found their wife—why not say something then? Or was it something weird where he hadn't experienced Heseda until after they'd arrived on Earth?

But he'd started asking in their second year of the assignment. Did it really take that long for men to know?

As she went about fixing their tea, she found herself wondering if it was this hard for everyone else, too. Even if they were still on Tilion, still in Agerius, would it take him just as long to say something?

She wished she could talk to someone about it.

Shaking her head, she steeled herself. All of this would have to wait. Until Lexa was less chaotic and more mature, it just had to wait. It was the right thing to do.

At least, that's the mantra she kept telling herself.

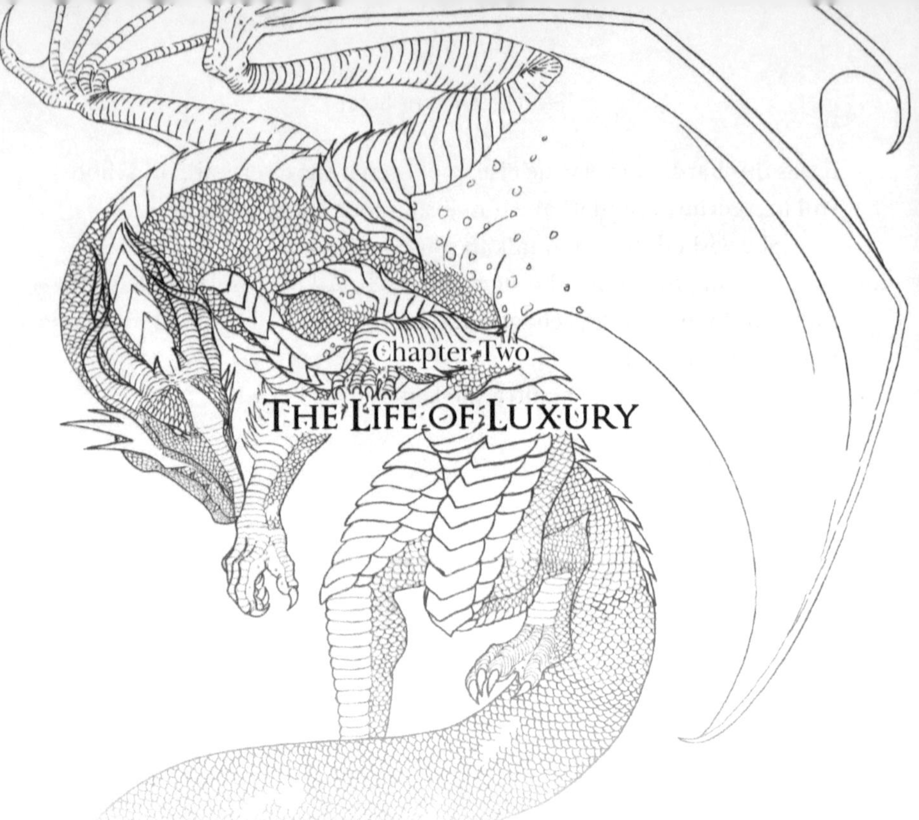

Chapter Two

The Life of Luxury

As long as she could remember, Lexa had a picture-perfect memory. It was why she loved architecture. A quick jaunt around a building, and she could remember with absolute clarity the layout and structure of the place. She'd always assumed it was proof she should be an architect.

But now she was almost positive it was something all Jumpers had.

Lexa liked being a Jumper. The ability to effortlessly shift from one dimension to another, almost magically appearing somewhere else practically instantaneously was something she had started using as soon as she knew she could.

And sometimes the walk to the train so she could head to the University took too long, and she preferred to enjoy her coffee rather than run out the door with it. All she had to do was appear in the less populated areas behind various buildings of the campus. Or in the less-frequented bathrooms.

Okay, so, yeah, she had gotten herself into some trouble a few times. Maybe several times. Maybe a dozen. Who knew? She wasn't keeping track. It wasn't like she immediately could master jumping. None of her Zaheri knew how to really train her.

Teneo had certainly tried. She would say that he had tried far harder than she liked. His lectures were just *so dull.* And that was all his "training" was—just him yammering on for what felt like an eternity about this or that. Over and over again, she was told that he knew exactly what he was talking about.

"Short of having a Jumper at your disposal, you should be thankful," Drogar would say in that grumbling, annoyed way he laced everything in. Like that somehow should encourage her. Like anything he'd say would ever be helpful to her.

Well, no shit, of course she'd prefer to have an actual Jumper help train her. She'd have to be an absolute idiot to say she wanted to figure it out on her own. It wasn't like walking or swimming.

She had to know where she wanted to go, how to get there, and carefully navigate to ensure she didn't pop inside someone or something. That was where her picture-perfect memory came into play. Knowing the exact layout of the room she was aiming for was practically required for jumping through dimensions. She'd been damn lucky the first time she'd accidentally clipped something, and it'd only been the edge of her jacket that materialized inside a wall. It'd been an honest mistake, just stepping out of the dimension a tad too soon and her jacket fluttering open a little too much, and *bam,* the bottom zippered portion of her jacket was stuck in the wall. Luck was on her side.

Even so, she'd been right furious. She'd loved that jacket.

And, on top of losing it, she'd had to spend the whole day walking around in a torn jacket. She. Had to walk around. With people seeing her. In a torn jacket.

It still sent a furious grumbling in her stomach at the reminder.

And yes, she had accidentally wound up jumping into a few stores ... and banks ... and the morgue that one time—totally not on purpose. She'd only been practicing. It wasn't like she'd *meant* to land in those locations. And even if she *had* meant to (which she most definitely did), it wasn't that big of a deal. Jumping right back out made the problem go away. In reality, it was a poof-now-it's-gone situation.

But her Zaheri always yelled. Every single time.

And she would roll her eyes.

Who would ever catch her? And if they did, it wasn't like they could actually restrain her. Nothing could hold her back.

It was something she reveled in. The first time Drogar had chained her to a desk, trying to force her to stay in one place, she'd been thrilled to find that jumping took her out of the restraints. Her freedom was hers, dammit. They weren't going to take that from her.

They kept forgetting she had basically been alone since she was sixteen. No one told her what to do. It'd been two years of her doing whatever she wanted whenever she wanted. Even with her Zaheri lying—which they always swore wasn't a lie, but that just totally meant it was and they were embarrassed about it—and pretending to be her "bodyguards," they'd always done what *she* wanted to do.

She wanted to go shopping, okay, fine, one of them went with her. She'd been young then. Gram had insisted she be protected. She didn't want to make Gram upset. So, she'd listened. She'd let her bodyguards go along with her, and she'd basically ignored them the whole time. Well, she ignored most of them.

She didn't ignore Ethran.

Then they'd gone and told her about who she was and what she could do. Were they dense? Of course she didn't need their protection anymore! She was a *Jumper*. She could phase through dimensions and go wherever she wanted. It wasn't like she had to worry about anyone hurting her anymore. Someone could raise a hand to try to hurt her and *poof*, she'd just ghost 'em. Literally.

So, of course she went wherever she wanted and did whatever she wanted. That was fricking logical. It wasn't her fault that her Zaheri were all braindead morons.

Well, she mostly did whatever she wanted whenever she wanted. Except when Gram showed up. Then it was a different story. She wasn't allowed to misbehave when Gram was around.

A large part of her did love the old bat. If it weren't for her, Lexa probably never would have existed. Lexa didn't know if her Zaheri knew that her parents had planned—actually fought—to abort her. She never brought it up. If she were honest with herself, she'd admit that the fact her parents never wanted her practically snapped her heart in half.

But she'd never be honest with herself.

Crying was for weak people. She wasn't weak. She'd never be weak.

She'd jumped to the train station near the University and waited in the Fifth Dimension. Just long enough to ensure no one would be around, and then she could move about her business.

It had felt really funny at first, standing in the Fifth Dimension and watching what happened on the Third. Like a ghost just silently observing things, watching vague outlines of people going about their day, completely unaware of her presence. She'd even recently learned how to practically autopilot to her routine jumping spots, like her brain had memorized the route, so it didn't even have to take an active running through the Fifth Dimension anymore. She just literally appeared where she wanted to go.

She didn't question it. All of it amounted to saved time, effort, and hassle.

If only all of life could be that easy.

Once the train platform was clear, she popped out of the Fifth Dimension with a small pulse of noise and a swirl of orange dust. She looked to the security camera and gave it a wink. At first, she'd been super worried that someone would say something, but now that it'd been a year of her doing this, she wondered if they even checked these stupid things.

And if they did, maybe they thought she was a ghost.

That actually was a really funny thought. She'd totally have to dress up as a corpse sometime and lumber around, scaring the shit out of random people. That would be hilarious.

As she made her way to the University, she took a long deep breath, a smile coming to her face as she admired the buildings she'd loved since the moment she'd seen them. Sydney was still her favorite place on Earth, and she was so grateful that Gram had let her live there the last two years.

The only downside to it had been the real goal of Gram's gift.

In order for Lexa to be allowed to stay in Sydney (under her bodyguard's watchful care), Lexa had to spend a month of her summers in Point Piper. That was where Gram lived, which was fine.

The reason Lexa hated Point Piper was because she wasn't allowed to stay with Gram the whole time. She had to spend time with Sheila and Rob. Maybe other people would have called them "Mom and Dad," but

Lexa figured they didn't deserve to be called that. And she definitely didn't want to ascribe any blood ties to either of those selfish pigs.

It sparked anger in Lexa's chest every time summer rolled around. Sheila and Rob didn't want her around, so why did she fricking have to spend time with them? They'd wanted to *abort her*, for Christ's sake. If she could figure out how to voice her anger about it to her gram, maybe then it wouldn't become such a deal.

But Lexa didn't acknowledge her hurt, or anger, or pain. Whenever any of those emotions surfaced surrounding Sheila and Rob, she just pushed it away. They didn't deserve any of her brain power or emotions. They didn't deserve to know what a fricking delight Lexa was. They didn't want her? Fine.

She didn't want them either.

But Gram was all dead set on forcing the three of them to spend time together. And the whole time she'd be with Sheila and Rob, Lexa thought about Sydney and her Zaheri. She thought about how great it would be if she could convince Ethran to come to Point Piper and go swimming at the beach so she could see him shirtless because ... damn. He was a snack, and she wanted to see him shirtless so badly.

Instead, she always got stuck with these adolescent boys who just fawned all over her. Duh. Of course they did. She was hot. Of course they stared. Of course they ogled. Of course they bought her things and tried to win her affections. Of course she played with them and made out with them. It was summer.

If she had to be somewhere she hated, she oughta at least have *some* fun.

The only reason Lexa had started enjoying it was because, one time, when she was thirteen, she'd left with a diamond necklace some boy had given her. Last summer, she'd been given a car. Point Piper was flowing with cash, but not much by way of brains. At least with the boys.

They certainly were worthwhile trips. She had mastered the art of using them then losing them.

But she wasn't in Point Piper; she was in Sydney, her favorite place in the world. Heading toward a campus that practically bowed when she walked down the halls. No more thinking about those asshats called Sheila and Rob.

Despite the fact that, five times a week, she walked up to the campus, she always found herself soaking in the rich architecture of the University. Its main wing was so regal that it made her want to burst with happiness. To think what it must have been like to be part of that team, designing that beautiful building. The trellises and peaks, choosing the right stones for each layer, telling the carpenters what type of wood to use for the detailed doors and entrances. Sometimes she liked to walk the campus when it was quiet, just to marvel at the masterpiece.

It was one of the reasons she loved Sydney. There was so much unique architecture that she could learn about. The Opera House, naturally, was one of the most recognizable landmarks of the city, despite it being located near the coast. Beyond that, almost every street held some fascinating building that stuck out.

One day, she would design palaces and mansions. She'd be the architecture genius behind a monument or a skyscraper. People would learn about her designs and try to mimic them, learn something from her special attention to the minutia of a project. She'd be wealthy not from her gram's money but from her own renowned name.

And one day, the whole world would know that she was a literal superpower not to mess with. That she could match someone not only in brains but in brawn. That she could pull raw energy out of the air and bend it to her will. She could fricking teleport.

They'd sing barmy songs about her. She'd be remembered for centuries. They'd probably even make statues and erect masterpiece buildings in her name. She'd be immortal. And not just because she was part dragon.

Her cocky arrogance oozed off her and could be seen to an outsider as confidence. She certainly saw it that way.

Marching into the building, her high-heeled boots clicking along the marble floor, she went straight for the architecture lab, ready to conquer her next assignment.

Halfway there, she was stopped as someone called, "Lex!"

She turned to see her friend, Anastasia, running toward her. The girl was convinced her name came from the old Romanoff story of "Princess Anastasia," and Lexa liked her enough to let her believe that. She dyed her hair, which Lexa found tacky, but whatever. She wanted to be a redhead, so be a redhead, you beautiful bitch. She was a dominator of the school, and people always seemed to follow her. Which made Lexa that much more powerful, because Anastasia followed her everywhere.

Looping her arm with Lexa's, Anastasia said, "I heard Damian invited you out to his yacht on Friday. What happened?"

A sly smile came to Lexa's face, and she said, "It's a small yacht."

"I hear he's heartbroken you won't see him again."

"I think we're above grade school gossip."

"Never," Anastasia said with a laugh. "What happened to you last night? I thought you were gonna join us at One22."

Dismissively raising her brow, Lexa answered, "Yeah, something came up."

Letting out a whining noise, Anastasia said, "You were with the hot guy again, weren't you? C'mon, Lex; you gotta spill. What's the deets?"

The rumors had been flying lately about Lexa and her "bodyguard" Ethan. She didn't dispel any of them, because they were just too good.

Ethran had met her after class about a month back and escorted her back to the flat. There'd been some alarm or something, and Asher wanted someone to guard her while they checked it out or whatever. But that's when everyone found out Lexa had bodyguards. And that's when Anastasia began pestering for details. She hadn't seen Ethran but had heard from some of her other friends that he was gorgeous.

Lexa chose to keep Anastasia in the dark to what Ethran looked like, because she wanted to watch Anastasia's reaction upon seeing him. She wanted to see the redhead give her an envying look. She wanted to see Anastasia wishing she had Lexa's life.

She even pretended to get text messages from Ethran and smile at her phone, just to make Anastasia think there was something going on between them. Because Anastasia was the gossip of campus, and she'd done a great job spreading the juicy rumors about Lexa and "Ethan."

And some of those rumors were filthy that Lexa loved hearing.

Gaining a coy smile, Lexa said, "He *is* a hot guy."

"You have got to bring him to One22 tonight." Anastasia gave her a pleading look. "C'mon, Lex; I've been dying to see this guy for myself."

Oh, that could work.

Lexa had never managed to get Ethran to go to One22. The only time he'd gone, the whole team had shown up looking for her. And she hadn't been wearing anything super sexy, so it wasn't even like she'd been able to really turn up the heat and get Ethran's attention.

But if she ran off tonight, Ash would totally send Ethran. She'd played her cards right, she knew it. After last night, they all knew she listened to him and only him. If anyone else went to collect her, she'd make a scene. And they didn't like scenes. So, Ash would send Ethran.

Which meant that all Lexa had to do was pick the right dress. Maybe even convince Ethran to have a drink or two to loosen him up. Because maybe that was all it'd take for him to realize that Lexa wasn't a little girl anymore. That she hadn't been since they'd met.

Mulling it over, Lexa asked, "What time tonight?"

"I don't have classes until tomorrow afternoon. I'll probably go over there around ten."

Lexa pursed her lips and pretended to stall.

Gently pulling on her arm, Anastasia begged, "C'mon, Lex, please? All the hot guys will show up if they know you're coming."

She pretended to not love that all the other girls struggled to get the guys' attentions. Even if anyone Anastasia called hot now would look like trash heaps once she saw Ethran.

"Fine. I guess I'll come."

"And you'll bring the bodyguard?" Anastasia asked with a knowing look.

Giving her a smile, Lexa answered, "I'll see what I can do." She glanced at her watch. "I gotta go to class. I'll catch you after."

"Okay, I'll meet you on the greens by Newtown." They waved to one another and parted ways.

This would be a night to remember. She could feel it in her bones. The anticipation was nearly palpable.

Working to brush off the jittery excitement she felt, she dropped her small bag onto the stool next to her drafting board and began to set up for her lecture.

Maybe if Teneo lectured like her professors, she would actually learn a thing or two from him.

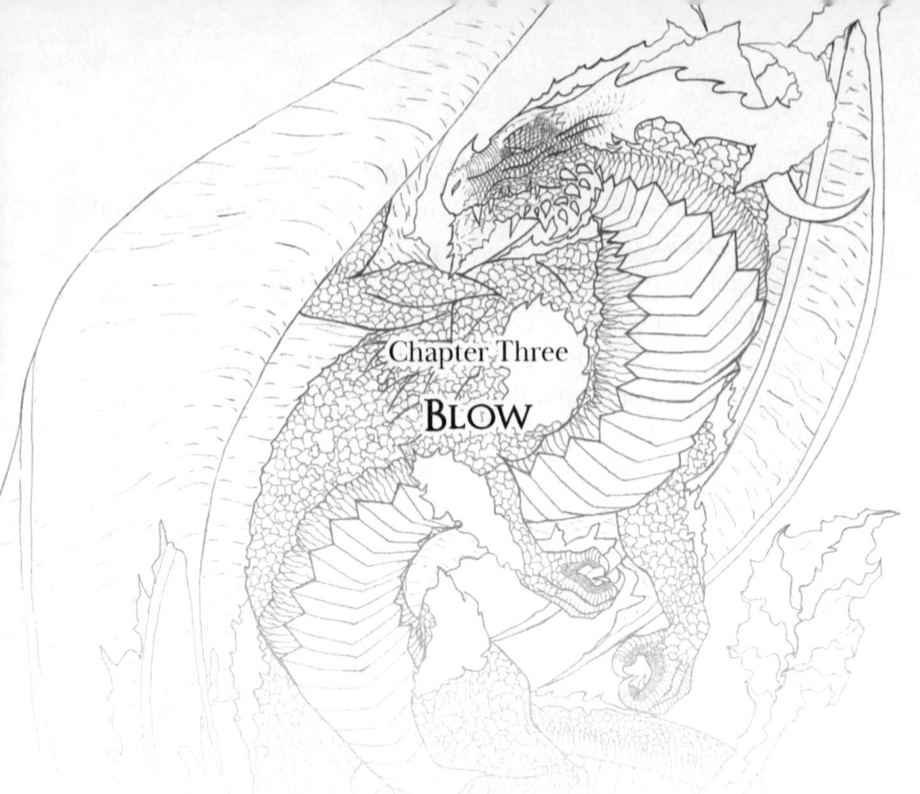

Chapter Three

BLOW

"And you're sure you checked everywhere?" Drogar asked as Ethran came down the stairs of the apartment.

Holding up his hands with an exasperated expression, Ethran responded, "It's not like the flat is that big. What am I supposed to do? Check under the bed?"

"I wouldn't put it past her to be that obnoxious."

The elevator let out a *ding* as the doors slid open. Asher and Teneo stepped into the flat as the former said, "She's not at the University."

"Nor was she at any of the late-night coffee shops," Teneo added.

"That only leaves one place," Ethran said. All eyes turned to him. "One22. She probably went there."

A round of groans circulated the group.

"Great. Who gets to go?" Teneo asked with mock enthusiasm.

Crossing her arms over her chest, Asher reluctantly looked to Ethran. Slowly, the other two men swept their attention to him, as well.

"Aw, c'mon, guys. Really?" Ethran whined.

"Let's face it. Teneo's right; you're her favorite. She listens to you," Asher said with a frown. "I would bet anything if any of us went"—she swept her hand out to indicate herself, Drogar, and Teneo—"she'd throw a huge fit and cause some kind of ruckus. We don't need that kind of attention, especially at One22."

"Remember what happened the last time we all went to collect her?" Teneo asked.

Ethran scrubbed a hand through his hair and lumbered down the remaining steps, as if throwing a temper tantrum. "Fine. But if I can't hear later, it's not 'cause I'm not listening. It's 'cause I'll be deaf."

"Wait," Drogar started with a labored sigh. "I'll go, too."

"You will?"

"You will?" Asher asked with narrowed eyes.

Holding up his hands, the elder hybrid continued, "I'll head over a little bit after you. Give you time to convince her to leave. If she doesn't, I'll come in and drag her out of there myself."

"That's ... actually a good idea," Teneo said.

"Why *actually*?" Drogar asked with a small glare.

Ethran squinted at the elder hybrid. "Do you think I can't drag her out of One22 or something?"

"I don't trust you to not fall down."

Asher laughed a little, and Ethran deflated.

"He has a point. The flatter the surface, the more likely you are to trip," Teneo said.

Fixing a determined look on his face, Ethran marched to the wall. He angrily smacked the little pressure release to reveal a hidden compartment holding his golden energy glowing battle axe. Snatching the weapon, he expertly worked to fold the appropriate portions of the handle so he could better conceal the axe. "I'm taking my axe, and I'll prove to you guys that I'm not gonna trip over a single thing tonight."

Drogar smiled at the young warrior. "I'll take that bet."

With a bit more effort than it should have, Asher worked to quell her giggles and gave Ethran an understanding look. "Just don't let anyone see it, okay?"

He flashed her a dashing smile and nodded. "You got it. Stealth, that's my name." As he started with purposeful steps toward the elevator, he slightly skidded and was quick to scream, "I didn't trip! That doesn't count!"

Once he was gone, Teneo gently shook his head and whispered, "Truly baffling."

Ethran hated One22. He didn't need to go inside to know the music was too loud and the people too chaotic and drunk. The smell of alcohol radiated off most patrons, and the noise—well, music, he guessed—thumped and thrummed against the walls when you passed by. If there were words to those songs, he couldn't hear them above the throbbing bass.

He glanced at his watch and rolled his eyes at the fact that it was nearly ten thirty and there were this many people out. On a Tuesday night. The week had only started; what did these people have to escape so quickly come the beginning of a week?

Tapping his small Bluetooth headset, he said, "Just got here."

"Yeah, I kind of figured," Asher said. "The music's always so loud."

He nodded and raised his brow. "Good, it's not just me."

Asher scoffed. "Drogar said he's surprised Lexa can hear anything after going there." She let out a small sigh. "He's leaving now. You've got five minutes or so to get her out of there before he shows up."

Parking his motorcycle, he pushed the urge to grab his battle axe aside. He had to leave it behind.

Whether there was validity to his insistence on his axe helping with his balance or not, he couldn't say. There certainly seemed to be some correlation between his lack of falling down and whether or not he was holding his weapon. Maybe he thought too much, or not enough, or something.

When he had to fight, even during spars, he didn't have to think through things to the tiniest detail. He let his instincts guide his actions. So, maybe that was the key—he just had to stop thinking.

He let his hand skim across the concealed weapon, feeling the energy thrum against his fingers as he touched the blade. Drogar had griped about it, but Ethran was grateful for the elder hybrid's assistance in modifying the motorcycle's frame to allow for a compartment where his axe could fit. It had required a modification to the handle and shaft so that it could fold, but it was still definitely the same weapon Ethran had made as a young Defender all those years ago.

Bern, his go-to swordsmith in Agerius, had been all sorts of grumbly about the concept of making the long, sturdy shaft fold into a neat fashion against the flat blade. Rightfully so, Ethran guessed. If he'd had his way, nothing would've ever changed about his well-loved axe. But he really didn't love using pistols and rifles all the time. There was just something about actively holding a weapon that held a storehouse of his own energy that he couldn't let go of.

Getting off the bike, he checked to make sure his pistol was fully concealed. Didn't want anyone screaming and freaking out about the weapon if they caught sight of it.

"I'll call if we need backup," he said as he neared the door.

There wasn't an absurdly long line, so maybe that meant it wasn't as crowded as it usually was on the weekends.

The bouncer looked at him, and Ethran nodded toward the door. "Any chance I can get in?"

Glancing at the line, and then back at Ethran, the bouncer said, "You aren't the only guy tryin' to score tonight. Back o' the line."

"I'm here to pick someone up."

He was met with a doubtful look.

"Listen, I don't like it here. My head hurts from how loud the music is. I'm just here to get someone and leave."

For a few seconds, the bouncer gave him a placid stare. Ethran was about to start begging when the burly man rolled his eyes and stepped aside. "You got five minutes to get out, y'hear?"

"Yessir," Ethran said with a mock salute.

Even though he tried to prepare himself for the noise, he still winced when he stepped over the threshold.

Oh good. He wasn't even near the dance floor yet and already his ears hurt.

The club wasn't wall to wall filled, but it was pretty close. There certainly wasn't a ton of room for him to navigate the crowd.

He spied Lexa on the dance floor as he descended the stairs and started toward her.

It'd only been a few seconds that he'd been in the building and already too many gazes roved over him. He tried not to make eye contact.

Something about places like this always made him feel like he was an animal on display, that the onlookers didn't see a man as much as a piece of meat. The hungry looks in people's eyes made him uneasy, so he did his best to quickly move through the room. He heard more than a handful of comments as he tried to focus on anything but the pounding noise.

The bass hit his chest with each pulsing ring. He could swear he felt his eardrums breaking. He'd only been in the building a minute, and his head was already starting to throb. And there was a smoky substance hanging in the air that smelled sweet but made his nose wrinkle. Every now and then, a strobing light flew across the dance floor and made him avert his gaze for fear of hurting his eyes.

At this point, he didn't care if Lexa wanted to stay. He wasn't sure if he'd be able to withstand much beyond a few minutes before his head exploded.

The dance floor was crowded, and he had to push his way through. More than once, a rogue hand pulled across his shoulders or his chest as a voice would try to ring him toward them. He found avoiding eye contact helped lessen the blow. Or, at the least, it helped him feel a little better about denying any of these people their base pleasures.

It was moments like these when he wondered just how animalistic humans really were.

"Lexa!" he screamed above the noise when he was close enough to be heard.

She spun to look at him and smiled. Her dress was too short, and the neckline was too low. He started at the sight of her. He'd never seen something quite so ... revealing before.

It unnerved him that she didn't seem bothered at all about wearing something like that. Didn't she realize how small it was? Didn't she see how much of her body was on display?

Too many eyes were on her. Too many were hungry.

"Ethan! Come dance with me!" she squealed and took his hand.

He squinted and shook his head. "I don't think I'd last more than a minute here. It's way too loud."

There was another girl there, around Lexa's age, who stared at him, her mouth hanging open and her eyes drinking him in. Something about the way she looked at him made him feel uncomfortable.

Lexa pointed to her and said, "Ethan, this is Anastasia. She's—"

"One of your classmates, I know." He nodded an introduction to the redhead.

"God, Lex, you never said he was a damn model!" Anastasia screamed with a wide smile.

"I'm not," he said with a shake of his head.

The redhead smiled deviously. "You totes could be."

Ethran turned away from the girl whose eyes were already undressing him and making him feel all the more anxious to leave. The music was boring into his brain, and he felt the pressure mounting on his temples. "Lexa, we really shouldn't stay here."

She pouted. "But you just got here! Come on; one dance. It'll be fun!" She tried to pull him to her. His feet stayed planted.

"Lexa ..." He tried to convey how inappropriate it would be for him to dance with her with the stern look he gave her. Especially in this setting, in this manner.

He could feel the hormones in the immediate area vibrating off of everyone around them as they practically ground themselves into one another.

It had never occurred to him that Lexa might be attracted to him. And it hadn't even remotely occurred to him that this might've been some ploy or game until just that moment.

But ... Lexa wasn't like that. She wouldn't try to rope him into something like this, right?

"Don't be such a prude, Ethan," Anastasia coyly said as she playfully smacked his arm. "Just dance with the girl! I promise I won't mind."

He opened his mouth to remind Anastasia that her feelings weren't even remotely on his radar when he saw a flash of a uniform out of the corner of his eye.

In the crowd, he could have sworn he'd seen ...

Lexa pulled on his arm, but he didn't move. He did, however, grip her hand and start pulling her toward him. He didn't see how giddy she looked; his focus was on the crowd. There was something amiss.

The gray uniform caught his eye again, and he swept his gaze across the building. Another uniform. And another.

His hand came to Lexa's waist, and he started to pull her behind him when he saw Avemod's face flash in the crowd as a strobe light passed overhead.

Not here.

Crap.

He'd never thought about it happening here. So quiet. So underwhelming.

Too crowded. Too many people. How should he do this carefully?

There wasn't a good way. He'd blow their cover. He had to, or people would die.

"Get down!" he screamed and quickly threw his hands up as gold energy surged from around his waist, across his chest, and down his arms.

A shield appeared above the crowd just in time as a gray blast tore at them. The collision against his shield sparked white in a flash and ricocheted off into one of the speakers. The music continued to play, but screeching filled the air from the speaker.

Screams erupted around them, and Ethran pulled the shield down as it splintered into several pieces and flew to meet opposing attacks. He had four to worry about, plus Avemod. He called for his battle axe, grateful he'd chosen to bring it.

He pushed Anastasia and Lexa behind him as people fled. Moving with assured swiftness, he pulled his pistol out to quickly take out the Caligan on his left.

Anastasia screamed and turned to run, only to trip in her heels and fall.

As the Caligan behind them ran for her, Ethran had two of his shield shards surge at it, slicing into its body and tearing at its limbs before it fell to the floor with a *thud.*

He dropped the pistol, and it hovered at his side, the gun handle cloaked in his gold energy. That was when his battle axe crashed through the wall, flying into his waiting grasp.

With an upswing, he met Avemod's gray-cloaked arm. The gold energy in the blade met its opposition and pushed back, sending the general staggering backward. Despite the momentary advantage, Ethran only had a few seconds to gauge the situation as Avemod lunged toward him again.

Not willing to let another rebuttal happen, Ethran swung his battle axe across his body. Gold energy surged from the blade like a slice of light, crashing into the general and the remaining two Caligans.

The force of the attack sent Avemod crashing through the rear wall. Timber clattered, and a small plume of dust came from the hole the general had left behind.

One22 was still loud, with an abandoned track bleeding into the next wave of sound. Screams sounded behind them. There was likely a bottleneck at the door. Everything led to one staircase and one entrance that way. The rear exit hopefully wasn't where anyone ducked to, given that was where the bulk of the fighting came from.

Quickly scanning the room, Ethran ensured there were no other attackers then turned to the girls.

Lexa was helping Anastasia to her feet, the redhead holding her half-ruined shoes in a loose grip.

He holstered the pistol that floated nearby, its grip still coated in golden energy, and kept a tight hold on his battle axe. "We have to leave. Now," he said to Lexa.

Anastasia sputtered some whimpering sort of noise as she hobbled to her feet, tears starting to form in her eyes. Lexa couldn't seem to grasp her friend well enough to actually help, her dress restricting her movements.

Effortlessly scooping Anastasia's stumbling weight upright, Ethran started to drag her toward the door.

Within a moment, they made their way onto the street. People ran everywhere, quickly vacating the immediate area. So that was good, at least. Hopefully, the commotion would keep people away.

Quickly tapping his headset, Ethran waited with a growing tension in his stomach.

The call connected, and Asher's panicked voice practically screamed, "What's going on?"

"We need backup down here," Ethran shot out, his gaze continuing to scan the area.

A curse fell from Asher as she muttered, "Elders, I was worried you'd say that."

"Ash, Avemod is here—"

"You know that douche?" Lexa snapped with a glare as Anastasia continued to whine out noises of confusion.

"—I took out the few Caligans with him, but something tells me he's not alone."

"He isn't alone. The portal's open. Drogar should be there any minute. I'm leaving now," Asher said.

"Wait, no, Lex has to go back to the flat."

"What? Why?"

"She"—he glanced at the teen then lowered his voice—"let's just say, she's not dressed for battle."

"Something tells me the stuttering redhead isn't your precious Human-Born," a smooth, light voice said.

Ethran spun around and shoved the girls behind him as a figure sauntered from the side of the building.

Lexa gripped his hand and scowled at the man methodically approaching them.

"Ethran?" Asher asked in a panicked voice.

"Don't worry about me," he hushed in a determined voice.

Avemod was a handsome man with softer features. A coy smirk was on his face, and his eyes held a playful glint. His hair was light blond and mid-length, falling in gentle cascades around his face. Of all the generals, he was fairly easy to pick out at first glance. His garb was made up of leather with metal accents.

Ethran wanted to count their blessing that they weren't up against someone like Akeno or Caedex. But at the same time, he knew that Avemod wasn't someone to be taken lightly. Those who were foolish enough to do so regretted it.

Keeping his gaze fixed on the Caligan, Ethran said, "Lexa, get Anastasia out of here."

"I'm not leaving you," Lexa shot back to him.

"Oh, that's adorable," Avemod said with a pouting smirk. "The brave little princess wants to stand by her Defender."

"Lexa, you have to get out of here. Get changed and get the others. You can't fight in that outfit," Ethran said, refusing to look away from their enemy.

"Don't change on my account, dear." Avemod's gaze roved over Lexa's body, drinking in every curve she had on display. "The dress is rather fitting. Don't you think, Agerian?"

Ethran simply glared.

Avemod shrugged. "Think she's too young for you? Too bad. The young ones are always the most delicious." A sharp look filled his gaze, and his voice dropped. "I've always loved making little virgins beg for it." In a flash, the Caligan surged forward at alarming speed.

Lexa almost yelled, if it wasn't for Ethran's quick reflexes.

A clashing *clang* hit the air as Avemod's gray-cloaked fist impacted Ethran's axe. With ease, Ethran shoved the general back, awarding them some space.

"Lexa, leave," Ethran snapped as he pushed her back.

Lexa scowled at Avemod before looking to Ethran. "I'll be right back."

Swinging his axe with practiced dexterity, Ethran fell into a readied stance. His axe blade flared golden light. "Counting on it."

"*Ooo*," Avemod said as though he were getting ready to savor something. "This could be fun."

The teenager disappeared in a pulse of orange dust, taking Anastasia's completely dazed form with her. Though it looked as though it was now a standoff between Ethran and Avemod, the Agerian knew better. He could hear the thundering footsteps and charging paws of bratak'ra and werewolves. Any second, he'd be overwhelmed.

It was a good thing Ethran didn't get overwhelmed.

Avemod charged forward, gray energy filling his hands like flames.

Simple dodges were all Ethran had to do to avoid getting hit. Swipes of his hands to deflect Avemod's furiously quick blows. All meant—he assumed—to throw him off guard.

Ethran hadn't spent all those years sparring hand-to-hand melee fighters and deflecting gunshots from snipers for nothing. He'd learned how to anticipate actions and make his opponent stumble.

Because stumbling was all he needed to get Avemod to do. Stall long enough until his backup arrived.

So, when Avemod changed up his tactics and moved to land a kick instead of a punch, Ethran swiftly landed a kick off the general's chest, propelling himself into the air enough that he could release the grip on his axe and instead snatch his pistol. Because a bratak'ra lunged over Avemod's skittering form, its large paws spread out with the intent to smother Ethran.

The beast's maw was wide open, as expected. Ethran fired a shot down its gullet, dropped the golden energy glowing pistol, spun in the air, and snatched his awaiting axe. Swinging up, he deftly deflected a strike from an approaching Caligan. Then another blow from Avemod.

It was a fast-paced dance with a sure-footed dexterity that Ethran couldn't have anywhere but in the thick of battle. He dodged and deflected, striking down as though he saw every intended movement from each approaching foe.

Avemod was tough, no doubt. The Caligan general was swift, agile, and cunning. He wore a sly smirk, even when he got hit or was sent skittering backward. There was a sort of captivation in his eyes as he watched Ethran, and that threw the Agerian off more than anything.

With his fluid ingenuity, Ethran dispatched a fair number of Caligans, creating a near ring around himself of slumped bodies. Bratak'ra and werewolves among them.

Just as a Caligan managed to catch a small opening in Ethran's movements, it got shot by a bright blue bullet.

Spinning in the direction the bullet had come from, Ethran saw Drogar on top of a truck, his sniper rifle in hand. Shots rang out, hitting their intended targets with Drogar's expert accuracy.

"Don't take your eyes off your opponent," Avemod crooned, leaping over a fallen Caligan and landing a blow against Ethran's face.

Though Ethran stumbled back a few paces, he recovered swiftly and fell into a back and forth against the Caligan general. Ethran's battle axe spun and swayed, moving into and out of his grasp with all the practiced skill he'd acquired.

Avemod nearly landed an attack on Ethran's chest when a golden shield appeared across Ethran's body. Fury etched onto Avemod's face, and he unleashed a stream of gray against the shield, shoving it into Ethran and sending him sliding back until he hit a nearby car.

In a blink and you'd miss it moment, Asher appeared in front of Ethran, her thin, nimble wings quickly folding into her back as she landed and threw up a shield that deflected another attack from Avemod.

Wearing a grin, Ethran said, "Thanks, Ash."

She threw him a knowing smile over her shoulder.

Avemod straightened and eyed Asher. "Well, well, what have we here?"

Ethran's jaw tightened, and he glared at the Caligan general.

"I always knew there was beauty in Agerius, but my, you're a spectacle."

Wrinkling her nose in disgust, Asher shifted closer to Ethran.

Languidly surveying Asher, the Caligan general slyly said, "I may have to do something about you."

"You'll have to go through me," Ethran said darkly, wearing a furious glare.

Avemod didn't move. Just shifted his gaze to Ethran. The corners of his lips turned up in a smirk.

"Let's take out the trash," Asher said quietly.

"With pleasure," Ethran growled.

Slightly lifting his head to look down on them, Avemod hushed, "Well, that could change things."

Ethran and Asher ran forward, expertly moving together as they parried attacks from Avemod and took out other opposition as they went. Golden shields flew about them, appearing in flashes and sparks. Drogar continued to provide cover from his roost on the truck roof.

A pulse of noise sounded, and a dash of orange dust popped near Avemod. Lexa appeared midair, looking as though she intended to land a kick on the general.

Though Avemod wore a small look of surprise, he recovered quickly enough to snatch Lexa's ankle and hurl her at Ethran's approaching form.

With a yelp, Lexa collided with Ethran. Her Zaheri had collected himself in an instant, catching her with ease.

"Oh, little girl, you just love to play, don't you?" Avemod's silky voice cooed. He drank in her exposed skin from the low-cut top she'd chosen and the fact that it barely covered her abdomen. At least her pants were an appropriate length, and she was wearing practical shoes. "You looking for someone experienced?"

"She isn't looking for anything!" Ethran snapped.

Letting out a scoff, Avemod smirked. "Sure she isn't."

"That's enough," Ethran growled, pushing Lexa aside as he charged forward. He began hurtling attacks at Avemod, striking with a ferocity that had the Caligan forcing a step back and losing ground with each hit. "No one is here for your amusement!" He landed a kick that sent Avemod soaring, hitting the ground with a *thud*.

A group of fighters filled the empty space where Avemod had been.

Without a second's hesitation, Ethran swung his battle axe along the ground then flicked it up forcefully. A large blast of gold shot from the blade, growing in size the instant it left the blade. Like a large, curved attack that mirrored the curvature of the axe blade, it slammed into the approaching fighters and nullified the threat instantly.

Avemod got to his feet and continued to watch Ethran's movements as he slowly ambled the way he'd come. "Well then..." he mused, gaining a dark look in his eyes as he fell into the shadows between the buildings.

A Ferveos landed with an explosion that was buffered by a golden shield. Asher landed a second later and marched to Ethran's side.

"You okay?" he asked the Team Leader.

"Yeah, I think we're all okay, but we've still got lots of them in the city heading this way," Asher said, whipping her gaze around to assess the situation.

Lexa wiped her hands on her pants and let out a disgruntled noise. "That douche thought he was so cool. What? Does he know Jumpers or something?"

"Lexa, now isn't the time to discuss that," Asher started, throwing the girl a disappointed look. "But we're going to talk about your choice of clothes."

Rolling her eyes, Lexa sneered, "Oh, c'mon, Ash. Don't be such a prude. I'm allowed to wear this."

Before Ethran could snap at her, Asher caught his arm and whispered, "Later, Ethran, we gotta keep our heads, right?"

"Right. You're right," he hushed back.

Teneo ran up to them, Drogar at his side.

"Excellent job with the shields, Ten," Asher complimented.

Drogar looked down the street where more fighters were still coming. "Looks like we've still got a fair number of them." He shook his head and grumbled, "I hate that we're dealing with this in the city. There's so much potential for damage."

Whipping his head to Teneo, Ethran said, "Unless we could somehow get all of them above the buildings."

For a few seconds, no one said anything as they all looked to Teneo, whose eyes were distant as he muttered out rambling thoughts.

Lexa scoffed. "What? You think Teneo can actually do something like that? He's weak."

"Teneo isn't weak, Lexa," Ethran scolded softly.

"I'll make a shelf," Teneo said, his gaze still locked away from any of them.

"A shelf?" Drogar asked, darting his attention from the squat man nearby and the enemy fighters growing closer.

"I'll make three or four large shields. Large enough to encompass the street, and propel them up into the air, along with any Caligans." His gaze was still stuck in the middle distance, as though running calculations or something. Even so, he pointed toward Ethran and Asher. "You two can stand on them, and I'll track your movements. Once you pass one of the panels, I'll have it fall down to the ground and move to the next section."

"We'll have to move fast," Asher said with a stern look to Ethran.

Nodding quickly, Ethran answered, "Got it."

"What about me?" Lexa asked incredulously. "You didn't even let me fight just now—"

"You'll keep an eye on things and move Drogar when necessary," Asher said.

Though he glared a little, Drogar said, "Makes sense. Teneo's gonna need cover, but you'll need me up there, too, for any fighters you can't get rid of."

Lexa shrugged in an exaggerated fashion, "But what're we gonna do? We can't just kill 'em all and then let 'em fall to the ground, right?"

"I don't have time to discuss the particulars; we need to do this now," Teneo said. Without warning, a flash of gold filled the street beneath their feet. Then, like an elevator, everyone save Teneo started to rise with the golden shield. Lexa clutched Ethran's arm, and Ethran grabbed Asher to help keep her upright as they rose.

Once the shield partition settled, they all turned to face the next rising partition, filled with stumbling, stuttering Caligans that clearly weren't expecting to rise fifty feet into the air.

"Okay then ... this is different," Ethran muttered as he swung his axe into a better grip.

PLANET HELL

Teneo ran down the street and did his best to keep pace with the group fighting in the air above him. In all truthfulness, he'd gotten the idea of how to do this from Earth's video games. Not that he played them, but he'd seen videos of what they were like.

He used his shields to set up a window of sorts that he could monitor with clear indications for where each partition ended. With each footfall of his comrades, he could sense the vibrations against his shield. Their energy was different than the Caligans, so it was easy to differentiate friend from foe. If he just tracked that, he could sense when they reached the end of one partition and moved on to the next.

Then he just made a net underneath each partition that would move forward as they went. It could catch the falling bodies as he moved the finished partition to the next section of road they had to cover.

He'd always hated Drogar and Ethran's running games, and how they'd forced him to join them. Even now, he had to pant and gulp in breaths as he ran along. Ethran and Drogar were both taller than him, and both had much longer legs. For every one long stride either of them took, Teneo felt he had to take two. It wasn't quite that drastic, but in times like these, it certainly felt that bad.

A pulse of noise startled him, and he leaped aside as Drogar appeared with Lexa. Barely missing a beat, Drogar found his footing and ran at Teneo's side, his rifle up and firing within seconds of his arrival.

Lexa, however, stumbled and screamed, "Hey! Wait up!" before she frantically ran after them.

Drogar had to get higher.

Teneo threw his hand toward the ground, and a golden ramp appeared nearby.

"Don't expend yourself!" Drogar reminded him as he leaped onto the ramp. And like a crazy trust exercise, he kept running, despite there being no guarantee that Teneo could keep up with making sure footing remained underneath Drogar's feet.

They might've been crummy teammates sometimes, but there was one thing Teneo knew without a doubt: they trusted him and knew what he was capable of. Lexa, for all her faults, hadn't seen him in action. She only knew him as the teacher of the group. Perhaps this whole mess would actually help her have some respect for him.

At least it was easy to see where their opposition was. With the golden shield beneath their feet, Asher could see everything with clarity, despite the late hour.

In the handful of times she'd been able to fight with Ethran at her side, she'd liked it. There was a fluidity to his movements she could play off of with ease. Barely any thought went into her actions when he was her partner in battle. And here in this chaotic fight in the sky, she found his powerful energy at her side a supreme comfort.

Every action was swift and decisive. Every blow was as strong as she could muster. Ethran was the stronger of the two of them, without a doubt, but she knew she wasn't someone to laugh at either. Despite that knowledge, she still relied on her assault rifle. There was no telling how long this incursion was going to last, and they had a fair number of fighters to deal with as it was.

She cloaked her wings in her energy, letting them be a shield and a weapon whenever possible. That made it so, with every movement, she could inflict damage on whatever might be nearby. And since they had to deal with werewolves, she could quickly blanket herself in a shield for protection if necessary.

When an enemy fighter got too close, she used the bone spikes in her elbows as a quick way to dispatch her opponent. After all these years, she'd learned exactly what angle to swiftly raise her arm and swipe down to catch a Caligan in the neck and rip at their skin in a fairly painless death.

Truthfully, she hated those times. They were too close in those moments. Blood could splatter. She could see faces.

There would be nightmares.

Steeling herself against the reality of her crimes in that moment, she knew these were things that had to be done. If they sat back and did nothing, Lexa would die. Innocent humans would die. The Caligans were leaving them no choice. This wasn't what Asher wanted to do, but it was what she had to do.

Despite Ethran's bulk, she was amazed at how nimble he was. His wings were large enough to propel himself nearly instantly into the air, slice through a Ferveos, and then rocket him back to the shield where he would squash someone intending to hurt her. It was as though he danced around her, swinging his charged battle axe with ease.

Though she wasn't trying to do it, she still paid attention to where he was. To what was nearby. They pulled one another aside when something got too close. They swiftly leaped back when a Ferveos landed with a bellowing roar, and then unwaveringly leaped into action and took it out.

Ethran landed and took out their last opponent, nearly flailing right off the edge of the last platform. She was grateful she was close enough to snatch his arm and yank him back to safety.

Resecuring his footing, he gave her a smile. "Thanks, Ash."

"Can't have you tripping. Otherwise, you'll lose that bet," she joked.

"For the record, I never officially agreed to that."

Like a train, the platform moved across the rooftops.

"Where're we going?" she mused, looking around to figure out what Teneo's thoughts were.

He squinted ahead and gently tapped her arm. "I think he's taking us to the secondary portal activation."

Asher did a double take. "We can't go back to Tilion. This screams of—"

"A full blown incursion, I know. Ten's probably thinking the same. He's smarter than me, and if I figured it out—"

"He would, too; you're right."

Looking beneath them at the large net filled with dead enemies, Ethran whistled. "I always figured Teneo had to be strong." He whipped his head up to look at Asher. "He had to be, right? Otherwise, why would he get named an Elite?"

"I know what you mean."

"I mean, I've heard stories of what Bulwarks could do, but this"—he gestured beneath them—"is really cool."

She couldn't stop the smile that came to her face.

A pulse of air came from behind them, and they turned as Lexa appeared with Drogar and Teneo.

"We were just talking about you," Ethran said with a smile to Teneo.

The squat Zaheri blinked a few times and had to struggle to focus on Ethran. "What?"

Before Ethran could say anything, Asher held up her hand toward him and asked, "You're taking us to the second portal activation, the one outside the city, right?"

"Makes sense," Drogar said as he eased his grip on his rifle. "It's not open right now. We dump the cargo and then regroup."

"That's the thought," Teneo said with a shaky nod of his head.

Lexa wore a glare as she tightly held her arms across her chest.

Squinting at her, Ethran asked, "What's with the look, Lex?"

"I didn't get to do anything! Again!" she fumed as she flung her arms out in exasperation. "It's like you guys don't trust me!"

Drogar opened his mouth to answer when Asher swiftly said, "We had to take care of this quickly, Lexa."

Barely concealing his rolled eyes, Drogar nodded ahead of them. "Portal's coming up. I'll go open it."

Ethran held his hand out toward the elder hybrid. "Don't go through, 'cause—"

"I wasn't gonna."

"C'mon; let's get off this so Teneo doesn't have to worry about dumping us," Asher said. She looked at Lexa. "Mind if you give us a lift?"

With a scoff and a roll of her eyes, Lexa snapped, "It's not like it's hard."

Refraining from commenting on Lexa's snide remark, Asher simply took hold of the girl's hand.

This night was far from over, and Asher wanted to keep arguments to a minimum. If that was possible.

"What the hell is going on?" Lexa asked when they all reappeared back the flat.

Ignoring the girl, Drogar marched for the surveillance tech. "We should see if any of the sensors picked up numbers."

Teneo flopped onto a seat and rubbed his forehead. "That's wise. We can determine when they'll strike next."

"Hello?" Lexa snapped with a flabbergasted look.

"You should swap your pistol for a rifle," Asher told Ethran.

With a wince, Ethran shook his head. "Do I have to? Rifles are too bulky and slow me down."

"Yo, assholes!" Lexa screamed. "Answer my question!"

"Lexa, now isn't the time," Asher snapped with a stern look.

"Uh, seems like it is," the teen threw back. Her body language was flippant and screamed *"how dare you?."* "Danger's gone. Woohoo!" she let out as though mimicking a cheerleader. "Now's the time to answer my fricking question."

"We don't have time for this," Drogar grumbled, throwing a glare at the teen from over the screen in front of him.

"Lexa, we'll answer your questions once we know—"

"I don't care what you say, you're answering my questions *now!*" Lexa demanded, cutting Teneo off.

"Lexa!" Ethran hollered. "Enough!"

The teen stuttered back, her eyes wide as her mouth fell open.

"There is very real danger here and very little time to respond to it!"

Swallowing hard, she fixed a glare to her face and stepped up to challenge Ethran. "I deserve to know what's going on!"

"This isn't a game, Lexa! That guy was here to kill you!"

"Yeah, and seems you knew him. What? He a buddy of yours?"

Ethran reined in his frustration before he sternly said, "You don't know what you're talking about."

"Exactly," she snapped, keeping her glare fixed. "And I'm not letting anyone go anywhere until you tell me what the hell is going on."

Throwing Asher a look of frustration, Ethran sighed.

Drogar straightened from his hunched position over the computer. "Avemod left early. He was likely a scout, so it's possible we have time."

Still giving Lexa a frustrated look, Asher ground out to the teen, "You stay right here."

"Wh—"

"We"—Asher gestured to the team—"need to discuss things. And then we'll let you know whether you get your questions answered."

With a *humph*, Lexa dramatically crossed her arms and pinched her face into a foul look.

Asher grabbed Ethran and yanked him toward the kitchen. He, in turn, pulled a stumbling Teneo along as Drogar brought up the rear. Once they were in the farthest area of the kitchen, Asher hushed, "How bad do we all really think this is?"

"Avemod showing up?" Drogar asked. "Doesn't bear good will; that's for sure."

Rubbing his temple, Teneo answered, "Coupled with what we encountered last night, I genuinely fear the worst."

"Which is?" Ethran asked.

"That there has been a full-scale attack against all of them, not just Lexa."

"Right. Because if they were only coming after Lexa, we'd have seen Cregorous," Asher mused with a small nod of her head.

Easing back slightly, Ethran looked to Drogar. "We would've gotten backup of some sort by now, wouldn't we?"

With a small nod, Drogar hushed, "And that's a clear sign that things are sideways."

"But we aren't downed. We're all okay. So, the others probably are, too, right?"

"That's the hope, but there's no way to know. Especially if we can't use the portal."

"Okay, what'll we tell Lexa? I know she's not supposed to know about the others, but ..." Asher looked around to her teammates.

Teneo let out a sigh. "I think we should tell her what we know."

"Seriously?" Drogar asked as he scrunched his face.

"If we only tell her a little bit now and leave her in the dark about other things, she'll be furious later. Especially if she finds out some other way."

"Someone should watch the portal, though," Asher said.

Flicking his wrist in an informal wave, Drogar volunteered, "I can do that." As Ethran opened his mouth to respond, the elder hybrid added, "Teneo needs to rest after all the strength he exhausted, and you need to do likewise."

"Thanks, Drogar," Asher said with a small smile and a nod.

"You kidding me? This is selfish." He rolled his eyes and grumbled, "I have no willpower to handle that brat tonight."

"She probably doesn't like you 'cause you call her stuff like that," Ethran said with a smirk.

Letting out a scoff, Drogar answered, "By all means, be her favorite. It saves me headaches."

Asher took in a deep breath before she muttered, "All right, let's try to get her to meet us halfway."

"How're you gonna do that?" Ethran asked.

"Give her an ultimatum."

When they stepped back into the living room, they found Lexa in the exact same position as when they'd left. Her shoulders hadn't budged from the hunched fury of her crossed arms, and her scowling expression hadn't shifted in the slightest.

"That's dedication," Ethran muttered under his breath.

"Yeah, I'm leaving," Drogar said, marching for the elevator.

As he went to pass Lexa, the slender teen nearly exploded as she went to snatch Drogar's arm and stop him from leaving. "Excuse you! I said no one—"

"Lexa!" Asher commanded, grabbing the girl's hand.

Drogar didn't pause in his march and continued to the exit.

Fuming at Asher, Lexa held her Zaheri's stern look.

"We made a decision that is necessary given the situation, which includes Drogar going and watching the portal for the safety of *all* of us. Now, we will answer your questions. On one condition."

Lexa ripped her hand free and snapped, "Which is?"

"You listen to us. And I mean *actually listen* and *follow through* with what we say for the remainder of this incursion."

"And why should I?"

Deflating a little, Ethran let out a sigh. "Lexa, please, just ... drop the anger for a sec."

The teen flicked her glare to Ethran, losing the harder edges just a little.

"Everything that just happened was *bad*. All of those times we talked about something bad happening? That was tonight. That was One22. People probably got hurt tonight, and if we aren't careful, more people could get hurt. Or worse."

Lexa looked to the floor, her glare melting into a frown as she chewed on her lip.

"Hey, c'mon; look at me," Ethran said as he came up to her, placing his hand on her shoulder. When she met his gaze, he begged, "We're not trying to belittle you. We're trying to keep you safe. But you're making that really hard by acting like you're in control of this situation. Okay? None of us are in control of it right now." He gave her an imploring look. "Especially you."

She shrugged him off and stepped back, going back to crossing her arms over her chest as she grumbled a reluctant, "Fine."

Ethran cast Asher a look.

"I'll do what you say," Lexa added with a roll of her eyes.

"Okay," Asher said, sounding like she'd just convinced someone to not set off a bomb. "Then let's sit down and take a few breaths, because this is probably going to be a really long night, and we have a lot to tell you."

Wearing a look of barely contained anger, Lexa flopped onto the chair and shrugged. "Sounds good. Why don't you start with what the hell is going on?"

Teneo rolled his drooping eyes and grumbled, "I'm gonna make some tea."

Asher and Ethran both mumbled requests for some, as well, as he walked off. They were going to need all of the caffeine to get through this conversation.

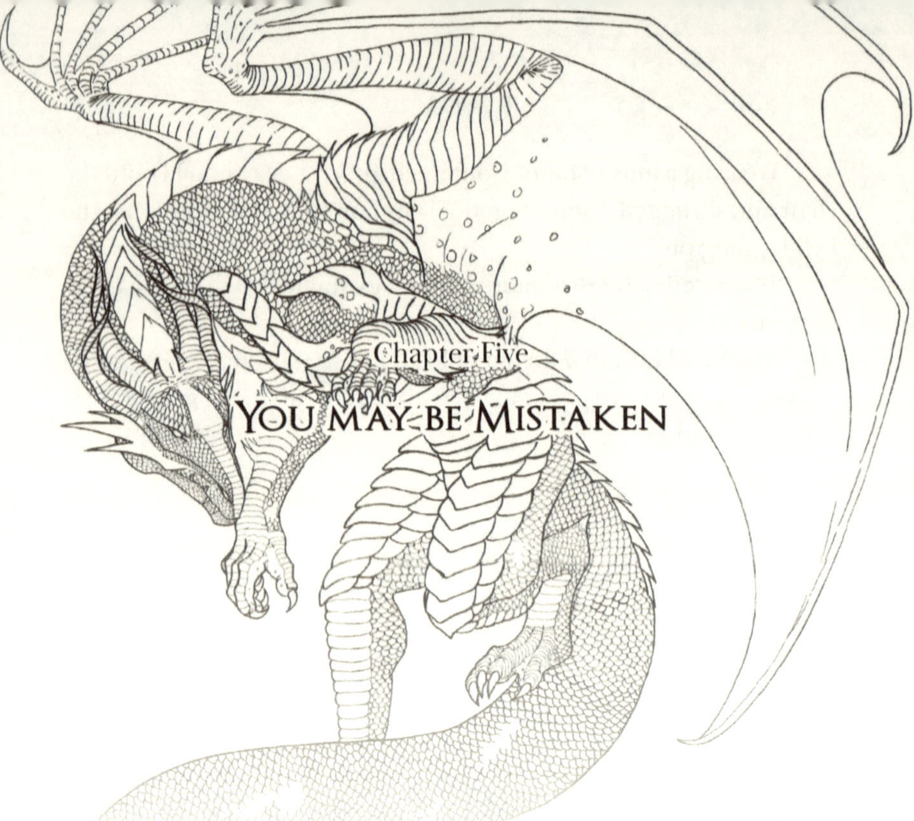

YOU MAY BE MISTAKEN

"What do you *mean* there are more Human-Borns?" Lexa snapped, gripping the edge of her chair as she glared at Asher. "How many more? Where are they? Why didn't you tell me about them sooner?"

"There's seven total, and—"

"Seven!" Lexa cut Teneo off. "Fricking seven? I thought you guys said I was special!"

"You are, Lexa," Asher tried. "Now, if you could—"

"I thought the whole point of me being a Human-Born was to take down some bastard named Cregorous? What do I need a bunch of other Human-Borns for?"

Ethran started, "The prophecy wasn't super specific about how—"

Lexa stood and started gesturing wildly. "Why didn't you tell me about this sooner? You've had me thinking this whole time that I was the only one, and now I gotta—"

"Lexa, *shut up!*" Asher shot to her feet and bellowed, unable to contain her fury any longer.

"No! I—"

"*Yes!* Shut up right now!" Asher pointed rigidly at the chair Lexa stood in front of. "Sit down and be quiet for longer than a second! You asked us to answer your questions and demanded that we treat you like an adult, *despite* the fact that you're acting like a whining child! Sit down, shut up, and *let us talk*!"

With a huff, Lexa dropped into the chair and crossed her arms, glaring at Asher.

"That's better," Asher said in an authoritative tone. She then calmly sat back down. "Now, you're going to keep that huge mouth of yours quiet while we tell you what we know, or I swear I will chain you to me for the night and refuse to answer a single question. *Do you hear me?*"

Glaring at the wall, Lexa grumbled, "Yes."

Ethran sat next to Asher, pinching the bridge of his nose as she reprimanded Lexa. Teneo sat across from him, gently shaking his head with heavy eyes that drooped occasionally, forcing himself to snap back to attention.

"We don't know where the other Human-Borns are," Teneo muttered through half-lidded eyes. "We were only told your location. Other Zaheri watch over the other Human-Borns."

"The prophecy that told us about you—all of you—talked about how each of you is important for seeing the end of this war," Ethran said. He glanced at Teneo. "Now, Ten's an Archivist back home, so he'd understand the theories around you all a lot better than us."

Lexa waited for a short few seconds before she looked to Teneo. "Okay. So, why do I need a bunch of other Human-Borns to help me beat up Cregorous?"

Ethran and Asher shared a look.

Sitting up, Teneo said, "Lexa, the thing of it is, you aren't the one who Cregorous is coming after."

She scoffed. "Please, like he'd go after anyone else. They're all probably super weak and useless." Sitting up a little, she added, "I can phase through dimensions, remember? How many other Human-Borns can do that? Hell, how many other *Agerians* can do that?"

"Only one that we know of."

"Lexa, Cregorous probably isn't coming after you," Asher said.

"Why not? I'm obviously gonna be the best of the Human-Borns."

Giving the teen a hard stare, Ethran said, "If Cregorous was only interested in you, he'd have attacked you himself and probably wouldn't have made a show about it. He isn't above killing people, and you'd be—"

"What? Easy for him?"

Ethran slumped a little and said calmly, "I was going to say defenseless against him."

She threw him a snide look as she scoffed, "Remember, he can't hurt me if he can't catch me."

"Cregorous is a Jumper, too."

Lexa's brow twitched, and she jerked back a little. "What?" she asked quietly.

"And there's evidence that he's also a Telepath. And he's incredibly powerful," Teneo added. "Not to mention any other number of abilities he might control that we don't have any confirmation on."

She'd always known she was strong. Lexa was sure of it. She had to be. Otherwise, why be some special Human-Born hybrid?

Working to brush off the growing thought that maybe Cregorous was a lot bigger of a threat than she had given him credit for, Lexa shrugged. "So I just need to spar more and get stronger. No big."

"Lexa, he's probably not going to come after you," Asher said.

With a scoff, Lexa felt the momentary start of fear for Cregorous completely disappear. Instead, she immediately was annoyed that he'd blow her off so easily. No one blew her off easily. That wasn't how this worked.

"C'mon, please, like he'd bother with anyone else."

"Lexa, I don't think you understand," Ethran said.

"Understand what? That Cregorous is powerful? Nope, got it. According to you, he's the biggest bad out there. So, of course he'd come for me."

"You aren't the most powerful Human-Born," Teneo quickly said.

Disgust filled Lexa's features as she slowly looked to Teneo. "What?" she asked, like a queen demanding a subject explain themselves.

"You're the Fifth Human-Born, the Shifter. You're likely still very powerful, and that's evident by the fact that you hold a powerful ability, but—"

"So, you're saying there's some Human-Born out there who's stronger than *me*?"

Ethran averted his gaze as Asher said, "We know for a fact that the First Human-Born is stronger than you. Because they're stronger than Cregorous. They have to be, given the circumstances that showcased their arrival."

Falling back into her seat, Lexa felt everything go wonky for a minute.

This wasn't how it was supposed to go.

She was supposed to be a hero. Go to some other world, vanquish a monster, and become the queen of Agerius or whatever. Go down in history and be seen as the greatest hybrid ever. Have people worship her and sing her praises. Have servants who went out of their way for her 'cause she was Lexa, *the* Human-Born who would take down Cregorous. The only Human-Born. The only person who would take him out and become a hero.

And, even now, she felt her Zaheri already felt this other stupid Human-Born was better than her. No one was better than her. No one was stronger than her. It all had to be wrong. Their stupid prophecy thing *had* to be wrong.

Feeling her resolve cracking, Lexa asked, "So, what're all the titles?"

"What?" Ethran asked.

"You said my title was Shifter, right? So, what're the others?" She was hungry, eager, insistent to know. This First Human-Born's title was probably meant for her, not some pompous jackoff who just got to swoop in and steal all the limelight.

"Oh. Well, the prophecy states them in order—Raidin, Protector, Warrior, Healer, Shifter, Scholar, and Requisite," Teneo said.

Lexa's face scrunched. "Raidin?"

"It means 'Elder's Warrior.'"

"That's stupid," Lexa said, wearing a look of disgust. "Why does the First Human-Born get some special title that means something super epic, and the rest of us just get stupid ass basic titles?"

"Well, they were given by the Elders, and I'm sure there was a reason why they assigned the names like they did. It's a question other Archivists have raised, too, but no one could ever find any specific reason ..." Teneo droned on.

She drowned him out. His rambling only made fury boil in her gut.

There had to have been a mistake. The Fifth Human-Born? Did that mean she was seen as the fifth strongest? What the hell? Who got to decide this? They were wrong!

She'd prove them wrong.

She'd prove them all wrong.

As she shook her head, Lexa glared. "I'll prove it's wrong."

"What?" Ethran asked as he furrowed his brow.

"You'll see. That stupid *Raidin* will see. I'll prove all of you and your stupid Elders wrong. I *am* the strongest Human-Born, and I'll prove it. I'll show that stupid Raidin just how strong I am. He'll see."

"Lexa, no one thinks you're worth less," Asher said, trying to give as much sympathy for the girl as possible.

"Yeah, sure," Lexa grumbled, slumping back in her seat.

Her Zaheri kept talking, telling her stuff about how they found out the Human-Borns had risen and all this other nonsense. Something about getting called before their Council. Being assigned to the team and told that they'd be her Zaheri. Whatever. She didn't care about any of that.

She was trying to figure out how to make herself shine as brightly as possible.

Apparently, this jackoff Avemod was a general or something and blah, blah, blah.

Lexa didn't care.

She just needed to figure out how to get Cregorous to see just how wrong he was to only focus on the First Human-Born. 'Cause Lexa was strong, too. And everyone would rue the day they thought they could belittle her or make her feel smaller than this stupid Raidin.

And whoever that Raidin asshole was could just go to hell. He was probably some guy who would try to mansplain everything and tell her how to do stuff. He'd probably be some arrogant asshole who would just tell everyone what to do and where to go, and not let anyone else do their own thing. He'd probably be some stupid jerk who waved his power in other people's faces.

She hated him already.

But she couldn't wait to shove it in his face just how much he underestimated her.

Chapter Six

WHERE DO WE GO FROM HERE?

Lexa didn't love the idea of taking everyone to the portal so they could talk with Drogar about plans going forward. So, she'd had a small outburst at them about their request to have her take them. It ultimately ended with Lexa being told that it was either that, or they were all going to walk to the portal, because no one was letting Lexa stay alone until this was over.

Begrudgingly, Lexa "offered" to take everyone to the portal.

When they arrived, Drogar glanced to his watch and commented with a snark, "Wow, that only took two hours. I thought for sure it'd take longer."

"How're you doing, Drogar?" Asher asked.

Not caring in the slightest whether it made anyone angry, Lexa snidely said, "Yeah, you're like eight hours past bedtime, right?"

Ignoring Lexa's comment, Drogar looked to Asher, "Fine. Nothing's happened here."

"Yeah, and none of the tech picked up anything either," Ethran said.

"That's ... weird," Asher admitted.

—~~— 409 —~~—

Resting his hands against the butt of his rifle, Drogar said, "It could be there's too much resistance on Tilion. Maybe that's delaying any second wave."

Rolling her eyes, Lexa grumbled, "You really think they're coming after all this?"

"Yes," Asher said with a sideways look at the teen.

"It's gotta be, right?" Ethran asked with glances to his teammates. "Otherwise, the Council would've sent Defenders to check on us."

"Of course they would," Teneo said confidently. "After a strike like we faced? They wouldn't just sit back and assume we were fine. Not with a Human-Born threatened."

"So, it has to be that something is barring them from the portal," Asher said with a nod. "Or someone."

Drogar gave her a grave look. "It has to be Cregorous. It's the only thing that makes sense."

Closing her eyes, Asher gained a slightly pained expression. "It's hurting my stomach that we haven't seen a retaliation yet."

"That's called anxiety, Ash," Lexa said flippantly.

"Well, whatever it's called, it doesn't feel good."

"I just wish we could know if the others were hit or not," Drogar said with a shake of his head.

Pulling herself from her moping for five seconds, Lexa rolled her eyes. "You guys are hopeless." As she pulled out her phone and started navigating to the right app, she added, "There's this amazing thing called the internet. We can just check social media."

Ethran offered her a smile. "Hey, good thinking, Lex."

She was still a little mad at him for how he'd yelled at her earlier, but she couldn't stop the smile that came to her face. Returning her attention to the screen, she nodded. "Yep, looks like a bunch of other places had"—she scoffed—"'pillars of light' is the trending hashtag. So is 'apocalypse.' That's hilarious. People really think dragons are gonna be part of the end of the world."

"Um, Lexa, they could be," Drogar reprimanded.

She ignored his comment and continued scrolling. "Something here about dragons loose in the USA. Serves 'em right. And—oh, this is rich. Some British royal twat is supposedly connected to some pillar of light thing in England. And something about monsters in Tokyo." She shrugged. "Nothing else I'm seeing."

"It could be that the other Human-Borns live in less populated areas," Teneo offered.

"Or that their communities don't use the internet as freely as others," Asher added. She let out a sigh. "Okay, Drogar and Teneo, I want you two to go back to the flat and get some rest for the next hour."

"Ash—"

The Team Leader held up her hand to silence Drogar's comment. "I know you'll say you don't need the rest, but you do. We all do. I figure, if Ethran and I take the first watch, you and Teneo can come back and take the second. We'll just have to deal with broken sleep until we know that we're clear and safe."

"Do I get to do anything today?" Lexa snipped.

"Yes. You can go rest, too."

Lexa rolled her eyes and let out a frustrated scoff.

"Lexa, you should rest up. You've done a bunch of jumps today. That has to—"

"Oh, please, that's all nothing. I can totally do more. It's not like they take that much strength."

Asher threw Ethran a look. For a second, he just stared back at her. Then he jolted a little and looked to Lexa. "Resting isn't bad, Lexa. We'll be doing our turn of sleeping later."

The teen looked toward the sky for a moment before she asked, "Well, how're you gonna do all the back and forth with the portal?" She gave Asher a knowing look, as though she'd outsmarted her Zaheri. "Don't'cha think that'll take a lot more out of you guys than necessary? I could stay with you and Ethran and rest when you guys do."

Rolling her eyes, Asher conceded, "Fine. Go take Drogar and Teneo back, and then come back here." She looked to Drogar. "We'll say an hour and a half."

"Sounds golden," Teneo said as Drogar nodded.

Throwing Asher and Ethran a smile, Lexa took a hold of the other two and said, "I'll be right back."

Once they were gone, Asher grumbled, "I really had hoped she wouldn't bring that up."

Ethran offered a small smile and said in an upbeat voice, "Hey, it's probably for the best."

She walked over to a nearby tree and leaned against it, letting out a heavy breath as she stared at the unassuming portal. Shaking her head, she whispered, "I just wish Lexa didn't make all of this so much harder."

"Yeah, well, she isn't," he said as he came to stand next to her. He glanced to where the others had been and hushed, "Look, Ash, before she comes back—"

"I'm fine."

Ethran looked at her and said, "You don't know what I was gonna say."

Slowly meeting his gaze, she turned to him and whispered, "Ethran ... I ..."

His eyes searched hers, brimming with hope. They veered slightly toward one another, just enough that it made his heart leap into his throat at the prospect that maybe, just maybe, Asher would finally let her walls down and let him in.

They'd barely wavered toward one another, no more than an inch, when Asher swayed back and shook her head. "Now isn't the time," she said for the millionth time.

He was a hairsbreadth from grabbing her arm, pulling her to him, and kissing her when the pulse of a jump alerted them to Lexa's return. Drawing his hand back to his side, he eased his weight so he would straighten.

Lexa almost immediately started to argue with Asher about what she could and couldn't do later, whenever the second wave hit. Usually, he would be a mediator for them, try to temper Lexa's indignation and Asher's fury. And maybe if he tried harder, he could've.

But in that moment, he didn't want to be a mediator. In that moment, he wished Lexa had just listened to Asher and stayed back with Drogar and Teneo at the flat. It would've given him a chance to try to explain himself.

What if something terrible happened? What if Avemod stole Asher away in some sick game? What if he did all the painful things Ethran had heard he was capable of? What if he killed her just because he could?

Never in the time that Ethran had known her had he questioned whether Asher could take care of herself. She was beyond capable. She was strong, independent, talented, and resourceful. She was beautiful, spunky, and full of life. She was a strong fighter and knew how to defend herself and those she cared about.

But ... this was Avemod. The sick pervert who stole from people things they couldn't get back. The general who everyone was warned about, because he'd hurt so many Agerian women that they'd lost count. And he'd clearly made comments about Asher that were just ... wrong. The things the Caligan had said had set Ethran's muscles to quake in tension and anger that anyone would talk to her like that.

Lexa suddenly smacked him, ripping him out of his thoughts. "What're you all mopey-mopes about?"

Sucking in a breath, he blinked a few times and tried to wipe away the frown that had formed on his face. He managed to pull a more resigned look as he said, "Ah, sorry, just ... lost in thought."

"Oh please," Lexa scoffed as she rolled her eyes. "There's nothing to worry about. You guys have me."

"You still should be careful, Lexa," Asher warned, trying to maintain a calmer, more motherly tone. Sometimes that worked.

It only sort of worked as another small spat started between the two of them.

Ethran couldn't stop looking at her.

Elders help him, he prayed this wouldn't be the last time he saw her. He prayed he wouldn't lose her. He prayed they'd get their "maybe later."

He just wanted to have that chance to be her hero.

Chapter Seven
THE DESIRES OF THE FLESH

Avemod lurked in the shadows, silently watching the Human-Born, Asher, and *him*. To say Avemod was distracted would be a massive understatement. Every time that mighty specimen moved or spoke, Avemod felt his hunger grow. The Agerian was tall, built like a champion, and was strong.

Sure, at first, the redhead, Asher, had been his target. She certainly was a figure to behold. Short and spunky and so in need of breaking.

But then that man had gone and shown just how powerful he was, and darkness—

The decision was made instantly. Avemod had to take him.

It might make Kelek angry, but if there was one thing they had in common, aside from their sick games, it was breaking Agerians. Admittedly, Kelek didn't take to the whole kidnapping and raping thing, but he certainly was one to let his eyes stray. Avemod knew who caught Kelek's eye: strong brawlers with impressive strength.

And if the Agerian resembled the Master in any way, well, then Kelek was all too swift to pinpoint a target. The target might never be grasped, because Kelek didn't go out of his way to satiate his hunger. He didn't need to; that's what Avemod was for.

That was where they were wildly different.

Avemod would always go out of his way to satiate his desires.

He waited patiently. Gleefully listened in on the arguments with the Human-Born. The girl was far too spirited, convinced she knew all the answers and had the ability to sway the war. Arrogant. Conceited. Foolish.

The darkness within this girl was palpable. She was more Caligan than anyone would wish to admit.

Several times, Avemod wondered if the Master might like a new toy. This Lexa would prove a fun stone to crumble, he was sure.

Every now and then, his target—Ethran, he learned—would speak up and intervene between the arguing Zaheri and her charge. Each squabble grew more ridiculous than the last. Finally, about an hour and a half later, the prickling hit Avemod's skin just before the girl jumped them all away.

That was his window. He had a few moments at least to grasp the portal and return to Caliga. As he snatched the white sphere, fear clutched his throat.

Be calm. Explain your plan. The Master will see the value of the time spent, he thought. He reminded himself of his plan: return ahead of the next wave, have the portal deposit him closer to where the Human-Born lived (as he had silently followed them to their little resting spot), drug Ethran, take what he wanted, destroy the only line of defense the Fifth truly had, and then annihilate the little girl who pretended she was fine. He told himself the plan over and over again. Reassured himself. Convinced himself.

Deep down, he knew ...

He was likely about to die.

Perhaps Kelek would intercede. He had before. The Master listened to his Right Hand. Could be convinced of Avemod's value. Reminded of their past. Reminded of all the little pillars of Agerius that Avemod had personally destroyed.

Gripping the portal tight in his grasp and watching the white orb flash red, Avemod swallowed hard.

Just be calm.

Swiftly marching to the door, he ripped it open and nearly barreled right into Kelek, who immediately snatched the belt across Avemod's chest and harshly shook him.

"Where were you?" Kelek hissed, his face tight with fury.

"Plotting," Avemod said quickly, grateful he didn't tremble.

Trembling could come later.

A pulse hit the air, and Kelek released Avemod in a stuttering shake. Red mist flicked the air.

He'd made his fate. Resignation filled him, and Avemod didn't shake. At least in his death, he would appear noble.

"Were you now?" Cregorous' smooth voice seethed.

Pain flashed across Avemod's frame, and he crumbled to the ground, harshly spun to be on his knees before his Master. Red cloaked his body, skittering about. He shook under the jabbing stabs and glanced up at the Lord of Caliga.

Cregorous glared at him, red flashing across his eyes. "How nice for you," he growled.

The intrusion impaled Avemod's mind, and he gave no resistance. There was no point. No use. To resist the Master was to resist a god. He knew that.

His intentions would be laid bare. The Master would see that.

The Master had allowed his toying with Agerians in the past. Surely, he would see the value of breaking the Fifth's strongest defender. Surely, he wouldn't kill Avemod now. So he told himself. So he lied to himself.

Deep down, he knew.

This might be his last breath.

An annoyed grumble came from the Master, and Avemod felt his mind released from Cregorous' inspection. The general gasped, still held tight under the powerful telekinetic hold of his lord.

"A selfish plan," Cregorous said, giving Avemod a condescending stare.

Avemod didn't respond. There was no point. It wasn't like he could say something the Master didn't know. The Master knew everything.

"But one that will bear the best results," Cregorous sneered, releasing his invisible hold on Avemod.

Sucking in a surprised gasp, Avemod fell back slightly, his shoulder blades hitting Kelek's legs. Avemod could tell how tense Kelek's muscles were.

He would be punished. Harshly.

Cregorous stared down at Avemod with a patronizing smirk. "Amazing you were smart enough to design such a scheme." He flicked his gaze to Kelek before he spat, "Two hours."

"Master," the two generals said with bowed heads.

A popping pulse filled the area as Cregorous jumped away.

For a moment, neither of them moved. Avemod knew any attempt to explain himself would be shut out. He had to wait for Kelek to vent his anger, and only if Kelek asked would he be permitted to tell his plan.

In a flash, Kelek grabbed a fistful of Avemod's hair and glowered down at him. "I told you not to be foolish," the Right Hand growled.

Letting out a whine as he grimaced at Kelek's tight grasp, Avemod tried, "I couldn't help myself."

"Today, of all days, you choose to be a blighted idiot?" Kelek snapped as he threw Avemod to the floor. He towered over the fair-faced general, his fists tight at his sides. "What are you scheming?"

Carefully lifting his gaze to Kelek's, Avemod answered, "There's an Agerian."

"There are always Agerians. You can have your fill another time."

"This one is different—special. I can tell. He has power that rivals Tyron's, I'm sure of it."

Kelek's face pinched in annoyance, his gaze flicking to the wall for a moment. Swinging his attention back to his lover, he spat, "You don't have much of Morgan's drugs left. You'll waste one here?"

"We win today, you know that."

"You're growing bold, Avemod," Kelek seethed, marching a few steps forward so he could pin Avemod to the floor with his foot on Avemod's chest.

Avemod wanted to say that if Kelek had seen this Agerian, Kelek would want him, too. He knew his partner all too well. And that meant he needed Kelek's approval for this. Yes, he'd gained the Master's blessing to accomplish his task, but it was a two-fold acceptance. He needed Kelek's approval.

Carefully considering his words, Avemod stared up at Kelek. A part of him already wanted to tremble. The power Kelek possessed radiated from him, and the pressure against Avemod's chest was gentle in comparison to what would await later.

"It will be worth it," Avemod finally said.

Silence fell between them for a moment as Kelek barely moved. Aside from angry breaths tumbling from the Right Hand, his attention didn't waver from the man under his foot. Eventually, he flinched his brow a bit and grumbled, "You have two hours to earn it."

A sly grin came to Avemod's face. "Two whole hours, huh?"

"Yeah," Kelek said with a smirk. "You better start working on satiating *my* needs before you fill yours."

This worked out better than Avemod ever could have hoped for.

Chapter Eight

Don't let Your Guard Down

The flat was quiet as the dawning day slowly filtered light in through the large glass windows. Despite his best efforts to stay awake, Ethran had nodded off over an hour prior, his sleep now deeper from deprivation as he snoozed on one of the comfortable leather chairs in the living room. His axe had fallen at some point and lay on the floor, its golden energy dancing brightly in the darkened flat.

The elevator dinged faintly, the doors sliding open to reveal Avemod as he silently stepped into the flat. He ambled into the living room, glancing to Ethran's sleeping form before continuing toward the technology against the far wall.

He grazed his energy-skittering fingers across the surveillance tech, short-circuiting the equipment. Turning back to survey the flat, he let out a quiet hum of appreciation for the layout and furniture. Silently, he moseyed toward his target.

Stopping as he neared Ethran, his hypersensitive hearing picked up the voice coming from the fallen earbud radio on the floor by Ethran's seat. He languidly took the earbud into his grasp, rolling it around his fingers.

Drogar's voice was frantic on the other end. "Ethran! Asher! They're—"

A spark of gray energy flew across the small tech, and Avemod smirked.

Ethran twitched a little as he started to wake.

The Caligan quirked his head inquisitively at the action.

Blearily realizing he'd fallen asleep, Ethran looked up in time as Avemod stuck some long needle into his neck. On impulse, Ethran sprang into action and slammed Avemod against the far wall.

Wearing a sly grin, Avemod said, "*Mmm* ... just as I expected. Quick reflexes."

Ethran scowled. "You're gonna answer my questions, or I'm gonna kill you."

"Oh, now aren't you being all naughty?" the Caligan general mock chastised, still smirking.

"You're going to tell me what your master's plans are right now," Ethran snapped. A jarring hit his brain, and he blinked a few times. It began to feel as though he were losing communication with his limbs.

Avemod gently tilted his head, giving Ethran a bemused look. "No, I'm not."

In spite of the fact that Ethran was the stronger of the two, Avemod easily pushed him off, leaving the Agerian wavering as he stumbled back. A second later, Ethran's legs buckled, and he fell to the floor.

With deft movement, Avemod snatched Ethran's arm and started to drag him back toward the seats. "You know, I've always loved Agerians. How much fight you have. It's so predictable, but I can't help myself. It's always so much fun to watch the surprise on your faces."

The room spun and swayed in Ethran's vision. Avemod's words were slurred and a little jumbled in his ears. His heart felt strained, as though it could tear.

Avemod's path to cross the distance to the seating was slow and methodical, dragging Ethran along with ease. "I've had my prizes, of course, but I didn't know about you. I just had to add you to my list. And then I found you here, sleeping away the day."

He threw Ethran into the chair, the prisoner letting out a small gasping noise in the process.

Everything was blurry and unconnected in Ethran's mind. He could barely feel his fingers and toes. His head lolled around, lacking stability.

A dark, possessive look filled Avemod's face. He towered over Ethran, his knees hitting the edge of the chair's arms. Avemod took hold of Ethran's jaw and began to stroke his fingers along his throat. He inspected Ethran's features, a playful fascination on his face.

"You're no Tyron, but he's marked for Kelek. And I've had my eyes on that pretty Jumper of yours for a while. But my, you are *something*." His lips parted, and he let out a long sigh as he slowly ran his agile fingers across Ethran's Adam's apple. "All that strength I saw earlier, I just had to get a taste of it." He smirked devilishly at Ethran's disconnecting eyes. "You can't show off power like that and not expect it to get you attention, after all."

Just as Avemod was moving his clawed hand to rip Ethran's shirt off, a blast of orange energy smashed into the Caligan general.

Shock radiated in Lexa's eyes as her fingers trembled. Tears began to well as she screamed, "Leave him alone, you asshole!"

From the floor, Avemod laughed and propped himself up on his elbows. "Sure you don't want to watch, pretty thing?"

A sharp breath escaped Lexa, and she twitched a little, her orange energy skittering around her arms in a pop.

Avemod licked his lips and smirked at her. "Better yet, why don't you join us?"

The flash of the image in Lexa's mind sprang heat onto her face.

"Ethran!" Asher bellowed as she leaped off the landing of the stairs and over Lexa. A charged blast of gold surged from her and smashed into Avemod, sending him soaring out the windows.

Without missing a beat, Asher ran straight to Ethran and gently took hold of his face. "Ethran. Ethran! C'mon; look at me!" she commanded.

His eyes continued to roll back into his head like a porcelain doll.

Snapping her attention to Lexa, Asher hollered, "Lexa, go get Drogar and Teneo! We have to regroup!"

Lexa's gaze was fixed on Ethran's nonresponsive state, her eyes wide.

"Lexa!" Asher yelled again in her booming voice.

It startled Lexa to look at her.

"Go get Drogar and Teneo! Now!"

Shakily, Lexa nodded. "Yeah. Right—right away." A pulse sounded as Lexa disappeared into orange dust.

Asher returned her attention to Ethran. She slapped her hand onto his chest, finding his heartbeat rapid yet weak. His breathing came out ragged and rough, his whole body limp. Desperately, she grabbed the back of his neck and forced his head to pivot so his face was looking at her. His eyes continued to stare blankly, rolling about here and there.

"Elders, Ethran. Look at me!" When his condition continued much the same as before, she took hold of the sides of his face and pleaded, "C'mon, you idiot! I'll go on a blasted date with you if you just look at me!"

For the longest few seconds of her life, Asher stared at his still disconnected gaze.

She bit back her fears and stroked his cheeks. "Please," she whispered.

Glacially, Ethran's eyes met hers. There was a dullness there, but at least he'd connected. An unsteady breath escaped him as he barely croaked out, "Ash ..."

She let out a shaky breath of relief. "Hang in there, okay? We're gonna get you through this."

A pulse hit the air, and Asher whipped her head over to see Lexa appear with Drogar and Teneo in her grasp.

"What—" Drogar growled then stopped short. "Ethran ..."

"I don't know what happened to him," Asher said, briefly meeting her teammates' concerned expressions before looking back to Ethran. "But Avemod was here."

"Oh, Elders burn it," Drogar muttered. "He could've used one of those things. Those concoctions of his."

"What? He drugged him?" Lexa asked with disgust.

"Avemod has a reputation," Teneo answered with dismay. "He's raped an absurdly high number of Agerians during raids and combat." The squat Archivist glared at the ground and fisted his hands. For a moment, he looked unlike himself. "It's disgraceful what he does to people."

Lexa looked to Ethran and assessed his condition. He certainly acted like he'd been drugged. Some sort of paralytic maybe? Or maybe it was some kind of date rape thing, but way worse. How long had Avemod been here? And when had he injected Ethran? These things usually took time; they weren't usually instantaneous.

Asher had been asking about what was going on at the portal. More Caligans had shown up; some dragons, too. They'd done their best, but it was only Drogar and Teneo. They'd called for Ethran and Asher, but when no one had responded, they'd gotten worried. Then, when Lexa had shown up to get them, it had made them even more fearful.

They could handle the problem of Caligans invading the city later. She had to figure out how to save Ethran. Depending on what Avemod had put in him, Lexa wasn't sure what she'd need.

Cutting into the conversation, she abruptly asked, "How fast is his heartbeat?"

Snapping her gaze to Lexa's, Asher looked bewildered for a few seconds. "Why's that—"

"Because humans suck balls, and we have drugs that hurt people, too. But we also have drugs that help people. Is his heartbeat fast but weak?"

Asher nodded. "Getting weaker."

Lexa began to pull her hair into a ponytail and gained a determined look. "Okay, I'm gonna go snag some adrenaline from the hospital."

"Adrenaline?" Teneo asked with wide eyes, his voice back to its usual higher pitch. "You can't just put that in him! Who knows what it'd do?"

"It'll save his ass, and that's all that matters right now!" Lexa snapped with a scowl.

Looking between Lexa and Teneo, Drogar asked, "What's adrenaline?"

"It's the stuff that kicks in when your body gets scared or goes into shock," Teneo said, still keeping a hard look on Lexa. "Humans use synthetic versions of it when their system gets weakened and they gotta push through. It's a last resort thing."

Lexa started, "Exactly—"

"Hybrids already produce more adrenaline than a human during heightened situations." Teneo clenched his jaw, flinging his hand toward his drugged teammate. "Ethran probably had his system full of it when he got injected with whatever drug Avemod gave him. It could've even played into why he's in this state. If we put more into him, he could overload."

"Overload?" Asher asked quietly.

"He could lose his reasoning skills; all of the things that keep him from overusing his energy. Ethran's no pup; he's a powerful wielder. It's why he pushes energy into his axe." He gestured loosely toward the glowing weapon on the floor. "He has a lot to work with. But he keeps it in check." He looked to Lexa, keeping his gaze firm. "If he lost his reasoning, even for a little while, he could cause damage to his body because he wouldn't know how to stop himself."

Lexa angrily gestured toward Ethran's limp form. "He could die!"

"We have to get him back to Agerius. They're the—"

"Lexa's right," Drogar mumbled.

Shooting the elder hybrid a glare, Teneo snapped, "What? How could you say that?"

With a defeated expression, Drogar sighed. "The portal is active from Tilion. Even if we could get to it right now—which would be a tricky task as it stands with how many Caligans have likely come through since we left—we can't force it to take us back to Tilion until it shuts down and we can open it from this side. And"—he slowly looked toward Ethran—"I don't think he has that much time."

Teneo glared at the ground and fisted his hands again. Letting out a long, slow breath, he eased a little before looking to their Team Leader. "Asher?"

Asher hadn't stopped staring at Ethran. His eyes had closed during their conversation, and his breaths kept coming out in short, gasping noises. His chest shuddered here and there.

She gripped his forearm and pinched her eyes shut. "Lexa."

The teen looked to Asher expectantly.

"Go get the adrenaline."

Chapter Nine

THE SHIFTER ALIGNS

The hospital was chaos and noise. It appeared that the damage caused earlier in the night had resulted in a number of injuries. Lexa hadn't even considered the collateral damage of it all. Somewhere in the back of her mind, she briefly admired how Asher and Teneo had found a solution to ridding them of the remaining Caligans earlier and removing them from the streets at the same time.

She'd learned a long time ago that if you just acted like you knew what you were doing, and acted like you had a right to be wherever you were, it would take people a little longer to recognize that you didn't belong. Ironically, it was one of the first things Drogar had reinforced for her after they'd first met over two years prior.

Lexa had always walked with determination and arrogance, so it wasn't like it took any active thought on her part to walk through the hospital like she owned the place.

Marching through the halls, she did her best to keep an eye on the nurse she was tailing while keeping her distance. There was so much going on that no one had noticed her yet. And the doctors and nurses definitely had their hands full with the influx of injuries.

The nurse ducked into a room, and Lexa walked past, casting a sideways glance at the door. It appeared stockpiled with various medications.

Dammit, Lexa thought.

There was some person there. Probably the gatekeeper that handed out the meds. How could she get that guy out of the room?

If she had backup, she'd just play the sweet schoolgirl routine, bat her eyes a bunch, and distract him. But she'd come alone to try to keep them as unnoticed as possible.

Casting a quick glance at her watch, she muttered another curse. It'd been a minute and a half since she'd left. Ethran was only going to get worse. And they still had to deal with the fact that any minute now, the rest of those Caligans were going to fall onto the city. They might've already started.

And then there was that bitch Avemod.

It made her furious that he'd tried to rape Ethran. Then to insinuate that she'd want to watch? Pervert.

She rounded the corner and kept her gaze trained on the door. If she had just enough of a window, she could jump in there behind the gatekeeper and kick him as the nurse left, pushing both of them out into the hall. And if she moved fast enough, she could lock the door and snag what she needed before jumping again.

Her timing had to be great, or Ethran would suffer.

No.

Her timing would be perfect.

As the door opened, the nurse turned to thank the guy in the medication room.

Lexa jumped into the room behind the gatekeeper, yanking the scarf she had up around her face in the process.

"What the f—" the gatekeeper started. He'd visibly leaped from the pulse that preceded the orange, dusty form of Lexa abruptly appearing. She landed a hard kick to his chest, sending both he and the nurse sailing out the door.

The instant she got her footing, she slammed the door shut and locked it. She wasn't going to spare any further thought as she turned and focused on finding the adrenaline.

"C'mon dammit," she muttered as she rapidly skimmed the shelves.

She found one of the brand names she recognized from the list she'd quickly read before she'd left and snatched one of the syringes.

A second later, she was back in her flat.

"Did you—"

"Yeah, dumbass, I got it," Lexa snapped at Teneo as she thrust the syringe into his hand.

"Okay, from what I read, we put this into a vein, so his arm should do the trick ..." Teneo mumbled as he popped the cap off.

Lexa crossed her arms and wore a look of distrust. "In movies, they always inject it in the heart."

"Again, we aren't human," Teneo snapped.

Drogar snatched the Archivist's shoulder and shoved him toward Ethran's unconscious form. "Just do something already! Elders, we don't have time for this!"

"Right, yes, of course." With unease radiating in his posture, Teneo gently placed the needle onto the crux of Ethran's elbow. "I'm only going to give him a little, since we don't know how this will affect him."

As he started the injection, going slowly so he could stop when it seemed to take effect, the others stared at Ethran with worried anticipation.

Ethran twitched, and his eyes opened.

A relieved sigh escaped Asher. "Thank the El—"

In a flash, Ethran sat up. The action startled Teneo, who accidentally pushed the plunger all the way down.

With a grunt, Ethran pinched his eyes shut for a second before he slowly opened them and let out a long, slightly pained sound. An angry growling noise rumbled up his throat, and he snatched Teneo's shoulder, his grip tight as he hoisted himself upright, bunching Teneo's shirt in the process.

"Ethran! Wait!" Lexa started.

Drogar pulled the teen back, shoving her behind him.

"Where are they?" Ethran growled as he snapped a fierce glare at Drogar. Gold energy began to spark around his arms and chest. A flicker of gold snapped across his eyes.

Trembling on the floor, Teneo whispered, "O–o–overload ..."

His gaze sternly on Ethran's, Drogar answered, "The Caligans have likely breached the city. We need to push them back to retreat so that we can then return to Tilion safely."

Ethran's battle axe flew up into his grasp with a slap against his skin.

"Okay, we need to formulate a plan," Asher started, slowly reaching for Ethran to try to slow him down.

Without a word, Ethran's wings burst from his back, and then he soared out the broken windows. Golden energy trailed in his wake.

Drogar turned to Lexa. "You have to get us to the portal now."

"What about the city?" Teneo asked incredulously, staggering to sure footing. "We have to keep people safe."

"And we will," Asher said. "Ethran's likely going to latch on to the first group of Caligans he sees and form a wall there. But we have to try to bottleneck them at the portal, or we'll be downed. Drogar, Teneo, I leave that to you two." Her thin, razorlike wings took form. "I'm going to try to keep an eye on Ethran and provide support, if it's even necessary. Lexa, once you get them to the portal, you get back to the city and stay with Ethran and me. Avemod's bound to reappear, and he's fixated on Ethran for some reason."

"So we have to watch his back," Lexa said defiantly. "Got it. C'mon, DT."

"For the last time, we have names," Drogar growled as he strapped a sniper rifle to his back and readjusted the assault rifle in his grasp.

Lexa gave him a mocking smile and grabbed both of their arms before she whisked them away into the Fifth Dimension.

When they neared the portal, Lexa felt her confidence waver a little. Against the oily smear of the Fifth Dimension, she could make out the spiraling cylinder of the portal as it bled white streaks against the morning sky. And from it exploded enemies. Like a waterfall of browns, grays, and blacks, smeared figures seemed an endless stream from the white portal.

Steeling herself, she asked, "So, where am I putting you two?"

Both Drogar's and Teneo's gazes were clicking across their opposition. If Lexa had looked at them as they were, she would have been awestruck at how quickly they could assess the situation and determine solutions. But her mind was wrapped wholly around Ethran. In that moment, all she wanted was to dump Drogar and Teneo so she could get to Ethran's side.

"It's a shame you can't make Paths," Teneo muttered.

"What?" Lexa asked as she scrunched her face in annoyance.

"Nothing. Put us there." He pointed toward the right of where the portal was. "Does that work for you, Drogar?"

Nodding a bit, the sniper said, "Yeah, that'll do." He looked to Lexa. "And remember, right after you get us there, you head back to Asher."

Well, that *was* the plan.

But now she wanted to show him up.

So, she didn't respond. Instead, Lexa dumped them where they had indicated then immediately jumped back into the Fifth Dimension. While she hadn't done anything like what she was about to attempt, she was fairly sure it could be done. At least, it felt like it should be done. It was stupid if it couldn't.

Lexa ran toward the opposition that poured from the portal. Many of them started to drop as gunfire opened behind her. A shield appeared, and the charging Caligans ran straight into it, bones crushing as they slammed their bodies into the suddenly appearing wall.

She should have gone after the Caligans that had already made it past Teneo's shield. But if she did that, Drogar wouldn't see what she was about to do. And that was what mattered in that moment—showing them how badass she was. Reminding them that she was the best. That *she* was the one they should hold reverence for. That *she* deserved some special title, too. If not a better one than that stupid *Raidin*.

The Caligans that emerged from the portal pivoted and avoided the golden shield, turning toward the gunfire. Teneo was using shields expertly. And again, if Lexa bothered to like him at all, she'd acknowledge just how impressive Teneo was—and had been—during this whole incursion.

But she ignored all of their efforts, because this was about her.

Caligans ran at her, and she didn't consider any potential consequences as she snatched a werewolf by the leg, forced it into the Fifth Dimension, and immediately let go of it the moment it was through.

With a yelping howl, the beast splattered into an oily smear, as if it had been a balloon of paint and a dart had impacted it. Within moments, the pocket of the Fifth Dimension around Lexa looked like a Jackson Pollock painting. Smears and splatters of enemy fighters surrounded her, and she was deaf to their wails and cries of pain as they were torn apart in the Fifth Dimension.

Once she was confident that she'd caught Drogar's and Teneo's attention, she jumped out of the Fifth Dimension long enough to literally land on a bratak'ra's back, hop into the air, and mock salute Drogar and Teneo. "Have fun!" she said before sticking out her tongue and jumping into the Fifth Dimension.

There was a faint curse from Drogar that followed her into the jump, and Lexa laughed at it.

Ethran's form tore through the city, making the glass in the towering buildings shutter as though a harsh wind had gone by. Streaking golden energy trailed behind him, leaving an easy path for Asher to follow. Of the two of them, she was typically the faster flyer.

And she was having trouble keeping up.

Panic gripped her heart at the ramifications of what was going on with Ethran and what sort of damage he might be inadvertently doing to himself. They had to squash this invasion quickly and get him back to Agerius for help from the Caretakers. No matter the cost. Even if she had to distract Cregorous and his generals herself, she'd do it.

It wasn't until Ethran had been slipping away from her that Asher had finally acknowledged she did feel something for him beyond friendship. Maybe her reasons for keeping him at arm's length were just. Maybe trying to keep her focus on Lexa and ensuring her safety was the top priority. Maybe all of that was perfectly right and unfaulty.

But her emotions screamed at her for letting it come to this.

What if something terrible happened because of this whole adrenaline thing, and Ethran di—

Sorrow hurtled into her throat, and she had to gulp the emotion down. It felt like a lump in her stomach and made her queasy.

No. No. He wouldn't die. They couldn't let that happen.

No matter the cost, they would get him back to Agerius and to people who could help him, and he would be all right.

He had to be all right.

Elders, please, let him be all right.

Because, quite suddenly, she really wanted to see what "going on a date" with Ethran would look like. What that could be the beginning of.

The sounds of screaming and destruction met their ears, and Ethran threw himself to the ground. He landed with an earthquaking *thud* that rippled the asphalt under his feet. Gold energy slashed out on impact and cut through the Caligans nearby.

There was a definite quaking in the Caligans that hadn't been hit, but they recovered when Avemod leaped into action. For half a second, Asher was worried about what the general might do.

But all Ethran did was kick Avemod in the chest and send him soaring before he continued his rampage. Every action he made was charged with a brutality that was completely unlike him. Golden energy pulsed from his body and flew with every punch, kick, or swing of his axe.

Caligans were completely caught off guard. They tried to fight him, get near him, throw attacks from a distance—anything to make the golden flaming Agerian falter.

Gray attacks impacted him and sparked white against the golden energy that continued to spiral around his form, but each hit did nothing to faze him. He just continued fighting as though he had no other thought or desire.

Asher did her best to keep her distance but stayed close enough to watch his back. It felt ridiculous that she didn't even worry about her own safety in that moment. And rightly so. Ethran wasn't leaving anything for her to have to take care of. The Caligans didn't even have a chance to consider attacking her.

Lexa appeared in a popping blast of orange, falling into step with Ethran a few paces from his side.

"Wh—what are you doing!" Asher cried as she ran toward Lexa.

The girl didn't respond. Whether that was because she couldn't hear Asher, or whether she was blatantly ignoring her was anyone's guess. She threw attacks, and punches, and kicks. But she didn't seem to realize the danger of how close she was to Ethran. How dangerous he was in that state.

Asher reached Lexa and tried to snatch the girl's arm to pull her back.

"Let go of me!" Lexa snapped, ripping her arm free.

"We need to keep our distance from Ethran right now. He's like a livewire and might not recognize us as friends," Asher commanded.

A crackle of energy caught their attention, and Asher shoved Lexa aside just in time to throw up a shield as Avemod barreled down on her.

With a yell, Lexa moved to try to kick Avemod, only for the general to leap back off Asher's shield and avoid the teen's attempted attack.

Undeterred, Lexa sprang into action and started to wildly throw punches at Avemod, doing her best to one-up him. A bemused smile played on his face as he deflected each of her attempted blows with ease.

Asher charged for him, intending to push him away from Lexa. When, in a swift movement, he caught Lexa's wrist, swung her around, and pulled her tight against him, locking her in a captured hold. His hand greedily splayed across her exposed abdomen, and he purred, "I do love a girl with fight."

"Let her go!" Asher yelled as golden energy swirled around her arms.

Writhing in his grasp, Lexa tried to push his arms off her. He'd secured her wrists against her waist, his other hand around her throat. Panic tightened her lungs. She couldn't just jump to get away from him, not with how tightly he held her. He'd come along for the ride, and she'd have little to no maneuverability, not with how he'd managed to catch both her wrists in his grasp. But, maybe if she jumped, would that throw him off enough that she could push off him? Or would he expect something like that?

As if he could read her mind, he smiled against her and hushed, "Don't try any of that jumping nonsense, dear. I'm far too well versed in that."

"I said let her go!" Asher commanded again, stalking forward, wearing a fiery look.

"Or what?" Avemod teased. "Are you gonna try to stop me?" He drilled his gaze into her. "Like you stopped me before?"

Thudding footsteps met their ears, and they turned as Ethran's sparking form lumbered toward them.

"Let. Her. Go," Ethran demanded, his voice dark, gravely, and cruel.

A wanting sort of breath escaped Avemod. He pushed Lexa against him as he groaned, "Let's trade then."

Lexa wanted to gag at the lewd actions of the general holding her captive.

"No." Ethran threw his arms out, and a charging blast of gold tore from him like a beam.

Without hesitating, Avemod threw Lexa at the attack.

She had half a second to react, and the only thing she could think to do was jump through the charging gold. A second later, she felt Ethran's form pass through her. The weight of his out-of-control energy pulled at her as though she'd had something push at her organs.

Lexa had only ever had one time when someone had walked through her while she was in the Fifth Dimension. It was unnerving, but it hadn't caused her any physical sensations.

This time, though, she had felt Ethran's body—or maybe it was his energy—pass through her.

She stumbled out of the Fifth Dimension and turned as she saw Ethran barreling down on Avemod, the two of them throwing furious attacks at one another. His attention diverted, Ethran wasn't taking out the remaining horde of Caligans. Asher sprang into action, taking out what she could.

But there were too many.

Just as Lexa was getting her bearings again, she felt a pulse hit the air. It wasn't like the pulse from another Jumper. At least, she didn't think it was. It didn't feel like another Jumper. But ... there was something oddly familiar about it. Like a small push of air had impacted her and gently swayed her body.

Her fingers started to tremble as her vision blurred and overlapped, swaying this way and that, as if she were on turbulent waters. Blinking furiously, she tried to get her vision to realign.

Flashes tore at her sight with each blink, as if she were clicking through scenes of other worlds. The Fifth Dimension's oily smear. A glassy, shatteringly fragile white overlay to the world. A screeching, frost-covered dark space. An airy overlay, where everything felt lighter and farther away.

And then they all aligned and righted in her vision, as though she could see through layers of a diorama. She felt the air around her grow strangely still, but it was somehow terribly loud at the same time.

A bratak'ra lunged at her, and for no good reason, Lexa didn't flinch or even worry that it would impact her.

Because it didn't.

The bratak'ra soared through her and landed, whipping its head at her in confusion. It growled, "What is this trickery?"

Suddenly, the ground beneath the bratak'ra disappeared, a circular hole underneath its feet ringed in orange, flitting dust. It snapped shut once the beast was through.

Lexa turned and looked at all the enemy fighters running toward her, intending her harm. And though she didn't have any understanding of what she was doing, she knew how to do it.

Letting out a smooth breath, she gently swirled her arms out. With the action, more of those strange holes appeared, all ringed in orange energy that flitted in the breeze. Caligans, bratak'ra, werewolves, and—though she couldn't see it directly in front of her—in the sky above, the Ferveos, too, got caught in these suddenly appearing holes in the world. They fell into the strange rifts as if they were nets being swung around to ensnare butterflies.

Avemod looked to Lexa before fixing a glare on Ethran. With a frustrated sigh, he pouted. "And I didn't even get to have any fun." He pushed against Ethran and let himself slide back before he darted down an alleyway.

Ethran nearly followed him, had it not been for a werewolf charging at him. He snapped his attention to the other fighters and returned to decimating the Caligans nearby.

In her trance-like state, Lexa continued to use her multiple dimensioned nets to sweep enemies away with ease.

But just as quickly and abruptly as it had come on, so, too, did it snap away, leaving her stumbling for stability. Her body felt heavy again and wholly grounded, only now making her realize that she had felt weightless before.

Ethran swung his battle axe, releasing a trail of violent golden energy that slammed into the last group of Caligans stupid enough to be anywhere near him.

Shakily holding a hand to her temple, Lexa felt her world teeter slightly. She stumbled a bit but was able to secure her footing. As she blinked to get her vision to stop tilting this way and that, she focused on Ethran's hulking form.

His shoulders were taut, the muscles on his arms rigid and painfully flexed. Gold energy skittered around his form like livewires. His shirt was torn in places, one of the sleeves dangling by a few threads. Hauntingly heavy breaths escaped him, his whole body rising and falling with each growling gasp.

When he turned toward her, Lexa's heart lurched into her throat.

All of the neat and orderly nature to his features were replaced with an animalistic glare. His jaw trembled around a snarl, and his eyes were nearly eclipsed by his sparking energy. There was a brief pause, as if he was trying to assess her.

Without warning, he swung his battle axe into a ready grip, his knuckles white as he clutched the weapon. He charged forward, raising the suddenly golden flamed axe as though he intended to hurt her. A furious yell was in his throat.

Drogar swiftly sprang into action, jabbing the butt of his sniper rifle harshly into Ethran's temple. The overloaded Agerian collapsed to the ground, his axe falling with a clamor.

Completely forgetting that Ethran had been on a collision course with her, Lexa gave Drogar an aghast look and snapped, "Wh—you hurt him!"

Ignoring the teen, Drogar moved to scoop Ethran's unconscious form off the ground.

Golden energy continued to flit here and there around Ethran, sparking in a wayward dance. There were deep, spiderwebbing gouges across his skin, from the tips of his fingers and climbing up his arms. Blood began to seep through his shirt, more along his shoulders than anywhere else.

"We need to get him to Agerius," Drogar said with a grunt as he draped one of Ethran's arms across his shoulder.

Asher moved to Ethran's other side to take some of his weight off Drogar. "Teneo, you and Lexa need to get back to the flat and stay there until we get back."

The squat Zaheri nodded as he took Drogar's rifle and, in turn, handed him a pistol. "Understood."

"What—no! I'm going with you!" Lexa snapped as she started toward Drogar, intending to shove him away so she could take his place.

"No, you aren't," Drogar commanded, placing a large hand on Lexa's shoulder and shoving her back.

"Ye—"

"Lexa, you're staying here!" Asher shot, fixing a stern look on her face. "The Expanse will still be filled with Caligans. If they've retreated, then it means the Council got control of the portal, but there will still be a battle on the other side."

"But—"

"Go home. Now."

Fear gripped Lexa's heart as she lost her scowl upon looking at Ethran's unconscious form. Sure, he wasn't graceful or always super steady on his feet, but he was never limp. He was never boneless.

Seeing him like that, and with those injuries, sent a clutching sort of tightness to her stomach that made her want to be sick.

Before she could utter any more arguments, Drogar's and Asher's wings burst from their backs, and they flew off with Ethran in tow.

Lexa watched them go, feeling as if a part of her had gone with them.

Chapter Ten
LASTING SCARS

Lexa kept rolling her phone around on the table, fidgeting with the case as she checked the clock for the twentieth time.

Drogar had said they'd return when they could.

It'd been a day and a half since Asher and Drogar had dragged Ethran's unconscious form off through the portal. Drogar had returned a few hours later. The only thing either of the remaining Zaheri would say was that Ethran would be fine.

It didn't feel like he'd be okay. Her whole body trembled at the prospect of what the longevity of their stay in Agerius might mean.

She glanced over her shoulder at Drogar's lounged position on the couch, opposite the bar. Both he and Teneo had been so relaxed since the attack, like they weren't concerned about anything.

So, maybe she was just overthinking it all.

That was possible, right?

Just the thought of brushing off Ethran's condition sent a knee-jerk reaction of freaking out. She wanted to scream for them to take her to Agerius so she could see him. They had to know something more than what they were telling her. Hybrids healed fast, which meant that anything longer than a few hours meant there was something really wrong with Ethran.

Chewing on her lip, she resolved to make her demand and got up from her spot at the counter. As she turned to hurl her command at Drogar, the elevator dinged and the doors slid open.

She spun toward the elevator and saw Ethran wince as he stepped over the threshold. There were bandages that ran down the length of his arms and covered the bulk of his palms and fingers. The V-neck shirt he wore allowed for her to see the spider-web-like injury that stopped around his collarbone. His face was scratched up and marred, and his eyes were a little bloodshot.

Without thinking, Lexa ran to him. Throwing her arms around his neck, she heard him let out a grunt as he brought a shaky arm around to stabilize her against him.

"You're okay," she hushed.

"Yeah," Ethran wheezed. "Barely, but I'll take it."

Lexa knew she had to let go. Continuing to make him hold her up wasn't good for his condition, she was sure. But, even though her toes barely touched the ground, and she knew he supported most of her weight, she found herself unwilling to step back.

"Okay, Lexa, you gotta let him sit down," Asher said as she gently pulled the teen off.

Reluctantly, Lexa obliged but kept a hold of his hand. "C'mon; I'll help get you settled," she said as she led him toward the couch.

Ethran let out an unsteady scoff. "I'm not totally broken."

"No, only mostly," Drogar said with a placid expression.

"Nice to see you, too, D." The overtaxed Zaheri fell onto the couch ungracefully and let out a heavy sigh as his eyes slid shut.

Lexa whipped an accusing stare at Asher. "You should've called me."

Asher opened her mouth to respond before she settled on letting out a short breath.

"Her phone got busted the other day," Ethran mumbled sleepily. "And mine's here somewhere."

"Can I get you anything? Water. I'll get you some water," Lexa said hurriedly then made for the kitchen.

Teneo looked to Ethran, a relieved smile coming to his face. "It's good to see you back here."

"Mmhmm," Ethran responded without opening his eyes.

"We'll leave you to rest," Drogar said and waved Teneo to follow his retreat.

Once they were alone, Asher walked over and gently stroked her hand through Ethran's hair. He leaned into her touch and let out a soft hum.

Despite herself, she smiled at the reaction. "Take the time you need to rest, Ethran," she whispered.

As she turned to walk away, he raised his hand and barely managed to hook his fingers against hers.

When she turned to ask him what he needed, he forced his eyes open and smirked at her. "Don't think I didn't hear you."

A tint similar to the shade of Asher's hair flared across her freckled cheeks.

"You owe me a date."

Curling her lips into her mouth to hide her smile, Asher stepped back to him and hushed, "Yeah, I do." Then she leaned forward and pressed a light kiss on his temple.

Ethran let out a contented sigh and smiled as his eyes drifted shut. He let her step back and eased into the cushions of the couch.

Lexa returned a second later with a glass, settling next to him. Holding the glass out to him, she asked with a frown, "Is there anything we can do?"

"He just needs time to rest," Asher said. She walked to the teen and gently held Lexa's shoulder. "We should let him have some quiet."

"Can't I just sit with him?" Lexa asked, giving Asher a pleading look.

Letting out a small sigh, Asher deflated. "You promise you'll let him rest?"

The teen responded with several rapid nods.

"Okay," Asher said as she straightened. "I'm going to get a shower, and then you can help me get him into bed."

As Asher walked off, Ethran cracked his eyes open to look at the girl at his side. "I'll be fine, Lex."

She studied him, chewing on her lip before she scooted closer. Gently resting her head on his chest, she whispered, "I was really worried about you."

A smile tugged on his lips. "Ash is gonna kill you if you don't let me sleep."

"Then she can kill me."

"Kinda defeats the purpose, don't you think?" He looked down at her and blearily focused his eyes. "Hey, maybe you can help me out."

Lexa smiled at him and sat up. "Sure! With what?"

Gingerly lifting his arm to rub his temple, he groaned, "Well, whenever I can stand and not fall over—"

"So, never."

"Oh, shut up."

She smiled back at him in response.

Pinching his eyes shut, he continued to gently rub his forehead. "You've been to every restaurant in town. What's a good one? That's classy, I mean. Good for a date."

Lexa's brows pulled together. "Wh ... Who're you taking on a date?" She'd tried to make it sound teasing, but it definitely came out more accusing.

He didn't seem to catch the inflection. "A good thing about this whole—" he gestured vaguely to his bandaged state "—near death thing is Ash finally agreed to go out with me."

"Ash?" she whispered, giving Ethran a look of mild betrayal.

As if on cue, Asher appeared at the top of the stairs, hands on her hips as she said, "I thought you agreed to let him sleep."

Lexa slowly looked to the woman on the stairs. She had to actively tell herself to not glare at Asher.

She got up and muttered, "Yeah, I'll just ... leave you alone." Swiftly ascending the stairs, she grumbled, "Wouldn't want to get in the way."

"What do you mean, 'things phased through her?'" Drogar asked in a hush.

Ethran was passed out in his bedroom, and Lexa had holed herself up in her room, leaving the three of them some privacy as Drogar and Teneo worked to revitalize their damaged surveillance tech.

"That's what it looked like," Asher said with a shrug. "A bratak'ra went right through her"—she sailed her hand across her to try to visualize the action—"like she wasn't even there. But she *was* there. I could see her. But nothing touched her. And then all of these random ... holes just appeared."

"Holes," Teneo reiterated.

"All of them had these orange borders, and they definitely weren't like rings of energy for weapons or defensive purposes. Because each of those holes looked different and kind of ... strange."

"Strange how?"

Asher helplessly shrugged. "The only one I got a clear sight of was the one that looked a little like the dimension that Lexa jumps in."

"Oily, like paint," Drogar said as he nodded. "Maybe they were tears into other dimensions."

Smacking Drogar out of misplaced excitement, Teneo burst, "Dimensional Paths!"

"What?" Asher asked as she gave him a confused look.

"I've read about them! They aren't very prominent in the Archives, but there's mention of these things Jumpers can make. They're called Dimensional Paths. But I've only ever read of them being used for Jumpers to make short doorways for non-Jumpers to step through, not to send things into other Dimensions."

"Well, she wasn't sending anyone anyplace fun, from what I saw."

Straightening from his task of messing with wires, Drogar asked, "What does this mean?"

"It means there's the potential for far more to Lexa's jumping than we thought," Teneo said, wearing an excited smile. "I wish I knew the Jumper in the Elite. I might be able to ask him questions about it."

"That's not likely," Drogar grumbled as he quickly returned to his task.

"Why?"

"Because he's a moron."

Asher gave him a disapproving look. "That's not very nice."

Flashing upright again, Drogar waved the screwdriver in his grasp at her. "You try talking to him then. He's a blasted idiot! I'll be shocked if he's still alive after being assigned to the Alpha Team alongside Ar'on."

Letting out a guffaw, Asher asked, "Wait, what? He's on the Alpha Team?"

"Yeah, Ar'on told me about it after we were all assigned. He was *not* looking forward to it."

"There's a chance the Jumper has grown in his assignment to the Zaheri," Teneo said hopefully.

Wincing, Drogar said, "I wouldn't hope for that."

Asher sighed and looked to Teneo. "Any thoughts on how we help Lexa work through this advancement in her ability?"

"You think it's persisted?" Teneo asked with a small raise of his brow.

"It did seem to come and go," Asher admitted. "But maybe it was like a jumpstart or something."

"Which means ... what?" Drogar asked.

"Perhaps an outside force?" Teneo mused, glancing between them. "Something that spiked her ability?"

Slowly, Asher nodded. "There might be some validity to that."

"How so?"

"When we were in Agerius, Gaeor was brought in with some major injuries. So was Zelek." She gave Drogar a sympathetic look. "Gaeor lost an arm."

"Oh, Elders," Drogar said as he angrily put the screwdriver down on the table.

Still wearing a concerned look, Asher continued, "But to your point, Teneo, both of them mentioned that they witnessed their Human-Borns do some pretty amazing stuff suddenly toward the end of their battles."

"Well, what happened?" Drogar asked. "Was everyone hit at the same time?"

"Seems that way. And everyone went up against different generals by the sound of it. The Eta Team had to deal with Kelek, and the Gamma Team had Caedex barreling down on them."

Teneo winced and sucked in a sharp breath. "I don't envy them."

"I know what you mean."

"Wait, so"—Drogar leaned against the computer in front of him—"does this mean ... Cregorous was controlling the portal to dump warriors into seven different locations? At the same time?"

Asher gave them both worried looks before she nodded. "It seems that way."

"Elders," Drogar cursed as he closed his eyes.

"We always knew he was powerful, but that?" Teneo asked, his face going pale.

Drogar clicked his gaze to Asher. "Everyone dealt with generals?"

"Yeah," Asher said.

"So, who got Cregorous?"

Raising her brow, Asher said, "I overheard Tyron say the First Human-Born went up against him ... and is fine."

Drogar gagged as Teneo went paler still.

"Elders, how strong is that kid?"

"Let's just say, I don't envy Tyron."

Chapter Eleven

A Shift in Focus

"So, his name is Ethran, not Ethan?" Anastasia asked as she hung on every syllable that left Lexa's mouth.

"Yeah," Lexa answered.

"*Please* tell me you're sleeping with him."

Feigning disinterest, Lexa said, "*Ew*, Stasia, no."

"What do you mean *ew*! He's one of the hottest guys I've ever seen!" She playfully smacked Lexa. "I know you think he's hot. I saw how you looked at him." Wiggling her brow, she slyly added, "And I saw how he looked at you."

Rolling her eyes, Lexa tried not to think about it.

"C'mon, you looked sexy! I know he was checking you out." She let out a whimpering sort of noise. "And he is damn sexy. How decisive he was, and God he was so solid. I wish he'd touched me more that night."

"Yeah, you left quite the impression on him, huh?" Lexa mocked.

"Oh, come on, Lex," Anastasia said, quickly trying to defend herself. "I wasn't expecting any of that!"

"Yeah, that was obvious."

"Anyway, it's not about me; it's about you and Ethran."

"There isn't a me and Ethran."

"There totes is, and you shouldn't be embarrassed about it!" Giving Lexa a knowing grin, she added, "Hell, I'd tell the world if I got to sleep with an Adonis like him."

Lexa let her continue to drone on about Ethran. A part of her wanted to let Anastasia make up as many stories and rumors as she wanted, if only for some strange dream satisfaction. But it kind of felt strange how disinterested Lexa was in gossiping with Anastasia.

It'd been three days since the attack, and the city was still reeling. Lots of property damage had occurred. One22 was closed for the foreseeable future as they went about repairs. Whole swaths of downtown were broken or, at the least, scratched up. There were a handful of bratak'ra, werewolf, and Ferveos bodies that had been snatched up by the government before the Agerian reinforcements could haul them back to Tilion.

And, according to her Zaheri, all of the Human-Borns had been fine.

Lexa still hated the phantom *Raidin* and wanted to show him up something fierce, but she had to admit she was a little intrigued. Since Ethran had gone and crushed her heart, she kind of wanted to make him jealous.

Maybe cozying up to this super strong Human-Born would make him realize what he was missing and dump Asher.

She couldn't fault Asher. Too much. 'Cause it wasn't like Asher had tried to weasel Ethran away by being pretty or anything, which was kind of why Lexa sometimes hated her. Asher stuck out because of her vibrantly red hair and freckled face. Maybe there was something Lexa could do to stand out, too, so Ethran would notice her.

She'd had trouble sleeping. Seeing Ethran's unconscious body slumped against Drogar kept making her panic. The memory of it would spark at the worst times, sending her stomach convulsing.

In a real way, she wanted to pull Ethran aside, kiss him full on that beautiful mouth of his, and tell him that she wanted them to be together. But he was still recovering, and he had revisited the question he'd asked her, wanting to know what restaurant to take Asher to.

Lexa had nearly yelled at him. Didn't he see her? Didn't he realize she liked him? Why didn't he respond to her affections? Asher had always been so indifferent with Ethran.

Maybe that was it. Maybe Ethran was all about the girls who played hard to get.

Even so, those thoughts weren't the most prevalent in Lexa's mind anymore. They were there, no doubt, but they weren't where her mind drifted to most often.

Sydney suddenly seemed so small.

The city she so adored and wanted to spend her whole life in had, in the blink of an eye, become a speck. She'd always known there was another world. That Tilion was where her Zaheri came from. That their nation was called Agerius. That they fought against a group from some place called Caliga. That someday, they might try to hurt her.

All this time, she'd thought she'd understood the gravity of it. Because she could jump, she could just flit herself away from danger and *voila!* she'd be safe.

It was all that bastard Avemod's fault. The way he'd grabbed her and yanked her against him, making her unable to simply jump away from danger.

It hadn't been the first time she'd been in the presence of some idiot who tried to get with her. It hadn't even been the first time she had to be prepared to dodge a slap or kick some douche in the balls for getting too handsy.

But how quickly he'd managed to snatch her and render her unable to fight back. How easily he'd captured her in his grasp, keeping her pinned against him. Sure, he was handsome, but clearly bat shit crazy. And she didn't play with crazy.

So, no, she hadn't enjoyed being that close to that maniac, especially after what he'd tried to do to Ethran.

And there were probably lots of people in Caliga just like that freak.

Ethran had almost been taken away from her. Even if she could never convince him to be her Ethran alone, she'd take him in whatever limited capacity she could get him. That was better than nothing. That was better than him being killed or abused by some asshole who thought they could hurt people without consequence.

She didn't necessarily want to get to know the Human-Borns or have anyone lord their power over her, but she did have to admit that if they would help her rid the universe of people like Avemod, then fine. She'd work with them.

It wasn't until she was in her classroom and taking out her sketchpad that she realized she hadn't admired the architecture of the building.

Quite abruptly, everything she used to stare at in wonder held no luster.

And she hated it.

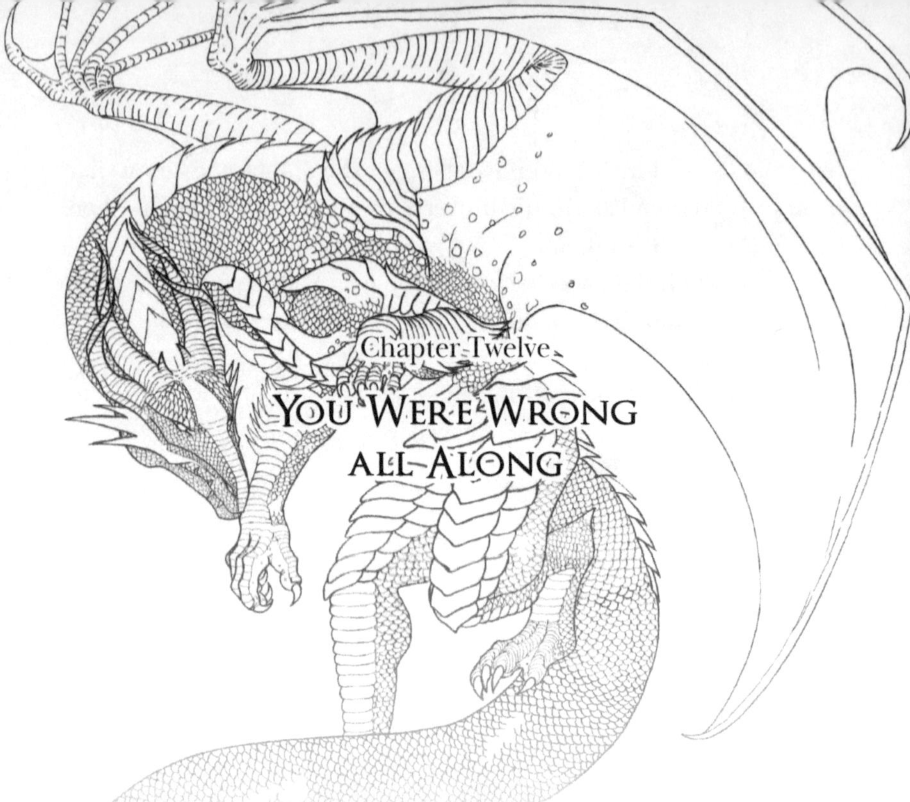

Chapter Twelve

YOU WERE WRONG
ALL ALONG

About a week after the attack, Lexa went to Point Piper to tell her gram what had happened and that she was planning to pause her studies at University after the fall semester. Asher and Ethran went with her to help with explanations.

Gram had been furious at first. Furious at Asher and Ethran for lying to her. Furious at Lexa for keeping the secret. Furious that she had trusted any of them. But then, as things were explained, her anger slowly shifted into gratefulness for the Zaheri and their dedication to keeping Lexa safe.

Lexa got a scolding for misbehaving and was charged with doing better when it came to obeying the people trying to protect her. She'd reluctantly agreed to try.

Gram then asked a lot of questions, like what was expected of Lexa and would she be forced to move to this other world. It sparked a foreign emotion in Lexa. Or, at least, one she thought she had buried.

As her Zaheri discussed the particulars with Gram, and the possibility that Lexa might one day have to move to Agerius, Lexa felt something begin to cripple her chest.

Gram was old. Getting older. Even if this Agerius was such a utopia, like her Zaheri seemed to make it out to be, the old woman wouldn't have a home there. And she wouldn't want to leave Earth, Lexa was sure of it.

Which meant Lexa might have to leave her behind.

That was good, right? It meant she wouldn't have some old hag nagging her about manners, or about dressing appropriately, or about being a lady. It meant she could be her own person and not have to worry about disappointing someone. It meant freedom. Right?

So, why did it spark pain in her lungs and make her heart pound madly in her chest? She didn't like the feeling. So, she pushed it aside. Told herself to stop it. Pretend like it didn't hurt. Ignore it until it went away. And when she managed to shove the painful feeling aside, she moved on.

Everything was fine.

In the end, she was told to visit Gram once every other week, at least. If she wouldn't have studies to fill her time, Gram wanted to see her more often.

She understood why Lexa was taking a break. Given the drastic nature of the attack, it made sense that the girl should lie low. Gram used some connections to ensure Lexa wouldn't be tied to the events and went to fairly great lengths to eradicate any photos that might have said otherwise.

Being rich had its benefits. And one of them appeared to be that they could make their own version of events that the world just had to agree were true.

The fall semester ended, and Lexa spent a month or so with Gram in Point Piper. Her Zaheri came along, of course, and Gram insisted they stay with them at her mansion. Much to Lexa's pleasure because she did finally get to see Ethran at the beach. It meant she saw Teneo shirtless, too, which wasn't a pleasant sight. The squat Zaheri had nothing trim about his physique. But Ethran's toned chest and boyish grins were more than enough to make up for it. Even if those grins were almost always aimed at Asher. Lexa tried to pretend like it wasn't happening. Or that, if it was, it was some sort of fling that Ethran had to get out of his system.

She must've reminded them a dozen times on that trip that she wasn't a child, if only in the hope that maybe Ethran would look at her differently.

Knowing the fullness of Lexa's importance, and the danger she faced, Gram was hard pressed to let the girl be without her Zaheri at any point. It was like she was sixteen again, being reminded over and over again that she needed someone to protect her. And though she rolled her eyes, and grumbled, and bemoaned how Gram treated her, she also found herself grateful for the knowledge that her Zaheri were always there.

Every time she turned around, one of them hovered nearby. Whether she was out shopping or grabbing a meal with Anastasia, who was quick to try to dig any information she could out of Lexa as to what was going on, her Zaheri were always nearby.

Until that day.

This guy—Rowboat or something, Lexa didn't care to remember his name—showed up and said something about the Zaheri being disbanded, removed from the Human-Borns' training. That Ethran, Drogar, and Teneo needed to go back to Agerius with him. There were hushed conversations. Asher spat several angry comments. Drogar griped remarks. Teneo squeaked out shocked statements. Ethran kept throwing Lexa worried glances. And then they'd left. Hasty goodbyes, and then *poof*, off to the portal. Gone. Just like that, it was only Asher and Lexa.

That had been four days ago.

Nothing had happened. That random dude had made it sound like any minute now the rest of the Human-Borns would be coming to Sydney to meet them. And here they were, almost a week later. Not only had nothing happened, but on top of that, she'd been stuck with Asher the whole time.

In the last three months since the attack, Lexa had been trying a little harder to listen to her Zaheri. Even Teneo, for all his boring lectures, and Drogar, for all his snarky comments, she had tried, dammit. And *this* was how she was being repaid?

The flat was horribly quiet, but strangely stuck at the same time. Ethran's bed was still messy from the morning they'd all left. Teneo's books were still on the shelves. Drogar's second sniper rifle still hung on the rack with a couple pistols and spare ammo. All these ghosted pieces were all that was left behind of the team.

It was as if every little piece of the guys left behind unvoiced questions. Would they come back? Would things ever be the same again? Was this the sign of Lexa being forced into something by the Agerian's Council? Could this be the last few days Lexa had in Sydney?

Despite the possibility of that last question being true, Lexa found herself unable to leave the flat. A part of her felt the moment she did, it would all disappear. Ethran's shoes. Teneo's notebooks. Drogar's jacket. That somehow, if she left, some phantom would appear and rip it all away.

And she couldn't stand the concept of that.

She didn't know why it hurt so much to think that she might never see Teneo or Drogar again—they annoyed the shit out of her. Teneo was so boring and know-it-all. Drogar was old and crotchety. Neither of them had been her favorite people.

So, then why did she miss them so much?

Asher had tried a few times to get Lexa to talk about it, but the teen had simply snapped comments at her Zaheri. No, she didn't want to talk about it. She didn't want to discuss any of it. She just wanted it all to go back to normal.

But that wasn't happening.

With each day that passed, it became painfully apparent that nothing was going to be the same again. No matter how much Lexa wanted it to be different, she was stuck at the mercy of some unseen force that wouldn't let her have happiness. Or so it felt.

Lexa sat on the couch, angrily tapping her foot against the coffee table as she glared at the clock. Almost another day gone, and still nothing. If one more day passed without incident, she was going to demand Asher take them to Agerius so she could see the others.

An alarm blared, and Lexa nearly leaped out of her skin at how loud it was. She whipped her attention to the computer rigged to all of their sensors.

Asher ran to the screen as Lexa vaulted over the couch and asked, "What is it? What's going on?"

"It's a portal activation," Asher said evenly, her expression sharp as she took in the information on the screen. Her brow twitched as she said, "In the Opera House."

"What?" Lexa asked as she furrowed her brow.

Glancing to the teen, Asher said, "Technically, it's the more stable activation point in the area, but we never use it, 'cause ... y'know, it's the Opera House."

Lexa's gaze flitted between the screen and Asher a few times. "'Kay, so ... the Caligans came from north of the city."

"Right." Asher went to where the pistols were kept and grabbed one, quickly holstering it. "We need to go investigate it; see what's going on."

"Okay, but where in the Opera House can I jump that we won't immediately be seen?"

With a quick look at her watch, Asher answered, "The east stairwell. This time of day, there should be less security on that side of the building. We can get into the auditorium from there."

"East stairwell," Lexa muttered as she glanced toward the ceiling, doing her best to remember the layout of the building, and the stairwell in question. After a second, she nodded. "Right, gotcha."

As Asher took her arm, she added, "And you'll listen to my orders?"

Wearing a resigned look, Lexa nodded. "Yeah."

"Okay. Let's go."

A moment later, they appeared in the stairwell in question with a soft pulse of orange mist.

For a few seconds, they remained still, listening for any indication that their arrival had been heard. Asher then nodded to Lexa and exited the stairwell, checking the halls as they went. They carefully made their way to the auditorium doors and could faintly hear voices inside.

"Stay behind me," Asher hushed to the teen.

"*Okay,*" Lexa hissed in exasperation, giving Asher a look that said, "*I get it. Stop saying that.*"

Ducking into the auditorium, Lexa followed Asher as they carefully made their way to the stage.

There was a group of people there. Maybe a dozen total. All of them looked worse for wear, with clothing either dirty or askew. Several bore the echoes of battle, with either blood splatters or visible injuries.

"It's a national landmark, at least," some Japanese-looking kid said.

Some old guy grumbled, "Okay, so we should probably find a way out of here before someone comes in and starts screaming." He sounded a lot like Drogar.

Relief flooded Asher's features, and she let out a small sigh as she said, "No need to go looking."

Everyone on the stage sprang into action. A couple of the teens got shoved behind adults as guns were raised to the ready. Two large creatures let out growls as they turned to survey who had spoken.

Stopping mid-step, Asher threw her hands up. "Whoa, what a way to greet someone."

"Asher," the grumpy-sounding one got out through a strangled sigh, lowering his rifle.

"We've just been through a rough morning," an older woman said, her darker skin a beautiful complexion, in Lexa's opinion.

"I can see that," Asher said as she continued walking down the aisle. Lexa followed behind, trying to take in everyone on the stage.

Clearly, these were other Agerians. And the teens must've been Human-Borns. Lexa scanned them, trying to figure out which of them was the Raidin. Trying to size up her competition.

Two boys and two girls. One of the boys was Japanese and clearly a fighter, with a wider frame and plenty of muscle. Kinda cute but looked like he was chaotic. He was probably the Raidin. An empty sword sheath was strapped at his side. Then there was—*ugh* that was the Brit, wasn't it? He looked every bit like some snob who probably had tea preferences. Great.

One of the girls was definitely African. Her garb reflected what Lexa would've expected from some tribal girl, and her dark skin a stark contrast against the vibrant fabrics. She was pretty but looked fragile, like she didn't have a lot of physical strength to her body. Lexa liked her dress.

The other girl stood behind an imposing-looking man who clearly kept himself planted in front of her. She wasn't built too much differently than Lexa. Shorter and less thin. She was dirty, and her jacket was torn. Whoever she was, she looked like hell.

Pointing toward the ceiling, the man guarding the second girl asked, "Are we where we think we are?"

"Well, if you think you're in the Sydney Opera House, then yes," Lexa answered.

"Where are the guards?" a slender, beautiful blonde asked. Lexa liked her already and thought they'd probably get along famously.

Asher waved them down. "Busy, but not for long. They take rounds, and currently there's a gap in their security. We can slip back out of the building if we're quick."

Some guy with jet-black hair muttered something Lexa couldn't pick up. *He* was cute. She'd have to get to know him.

Voices came from the entrance, filtering in from the hallway outside. It'd be faster if Lexa just jumped them all to the flat. They could talk there.

She tugged on Asher as she got onto the stage. "C'mon, I can get us out of here." She walked up to the group.

The second girl pointed at her and said, "You're the Shifter."

"I'm a Jumper," Lexa answered. She took a step toward the girl and held out her hand. "My name's Lexa."

Shaking Lexa's hand, the girl said, "Jen. We can do the rest of the introductions later. Can you handle everyone?"

By the time they got to the flat, Lexa found that she hated the Raidin even more.

Because now it wasn't some boy she had to impress. It wasn't even like that had been a requirement.

She'd been overshadowed by some plain-looking bitch.

The SCHOLAR'S SCARS

Sixth brings the
Scholar,
seeker of wisdom,
whose gifts allow
truth to chime.

Chapter One
HIDDEN DREAMS AND
SECRET MEANINGS

Mendoza was a town rich in culture, scenery, and wineries. Tradition and familial expectation bathed even the most unassuming homes, and the most unassuming lives. Children had certain roles they were expected to fill and certain things that everyone assumed of them.

Sophia Gonzalez met none of those expectations.

Hurriedly getting her boots on, Sophia did her best to be out of the house before daylight snuck into the house. She hastily threw her brown hair into a fat, messy braid before snagging her falling-apart bag. Glancing over her shoulder, she took note of the dawning light.

Panic clutched her chest as she carefully cracked her bedroom door open and peeked into the hallway.

Faint snoring from down the hall. No lights on. Diana's door was ajar. But no movement.

Gently stepping out of her room and pulling the door shut with absolute silence, Sophia creeped through the dark house. She just had to get outside before anyone else woke up. If anyone caught sight of her, there'd be consequences.

This was the one thing she could almost always get right. But lately, she'd been failing at that, too. Her wildly vivid dreams kept her in bed longer than she knew she was supposed to be, especially on workdays. There was something about her dreams that she couldn't let go of, even after she woke. They were chaotic and messy, and never lined up with anything she'd ever concocted. If dreams truly were her subconscious linking together random events from her day-to-day life and putting together a story, then she was living a double life.

Well, she *was* living a double life, but her double life would've had to be much more fantastical than her current double life.

And she couldn't blame the books she devoured either. While many were fantastical and brought to life other worlds, creatures, and concepts, her dreams were never like any of her books. They were always most vivid just before she woke, or just as she drifted into slumber. Which was why she was in such a rush today. She'd tried so hard to hold on to the already blurring details of her dream and had laid in bed too long.

Her parents knew her schedule better than she did, and they knew which days she was supposed to be gone before they woke. And if Diana caught sight of her after she was supposed to be on her way to work, even if it was only a moment, that'd be worse. Because Diana was, as her name suggested, the princess.

About a year prior, right about when the dreams started, Sophia had been unable to stop talking about their fantastical nature. It was like the logical part of her head had just shut off and she'd babbled on and on about what she'd dreamed. Diana always plugged her ears and called Sophia a crazy little thing. She'd even once tried to convince the priest of their local parish that Sophia was possessed. Later, after a harrowing day for Sophia, where she was questioned and treated like a monster, Diana had admitted it was only a joke and batted her pretty eyes in apology. And, of course, forgiveness was granted to her immediately.

Diana never got in trouble.

It was Sophia's fault. If she'd just shut up and not been so annoying, none of it would have happened.

Her parents had been furious, and taken their frustration out on her, and then one another. That was when Sophia had stopped talking about her dreams. And it was the last time she'd really talked with Diana. Though, "talked with" was a stretch.

Truthfully, Sophia couldn't recall a single genuine conversation she'd had with her sister. The warmest memories she could remember were of the times Diana gushed about dates or lauded her superiority over Sophia.

Sophia couldn't blame her. After all, Diana was the pretty one who did all the things expected of her. She was the one who had the boys fall over one another to try to get her attention. She was the one who had several boys begging to be her boyfriend once she'd turned fifteen and could officially start dating, which Sophia had known was all a farce. Diana had been dating a seventeen-year-old for at least a year.

Even so, a tiny part of Sophia felt that Diana wasn't that worthy of praise. Not that she'd *ever* say it out loud. But, seeing as Sophia was the one who got reprimanded for being too quiet, too nervous, too anti-social, and had been forced to witness many of her beloved books ripped from her hands and thrown aside as she literally got shoved in front of some boy, Sophia knew, beyond a doubt, that she was wrong.

Diana was the good child, and Sophia was the bad one.

Diana never got reprimanded. She was beautiful, and flirtatious, and outgoing, and social.

Once Sophia had turned fifteen, her parents seemed to have been under the impression that some switch would flip and Sophia would suddenly become a ball of socialness. Instead, quite the opposite had happened.

Sophia knew she was expected to go find a boyfriend and start seriously dating, working her way toward marriage. She knew she was supposed to be out partying or spending time with friends. She knew their culture would only see her as strange if she stayed cooped up in her bedroom or the small local library, reading yet another new book.

Books were the only thing she felt comfortable around. Their smell welcomed her as though a comforting blanket for her soul. The feel of the pages under her fingers. The intricate designs of antique books and the smoothness of leather spines sent her an unquantifiable level of serenity that simply couldn't be achieved anywhere else.

Boys were weird.

Why would she ever want to trade one of those glorious, wonderful, captivating books for a boy?

As she made her way through the kitchen, a note caught Sophia's attention. The words on the page were simple. Even so, they sent her stomach into a clenching knot.

Juan tomorrow 6pm

That was it.

Gripping the strap of her bag tighter, Sophia tried not to quake at the idea of another date. She knew exactly who the note referenced and knew exactly what she had to be prepared for. Juan was one of the many boys who had tried and failed to get Diana's attention. They all saw Sophia as a leftover, and they weren't nice.

Sophia had tried. She really had. But every time things moved too fast, and they grabbed too hard, she just couldn't go along with it. And every time she came home with a bruise and crying, if her parents saw her, it all got worse.

Once she was outside, a sigh of relief tumbled from her. She'd made it outside without being seen. It could be a good day. She could stay out of trouble.

Making her way across town to the diner she worked at, Sophia tried to shove the reality of her planned date the next night out of her mind. Most girls were happy to be doted on and treated like princesses. Date and marry, be taken care of. Sophia didn't necessarily find it intolerable; she just ... kinda felt like she wanted to learn.

Learn what? Well, learn everything. Especially if it had to do with words. Words and language were her favorites. Not that she knew many languages. She could read English nearly without issue, but speaking it? She had yet to conquer that. A few small phrases she could muster, but she typically messed up tenses. Why was English so difficult to learn?

But if it was a written language, she could learn it. She'd taught herself how to read French alongside English and had learned Latin before either of those. She couldn't speak French or Latin, but she'd read whole books written in both languages without issue.

Truthfully, the only reason she could read English as well as she did was because of her Zaheri, Salan.

A small smile came to Sophia's face as she neared the diner. Just a few hours of work, and then she could go to her favorite place.

When she reached the diner, one of the older women immediately barked, "About time! Get moving!"

"I'm sorry," Sophia said, scurrying to drop her bag and snatch her apron. Glancing at the clock, she bit her tongue. Fifteen minutes early still wasn't enough. She'd have to plan to get to work earlier.

Once she got working, things went by quickly. She never got orders wrong, so that helped. But, as most of the patrons were locals, Sophia didn't get any praise. None of them really liked her much. She caused too much trouble, and everyone knew it. Her parents weren't quiet about every mistake Sophia made, so the whole town saw her as the child who constantly messed up.

It made her yearn for somewhere new. A place where no one knew her so she could start over. Maybe in a new place, she could leave her mistakes behind her.

If only she could go to university. Maybe there she wouldn't be looked at as weird. Well ... she probably would still be weird. It wasn't like she could ever fathom going to university in some faraway country, no matter how much she wished she could. Her family couldn't even afford for her to go to a university in Argentina, let alone some other country where no one knew who she was. Or where girls studying weren't quite so different. Not that it was impossible or frowned upon; it was just ... different.

Her shift was a blur of commands for her to be faster. To be more friendly to customers. To get out of the way. She didn't drop any plates today, so at least she hadn't messed that up. And it was payday, so her parents would be happy about that.

When she was handed her check, Sophia realized it was a little less than last week's amount. A frown came to her face as her boss grumbled, "Be here on time, and I won't have to dock your pay."

Right. She had to get there earlier. This was her fault.

Her parents wouldn't like the pay cut.

Timidly lifting her head, she asked, "Could I ... maybe work a little longer right now? I'll clean the dishes or scrub the floors to make up the extra money."

Her boss gave her a condescending look before he rolled his eyes. "Fine, sure. But be quick about it," he said dismissively, waving his hand as if Sophia was a pest.

She didn't respond. Responding wasted time. She had to be swift and get a lot done in a short amount of time. He'd probably only let her work for fifteen minutes or a half hour. Could she get enough done to make up the missing pay?

Her arms were sore when she finished her extra time in the kitchen. She'd never scrubbed so frantically, or cleaned quite so many dishes, as she did in that short twenty minutes. But she made up the extra pay, so she smiled and thanked her boss profusely.

Hopefully, Salan wouldn't be upset with her. By now, her Zaheri was probably situated at the library. Though she'd never seen Salan look annoyed or irritated, Sophia could imagine her Zaheri glaring at the clock and grumbling to herself at Sophia's tardiness.

Just under a year ago, Sophia had been introduced to her Zaheri. She'd been told a little bit about who she was to them and why she needed their protection. They kept their distance, mostly at Sophia's insistence.

She was almost positive that her parents would have none of it if Sophia came home with three aliens and a large, talking, four-legged creature in tow. And, while she wished for her two worlds to mesh well, there was a nagging doubt in her mind that it wasn't possible. That her parents simply wouldn't acknowledge it as reality.

But it was reality. It was the truth. It wasn't as though Sophia had chosen to become this special person, a Human-Born, for her Zaheri.

All she had been told was that she was a Human-Born, a warrior foretold in a prophecy on her Zaheri's home world, Tilion. That her title was Scholar, and that, one day, she would help rid her Zaheri's nation, Agerius, of a foe they fought called Cregorous.

That was it.

On one hand, she was content with that information. For the time being, that was all she needed to know. It explained why she didn't get sick easily. It explained why her bones never broke, even when she should've suffered a major injury (like when she was pushed down as a girl and caught her fall on her wrist. She should've broken it, the doctor said. A miracle, he'd said). It explained why she could hear things better than normal people. Why she could see things better than normal people. And she was almost certain it was why she could remember things better than normal people.

However, there was no doubt that she wondered how *she* was supposed to be a warrior.

She couldn't even walk in a straight line sometimes.

Would her ability to devour and retain knowledge really be that helpful in a war? It felt like that wasn't possible. Yes, knowledge had its value, Sophia knew that. She cherished that. But in war? Especially a war on another world? Another world Sophia knew little to nothing about? Against a foe she knew even less about?

As she ran to the library, she wondered what Cregorous was after. What he really wanted. Maybe if she could figure that out, and give him whatever he wanted, the war would be over. But if she couldn't, how was she supposed to stop him?

Begging and saying please probably wouldn't do it.

The bell tolled the hour, and Sophia pushed her legs faster, narrowly avoiding a car as she went. Swears came from the driver as he yelled at her to watch where she was going. She panted back a flimsy apology.

Hopefully, her parents wouldn't hear about that.

I just have to get to the library. Salan's already been waiting. If she left, then I won't get any teaching today. Just move faster, she told herself.

This was the only thing she wanted. She had to get to the library on time. If she missed Salan, if she didn't get to learn anything today ...

When she reached the library, she sucked in gasps of air. Leaning against the wall of the small building immediately made her feel better. If she believed buildings could restore the soul, she'd be convinced the library was her hospital.

Another chime from the bell tower, and she let out a heavy breath. She'd made it on time. Salan might still be here. Her heart stopped pounding and her breathing soothed as she sank back a little.

Walking into the library, she smiled shyly at the old man behind the counter. Mr. Rivera was a kindly old man with lots of wrinkles that adorned his features. His head was covered in tight, short curls that barely helped mask the thinning of his locks. She'd wondered often if he had spent the majority of his youth in the sun, as his skin was tough and dark, and there were a few tattoos that she caught glimpses of from time to time.

He was one of the few people in town who she thought liked her. He smiled warmly at her whenever she entered the library and never bothered her when she left with an armload of new books to read. Truthfully, she liked him very much, even if she knew little about him.

The library was usually empty. Occasionally, there were families who came looking for books for their children, and those studying in university might be seen roving the stacks for research material. Most days that Sophia visited, there was maybe one or two other people who came and went during her hours-long stay in the quiet building.

Sophia liked quiet, and she liked being surrounded by all of those books. Every now and again, she would look up and marvel at the sheer number of volumes filling the shelves. It would take a lifetime to read them all. More than that, most likely.

Even though she read at an alarming speed, Sophia wished she could consume books faster. Then maybe she would be able to take all of them in, no matter the subject matter.

Well, that wasn't true. She really didn't like horror novels. But everything else she'd read so far, she'd loved. That included textbooks.

As she neared her normal corner, she prepared herself to be disappointed. Though she knew that Salan should be there based on the hour, she'd been late. Her Zaheri was bound to have angrily left after Sophia kept her waiting for over an hour. Anyone else would.

To her great relief, Sophia came around the corner and found Salan huddled over a book. The older woman whipped her head up and immediately smiled sweetly to Sophia.

"What a relief. I was getting worried," Salan said, closing her book and setting it aside before gently patting the table next to her.

Sophia couldn't rightly say what made her straighten at the sight of her Zaheri. Why smiles always came unbidden to her face and why warmth spread in her chest. There was just something about Salan that made Sophia feel ... happy.

The woman had a confidence and fierceness that Sophia admired greatly. That Salan could go from bright, warm smiles that were infectious to stern and serious in an instant, if necessary, only resolidified just how assured the woman was in herself. She was gorgeous, Sophia thought. With a softness to her cheekbones and a natural kindness in her eyes, Salan held this ability to see through people, as if reading their every action without actively trying. Her long, thick hair was always down, falling in cascades around her features. If Sophia had to guess, Salan and her husband, Neri, were both in their forties or early fifties, as they had wrinkles to show for their age; otherwise, they were aging very well. There was a weathered-ness to their stances, as though they'd seen enough to know when to be aggressive and when to be soft.

In a moment, they settled into their rhythm for study. Salan had leaped at the opportunity to aid Sophia in her study of English, and by this point, they had a system down. There wasn't a lot of small talk. Sophia's hours were limited between work and her family's insistence that she be present at evening meals and at least a little engaged with the almost daily get togethers of friends or family in the house.

As much as Sophia wanted to talk with Salan about many different things, she greatly appreciated that the Agerian was willing to keep their study time streamlined.

Per the norm, when the hour chimed from the church nearby, they finished up the English tutoring and began to slowly pack their things.

"I believe you've learned all you can from me on this subject," Salan said.

"Really?" Sophia asked. She was about to put her notebook away, but instead opened it again and studied her most recent notes. "I would have anticipated that I still had several weeks of practice left."

With a small shake of her head, Salan smiled. "No, dear, I think you're fully capable of reading English fluently. Which is why"—she produced a small, leatherbound, unmarked book—"I thought you could start reading this."

Her eyes flicking between the book in Salan's grasp and her eyes a few times, Sophia gingerly reached for the offered book. "What is it?" the girl asked.

Salan rested her elbows against the table as she answered, "It's one of the books from Agerius' Archive."

Snapping her gaze to Salan's, Sophia felt excitement shoot through her body, her fingers clutching the leatherbound book in her grasp.

"I thought you might like to read something from our world."

Ripping the book open, Sophia began searching the first page for information. She wouldn't have expected to feel so ravenous over an Agerius book but, in that moment, she couldn't imagine putting it down.

"I can't promise I chose the best option." Salan grimaced but kept a small smile on her face. "It was hard enough to get some of the Archivists to let me leave with it." When Sophia remained silent, her wide eyes, drinking in the words on the page, Salan asked, "So, what's this volume talk about?"

"This volume? You mean there's more!" Sophia squeaked in a louder voice than she'd intended.

Wearing a joyful glee, Salan smiled back at the girl. "There's a whole portion of Agerius set aside for our Archives. Some of the records might be a bit dull. We record everything from birth dates and Defenders' promotions to major events."

Sophia nodded a little, her gaze still glued to the pages. "This appears to document the—" She sucked in a breath and incomprehensible words tumbled from her mouth. It took her a few seconds to recover, her eyes alight with excitement as she looked between Salan and the book. "This ... this talks about the appointment of the Zaheri!"

Relief flooded Salan's features as she sank back with a heavy breath. "*Whew*! I got the right one! I was almost worried the Archivists gave me something that just documented some birth records."

Slowly looking away from the book in her grasp, Sophia met Salan's gaze. There was something about this gesture—this gift—that Sophia couldn't put a word to. It made her feel ... like she'd been seen for the first time. Like someone understood her.

The knowledge that Salan had gone out of her way to procure a book from Agerius' Archive sent a strangely wonderful feeling in Sophia's chest.

"Thank you," Sophia finally whispered.

Offering a smile in return, Salan nodded. "Of course, sweetie."

Then the bell from the church chimed the quarter of the hour, the alert that Sophia had to be making her way home, which meant this cherished book of history would have to wait.

"You'll have to tell me all about what it says tomorrow," Salan said as she rose to her feet.

"You haven't read it?" the teen asked as she gathered her old messenger bag.

Shaking her head, Salan answered, "No. I thought it would be good for you to read it, and then tell me what it says. Then I can check whether you got it right."

Perhaps someone else might have seen that as a groan-worthy test. For Sophia, however, she was thrilled with Salan's choice. It was a fantastic measure to determine whether Sophia had officially mastered reading English in its written form.

She could think of no better test than to check her understanding against a piece of Agerius' history.

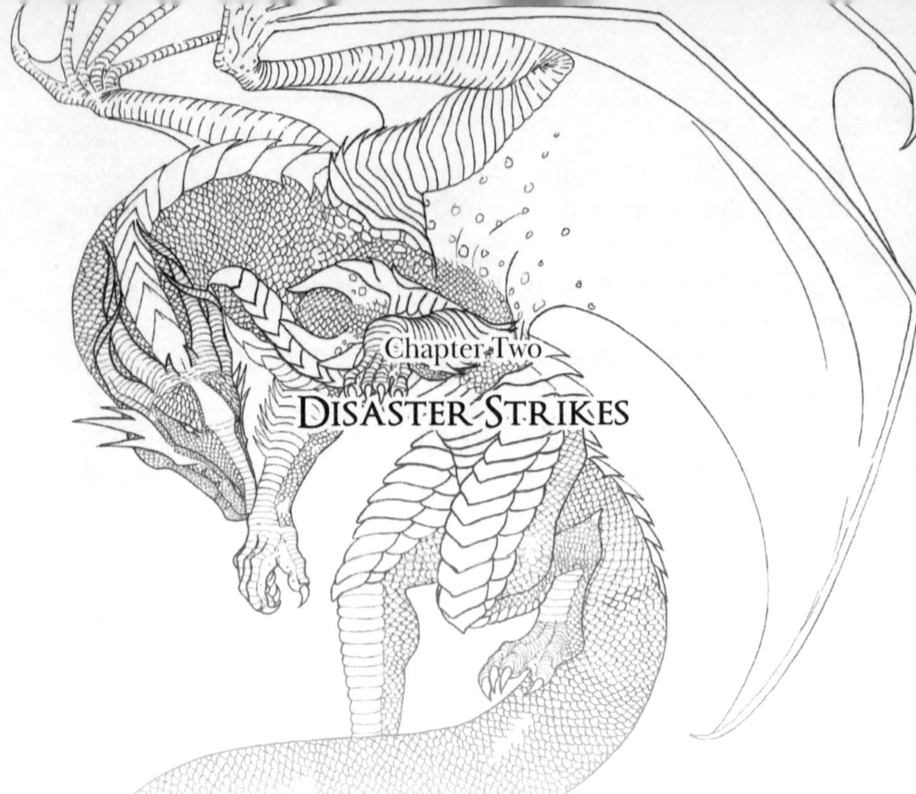

Chapter Two

DISASTER STRIKES

A man's outline loomed ahead of her, a bloodred mass with sharp teeth and black smoke-filled eyes. Behind it was a massive dragon. She felt as though, in that instant, she could connect with no one and was completely untethered from everything. Just a glance at this being sent her to heart palpitations, instilling a feeling of dread that sank into her bones.

With a sadistic smile on its face, the man hurled an attack toward her; a red, crackling beam, looking like a spear with smoke and lightning flying behind it like blood. She turned and followed the attack as it collided with a small figure, its whole being a white light.

Sophia felt chained to the events playing out before her as she followed the aftermath of the attack. The white figure's form conveyed extreme pain as it flew from its original spot as though struck. Within a few seconds, it turned into a singular white ball of light, with white smoke all around it. The light smashed into another white figure, and the orb of light grew larger. It continued on its path, pummeling a third white figure. Again, the light assimilated its form. It hit a fourth figure, then a fifth. Each time the orb of light collided with one of the figures, it pulsed in vibrant light and grew ever more powerful.

As it flew, the ball of light gained sound, starting softly like a screaming firework. It grew in volume and pitch, striking anxiety in Sophia's chest as she waited for the catastrophic boom.

On its unseen path, the orb soared toward a sixth white figure. Six sounds converged, creating a harmony as it neared this next, seemingly unsuspecting person. The harmonious sound grew louder and louder. When the light smashed into the sixth form, it recoiled, staggering back as though it had been shot. The white dispersed through its being, splaying light that radiated along its veins.

A ringing sounded as the sixth planted itself and stretched out its arms, fists clenched, and its light grew and grew to a blinding level. The tones, though harmonious and beautiful, rose to a deafening ringing.

The red attack from the shadowy figure hurtled at the sixth figure, screaming its outrage as it went. When the attack collided with the blinding white, an explosion tore away from the sixth figure. Its form turned brilliantly blue.

A shockwave tore the red attack apart, cutting straight through it and smashing it into a million pieces. Then a blast of rainbow colors slammed into the shadowy attacker, hurtling it back to where it had come.

Her alarm began to blare, and Sophia felt herself get yanked out of the dream in a snap. Without moving, she slapped her hand in the direction of her alarm and managed to hit the *off* button.

She lay in bed, staring at the ceiling, trying to commit this dream to memory. Even if it was horrible.

She'd tried dream journals before, but they always became jumbled confusion for her when she went back to reread them. Like she couldn't even dictate properly what she had dreamed.

The book Salan had given her had fallen to the floor, and Sophia wanted to snatch it up. She'd read it before she fell asleep the night prior.

Something about her dream was clinging. Grasping at her consciousness and almost begging her to connect dots. But what dots?

Sophia didn't understand why her mind thought it understood something. As if she grasped some deeper, hidden meaning to a question she hadn't been asked. She wanted to figure out what question she needed to ask that would suddenly click her subconscious answer into place.

But her dreams were just dreams. Chaotic, crazy, unconnected dreams.

A *bang* sounded on her door as her father yelled, "Get up!"

Snapping upright, she clutched her blanket, staring at the door in fear. He'd banged angrily. She could tell it wasn't just a gentle *tap, tap* to let her kindly know she might be late.

He was already angry about something.

Which meant her mother was already angry about something.

She'd need to tread especially carefully.

Already, her dream was forgotten. The real danger of her parents' ire and the ramifications of that had stolen it away.

Within a few moments, she was dressed and in the kitchen, throwing together a small meal. There was a fifty-fifty chance she'd actually eat it. Some days, she was so nervous and worried about stepping out of line that she couldn't bring herself to put anything into her system.

Almost all of her money went toward her family's cost of living, leaving her a miniscule amount to tuck away to maybe one day put toward university.

So far, she'd managed to avoid her parents. That was good. If they were angry about something completely unconnected to her, and she kept out of their line of sight, that meant they couldn't associate their fury with her. But if they did see her, and they did associate their anger with her, well …

She didn't want to have to change into a long-sleeved shirt.

Her mother always managed to strike her blows so no one would ever see them. Her father, for whatever reason, always veered toward harshly shaking Sophia by her arms, leaving rough bruises.

At least, as a Human-Born, she healed fast.

It must've been that she did something really wrong when she was little, and it had carried over into her older years. And it probably was her fault. If she just would be more outgoing and do what they said, maybe they wouldn't be so angry. If she didn't mess up so much, they wouldn't have to carry her failures.

Just as she started for the door, she stopped in her tracks. The Agerian book! She couldn't leave that behind. She'd left enough books at home only to find them missing upon her return later to know that she couldn't risk it. Where her other books got to, she couldn't say. But she'd never dare ask.

It was her own fault for leaving them laying around. Her parents—maybe even Diana—were tired of cleaning up after her.

Her bed wasn't made, either. And she had left a dirty dish in the sink.

Don't freak out. Just move quickly! she told herself.

As she hastily put her bed together and realized she was making too much noise, she reprimanded, *Move quickly, but get it right. Don't make too much noise. Don't disturb anyone. Just get it done and get out of the house.*

Snatching up the Agerian book, she carefully put it into her worn messenger bag then scurried to the kitchen to clean up her dirty dish. She couldn't leave a trace of her mess.

A surge of relief swam in her chest as she grabbed her bag and made for the door.

She'd almost made it out the door without seeing her parents. Her hand was on the doorknob and everything.

"Sophia," her mother snapped.

Before she could defend herself, the barrage started.

"I thought we told you that you were to accept Juan's invitation for tonight!"

The note yesterday.

Oh no, she thought. She hadn't realized—

This had to be the biggest blunder she'd ever made.

She'd been so wrapped up in the Agerian book, in her excitement to read it, in her eagerness to get lost in the pages ... she had completely forgotten about the date. And to top it off, the note had been left for her to confirm things? How stupid could she be!

Quick, come up with an answer! Say something!

"Oh, um ... well ..." Sophia said, grabbing her arm and rubbing her skin awkwardly.

"This is unacceptable!" Her mother slammed her hand down onto the rickety kitchen table. A few utensils hopped from the force. "We have told you again and again what you should be doing!"

"But, Mama, I—"

Slap.

She should've known better than to talk back. Why did she always have to try to talk back?

Her mother launched into a furious stream of words so fast that Sophia found herself just nodding a lot, doing her best to ignore the stinging pain on her cheek.

It was the same string of commands she'd heard before. She shouldn't talk back. She shouldn't slouch. She needed to wear better clothing. She needed to do a better job catching the boys' attentions. She *must* say yes to Juan, because no one else was asking about the shy girl who didn't talk. They refused to take care of her and let her abuse their kindness.

"You stupid, forgetful child!" her mother hollered.

Sophia clutched the strap of her bag. "I'm sorry, Mama," she said meekly.

Her mother snatched her by the hair and yanked hard. "You had better not—"

A frantic knocking at the door startled Sophia so much she staggered away from it.

"What is it now!" her mother exploded in exasperation, ripping the door open and glaring at whoever was there.

Salan and Neri stood on the small stoop.

Neri wasn't an overly tall man, only having a few inches on Salan. His face was long, and his skin was sun-soaked, but it wasn't a caramel color normal for Argentina. He had soft, caring eyes and a stern brow. Often, he was cleanshaven; but today, there was evidence of scruff, making Sophia wonder why he'd changed his appearance. His short, dirty blond hair was never styled but always fell the same way.

Offering a sweet smile, Salan said, "Hello. I'm so sorry to intrude."

"Who are you? What do you want?" Sophia's mother snapped.

Trying again to smile warmly at the shorter woman, Salan answered, "My name is Sabina. I've been tutoring your daughter at the library."

Sophia's mother crossed her arms and gave Salan a hard stare. "You're the one filling her with fanciful ideas of some expensive school!"

A little caught off guard by the hostility of the woman, Salan defended herself. "I'm merely trying to help your very talented daughter—"

"Leave! We have no need of your services! And I won't be paying for them."

Gently pushing Salan aside, Neri gave Sophia's mother a stern look. "I'll ask you not to speak so harshly to my wife."

"I don't care who she is! Or who you are! Leave! Now!"

"What's all the noise!" Sophia's father boomed as he lumbered into the area, shoving Sophia back so he could tower behind his wife. He had a wide girth but was broad and proud. Years of working manual labor had earned him a reasonable strength that was buried underneath a beer belly.

He eased a bit at the sight of Neri, who wasn't much taller than him but appeared weaker based on his looser fitting clothes that hid his strong torso.

"Ah, I've seen you around. You're the ones've been pulling our daughter astray."

Clenching his jaw, Neri said, "We haven't been doing anything of the sort. But right now, we don't have time to discuss your distaste for us."

Rising as tall as he could, Sophia's father gained a dark look as he growled, "You come into my house—"

"Technically, I'm on your stoop."

"Neri," Salan hushed with a frown as she pulled him back. "Please, forgive us. We didn't intend to cause—"

"You are to leave our home immediately!" Sophia's father yelled as his wife nodded approvingly, reiterating her own frustration in quick, angry phrases.

"Not without Sophia," Salan said simply, gaining a defiant look in her eyes.

"She is our daughter! You have no right—"

"We have every right," Neri challenged, getting in Sophia's father's face. "You don't realize it, but we need her to come with us now. It's a matter of life or death."

Sophia's father moved to try to shove Neri back, only to be unable to move the slender man.

Neri quirked his head, gaining a confused look as Sophia's father seethed, "Leave this instant!"

"Are you trying to shove me?" Neri asked.

A perturbed sigh escaped Salan as her shoulders slumped and she covered her face with her hand, muttering something to herself.

Before an all-out fight could start between the two men, a loud, bellowing roar filled the air. A second later, a dragon flew overhead, no more than twenty feet off the ground. The gust of wind it created in its passing sent a plume of dirt flying into the house from the open door.

Sophia caught a glimpse of the beast and knew that it wasn't one of her Agerian's dragons. The scales were dark, and spikes littered its body. Agerian dragons were more regal and sported bronzes and golds in their scale colors. This dragon was clearly an enemy one, called a Ferveos.

Salan and Neri were right to be so concerned. Clearly, something had gone really wrong.

"We don't have time for this," Neri said, shoving Sophia's parents aside to get into the house.

"Neri—blast it. So sorry," Salan said with an apologetic look toward the bewildered couple.

Sophia timidly took Neri's outstretched hand and let him pull her from the house. She turned to say something in apology to her parents, but her words were all stuck in her throat. The stinging mark from her mother's slap was still on her skin, though it would fade in another moment. However, the reality of the situation created fear of her misspeaking, or saying the wrong apology.

And one look at her parents' expressions told her that they were absolutely fuming in rage.

It sent a sick feeling in her stomach, as her insides turned into knots.

"Wh—what's happening?" Sophia asked as she ripped her attention away from her parents and fell into a quick step between Salan and Neri.

"We aren't entirely sure, but it seems we may be under attack," Salan said as she gently held Sophia's shoulder. "It's going to be okay," she added with a comforting smile. "We won't let anything bad happen to you."

Despite the assurances, and even the calming that Sophia felt at

Salan's words, the girl still wound up clutching her messenger bag to her chest.

What did an attack mean?

Once they got outside of town, Sophia caught sight of a strange light on the side of the Andes Mountains. "What is that?" she asked.

They continued at a brisk pace toward the hills. Sophia knew that her Zaheri lived somewhere in the hilly country toward the mountains but had never been to their home before. She assumed they were heading there.

"That's the portal," Salan said with a nod toward the light. "The gateway to our world."

Neri threw his wife a concerned look while telling Sophia, "It doesn't normally look like that."

"It doesn't?" Sophia asked. His tone made her draw in on herself.

"We'll consider the ramifications later," Salan said.

Though it was cloudy, Sophia could make out the rough outlines of dragons as they flew toward them. There was an uneven thundering in the air, like footsteps, but not rhythmic and disciplined.

A moment later, they were joined by the rest of the Zeta Team. On the ground rushed Specter, the Warrior grovix. She was a lean but muscular beast. Her coat was mostly black, with speckles and stripes of white across her body. Her face reminded Sophia of a panther, but her maw was wider, and her ears were more pointed than round, and longer. She had white claws that looked feline more than canine, with more curvature than that of a dog's claws. Her armor glittered in the rays of sun that poked through the clouds, the metal plating adorned with spikes. Sophia had always thought she was a beautiful creature, but donned in her armor, Specter looked like an imposing enemy.

Dalia flew, her wings thin and razorlike. They reminded Sophia more of a bat's wings than a dragons'. The Agerian landed gracefully and skipped a bit as she made her way toward them.

There was a childlike nature to Dalia. Brightness in her eyes and a swiftness in her gait. She was more slender than Salan, and at first blush could be mistaken for a peaceful merchant, not a warrior. Though she was thin, she was a reasonable height and towered over Sophia's diminutive five-foot-two height. She had reddish brown hair that was pinned up in beautiful braids and kept close to her scalp to not get in her way while flying. Strands of hair always escaped her best efforts, and she'd wrinkle her button nose whenever a stray one swiped across her face.

"Sophia. It is good to see you, child," Specter said, gently nuzzling the tip of her nose against the teen.

It had taken Sophia some getting used to looking eye level at Specter. The grovix stood at nearly the same height as Sophia, making for a harsh reminder of just how powerful the creature before her was.

Undoing a belt across her chest, Dalia said, "I brought ya your scythe, Neri." She swung the belt around, producing the large scythe she had strapped to her back.

"Thanks, Dalia," Neri said as he took the weapon into his grasp. Then he nodded toward the portal. "What's it look like?"

"Not good," Dalia answered with a shake of her head. Wearing a frown, she continued, "Lots of 'em. Looks like a quarter of a legion maybe."

Salan gave her a motherly look. "You comfortable taking care of the Ferveos?"

A smile rose on Dalia's face, accentuating her big cheeks. "I'm your girl."

With a small chuckle, Neri patted her head. "Wouldn't expect anything less."

Nodding, Salan said, "All right. Neri, you and Specter need to cover the ground fighters. Dalia, I'm going to leave the Ferveos to you. I'll be staying with Sophia and keeping her guarded until this is over."

Dalia saluted. "You got it!" She hopped into the air, and her nimble wings gave a mighty push, rocketing her into the sky.

Sophia was struck by the smoothness and agility Dalia possessed, watching her seemingly effortless movements.

"You will be all right?" Specter asked with a nod toward Salan.

"I'll be fine. Now, come along. We need to meet the opposition before they reach the town," Salan said before jogging in the direction of the portal.

Scrambling after Salan, Sophia gave her a fearful expression. "Um ... what should I do?"

"Nothing right now, sweetie," Salan answered with a small shake of her head. "I just need you to stay right next to me so you can stay safe."

The concept of someone wanting to protect her made Sophia's mind short-circuit for a moment. What the action meant, and whether it was fueled by anything other than duty, made Sophia want to sit down and analyze it all to find the truth behind her Zaheri's actions.

But it couldn't possibly be anything more than duty.

All Sophia brought, and all she ever made, was trouble. And today was proving that tenfold. Even her role as a fabled Human-Born wasn't free from her clumsy blunders.

It took everything in Sophia to not cry at the reality that this one last tendril—this one last string of hope—had snapped.

She truly was a walking mistake.

Chapter Three

BATTLE LINES

Dalia surged through the air with her practiced dexterity. She missed fighting alongside the Scouts—the smaller dragons of Agerius—but knew that, for the time being, she had to be all right with flying solo. She would be among other Skycaptains and their Scouts before she knew it. Already the nineteen years on Earth had gone by quickly.

She came up on the first Ferveos and nearly rolled her eyes at the beast. They all did the same things—snapped wildly at first, and then blasted fire, like they didn't know how to do anything differently. All she had to do was push herself back with a flap of her wings, avoid the snapping jaw, and then she would kick it in the snout. It was antagonistic, and she knew that. But it was also a really easy way to get their attention.

Once she kicked the beast, it let out its grumbling annoyance and she landed on its brow. Cupping her hands around her mouth, she looked to the Ferveos next to them and hollered, "Hey! You there!"

The Ferveos she stood on tried to look up and see her but couldn't with where she stood.

But the Ferveos she had called to whipped its head over and looked at her with a growl.

She waved and said, "Hi!"

With a roar, the second Ferveos moved to slash at her. Though, to a passerby, her narrow escape through its talons would've looked dire, it wasn't a concern for Dalia. She avoided the beast's attempt with ease as it started to brawl with the first Ferveos.

On to the next one, which was easy, because it had turned to try to get at her, too. A few quick, well-aimed blasts from her pistol awarded her a dead beast that began to plummet toward the ground.

It seemed some things never changed.

Ferveos fell from the sky, explosions ripping the landscape where they collided with the earth. Caligans, werewolves, and bratak'ra alike were caught up in the mess. It left Neri and Specter less to worry over as they worked at stopping anything that came near them.

In his earlier years, Neri wouldn't have anticipated enjoying fighting alongside a grovix as much as he did with Specter. She was attuned to his position in the battle and would watch his back just as easily as he could watch hers. They paired well together and bounced about the field with relative grace, never impeding the other's attacks.

Gold energy surged from Neri and his scythe, taking out swaths of enemy fighters. He was grateful he'd stored up as much energy as he had in the weapon. It meant he didn't have to rely as much on the energy in his body right away. It kept his stamina up and allowed him to keep fighting without tiring.

Salan kept relative pace with them. A domed shield protected her and Sophia, enemies bouncing off the barrier, and attacks striking off with white sparks like hot lead. Keeping a hand on Sophia, Salan had to pull the girl along.

She'd gone quiet, gripping Salan's arm, and her legs staggered under her—she'd nearly tripped a few times.

If she could trust things enough to stay still, Salan would. But, as it stood, she had to keep a pulse on what was happening with the rest of her team, and whether they needed her assistance.

Dalia was doing a fantastic job taking out the Ferveos, which was to be expected. The younger hybrid was skilled in aerial combat and had proven on more than one occasion that, though she was young, she knew how to handle herself. And she didn't balk in the face of great opposition, a trait that Salan admired greatly in the redhead.

As she anticipated, Specter was dominating the battlefield. She was a limber Beta Warrior and had clearly solidified her role in the pack by being such a valiant fighter. Swift and decisive, Specter used her leaner form to charge through the battle and catch the bulkier bratak'ra off guard. The werewolves didn't seem to know what to make of her as they lumbered toward her with their lanky frames and sunken features. She made quick work of anything attempting to take advantage of Neri's blind spot, leaping over her fellow Agerian when necessary so she could squash an attempted blow.

And Neri, well, Salan knew her husband was beyond capable. He'd seen his fair share of battles and knew exactly when to use the fullness of his strength, and when to play it safer. She didn't fret over him much.

Though, in fights like this, she couldn't help but glance his way. Just in case.

If they had additional fighters, she wouldn't spare the time or attention. But four of them against at least two hundred meant she needed to stay alert. Her shields could mean the life or death of one of her teammates. And she had a feeling that Sophia feared such a thing.

The girl clutched on to her and trembled. After several minutes passed, Salan found herself practically dragging Sophia along, keeping her upright as best she could with one hand.

She sent shields into the field when necessary, being sure to watch her teammates actions so she wouldn't unintentionally impede them. Salan had learned that sometimes shields could do more harm than good, if a fighter was planning to use an attack or attempted blow to their advantage.

A handful of Caligans remained and worked to overwhelm Neri. With a swirl of his scythe, he slammed the weapon into them, sending them stumbling backward. Salan shot a slicing blast of gold at one. Specter pounced on another. As Neri dispatched a third, Dalia landed on top of the fourth.

They all straightened and got their bearings, finding no further opposition.

"Go team!" Dalia said with a smile as she hopped in the air, swirling a little before gracefully landing again. "That wasn't so bad."

Catching his breath, Neri planted his scythe in the ground and rested against it. "You did well, Dalia."

As Specter stepped up to him, he nodded to her. "Thanks for watching my blind spots."

Specter nodded gracefully in a bow. "As I must thank you. I appreciated your efforts to keep me safe."

None of them were unscathed. They all had cuts or nicks here and there. Smudges of blood where wounds had already healed. Patches of blood on clothing where the fabric had already restored.

Sophia continued to clutch Salan's arm, her eyes unfocused and her breathing sharp and fast.

Gently cupping Sophia's face, Salan hushed, "Sweetie, it's okay. Breathe."

"S-so many ..." Sophia managed to squeak out.

She'd never seen a fight. Not like that.

There had been odd fistfights here and there. Boys getting into scraps. Her father and uncles roughhousing and getting carried away with their drunken punches. Strangers getting into brawls over stupid things. Even violence between her parents and hits aimed at her.

But ... these were dead bodies. And there were ... so many ...

Looking to the others, Salan said, "We should get her home and away from here."

"Agreed," Neri said with a few nods. He came up to Sophia and blocked her view of the bodies strewn around them. "Hey, don't look at them, Soph. Look at me," he said softly, bending down a little to let her see his face.

She blinked a few times and connected her gaze with his.

"It's okay. It's over. You're safe, and everything's gonna be okay."

Sophia swallowed and nodded shakily.

"Do you want me to carry you?"

Biting her lip, she responded with a few nods as tears started to gloss her eyes.

"Shut your eyes, sweetie," Salan said as Neri easily scooped her up into his arms. "It's okay."

Sophia couldn't recall the last time someone had carried her. She could remember distant memories as a child, likely due to her hybrid genes. Faint memories of sitting on the floor and crying for her mother to pick her up, and being told no, that she was fine.

To have Neri lift her up so easily into his grasp and hold her as his wings formed, Sophia felt unbelievably safe. There was a comfort in that action that she hadn't expected and didn't know how to voice just how much she liked being that well cared for.

The rush of air made her squeak, and she clutched Neri tighter. They were flying, which meant it might be safe to open her eyes again. With trepidation, she did so and saw clouds whipping by. A second later, they rose above the cloud cover, and Sophia felt all of her fear disappear.

It was as though they'd left the world behind, the clouds were now the ground. They couldn't have been too high up, because the air wasn't too thin, which meant the clouds must've been hanging lower than she'd thought.

Dalia and Salan poked out the clouds behind them. Dalia giggled as she danced in the breeze, letting her wings skim the cloud cover. Salan smiled at her.

"Like the view?" Neri asked with a smile.

"Yeah," Sophia hushed, taking in the clear view. It was so quiet. So serene.

Neri looked forward. "Take it in. We'll be home in a little bit."

Easing in Neri's grasp, Sophia did just that.

Chapter Four

THE ENVY OF SOME

Izel watched the group fly off, the grovix tearing after them with a swiftness uncommon for a Warrior.

It was a strange group, he thought.

The girl who had taken out the Ferveos was bubbly and a bit flighty, bouncing about like it was a game. There was a cheerfulness in her face he envied. Even in the face of two dozen Ferveos, she'd been quick to smile. The way she flitted on the breeze and hopped in place. He hated that she had the gall to be that happy.

It was something he'd get to experience when the Agerians finally felt what they felt. What they'd experienced. All those years, safely hidden behind their stupid barrier. Untouched by their master's power. Hiding from his justice on behalf of them all.

If he could get his hands on that scythe, he'd happily take it for himself. A formidable weapon and deserving to be in better hands.

Neri seemed powerful enough, and might even prove a good fight. But a weapon like that was reminiscent of old weapons. Ancient weapons. The types he'd wanted to wield someday. And now this Neri got to hold something like that? It wasn't right, and Izel would be sure to rectify it.

He'd wished Salan hadn't hidden behind her stupid shield the whole time like some coward. She was the Team Leader, according to their contact, which meant she should be strong. While her shields never broke during the combat, that didn't mean she was powerful enough to really prove a challenge. She'd only let out a few small blasts here and there when covering her teammates.

Clearly, she'd been more focused on the girl than anything else.

The girl.

Izel had expected more of a fabled Human-Born. All these years the Master had been preparing for them. Building an army of fighters to decimate them and finally lay claim to Agerius, and with it, all of Tilion. Waiting for the right moment to strike, to hit them when it would hurt most.

And now to find that this Human-Born was some weak, sniveling little child? One that hadn't even raised a weapon in defense? Just stood there like a pup for slaughter, expecting someone else to take care of her.

It was pathetic.

These were the Human-Borns the Elders thought would strike fear into Caliga's heart?

It was laughable.

That girl would snap like a twig in Izel's grasp. He wouldn't even have to use his energy against a weak, little thing like that. His hands were easily as big as her face. How easily he could crush her under his fingers.

He wasn't like Akeno; he didn't purposefully go out of his way to make others suffer just to watch them cling to life. But clearly, this little girl was one who, when he snapped her neck, it would be a bit satisfying to watch her Zaheri stare in shock as their hopes and dreams all went out with the girl. He kind of understood Caedex's thirst for carnage at times. This was one of them.

If he knew how to feel pity, he might feel it for her. After all, she was just some child who had clearly never been meant for anything great. Even as a fabled Human-Born, she would prove nothing more than a vapor in history.

Truthfully, he didn't delight in the idea of crushing a child. He understood why the Master was striking today, and why he was striking while they were still children. It was a symbolic thing, to remind Agerius that nothing was safe, not even children.

After all, they'd learned that a long time ago.

It wasn't their fault that the blighted Agerians had forgotten what trauma really meant. They were simply the hands of remembrance. The harbingers of history.

This would be over quickly.

Traversing the mountainside to get back to the portal was annoying, to say the least. Izel came across a few Caligans who had managed to not die in the first wave. Unfortunate for them that he found them, as they were fleeing the battle in fear. He made sure their cowardice was rewarded with the death they deserved.

His wings easily lifted him to the mountain pass that would lead to the spherical white orb of the portal, although he hated to admit that the cold wind made his muscles tense up. He purposefully took several moments to get his body acclimated to the cold before he continued to the portal.

Once he reached the gateway, he was grateful for the mountain terrain changing to the empty, sloping room. The portal's red appearance flashed out as he arrived, splaying wisps of red about the whitewashed space.

The mountains surrounding the Sixth Human-Born made his back tight, and he kept finding himself glaring. He hated mountains. They always towered above, as though forcing those below to gaze upward at their haughty "majesty."

Caliga's flat, equal ground was the only terrain he liked.

He passed Kelek on his way to the war room, the Right Hand taking no notice of him.

Every part of him was furious about that. It made his teeth itch and his arms tremble, and all he wanted to do was slam Kelek against a wall.

He watched Kelek stalk off, reining in his jealousy.

Of all of them that Kelek had chosen, he'd chosen *Avemod?* Avemod. That whelp of a man. It was downright insulting.

Caedex didn't get it. Caedex thought he was stupid.

Caedex could rot in darkness, for all Izel cared.

He prepared himself for the echoed harmonies that hurt his ears when he hit the basement. Izel hated going down there. The amassed, mutated creatures felt like shadows of something, and it all reminded him of the darkness in Niveus. He didn't like thinking about that, and he didn't like hearing that clashing harmony.

It felt like it kept trying to whisper something to him. Something he shouldn't know.

The Master's experiments cried out in similar clashing harmonies, at least to Izel's ears. He could swear that behind all the noise was a voice that knew him and sought him out. The airy background to the chaotic monsters' cries was both unsettling and disturbingly comforting. He chose to ignore it.

A mistress was a few paces ahead of him, about to enter the war room. She saw him, whipping her gaze into the war room and back to him, uncertainty in her eyes.

She took a few steps back into the hall and ducked her head as Izel passed.

The Master stood over the ancient table and rolled his hand toward Izel in an impatient manner.

Casting a quick glance back toward the door, Izel figured the faster he was, the happier Cregorous would be. Because the Master clearly was hungry for release. Hence, the mistress.

With a quick bow, Izel rattled off, "The Sixth is well guarded, but the tactics of her defenders are easily recognized. There should be little need to adjust your plans of attack with the second wave."

"Leave," Cregorous simply said with a few curt flicks of his hand.

Izel bowed and stole into the hallway, the mistress quickly gliding into the war room.

As he marched up the stairs, he went the long way to his chambers, snatching a couple of the mistresses as he went. Both women were all too happy for his attention, and neither of them flinched at his rough grip.

The mistresses knew he was one of the rough generals. He kind of hated that neither of them quivered at his iron grasp. Trembling was exactly what he wanted, and he wasn't getting it. Yet.

That would change once he unleashed his fury.

Fury over his assignment. Fury over his placement among the generals. Fury over Kelek's dismissal.

And he'd give anything to be able to pummel something else into oblivion.

These two mistresses would have to do.

"You sure you want to tell her everything?" Dalia asked with a look of concern to Salan.

With a quick glance back at the girl in their little living room, Salan hushed, "I think she deserves to know everything. And she's mature enough to handle it."

"Hey, I'm fine with it. It's ... y'know ... the whole thing about the Council."

Shuffling his weight slightly, Neri admitted, "That's a valid point."

Salan looked to Specter. "What do you think?"

The grovix looked to her Team Leader before she shrugged. "I have no opinion."

"Really?" Neri asked with a smirk.

She threw him a perturbed look. "I mean to say, I don't think we'd be wrong or right either way."

"Even though the Council made it clear that there are some things we shouldn't tell them?" Salan asked, darting quick glances to the others.

There was a small pause.

Neri let out a breath then said, "I'm fine either way. Whatever you think is best, I support it."

Elbowing Neri, Dalia gave him a cheeky grin. "Aw, look at you being such a good husband."

He ignored her jabs. "If we tell her everything, she can probably handle it. And given the situation, it's possible the other teams are going to do likewise."

"Okay, and if they don't?" Salan asked as worry ghosted her usually confident features.

With a glance to the ceiling, Neri smirked. "C'mon; let's think about it. You really think Kedar, Streya, and Asher wouldn't tell their Human-Borns?"

"That's assuming they are all under attack."

Dalia shrugged. "Makes sense, right?" She flipped her hand around in the general direction of the portal. "The portal was huge. Plus, it's not like the Council to be all, 'Oh hey, they were attacked. They're fine. It's only the Human-Borns. We don't need to check on them.'"

Letting out a short breath, Salan nodded. "Okay. I think we should tell her."

As Salan walked toward the living room, Neri looked to Dalia. "Hey, mind making up some coffee?"

With another informal salute, Dalia responded with a smile. "Can do."

Their house was a small place. A single story, with only a small attic for storage, its slightly disheveled exterior hid the comforting hominess of its interior. With a rustic feel to the place, it had a fairly open floorplan when you first stepped into the building. A well-sized living area to the right, a small dining area to the left, and a half wall looking into the kitchen was all visible from the front door. A single hallway pushed back into the building, presumably leading to bedrooms and bathrooms.

As they walked into the living room, they found Sophia clutching the book from the Archives. She slowly lifted her gaze to them. There was a small lull of silence before the teen whispered, "There's more than one Human-Born, isn't there?"

Neri's brow pulled together. "How'd you know?"

Sophia looked back to the book in her lap. "I ... read this last night before I went to bed."

Deflating a little, Neri whined, "I thought we were gonna give that to her together? On her birthday."

"Shh ..." Salan said with a gentle wave of her hand toward her husband.

Specter walked up to the girl and sat next to her. "Is that significant?"

"I ..." Sophia chewed on her lips, playing with the edges of the book as she worked through her thoughts. "I don't know. But ... I had a strange dream this morning. I mean, I always have strange dreams; that's not weird. Maybe it is. I don't know. I have strange dreams all the time. So, maybe having a strange dream last night isn't anything to talk about. But I have this feeling that it is, even though I can't explain it."

"How does the book from the Archives tie into that?" Neri asked.

"At first, I didn't think it did," Sophia whispered. She stroked the cover of the book. "But ... while you were over there talking, I started reading where I left off, and ..." She lifted her gaze to Salan and Neri, carefully clicking her eyes between them. "It talks about a prophecy."

Salan looked to Neri before she moved to sit next to Sophia. "Yes, it does."

Hope rose in Sophia's chest. "So ... I'm not the only one?"

Shaking his head, Neri answered, "No, you aren't the only one."

A heavy sigh stole from the teen as she slumped back. Relief flooded her at the thought that she wasn't expected to stop Cregorous. At the least, she wasn't expected to do it all alone. The weight flew off her shoulders, and she felt she could breathe easier.

Maybe one of the other Human-Borns wasn't a walking mistake.

"So, you've read it then?" Neri asked, nodding toward the book.

Sophia nodded. "Yes. And ... according to this, I'm the Sixth. The Scholar, right?"

"Right."

"So ... the others, they all sound like they have really specific names." She sat up a little and searched the three with her. "Like Warrior and Protector, they're probably really good fighters and defenders."

The three shared glances.

"Right ..." Salan said, carefully gauging where Sophia was going with her thought.

"So ... Raidin ..." Sophia gained an unfocused look as she muttered, "It means 'Elders Warrior.'"

Neri straightened and furrowed his brow, quickly looking to Salan with question.

She met his confusion with her own.

Specter squinted at the girl and asked, "How did you know that?"

Blinking a few times, Sophia's gaze refocused, and she admitted quietly, "I don't know. I just ... did."

"Well, that could play into your ability," Neri offered.

Sophia snapped her attention to him, eyes wide and eager for answers.

"Which, admittedly, we don't know what your ability is," Salan said quickly, catching the girl's attention. "Scholar is a title that led many to question what exactly your ability might be. It's been long believed that each of the Human-Borns will possess some heightened ability. Warrior as a fighter, possibly able to make Masks—"

"Masks?" Sophia asked.

"Uh, simply put?" Neri started. "They're basically clones made from the wielder's energy. There's only one Defender in Agerius who can make them."

"The Protector," Salan continued, making Sophia look to her, "has always been believed to be a shield-bearer. A powerful one. The Healer, well, that's self-explanatory."

"So, there are Healers in Agerius," Sophia said.

"Maybe before the war," Neri admitted with a shrug. "There aren't any now; that's for sure."

Dalia walked in with two mugs of coffee. "Lots of Archivists think that Healers were really prevalent in the days before the war." She went back to the kitchen without further explanation, leaving Neri to give her a confused look as she walked off.

"The Shifter," Salan brought the conversation back to the other Human-Borns, "Archivists believed would be a Jumper, someone who can phase into and out of other Dimensions."

"But when it comes to the Scholar, the Requisite, and ... even the Raidin ..." Neri started.

"What their talents may be is mired in speculation," Specter finished for him.

Nodding absentmindedly, Sophia muttered, "But we're all needed. Like pieces to a puzzle."

"Exactly," Dalia said as she returned with two more mugs. She offered one to Neri. "We may not know how you'll end the war, but we know that you're all going to play a role, somehow."

"'*Sixth brings the Scholar, seeker of wisdom, whose gifts allow truth to chime*,'" Sophia whispered.

She mulled on the concept of truth. What might that refer to? Sure, truth was absolute. There was true and false. The idea that you could have both at the same time in all instances wasn't possible. Sometimes? Sure. Muddy gray in-betweens happened from time to time. But most truths were unquestionable. Up is up, down is down. Wrong is always wrong, and right is always right. No matter what the world might say otherwise.

But ... how would that factor into a war?

Gripping the book again, she said shakily, "But ... the prophecy also talked about ... five that fell ..."

"Yeah," Neri hushed, his shoulders falling a bit as his gaze fell to the floor.

"It's something you have to understand about Cregorous," Salan said carefully, gently placing her hand on Sophia's shoulder.

The girl lifted her head to meet Salan's eyes.

"All we know are his actions. And his actions have been ... cruel. The prophecy did speak of five that would fall, and honestly, we don't know why that had to happen, or when the five fell. But..." She looked to the other team members. "From what we figure, based on your birth month and when we left—"

Sophia sat up a little and furrowed her brow. "My birth month? Why is that important?"

"We ... wonder if all of the Human-Borns were born in the same year. Given when this all started."

"When what all started?"

Specter glanced around apprehensively. "Well, you know we've been here for nineteen years."

"Right. But what does that have to do with anything? That just means you've been here longer than I've been alive."

Neri nodded slowly. "Right. Well ... best we know, the First Human-Born was still a baby—an unborn baby—when they pushed Cregorous back to Tilion." He blinked a few times and hushed, "Nineteen years ago ..." He looked to Salan. "To the day."

"He *chose* today?" Dalia asked in thinly veiled disgust. "Ugh. Talk about a terrible choice for an anniversary."

"What happened nineteen years ago?" Sophia asked, looking to her Zaheri with worry written in her features.

Pulling herself from her thoughts, Salan said, "Um ... well, we don't really know. But we do know that nineteen years ago was when we learned that the First Human-Born had shown themselves. We all thought they'd be an adult. Someone who knew what they were doing. But, like Neri said, they were an unborn baby."

"Wait, wh—" Sophia's voice caught in her throat and panic filled her eyes. "Cregorous, he ... he attacked a *baby*?" Her voice got progressively smaller, and her eyes grew wider at the concept.

Letting out a slow breath, Neri nodded. "From what we can gather, yes."

The idea of "monster" grew greater in Sophia's mind.

No wonder the Agerians feared this Cregorous. He didn't have any issues attacking unborn children. All because some prophecy said they might be a threat to him. They hadn't even had the chance to live yet, and he hadn't hesitated to attack them? What of their mothers? Or their fathers? What might that loss have done to them?

A sickening feeling filled Sophia's gut.

Her dream barreled into her mind. Of the white lights crashing into white figures and gaining their strength, compounding on one another. Until they hit the sixth light, and ...

Shakily, Sophia put her mug down on the table, feeling her world spin.

"Sophia?" Salan asked, concern etching her brow.

The question she already knew the answer to. The question she didn't know to ask earlier. The question she never would have considered until just now.

"Are my dreams visions?" she whispered, her face growing pale.

"Visions?" Dalia asked as Neri moved to Sophia's other side on the couch. He and Salan held her upright as she looked like, at any second, she might pass out.

Specter looked to Salan. "Visions? Of what?"

Shaking her head, Salan looked to Sophia. "I don't know. Sweetie, are you okay?"

A heavy breath racked from Sophia, and she sputtered out, "I think ... I think I might be ... seeing things ... in my dreams."

Quickly moving the mugs out of the way, Neri sat on the coffee table and gently took hold of Sophia's face. "Hey, shh ... it's okay. Breathe, Soph. Just breathe. It's okay."

Salan gently rubbed Sophia's shoulders, soothing her with her touch. "That's it. Gentle breaths. It's going to be all right."

After a moment, Sophia's breathing returned to normal, her mind no longer spinning into chaos. It still spun, but not as quickly.

"That's it," Salan said, holding the back of her hand up to Sophia's forehead and feeling the sweat that the girl had built up from her attack. "It's okay. We're here."

Dalia stepped up with a large glass of water and set it down on the table. She awkwardly shuffled her feet, glancing to Specter as she fidgeted with her hands.

Looking between Salan and Neri, Sophia whispered, "My dreams, I ... I think they might be visions or something."

"Visions of what?" Neri asked calmly.

"The past?" Sophia guessed. "I don't know. But ... last night, I ... I had a dream about ..." She shied back, retreating from both Salan and Neri's comforting gestures. A part of her wanted to lean into their soft attention, but the bulk of her didn't know what to do with their softness. "There was a ... man. And he attacked ... someone, I guess. And their light went to someone else. And it did that five times until it finally reached a sixth person."

She lifted her gaze with trepidation, fearing that they'd call her crazy. Waiting for them to call her crazy. Instead, she found them giving her those same calm expressions, listening attentively to what she said. Their expressions made her feel ... something. She awkwardly looked away.

"When the man attacked the sixth person, they pushed him back ... and then I woke up."

Sitting back a little, Neri muttered, "Well, it would align with the prophecy."

"And could explain what we saw," Salan said to her husband.

"Which was?" Dalia asked, rolling her hand toward the couple.

"Cregorous pushed back through the portal," Salan answered absently.

"If ..." Sophia's small voice squeaked.

They all turned to her.

"If ... I am seeing visions of the past ... then"—She looked to them with terrified eyes—"what does that mean?"

Salan laid a hand on Sophia's shoulder. "It means you're one of a kind."

"She's right," Neri said with a smile. "There's not a single person in Agerius who can do that."

"So ... what do we do now? What's happening?" Sophia asked, slowly looking to each of her Zaheri.

"We were discussing that," Specter said as she shifted her weight between her paws. "Seeing as we have yet to receive any sort of reinforcements or communication from the Council, it sends warning into my heart."

"Mine, too," Salan said with a nod. She looked back to Sophia. "Cregorous is very powerful, but we wouldn't have anticipated that he could do what he may have done."

"Which is?" Sophia and Dalia both asked.

Glancing between the two of them, Neri said, "He may have control of the portal in the Expanse—on Tilion"—he added for Sophia—"meaning that he may be doing something to it that would award him the ability to send Caligans to attack all Seven Human-Borns at the same time."

"That would explain the fact that the portal was bigger than it normally is," Dalia said with a bobble of her head.

"Will they be all right?" Sophia asked as she sat up. "The other Human-Borns, I mean. They'll be okay, won't they?"

"I'm sure they will, Soph," Neri offered with a reassuring smile. "They all have Zaheri, just like you do."

That was comforting. If the other Human-Borns' Zaheri were as good as hers, they were bound to be fine.

Faintly, she heard the church bells from town toll the hour. Alarm shot through her body. "It's nearly lunchtime!" Frantically shooting to her feet, she added, "I should get home! My parents will—"

"Okay, relax. It's okay, Sophia," Salan said as she calmly rose to her feet. "I'm sure it's fine. We'll go to your house together, and we can explain the situation to them there."

Dread slammed into Sophia's stomach. The image of her parents' furious expressions earlier flashed in her mind.

She knew she needed to go back home and check on them, make sure they knew she was okay. That things were going to be okay. That she was sorry for any problems she'd caused. But fear eclipsed her for a moment.

Because all she could imagine was fury from them.

Salan offered another one of her warm smiles. "It's okay. We'll all go with you."

Though she was still scared, Sophia was less scared knowing her Zaheri would be with her. That they would help her explain it all.

It would be okay.

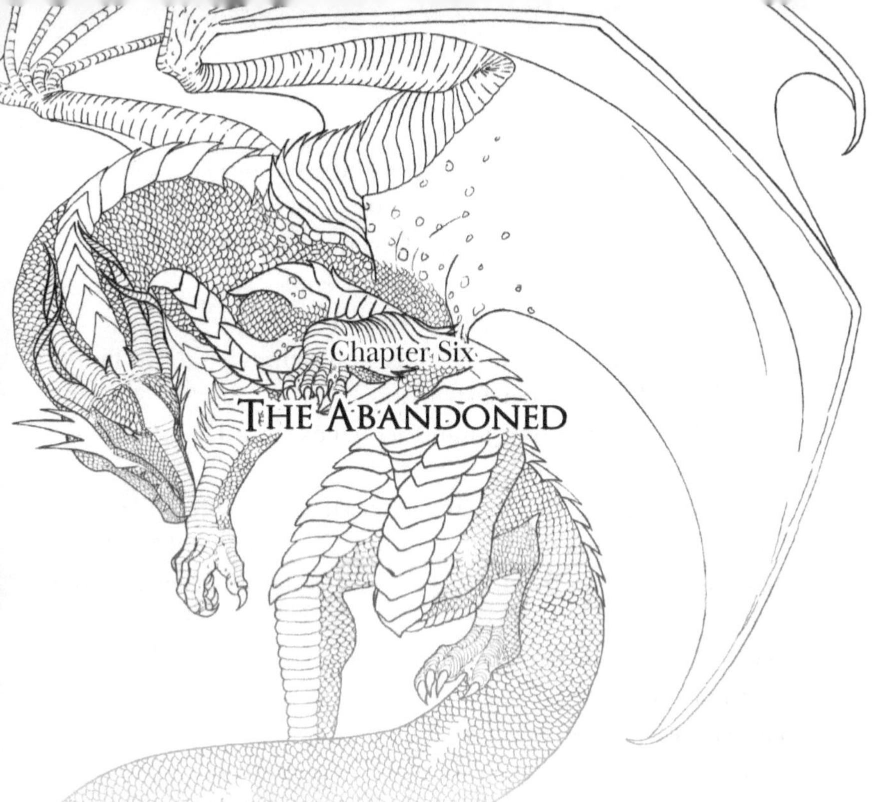

Chapter Six

THE ABANDONED

It felt as though all eyes were on them as they entered the town. Sophia saw faces poking out of windows and cracks in doors. Neri kept his scythe on him, Specter was armored, while Salan and Dalia both had a pistol strapped to their thigh. She'd understood why they remained armed. With the knowledge that the first wave had been a scouting party of sorts, almost like a sick warning, another wave of fighters could fall on them at any moment. It was better to be prepared.

But that didn't mean she felt comfortable with the many suspicious gazes taking them in from a distance. There was a thick feeling of distrust in the air, and it made Sophia wish to retreat. If this was how the townspeople were reacting, how would her family be?

There was commotion the moment they neared Sophia's street. Voices hollering and people running away from them, toward her house.

A twisted, pained feeling began to wind in Sophia's gut, and her pace slowed.

Salan noticed her glacial movements and asked, "Sweetie? What's wrong?"

Before Sophia could voice the fact that she didn't know what was wrong, just that she was suddenly feeling ill, her parents charged out of the house and began stomping toward them.

Shoving the feeling aside, Sophia forced her legs to move as she gently pushed past Neri to try to meet her parents.

"Papi, Mama, I'm so sorry about earlier. I—"

"What have you brought on us?" her father thundered. His face was pinched and cheeks reddened with anger.

Sophia shook back a little, pulling her hands toward her stomach slowly. "I ... I didn't mean to—"

"Monsters destroyed some of the homes in town! This is all your fault!" her mother snapped, scowling disapprovingly at her daughter.

Diana stood behind them, arms crossed as she gave her sister a disgusted look.

Her words were stuck in her throat. Her thoughts swirled. What were the right things to say?

Sophia stuttered out, "I'm s-sorry."

"*You're sorry?*" her mother shot with a scoffing noise while she glared at her daughter. "That won't bring back homes!" She flicked her wrist dismissively. "You've always brought problems everywhere you went."

"Diana was right all those years ago! Demon possessed! That's what you are!" Her father snatched her wrist, jostling her. "We should have—" he started, raising a fist, intending to hit Sophia.

A squeaking whine tumbled from Sophia as she tried desperately to find the right words to apologize, to make it all stop.

But they were right. It was all her fault. If she hadn't—

She pinched her eyes shut, bracing herself for the punch coming for her.

Abruptly, she was ripped out of her father's grasp.

Whipping her eyes open, she saw Neri shove her father back, and he snapped, "Don't you *dare* hurt her." He took up a protective stance next to Sophia, holding her arm and glaring at her parents.

Salan stayed behind, eyeing the parents warily. Her usual smile was absent.

"I always knew there was something wrong with you," Diana spat, giving Sophia a look of disgust.

"B-but I didn't mean to ..." Sophia started, her voice trembling just as much as her hands.

"All of this destruction! It's your doing! If you hadn't brought it upon us, none of this would be happening!" Her mother's scowl deepened before she spat a curse at her daughter. "Monster."

"Mama," Sophia whimpered past mounting tears.

She'd always known her parents were quick to be angry with her. She'd always known they didn't like her withdrawn personality. She'd always known she wasn't the favorite daughter. None of that had been a secret. Everyone in town knew that Sophia was the problem one. Everyone knew that Diana was the princess, the favorite, the one gifted with all of the talents of value.

She'd never blamed them. She knew she made mistakes. She was okay with the way things were. Because she had always assumed that just because her parents didn't shower praise upon her, that didn't mean they hated her. Every time they lashed out, it had been because she made a mistake, so that didn't mean they hated her.

That didn't mean they didn't love her.

After all, she was their daughter. They had to love her, right?

Right?

Looking at their furious expressions. Hearing their words strike her and lodge as though arrows, Sophia was finding it hard to breathe. Her vision blurred with tears. She swallowed them back as her father continued to throw the blame on her. That it was all her fault. If she'd never been born, none of this would have happened.

They were right, of course.

It was all her fault.

If it wasn't for her, then—

Salan shoved Sophia behind her, and Neri stepped to his wife's side. They were suddenly a wall of defense for the teenager, placing themselves directly between Sophia and her outraged parents.

"You do *not* get to talk to her like that," Salan commanded, a glare etched on her usually sweetly smiling face. Every edge was hard, and her eyes had gone cold.

"We can speak to her however we want!" Sophia's mother shot back, working to rise to Salan's height and still falling short.

"No mother should *ever* speak to their child the way you are!" Salan fired back. No part of her wavered. "This is *not* Sophia's fault. She didn't ask for anything to befall your town!"

"And yet it did!" Sophia's father said, glaring at Salan. "It's obvious that you knew something like this would happen!" He pointed an accusing finger at Sophia. "She's the cause of all this!"

Neri smacked his hand away again and fumed, "That's your daughter you're addressing." His jaw was tight as he stared the large man down. "Give her the respect she's owed."

With a guffaw, her mother said, "Respect? That child has been nothing but a problem since the day she was born!"

A sob tore from Sophia. The girl quickly slapped her hand over her mouth, trying to repress the sorrow that welled in her chest.

Dalia draped her arm across Sophia's shoulders, joining the others in glaring. Specter fell into a defensive stance, her fur bristled as a snarl formed on her snout.

"Sophia is a wonderful girl!" Salan fired back. "Anyone would be lucky to have her as their daughter! You should be ashamed of yourself!"

"You want her so badly?" Sophia's mother flung her hands as though actively trying to rid a pest. "*You* take the brat!"

Neri clenched his fists and let out a heavy breath, shooting daggers with his glare.

Salan lost her glare for a moment. A touch of softness in her brow as she blinked and hushed, "I would be honored to have her as my daughter." Tears rose in her eyes, and she straightened. With a scoff, she said, "You don't deserve her."

Raising a fist to strike Salan, Sophia's father started to say, "Don't you talk to my wi—"

Neri landed a harsh punch against the man, sending him falling. Wisps of gold energy sparked around his clenched fist. He then snatched the man's shirt, tearing it as he immediately yanked him upright again to get in his face as he seethed, "You don't touch *either* of my girls, you hear me?" He shoved him back harshly, letting the rotund man fall to the pavement as Neri towered above him.

A burn-like abrasion ran across the fat man's face where Neri had punched him.

Shaking his head, Neri nearly spat, "Salan is right. You don't deserve her. You never have."

Sophia's mother whipped her head between her husband on the ground and the Zaheri surrounding Sophia. She fixed a glare on her face and stared hard at Sophia. "Don't you ever come back here. You hear me! Take your cursed life with you, monster!"

"You're the monster!" Dalia shot before sticking her tongue out. "Old hag!"

Giving Sophia's parents a parting look of fury, Salan took hold of the girl's shoulders and said, "C'mon, Sophia; let's go home."

Neri remained glaring at the family. His hard edges daring them to consider striking any of the Agerians or Sophia as his wife led the teen back the way they'd come.

Tears stained Sophia's face, her jaw quivering as she tried to restrain her sobbing. Everything in her ached. A pain she didn't think was possible had struck her heart, and she felt her lungs collapsing in her chest as she racked shuddering breaths.

Her world spun, and her legs felt disconnected as she leaned against Salan. She knew her Zaheri had said things. Had come to her rescue and fired comments back at her parents. But it had all been deaf to her.

Her heart pounded painfully in her chest, and she was sure at any moment it would burst from her body with how wildly it thumped. Everything was silent except the beating pulse that *ker-thunked* to the point where she seriously wondered if she was about to black out. Her feet were unstable, stuttering along, just like her trembling mind. What ...? What had just happened?

Was it all true? Could it be that she now was completely unloved? Unwanted? Discarded and abandoned by the people who were supposed to love her most unconditionally in the world?

Salan rubbed her arm and whispered calming words, but Sophia couldn't hear them past her raging panic.

She was alone.

The trip back to the Zaheri's house was littered with furious comments. Specter snapped her jaws and bit out every word that came from her snarling maw. Her fur was still bristled well after they arrived at the house.

Dalia rolled her eyes a bunch and dramatically flailed her hands around, unable to fully articulate the anger she felt and was trying to convey it with her wayward gestures.

Meanwhile, Neri silently raged in fury. His shoulders were tight, and he barely relaxed his hands enough to open the door to the house. He wound up storming into the kitchen and angrily went about making a fresh brew of coffee.

Salan quietly led Sophia into a rear bedroom and sat her on the mattress before closing the door. As she settled next to the girl, she gently rubbed Sophia's shoulders and asked, "Sophia?"

The teenager's eyes were bloodshot and puffy, her nose red and a little snotty as she sniffled before rubbing her nose again. She couldn't bring herself to look to her Zaheri. Her heart was still thudding, though not deafeningly anymore.

A small sigh left Salan. "Everything they said was wrong."

Sophia's mouth contorted as her face pinched, her cheeks going rosy as tears glossed her eyes again. "But ..." she cracked out, barely above a whisper, "they're right. It is all my fault."

"No, sweetie, it isn't," Salan said desperately, taking hold of Sophia's hand. "None of this is your fault."

"But, if I ..."

"Oh, sweetie, if you weren't here"—Salan's shoulders slumped as a frown fell on her face—"our lives would be so empty without you in it."

Blinking a few times to clear the mounting tears, Sophia looked to Salan. "W-what?"

Salan cupped her face, swiping the tears aside, even as new ones fell. "Sophia, you're a wonderful, lovely young woman. You're everything we could have ever dreamed for in a Human-Born. You're sweet, and gentle, and kind. I've known that from the day I first saw you." She smiled past her growing tears. "You were five and found a bird with a broken wing. You tried to get your parents to help you with it, but they brushed you aside. So, you took it upon yourself to go to the library and learn all about birds. You carefully kept it hidden in the park and nursed it back to health. You were so quick to tend to such a small creature." Salan pulled her lips into her mouth, blinking past her own tears. "Sophia, I've known from that moment that all I would wish would be to have a daughter like you."

Unable to stop herself, Sophia flung her arms around Salan's neck, bawling against her as Salan cradled her head and gently rocked her.

"You don't deserve any of what they gave you. None of it," Salan hushed gently as she continued to rock the teenager in her strong, warm embrace. "I'm going to do everything I can to make sure you never hear lies like that again."

Sophia continued to cry, clutching to Salan and her stable support.

"Shh ... it's all right. It's okay. I'm here. I'm here, sweetie. I'm never going to let you go."

They stayed locked in that embrace for a few long moments. Moments where Sophia felt for the first time a genuine connection with someone else. She couldn't recall a single time she'd been held so fiercely. So completely. Where promises uttered in those moments of tight embrace were bound to be true. They were wrapped in affection and softness. Bound together by an emotion Sophia wasn't sure she understood until just then. Because, for the first time, Sophia realized she'd never really, genuinely, actually known what it felt like to have someone care about her.

Salan gently closed the door and stepped into the hallway. Tears stained her cheeks, and she had to suck in calming breaths.

Neri had been sitting on the floor, his head up and resting against the wall, staring at the ceiling. However, he hopped up as she exited the room, wearing a look of worn worry. In a fluid movement, he cupped her cheeks and wiped her tears aside. Gently kissing her, he then brought her into an embrace.

As she wrapped her arms around his waist, he whispered, "You doing all right, soldier?"

A sad smile came to her face as she closed her eyes and nodded against him. "I'm doing all right, defender."

"How's our girl?"

Biting back her anger, her hurt, her frustration, Salan looked to the ceiling. She clutched her husband. "She's been hurt."

Neri's grip tightened. Tears glassed his eyes as his mind flashed back to those idiots. And they were. They were absolute *morons*. What other word could possibly describe parents who would throw away a child as wonderful as Sophia? He'd barely held back his energy when he'd punched that fat man. He refused to acknowledge either of them as her parents. Not anymore.

They would be her parents. They would be her family.

"When this is over, we're gonna take her away from here," he hushed to his wife.

Salan nodded against him and sniffled.

"We're gonna take her home so she never has to be reminded of those ..." He wanted to call them something harsher than idiots, but he didn't know the words. He knew there were curses, and he felt that those monsters were deserving of incendiary descriptions. "Blasted fools," he finally landed on. "Back to our place in Agerius, where she can be happy. Where she can be herself, without any of this to hold her back."

Screwing her face to keep herself from crying outright, Salan nodded against him again and let out a small laugh. "I like that plan."

Gently pulling back to cup her face again, he smiled at her. "I thought you might," he said softly, studying her as he worked to wipe her tears away.

Another small laugh escaped her. "I'm surprised you didn't kill her fa—"

"He doesn't get that title anymore." He gave his wife a grave look. "And that woman doesn't get the title of her mother. They don't deserve that."

"Neri, we can't just say we're her parents now," Salan whispered desperately.

"She might not call us that, but ... Salan, I know you love Sophia." He shrugged helplessly. "I know I do. And I'm not afraid to admit that. Elders, I'm *proud* to say that I love her as if she were ours."

She rested her hand on his chest, fighting a smile as she considered his words. "Do you think we can ... love her the right way? So that she can heal from all this pain?"

"I don't think I can do it alone, but us? Together?" He offered a warm smile. "I can tackle mountains with you."

Letting out a small, contented sigh, she smiled broadly at him. Pulling him to her, she kissed him for several long seconds, letting her actions convey just how much she loved him.

He gripped her a little tighter and mumbled against her, "Elders, why'd you have to do that?"

Giggling amid their kissing, she wove her fingers through his hair.

"We need to talk about next steps," he hushed against her but made no action to move from their embrace.

Footsteps came from behind them before Dalia grumbled, "Oh, *ew*, you guys."

Neri pulled back and let out a small laugh before awkwardly looking over his shoulder at the younger woman.

Salan bit her lip and hid her red face in Neri's chest.

"Aren't we sorta in the middle of a situation?" Dalia asked, pinching her round face in discomfort.

"Yeah, you're right, sorry," Salan said a little breathlessly as she stepped back from her husband.

"And hey, don't we have a rule about this? I thought I told you I didn't wanna see any of ... y'know"—she flailed her hand around in a loose gesture to them—"that."

Waving his pointed hand a little, Neri said, "In our defense, it *has* been a crazy day."

Dalia looked away and pinched her eyes shut, flipping her hands in front of her like a t-rex in a slapping contest. "I don't care. I don't wanna see it."

Salan held up her hands and said, "All right, we apologize. Sorry for getting carried away." She took Neri's hand, and they walked into the living room.

By the front door, Specter rose to her feet. "How is Sophia?"

"Upset," Salan said with a sigh. "But hopefully, as time goes on, she'll be able to heal from it all."

A scowl came to the grovix's face. "Beasts," she spat. "Bratak'ra would be more kind to their own."

"She's here now. At least there's that," Dalia offered.

"Has there been any further activity from the portal?" Salan asked.

Shaking her head, the redhead answered, "No. None of the sensors have gone off. I guess it's possible they got damaged at their arrival."

Specter lost her snarl and sat down. "I have not sensed any bratak'ra or werewolves. I believe, at the moment, we are still awaiting a response."

"That's weird," Neri mused as he crossed his arms. With a shrug, he added, "Why so long between attacks? By now, we ought to have seen something. Even if the Defense threw everything they had at Cregorous in the Expanse to try to win back the portal, that would just cause him to come to Earth right away, right?"

"The only thing I can imagine is that something has forced Cregorous to pause," Salan said. "Though I cannot fathom what that something could be."

"The First Human-Born maybe?"

"Perhaps. We may never know."

"So, what do we do now?" Dalia asked, rocking her feet. "Are we seriously just going to sit back and wait all anxiously for them to strike again?" A small rumble came from her stomach, and her eyes widened as she sank in on herself.

Wearing a cheeky grin, Neri asked, "Someone a little hungry?"

"Maybe," Dalia muttered.

Throwing the girl a look, Specter said, "For someone so small, you certainly consume a lot of food."

"Well, for someone so big, you ... do, too," Dalia tried to fire back with tenacity, only to mutter off some string of weak defenses and look to the floor.

"Kinda fell apart on you there, huh?" Neri asked with a smirk.

"Shut up," Dalia grumbled, a sour look pinching her face.

Neri rubbed Salan's back as he placed a quick kiss to her temple. "I'll whip up some lunch."

"Can I help?" Dalia asked as she perked up.

"Dalia, you're a dear, but I think it's time you accept that cooking isn't your strongest talent," Salan said with a small smile.

With a huff, the redhead conceded, "Okay, that's fair." She started for the door. "I'm gonna go check the sensors by the portal, just in case."

"Be careful."

"Always am!" the nimble flyer said as she hopped out the door with her usual bubbly gait.

Specter rose to her feet and approached Salan. "Are you doing all right?"

"I'll be fine. I just wish ..." Salan sighed as she looked toward the bedroom where Sophia rested. "I wish I could take away all the pain."

Gently nudging Salan's arm with her snout, Specter smiled softly at her. "Give it time. One day, you will."

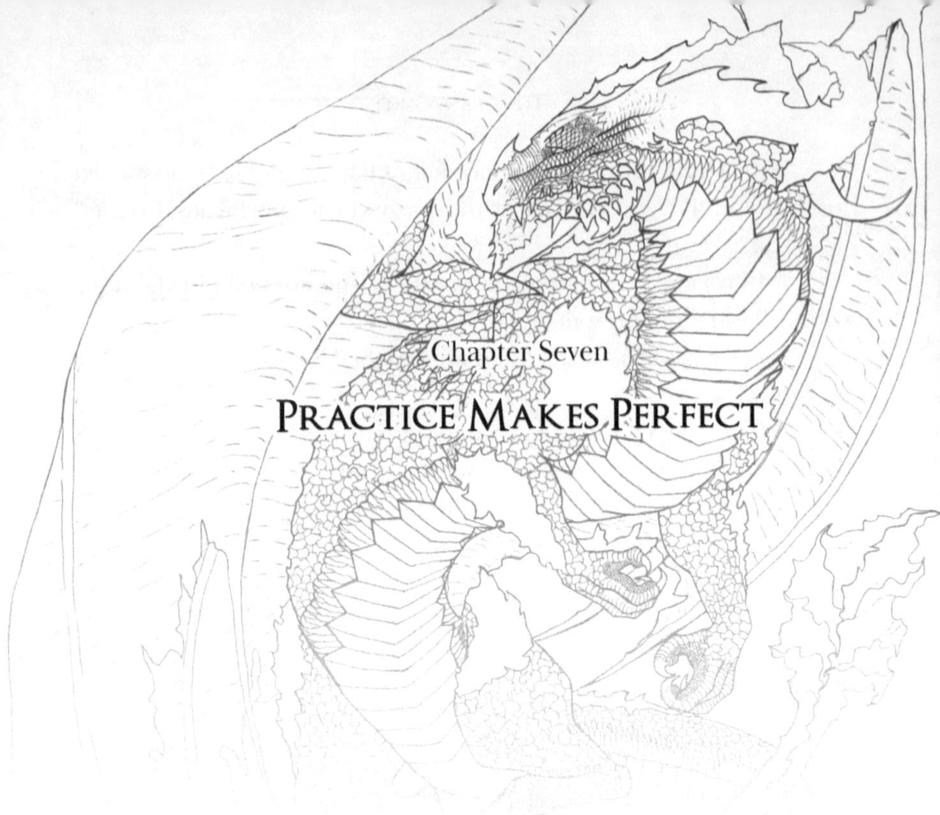

Chapter Seven

PRACTICE MAKES PERFECT

A screeching filled the air as the skittered vision of a decaying dragon splayed in her mind. Jarring noise blasted her thoughts with each fragmented skip, as though she were looking at a video frame by frame. Everything was spread, as if depicted in a messy oil painting. Panic surged within her, even though she couldn't say she was actually "there."

There was a white cylinder that waved and warbled. Gray-smudged figures tumbled from it, falling atop one another as though they'd suddenly been cut down. Chaos erupted in nothing but fragmented noise.

A blast of blue tore out from her, and her vision followed just behind it, soaring through the white cylinder, screaming a cry of fury as it flew. It smashed against other gray-smudged figures that yelped and yelled in surprise at its appearance.

The blue pushed without any sign of hesitation or resistance. It tore through the other side, shoving everything that had been within the cylinder aside, and charged heavenward. Red marred the world, tainting everything in its blood-like glow. Black swam around the edges, creating clouds of death just outside of the red.

Undeterred, the blue blast tore straight through the wall of red, shattering a broken hole in the wall. The blue then spun in the air, growing in a feverish scream of unbridled pain before exploding. Its resulting shockwave rendered the rest of the wall obsolete, obliterating it into red, sparkling mist. Even the black clouds fled, wrapping back to a lone figure from whence it had come.

Sophia's eyes snapped awake, panic tightening her chest as her heart thundered again.

For half a second, she was confused.

This wasn't her bedroom.

Then it came back to her.

Never mind that, she thought. *The dream! The vision! Hold on to it!*

Frantically searching for a pen and paper, she knew she had to scrawl out what she could remember of the vision. It had to have been a vision. She wished she could realize just how far into the past these events could happen.

As her pen neared the paper, she found herself faltering.

How should she describe it? What had she even really seen?

A decaying dragon. Screeching. A blue light that shot through the pillar of white.

Blue light!

Was it the same blue light from her other vision? She couldn't remember. What if it wasn't exactly the same? What if it was? What did either of those possibilities mean?

Perhaps it was simply a replaying, or a continuation, of her vision from that morning. The blue had pushed gray things back, and ultimately hit a red thing. That lined up with what little she could remember from her dream ... vision ... thing from that morning.

A huff of frustration left her. She wished she knew more about what these random things were that she was seeing. That she could just know more about them without it being outright said or explained in the vision itself. If only she could just magically know whether this was a continuation of the earlier vision, or something else entirely. If only she could know whether it was a recent event or an ancient one.

Maybe she could consciously experience a vision.

That thought hadn't occurred to her. Granted, she hadn't really had a chance to consider any of what being a vision-seeing-person could mean or what she could do. That realization had been made just before … well … the thing she wasn't going to focus on.

Maybe it was possible for her to choose to see a specific thing. So far, all of her visions had happened just before she'd woken up. That was why she'd always assumed they were dreams.

If this was an ability, like Salan's shields or the Masks her Zaheri had mentioned, then perhaps there was something to the "active thought" theory. That if she just concentrated, perhaps she could dive back into her vision and discern the meaning behind it, or more of the truth within it.

Quickly plopping to her feet, she sat cross-legged and settled, trying to get into a position that might help her focus. Letting out a long breath, she closed her eyes and gripped her knees. *Focus, just focus,* she told herself. She tried to imagine the last clear thing she could see about the vision: the blue light swirling in the air.

Annoyance bubbled in her chest. She rocked her weight and shimmied her shoulders, trying to readjust. Maybe she just wasn't sitting correctly.

The blue light swirling in the air above a red wall.

A flash of an image tore at her mind.

Her eyes ripped open, and she scrambled for the paper again to jot down what she had seen. It wasn't simply a red wall. It was a red dome. Black clouds hung around it, like veins against the red dome. It must've been a shield! The blue light had torn through the red shield, and then destroyed it.

For a second, Sophia smiled down at her scribbled notes, proud that she'd managed to remember more of the vision, and that she had managed to make her notes semi-coherent.

Then she slumped and frowned at the note.

It didn't align with what her Zaheri had said of the First Human-Born's encounter with Cregorous. They'd said that Cregorous was pushed back to Tilion by the First Human-Born. There wasn't anything about a red shield.

So, this was a different event entirely. It must've been.

Pursing her lips and staring hard at her notes, she practically demanded that the notes reveal to her when these other events had happened, and between whom.

Nothing came to her.

She slumped again and released her hold on the paper. For a second there, she thought she'd suddenly grasped the concept of what her ability could do. Clearly, that wasn't the case.

Though Salan's soft encouragement earlier was something she tried to cling to, she couldn't deny that, in that moment, all she felt was the weight of crushing reality. She was good for nothing. She was a failure.

If this ability was truly so unique to her, why couldn't she navigate it better? Why couldn't she be good at something, just once?

A soft knock sounded at the door. Inadvertently, Sophia tensed and timidly looked to the door.

But that was a gentle knock. It wasn't a furious banging.

"Sophia?" Salan's voice called.

"Oh, um ... I'm awake," Sophia responded.

Salan carefully opened the door and asked, "How're you feeling?" She stopped and took in Sophia's sitting position and gave her a bemused smile. "What are you doing?"

"Oh!" Sophia shot to her feet, awkwardly flailing for her paper. She teetered her weight between her feet. "I uh ... had another vision. And I thought maybe I could look at it again, or continue it, or something."

"Were you successful?"

Shaking her head, the teen answered glumly, "No. At least, not beyond a small picture that filled my head." She lifted the paper to Salan. "Does this mean anything to you?"

Salan took the paper and read over the few lines Sophia had written. With an apologetic smile, she answered, "I'm sorry, sweetie, no."

Sweetie. Salan had always called her that, but why did it sound different now? Why did Sophia want to smile at that little name?

As Salan handed the paper back to the girl, she added, "But I'm not at Archivist. It's possible that one of them would be able to supply you with assistance navigating all of this. Especially your visions."

A sting of panic caught Sophia's chest, and she snapped her eyes to Salan's. "What time is it? Was there another attack? Are we okay?"

"Shh ... sweetie, it's okay. Take a deep breath." Salan gently laid her hands on the girl's shoulders. "It's all okay. It's been an hour or so since you fell asleep. We haven't seen any retaliation yet."

"But ... there is one coming."

"Unless we see members of the Defense come to check on us, we have to assume that another strike will come."

Sophia frowned, despite her best efforts to look brave.

"Are you hungry?"

Her frown deepened. "Not really."

Salan offered an understanding smile. "That's all right. If you aren't hungry, you don't have to eat. We made lunch and left you some. It'll be available if you want it."

Truthfully, Sophia couldn't stop thinking about the concept of another attack. She didn't want to just stand there useless next time. But she didn't think she'd be able to do much. While she could manifest a small wisp of her yellow energy, she couldn't seem to make it conform into anything larger.

Chewing on her lip, the girl slowly met her Zaheri's gaze. "Salan?"

"Yes, sweetie?"

"I want to learn how to fire a gun."

The pistol felt heavy in her small hands.

Though Dalia had a good six inches on Sophia, her hands weren't much bigger. However, she showed the girl how best to hold the pistol to keep it secure in her grip.

"That's it," Dalia said with a smile as Sophia mirrored her grasp.

"With all guns, Agerian or human made, you have to remember these things," Neri said. He held up his hand and started counting. "One, never keep your finger on the trigger. Near the trigger, that's fine, but it should never be resting on the trigger unless you're intending to fire it. Two, always point the weapon toward the ground if it's in your hands. Don't point it at someone unless you want the possibility of shooting them—this is a lethal weapon and can hurt people. Three, when it's going into your holster, flip it into safety. That'll ensure that even if you happen to get hit by something, or something hits the trigger just right, it won't go off." He gestured to Sophia. "Now, show me where the trigger is and where the safety is."

Keeping the weapon pointed toward the ground as instructed, Sophia pointed to both parts of the gun in turn.

"Good. Now"—Neri nodded a dozen feet from them, where a makeshift target had been constructed—"pull the pistol up and look down the barrel." He moved to stand behind Sophia, ducking his head to make sure she was pointing it well. "See that little point on the tip?"

"Is that the sight?" Sophia asked.

"Good girl," he said with a smile. "That's gonna help you line up your target. Like we talked about earlier, you may need to determine whether closing your left eye is best or not."

Lowering the gun, she looked over her shoulder at him. "Dalia fired her gun with both eyes open."

Shuffling her weight awkwardly, Dalia said, "I can't close just one eye."

"Oh," Sophia said. She wanted to comment how strange that sounded. It was easy for her to close both of her eyes independently from the other.

"And it may prove best for you to fire with both eyes open. But, for some people, it's easier to aim with just their dominant eye," Neri said. He patted her shoulder. "Let's get your target shooting posture down."

She gave him a confused look. "But I want to learn how to do this so I can defend myself."

"Target practice first, Soph. You can't fly before you can stand."

She nodded and faced the target, slowly raising the pistol. Though none of her Zaheri were in the line of fire, she was terrified she'd somehow pull the trigger and hurt one of them. But so long as she was careful and ensured that, as Neri said, she kept her finger away from the trigger until she was ready to fire, that wouldn't happen.

"Learning how to stand still and fire your weapon will give you the muscle memory for when you need to focus and aim in combat," Neri instructed.

He and Dalia gave her some pointers on how to stand to best prepare for the kickback of the pistol. It was about as powerful as a

9mm pistol, so Neri gently placed a hand on her shoulder to give her support for her first shot, just so she'd know what to expect.

It was powerful, and Sophia startled a little by the feel of the weapon firing and the ripple it made in her arm. How it made her hand vibrate a little with warmth. But it wasn't as bad as she had expected.

She let out a soothing breath.

"You okay?" Neri asked.

Nodding, she said, "Yeah. But"—a frown came to her face—"I didn't hit the target."

"You were really tense," Dalia said, flipping her hand dismissively. "Probably 'cause you were worried about the kickback. You know what it feels like now, so try again."

It felt a little strange to fire the gun and not see a shell discharge. Not that Sophia watched many of them, but the few action movies or TV shows she'd watched showed bullets flying and shells falling from guns. The little blue light that tore from the barrel sang a banging shot, but it wasn't as startling as a human-made gun. Or, at least, not as startling as Sophia would expect a human-made gun to sound.

After she fired several shots, Dalia made suggestions on how Sophia could hold her shoulders. She'd hit the target, and each shot got progressively better. After twenty minutes or so of firing between instructions, she felt much more comfortable with the weapon in her grasp. It still felt heavy, but at least she'd reached the point where she didn't want to recoil at the thought of touching it.

The whole exercise had started with her assembling the pistol under Neri's instruction as Dalia went through the motions next to her. Once they'd practiced for nearly a half hour, they ended the session with the dismantling of the pistol and how she should clean it.

Once they were done, and Dalia had clicked her pistol back into place, holstering the weapon, Neri handed Sophia a thigh holster. "That pistol's yours now. Better have a place to hold it when you're out there," he said.

Sophia had never anticipated that she'd like having a gun. Truthfully, she'd been fairly ambivalent about weapons in general until now. The only reason she wanted to learn was so that she could protect herself, and hopefully afford some assistance should another attack happen.

But, as Neri handed her the holster and Dalia instructed her on how to attach it to her belt and strap it to her leg, Sophia found herself smiling as she took up the Agerian weapon. It was hers. Given to her by her Zaheri.

It wasn't like gifts were foreign. She'd been given many things from her family in the past—mostly clothes handed down from her sister—but they'd never given her anything that she found herself wanting to cherish.

This was a weapon, something that could hurt people. She knew the gravity of the thing she now had weighing down her right leg. And she wouldn't take it lightly. But it had been given to her because the people who gifted it wanted her to be safe.

And there was something about that action that warmed her heart.

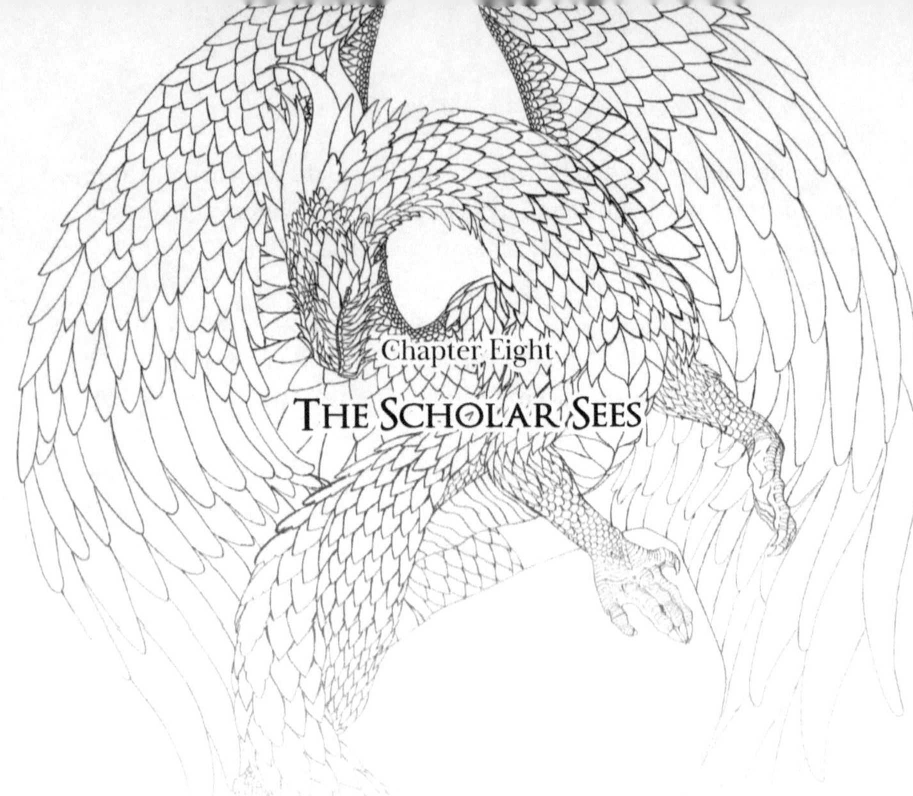

Chapter Eight
THE SCHOLAR SEES

Sophia sat in the living room, continuing to read the small book from the Archives. It appeared to be all about theories surrounding the Human-Borns and what they might be like. The prophecy spoke of them all with such greatness, as though they were truly amazing.

She wondered if Agerians had been shocked when they found out that their famous Human-Borns were children. Had they known that it was a bunch of teenagers that this prophecy spoke so highly of?

Lifting her gaze from the page, she wondered who the other Human-Borns might be. Where were they right now? What sort of problems were they going through? Were their families just as broken as hers? Were they just as broken as she was? What if they were all really mature, and all put together, not needing a ton of help from adults? What if they were confident and assured? What if they were all really smart and had attended university?

Would they think less of her? Would they see her as this tiny, weak thing? Would they look down on her because she didn't have any great ability? Would they see her as a weak link? Would they like her at all?

Or would they want to discard her, too?

Looking toward the kitchen, she saw Salan and Neri smiling at one another as they spoke of something. Dalia and Specter were outside, keeping watch.

She clutched the book to her chest. It suddenly felt heavy, just as heavy as the pistol at her side.

Salan had said she wasn't going to abandon her. That she was going to be there for her.

But ... what if that changed?

She knew that Neri and Salan were married. Did they have children back in Agerius? Would they run back to them, taking all of their smiles and warm hugs with them? Would they pat Sophia on the head here, offering comfort while on Earth, only to leave her behind once they returned to Agerius?

Would she be doomed to be forgotten forever?

She wanted to find comfort that there were other Human-Borns. That they were all her age. That they were, by all accounts, a team meant to work together to end the war.

But fear clutched at her heart.

There was no telling where the other Human-Borns were. No telling who they were, what they were like, or whether they were nice at all. Humans weren't exactly well known for getting along, especially across cultures. Sophia wondered if perhaps that was the case. After all, the world was large, holding many different groups of people. The chances of all seven Human-Borns residing in South America were slim.

Would they understand her? Would they mock her for how her family treated her? Would they give her looks of pity and remain silent? Or would they brush it aside, saying that it wasn't that bad?

And maybe it wasn't that bad. Maybe Sophia's hurt feelings were all childish. Maybe she had to just forget the pain and move on. Even as it dug deeper and stabbed at her mind in ugly reminders.

She tried to shake the memories away but wasn't fast enough. The reminder that her parents had disowned her. That her sister had spat at her. That she'd been abandoned when she'd needed them most.

No. Stop it. Don't cry, she told herself. Crying wouldn't change anything.

So then, why did it sound like such a good idea?

An alarm sounded, and she flinched, nearly throwing the book into the air.

The door opened a few seconds later, and Dalia said, "The portal's open!"

Neri and Salan had both lost their smiles, marching for the door as Sophia hopped quickly into step with them.

Once outside, Salan commanded, "Same as last time. I'll keep Sophia close to me. The rest of you see to watching out for one another. We can do this. We just have to stay levelheaded."

With a smirk and a nod, Neri said, "Yes, ma'am."

They ran toward the mountain range, maybe two or three miles away from the house. They stuck next to Sophia, keeping pace with her shorter legs as they went. Within a few moments, they spied the portal moving down the mountain, getting closer to them. Ferveos began to fly from the white cylinder, and they could see figures emerging from the base of the light.

"Dalia, be care—"

"I will, I will," the redhead said impatiently with a salute to Salan before she pushed herself into the air.

Neri stopped and took hold of Salan's arm. "*You* be careful." He looked to Sophia. "Both of you."

"We will," Salan said before he kissed her quickly.

In a second, he rocketed himself into the air, his scythe trailing golden energy as he pulled it into his grasp. He and Dalia began to make quick work of the Ferveos above them.

War would be upon them at any moment.

The thundering of footsteps had Sophia reaching for her pistol, hoping the weapon might bring her some comfort.

It didn't.

Specter charged toward the mass of fighters coming for them. Bratak'ra and werewolves were first. Their numbers were great, but not as great as Sophia had expected. Even the number of Ferveos and Caligans seemed thin from what she would have thought a second wave would look like.

Perhaps they thought she wasn't worth great numbers and legions of warriors.

Was she really that weak that even the enemy thought she could be swallowed by a couple hundred fighters?

Salan didn't use a domed shield this time as they slowly marched forward. Instead, it was a wall that protected her and Sophia. Meanwhile, she shot blasts of gold from her energy-gauntleted hands. That fierceness was in her eyes again, as if she dared anything to challenge her.

It was a look Sophia marveled at. A look she felt she'd never be able to replicate, no matter how long this journey might be.

Her accuracy was reasonable. Considering she'd only had the one lesson, she was happy with the mediocre aiming she pulled off. She couldn't bring herself to aim for heads. Chests, arms, legs, wings, those were fine. She didn't mind firing toward those.

Somewhere in her mind, she wondered if any of these people were fathers. Mothers. Did they have loved ones waiting for them back home? Did they care at all that they charged at a child?

One of them broke through and slammed a gray-cloaked fist against Salan's shield. He stood right in front of Sophia and, in that instant, Sophia got the answer to her last question.

They didn't care *at all* that they were attacking a child.

The hatred that was etched in his eyes as he glared at her, it held a hunger for her blood. He didn't even have to say anything for her to feel that monstrous want. It made her quiver.

A blast of gold tore through the shield and sent him falling to the ground with a dull *thud*. Sophia couldn't look.

Even though he'd clearly been willing to kill her, it made her stomach twist and bile rise in her throat at the concept that he'd been breathing a second ago, and now he was dead. Even if he was an enemy ...

She was having trouble understanding how to justify it all. How to wrap her head around it all. These were people, right?

Suddenly, a tower of a man tore from the ranks and surged for Salan.

The shield wrapped around Sophia, encasing her in a domed protection as the large man landed a blow against Salan's golden-cloaked arms. His whole build was blocky, his head square shaped, and every edge of him was hard. The clothes he wore were different than the other

Caligans. Theirs were all a drab, unimpressive gray with no special markings or symbols to distinguish one from the other.

This man, though, his uniform was a mixture of chainmail, leather, cloth, and metal. There was an icon embossed on his leather gauntlets, accentuated by red ink that streaked. Something about the symbol flashed the word "*Caliga*" in Sophia's mind.

His hands were big, his arms were big. Everything about him made Salan dwarfed.

Even so, the smaller woman deftly deflected his blows, parrying and landing a few of her own. Despite his bulk, he was fast. And each punch he threw sparked gray energy that shot away with every impact against a shield or deflection of Salan's.

Between the two, Salan was more adaptive, Sophia thought. She dodged, and kicked, and punched, whereas this man seemed to barely dodge and only punch. Something about him was cunning, though. The way he squinted and how he sized Salan up, as though he was studying her movements and analyzing her. Salan seemed aware of that because she was barely repeating movements and attacks.

She pushed the hulking attacker back and swung her arm around her.

With a yelp, Sophia felt the shield around her move, taking her with it. A dead Ferveos landed where she'd been a second later.

Salan abruptly dove aside, and Sophia wondered why, when Neri tore from the sky and slammed into the hulking warrior.

Leaping back into the shield, Salan panted, "Are you okay, Sophia?"

"I ... I think so," Sophia shook out. Her pistol was still in her grasp, but she barely held on to it. She wasn't even using it. Shakily, she had to try three times before finally getting it holstered. "Wh-who is that?"

Salan sucked in heavy breaths, her body defensive as she glared at the man battling her husband. "He's one of Cregorous' generals. His name is Izel."

Every movement Neri made was precise and swift. His scythe would be in his grasp one second then flying through the air the next. He'd use it to deflect an attack then push back, blasts of gold shooting at Izel and sending him skittering backward.

"Enough," the general commanded, landing a blow to Neri's face.

With a grunt, Neri clamored to the ground, his scythe falling from his grasp.

"We only want the girl," Izel said simply as he looked to Salan.

A dark look filled Salan's eyes as she growled, "You'll have to kill me first."

Cocking his head, Izel said, "That can be arranged."

"Salan," Sophia whimpered, grasping her Zaheri's arm. She didn't want to lose her. Not when there was a small chance this woman could care about her, maybe love her. Really show her what it meant to be cared for and protected.

In a snap, Salan tore through the shield at the same instant that Neri sprang back into action. The two began furiously attacking Izel, forcing the general into a retreating stance as he continued to be pushed backward. Each blow from Neri and Salan was hasher than the last, as though fueled by something other than their energy. As if they were feeding off one another.

Every blow one sent, in the small pocket that would follow, the other would be there with their own attack. They moved like a practiced routine, in perfect synchronization. Not a single instant were they out of step. Their unity was fully evident in that moment as they stood, flaming gold defenders of the girl they both loved with a devotion Sophia couldn't fully grasp.

And she was in awe of the scene. Standing there in her shield, untouched and unscathed as her Zaheri gained cuts, bruises, and abrasions.

They took the beatings and the blows. They didn't flinch when they got hit. They didn't waver when the enemy growled. They just continued on.

They had to be exhausted. They had to be feeling the effects of the day. But they weren't showing a single lick of it. Not a crack in their resolute stances. Not a glimmer of fear. And if they felt anything other than assurance, Sophia couldn't see it.

Something pulsed from the portal, and Sophia felt her vision go fuzzy. For a second, she couldn't see straight. Everything doubled.

And then she wasn't there at all.

She could still feel the hum of the golden energy that protected her. She could still hear the faint sounds of battle. She could still smell the grass of the hills and the blood of the battle. But it was all layers deep, behind the scenes that splayed across her vision in an array of moments, and she couldn't grasp any of them.

A forest where a large, imposing grovix snapped some furious comment. A blond-haired boy dueling against a man wielding red energy. A sword clamoring to the ground as a body fell nearby, the sword disappearing into a flash of light a second later. A man with red energy in his grasp shoving a hazel-eyed woman aside as an attack slammed into him. A pregnant woman on the ground, pleading as she cried. A massive, mountain of a dragon made of stone and rock thundering a furious roar. A group—herself among them—all suddenly swept into a hole as the floor beneath them gave way.

A room filled to the brim with books, and a young man seated across from her, lifting his blue eyes to her, wearing a small smile on his face. A black grovix skulking into a town, blackness billowing from its fur. A hazel-eyed woman giving her a condescending look as she twirled blue energy in her grasp. a man with red energy dancing in his eyes standing behind her.

These and seemingly hundreds of other small moments soared through her mind, none taking root. Even as she groped and grasped for them, trying to snatch even one and discern the meaning behind them. In that instant, she knew she was seeing visions—many, many visions. She knew some were the past. Some were possible futures. Some were futures of pain and suffering. Some were futures of righteousness and healing. But which were which, she could not know.

With a snap, it all disappeared. She felt her legs buckle just before her vision swirled and she blacked out.

Izel's gaze snapped to Sophia, and he threw both hands out. A surge of gray energy divided Neri and Salan, creating a small path for him to charge through. They skittered around, right on his heel, aching to stop his advancement.

The Caligan general barreled toward the girl. Her gaze was distant, her eyes filled with yellow energy, her face slack.

He leaped into the air and raised a gray-cloaked fist, intending to slam it into the golden shield so he could blast an attack at Sophia.

A whipping of leathery wings hit the air as Dalia appeared and landed a harsh kick against Izel, sending him flying to the side and away from Sophia. She then fell into a defensive stance in front of the shield as Neri and Salan quickly took up their position in front of her.

With a grunt, Izel lifted his head off the ground and spat out a small bit of blood. He glared at them as he pushed himself up. Then, with a low growl, he muttered a curse before his wings shot from his back. Without a word, he blasted himself into the air and made for the portal.

They watched Izel go, not trusting to take their eyes off him for fear that he might turn around and come back.

Specter ran up to them and didn't stop, going straight to the shield. "Salan! Drop your shield!"

Salan spun toward Sophia, finding that she'd collapsed and was unconscious. In a frantic movement, her shield fell, and she leaped to Sophia, cradling the girl in her grasp as she gently took hold of her face.

Before Neri could ask, Salan let out a heavy breath and shook out, "She's okay. She's breathing. She passed out."

Dalia slapped a hand to her forehead. "Elders, why! What happened?"

Neri turned to Specter. "Do we have stragglers?"

Glancing back the way she'd come, Specter said, "Perhaps. I am unsure. I witnessed Izel's charging and abandoned my attacks to ensure I could render aid in fighting him."

"You've got her?" Neri asked his wife, his chest heaving as he continued to swim in adrenaline.

Nodding, Salan hushed, "Yes. Please go make sure we chased them off."

"Dalia, stay with them."

"Neri, th—"

"Salan, I'm asking for you to be protected while you watch over

Sophia." He spoke with sternness, but his eyes were soft and worried. "Please."

Salan slowly looked to Specter. "You'll watch him?"

"As always," Specter answered with a nod. She and Neri took off a second later.

Her gaze flicking between her departed teammates and Salan, Dalia asked, "What do you think made her pass out?"

"I don't know," Salan hushed, gently moving some of Sophia's hair aside. A watery smile fought its way to her face as she said, "I'm just relieved that she's all right."

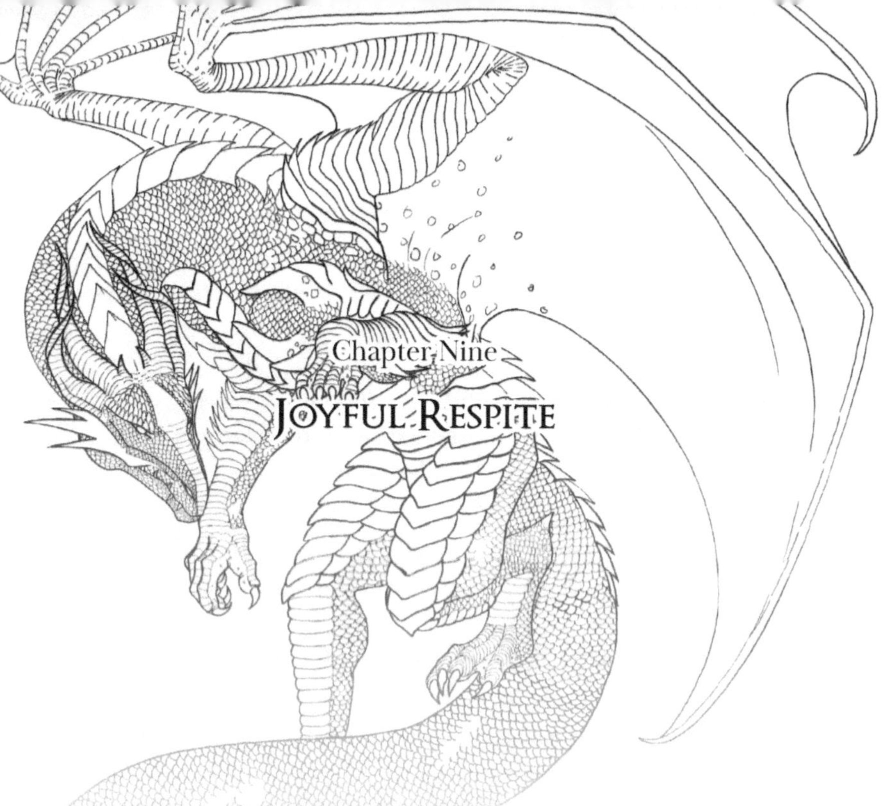

<h1 style="text-align:center">Chapter Nine
JOYFUL RESPITE</h1>

The man with red energy rolled his eyes as he crossed his arms over his chest. He grumbled something in a language Sophia didn't understand.

A hazel-eyed woman gave him a stern look and said something in response, her stance defiant against his grumbling.

He flashed his eyes to her and held her gaze for a moment. Sadness ghosted his features before he frowned and responded in the garbled words Sophia couldn't discern.

Sophia woke and immediately registered a pounding headache. Her sinuses were under pressure, making her wince and shut her eyes. The room spun a little as she slowly worked to sit up. The bedside light was on. She slowly looked toward the window, finding that it was nighttime.

She tried to recall what had happened. The last thing she could remember was watching Neri and Salan fighting Izel, the Caligan general.

She must've blacked out.

But, why?

Rubbing her pounding temple, she closed her eyes and tried to think through it all. Something must've made her black out. It wasn't like she was prone to just falling down and fainting. If she were, then this wouldn't be so weird.

She'd been watching Neri and Salan, marveling at their fighting, when she'd glanced to the portal, and—

Her eyes snapped open. She'd seen visions. Lots of them. She knew she'd seen many but couldn't say how many, and she couldn't recall any details from them. Already, her vision before she'd woken was gone.

Disappointment flooded her. She'd been so close to so many fragments of moments, and she couldn't remember a single one. Not even faint memories. All she could remember was that she had witnessed many visions, that they were events in the past and in the future. Maybe even multiple futures.

Unlike before, she didn't even know what details she could focus on to try to glean further insights. It was as though her mind said, *"Yes, we saw them, but we won't actually remember anything of importance."*

Which felt absolutely useless.

A sigh tumbled from her, and she deflated. Was this how it would always be? Would she constantly be wondering whether there was anything worthwhile in her visions? Would she always suffer from a lack of understanding?

Some great Human-Born she was turning out to be.

The door opened, and Salan did a double-take when she realized Sophia was awake. "Oh, thank the Elders," she said quickly before practically falling on Sophia and hugging her fiercely.

Without any active thought, Sophia returned the embrace just as tightly, clutching on to Salan's affections.

Pulling back a little, Salan grazed her hand across Sophia's face. "Are you all right?"

Sophia went to nod but felt her mind scream in protest at the action. She winced. "I'm fine, but my head hurts."

The Zaheri smiled. "I'll get you some food. You should rest."

"Wait, Salan." Sophia caught her arm before she could walk off. "What happened? Is ...?" She quickly pulled her hand back. Fear suffocated her for a second before she gulped it down, doing her best not to tremble. "Is everyone else okay?" she asked in a quiet voice.

Running a hand through Sophia's hair, Salan smiled at her. "Yes, sweetie, everyone else is fine. A few cuts and bruises, but nothing that won't heal."

Relief flooded Sophia, and she relaxed against the mattress. They were all okay. Despite her blacking out, it hadn't affected her Zaheri in their fight.

"I'll be right back," Salan said with a gentle swipe of her hand across Sophia's cheek.

Sophia slumped back, the weariness of the day taking root. Though she was confused about her visions and why she couldn't recall any of the myriad that she *knew* she had seen, she was terribly grateful that her Zaheri were all okay. She wasn't alone. They hadn't abandoned her. And though a part of her knew this was just the beginning of the war, as she saw it, she knew she would be okay. That they would all be okay. Because she had them to help keep her safe, no matter what happened.

The months that followed were blissful for Sophia. At first, she had been worried that, after the attack, her Zaheri would want her to go back home and live with her parents again. When she voiced that fear, Neri and Salan had been adamant that she would never go back to that wretched house again. That this was her home now. Then they started to ask profusely whether Sophia was okay with that. Did she want to stay with them? Or did she want to go back home to her family?

They'd seemed relieved when Sophia had assured them that, no, she would much rather stay with them. That she had no desire to return to her parents' house. Even with the handful of personal items she might want, she judged them a reasonable loss. Considering what she'd gained, Sophia felt it was a perfectly acceptable trade.

Because she was hugged here.

She was listened to here.

She was shown affection here.

A small part of her wished she'd been allowed to move in with her Zaheri a year prior when they'd revealed themselves to her. How much better her life might have been.

But it wasn't like she was suddenly all better. Like this one change led to her never second-guessing herself. If anything, it made her all the more concerned about making a misstep.

What if she said something that made them angry, and they started to resent her? What if it was only a matter of time before they realized how much of a pain she was, and they, too, kicked her out? What if her parents were right, and she was a monster, a curse, a burden, and they were right to have disowned her?

Each of those questions was usually met with Neri grumbling curses while Salan quietly and carefully spoke with Sophia, trying to affirm the girl's worth.

Sophia didn't fully believe them.

She wanted to. She wanted to believe that her Zaheri were being honest. That they were saying truthful things about her. That they were working to build her self-esteem for her own good.

But there was always this nagging doubt in the back of her head. And it sounded a lot like her parents. Of the comments they made. Not only the ones on the day they'd been attacked, but ones from before, too. Of how difficult she made life. How problematic she was by not conforming.

She'd heard these sorts of things most of her life. She believed many of them to be the truth about her. It wasn't like some kind words from her Zaheri would suddenly make her change her self-image.

But she saw how upset it made them, so she tried to at least pretend like she wasn't struggling with the negative voices in her head. It didn't always work.

Salan was always so patient with her. So gentle. So kind. She gave her so much time and energy, pouring hours into conversations and struggles.

It was a welcome change to be so seen by people. But Sophia couldn't stop herself from wondering when they'd say what they really thought. And when those real thoughts would come out, revealing that her parents had been right all along. That she was the problem.

That didn't stop her from loving every minute of her life with her Zaheri.

Even if it would all one day go away, it was still a happier home than her parents' house had ever been. There was laughter and stories. There was learning and growth. She got to explode in excitement about something, and no one would tell her to shut up.

Her room was smaller, but she didn't care. She shared it with Specter, which was probably one of her favorite things about moving in with her Zaheri. Snuggling with the grovix on the bed that was barely big enough for them both, Sophia slept incredibly soundly. She never worried over the possibility of another attack with Specter so close by.

About a week or so after the attack, Sophia's birthday had rolled around. She'd had a cake once, she thought, when she was little. She couldn't remember if it was hers or if it was Diana's. But she did remember cake. Not that she could recall one in recent years.

So, when she'd woken to her Zaheri fussing over a breakfast of her favorite foods, and later when they had given her two different cakes because they didn't know which she liked more, Sophia hadn't known how to respond beyond wide smiles.

Gifts had been eagerly given to her. Dalia had proudly given her a horridly wrapped notebook (Neri had poked fun at Dalia's poor job of wrapping the gift). And then Neri and Salan had given her a gift—one of the books from the Archive. This one, however, was written in a language no one could speak or read in Agerius.

Excitement had nearly burst from Sophia as she looked over the flowing script, already hungry to discover its secrets. Why could no one read it? What had led to it becoming a dead language? How many books did they have written in this script, and why so many if they couldn't read it? All questions none of her Zaheri could answer. But they again mentioned Archivists, who Sophia asked to know more about.

And when she learned that two Archivists were Zaheri themselves, protecting other Human-Borns, Sophia became eager for the day she might meet them. What they might be able to talk about. What Sophia might be able to learn from them.

Dalia taught her some about fighting and basic defensive combat skills. Even if Sophia couldn't manifest strong enough energy for offensive attacks, she could still learn how to use what little energy she had to deflect attempted blows.

At first, Sophia hadn't looked forward to such practice. But after about a month, she found herself enjoying the one-on-one time with Dalia. The redheaded Zaheri's bubbliness was infectious and, inadvertently, Sophia started to hop a little in her gait. Dalia found it adorable.

Specter, meanwhile, had taken to leaning against Sophia, or at the least being right by her side. As if she were a comfort blanket for the girl. Sophia didn't mind. She found Specter's displays of affection incredibly welcoming and loved when the large, intimidating grovix would snuggle up against her wherever she was.

She and Neri cooked together. He taught her all sorts of different things, which was when she learned that of them all, he was the best cook. Salan would joke that she was the luckiest woman in the world.

Sophia's parents didn't display affection around others. In fact, Sophia couldn't recall a single time when she had heard them say they loved one another, let alone kissed. Which was why, at first, she didn't know what to make of Neri and Salan's interactions.

Every night, if one of them went to bed before the other, they would say goodnight and land quick kisses. Whenever one left for groceries or other errands, there would be quick pecks to foreheads or cheeks, as though it was second nature. They smiled at one another and held hands. They snuggled on the couch as they read books or watched movies.

When Salan would brave the kitchen and go to make something, Neri wouldn't hesitate to come up behind her, wind his hands around her waist, and rest his head on her shoulder, looking over whatever she was attempting to make. When he would puzzle over something he was reading, she would come up and drape herself against him, peering over his shoulder as she hugged his chest.

Those natural, innocent, quiet gestures to each other made Sophia smile more and more. It became painfully obvious that the two had a deep love for one another, and they weren't afraid to show it. They doted on each other, taking on tasks or coming to render assistance without any request being made.

Dalia would make faces and cover her eyes, telling them to stop being gross. Specter would admonish her, telling her that it was perfectly normal. That someday she would wish to shower her husband in similar affections.

In one such encounter, Neri joked that Dalia probably already had someone she admired and just didn't want to admit it. When the bubbly Zaheri went quiet, Neri spent the better part of the next few days rattling off names, trying to see if he could get her to blush, tell him to be quiet, or leave her alone.

When he said the name Eccio, Dalia had bit her lip and scrunched her face before muttering, "Shut up, Neri. You're being mean."

Sophia suddenly wanted to meet this Eccio and know what he was like.

The days passed without incident. Sophia learned how to tend a garden alongside Salan. She continued studying languages and started to conquer more of English, though she was still struggling mightily against the language. It just didn't make a lot of sense.

For the first time, she understood why people took pictures of their family, so Sophia scrounged together enough money to buy a cheap little camera that she could capture moments with. It took some time for her to be comfortable being in some of the pictures, but she eventually admitted that she liked seeing herself among the people she was beginning to love.

It was the happiest Sophia could ever recall being. And that was all she wanted life to continue to be like. Her and her Zaheri, happy, and together, and safe. Laughing and making memories. Learning about one another and learning to help one another as they went.

Which was why when the gray, armored grovix showed up about three months after the attack, Sophia hated the words that came from him.

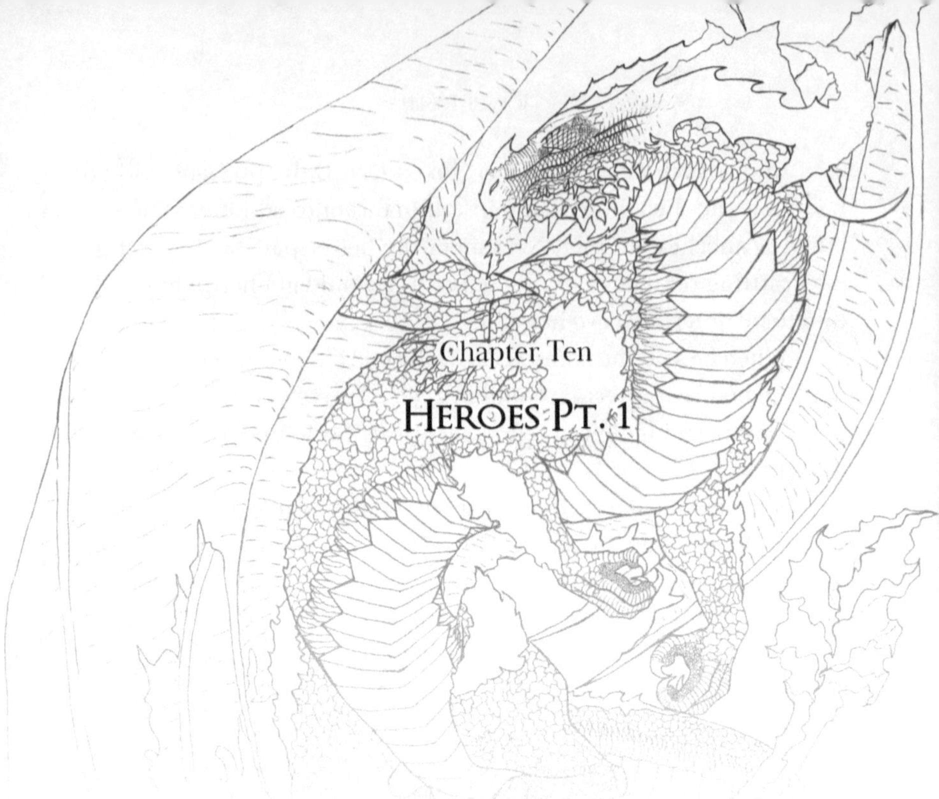

Chapter Ten

HEROES PT.1

"Disbanding?" Neri asked with an incredulous look.

Dover, the grovix from the Gamma Team, let out a small sigh as he frowned. "I don't think any of us like the concept."

"You would be right to hate it," Specter said with a small snarl. "The Human-Borns should require more protection, not less."

"You said they're on their way here," Salan asked Dover.

With a nod, Dover answered, "Yes. I'd imagine they would be here within a couple days, at most. They were eager to gather everyone together as quickly as possible."

"B-but what does this mean?" Sophia asked, still not fully grasping everything they were saying. She knew enough English to follow most of the conversation, but not all of it.

Dalia crossed her arms over her chest. "I don't like it. Leaving just Salan here? What if another attack comes? Do they seriously think Cregorous wouldn't take advantage of something like this?"

Ears flattening, Dover shied back.

Specter let out a snort and looked to the redhead. "We all agree that this is wrong, Dalia. Dover is only doing what he can to keep us informed."

"Wait. So, if Lorn went to the Delta Team, and Rowan went to the Epsilon Team, who's going to the Eta Team?" Neri asked. "I can't imagine Zelek abandoning his Human-Born."

Snapping his gaze to Neri, Dover bristled a little. "He would never."

"Relax, pup," Specter said, stepping into his eyeline.

Dover shied back again. "Zelek is still with Takeo—the Third Human-Born," he explained quickly. "Another Defender was assigned to go collect them."

"This is all so strange," Neri muttered to Salan, who had remained silent since Dover had shown up and told them the news.

Dalia looked to their Team Leader. "What do you wanna do?"

A frown sat on Salan's face. She looked to Sophia and studied her, taking in the terror behind the teenager's eyes.

The poor girl had already been through so much. She was just starting to smile more freely, and the days of questioning her value were growing fewer the further they got away from the whole horrible incident.

Should they all just go back to Agerius and await the Human-Borns there?

No. If they did that, the Human-Borns would come for Sophia and find her missing. That could send them into fearful chaos. Even if that might be the safest step forward, Salan wasn't sure if that would be best overall. She had to consider all of the Human-Borns now, and their Zaheri.

If they all showed up here, they'd likely head into town. Ask questions. Search high and low. What if that delayed them? What if that put a target on them, and Cregorous took advantage of their distraction, and one of the Human-Borns was attacked? Or a Zaheri was lost?

With a glance to Neri, she already knew he would refuse to go. Even if she tried all of her persuasion to convince him, he would sooner lose every right he had to Agerius than leave her and Sophia alone. He cared about them too much.

But, what would that mean for him? Would the Council truly be so cruel as to pardon her but banish Neri? No. No, the Council wasn't like that. This wasn't a decision being done of out of malice. It couldn't be. They weren't dictators who demanded things.

Though there was great warning in her heart about it all.

It was so unlike the Council to make a decision like this. At least, the Council she'd known nineteen years ago.

Was it truly possible that they could have changed so much in their absence?

Sure, the Elemental grovix were no longer actively sitting on the Council. But it didn't add up that the loss of two voices was somehow capable of creating such a dissonance in the Council's decision making.

These were the Human-Borns. Everything surrounding them had always been approached with the greatest of care and forethought. Elders, thirty warriors had been stationed on a foreign world to watch over the burgeoning Human-Borns for nineteen years. The Council had practically stripped the Defense bare of their most seasoned warriors all for the Human-Borns' sakes and safety.

Were they simply terrified of another attack? And wanted them all safely in Agerius? But then, why disband the Zaheri? The Human-Borns were still children. The Council had to be aware of that.

Was it possible they were aware of the emotional attachment that she and Neri had gained for Sophia? Was that part of their reasoning? Were other Zaheri put through similar things, and they, too, were now emotionally entangled with their Human-Borns?

Even so, it didn't make sense.

"Salan?" Neri hushed, gently rubbing his hand along her back. His brow was dipped in worry.

He always knew when she was falling into a hole and her thoughts spiraled.

Taking in a deep breath, she said, "I would leave it up to each of you, but it stands to reason that the Council must have a purpose for their decision." She gave Neri a serious look. "There would be consequences if you disobeyed."

"Then I disobey," Neri said with a shrug. "It's not a question, Salan. I'm not leaving you and Sophia here alone."

Dalia shifted her weight. "I don't want to leave you guys here, either. What if something happens?"

Salan gave the girl a soft look. She was barely over a hundred years old and already was so promising in so many ways. Such a lively spirit and tenacity that could put even the highest-ranking members of the Elite to shame. She might've been a Knight Commander, but she was brave.

"If you stay and they demote you, you won't be an Elite anymore," Salan said gently.

Dalia pouted and looked toward the ground.

Looking to Dover, Specter asked, "It's only you, another pup, and Warden to plead to the Betas, isn't it?"

"Uh, yes," Dover said with a nod. "Alpha Blaze has insisted that she stay with the First Human-Born."

"Then it is likely that Alpha Frost would stay with his Human-Born, as well," Specter mused.

She looked to Salan. "I will return, though I wish I could stay. In Agerius, I can assist Warden with swaying the Betas to our cause." She gave Dover a sideways look. "Two pups would not be well heard among them."

"Yeah ... I was afraid you'd say that," the other grovix said, his ears flattening and his whole demeanor shrinking a little.

"I was thinking similarly," Salan said with a nod. "I think that's the best place for you, Specter."

A frown came to the elder grovix's face. "You must insist that you will be on guard. That is my only request."

"We wouldn't do anything less," Neri said with a small smile.

Dalia looked between Specter and Salan, a look of discomfort on her face.

With a warm smile, Salan stepped up the redhead and embraced her. "There's no need to fear, Dalia. It'll all be fine. You'll see." She stepped back and gave her an encouraging smile. "If you go back, you can assist with convincing the dragons to join the cause. You and Taesir have connections among them that will be sorely needed."

"But," Dalia said, frowning as she flicked her gaze to the ground before meeting Salan's assured expression, "it just doesn't feel right."

"I know it doesn't," the Team Leader said as she raised her brows. "I wouldn't wish for either of you to go. But, given the current situation, your place is best suited in Agerius. We'll be together again soon. Once all of the Human-Borns have united."

"You're right." Dalia smiled to her, losing some of her worry. That bubbly nature eked through. "Of course you're right."

"We should be off," Specter said. "It's possible, if we delay too long, the Defenders on Tilion will come for us themselves." She bowed to Neri and Salan. "We will see you soon."

Dalia and Specter stayed until Sophia was given the rundown of what was going on. Though the teenager clearly didn't want either of them to go, she let them give hugs and offer "see you laters" before they were off to the portal.

Sophia didn't like seeing them go, but she had to admit that the knowledge that Neri and Salan weren't going anywhere eased her worry. She would always be safe so long as she had them. They would never let anything bad happen.

Because they both loved her.

She hadn't said it to either of them, because she wasn't entirely sure if she understood what love felt like in a familial sense. She used to *say* she loved her family, but it was just something she said. She used to think it was true, but as the days had stretched on and her attachment to her parents and sister disappeared to nearly nothing, Sophia wondered if she had been trying to lie to herself and to everyone else every time she'd said it.

It was different with Neri and Salan. There was a definite feeling in her chest whenever she was with them. Every night when she went to bed and they said goodnight and that they cared for her and loved her, she knew there was a swelling within her to echo their sentiments.

But did she really love them?

Did she know what loving a family member was?

She didn't want to say it just to say it. Not with them. Because she was sure if she did utter those words to Neri and Salan, it would create something that could be broken. Just like with her parents. And she didn't want to go through something like that again.

Sophia had gone to bed a while before Neri and Salan sat down to discuss the situation.

Rubbing his jaw, Neri mused, "It's not a bad idea—just going to Agerius. She would be safe there."

"But the others," Salan cautioned.

"I know." He let out a disgruntled sigh and raked a hand through his hair. "I wish there was some way to inform them that we just went to Agerius ahead of them."

"Perhaps we can leave a note?"

"And leave it where? We can't guarantee that they would come here. What if they go into town? Who would we leave it with?"

"If the mountain's path wasn't so problematic, I would just leave something there for them to find."

He shook his head. "They'll probably immediately fly down to solid footing. Maybe at the base of the mountain?"

"Like you said, where? Goats roam the fields freely, as do the chickens. The only type of note we might be able to leave would be paper. And the livestock could easily destroy something like that."

Darting his gaze between the table and his wife, Neri admitted, "I think we should just wait for them."

She sat forward and took his hand. "I agree."

He smirked and said with a shrug, "After all, it's only a day or two, right?"

"If all goes to plan." She perked up a little and hushed, "How do you think the First Human-Born can manage it? Making the portal connect to two Earth activations?"

With another shrug, he offered, "Well, we always figured the First would be powerful. And we know energy strength plays a role in the portal. Otherwise, humans could see it."

"Plus, there's the fact that Cregorous clearly was manipulating the portal in a way outside of its normal function on the day they were attacked. You're right; the First Human-Born must be capable of producing enough energy to make the portal function differently. That must be it." She shook her head in wonder. "It's just so fascinating—that one person could be that powerful."

Salan grew quiet, her gaze drifting as she absentmindedly rubbed her thumb against Neri's hand.

After a few seconds, he asked, "What're you thinking?"

Slowly, she met his gaze. "I wonder if the First is scared of that much strength."

"Would you be?"

She gave him a smile. "Without you? I know I would be."

Gently pulling her hand to kiss the back of it, he said, "Well then, I guess we Zaheri just have to do everything in our power to help them."

After the second day passed and there was no sign of the Human-Borns, Neri and Salan began to worry.

What did that mean? What might have delayed them? Were they overthinking things? Was it just a matter of bad timing? Perhaps there was something one of the other Human-Borns needed to do that would slow them down. Perhaps it was as simple as the First needing to take breaks between the use of the portal in the way they were using it.

Neither of them voiced the fear that churned in their stomachs.

That something terrible had happened.

They reconsidered going to Agerius, but again were brought back to the reality that, if they left without any way to alert the Human-Borns to where they were, it would cause panic.

Because what if everything was perfectly fine? What if they were simply trying to give the First some time to rest? What if the Fourth or Fifth Human-Borns had schools to step away from, or families who objected? There were any number of things that could be delaying them.

Without any way to contact them, they just had to be patient.

It would be fine.

It was barely dawn four days after Dalia and Specter had left when an alarm blared. The portal was open. Sensors picked up a similar number of enemy fighters as the initial scouting party on the day of the attack.

They leaped into action and went into the field, knowing it would be better to be there and be prepared. It was early, but not terribly so, around six in the morning.

Neri rejoined them, landing as he said, "No Ferveos. But we've definitely got a fair squall coming our way."

"What should we do?" Sophia asked as she clutched Salan's arm.

Salan offered a reassuring smile. "It'll be all right, Sophia. We'll be fine. Neri and I won't let anything bad happen to you." Giving her husband a pointed stare, she added, "I'll stay here with Sophia, just like last time."

"I'll handle the mob," he said with a smirk before he leaned toward her and kissed her. "Be careful," he hushed against her.

"You, too," she whispered back before giving him another quick kiss.

"Be careful, Neri!" Sophia called as he stepped away.

He threw her a confident grin. "For you? You got it."

Sucking in a determined breath, Sophia took hold of her pistol. She'd been practicing in the months since the attack, and her accuracy had improved greatly. This time, she would be able to help.

As she watched Neri fly off, she felt the urge to cry out that she loved him. That she wanted him to come back safely. That she didn't want to lose him.

Gently gripping Sophia's shoulder, Salan gave her a smile. "He'll be all right, Sophia. Neri is a great fighter."

"I know," she hushed in response.

But he didn't have anyone to watch his back this time. It wasn't like before when he'd had Specter on the ground and Dalia in the air. They'd kept one another safe.

There was a screeching noise, and Salan whipped her head toward the sound. A flash of gold tore across them, and Sophia shook back when boots hit the shield and kicked off, landing solidly a few paces away.

A confident smirk played on their attacker's face.

He had softer features and longer hair, a lean and relaxed posture. He looked a stark opposite to Izel. His jacket and pants were made of leather, and his boots and knee bracers were metal. The collar of his jacket accented the shape of his jaw perfectly, drawing attention to his charming features.

"Well, what have we here?" Avemod cooed in a smooth voice.

"Sophia, whatever happens, stay behind me," Salan hushed in

a commanding tone. Her gaze was hard on their attacker, her stance ready to spring into action at a moment's notice.

Licking his lips, Avemod looked at the teen. "Mmm ... Sophia. That's a lovely name."

Sophia shied back and shivered. She didn't like the way he looked at her.

"You should leave before I kill you," Salan demanded, a scowl fixed on her face.

Sliding his gaze to Salan, the Caligan said in his buttery voice, "Such cruel words from such a pretty face." He shrugged apathetically. "I have to say, I haven't had so many lovely ladies near me as I have today." His gaze grew dark. "Should I tell you what I did to Streya?"

"That's enough!" Salan commanded, her voice booming enough to rattle the shield that separated them from their attacker.

A sly grin came to his features. "I don't do well with commands, love. You'll have to come out of that little shield of yours and make me."

As a crackling hit the air, he whipped his gaze up and leaped back just in time to avoid Neri swinging his scythe into the ground.

Neri then straightened and swung his scythe around, ready to strike.

"Ah, another weapon wielder." Avemod quirked his brow and grinned at Neri. "You're quite the specimen, too."

"Leave," Neri growled.

"Sorry. I have too much riding on this," Avemod said simply, leisurely lowering his arms as gray swirled around his limbs, pooling at his hands.

Without a word, Neri surged forward, and the two began trading blows. Avemod was much faster than Izel, and his strikes were precise. With each deflected blow, he was swift to keep Neri on his toes, sending out small spurts of gray, making Salan create shields to protect her husband or forcing Neri to swiftly move aside.

Gold and gray swirled and spun. Flitted and stabbed. The air was alight with the sparks of the energies battling. It sent fear into Sophia's stomach.

On a dime, Avemod switched tactics. Neri swung his scythe out, and Avemod deftly dodged it, leaping into the air. Gray energy filled his foot as he landed a harsh kick to Neri's face, sending the Agerian soaring and crashing to the earth.

As he landed, he swiftly brought his hands up in time to deflect an attack from Salan. A blast of gray tore from him as he yanked his arms down, and the attack pummeled into a golden shield that appeared just in time to protect Salan.

The Team Leader landed and slid across the grassy hill, keeping her shield in place as she charged forward, slamming into Avemod. A crack tore the air and Salan pushed off the shield, sending shattered fragments of gold to slice at the general.

Avemod was sent tumbling backward, getting his footing after a few stumbling steps.

With a yell, Salan barreled down on him, a storm of gold in her joined hands. She threw her hands out, and a stream of gold tore at him.

A gray shield appeared, and Avemod shoved his way through her powered attack. Even as his shield cracked and strained, he kept going. Determination was fixed on his features. He was bleeding from multiple injuries, but he didn't stop.

From inside the shield, Sophia shook as she tried to figure out how to hit him with a shot from her pistol. He moved so fast that she was terrified she'd accidentally hit her Zaheri.

Neri leaped back into the fight, pinning Avemod between himself and his wife. Gold blows were traded, keeping Avemod moving. Neri sported a gash along his face, and blood dripped from his brow. Salan's arms trembled.

Cracks started to appear along the shield protecting Sophia, and she looked at them in panic. What did that mean?

A large splinter tore in front of her, slicing the air with its presence.

A swirl of gray exploded from Avemod, knocking Neri and Salan back. He tore from his spot at alarming speed. A broken blade was in his grasp, sparking blue energy.

Sophia fired off a few shots, shakily, furiously, unblinkingly hoping they would connect. And they did.

But they didn't deter Avemod from his goal.

There was a crack, a blast of air, and Sophia was shoved aside.

Then a sickening squelch.

Sophia ripped her gaze over her shoulder and felt everything tremble.

Avemod's gray-cloaked palm was splayed across Salan's face. In his other hand, he held the broken blade, now buried to the hilt into her abdomen. Then a blast of gray erupted from his palm, slamming straight into Salan's face.

If Sophia screamed—and she must have—she didn't hear it.

Yellow erupted from around her and careened into Avemod, sending him skittering backward as Salan hit the ground. Half a second later, there was a crackling charge and a furious yell from Neri.

Gold slashed across Avemod's body. The resulting blast against him sent him flying straight through the trees and into the mountains. He flew so fast from Neri's attack that it only took a second for the mountain to shudder a *thud* from the impact, despite its great distance from where they were.

Sophia scrambled, her hands and feet skittering grass and soil as she tried to not collapse, even though nothing connected in her brain.

Salan was crumpled on the ground, her back to Sophia. Blood dripped from the broken blade tip.

She wasn't moving.

Neri slid to her side, gently taking her into his arms. "Salan! Sa—" His breath caught as his hand kept swiping across her brow.

Without thinking, Sophia grabbed Salan's arm and tugged as she screamed, "Salan!" Her whole body clenched when she looked to her Zaheri's face.

Where was her smile?

Where was her warmth?

"No," Sophia shook out as tears rolled down her cheeks. "No! No! Salan! I love you!" She pinched her face in an attempted restraint as she felt sorrow eclipse every thought in her being. "Come back! I … I never said it! I never told you! I … I love you!"

Weeping overtook her, and Sophia fell forward, bawling into Salan's still chest. Repeating over and over again that she loved her. That she wanted her to come back.

"I'm sorry," she wailed. "I'm sorry I wasn't—"

Neri gripped her shoulder and yanked her upright. Through her blurry, tear-filled eyes, she saw his face racked with sorrow. She'd never seen Neri cry. And now that she had, she wished she could erase that image from her mind.

"It's not your fault, Sophia," he managed to croak out as his jaw trembled. His voice broke as he gently shook his head. "It's not your fault."

She flung her arms around his neck and sobbed. He clutched her and pinched his eyes shut as tears rolled sloppily down his dirt- and blood-stained face.

They didn't even get to say goodbye.

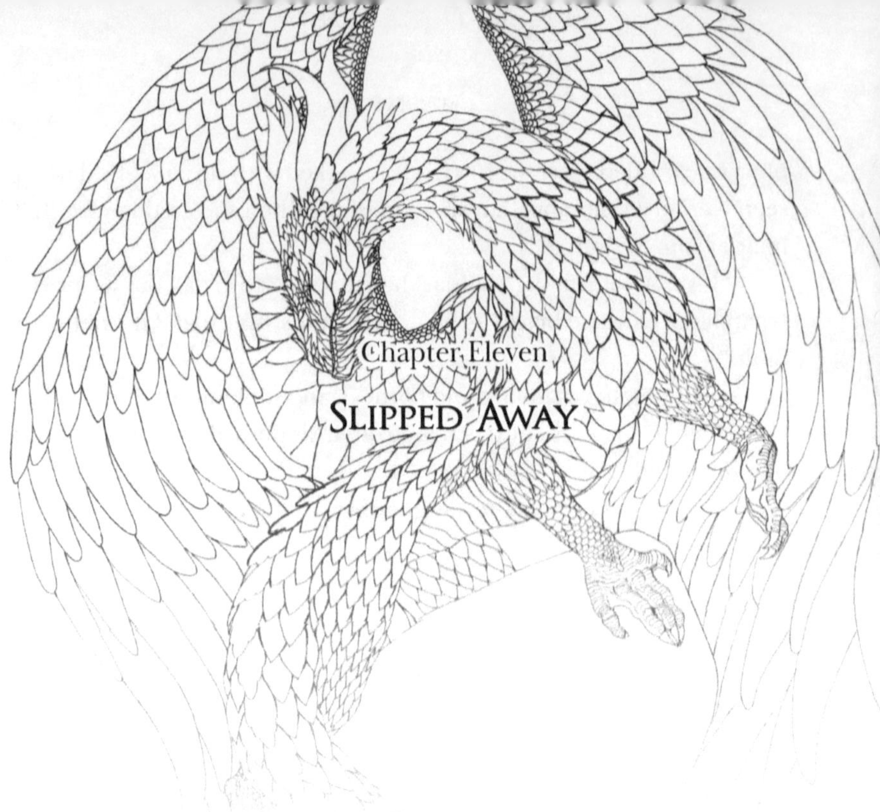

Chapter Eleven

SLIPPED AWAY

When Sophia finally cried herself to sleep in Neri's arms, he had to prepare himself for the worst thing he could have ever imagined he might have to do.

He'd have to be quick about it, too. And that made it hurt even more.

Neri didn't dare move Sophia into a bed, so he just gently removed himself from under her, leaving her on the couch.

He nearly wretched when he pulled the sword from her body. Then he doubled over and shook from restrained sobs. He had to be quick. He couldn't leave Sophia alone. Because if she happened to wake while he wasn't there, she could go into a terrified panic.

Forcing heavy breaths into his lungs, he lifted his wife's body into his arms and clenched his jaw to try to keep himself from weeping.

All he wanted to do was hold her and cry.

There was so much he wanted to say. So much he wanted to scream.

The trip back to the house was a daze. He honestly didn't know how he'd made it. His tears had run again, dripping down his jaw.

When he lifted his foot to step onto the porch, he found himself unable to stand anymore and fell to his knees. He doubled over her broken body and gritted his teeth so hard it hurt. His skull vibrated from how tightly he held his emotions back. The onslaught of it was enough to make his heart burst.

He laid her down as gently as he could, his arms trembling from the motion. The realness of it made it hard to breathe.

Stumblingly grabbing the blanket he'd taken before he'd left, he went to cover her.

He made the mistake of looking at her scarred face.

So many words wanted to tumble from his lips. Apologies. Begs. Pleas. Cries.

Agony filled his whole being.

Closing his eyes, he rested his forehead against hers. She wasn't supposed to be this cold. She was never supposed to be this cold. She'd always been warm. Bright. Smiling.

"I'm sorry," he said so quietly he could barely hear himself. "I was supposed to be your defender," he cried as wordless, silent sobs racked his body, shaking his shoulders. Gently caressing her face, he searched her and sucked in painful breaths. "I love you." He leaned back and couldn't bring himself to say anything else. He couldn't breathe out of his clogged nose.

So, he just shakily covered her.

Then he tremblingly stood and staggered into the house.

He collapsed on the floor next to Sophia and waited for the darkness of sorrow to swallow him.

Chapter Twelve

FATED MEETINGS

The day that followed was a daze of exhaustion and crying. Neri managed to keep himself from completely breaking down every time Sophia bawled into his chest. He managed to keep breathing. He shoved everything aside, forcing himself to focus.

Sophia was the priority. He could die later.

No. No, he couldn't.

He had to keep breathing. He had to keep going. Sophia depended on him.

She sought him as support. Stability.

The poor girl was traumatized, and he didn't know how to patch her together. Because he was barely holding himself in place. He couldn't sleep. Even when he thought for sure he couldn't cry anymore. He couldn't go on anymore. Exhaustion wore his body and strained his mind, but he kept reminding himself that he needed to keep it together.

The Human-Borns were coming. They had to be.

So, when the alarm blared two nights after the worst morning of his entire life, Neri took too long to figure out what to do. It had to be the Human-Borns and the other Zaheri. It just had to be.

If it was anything else, he didn't know what he'd do.

Elders help him.

Elders save him.

He was failing at everything in that moment.

Sophia gripped his arm as he kept his façade in place long enough to remind her to hold on to him. To get behind him if anything went amiss. Reminding her that he wouldn't let her get hurt.

She'd nodded absently, even as terror filled her eyes, and she silently begged him to not leave her, too.

They flew out to the group once he'd discerned that they'd broken up into two units. Enough sensors were left that he could determine there was one group with figures in size similar to a werewolf and two bratak'ra. Though the other group of all hybrids went to the town, he knew he needed to stop the group with the werewolf first. Just in case.

The flight there was just a mantra of a prayer.

Let it be them. Let it be help. Let it be Agerians.

Please, please, please.

Not Caligans.

He didn't want to let Sophia down again.

Fixing a glare on his face helped him lock away his pain. So, when he would land near the group that happened to be the remnants of the battlefield from days earlier, he would appear more collected than he actually was.

With a mighty flap of his wings, he landed, and Sophia unsteadily pulled herself out of his grasp. He swung his scythe around, ready to strike, when relief flooded him.

Sophia shakily raised her pistol and asked, "Who are you?"

Praise the Elders, it was Agerians.

Neri reached for her and gently lowered her arm. "It's all right. They're friends," he said.

She was grateful that he sounded so calm. Sophia knew he couldn't possibly be okay. He had to be burying his feelings for her. But his steadiness was helping her not fall over and immediately bawl.

"You recognize us?" a boy—she assumed Japanese, given his features—asked. She understood him without issue but didn't question it. It must have been all of her time studying English had paid off.

Her study with—

"They do?" a large, unarmored grovix asked, flicking his gaze between the teens and Neri.

"Thank the Elders for that," the werewolf among them said. He stood fully erect and wore clothing, so she barely recognized him as a Tilion werewolf. Not with how gentle he looked, despite the fact that he towered over her.

Sophia shuffled closer to Neri. She drew her arms in and bit her lip, trying to will herself to not cry. Her eyes had to be puffy, and she simply had to look awful.

Neri was focused on her, his hand still on her arm. He quickly glanced toward the group. "I'd be a fool to not recognize the Council Member among you."

The white grovix in the group bowed her head. "Thank you, Neri. I appreciate the remembrance."

"Sophia, it's okay," Neri whispered to her, gently rubbing her back.

She nodded a few times and swallowed. Her terror was subsiding slowly. The group before them looked formidable. At the least, she wouldn't lose Neri.

She would still have him to cling to.

The pristine white grovix with striking red eyes glanced to the brown-haired girl in the group.

"Oh, uh ... he's reassuring her," the brunette said. She turned her attention to Sophia and, for a second, Sophia felt a jolt of remembrance. This girl looked familiar. Her hazel eyes, the way her hair fell, even the way she stood ... it all jabbed at Sophia's brain as though saying, "*We've seen her before.*"

Stepping forward a bit, the other girl said, "Yeah, we're the Human-Borns." She offered a small smile and added, "I'm Jen Monroe." Thumbing over her shoulder, she introduced the other girls, "That's Lexa Ackart and Eshe Balewa." She turned to the dark-skinned girl wearing a vibrant dress. "Did I pronounce that right?"

Eshe smiled broadly. "Very well."

The other boy among them came to the brunette's side, and Sophia felt her stomach flip.

If the girl was familiar, this boy was even more so. And she knew precisely where she'd seen his face before.

In a vision.

"I'm Skylar Mitchell, and he's Takeo Yoshi," Skylar offered, slowly taking a few steps forward. He wore a look of great concern, a small frown on his face as he took stock of her. "Are you all right?"

"*No,*" she wanted to cry.

At least they were nice. At least they weren't looking down on her and her fragile state. Perhaps they'd understand. Perhaps they...

Her heart grew tight, and she sucked back a sniffling breath. She had to introduce herself. Things were okay. Well, as okay as they could be. Neri wouldn't get hurt. No one else would get hurt.

She wanted to break down and bawl at the thought that someone she genuinely loved was gone. How did she still have tears left? Hadn't she cried her eyes dry by this point? Nevertheless, the desire to sink into sorrow crippled her chest.

"I'm Sophia. Um ... Sophia Gonzalez," she finally managed to say.

Skylar continued to stare at her with that look of concern.

Then the unarmored grovix asked, "What happened?"

Everything broke, Sophia thought.

Just as she feared it would.

Neri managed to catch them up on almost everything and not break down. Sophia didn't know how he did it. How was he still standing? She knew how deeply he loved Salan. Surely this cut him so much deeper than it did her.

In that instant, she wanted to blurt out that she loved him, too. That she would say it every minute of every day if it meant they wouldn't lose one another.

Her red eyes drilling into Neri, the white grovix asked, "Where is Salan?"

And Sophia lost it.

She blearily registered Skylar taking half a step forward, gently reaching toward her but pulling his hand back.

Lexa dropped her gaze and whispered, "Oh God."

Everything was blurry and disconnected. She wanted to sink into darkness and stop thinking. Stop breathing. Just stop. Because maybe then it wouldn't hurt so much.

It was all her faul—

Jen gently stepped forward and hushed, "I know it's not a comfort …"

She forced her eyes to focus on Jen. Right. The Human-Borns. She was one of them, right? That meant she wasn't allowed to just fade into darkness.

No matter how much she wanted to.

Wearing a frown and a crumbled expression, Jen said, "I almost lost one of my Zaheri yesterday, so … I'm … I'm sorry."

Wait—

One of the other Zaheri almost …?

But Jen seemed confident. Assured. She'd only started frowning and looking less than bold just now. Surely she was talented. Surely she was one of the other strong Human-Borns. She'd been the first to introduce herself, so … could that mean that...

Was she the Raidin?

Maybe. Just maybe.

It wasn't Sophia's fault. Just as Neri had said. Maybe this had happened because Salan had been doing what she lived for—protecting those she cared about. And maybe, as awful, horrible, and gut-wrenching as it was, it wasn't something Sophia needed to take the blame for.

Because if Jen could stand up despite whatever she had faced, maybe Sophia could, too.

Not today.

But someday.

The REQUISITE'S RISE

Then Seventh and last,
the Requisite true.
Without whom,
all would be lost.

A Frozen Start

It was a small miracle that Alaster O'Brien had adjusted so well to the massive differences in daylight. Even in Alaska, he had struggled with getting adequate sleep during the all-day season.

His sleep had been fitful, resulting in mediocre rest. Though his eyes were heavy, he could count it as gain that he'd managed nearly five hours of slumber. He lifted his arm and stared at his watch as the second hand ticked, revealing it was nearly five in the morning.

Better than some nights.

On the floor directly next to his bed was his slumbering Zaheri grovix, Frost. Alaster envied that the sentient, speaking animal never seemed deterred by the sunlight that would occasionally peek through the sides of the blackout curtain.

Releasing a sigh, Alaster sat up and made sure to place his feet over Frost's body. The grovix was long and slender, and in the confines of Alaster's room, he didn't have to worry about human eyes seeing his otherworldly form.

Frost stood around five feet tall, with a medium length, light blue coat, and sea-blue eyes. His ears were thin but long and ended in a point, much like a bobcat. His bone structure was more canine, with a narrow snout. He had sturdy legs and substantial paws, and his tail was long and fluffy. Despite being a creature of authority in Agerius, Alaster was perfectly fine reaching down and gently stroking the soft fur along Frost's head.

The grovix's nose twitched in his sleep, causing Alaster to smile as he got up. The seventeen-year-old Ireland native stretched. Even if he couldn't sleep any further, at least it had felt good to close his eyes and lay down.

Ruffling his blond hair, he shuffled over to a simple dresser with a small mirror on top and pulled out a change of clothes.

Glancing at his reflection, he caught the bags under his green eyes and the scruff appearing along his chin. He shook off his weariness and changed.

Before he left the room, he snatched the military dog tags off his dresser, the metal chain scraping across the wood.

When he stepped out of his room, he was met with the sight he had grown accustomed to for the past two and a half years—white cinderblock walls, a black floor, and an exposed ceiling of metal stretched down the hall. At the end was one of the entrances of the Amundsen-Scott Station.

Tucking his dog tags under his shirt and pulling on his light jacket, he walked to his right, trying and failing to keep his footfalls quiet. That was nearly impossible with no one else in the hallway.

Daylight streamed through the windows along the corridor. It was cruel to think that it was five in the morning. One of the crazy phenomenon to observe in Antarctica: the sun rose in September and didn't set until March. It was a shame that most people couldn't witness the beauty of the continent, but the cold was a little unbearable at times.

Alaster walked a short way down the hall and came to a set of doors. They led to the dining hall, or the galley as the residents called it. Stifling a yawn, he entered the empty room. He wasn't expecting to find many people here. Even though it was hard to sleep during the all-day season, many still tried and a few succeeded.

Only one thing was on his mind: coffee. He preferred tea, but the only offering was a really generic brand of basic black tea, and

Alaster hated that he couldn't get himself to drink it. He didn't like being picky and, truthfully, couldn't afford to be. But tea, it seemed, was the exception.

None of the chefs would be serving anything until at least six, when the others would blearily stumble out of their beds and work for another light-filled day.

Pouring himself a cup of coffee and letting the scent of the fresh beans fill his nose, he felt a little more aware.

The door opened off to his right as he poured a bit of cream into his mug.

"Couldn't sleep?" he asked before turning around.

One of his other Zaheri, Kedar, barely registered the Human-Born before falling into one of the chairs at a small, round table. Lifting his head, Kedar glared at the teenager. "How have you done this for the past two years?"

Taking the few steps toward his Zaheri, Alaster offered the coffee. "You get used to it."

Kedar spied the coffee suspiciously before taking it in his hand and smelling it.

Turning back to get himself another mug, Alaster shook his head as he heard the Agerian take a sip. He could just imagine Kedar grimacing. After all the time Kedar had spent on Earth, it surprised Alaster that none of his Zaheri had acquired a taste for coffee.

As the teenager sat down, Kedar asked, "What're you doing up?"

Kedar was a tall, lean individual. Short, deep brown hair with lighter brown patches sat unevenly on his head, and his dark brown eyes looked almost black from the lack of sleep. Kedar's years with the Agerian Defense had helped him maintain a strong musculature that he relied on whenever he got into a scrap of trouble.

"I couldn't sleep. Thought I would go check on my parents," Alaster said before taking a sip of coffee and feeling the warmth fill his bone-cold body.

Setting the mug down and crossing his arms, Kedar said, "Seeing if there's anything their brilliant son can help with?"

"Trying to find something to take my mind off of the fact that I couldn't sleep more than five hours."

"Yeah, I can't say that I'm happy we're here," Kedar grumbled with a glance around the room. The myriad of windows along the walls showed the icy landscape and swirling powder just outside.

"You have to go where the science is," Alaster answered with a smirk.

Giving the teen an unenthused expression, the Zaheri said plainly, "Science can't be found somewhere not desolate?"

Alaster considered the question before he shrugged. "Not deep space science. Desolate's kinda the point."

The two of them finished their coffee or, at least, Alaster finished his coffee while Kedar swirled his spoon around in the drink, and then parted ways. Kedar had to continue to pretend to be part of a National Geographic team doing a piece on Antarctic living. All of the moving Alaster's family had done in the past five years had made training the teen rather difficult.

A Human-Born hybrid. That's what Alaster was. Part human, part dragon, awarding him abilities like rapid cellular regeneration, wings, and the power to pull "energy" into a tangible force.

Energy was so broad, and Alaster wanted to understand a more specific sense of what the green, misting, staticky substance was. Raw energy from the world around him? Was he manifesting the heat or water from the air and converting it into something tangible? Or was he legitimately taking molecules of nature, atoms themselves, and making them swirl into his grasp and poof away like dust?

Kedar had rubbed his head a bunch and told Alaster to stop thinking so much about it. But thinking about things was exactly what Alaster was good at. It was the chief reason why he was allowed at this station at all.

Kedar and his teammates were a group of four—three hybrids and the grovix, Frost. They were charged almost nineteen years ago with the task of protecting Alaster from their enemy, a man named Cregorous. Some terribly powerful man who wished death and destruction.

To what extent Alaster was supposed to stop some monstrous force, the teenager couldn't say. And if the fate of some other world connected to Earth truly did rest on Alaster's shoulders, then that world might be doomed.

Because, so far, Alaster hadn't seen much of what his energy could do. His parents had forbidden any training whatsoever. And it wasn't just because they were on a research station in Antarctica.

Five years prior, when Alaster's parents had moved the family to Alaska, Kedar had made an executive decision and approached the boy and his family.

Things didn't go well.

Despite the demonstration of his own energy, Kedar was unable to convince the O'Briens of the severity of the situation. Even though they were told to leave the family alone, the Zaheri followed them to Alaska, anyway, and continued their duty of protecting Alaster.

From a distance. The parents never knew the Agerians had followed them to the States.

Things could have stayed that way until two years later, when the O'Briens' application for a three-year expedition to Antarctica was approved. The Zaheri definitely had to be with Alaster to make sure he was guarded.

So, they paid their way to Antarctica and had finally arrived six days ago. Despite Alaster's parents discomfort with the situation, Alaster had pleaded for his Zaheri to stay so he could learn from them. Ever since he had been told of his Human-Born status by Kedar those years ago, he had been randomly doing things he didn't know he could do, like conjuring sparks of green energy between his fingers and growing wings.

Frost had been with Alaster since he was twelve, disguised as a German Shepard that followed him home one day from school in Alaska. He revealed himself to the boy shortly after he was brought into the family. And, while it grated against Alaster to keep the secret, he understood why he couldn't say anything to his parents.

Now that all four of them were at the Antarctic base together, secretly trying and failing to train Alaster in his fighting skills whenever possible, Alaster knew his parents were furious about the situation.

He wished he could explain it to them, but he could barely explain it to himself. When he saw his energy flit in his grasp, he knew there was more at work in his life than he ever could have thought.

Alaster walked past his room and poked his head in to make sure that Frost was still sleeping and to grab his heavier coat. As he took the fabric into his grasp, he gave the article of clothing an unenthused stare.

One of the many things his hybrid gene allowed him to do was adapt to and survive brutal temperatures. After two and a half years, he could handle subzero temperatures like it was thirty degrees outside. But he couldn't let on to what he really was. The reactions from the other scientists was unpredictable, and he didn't want to risk something bad happening because of his carelessness.

Walking to the other end of the long station, Alaster reached an elevator. Glancing around to make sure no one was nearby, he grabbed the elevator doors and pried them open enough to fit in. He stripped off his light jacket and threw both coats down into the elevator shaft before sliding through the gap.

Once inside, he turned and kept his toes gripping the edge of the floor as he pulled the doors shut again. Darkness enveloped him, but after blinking twice, he could see just as well as if the shaft were lit.

Now that he was only wearing his shirt—a self-replicating one from Tilion—he took a deep breath and felt wings begin to expand out of his back. Two thick bones jutted out, tearing through his shirt, and his skin molded with the bones, forming into dark leathery wings that were vast enough to easily fill the elevator shaft. The moment his wings formed, his shirt patched itself back up and sealed around the wing joints, as though the holes were made specifically for this purpose.

Letting a small grin come to his face, he let go of the wall and let his wings skim the sides of it. He carefully glided down to the bottom of the shaft and landed gracefully.

Standing still for a moment, he closed his eyes and rolled both his shoulder and wing joints, trying to stretch out the never-used muscles. He almost wanted to propel himself back up the elevator shaft just to let his desire to fly be somewhat fulfilled. But that would be heard, and his wings were so strong that the pressure of them might knock out one of the walls.

No matter how much he wanted to fly, it would be careless.

Letting out a sigh, he forced his wings back into his skin, and his bones complied, folding back the way they had come. Once they were gone, his shirt blended back together and looked as if nothing had happened to it at all.

In a way, he wished he could go through a full body x-ray. He knew his wing bones folded against his internal organs and skeletal structure, but he would be intrigued to see how.

Snatching his jackets, he pulled open the bottom floor elevator door and poked his head out into the hall.

Once he knew it was clear, he quickly squeezed through the crack in the doors. Zipping up his jacket, he made his way to the Arches, which would lead him outside to the IceCube, the drilling platform where they pulled out long, pipe-shaped ice sticks that would show thousands of years' worth of information upon study.

Warring emotions hit his chest as he neared the entrance. He loved the cold of Antarctica and the beauty seldom appreciated here, but whenever he went outside, all he wanted to do was take off and fly. It was early enough that maybe no one would notice. But, during the all-day season, there were always people everywhere.

He was stuck on the most isolated continent on Earth and still couldn't be who he wanted to be.

His parents weren't biologists or geneticists. If they were, perhaps they would try to delve into his genetic makeup and figure out what made him have the powers he had. It would provide an answer for the science side of their minds.

And he couldn't appeal to the faith side of his parents. Maybe before. Maybe if Cam hadn't—

Alaster shook his head to rid the reminder.

He reached the entrance and pulled his hood up to begin the long walk out to the IceCube. He could have taken one of the Ski-doos, but he really wanted to take the walk out there. Even if he was slotted and fell into one of the crevices in the ice, he'd be fine. He could just blast his way out of the ice with his energy.

Just the thought of using his strength like that sent a sparking tingle in his fingers underneath his heavy gloves.

One day, he'd be able to figure himself out.

When he reached the IceCube, he climbed up the stairs and felt the vibrations from the large machine working. When he reached the platform, he saw his parents, both bundled in God only knew how many layers of clothing, with one of the operators. It was mandatory for the scientists to be supervised, just in case something went wrong with the equipment.

They must have just finished drilling because the machine turned off and Alaster could see the deep hole stretching down into the ice. It was a warbled, circular shape, as all of the drilled ice looked, and reached down hundreds of feet.

With the noisy machine silenced, Alaster's approaching footsteps were heard and his parents turned around.

"Alaster! What're you doing here?" his mother said.

A smile came to his face as he said, "I couldn't sleep. Thought I'd come out to see if there was anything I could do to help."

His father waved a heavily clothed hand dismissively. "Not now. We've already done the hard part."

"How much sleep did you get?" his mother asked.

"Five hours. I'll be fine," Alaster answered.

Giving her son a concerned look, she opened her mouth to respond, when his father chimed in, "He'll be fine, lass. Not the first time he's gone with little sleep."

Alaster's ability to be allowed on the base was as simple as it might seem—his parents were his only relatives, aside from extended family. Additionally, he was exceptionally bright and qualified to have the expedition count for graduate-level classes, despite currently only being in his undergrad studies in university.

Placing her heavily mittened hand on Alaster's arm, his mother said, "C'mon, honey; let's get you inside and get some breakfast."

Until they moved the ice out of the drill, which would happen once they left, there wasn't anything to do. That process took a little while and a good deal of coordination so you didn't break the long pipe of ice. If that happened, they'd have to drill all over again in a whole new spot. No one ever wanted to do that, so they were always incredibly careful not to have that happen.

When they reached the ground, Alaster's father gestured toward the few ski-doos sitting nearby. "Why don't you grab the other one, and your mother and I will take this one?"

"I don't need to. I can walk back," Alaster said without thinking it through.

When he turned to them, he could tell by the shape of his mother's slumped shoulders that she didn't approve.

Nodding, he pointed to the ski-doo. "Right, I'll take this one."

Back in the galley, Alaster and his parents sat at a small table together, waiting for the food to be put out. The smell of cinnamon buns and pancakes wafted into the area. It was one of the good days for food. Usually, you got choices of cereal, soggy sloppy eggs, and frumpy looking bacon.

Frost walked into the room, fully disguised as a German Sheppard. It was one of the gifts Elemental grovix like Frost had—they could mask their appearance, seemingly for as long as they wished. Coming up to their table, Frost panted like any other dog and played the part well enough. To everyone on base, Frost was Alaster's therapy dog.

"How're things coming out there?" Alaster asked his parents as he absentmindedly patted Frost's head.

"Well, assuming that a beaker like Johnson doesn't get a hold of it first," his father started.

"Keegan," Alaster's mother said under her breath.

Grunting and looking at Frost, who just stared back at him and panted, Alaster's father changed the subject, "How're your classes coming?"

"Fine. I've finished most of them. In a week, I anticipate to be done with them all," the teenager answered. He had been taking online classes since he was fifteen and was set to graduate from college by the end of the semester, four and a half years early.

Before he'd known about what he was, Alaster had had every intention of becoming an astronomer or astrophysicist. He'd always been fascinated by space and the mysteries it held. Truthfully, he still loved his studies and the times he'd devoured information on the heavier parts of astronomy. Especially black holes. Despite his deep love for the stars, he had to admit a growing unrest.

He'd tried to blame it on being stuck in Antarctica. After all, most teenagers would have gone batty spending their formative years surrounded by insanely smart adults and no one their own age to spend time with. But Alaster had always liked adults, insanely smart or otherwise.

Probably Cam's doing. A six-year age gap hadn't meant a thing to Cam. He'd let Alaster tag along with him to everything. And Alaster was smarter than the average kid, though he didn't like to think of himself like that. It was bad enough that his da kept reminding him of how smart he was, practically shoving it in other scientists' faces sometimes.

Maybe that played a part in the unrest. Plus, the knowledge that he was a Human-Born, that there was a destiny out there just waiting for him to take part in, that someday everything would fall into alignment.

He hoped he'd notice when it happened. That he'd have the courage to follow it.

"Things are all set, then?" his mother asked.

"Aye, graduating in December," Alaster answered.

As they talked, his father continued to stare at Frost. Keegan knew full well what was under the façade of the happy-looking dog. There'd always been something about the absurdly well-trained stray that made him wonder if something more was going on. He'd put things together when the other three arrived. He hadn't voiced it, but he was convinced Alaster had known all along.

"Then onto graduate school and your PhD," Keegan said.

Alaster stilled in his actions, and Frost looked at him. The teenager swallowed and said, "What if I decided to take some time off?"

"And do what?" his mother asked.

Glancing at Frost, Alaster said, "Um ..."

"No," Keegan answered quickly.

Alaster spun to look at his father, a plea forming in his head but not on his lips.

Keegan shook his head. "Absolutely not."

Frost whimpered, and Keegan shot the dog a glare.

Well, that had been dismissed faster than Alaster had thought.

A clang came from the serving area, and one of the chefs called out that the food was ready. The family was still for a moment before Keegan got up, his wife following a second later.

Alaster looked over at his Zaheri. "I guess this'll be harder than we thought."

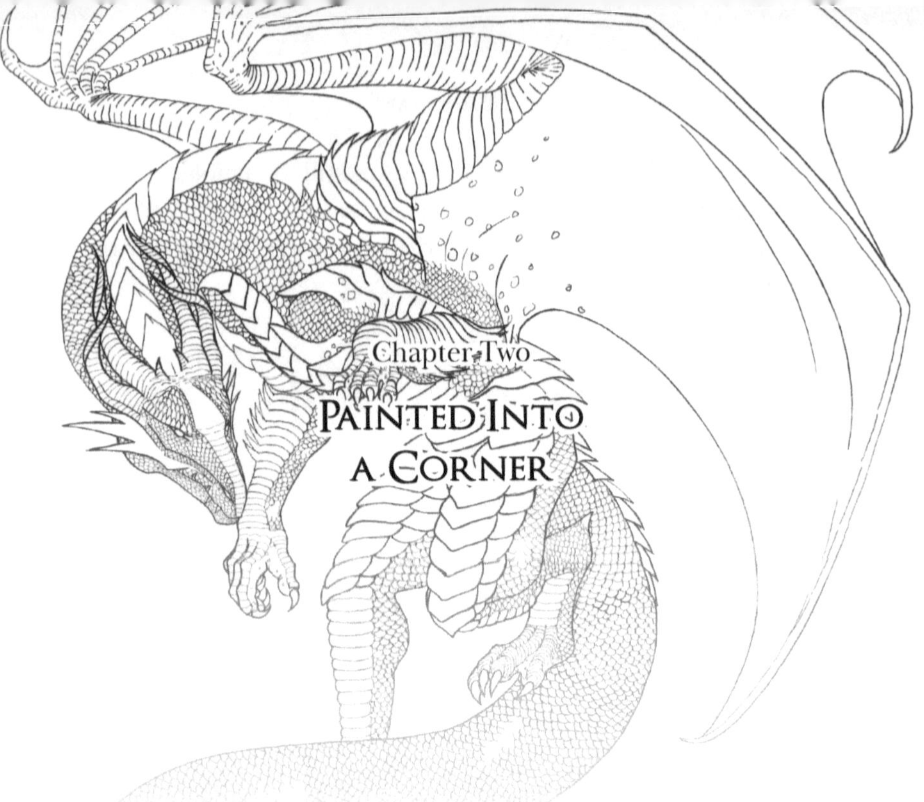

Chapter Two

PAINTED INTO A CORNER

Anger churned its presence in Alaster's stomach. It wasn't like this was the first time his da had outright said no. He should've seen that coming.

It was an emotion Alaster couldn't quite name. He felt caged, trapped maybe. But he also knew why his parents were so quick to keep him closely guarded. He could understand their emotions, their motivation for the staunch position they took concerning his training. So, "caged" or "trapped" weren't proper descriptions of what he felt.

His inability to name the feeling in his chest poked and prodded at his mind, dredging itself into his thoughts and begging him to find the answer. But emotions were tricky. Answers to them were seldom easy.

Pushing his frustration—both at his own inability to name his feelings and at his father's inflexibility—aside, Alaster made for one of the science labs.

He and Frost were on a hunt for the rest of the Zaheri, which was proving a little difficult.

There were so many rooms and places people could hide on the station that searching for anyone was time consuming. Sometimes it could take an hour before you tracked down who you were looking for, especially during the all-day season when people grabbed sleep where they could.

Searching might prove useless. If that were the case, Alaster would head back to Wing A-1, where all of the dorm rooms were located. There were two lounges with books and movies, so he could just hang out there if tracking down his Zaheri on his own didn't work out.

As they came into Wing B, they could hear a commotion that could only be caused when scientists felt like they weren't being listened to. In actuality, it often was that they were having the utmost attention paid to them. They just weren't explaining things for not-science-minded people to understand.

Alaster felt like a missing link sometimes because he seemed to be one of a few people capable of explaining scientific babble into something everyone else could comprehend.

The most likely cause for the commotion was his Zaheri. Not that they were trying, but it seemed the Agerians had managed to get on every single researcher's last nerve when they spoke to them. Likely due to that misunderstanding that occurred.

Best Alaster could tell, his Zaheri—and perhaps Agerians in general—weren't well versed in advanced science.

Coming up to a door to one of the labs, Alaster poked his head into the room and saw three people standing with one of the lead scientists who was waiting for the dark months to appear so he could work in the dark sector and study stars.

Kedar was one of the three talking to the scientist. With him was Taesir, a woman who stood a few inches shorter than Kedar, with short, chestnut colored hair that fell just below her ears. She was thin, but in a fit and muscular sense, and from where he stood, Alaster could tell that her patience was waning. She tapped her foot as quietly as she could and thrummed her fingers against her side.

The other person standing with them was Gaeor. If Gaeor was a soldier, Alaster didn't see it right off. He'd been told Gaeor was a Sniper. So, perhaps that had attributed to the lankier build of the older man. He had a warmth to his skin tone that didn't reflect in his dark blue eyes. Alaster couldn't be sure, but it seemed Gaeor was constantly looking at the world with a bland enthusiasm.

Maybe he just didn't like Earth.

All of them wore thicker sweaters, still adjusting to the bitter cold of Antarctica. Though Alaster knew his da didn't like it—because he gave a disapproving look whenever any of the Zaheri walked by—they all wore Aran sweaters common to Ireland. Alaster figured they'd just purchased the sweaters when they'd lived on the isle and had chosen to keep them during their moves. He highly doubted it was a choice made just to spur his da's fury.

Seeing Alaster's head in the doorway, the scientist flung his hand toward the teenager. "Well, maybe he can explain it to you."

The three Zaheri turned toward Alaster as the teenager stepped fully into the room.

"Explain what?" Alaster asked.

"Dark matter. It's an easy concept to grasp, but these reporters seem to understand *nothing*," the short scientist said with a frustrated look.

One of the problems with working alongside brilliant people was that they tended to have no patience for anyone who didn't grasp their research right away.

Alaster nodded slowly. While, yes, for him dark matter was an easy concept, he could see why someone else wouldn't get it.

Shrugging a little, he said, "I can try. It's basically everything in the universe that we can't account for. It has to do with gravitational distortions. Dark matter used to be used specifically as a way to justify various calculations regarding planetary mass and gravitational fields."

"Yes, yes, yes," the scientist cut in. "Over eighty percent of the entire universe is made up of dark matter, and there are varying kinds of dark matter which can compensate for ..." He turned and began scribbling things down on a white board frantically, his rambling devolving into nonsense to the Agerians.

As he continued his bombardment of information, the Zaheri turned and began to slowly move out of the room, none of them wanting their escape to be noticed.

Once out of the room, Gaeor said under his breath, "Keep moving. I don't want him to follow us." He quickly marched down the hall.

"Things are going that badly?" Alaster asked with a small smirk.

The other two Zaheri fell into step with him as Frost picked up his pace to stay with Gaeor.

Kedar rubbed his forehead. "I've never understood why humans feel the need to find the answer to everything."

Nodding, Taesir said, "Does it matter what the universe is made out of? Why can't humans just be happy with the fact that the stars are on display every night as light in the darkness?"

With another shrug, Alaster answered, "I think it's just the way we are. Probably our curiosity."

"Y'know, Agerians are plenty curious, too," Kedar grumbled. "We just don't have to know everything about everything."

When they reached the residential wing, Taesir asked the teenager, "What's wrong?"

Kedar snapped his head up and looked at Taesir before he looked to Alaster.

Taesir shook her head and smiled at him.

"Da won't allow me to take time off school to train with you," Alaster said, more glumly than he'd intended.

Maybe disappointed was the right emotion.

The two Zaheri shared a look before Kedar hushed, "This is a conversation to have under stone."

Alaster nodded and, a few moments later, they stopped at one of the lounges. When they reached it, Kedar whistled to Gaeor and Frost. The other two members turned, and Kedar pointed into the lounge.

"What's going on?" Gaeor asked once they gathered in the lounge.

"Keegan won't let Alaster train with us," Taesir said with a gesture toward the Human-Born.

Furrowing his brow, Gaeor said, "Why? What's the human afraid of? His son surpassing him?"

"Gaeor," Kedar said, as though trying to remind the elder hybrid of something.

"I doubt that is the case," Frost said as he moved to sit near Alaster, who had plopped down onto one of the couches in the room. "I believe that Keegan still has concerns surrounding our intentions."

"He definitely isn't happy that you lot're here," Alaster said.

"That can't be the only thing," Taesir said. "Even your mother seems disgruntled." She sighed and looked at Kedar. "Maybe it wasn't such a good idea to follow them here."

Kedar shook his head. "No, this was the one thing we've done right in the past year."

"What if Taesir is right?" Gaeor asked. "His parents don't trust us. I can feel it in their eyes whenever they stare at us."

Smiling, Kedar said, "Tae has been right about a lot of things, but I don't think this is one of them."

Alaster looked up to Taesir and saw her staring at Kedar, wearing a mix between frustration and flattery on her face.

"I would just take it as a compliment," Alaster offered.

"How are we to train him here?" Frost asked. "People perpetuate every inch of this compound. I will admit that I have imparted what knowledge I could over the past five years, but I can do little to help him in practical ways surrounding his energy."

"Why don't we just take him with us to that other base? Stop and train him somewhere along the way?" Gaeor suggested.

"What? McMurdo?" Alaster asked.

Nodding, Gaeor said, "We could say that we need a translator for scientific babble, and he's the only one who knows how to help us understand."

Alaster shook his head. "There's nothing in McMurdo that reporters would need to see or ask questions about. It's a military facility." He sat up and added, "And speaking of the whole undercover thing, you are aware that this is a limited engagement situation, right? They won't let you stay here forever."

"We don't need to stay forever," Taesir said. "You and your parents aren't allowed to stay past March, right?"

"Well, yeah," the teen answered, "but that's four months away. Why would reporters need to stay in Antarctica for four months to write one article?"

The Zaheri looked at one another before Kedar said, "We'll think of something."

Inclining his head to Alaster, Frost said, "Again, how will you train him in his skills and abilities, if he should have any? What if something is to happen, and he is left to fight on his own?"

"What makes you think he'll need to fight on his own?" Gaeor asked. "It's not like this continent is crawling with Caligans."

Frost's expression grew stern. "There will come a day when Alaster's skills will be required. Are we to wait until that day dawns to act?"

"How are you supposed to act?" Alaster asked. "There's nowhere we could go that we wouldn't be seen. And if I left beyond the sight of one of the expedition members, my parents would notice, and then forbid me to even speak with you."

"We need to find a way around his parents," Gaeor said. Everyone turned to him, and he rolled his eyes. "Let's be honest here, they're the ones getting in the way."

"That may be, but it is not our place to interfere with the inter-working of a family unit," Frost said.

Taesir looked to Kedar. "Do you have any ideas?"

Wearing a look of disappointment, Kedar shook his head. "Not at the moment."

"Then, for now, there isn't anything we can do," Alaster said as he stood. "I'll just have to figure things out on my own."

"Well, that's not entirely true," Kedar said with a quick glance to the others. "How much time do you think you can spare now? Without being looked for, I mean."

Alaster shrugged. "I don't know. Maybe another hour?"

Kedar stepped closer to the door, placing himself so that the others would be able to look out the little window behind him and warn him if someone were about to enter. He looked to the teenager. "We've explained the basics of your energy."

"Right. What about it?"

"Have you felt it getting out of control at all? Or any sort of itching or trembling in your muscles?"

Glancing to his hands, Alaster thought it over. "I sometimes feel a little restless, like I want to go for a run." He gestured toward the door. "I've just gone to the gym and used the treadmills when that happens."

Scrubbing a hand through his hair, Gaeor grumbled, "If he could discharge some of his energy, that would help."

"We don't have any Agerian weapons on us, outside of a few smuggled pistols. Nothing for him to push excess into," Kedar said.

"And it's not like we can even spar with him so he can just push it out of himself naturally," Taesir mused.

His gaze flicking between his Zaheri, Alaster asked, "What're you on about?"

Kedar let out a small sigh. "It wouldn't be a problem if you weren't a powerful wielder. I was hoping you'd say you'd never felt anything. But when someone with strong energy can't fully discharge what spirals in them, it can cause a feeling of restlessness."

"So... what does that mean?" Alaster asked, concern beginning to take hold in his chest.

Taesir quickly flashed her hands out and waved them. "Oh no, no, don't freak out. It's not like you'll explode or anything."

Alaster gave her a concerned look. "...Exploding is an option?"

Throwing Taesir a look of exasperation, Kedar said cuttingly, "No. Exploding is not an option." He gave her a look that said, *What even was that?*"

She offered an apologetic smile and shrugged.

"You'll be fine," Gaeor said to the teen. "You just might start to feel that restlessness more often as you become more aware of your energy."

"If we were to train you properly, it would likely have come on sooner. And could be remedied more effectively," Frost added.

"So, should I plan to do anything different?" Alaster asked.

"The treadmill's working?" Kedar asked.

Alaster nodded.

"Then stick with that for now. If you find it's not satisfying the itch of your energy looking for release, well"—gently shaking his head, Kedar looked to the ceiling before he met Alaster's gaze again—"we'll deal with it then."

The situation was swiftly switching from annoying to infuriating. All Alaster wanted to do was explore who he was and what he was. But he couldn't. His parents had point-blank forbidden him from any sort of engagement in what being a Human-Born hybrid was.

If the world of Tilion really did rely on Alaster, he feared he'd prove a poor hero.

He was on a battlefield. The ground shook. Alaster fell to his knees and gripped the ground as the arid desert made him cough. Bullets whizzed past him, and he felt the sting of them graze his shoulder. Staggering to his feet, he began to run. Buildings were in the distance, and a tank rolled beside him.

An explosion blew him off his feet. He used his wings to adjust his trajectory as he glanced to his side. The tank was a mangled mess of metal.

Landing ungracefully, he ripped a piece of shrapnel out of his skin, frantically shooting to his feet.

A scream of agony hit the air, and he turned about wildly.

"Cam!" cried desperately from his lips. Panic thudded in his heart as he suddenly was flying, tearing through the sky in the direction of the screaming.

He ran through a shabby building, the frame wobbling from the gunfire and explosions. Dirt rained from the ceiling.

Without hesitating he took out anyone who staggered into his path. He had to get to Cam. He knew Cam was there, somewhere. He couldn't hear him anymore. His green energy skittered around his body, shaking and trembling.

He called his brother's name frantically, desperate to hear Cam call back. Needing to hear his voice.

Coming to the only door, Alaster shoved his way inside, nearly blowing it off the hinges. His stomach clenched upon entering. There was a man strapped to a chair in the middle of the room. His hazel eyes were bloodshot, and he was bleeding from a cut along his scalp. Short, strawberry-blond hair was matted with sweat and blood. His shirt was ripped, bearing the tells of his injuries. He was gagged, so Alaster quickly moved forward and removed it.

"God, Cam," Alaster whispered, the urge to cry prickling his eyes.

"Hey, Alaster," his brother coughed out. "Thanks for coming to get me."

Undoing the ropes holding Cam to the chair, Alaster said, "Well, someone had to." He looked up just in time for a bullet to shoot through Cam's forehead. Blood splattered Alaster's face as his eyes widened.

But he'd gotten there. He'd been so close. He ...

Everything swirled into fury as he felt a storm brew inside his chest. Flashes of faces unknown screwed in screams and pain, yelling their crescendo of torment that he felt hit the recesses of his soul.

With a jolting gasp, Alaster woke, his heart hammering in his chest. Shakily slapping his hand to his face, he felt moisture meet his touch. Yanking his hands back, he stuttered out a few shaky breaths, relieved to only find sweat.

"Alaster?"

The teen looked over and saw his Zaheri staring down at him. The grovix's light blue coat glimmered from the shaded light. His ears were drooped and pulled back as he asked, "Is everything all right?"

Starting to get his breathing under control, Alaster shook his head and pulled himself up, sitting cross-legged on his bed and resting his head in his hands. Shakily, he raked his left hand through his hair as he wiped his fisted right hand under his nose and inhaled loudly.

The dog tags around his neck were heavy.

He could feel tears beginning to work their way to his eyes, so he blinked a bit and took some deep breaths. A trembling laugh left him that was short-lived before he said, "You'd think I was too old for nightmares."

Frost's large paw fell onto Alaster's forearm. "There was nothing you could have done."

"I could have joined," Alaster said as he made eye contact with his Zaheri. The two were silent as Alaster swallowed. "I'm a perfect candidate. I can't even get hurt."

The grovix pinched his eyes shut.

"I could have saved him, Frost. I know I could've if I was ... if I had been there."

Shaking his head, Frost said, "But you were not there. There is little that can come from sitting in the aftermath and wondering of all the roads we may have taken and how it may have changed what is. Little aside from guilt."

Looking away from Frost, Alaster asked, "Have you lost anyone in the war?"

"We have lost many in the war," Frost said as he looked down and removed his paw from Alaster's arm. "I regret to say that there were few I was close with." When Alaster said nothing, Frost leaned in. "Your brother would wish you to remember and honor him, not to mourn in his passing."

There was truth in that. Cam would want Alaster to move on. Eventually. It was unlikely that Alaster would suddenly be okay with the fact that his older brother was dead after only a few short months.

But wasn't it wrong to just pick up and forget about those who had sacrificed so much? Wasn't moving on an act toward forgetting?

Not that Alaster thought he could forget his brother—he couldn't. Cam had been the one to teach Alaster how to ice skate, and how to track animal prints, and how to hunt for the right kind of bugs for fishing, and where the perfect places were to climb trees.

The last time Alaster had seen Cam, his brother had been at the station. He'd worked his way to be able to spend his leave in Antarctica. Even managed to stay at McMurdo for nearly a month. He still had all his military duties to perform, leaving him little time to regularly spend with his family. But it wasn't out of the question for him to come to the Amundsen-Scott station during that time.

They'd talked about Alaster's studies, and Cam had tried to get him to talk about girls, like Alaster had any prospects. He'd teasingly said that Alaster would be old and crotchety before he ever found someone who could keep up with him. It'd devolved into a more serious discussion, with Cam trying to warn Alaster about getting involved with the wrong kind of woman. Not just following his hormones and actually seek out someone of substance and quality.

He'd laughed and rubbed his forehead, giving Alaster a cheeky grin. "Like you'll find someone like that hanging around dusty old labs like this."

Alaster had always liked Cam's wide smiles. And he could never stop himself from smiling back.

He'd shoved Cam playfully. "Shut up! Someday, I won't be living in a lab."

"Sure you won't. And someday, you won't be curing cancer or saving the world."

When Alaster had fallen silent, staring toward the table, Cam's brow had twitched as he surveyed his brother.

"Hey, what's the story?"

Fidgeting with his fingers, Alaster had asked, "Were ...? Were Da and Mum angry with you? When you decided to join the military?"

Cam had leaned onto the table and let out a scoff. "They were right furious. But c'mon, Alaster. I'm not cut from the same line as you. I take after Uncle Max, remember?" He had shaken his head a little. "I'm a tank, mate. I'm not cut out for all this." He'd flitted his gaze around the galley. "It's grand, and I'm all for you doing it. But me? I dunno. I guess I'm more a fighter."

Alaster hadn't responded.

A frown had come to Cam's face, and he'd asked quietly, "C'mon, mate; what's the story."

"It's ... this ... thing. I kinda feel like I want to explore it. Consider it as an option, y'know? But, Da and Mum, they ..."

Placing his larger hand on Alaster's shoulder, Cam had given a reassuring smile. "Hey, don't worry about them. They're stronger than they give themselves credit for. They accepted my choice. Why wouldn't they eventually come around to yours?" He'd shrugged. "You don't wanna be a brainhead? Don't do it, mate. You're already ahead of the curve, y'know? What's the harm in exploring something different?" Cam had ruffled Alaster's hair and grinned a little stupidly. "The world'll still be there, waitin' for you to save it later. Da and Mum'll come 'round. They always do."

Aside from the goodbye a day later, that was one of the last things Cam had ever said to Alaster.

Those memories brought a smile to Alaster's face, and the fact that he wouldn't be sharing any others brought tears to his eyes.

Ashamed, he tried to stop crying, but he found that no matter his attempts, the sobbing just got worse.

Frost's eyes burned with sorrow, and he pushed forward and nuzzled the teen.

For a few seconds, Alaster thought of forcing Frost away, but when his hands touched his Zaheri's soft fur, he found himself pulling the grovix into a hug.

It was times like these that he was certain that, if he had only had his training, if he only knew how to be who he was, maybe his brother would be sitting alongside him and teaching him how to play *Call of Duty.*

Instead, there was nothing remaining of his brother except a few pictures, a tombstone in Arlington, and the cold metal that hung around Alaster's neck.

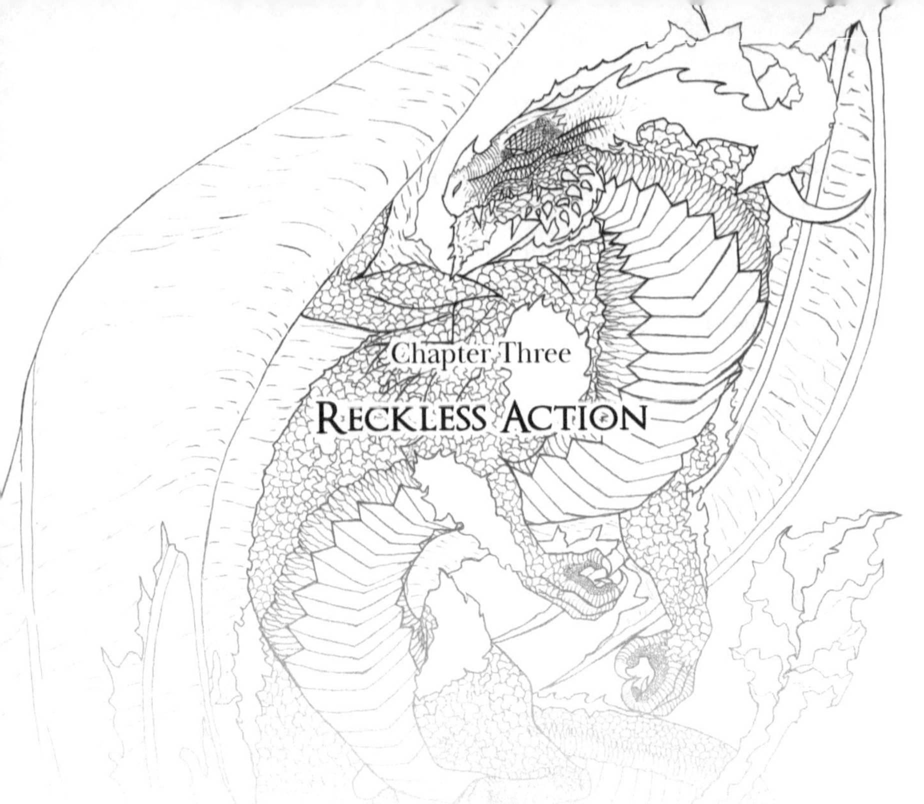

Chapter Three

RECKLESS ACTION

The nightmare plagued him. And though Alaster's crying had created a weariness in his body, he couldn't get back to sleep. Angrily checking his watch, he saw it was eleven-thirty at night. He was grateful he'd gone to bed just after dinner, even if it was terribly early. It meant that even though he was tired, he'd at least gotten some sleep.

He felt that restlessness in his body, worse this time. More like the twitching and aching in his muscles like Kedar had described.

Maybe it'd been brought on by the nightmare. Maybe it hadn't. It didn't change the fact that, at that moment, Alaster was positive he wouldn't be able to sleep.

In a fluid movement, he swung his legs over Frost's resting form and sprang to his feet, hastily changing.

Blinking a few times, Frost looked up at the teen and asked, "What are you doing?"

"I'm feeling that restlessness Kedar was talking about," Alaster muttered as he shoved the dog tags under his shirt.

Frost rose to his feet. "And?"

"And I'm going for a fly."

"You ...? You are what?"

Alaster grasped the door handle and looked over his shoulder at the grovix. "You coming?"

Eyes darting around the room a bit, Frost finally reconnected his gaze and said, "Allow me a moment to conceal my appearance."

When they left the room, Frost had to canter at Alaster's side. The teen marched swiftly down the hall, carefully sweeping his head to the doors of every room they passed. As expected, the station was basically dormant.

There were bound to be people milling around—some just preparing to go to bed; others fitfully sleeping. His parents usually didn't quit for the day until midnight. But he knew where they'd be.

They'd be on the other side of the complex, pouring over the data collected from the Ice Cube. Analyzing every little thing they could. They'd be nowhere near the main entrance, Destination Alpha, where the ski-doos were parked.

As Alaster hopped onto one of the bright yellow ski-doos, he went to turn it on when Frost asked, "Where exactly are you going?"

"Somewhere not here," Alaster answered as he turned the key. "I can't explain it, Frost. I have to stretch my wings. There's a weird ache there."

"And when your parents find you missing?"

Gripping the handles, Alaster clenched his jaw. "I know this is careless, flippant, and stupid. But y'know what?" He revved the engine. "I'm a teenager. Careless and stupid is supposed to go with the territory."

Frost sighed, and then Alaster took off. His Zaheri was right at his side, easily keeping stride with the fast snowmobile.

At first, Frost thought this was a terrible idea, but as he ran over the smooth snow and felt the cold powder cave into his paws, he began to feel rather glad Alaster had come up with this "careless and stupid" idea. It was a brash and sudden choice, but the farther they got from the complex, the freer they both felt.

After several moments, Alaster came to a stop. "You don't have to hide anymore. I don't think anyone will see you," he said.

Even though Frost panted heavily and steam rolled out of his wide mouth, there was strength waking in his muscles at the simple action of running. For far too long he had been sitting and confined to a small building, and he suddenly yearned for this ability every day.

Both of them knew Alaster was going to get into a lot of trouble for doing this. It wouldn't happen again. So, all the more reason to simply partake of the chance.

Taking advantage of the opportunity, Frost shook out his fur. As he did, it was like the German Shepard appearance had only been paint. The dark tans and blacks of the fur flew into the air, leaving behind a brilliant light blue coat that shined in the sunlight. He rose to his full height, looking every bit the majestic creature he was in nearly an instant.

A long sigh left him, and he opened his eyes, his fully blue eyes staring around at the plain horizon. This was his Element, and he felt more connected to it than ever.

He looked over and smiled at Alaster, who smiled in kind.

"C'mon," Alaster said as he got off the ski-doo and pocketed the key. Then he stripped off his heavy jacket, leaving him in his light coat and T-shirt. Draping the heavier clothing over the ski-doo's seat, he popped sunglasses on, straightened, and looked to Frost. "Let's be ourselves."

"That sounds like a wonderful idea," Frost said with a grin. The grovix didn't wait, turning and taking off into the white landscape at a great speed.

Alaster wasn't far behind him as he ran and leaped off the ground, his wings ripping through his clothes. He was thankful that Kedar had given him the two articles of clothing from Tilion; the self-replicating cloth wasn't something he had to worry about when using his wings.

Even though they were already at a high altitude as it was, Alaster flew higher into the air, a laugh tumbling from him. Twirling as he flew, he felt his energy bubble outward, swirling around his form before blasting into the atmosphere with a *pop*. A weight dissipated from his chest, and he let gravity catch him as he reveled in the momentary weightlessness of flight.

He spiraled down toward where he saw Frost's blue fur standing out against the brilliant white of the snow. Powder picked up like a storm behind Frost's powerful running.

Reaching the ground, Alaster flew parallel and caught up to his Zaheri. The two looked at one another before Frost surged ahead in speed and Alaster followed his lead. The weird ache in his muscles lessened with each flap of his wings.

Gently setting his hand out, he kept his palm just above the ground and felt the spray of powder flying between his fingers. A wonder-filled smile cracked his features as he admired the feeling of the snow flitting through his fingers.

This was living. This was who he was. It was now that he realized it more than ever before.

Rearing up slightly, he landed perfectly and stretched his wings, a content smile on his face.

Frost noticed the Human-Born wasn't beside him anymore and skidded to a stop a few feet away. Turning to face Alaster, the grovix said through gasps of air, "Oh, come now! You cannot be finished so soon!" There was a hopping canter to his gait as he went back toward the teen.

"No way," Alaster said with a shake of his head. "I just want to enjoy this while I can."

A laugh came from the Zaheri. "Yes, I anticipate your parents will be enraged when we return."

A normal human couldn't take deep breaths in the Antarctic. The air was too thin, and the human body couldn't handle that much cold air entering its system. But as Alaster stood there, he took a heavy breath and felt the icy air fill his lungs then escape back out in a puff of steam.

"Why can't it always be like this?" he asked Frost.

The grovix shook his head. "I wish I could say. This has been a happy change from what has become the normal exercise for my body." He glanced down at himself. "I fear I may have become lethargic in these past few years."

Alaster laughed. "If this is you lethargic, then I'd hate to see you in true form."

"I believe it is safe to say I could move like the wind in my best years," Frost said as he sat down. The action was simple, but already he wanted to spring back to his feet and romp around in the snow. Sitting seemed like a waste, especially as this little respite from reality was going to be short lived.

"Another sprint?" Alaster asked after his Zaheri sat.

Frost only grinned before he jolted out on a dime, tearing across the frozen tundra.

Another laugh tumbled from Alaster as he propelled himself into the air. He could feel the currents. The billows and rolls of the breeze. The way it pushed at his wings, gently swaying him this way and that. He could flex small muscles and maintain a steadier flight, letting the currents carry him if he wished.

He saw Frost slow to a canter and returned to the ground. As he landed and turned to tell Frost how nice it was to practice flying, his words got trapped in his throat. A sudden dread hit his stomach. The hair on his arms stood on end, and a shiver of anticipation surged down his spine.

He shook off the feeling as Frost approached. "Are you all right, Alaster?"

Ruffling his hair, Alaster said, "Yeah." He forced a happier demeanor, still feeling the tug of dread. "It's nice to finally practice flying. *Really* practice it."

Frost smiled at him. "You are quite overdue for flight training. I only wish we could afford you more time for such things."

"It's not as though you're to blame. It's the situation." Alaster chuckled sadly. "Can you imagine if someone saw me?"

The dread in his heart began to heighten. A panicked sense hit his mind, and he whipped around, suddenly feeling as if something was closing in.

"Are you—" Frost stopped, and his body went rigid. His ears shot erect, and his tail went straight. "Something comes."

"What kind of something?" Alaster asked, scanning the horizon. Nothing looked out of place. The wind rolled fluffy snow in the air. Somewhere in the distance, there was a faint shifting of ice.

"Bratak'ra," Frost growled. "We must return to the base and inform the others."

An image flashed in Alaster's mind at the mention of the creature. A large, four-legged beast lunged at him, its horns hooked around its skull, jutting toward him. Its maw wide and its breath foul. Cars lined the background, a ridgeline blurry farther back.

He flinched at the abruptness of the sight, ducking to avoid being hit.

Frost's head butted against his hand as his Zaheri asked, "Alaster, what ails you?"

Gripping Frost's head and pushing himself upright, Alaster said, "It's ... nothing. I ..." He looked to the grovix. "You're right; we need to get back and tell the others."

"Alaster," Frost's voice was laced with concern as his brow drooped. "You must tell me if something is amiss."

"I must be sensing the bratak'ra; that's all," Alaster said dismissively as he started to walk back the way they'd come.

"If you are, that would be quite the feat."

"Really?"

"Yes. Sensors are quite rare and exceptionally powerful. If you are exhibiting traits similar to them, then we must address it to see that you are trained appropriately."

A quick, slight, straining pain skittered along his back, as though someone had swiped a stick across his skin. It wasn't enough to make him wince, but it was enough to echo across his body, as though registering a ghosted injury.

He chose to ignore it and forced himself to not grimace. That would only worry Frost. And Frost was already worried.

"Come along; we must return with haste," Frost said as he cantered past Alaster.

"Right," Alaster muttered before he pushed himself into the air again. There would be time later to dissect what he was experiencing. For now, he'd do his best to ignore it. Especially if there were enemy fighters inbound.

The nagging in his mind on the return flight did little to convince him that ignoring it was the correct course of action.

Chapter Four

BATTLE STATIONS

Skidding the ski-doo to a jerking stop, Alaster hopped off the snow-mobile and ran for the Destination Zulu entrance at the center of the station. Frost was at his side, and as the two ran up the stairs to get to the main floor, Alaster felt anticipation and fear grow inside him. His arm hairs were standing on end, and it felt like something was constricting around his internal organs.

He ripped open the door and ran into the station, slamming into the wall of the hallway because of his miscalculation of speed.

"There you are! Your parents are—" One of the scientists started before letting out a sharp gasp.

With a glance to his left, Alaster saw that Frost hadn't disguised himself. That didn't bode well. Frost was so concerned with whatever was going on outside that he hadn't paid any heed to secrecy.

Pushing the anxiety away from his mind, he asked the grovix, "Where are the others?"

"I can smell them. Follow me," Frost said then picked up speed.

The two tore down the hallway, and the scientists and personnel shrank back or screamed at the sight of Frost barreling down the hall.

Alaster wanted to tell them it was okay, that the grovix wouldn't hurt anyone. But, on the flip side, he could see why they were frightened. Frost was the size of a lion and looked like nothing of this world. If this panic proved to be nothing more than a false alarm, then Frost was going to be in major trouble. Not from Kedar—knowing the Team Leader, he'd be glad to know Frost was so ready to leap into action.

No, Frost would be in danger from the many scientists who would want to study him. Worse still, the reveal to all these people that there were creatures called hybrids and grovix, and they could appear indistinguishable from humans and animals.

They weren't halfway down the main hall when they saw Kedar, Taesir, and Gaeor come out of one of the lounges, each wearing looks of concern.

"What's going on?" Kedar asked.

Coming to a stop, Frost answered, "I do not have exact certainty, but I fear that the Caligans are aware of our position here." He took up half the hallway with his bulk, making it a tighter squeeze than normal.

Through heaves of air, Alaster asked, "How would they know that? Is there even a portal activation in Antarctica?"

"Not that I'm aware of," Kedar said with a scowl and a glance out the window.

Gaeor stepped forward and asked Frost. "What did you sense?"

"Where were you two? The whole station's been on search," Kedar asked Alaster.

"I shall answer both," Frost said. "To your query, Kedar, Alaster needed some fresh air and, as it turned out, so did I. It was reckless, and we are aware of that, but our escapade yielded different results than we had intended. What I sensed, Gaeor, was bratak'ra. At the very least, I believe that I have. I will be the first to answer that it has been a great while since I have heard or even seen the beasts."

The group was so involved in their conversation that Alaster hadn't noticed the other scientists beginning to encroach on their meeting until one of them was practically on top of him. He turned as one of the animal biologists pointed at Frost with a shaking hand and a wide mouth.

"Um ..." Alaster said to Kedar.

Turning to the growing mass of scientists, Kedar said, "Don't mind us. Talk amongst yourselves."

"What is that thing?" the biologist asked.

With a glare, Frost growled, "I am a grovix, not a thing. And I would appreciate for you to remember that."

If it was possible, the scientist's mouth opened wider, and they said, "Did ...? Did you? He just talked!"

"We don't have time for this," Gaeor grumbled.

"Where is the expedition leader?" Taesir asked.

Pushing past them, Kedar said, "Alaster and Frost, you're with me." He looked over his shoulder and said to Gaeor and Taesir, "You two, get your gear and be ready to move. If what Frost sensed is real, then we don't have much time."

The other two members of the team nodded then turned to walk in the opposite direction but were met with a crowded hallway full of onlookers.

A stern expression on her face, Taesir said, "Okay, people, move aside! Serious business to attend to!"

"Return to your rooms and stay there!" Gaeor called as they pushed through the hall and began to make their way to their rooms.

"What do you mean we don't have much time?" Alaster asked Kedar.

"If Frost is right, then we have Caligans heading straight for us. Bratak'ra don't fight alone." The Team Leader didn't say anything more. He began jogging down the hall to the elevator.

"Where are we going?" Alaster asked.

"Destination Alpha," Kedar answered. "We just interviewed the expedition leader, and he was heading out to the IceCube. If we're lucky, we can beat him before he leaves the station."

"How many others are outside?" Frost asked. "It will be necessary to get them to safety quickly."

A groan came from Kedar. "We don't have enough people to designate tasks to."

"I can—"

"No," Kedar cut Frost off. "No one will actually listen to you.

They'd probably just stare at you and wonder how you can talk. And I need you with me in case we need to figure out a way to barricade the Caligans from getting here."

Just down the hallway, they saw a large, balding man putting up his hood and preparing to exit the station.

"Dr. Davis!" Kedar called.

"Wait!" Alaster said.

Dr. Davis turned to face them. He had a circular face and fairly jolly dark blue eyes. He pulled his hood down and said, "I'm grateful you found our renegade, Mr. Kelvin."

"Well, I didn't find him; he just—"

"And you, young man," Dr. Davis said to Alaster. "I expected more from you."

"Sir, you need to listen to us," Alaster said.

"I'm afraid I don't have the time at the moment. We'll discuss the repercussions of your actions when I'm finished with my duties."

A growl came from behind Kedar and Alaster as Frost pushed his way between them.

Before now, Dr. Davis hadn't seen the grovix, but once he did, he was startled into paying attention.

"Now listen here, sir, we have no time for your duties or anyone else's. We have little time at all until this whole station is compromised beyond our help. We require your understanding of our plight and your own," Frost snapped.

Dr. Davis's mouth opened to let out a yelp.

Kedar held out his hand to try to silence the human's comment. "Sir, I know this is a lot to grasp, but I need you to get everyone inside now. There is very real danger coming our way, and we need everyone as safe as possible."

Noticing a change in who he believed was a reporter named Mr. Kelvin, Dr. Davis's brow furrowed, and he said in a commanding tone, "Now, look here. Who are you? You obviously aren't a reporter. And what is that *thing?*"

Another growl escaped Frost. "I am a grovix, not a thing. And if I am subjected to such a name again, I promise you that whoever says it will regret that action immediately."

"I don't care what you say you are or the fact that you can say anything," Dr. Davis shot to the grovix. "I demand an explanation!"

"There will be one in due time, sir," Kedar said, trying to remain calm. "However, right now, I need you to—"

"You, Mr. Kelvin, will demand nothing of me!" Dr. Davis said. "You will either explain yourselves or you will leave immediately. I am doing nothing for you until I am told who you are and why you're here!"

"They're here because of me," Alaster said. "They're my Zaheri—uh, protectors, guardians—and right now, there's a chance that dragons are going to be attacking this station and killing everyone they find here."

"My boy, dragons are mythical creatures," Dr. Davis said with a scowl. "I have no time for your preposterous claims and, furthermore—"

An explosion rocked the station, and a hole appeared down the hall. A blast of cold air shot into the warmth. The three people grabbed the walls for support from the sudden movement of the lifted station.

"Frost!" Kedar hollered above the howling wind.

The grovix had been moving before his name was even called.

Running up to the hole in the wall, Frost stamped his paw into the floor. Ice shot out from the impact and up the side of the wall, encapsulating the hole and covering it in a solid sheet of ice. He then turned to Kedar and Alaster. "Time has run out. We must act without further delay."

A sound like a screech and a bellow mixed together came from outside.

Kedar walked up to the elevator and pulled the doors open. "Go!" he called to Alaster, who hopped down the shaft, followed by Frost.

Before he entered the elevator shaft, Kedar said to Dr. Davis, "We don't have any more time. Get people to safety or prepare for death. We can't offer anything else."

Without another word, he leaped into the open elevator shaft and let himself fall to the ground. When he landed, he felt the metal bow from his weight. Alaster held the door open for the first floor, and Kedar quickly maneuvered through it.

Once outside, Gaeor and Taesir pulled up on ski-doos before dismounting.

"Here," Taesir said as she handed two pistols to Kedar.

Taking the offered pistols, Kedar said, "Tae, take out the Ferveos. Do you know how many there are?"

"I've counted four so far," she answered. "But there's a chance that more are on the way."

"What's the likelihood of them not being able to withstand the temp?"

"Fair. They aren't used to extreme cold, so they might be slow, and their fire might not be as powerful. In fact, they might be reluctant to use it at all," she answered as she snapped her thigh holster into place.

With a nod, Kedar said, "Okay. Frost, I need you to cover the bratak'ra and werewolves, if they brought any. Once you've done that, I need you to find a way to barricade them out. Create a dam or a large fortress of ice—anything. Just something to keep them out so we can ensure everyone is okay."

Frost nodded before he took off.

Lifting his head to look at Gaeor, Kedar said, "Gaeor—"

"I'm gonna go kill some things," Gaeor said before he went off after Frost.

Alaster moved to follow Gaeor, but Kedar caught him. "No, you're staying with me. Have you ever fired a gun before?"

The teen looked at the pistol in Kedar's outstretched hand. "Uh ... Cam taught me the basics of firearm safety, and I shot a 9mm back in Alaska before he shipped out."

Thrusting the pistol into Alaster's grasp, Kedar said, "Then you're more equipped than I thought." He quickly pulled the pistol from his thigh holster and began indicating various parts of the weapon. "Safety's here. Yours is on. Flip this to turn it off so you can fire the weapon. Clip release is here. Don't ask about the science behind it, but the clip you've got oughta work for about five hundred rounds. Don't point it at anyone—"

"You don't wanna shoot. Firearm safety, remember?"

Kedar offered a smirk. "Humans call it friendly fire, right?"

Alaster nodded.

"Yeah. None of that." He indicated the empty tundra before them. "Fire it once, just so you can get a feel for the kickback. Keep your aim low, though, just in case."

The air was mostly clear, with only the occasional billow of snow. There wasn't a lot of wind today, which was a small miracle Alaster felt he needed to offer praise for.

He pulled the trigger and felt the gun rattle against his grip.

"Use two hands," Kedar instructed.

Alaster cast him a quick glance and saw his Zaheri sweeping his gaze at the horizon as if it were going to explode.

Steadying his racing heart with a few long, smooth breaths, Alaster gripped the pistol tight. *Brace for the kickback. Hold the weapon right,* he remembered what Cam had taught him.

It'd been a few years, but Alaster could remember it well enough. It'd been a warm spring afternoon. He and Cam had gone for a camping trip off into the wilderness of Alaska. Some brotherly bonding before Cam shipped out.

A fleeting question of whether Cam would've liked Kedar entered his mind. Alaster felt his brother would've gotten along famously with all of his Zaheri.

Another shot, and this time the gun didn't rattle. The weight of the weapon in his grasp was heavier than the target practice with Cam, and Alaster was pretty sure that was only slightly because of the weapon's actual weight.

Kedar looked to the teen. "How're you feeling?"

"Scared."

The Zaheri gained an understanding look as he placed his hand on Alaster's shoulder. "You can st—"

"No," Alaster said with a forceful shake of his head. "I'm going with you. I'm going to help."

With a quirk of his brow, Kedar let out a small breath. "Well then, you'll be grand." He slapped his hand on Alaster's shoulders a couple times. "Warrior spirits like that aren't in everyone, so you've got this, champ."

Kedar's encouragement steadied Alaster's fears a little. He had to remember that they did have the upper hand. The chances of their enemy being equipped for this level of cold was unlikely. Which meant they wouldn't be as responsive as normal. And his Zaheri wouldn't let anything truly terrible happen to him. That was why they were there.

Yet, as they took off where the others had gone, Alaster couldn't help but feel frustration ebb in his mind.

This was exactly why he'd wanted to train with his Zaheri. As it stood, he was woefully unprepared. He'd only just learned how to really fly with any stability.

Sure, he could fire a gun. But would that be enough?

He prayed it would be.

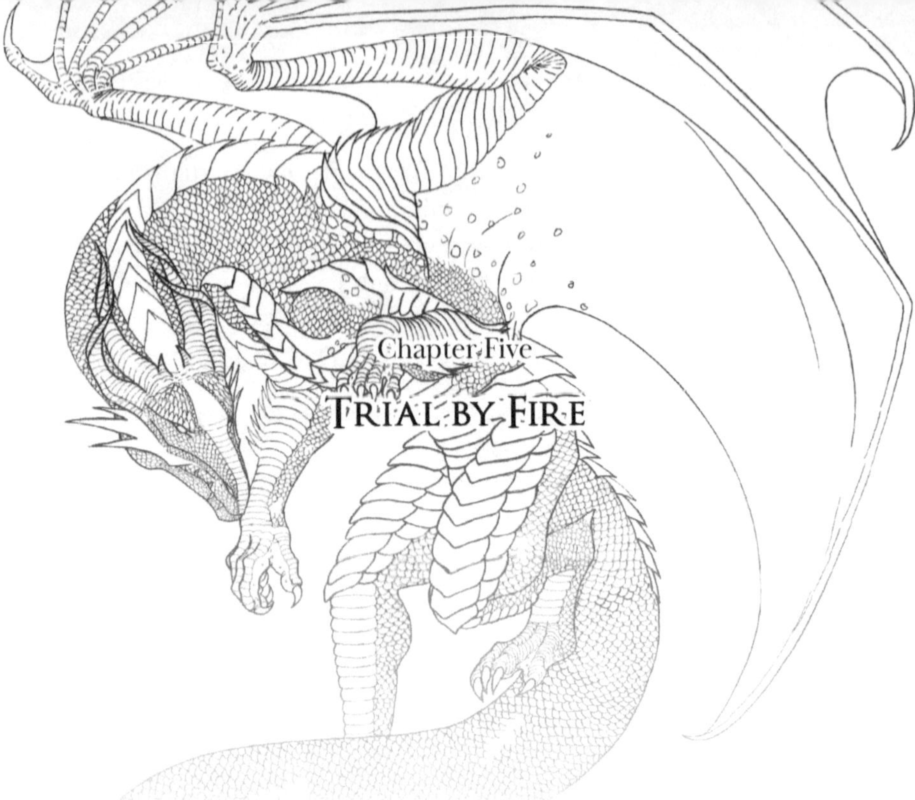

Chapter Five

TRIAL BY FIRE

Taesir could tell that the Ferveos were sluggish. Each flap of their wings was slower than the last, and their altitude fluctuated pretty wildly because of it. From her place in the sky, she could tell all of the other Caligans—bratak'ra and werewolves included—were struggling, too. Praise the Elders, that might be their saving grace.

Her wing muscles were a little tight because of the cold, but she knew she was moving better than the beasts. Therefore, her speed would still best theirs, even if she was a little slower than normal.

Surging forward, she coated her wings in her golden energy. It did two things. First, it caught the Ferveos' attention, making the four large creatures switch their attention from the flashes of gold on the ground to the beacon in the sky. Second, it prepared her for the attack she would use to take two of the beasts out.

Boy, she was moving a *lot* faster than them. In a few seconds, she was between the first two, their snapping jaws delayed, resulting in them pivoting well past the time she was near their faces.

Twirling her body, she released slashes of gold energy from the edges of her wings, effectively making layers of swords to cut at the sides and underbellies of the Ferveos. Cries and bellows tore from the sluggish creatures as scales were slashed off and gaping lacerations cut at their hides.

She righted herself and deftly dodged the jaws of the third Ferveos. Flipping herself, she landed on its brow before running down its spine. She'd rely on her pistols to preserve as much of her energy as possible.

Firing at the Ferveos's wings and joints, she tore massive holes in the leathery membrane and felt the dragon's stability quickly falter.

One left. Things were going smoothly. So far.

Frost ran swiftly toward the enemy. He was rather glad he'd had time earlier to warm up his muscles from the lethargy he had suffered from. If he and Alaster hadn't left, a number of bad things would have happened. He found himself thankful for the Human-Born's rash actions.

It had been so long since he had engaged the enemy that the faces of the bratak'ra had left his thoughts. Yet now, as he ran toward them, he remembered why they were worthy of fear.

A contingent of bratak'ra ran toward him, led by a tri-horned leader, their brown coats standing out against the white landscape. These beasts were easily half a foot taller than he was and twice his weight. Their paws were massive, as were their heads.

The tri-horned one was easy to distinguish, with its third set of horns jutting from its bottom jaw, like tusks. And this one looked weathered, bearing scars and cracks in its massive horns. It looked mountainous to his smaller form. He'd known that tri-horned bratak'ra were larger and fiercer than those they commanded, but seeing one was something different. Especially after all these years.

Forcing the worry about the beasts away from his thoughts, he charged on. A small growl rumbled up his throat, and he picked up his speed.

What he lacked in size, he could make up for in speed, and if he was quick enough, he could catch them all by surprise.

They likely didn't even remember his power or what he could do to them. After all, he had a great advantage to them.

His fur stood on end, and he felt it bristle against his skin, becoming rigid and solid. A multitude of growls and roars mixed with his own when he ran straight through them, crashing into the tri-horned one.

His concerns were put to rest instantly as he saw that one touch from his paw had made the beast freeze almost immediately. Fear had blanketed the yellow eyes before they froze over and the bratak'ra crashed to the ground, shattering into pieces of ice.

The others of the small contingent that had been unfortunate enough to run into Frost or their tri-horned leader froze just as quickly. The few mono-horned ones that were left turned to run at Frost out of desperation.

Facing them, Frost roared. The sound was similar to a lions, but a higher pitch.

His rigid fur had become encapsulated in ice, and as he roared, those ice shards shot out of his fur and toward the remaining bratak'ra. Like thousands of tiny needles, the fragments shattered into the beasts, cutting through them like butter, penetrating their thick hides and even thicker bones.

Watching his opponents fall, Frost turned his attention to finding any werewolves. He would engage any of the Caligans he came across but would not worry about them. Gaeor and Kedar would be sure to take care of those enemies. However, the werewolves were something Frost would have to take out on his own to ensure his team members would be spared from being bitten.

Finding the werewolves wasn't a hard task. They were never far from the bratak'ra, and they had an awful scent.

Frost ran toward the atrocious smell and guessed there were at least five of the cursed beings in this first strike. And he had to assume this was a first strike. Their numbers were few, and the Caligans never—unless during a raid—utilized their full force against the Agerians. Frost could also assume that many had already turned back to act as scouts and inform their master of the situation.

Warning clutched his heart at what a first strike might mean, and what might lay ahead of them.

Somewhere in Gaeor's mind, he knew his supreme distaste for Earth wasn't justified.

But being stuck on this frozen continent, met with a level of disdain by the humans they had to interact with for their cover, unable to train their charge and prepare him for stuff like what was happening right at that moment ...

It didn't bolster any warm and fuzzy feelings for humans.

Plus, he didn't like how they'd painted him. Or his friends. His mentor.

He didn't know how to verbalize any of that, though, so disdain, it was.

As he fired off shot after shot, slowly advancing on their encroaching enemy, Gaeor found himself grateful that the others had listened to his suggestion about the cold weather training. He didn't mind Kedar being younger than him. Gaeor wasn't someone to feel he'd been nullified simply because someone younger than him was in charge. He had great respect for Kedar. Sure, he was a Chief Master and plenty young, but he had a solid way to process and analyze.

If the Council had made Gaeor the Team Leader, things would've been a mess.

Well, a bigger mess.

Kedar had been the one to figure out how to get them to Alaska. How to get them to Antarctica. And Gaeor was almost positive that Kedar had somehow managed to buddy up to Alaster's brother when they'd all been in Alaska.

The post had been good for the younger man. And even Taesir, with all of her annoying pestering and trying to get him to open up, could be called tolerable. Likeable even. Maybe. If she'd settle down a little bit and stop being so annoying.

A bratak'ra surged forward. *Huh.* So, they weren't as unified as usual. Maybe the cold was messing with them so badly that they couldn't determine how to stick with their own.

It was easy to duck past the lumbering monster and shoot it without missing a step in his slow march forward.

Best he could tell, they'd fanned out well to ensure that nothing got through. Because nothing had come charging his flanks. It meant he only had to keep his attention trained ahead, doing his best to avoid any strikes of gray energy that soared toward him. He'd done well enough so far and had kept himself mostly hit-free. The attacks he'd suffered had been small and barely caused any damage.

The cold must've impacted their energy control, too.

Within a couple short moments, he'd nullified the fighters near him. Now to figure out where he could best help. Lowering his pistol, he stilled and swept his gaze across the icy terrain.

Flashes of gold and green were to his right. That was where he should go.

Frost could handle anything in this environment. He was surrounded by his Element, which meant the chances that he'd need help would be slim. And, though he didn't plan to ever voice it, he had to admit that Taesir was pretty effective at nullifying the Ferveos.

Kedar hated the situation they found themselves in. Fighting wasn't the problem; he knew he could hold his own in a fight. Plus, the group of enemy fighters seemed small compared to what he'd expected. It had more to do with the fact that Alaster had little to no training, and that fact kept Kedar's focus was divided.

As he and Alaster ran to meet a group Caligans, he sent up a brief prayer to the Elders and hoped they would protect them from any major harm.

I sure hope you learn best from example, Kedar thought.

He leaped over a gray energy attack before landing firmly. Swiftly throwing his hand out, a gold-walled shield appeared and shot forward. It skidded along the ground, kicking up snow and ice as it went. The shield was translucent, for the most part, with swirling patches of more vibrant golden energy here and there.

Other gray attacks slapped against the shield; some bouncing off like hot lead and others absorbing into the gold. It created a speckling pattern across the shield, making a dazzling array of gray swirling into gold.

Alaster watched in fascination as Kedar swiped his hand across his body. The shield cracked and shattered. Some shards tore outward and slammed into their enemy. Others flew around to them. Three of those large fragments danced around Kedar, and three danced around Alaster.

Shields. Of course that could be possible. Their energy could manifest as spherical orbs or sparks of lightning, so it made sense that shields would be a possibility. But the level of mastery to do what Kedar had done made Alaster have an awe-filled moment.

Caligans that either were untouched from the erupting shield, or not too badly damaged from the shards, leaped back into the fray, running at them. Gray attacks shot from various Caligans, each met with one of the shield fragments surging to where it was needed and protecting them.

Once the Caligans got close enough to them, it forced both Kedar and Alaster to resort to attacking on their own. Golden energy slapped around Kedar's arms and hands like gauntlets.

For a few seconds too long, Alaster was captivated by that concept. It could become like armor?

The blasts of gold tore from Kedar's gauntlet-like arms. So, maybe not armor. Maybe a sort of reserve?

An attack slammed into Alaster, sending him skittering backward.

Right, idiot. Enemy fighters, Alaster chastised. He was in the middle of a battle. Now wasn't the time to analyze anything.

There was a larger blast of gold from Kedar, and Alaster threw a quick, fleeing glance at Kedar's pose.

Hand out, a streaming blast.

Tearing his gaze away from Kedar, Alaster faced the oncoming attackers. Green energy roamed down Alaster's arm and concentrated in his palm as he threw his hand outward. The green flash flew from his hand and impacted an oncoming Caligan, forcing it to fly backward and smack into another one of its fellow soldiers.

A bone-like spike flew at Alaster, hitting him in the left arm around his bicep. The force of the hit sent him crashing to the ground.

Getting to his feet, Alaster looked down and saw a small spike, almost claw-shaped, impaling his skin. For a brief second, he was conflicted. As a boy, he had always been told not to take things like this out, but he also knew his hybrid genes would heal the wound once it was removed.

Not thinking on it any further, he ripped the spike out of his skin, and blood began to pour from the injury, completely soaking his shirt. Grimacing, he looked up to see a gray attack flying toward him. Out of instinct, he threw his right arm out, and green energy surged forward, meeting the oncoming attack.

The two energies impacted, and a pulse, high and loud, erupted from the spot of collision, followed by an explosion. Rocketed off his feet, Alaster hit the ground again, landing on his back.

A hand gripped his right arm and pulled him up. Gaeor was at his side.

"Hey, you okay?" his Zaheri asked. His voice sounded muffled, and none of the words actually reached Alaster's ears. If they did, he definitely didn't understand them.

Pushing Alaster back, Gaeor whipped his pistol up and, in three quick shots, nullified the threat.

Kedar ran up to them a second later. "Everything okay?"

"I think he may have lost his hearing," Gaeor said.

As they spoke, Alaster's hearing was returning, but slowly. The teenager shook his head and yelled, "I'm fine!"

The two Zaheri looked at one another before Kedar turned to Alaster. "Why are you screaming?"

"I think I may have blown out my eardrums or something," Alaster hollered back. Feeling his ears, he pulled his hands away and saw blood on his fingers. He nodded and said, "Yeah, I definitely hurt my eardrums! Give me a few minutes; I think I can heal them!"

"Stop yelling!" Gaeor screamed as he screwed his face in annoyance.

Alaster nodded before he plugged his nose and tried to pop his ears. It felt as though he had suddenly changed altitude a few times over. The pain from the process was more than he would have anticipated, but it really wasn't much compared to the small hole in his arm.

Taesir landed a second later. "The Ferveos have been taken care of, except for one. I assumed one of you took it out."

Gaeor shook his head. "I didn't encounter one."

"It was a scout, like many others," Frost said as he came to stand amongst them. "This was merely a first wave."

"My thoughts exactly," Kedar said. "Their numbers were too few to have been anything else."

"Are you all right, Alaster?" Frost asked the teenager.

Before Alaster could speak, Gaeor said, "He blew out his eardrums somehow, but he'll be okay."

"What do you suggest we do?" Taesir asked Kedar.

The Team Leader shook his head and looked at the ground. He had a few small cuts on his face, and his right leg was bleeding a little. Overall, though, he was unharmed. Turning to Frost, he asked, "What are the chances we could make it to the portal and back to Tilion?"

Frost grimaced. "I fear that if Cregorous has sent a wave to us, then it is likely ..." He looked at Alaster.

The teenager looked back at him, a finger shoved in his ear, trying to get his hearing back. "What is it?" he yelled.

"You think he has control of the portal?" Taesir asked quietly, worry filling her features.

The grovix nodded. "It's incredibly likely. Our chances of retreating through the portal are slim. Even if we made it there, if there is even the slightest chance that Caligans await on the other side, we would last mere seconds before destruction."

"So that leaves us with staying here," Kedar hushed.

"But, what can we do here?" Gaeor asked in an equally quiet tone. "What if they send a stronger wave?"

"We'll have to figure that out when the time comes," Kedar said. "There aren't any other options. We can't just run away—we're stuck here. We could try to head for McMurdo, but that wouldn't help. It would only put more people in danger, and it would leave the station without protection."

"I believe our best course of action is to head inside and explain things to the humans," Frost said.

Nodding, Kedar said, "I'll make a shield around the station."

"Is that a good idea?" Taesir asked.

"It's the only idea I got. It'll hold well enough, but it won't be strong enough to withstand a major attack."

Frost turned away from the station and planted his feet. The ice shifted under his paws and, a few seconds later, a moat of sorts appeared a few yards away from where they stood. Forcing the ice to dip several feet into the ground, Frost then shifted his weight and, along the side of the moat, a sheet of ice rose several feet into the air.

When Frost turned to face them again, he saw Kedar's straying eyes and said, "I assumed a few minor defenses would be helpful."

Gaeor guided Alaster and said, "C'mon, kid; we're heading in."

As they had been talking, Alaster had been trying all of the remedies he knew for getting his hearing back. He was currently smacking the side of his face as though he were trying to expel water from his ear.

"It would be better trying for patience, my friend," Frost said to the teenager, though Alaster still couldn't hear him fully.

Their expressions had been worrying. He hadn't been able to make out anything they'd said with clarity, but it was apparent that they were concerned.

Once they were nearly at the station, Kedar turned back toward the tundra. He knew a shield the size he was proposing would likely drain him. It was why he had been taking in as much energy from opposing attacks as possible earlier. He'd need all his strength if he could manage to keep everyone safe.

He took a deep breath and, as he exhaled, he imagined a domed shield rising from the ground and slowly blanketing the station in its protection.

Staring at the swirling gold colors, Kedar hoped it would hold better than he had said. This was their only defense, and if they lost it, he didn't know what they'd do.

Chapter Six
THE RIGHT HAND

Kelek couldn't wait to be back in Caliga. The frozen tundra was making his fingers tingle, and his toes were going numb. He'd need to change some of his clothes under his uniform to afford him more warmth for the final push against the Seventh.

Grasping the portal, he thought of the mansion then appeared in the circular room. It was a strange sensation to watch the white globe of the portal flash to red as his surroundings changed.

He released the portal and exited the sloped room, immediately turning right and venturing down the hall. A moment later, he appeared at the stairwell and descended to the basement of the mansion. The howling cries of his master's experiments thrashed against the walls to his left. The dull thumping of fists against unbreakable glass filtered into the hall as echoed drumbeats.

Taking the door on the right, he entered the large war room. Its ancient, wooden table at its center displayed an intricate map of Earth and the various portal activations across the world. The large glass windows across the room splayed dull light into the room, and cracked-over glass bulbs held cold white lights on the ceiling.

Cregorous sat on his throne-like chair, one of his mistresses sitting on his lap.

It'd been centuries, and still Kelek envied those women.

"You're back early," Cregorous growled, shoving the woman aside.

"I gathered all the intel required swiftly, My Lord," Kelek answered with a bow.

Cregorous flicked his hand as a dismissal, and the woman quickly left the room, throwing Kelek a slightly perturbed look.

Once they were alone, Cregorous said, "Speak."

Falling into an attentive stance, Kelek squared his shoulders. "The Seventh is unprepared. My guess is he's untrained."

"And the Seventh's location?"

"Where you said," Kelek answered as his master stepped up to the table.

Studying the southern pole of Earth, Cregorous said, "They will not move."

"Master?"

"From the station," Cregorous added. "They'll dig in where they are. The tundra won't afford them options."

"I don't believe so, no."

"Anything further?"

"Yes, Master. The Ferveos should not come for the second wave."

Slowly, Cregorous lifted his scrutinizing gaze to the Right Hand.

"They fared poorly in the scouting wave."

"How poorly?" Cregorous asked unblinkingly, his jaw tight.

Refusing to shuffle his weight, Kelek swallowed. "They fell within moments, My Lord."

A growling noise rumbled up Cregorous' throat as he glared at the map on the table. "Damned beasts." He pushed himself upright and let out an angry breath. "Very well. I'll allocate them elsewhere. But I will send additional bratak'ra and werewolves."

Kelek bowed. "My Lord."

With a dismissive wave of his hand, Cregorous turned back to the chair he'd been seated on.

Bowing again, Kelek quickly vacated the room. He'd have to wait for the other generals to return before the master gave them instructions.

For now, he had to prepare himself for the frozen climate.

As he reached the first floor, he nearly smacked into one of the younger mistresses.

"Lord Kelek, I—"

He simply shoved her aside and continued on his way. She was new and wasn't yet aware that he didn't care for them. After all, they weren't here for him. They were here for the master.

Sure, Akeno, Izel, Caedex, and Vorex certainly acted like the mistresses were their toys, too. And maybe they were. Kelek didn't really care.

The last time he'd been with a woman, a few days later, she'd betrayed him. She'd betrayed them all.

So, what good were they?

As he entered his room and stripped off his uniform, he began digging through his things to find something warmer to wear underneath the dark gray jacket. His search rewarded him with one of Avemod's left-behind clothes, causing him to pause for a moment.

After today, things would be different. Agerius would be theirs by tomorrow, and if the master so desired, so would Earth. Shortly thereafter, the Elders themselves would fall.

It was a momentous day.

Coupled with that assured victory was the knowledge that, soon, he would be able to breathe easy. He wouldn't have to fret over Avemod's security. Because, after today, the master would rip everything apart and put it back together the way it was supposed to be. And there would be no need to worry over Avemod's place among the generals.

So long as Avemod didn't screw up.

Fury coiled in his chest at the idea that the damned idiot might actually manage to get himself killed. And if Avemod did get himself killed, Kelek would find his corpse, bring it back to life somehow, just so that he could kill Avemod himself.

Damned idiot, he thought. *He'd better not get himself killed.*

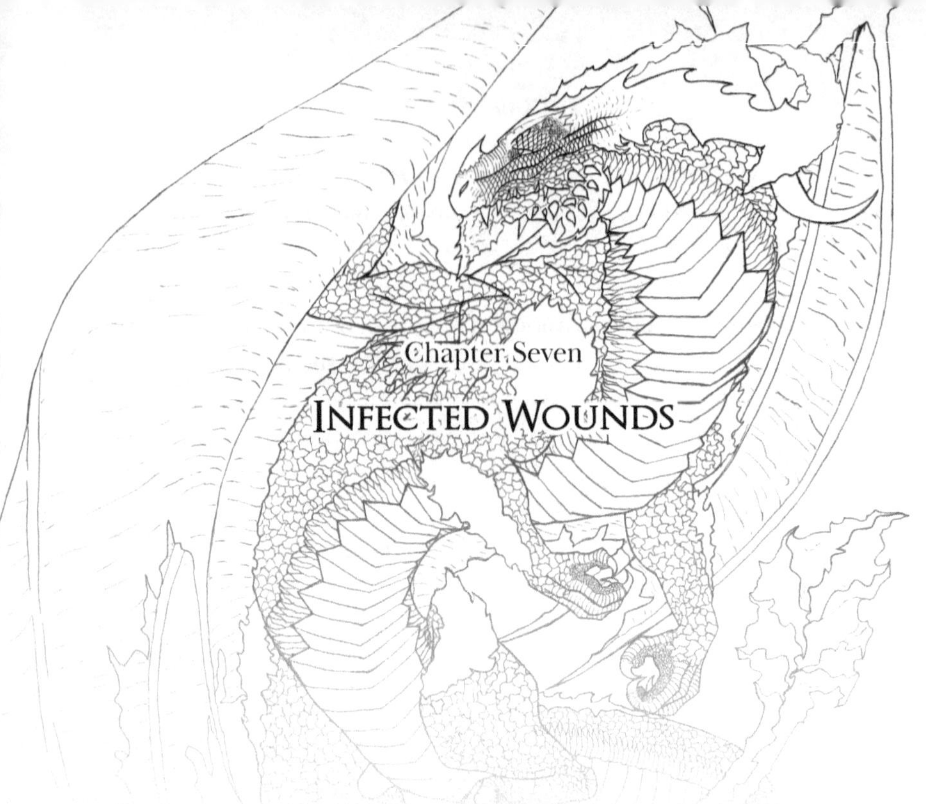

Chapter Seven

INFECTED WOUNDS

As they walked back into the station, they were almost immediately bombarded by Alaster's parents.

"Alaster Keegan O'Brien! What are you doing?" his mother yelled, in full panic.

Glancing to his Zaheri briefly, Alaster looked to his mother and said, "I'm doing what I'm supposed to do. If you had let me train—"

"Are you bleeding?"

"Young man, you are most certainly never doing that again," Keegan commanded.

Gaining a defiant look, Alaster swallowed back his urge to obey and challenged, "If another attack comes, yes, I am."

"This might be a conversation better for private quarters," Taesir tried to say.

"War doesn't solve anything! Did you learn nothing from Cameron?" his father boomed. A scowl was on his face, but his eyes were downcast and pained.

Throwing his arms out, Alaster shot back, "You're making it sound like I started this! I'm doing this to protect you!"

Keegan jabbed a finger toward his son. "You are forbidden to—"

"No!" Alaster cut in, refusing to let his da finish what he was going to say. He already knew what he was going to say. "You can't forbid me to do anything! Not in relation to this! For once, I'm right, and you're wrong! If I don't help, we could all die!"

Scientists gasped and started sharing rushed worries.

"Now, everyone calm down," Dr. Davis said, waving his hands down as though to distemper fears.

Undeterred by the unrest they were stirring, Keegan's face reddened, and he scowled. "You never would have had this kind of defiance before you got mixed up with that lot." He flung his hand toward the Zaheri. "Listen to me right now, Alaster! You cannot do this!"

"I can, and I will!" Alaster shoved back. "I have to!"

His father's jaw clenched as he pinched his eyes shut. He clenched his fists so tight that his knuckles turned white.

"I have to protect—"

"Dammit, Cameron!"

Alaster shook back. Their fears clicked in his head.

Ripping his eyes open, Keegan gave his son a look of sorrowful disappointment. The kind of disappointment that was wrapped in a frown, and tears, and fears, and pain. And that look felt like a knife that had lodged in Alaster's chest.

His mother gently placed her hand on her husband's arm, a frown etched on her face.

Before Alaster could figure out a response, before his father could shout again, a shuddered sigh fell from Keegan, and then he stormed off down the hall. The scientists parted for him in his marching gait.

His mother looked to Alaster before she took off after her husband.

Shock radiated Alaster's body, wrapping around his lungs and making it a little hard to breathe.

Taesir had been right. He shouldn't have pressed that argument here. In front of everyone. The scientists traded looks of fear and concern. Whether that was over their safety or over the outburst from the O'Briens, Alaster wasn't sure.

But these people knew his family. They knew his father. And his father never got that angry.

Shame coated Alaster's mind, and he shrank back a little.

Gently pushing Alaster back, Kedar stepped up to Dr. Davis. "We need to talk about the severity of things."

Dr. Davis let out a resigned breath. "Yes, we do."

Turning toward his team, he said, "Give me ten minutes. I'll meet you in the galley."

"Kedar, we need to—"

"I know," Kedar cut Gaeor off, "but we can't do anything until we give him the basics." He swung his attention to Dr. Davis. "You probably won't let us have authority unless I explain some things, right?"

The expedition leader's face contorted in a puffed stature. "Authority? That's out of the—"

"Sir, no, it's not. You'll understand once we talk."

Wearing a slightly frustrated expression, Dr. Davis turned to the scientists. "Treat this as an emergency situation. I'll provide information once I have it." He looked to Kedar. "With me, Mr. Kelvin."

Before he followed the expedition leader, Kedar grasped Alaster's arm, jolting the teen to look at him. "Your parents will calm down, and then you can talk to them."

"And say what?" Alaster asked, wearing a frown.

Letting out a small sigh, Kedar answered, "We can work that out." He patted Alaster's arm then walked off after Dr. Davis.

Frost nudged Alaster with his snout, and said, "Come along, Alaster. We have much to discuss."

Alaster nodded but said nothing. The knowledge that he'd have to confront his parents about everything sat like a brick in his gut. Meanwhile, his mind spun around his father's angered reaction, and what that meant.

The dog tags were only getting heavier.

Kedar joined them less than ten minutes later. He pushed the galley door open and said, "Dr. Davis isn't totally convinced we should be in charge, but he's at least acknowledging the danger we're in."

"He will not relinquish control of action?" Frost asked.

"Not at the moment," Kedar answered, crossing his arms over his chest, wearing a cheeky expression, and sounding like he was mimicking the doctor's tone.

Gaeor shifted his weight and asked in his gruff voice, "So what'd ya wanna do, Kedar?"

With a short breath, Kedar looked to Frost. He held the grovix's gaze for a few seconds before he asked, "Do I have the Council's permission to get him set?"

Alaster whipped his head up. He'd been silent, trying to process both the situation with enemy fighters and the strangled relationship with his parents. So far, he hadn't been able to come to grips with either and found no solutions that would result in peace on either account.

It'd been a crummy ten minutes.

Frost was quiet, his gaze falling to the floor as though it would hold an answer.

"Frost?" Taesir asked.

His ears flattening, the grovix slowly lifted his head, wearing a troubled look. "I am unsure."

"About what?" Gaeor asked a little gruffly.

"I think he can handle it," Kedar said.

"That is not the issue," Frost answered.

Agitation mixed with irritation bubbled in Alaster's chest. His face contorted, and a scowl sat on his brow. His tone was a bit cutting as he said, "I'd prefer you don't talk about me as if I'm not here."

"Sorry, champ," Kedar said with an apologetic wince. "We're just trying to figure out the next steps."

"That should be obvious," Gaeor said. He threw his hand toward the large windows. "We should be preparing for a second wave. It's likely to come at any minute."

"Wait. How do you know that?" Alaster asked. His frustration melted into worry.

"Frost?" Kedar asked, giving the grovix a pleading look.

The light blue grovix's muzzle wrinkled, and he closed his eyes before forcefully shaking his head. He rose to his feet and quickly said, "Alaster, listen well. Everything occurring stirs fear in us because of several things. The first of which is that we have not seen reinforcements."

"And you're sure you'd get some?" Alaster asked, glancing to his Zaheri.

Kedar nodded. "You're too important for the Council to just assume you're okay. They would have sent someone—anyone—to check on us if they knew you'd been attacked."

Shrugging a little, Alaster offered, "Maybe they just don't know?"

"That is highly unlikely," Frost muttered. He met Alaster's gaze. "What is far more probable is this: Cregorous has gained control of the portal on Tilion and is utilizing it to render attacks against all of you."

"All of ..." Alaster slumped in his chair, and his mouth fell open as he slowly looked to each of his protectors. "There are more Human-Borns," he hushed.

"Yes," Frost said with a single nod. "Seven in total. You are last."

Confusion hit Alaster's mind as multiple questions formed. His face pinched as he tried to figure out what to ask first.

In that pause, Kedar quickly said, "You've got questions, we'll address them. But let us talk for a minute."

The teen slowly exhaled and dropped his hands to the table with a small *thud*. "All right," he said in a resigned breath.

"There is a prophecy that we hold to. We do not have the time to delve into the details. Simply know this: seven Human-Borns were prophesied, each holding a title. Requisite is yours," Frost said.

It felt like a stupid title, but okay.

"The numbers that attacked us were too small to be a genuine strike. So, it holds that it was a scouting party to gauge our defenses," Kedar said.

"Which means they'll likely be back, and soon," Taesir quietly said. She quickly placed a hand on Alaster's arm. "We'll be fine. We just have to stay calm."

Biting his tongue, Alaster didn't say what burned in his mind. How could they possibly be fine? He wasn't trained, and there were only five of them.

"The problem is, we don't know to what extent to prepare," Gaeor said with a sigh. "Cregorous himself might be coming for you."

"Probably not," Kedar said.

"Why?" Alaster asked, only feeling slight relief that the monstrous enemy might not come after him right away. Then fear gripped his heart. "Wait—do you think he'd go after another Human-Born?"

"Maybe. We don't know."

Frost winced. "It stands to reason that Cregorous would choose to go after the First Human-Born rather than another."

Raising his brow slightly, Gaeor shifted his weight again. "And he does have six generals."

"Generals?" Alaster asked.

"Loyalists. Powerful men he's put in charge of other lesser Caligans. They lead a lot of the raids in Agerius," Taesir said. Then she looked to Kedar. "And I think I might have seen Kelek earlier."

"What? In the sky?" Gaeor asked a little snidely.

"No, on the ground," she said with a small roll of her eyes. "He wears a different uniform, right? Similar to the others, but darker in color?"

"That could have been Akeno."

Shaking her head, she answered, "No, it didn't look like leather."

Rubbing a hand through his hair, Kedar let out an even breath. "Okay, so ... if Kelek came with the first wave"—he picked up his head and studied the wall, a dawning realization in his eyes—"then that would mean Cregorous might have sent them as his scouts and will wait for them to report back."

"Still sounds like a bad thing," Alaster said.

"It might not be as bad as it could be."

Alaster narrowed his eyes and asked, "Huh?"

"It means we might have time," Taesir clarified.

The teen shook his head before he flicked his gaze around the group. "Okay, can I ask questions now?"

"Sure," Kedar said with a nod.

"So, wait ... the other Human-Borns. Where are they? Who are they? Are they all my age, or ...?"

"Best we're aware, you were all born in the same year. We can't say anything about who or where they are. We were only told where *you* were," Kedar answered.

"What do a bunch of teenagers mean to Cregorous? Why is he all fixated on us?"

"Part of the prophecy states how you seven fit into his downfall," Frost answered. "He is 'fixated' on you because the First already bested him nineteen years ago."

Alaster swallowed. "Wait, nineteen ..." A breath rattled out of his mouth. "Are you saying he attacked a *baby*?"

With a sigh, Kedar nodded sadly. "It certainly seems that way."

Covering his mouth with his hand, Alaster felt he might be sick. "Good Lord."

Monsters were real in many senses. People hurt other people just because. They took advantage of the weak. Sometimes people could do truly atrocious things to other human beings. And it had always been a point of spiraling confusion for Alaster. What was the point? Why hurt someone else? What was to be gained?

"Is he just that power hungry?" he hushed, staring at the table. "To attack a baby ... something so defenseless ..." A new question barreled into his thoughts, and he shot upright, waving his hands. "Wait, wait. A baby? *A baby* bested him nineteen years ago?"

"Yeah, that was basically our reaction," Gaeor said.

But the First Human-Born was being attacked again. Targeted by Cregorous. Sure, he was being targeted, too, but, apparently, by someone less powerful.

It was the First Human-Born everyone should be concerned about. It didn't matter if they had survived when they were a baby. What mattered was a powerful man was threatening the life of a teenager.

"And you think they might all be getting attacked?" Alaster looked around the room helplessly. "How do we help them?"

"Alaster, we have to focus on helping you," Gaeor said crossly.

"He's right to be worried about the others," Taesir admonished.

Wincing a little, Kedar looked between Gaeor and Taesir before he said, "The others have their own groups of Zaheri. And those Zaheri aren't going to let any harm come to the other Human-Borns."

"If they are under attack," Frost stressed.

"Right. If they're being attacked," Kedar said with a loose gesture toward the grovix.

"Okay, so ..." Alaster sighed. "Then, what do we do?"

Looking to the group, Kedar asked, "What are our options?"

"Didn't we already discuss this?" Gaeor asked.

"Let's discuss it again. We need to examine every possible course of action."

Gaeor groaned as Taesir said, "We could try to leave."

"That's impossible," Alaster said. "The only way to do that is if we got a plane here, and if there are dragons flying about, then it's likely that it'll get taken down."

"What about McMurdo?" Gaeor offered.

With a shake of his head, Frost said, "It would require for the humans to be unprotected."

"What about the other bases?" Alaster asked. "There are dozens of them all across the continent. What if the Caligans go to one of them? They won't be able to last a few seconds, let alone fight back."

Kedar rubbed his forehead as he said, "We can't spread out, we're already too thin here as it is."

"It is possible that Cregorous knows of Alaster's location, and therefore will not waste any time with the other bases," Frost said.

"How would he know that?" Taesir asked.

"Perhaps he was told," the grovix answered simply.

Looking crestfallen, Kedar said, "That's assuming a Zaheri was feeding him information. That wouldn't happen."

Frost looked doubtful as he said, "It may not have been voluntary. You must remember, there is enough proof to suggest that he is a Telepath."

Alaster's eyes widened in surprise, and he stuttered out, "What?"

"We'll address abilities later," Kedar said dismissively. "Let's figure out our next steps first."

Shaking her head, Taesir said, "Assuming the other bases on the continent will be safe, where does that leave us with our options?"

"With one," Kedar said. "We stay and fight."

"Four against a legion? Those odds are not favorable," Frost said.

"Five," Alaster corrected.

Kedar pointed to Gaeor and said, "A top ranking Sniper"—he pointed to Taesir—"a Preliator breeder"—he pointed to Frost—"an Elemental grovix whose Element is water"—he pointed to himself—"and me."

"The Paragon Team Leader," Taesir said with a smile.

Alaster pointed at himself. "And a Human-Born."

"You're staying here," Kedar said.

Alaster sat up a bit and furrowed his brow. "No, I'm not. I didn't just yell at my parents for nothing. Everything I said, I meant. I'm helping you guys."

"By getting yourself killed?"

"Wait a second, Kedar, we might him," Gaeor said.

Nodding, Taesir added, "We need every source of resistance we can find."

Looking at his Team members, Kedar said, "He's had next to no training." He quickly looked over at Frost. "What do you think?"

The grovix looked at the Team Leader and shrank back. "This is not among my area of expertise."

"Frost! C'mon; I can hold my own—I just did a few minutes ago!" Alaster said.

"And if Cregorous does come here?" Kedar asked, turning toward the teenager.

Alaster picked up his hand, only to let it slap against his knee in defeat as he said, "Well ... I mean ... what would you do if Cregorous did come here, and I wasn't out there?"

"I'd—" Kedar looked down at the table with a scrunched brow.

The demanding expression on Alaster's face melted away. "You can stop him, can't you?"

A choke of a word left Kedar as he looked at the boy. "We could try."

He looked around at his Zaheri and realized that this was far more disastrous than he had thought. "You mean, if Cregorous comes ..."

"If Cregorous comes, you might be the only one to survive," Frost said, his ears flattening against his head.

"Might," Alaster repeated in a whisper.

Taesir looked around desperately and said, "But the chances of him coming are—"

"And he's going after the First Human-Born?" he nearly exploded. He didn't even know the other six Human-Borns, but out of nowhere, he was worried for their safety. What if one of them did die?

They were teenagers, just like him.

What if the First Human-Born was scared and untrained, just like he was? Would they be able to survive against Cregorous?

A tremor of worry rattled his chest, and Alaster could've sworn he heard a voice echo similar, scared thoughts. Not in any words he could make out, but the context was there, nonetheless.

He shook it off.

Frost started, "The First Human-Born has already—"

"But what about their Zaheri? And if none of you can—"

"We can try, and that could be all we need," Kedar said.

Alaster's shoulders slumped as he shrunk a little in his chair. He took a few calming breaths before he said, "Well, if you're going to be risking your lives, I'm not going to let you do it alone."

"While that's a brave sentiment—"

"I don't care if it is or if it isn't," Alaster said. "One day, I'm going to have to fight and defend those whom I care about. And apparently, today is that day. My family is here, and you guys are here. I'm not going to just sit idly by and hope that none of you get killed. Not if there's something I can do about it."

There was a funny echo again, as if he was saying the same thing to a different group of people. It made his brain itch.

Again, Alaster pushed the foreign emotion aside.

The Zaheri all looked at one another before Frost shook his head as he looked to Kedar. "He will not back down from this. I believe we should allow him the chance."

Kedar stared at the table again as he thought this through. The idea of Alaster going out to fight against a greater horde of enemy fighters didn't sit well with him. However, the others did have a point. They were only four warriors strong. Even with Frost's advantage with his Element and with Taesir's skill in taking out Ferveos, that only left Gaeor and himself to take out any remaining fighters.

It only raised their chances of survival a bit to add Alaster to their team, and it greatly diminished his chances of survival. Wasn't that why they were here? To keep him safe? How was letting him fight safe?

On the flip side of that coin, though, was the fact that Alaster had done a good job holding his own against the enemy fighters earlier. They couldn't have asked for more when he had so little training.

He really regretted not being more proactive about the importance of the boy's duties and responsibilities. Maybe if he had tried harder to appeal to Alaster's parents ...

There was nothing to do about that now.

With a sigh, Kedar looked over at Alaster. "Fine. But you had better keep yourself safe out there."

"Safe on a battlefield," Gaeor chuckled. "That'll be the day."

Nodding, Alaster answered, "I'll do my best."

"We only need to last long enough for the Council to send reinforcements," Taesir encouraged.

"Taesir is correct," Frost said. "Once the Council can find the ability, they will send us aid."

"Let's hope that happens soon," Kedar muttered. He glanced outside and saw the gold glow of his shield swirling about. They could survive this, couldn't they?

A resolute feeling filled him. Just as he'd said to Alaster, they would try, and that might make all the difference.

Chapter Eight

THE ROAD TO HEALING

While Kedar and Taesir went to go speak with Dr. Davis, and Gaeor looked into "adjustments" for his pistol, it left Alaster to track down his parents and discuss things in a calmer manner. Frost went with him, and while his presence comforted Alaster, he couldn't deny that Frost being there might only stoke his father's ire further.

They wandered down the hall, Frost following Alaster's lead. And they weren't walking in the direction of his parents' quarters, or their lab. Even so, the grovix allowed the teen to amble and gave him silence to process.

After several minutes of their slow march, he softly looked to Alaster and asked, "Do you wish to talk of it before speaking with your parents?"

Alaster came to a stop, his gaze fixed on the floor. "I don't really want to find them."

"Because you fear their reactions?"

"Mum's scared 'cause I got hurt," the teen muttered to the floor. He blinked a few times, continuing to speak more to the walls than to his Zaheri. "Da might be, too, but ... he got so angry. And he called me

Cameron." He pinched his eyes shut and tried not to clench his jaw. It was a failed attempt. Though he already knew the answer, he wanted there to be a *different* answer, and angrily asked, "Why is he bringing Cam up? He hasn't talked to me at all about it. Neither has Mum." His fists clenched. "So, why now?"

Letting out a small sigh, Frost said, "Alaster, you know the answer to that query."

"I'm not Cam. I—" His words caught in his throat as a strangled noise.

He was about to say he wasn't going to die.

Cam was dead.

Cam was dead.

Sorrow surged through Alaster like a geyser, and before he could stop himself, before he could suck back a breath to force the tears away...

He started sobbing.

Without any logic behind the action, Alaster spun on his heel and began running toward his parents' lab. That was where they'd be. They wouldn't go to their quarters. They'd bury themselves in a distraction. Because that's what they did.

But Alaster couldn't take it anymore.

He couldn't not acknowledge the truth.

Frost called his name and ran at his heel, trying to get him to stop and explain himself. To talk.

No. Talking would make Alaster stop. Talking would make him rein in his emotions. And that was all he'd been doing.

For months since they'd gotten the news that Cam had died, all he'd been doing was snuffing his emotions. Shoving them aside. Pushing them away. He only cried in brief moments, when he let himself, and always in the confines of his room. Because he hadn't seen his parents cry. He'd seen tears escape, but there hadn't been sobbing. And they didn't talk about it.

Whether it was because they hadn't had a memorial service for Cam yet or not, it was like his parents just wouldn't acknowledge it. And sometimes, yeah, it didn't feel real to Alaster.

But then the dog tags would clink, or he'd shift and feel them press against his skin. Like a cold tribute.

Why did he wear them? All they did was serve as a reminder that his brother wasn't coming back to them. That his brother was gone.

Today was the first time his father had mentioned Cam since he'd died.

Bursting into his parents' lab, he found them exactly where he'd expected—hunched over notes. His mother looked weathered and beaten, as though she'd reached the same limit Alaster had. His father looked weary and pained.

"Alaster," his mother started.

Without saying anything, he flung himself at them, gripping them tight and pulling them into an embrace. His father was too tall, and his mother was too short, but he tugged them close.

And he cried.

It was his father who started crying first.

And that made Alaster cry more.

Minutes or hours or seconds passed of sobbing as the family finally mourned. Finally laid bare their grief. It was gut-wrenching sorrow, the kind that spills tears and makes noses run and bodies rack in anguish.

His father slapped his hand onto the back of Alaster's head, roughly gripping his son's hair as he sobbed, "We can't lose you, too, Alaster."

"I know, Da," the son let out in a strangled cry. "You're not gonna."

"We can't, Alaster, we just can't," his mother cried.

Shaking his head a little forcefully, raking his chin across their shoulders, he said, "I'm not Cam, I ... I can do this."

A little forcefully, his father pushed him back. He gripped Alaster's shoulders tight and said, "You can't promise that, Alaster! War doesn't—"

"I don't have a choice, Da!" His mother squeaked a word of rebuttal, but Alaster quickly said, "No, please, listen to me!" Tears coated his cheeks, and his nose was clogged. He probably looked God-awful, but Alaster quaked in breaths to steady himself, even if everything about him was unsteady in that moment. "I'm not a normal human. I can do this."

Letting out an exhausted breath and wearing a look of lament, his mother said, "Alaster, that doesn't—"

"It does matter," he shook out. With no idea what to do, all he could think was to show them. His hands trembled as he shot them out and screamed, "Look at this!"

Green energy flew from his chest and into his grasp, swirling in a dance, as if moving with a breeze. Like how leaves would spiral and dance in autumn.

Jerking his hands, his energy moving with the motion, he said, "This is what makes me special, makes me different." He wildly looked between his parents. "I know I should have shown you sooner, but you'd been so against it—against this—that I didn't know how." Wearing a look of desperation, he practically pleaded, "You can't seriously look at this and expect it to mean nothing!"

His father's face was twisted and red, but everything about his posture conveyed devastation, not anger. His mother suddenly looked frail and fragile; her hands clutched tight at her waist as though that held her together.

In the dimly lit lab, his radiant green energy illuminated everything his parents feared.

"If you go out there," his father started, his voice cracking, "You could die."

A heavy sigh came from the doorway, and Alaster looked to find Frost standing there. Tears coated the grovix's eyes, and his shoulders were sunken.

"We completely sympathize, and empathize, with your concerns," Frost said as he walked toward the family.

Dropping his hands, his energy dissipating like green mist, Alaster stepped aside, allowing Frost some more room for his large frame.

"And I fully acknowledge that you do not care for me and what it is I represent. However, I must state the fact that of all of us, Alaster is the least likely to become injured if he were to fight."

Alaster's brow furrowed.

"How is that possible?" his mother asked.

"He is incredibly powerful." Giving the O'Briens an understanding and soft look, Frost continued, "Alaster is one of seven Human-Borns, and all are gifted with talents and abilities that can, and will, aid them in battle." His ears pulled back, and a sigh escaped him. "I truly wish I did not have to bring such a request to a family who has already suffered greatly. But there is no mistaking that Alaster is one of our Seven prophesied Human-Borns."

Swallowing and releasing his clenched jaw, Alaster's father asked, "And what does that mean?"

Frost gave the teenager a warm smile. "That he is more capable than even we might be able to imagine."

Silence fell for a moment, wrapping the space in the ambient noise of the equipment and computers whirring and trilling intermittently.

Giving his father a timid stare, Alaster said, "I'm sorry for my outburst earlier."

His father released a heavy sigh and ran a hand through his wiry hair. "I suppose I should apologize, as well. What I said was—"

"I understand, Da."

"We just ... we can't ..." his mother started, tears welling in her eyes again.

Alaster reached for her hand, giving it a gentle squeeze. "I know, Mum. But it's going to be okay. My Zaheri won't let anything bad happen to me."

Staring at Frost, his father flicked his hand toward the grovix. "Why don't they just leave? These monsters are only here because of them."

"They aren't here for them," Alaster said.

"Then what—" His father stopped abruptly and looked at his son. His mouth fell open slightly, and he said, "No, no, they can't be here for you. Why you?"

"You're just a boy!" his mother pleaded.

Holding his hands out, Alaster said, "I know this seems hard for you to grasp—I do—but—"

"Does this have to do with that prophecy that he mentioned?" his father asked with a scowl toward Frost, some of his harder edges returning.

Deflating slightly, Alaster shot out, "Da, prophecies worked in the Bible. Are we really going to dismiss the possibility of them working today?"

His father let out an annoyed growl as his mother reluctantly said, "He's right."

"That doesn't make it easy!" Keegan shook out. The exhaustion of the last fifteen minutes or so displayed heavily on his features, and he rubbed his bloodshot eyes. "The only peaceful place on this planet, and they come," he muttered.

"It's not just here," a voice came from around the corner.

Embarrassment shot through Alaster. He wanted the ground to swallow him up so he could disappear.

There'd been someone in here the whole time? Why hadn't they said anything?

"McKay!" Alaster's father thundered, his own flame of embarrassment soaking into his pale skin as he marched around to the cubicle where the doctor in question sat.

With a yelp and a look of sheer panic, the doctor nearly threw the headphones from around his neck and onto the floor.

He was a slightly rotund man, with just a few too many pounds wrapped around his middle. A receding hairline and round face didn't do much for his features, and almost beady eyes sat behind small, framed glasses. He'd only recently arrived, and Alaster hadn't met him yet. Some new scientist who was spending the winter on station to work on the black hole project.

Dr. McKay held his hands up and with wide eyes shrieked out, "I didn't hear anything! I was just taking my headphones off and heard you say—"

"What do you mean this isn't just here?" Alaster asked, relieved to hear that his family's first act of healing hadn't been eavesdropped on. The evidence of it must have been visible, though, because Alaster could feel the exhaustion of his eyes and the swollen nature to his nose.

Waving his fingers toward his computer screen, Dr. McKay said, "Well, it's ... it's all over the place. Reports that it's all over the world." He shook off his startled fear and waved his hands before saying, "Look at this." Turning back to his workstation, he started to cue up various reports across his multi-screened desk. The O'Briens and Frost gathered around as best they could.

"There was a spike of some untraceable radiation or energy or ... something right here"—he pointed to the map of Antarctica on the screen—"maybe fifteen minutes before those creatures showed up."

Shrugging, his father said, "That doesn't mean it's happening everywhere."

"I'm not finished," Dr. McKay said with a twinge of annoyance as he continued rigorously typing away. The map turned and zoomed out, revealing a map of the world. Other points lit up across the globe. "See? That same anomaly happened at the same time at these other six locations."

"Six other locations?" Alaster asked quietly. A wave of nausea rolled through him.

Dr. McKay nodded. "Yes, one on each continent. It's actually rather fascinating. Whatever is causing this is powerful. It might even be something utilizing fusion or zero space energy." He chuckled a little. "Whatever it is, it's something that could change the energy crisis if we could learn more about it."

"We must tell Kedar immediately," Frost said sternly.

"You think ..." Alaster started, anxiety eating at his stomach and twisting his gut.

Whipping his gaze to Dr. McKay, the grovix said, "You stated that each of these anomalous readings occurred at the same moment?"

"Uh ..." Dr. McKay stumbled out, staring at Frost in befuddlement. He then pointed at his screen again. "Yeah, at the same time."

"Then this is much more harrowing—for all of you Human-Borns—than we had originally anticipated. We must find the others."

The teenager took a step to follow Frost when his mother said tremblingly, "Alaster."

He turned to his parents, looking between them with a frown. Then, turning back to Frost, he said, "Go, I'll meet up with you."

"You are certain?" the grovix asked.

"I'll just be a minute."

The family walked back around the corner to afford some privacy as Frost hastened out the door.

"Da, Mum, I know what you're going to say—"

"You promise you won't get hurt?" his mother begged.

Alaster opened his mouth to reply, and a few strangled words escaped before he shied back, his brow dipping in concern.

Though a frown plagued his face, Keegan slowly looked to his son. "You promise you'll come back?"

Lifting his gaze to his parents, Alaster felt his heart crumble.

This wasn't fair.

It wasn't fair to them.

In that instant, he wished the burden of being a Human-Born was someone else's. If only to remove the fear that sat in his parents' eyes.

Mustering all the courage and assurance he could, Alaster nodded a bit and shook out, "I will." He swallowed back his own fears and concerns. He'd be sure, if only to give his parents comfort. Gaining a steely expression, he nodded more solidly. "I promise."

For a few seconds, his parents just stared at him. Then they stepped forward and enveloped him into a tight embrace, one Alaster returned readily.

"I love you guys," he whispered, clutching them as tightly as he could to let them know beyond a doubt that he would be okay. That it would all work out.

He prayed that simple gesture would be enough.

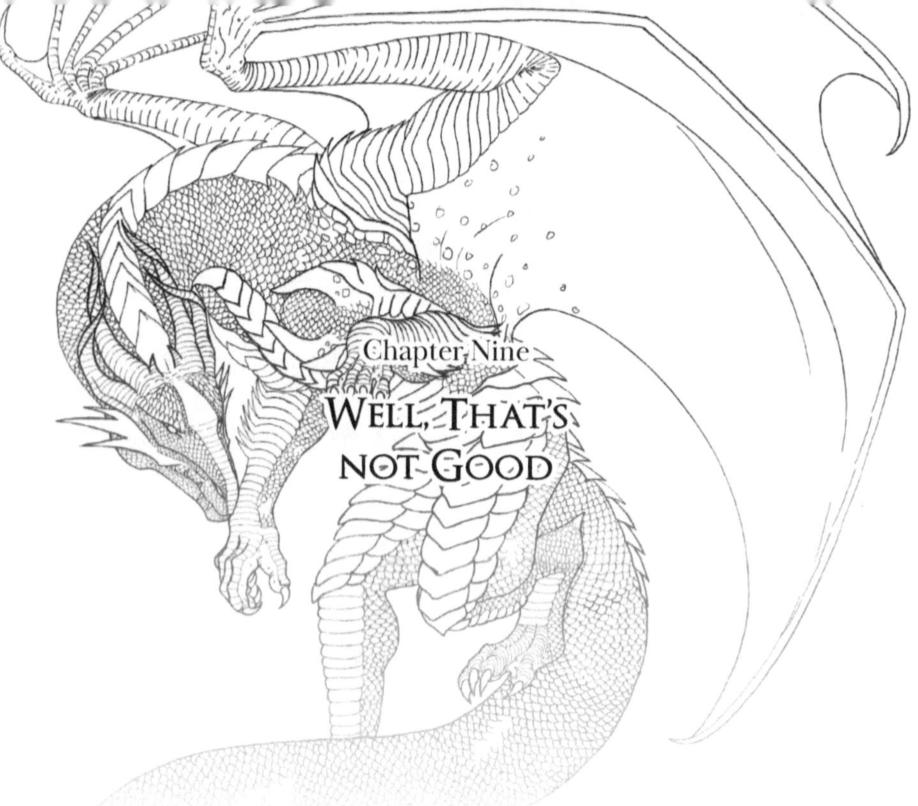

Chapter Nine
WELL, THAT'S NOT GOOD

Alaster was directed to find his Zaheri in one of the lounges, and as he entered, he heard Kedar say, "So, what does this mean for us? All of us, I mean."

"Cregorous has dominion over the portal which, simply put, means we cannot hope for reinforcements. Not timely ones," Frost answered.

"So, what then?" Gaeor asked, his face twisting in frustration. "We lay down and die?"

"Obviously, we can't do that," Kedar muttered, ruffling his hair. He let out a calming breath. "We have the upper hand here."

Taesir shuffled her weight and fidgeted. "How, exactly?"

"We've been able to adapt to the cold." Kedar gestured to the grovix among them. "Plus, we have Frost."

Ears flattening, Frost shrank back, letting his gaze fall toward the floor. "You should not put such trust in my abilities."

"Why not?" Taesir asked.

"The fight earlier was the first time in decades since I have utilized my Element. Even then, utilizing it as a weapon ..." He shook his head gently. "Millennia have passed since it was used as such. I am not confident that my skill will be enough to turn a battle."

"But you did well on the field before," Kedar said. "Why are you doubting yourself now?"

"Doubt is not what I am feeling. I suppose warning. I would not wish you to imagine me a winning piece. Because if I were to fail, it could doom us all."

"Maybe we should reevaluate our choice to stay," Gaeor said.

Kedar shrugged. "And go where? All that would do is strand us somewhere in Antarctica." He held his hand up uselessly then let it slap back to his side. "Unfortunately, we don't have any alternatives."

Glancing to his watch, Alaster tried to figure out how long it had been since the first engagement. Then he glanced toward the hall, wondering if Dr. McKay had a timestamp on the energy surge that they could utilize to determine when they might face a second attack. Because if there was time, maybe there was another option. At least, an option that might afford everyone else on base to flee.

He figured it had been nearing three hours since the Caligans had arrived. What did that mean? Was that a good thing, or a bad thing?

Alaster might've been smart, but he'd never been great at war-strategy games. Cam had taught him a lot.

What would Cam do in this situation?

Rubbing the dog tags through his shirt, Alaster knew exactly what Cam would do. He'd figure out a way to get innocent lives out of danger, and he'd hold the line to make sure they got to safety.

But Kedar was right. Where could they possibly send the scientists so they'd be safe?

He glanced to the window and tried to think outside the box. Objectively, what were their options. Taking his parents and any relational ties out of the equation, they were five people strong. Hundreds of scientists were in the crosshairs. Taesir had said she thought there was a Ferveos unaccounted for.

Did they miss any Caligans in the fight? Where might they hide if they were lying low? What shelter did they have outside of the station?

"The IceCube," Alaster mumbled.

Frost's ears pivoted toward the teen before he looked to Alaster and asked, "What were you saying, Alaster?"

"When did you join us?" Taesir asked.

Ignoring her question, Alaster stepped farther into the room. "Did we get all of the Caligans?"

Kedar glanced at the others before he shrugged. "Maybe. Maybe not. There's always a chance we missed some in the terrain."

"I still think I missed a Ferveos," Taesir said. She looked to Alaster inquisitively. "What makes you ask?"

"Just something I'm wondering. What if we took out whatever opposition remained and gave ourselves some breathing room? Maybe even got a window of opportunity to get everyone safely off the station?"

"And go where?" Gaeor asked, giving Alaster a look that conveyed he wasn't annoyed and was genuinely wondering where they might be able to flee.

A little helplessly, Alaster winced and shrugged. "I don't know. Maybe send the scientists to McMurdo. They'd be safe there, and then we wouldn't have to worry about them getting caught in the crosshairs."

Letting out a small sigh, Kedar admitted, "Maybe."

"Why only maybe?"

"It's been over two hours," Taesir answered.

"Maybe three since they landed in Antarctica," Kedar added. He gestured loosely as he continued, "Another strike could come any minute. Assuming that Cregorous did send each of his generals as scouts, I can't think of many reasons for why it would take more than two hours for them to report back to him. However they would do that."

"Then, shouldn't we take out whatever might still be out there?" Alaster asked with a vague gesture toward the window. "That would mean less fighters whenever the second wave comes, right?"

"Maybe, but that could also mean we might get stuck between the Caligans already outside and their reinforcements."

Alaster shrank back a little. "Okay, I hadn't thought of that."

Kedar held up his hands and said, "Let's spend whatever time we have right now trying to prepare ourselves for another attack. Then we can—"

A groan hit the air, and Kedar winced as he fell to the side. Taesir grabbed his arm, holding him upright.

"What was that?" Alaster asked, his gaze flicking to the ceiling in alarm.

"Something's hitting my shield," Kedar grunted. He grimaced as he held Taesir for support. He let out a pained rumble and tugged on her arm. "Quick, to the window; I need to see what's going on."

Slumping against the window, Kedar squinted past the fog appearing on the glass and saw a Ferveos rear back, a warm glow of fire at the back of its throat.

In a shaky movement, Kedar stuttered back and threw his hands down in desperation, begging his shield to listen to his hasty command.

Outside, the shield unwrapped from around the building, folding in on itself near the Ferveos just as it released a blast of fire from its gullet.

Kedar gritted his teeth and held his hands out, feeling a sparking flash of heat across his fingers that made his arms tremble. "Go!" he shook out in a command to his team.

A screech came across the announcement system, and Dr. McKay's frantic voice called, "Alaster, to my lab!"

The sound of a colliding explosion ripped the air, and Kedar was blasted backward, slamming against the far wall and dropping in his deadweight.

"Kedar!" Taesir screamed in terror.

Half a second later, the building shook and jostled, as though a train had gone off the rails.

Gaeor snatched Taesir's arm and shoved her toward the door. "Go take care of that Ferveos!"

"But—"

Alaster quickly put his fingers on Kedar's pulse point. He looked over his shoulder and said in a relieved urgency, "He's alive!"

The small woman fisted her hands and glared before turning on her heel and running down the hall.

"He will be safe here," Frost said, working to nudge Alaster away from the unconscious Team Leader. "We have little time until they hit the station again."

"He's right, kid. C'mon," Gaeor commanded, snatching Alaster's sleeve and yanking him out the door.

Just as they reached the Destination Zulu entrance, Alaster heard his parents cry out his name. He spun around to face them but continued toward the entrance. "I'll be fine! Keep everyone on the far side of the station!"

"Be careful!" his mother called.

Frost completely disregarded the many stairs and leaped right over the railing, three stories up. As he did, ice shot up out of the ground and appeared just beyond the railing, forming a ramp. He slid down expertly then charged forward the moment his paws reached the icy terrain.

Gaeor and Alaster followed the grovix's lead, each using the ice slide. The Zaheri's trip down the slide was fairly effortless. Alaster's was filled with some flailing and uneasy sounds as he slipped more than slid.

As the teen stumbled his way to surer footing off the slide, Gaeor grabbed his jacket sleeve again and tugged him along. "You're sticking with me, kid."

"Got it," Alaster said with a nod.

As Gaeor took off away from the direction Frost had run, Alaster asked, "Kedar's going to be okay, right?"

"He'll be fine, kid. Focus on the enemy right now."

He hadn't learned much from Kedar's actions, just that he relied a lot on his energy. And, as much as he hated to admit it, his lack of training was his greatest enemy in this fight. There had only been a few times he had experimented with it before today, but his parents were always around. He couldn't exactly stretch himself much.

But he had to try.

Gaeor was sure to take out any Caligans he came across, and Frost would take care of the bratak'ra and werewolves, while Taesir would focus on the Ferveos. That left only a small number of Caligans for him to take care of, right?

As they came over a snowbank, the two of them were met with twenty or thirty Caligans and a handful of bratak'ra.

Seeing the creatures in person jarred Alaster's mind back to earlier in the day, when he'd gotten a flash of an image of a bratak'ra in his mind.

But witnessing the sheer bulk of the beasts made him almost freeze.

Frost was tiny in comparison to a bratak'ra. These creatures must have had another hundred pounds or two on Frost. And the dual-horned one among them looked like a fury-filled monster. Scars adorned its body, and the sickly-yellow color of its eyes stood out against pale brown fur.

Without missing a beat, Gaeor leaped into the air and dove toward the thrall. Alaster opened his mouth to yell and ask him what he was doing.

Gold energy charged from Gaeor's chest and concentrated around his fist and forearm. Blasts of gray haphazardly shot toward him, but he remained undeterred. As he neared the ground, he slammed his gold-covered fist into the ice, and a splintering crackle tore from the impact. Shards of golden glass tore out, impacting everything nearby.

Alaster ducked to avoid a few then stutteringly realized a Caligan neared him. Concentrating on the spiraling energy in his core, Alaster begged it to help him, even if he couldn't figure out what to tell it to do.

The green energy tore down his limbs, and he thrust his arms out. Green erupted from his palms and surged at his attackers, striking them with a thunderous ferocity.

Not waiting too long, Alaster continued running, the urgency to act propelling him forward. If they didn't quell this fighting quickly, Caligans might reach the unprotected station. And there were too many people there he cared about. He had to do all he could to protect them.

There came a barrage of gray energy, all small and almost bullet shaped. He tried to dodge them, but a few hit him. Running despite the pain that filled his mind with each hit, he pulled green energy to skitter down his arm and pool into a softball-sized orb. He threw his arm across his body, releasing the attack.

As the orb shot away from him, it spiraled and shattered, little shards like glass flying in every direction, even back at him. Paranoia filled him as one of the shards almost hit his face, but it flew straight through him without a single problem. He could only assume that his own energy couldn't hurt him.

A body barreled into him, sending him to the ground.

The instant his back hit the ice beneath him, Alaster felt an echoing jolt shoot through his right side, as though something had rammed into his shoulder. A phantom echo of a wordless cry of pain tore through his mind before he registered the fist that impacted his face.

The Caligan had gotten Alaster underneath him and began wailing on his face, which Alaster tried to block with his arms. Glaring at the Caligan warrior, he yelled and landed a punch on his attacker's chest.

As he hit the enemy fighter, a green flash erupted, and the Caligan flew backward, a hole in its chest where Alaster's fist had landed.

Gingerly getting to his feet, his face feeling sore and bloody, Alaster turned to try to see what else he had to fight, but it seemed like that last Caligan was all he had left.

He winced as he felt his torn skin start to patch along his face, one cut at a time.

"Alaster!" Frost's voice came from behind him. He turned as the grovix ran up to him.

"Not bad, kid!" Gaeor said, jogging to join them.

"Where's ...?" Alaster started.

A Ferveos slammed into the icy ground nearby, a second crashing atop it a moment later.

The flapping of wings caused Alaster to look away from the decimated Ferveos to see Taesir land among them. She favored her left leg, where a deep cut was slowly healing. A branding red mark of inflamed skin remained in the wake of her healing body. There was a sour expression on her usually gentle features, and she said crossly, "No more Ferveos."

"Nicely done, Tae," Gaeor said with a smirk.

She let out a frustrated huff, not looking at all pleased with herself.

"Are you all right?" Frost asked Alaster.

With a grimace, Alaster answered, "Yeah, just really sore." He began to wipe away the blood on his face and could feel unhealed cuts sting at his movements.

"You held your own pretty well," Gaeor said to Alaster.

"I believe he is quite a talented fighter from instinct," Frost commented.

Alaster let his attention swing to the station. It didn't look good.

Destination Alpha looked as though it'd collapsed in on itself. Metal from the framing swung in the Arctic wind, twisting and swaying like an omen of things to come. A faint groaning was in the breeze, as if a support was under strain.

Hopefully, no one had been hurt.

Worry clutched his lungs. Alaster prayed they could find a way to get all of the humans out of the station safely. And soon.

Taking in deep breaths to calm himself, Alaster asked, "What do we do now? Kedar's knocked out and can't make another shield. Can one of you?"

Gaeor and Taesir looked at one another before Taesir said, "Kedar's the only one of us who has that ability."

"Okay, well ... how do you make a shield? Maybe I can make one."

Scrunching her brow, Taesir answered, "That's unlikely. Sure, there's a fifty percent chance you could have the ability, but it's more than just making a shield. They take the hybrid's energy and can drain them completely of physical and mental strength."

"That's true, but ... it's only happened once." Gaeor looked at Frost and asked, "What do you think we should do?"

"Why do you ask me?" the grovix asked.

"With Kedar knocked out, that leaves you in charge of the team. Unless, of course, you want Gaeor or me to take over," Taesir said.

Frost let out a sigh. "Very well. If I must be given the duty."

"You're a High Council Member," Gaeor reminded, wearing a look of confusion. "Wouldn't this be easier than anything you've ever encountered there?"

"You underestimate how difficult this posting has been," Frost said with a grin. He looked to Alaster. "If you wish to attempt to make a shield, then that would be our best option."

With a nod, Alaster said, "Okay. How do I make one?"

Scratching his head, Gaeor said, "My brother was skilled in shield creation. I think he said that it took a mental image and the desire to build it. But it may be different for you."

"Just a mental image?" Alaster asked doubtfully. That felt too easy.

Gaeor shrugged.

"Okay, I'll try."

He closed his eyes and thought of the station in front of him. He remembered what Kedar's shield had looked like. How it had domed the building, not conformed to it. Like a bowl placed upside down to catch an unwanted creature in a house.

Concentrating on that image, he felt the hair on his arms stand on edge and electricity surge through him. It felt a little funny, and he twitched a little to push the strange sensation aside. He felt something click into place and blinked a few times, taking in a green, domed shield around the station behind his Zaheri.

"I guess I'm part of that fifty percent," he said with a grin as he pointed behind his Zaheri.

The other three turned around, and it seemed as though they relaxed a bit once they took in the shield's solid state.

Frost cocked his head to the side. "I have always wondered: why is his energy green?"

"That's a good point," Taesir said.

"How 'bout we worry about that some other time," Gaeor grumbled. Inclining his head toward the station, he added, "Let's get inside."

Frost fell into step with Alaster. "Are you certain that you can keep this shield up?"

"I think so," Alaster said. "It feels strong. I can't describe it." He shrugged a little. "Kind of like tying a knot? How you have to secure it tightly to make sure it doesn't come undone. That's kind of what it feels like."

Frost looked to the shield, his gaze flicking across it.

"Is ... that okay?"

Quickly looking back at the teen, Frost nodded and offered a small smile. "Quite so."

They fell into silence as they went, leaving Alaster to wonder what Frost had really been thinking.

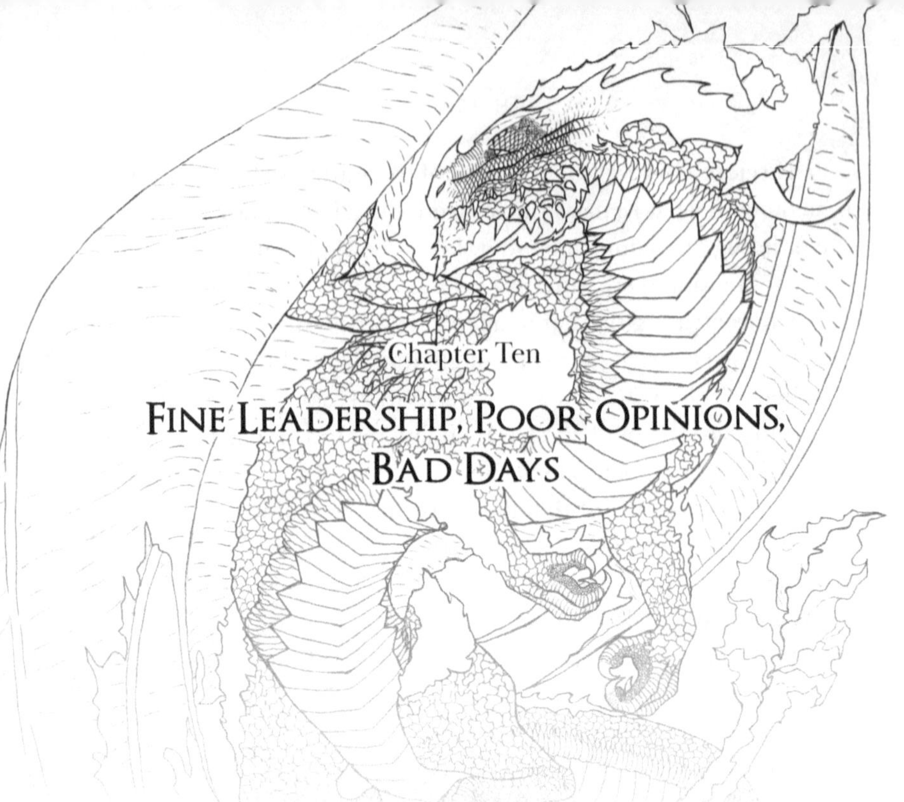

Chapter Ten

FINE LEADERSHIP, POOR OPINIONS, BAD DAYS

When they walked into the station, chaos surrounded them as people shuffled here and there. A large door was being sealed down the hall from where they stood.

With a furrowed brow, Gaeor asked, "What's going on?"

"Destination Alpha collapsed," Alaster muttered as he walked up to Dr. Davis.

"That must have been what caused the station to shift," Taesir said, her comment falling to the background as Alaster continued on his marching path.

"Sir?" the teen asked the expedition leader.

"Destination Alpha—"

"It's destroyed, I know. I saw it when we were outside."

The doctor nodded.

"Sir, how many—"

"Son, that isn't your problem."

Alaster swallowed back the bile that rose in his throat.

Dr. Davis gently placed his hand on Alaster's shoulder. "Don't take ownership of this, son. This isn't your responsibility."

"But ... this wouldn't be happening if—"

"You can't go blaming yourself for someone else's actions." A stern but soft look filled the doctor's bright eyes. "Especially when you've been acting so valiantly." He offered an encouraging smile. "I'm honored to have such a bright and brave young man at my station."

Alaster nodded a bit.

"We need to find Kedar and make sure he's okay." Taesir said.

"One of our personnel is with him. When we found him unconscious in the lounge, we called a doctor to look over him," Dr. Davis said.

Without another word, the Agerians walked the short distance to the lounge. The large door was finished being bolted, and Alaster stared at it in dismay before he followed his Zaheri.

Kedar was sitting up and trying to shove a woman's hands off him. "No, I'm fine. You don't need to worry."

"Sir, I don't think you understand what's happened to you," the woman said.

"It's okay, ma'am," Gaeor said as they entered the room. "We'll take it from here."

The woman looked at Gaeor then back at Kedar before she got up and left.

Kedar looked to them, holding his head in his hands. Seeing Taesir's injured leg, he jolted. "What happened?"

"I'm fine. Don't you dare worry about me," Taesir snapped as she came over and slapped her hand against his forehead.

"Ow," he whined with a wince.

"You've got a fever."

"And a pounding headache," Kedar nearly whimpered.

"I thought Agerians didn't get colds," Alaster said, flicking his gaze around at the others.

"He doesn't have a cold," Gaeor corrected. "His body's reacting to his shield breaking. It can manifest in all sorts of ways."

Gently pushing Taesir's hand away, Kedar asked through squinted eyes, "Did they get reinforcements?"

"If they did, it wasn't many," Gaeor said with a shrug.

"Any way we can find out if the portal activated?" Taesir asked.

Alaster straightened. "Actually, yeah, there is."

"There is?" Gaeor asked in bewilderment.

Nodding a bunch, the teen answered, "It turns out the portal creates some sort of radiation or ... something that's off the charts. There's a scientist here who was"—his eyes widened—"he paged me right before the attack hit!"

"You think it was about the portal activating?"

"What else could it be?" Taesir asked.

Frost's ears flattened, and his brow pinched. "That only serves to confuse me. Why would the portal open, only to provide no warriors?"

Closing his eyes and pinching the bridge of his nose, Kedar let out a long breath. "Okay, let's go—"

"No," Gaeor and Taesir said quickly.

Before Kedar could launch a rebuttal, Gaeor held his hand out. "You've gotta rest. You're not a Bulwark, so you're not used to having shields break on you."

"A Bulwark?" Alaster hushed in question to Frost.

"A shield expert. One of the specializations an Agerian Defender can obtain," the grovix responded.

Looking thoroughly unenthusiastic, Gaeor lumbered back on his heels and groaned, "I'll go with Alaster. And we'll talk to this scientist."

Kedar gave Taesir a look.

Before she could volunteer to go instead, Frost stood and announced, "Taesir should rest, as well. The Ferveos may have done more damage to your leg than you realize, and rest would be beneficial to you." He looked to Kedar. "I will go along with Gaeor and Alaster."

Carefully massaging the back of his neck, Kedar flinched at his gentle actions. "All right, fine. But let me know—"

"Of course we will," Gaeor said. "Now rest while you can."

Disappointment ghosted Kedar's expression before he flopped onto the couch, resting his head against the back and staring at the ceiling.

"C'mon," the older Agerian said, pushing Alaster out of the room.

The moment he entered the hallway, Alaster was met with his parents frantically looking about. They saw him and surged forward, calling in relief.

He was swept into his mother's arms quickly, and she hugged him as she said, "Thank God you're okay."

"Were you injured?" his father asked, gesturing at the dried blood across Alaster's face.

"Not badly. I'm fine. I healed already," Alaster said as quickly as possible in an attempt to calm their fears.

"You ... you healed already?" his mother asked in wonder as she pulled back from the embrace. "How?"

Stepping out of the lounge, Gaeor answered, "It's part of being a hybrid. We heal a whole lot faster than humans do."

"Rapid cellular regeneration?" Alaster's father whispered, fascination playing on his features.

Alaster shrugged and nodded. "Basically. It's why I can grow wings—"

"You can grow wings?" his father nearly shouted.

Shying away a bit, Alaster winced and rubbed the back of his head. "Uh, yeah ... I just haven't used them yet today. Well, I mean, I have, just not ..."

Though his father gained a reprimanding look, he let it go with a short breath. "Dr. McKay is looking for you. Something about the energy spike."

"Oh good, we were just going to go find him." He offered his dad a small smile. "Thanks, Da."

As he turned to walk off with Gaeor and Frost, his father caught him and pulled him into a tight embrace. "You know we love you," Keegan said quietly.

Gripping at his father, Alaster nodded. "Yeah, Da, I know."

And for the first time, those dog tags hanging around his neck didn't feel so heavy.

Once Kedar was sure that the others had left, he slowly sat up, resting his arms against his thighs.

He was the Team Leader. That meant he shouldn't be needing any rest at that moment, right? Wasn't he failing by being so useless? He couldn't even defend this station appropriately; how was he going to keep Alaster safe?

Making a shield that size had been stupid. He shouldn't have done it. Of course it hadn't been strong enough. He was a Paragon, for Elders' sake, not some equipped Bulwark. What had he been thinking?

And now he sat there, knowing that if he stood, he'd probably fall back down. His equilibrium was off, and he could feel the floor rock and sway under him. It made his stomach flip if he wasn't careful.

His gaze strayed toward Taesir's mostly healed leg.

Elders curse him.

One reckless action. One thoughtless attempt to be something he wasn't.

He had gotten one of his own team members hurt. And it'd been painfully obvious that Alaster had taken some hits. There was too much dried blood on the teenager's face to assume otherwise.

All these years, he'd seriously questioned his posting as the Team Leader. Gaeor was far more suited. He was wiser and had more experience in battle. Sure, he was a Sniper, but he was plenty powerful in his own right.

Gaeor never would have made such a stupid choice. Making a shield that size? How stupid could he be?

There had to be some way to verbalize his apology to Taesir. But all of them felt so worthless. Felt so small compared to the enormity of his misstep.

After Elders only knew how many silent moments had passed, he finally managed to croak out, "I'm sorry."

Out of his peripheral vision, he saw her whip her attention to him, sitting up straighter. "What?"

Blinking a few times, he nearly rolled his eyes at himself. "If I hadn't been so foolish and tried to defend from that Ferveos' attack, I wouldn't've passed out and left you three on your own." An angry sigh rippled from him. "I should've been there, and I—"

"Kedar, it's my fault," she shook out.

He moved his head as gingerly as he could, so as to not induce vertigo, and looked at her with puzzlement. "How is it your fau—"

"I missed the two Ferveos that attacked!" She pointed toward the window. "The Ferveos are my responsibility to take out, and I failed! If I'd just—"

"Tae, wait a second, this isn't your fault."

"Of course it is!" Tears brimmed her eyes, and she dropped her gaze in embarrassment. "That Ferveos was only able to attack because I missed it. And it ... it hurt you ..."

Forgetting about his wobbliness, Kedar stumbled over to her and snatched her into an embrace. She collapsed into him, shuddering out small cries as she held him tight.

"It's okay. It's not your fault," he hushed.

Burying her face into his shoulder, she whispered, "It's not yours, either."

He let out a sad chuckle. "We both know that's not true."

Landing a hard smack against his arm, she sat back and scowled at him. "If it's not my fault, then it's not yours."

"Tae," he said wearily.

She shrugged exaggeratedly. "What else were any of us supposed to do, Kedar? We don't have a Bulwark on the team. And we didn't have anywhere else to go to set up proper defense. We couldn't even run! What other options did you have?"

Though he wore a frown, he raised his brow a bit. "Okay, that's fair."

Tentatively, she reached out and grazed her fingers through his hair. His shoulders deflated at the touch, and he closed his eyes, letting out a beleaguered sigh.

"Your fever's still pretty high," she whispered.

"Yeah," he mumbled absently, slumping a bit.

Gently pushing him back to sit on the floor, she rose. "I'm pretty sure I packed some of the healing tea from Agerius."

"Oh, c'mon, really?" he whined. "That stuff is so gross."

"Yeah, well, too bad." She chuckled as she helped him up and got him to sit back on the couch. "It'll help you heal, and that's what you need right now, Team Leader."

Letting out a sad chuckle, he gave her a doubtful look. "You still wanna call me that after today?"

"Are you kidding?" she asked. Thumbing over her shoulder, she gave him a look that said, 'c'mon, really?.' "Gaeor would've gotten us killed years ago, and Frost is great, but he wouldn't've been able to do half the stuff you've done in this post."

He gained a small smile. "Something tells me that's all lies."

"Wow, now I know you're not feeling good."

She made it to the door when he said, "Tae." When she turned to face him, he gave her a warm smile. "Thank you."

Unable to stop herself, she smiled back at him. "Anytime."

Alaster, Gaeor, and Frost stepped into the room where Dr. McKay's workspace was.

The scientist in question looked relieved at their arrival and said, "Okay, good, you're here." He hurriedly walked over to his workstation.

"Was there another simultaneous energy surge?" Alaster asked.

"There was, actually. Just before the station was attacked and that gold shield fell, that same signature showed up again. All seven points were activated at the same precise time. It's fascinating, really. Whatever this thing is, it's powerful. Strong enough to connect to multiple points on the globe at the same time and using huge amounts of power to do so. It's just astounding! If we could study it, who knows what we'd be able to learn and make from it?" the scientist rambled.

Nodding, Alaster said, "Was there anything different from this time compared to the first one?"

"Uh ..." Dr. McKay said as he began to tinker around on his computer. "Well, actually"—he squinted at the screen—"now that you mention it, something strange did seem to happen."

"What?" Gaeor asked, turning away from the various equipment in the room.

"Well, it seems like there was a massive spike in energy the second time. It took a minute, but ... yes, there's a definite spike."

Alaster looked to Frost. "What could've caused that?"

Arms crossed and shoulders hunched, Gaeor's brow slowly pulled together, and he started to tap his foot against the floor.

Alaster squinted at him. Was that his thinking expression?

Meanwhile, Frost's ears swiveled on his head, and he hushed, "It sounds as if something may have interrupted Cregorous' second strike."

"What?" Alaster asked.

Ignoring the teen, Frost stepped up to Dr. McKay. "What transpired once the massive spike occurred?"

Dr. McKay shrugged and gave Frost a wide-eyed stare. "Nothing. It just snapped off, like the power cut off."

Frost slowly swung his gaze to Gaeor,

Alaster looked between them and asked, "Guys?"

"Are you the only person tracking this?" Gaeor asked.

Stilling in his actions, Dr. McKay timidly looked to the Zaheri and shook out, "Um ... are you about to kill me?"

"What? No," Gaeor said with a tone of annoyance as his face screwed in confusion. "In case we have other questions, I want to know who to talk to."

"It sounded like you were threatening me."

"He wasn't threatening you," Alaster quickly said.

"You'd know if I was threatening you," Gaeor grumbled.

Though he still looked a little scared, Dr. McKay said, "Look, all I can tell you is that the first time, there was a large amount of energy being transmitted to all of the points. The second time, it started with the same level of output, but then a massive spike happened of a different radiation—"

"Wait—so it was different radiation?" Alaster cut in.

Dr. McKay let out a sigh. "Yes, okay? It was a different signature of whatever this is. Radiation or frequency or ... whatever it is."

"You don't know?"

"I'm trying to," the doctor said with a raised brow, "but it's unlike anything I've ever seen before. And, while I am a genius, and am the foremost expert here, I'm not confident that I know what this is, or even how to label it."

Looking to his Zaheri, Alaster asked, "What could do that?"

"Something very powerful," Gaeor mused.

"Like the First Human-Born?"

"Perhaps, but we should not leap to any conclusions," Frost warned.

"Frost is right. Until we know for sure, we shouldn't assume anything," the hybrid said with a nod toward Frost.

"But the First Human-Born might have done it?"

Shaking his head, Gaeor said, "Even if the First Human-Born did push Cregorous' army back from here to Tilion, that doesn't mean we're out of danger. In fact, it'll probably just make Cregorous that much more likely to push back."

"But that means that the First Human-Born is strong enough to stop him, right?"

Gaeor shifted his weight and reluctantly said, "So we've been told."

Frost gave him an unreadable stare. Returning his gaze to Alaster, he said, "Alone? No, they are not likely to be strong enough."

"What? But I thought—"

"There are seven of you, Alaster." The grovix's gaze was heavy. "It does not stand to reason that the Elders would equip seven, if they only required one."

That was fair.

Blinking a few times, Alaster looked between his Zaheri. "Wait a second. If they didn't get any reinforcements, and we quelled whatever remained from the first attack—"

"Out with it, Alaster," Gaeor said curtly.

"We should take this chance to get the humans off the base and to safety."

"And send them where?" Frost asked. "We have discussed this; there is nowhere safe on this continent."

"You said that Cregorous was targeting this location," Alaster said, gesturing to Frost. "That means any other location on the continent is safer than here."

Gaeor looked to the ceiling and eased himself back a bit with a sigh. "Okay, assuming that's correct, what do you propose? It's not like it would be easy to get all of these people out of here. And if Cregorous is a Sensor, then he'd just move his target to wherever—"

"I think we should stay here."

Pinching his brow, Frost's ears grew a little more erect. "To keep his attention focused on this station?"

"Right. It'll mean that we can get innocent people out of danger."

"That's ... actually a good point," Gaeor said carefully, eyeing Frost.

Frost swiftly shook his head. "That is not our call to make. It would be Kedar's."

"So ...?" Alaster asked.

"We let Kedar rest. At least for a little while."

"And in the meantime?"

While giving Frost a sideways look, Gaeor said, "We should probably get something to eat to keep our stamina up." He nodded toward the door. "I'll go check on Kedar and Taesir. Why don't you two head to the galley and get something together?"

Alaster had to admit that food sounded positively excellent at that moment. The amount of calories he was bound to have burned so far that day were likely staggering.

In the wake of the two fights he'd been in, though, Alaster felt guilty. Kedar and Taesir were both injured, so going to make a meal felt like he was diminishing their current situation.

So much had happened in an alarmingly short amount of time that it made his head spin if he really sat down to think about it. Which, if he went to go eat something, he'd likely have nothing but time to sit and mull it all over.

As if reading his mind, Frost smiled at him and said, "Kedar and Taesir will not need long to rest. They will be capable of joining us soon enough. Come along, Alaster."

"Okay, yeah," Alaster said with a small nod of his head.

Maybe Frost would be able to help distract him from the potential silence of the galley, and the loudness of Alaster's thoughts.

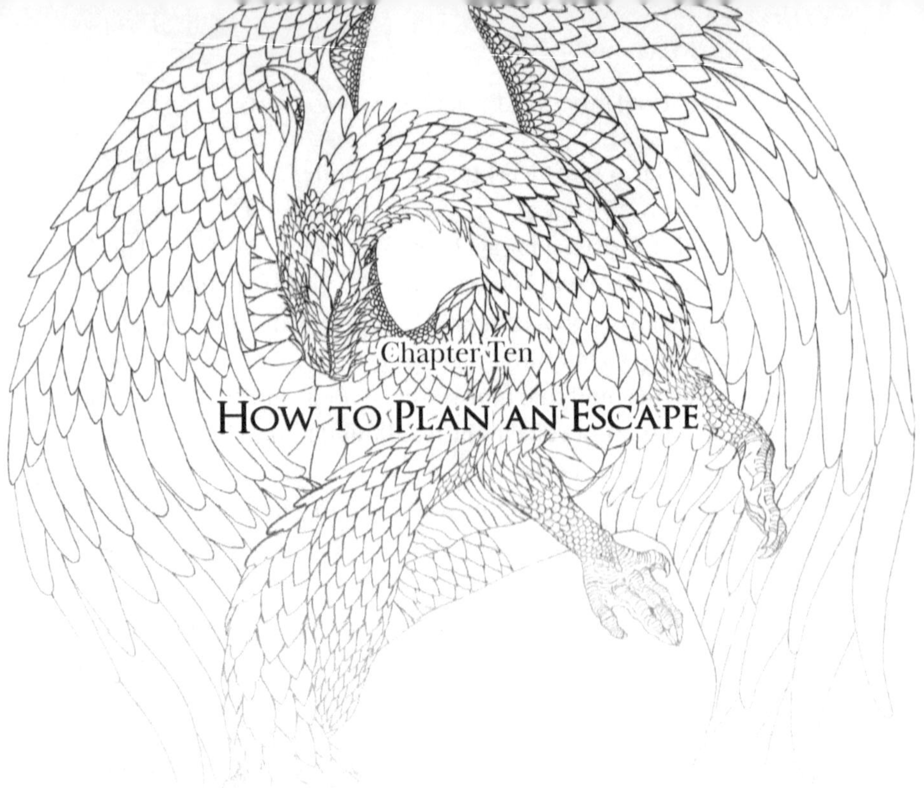

Chapter Ten

HOW TO PLAN AN ESCAPE

Alaster and Frost ate in silence, which only provided time for the teen with his thoughts about ... everything.

His Zaheri needed to recover from their injuries. But how long could they afford to sit idly by? How long would it be until the next wave hit? Would they be capable of holding off another attack?

He wanted to believe the five of them could. Glancing at Frost, though, he wondered if they really had that chance. While Frost did look untouched, there was dried blood on his snout, and some splattered blood across his frame. When he had run off with his Zaheri earlier that day, Alaster had no idea it would amount to this much trouble.

He wished he knew more about Tilion and Agerius. The world seemed like a floating abyss in his mind. Whether or not he had ever intended to go there was something he had debated about recently. With his parents pushing for him to continue his schooling, he hadn't been sure what to do.

Now, as he sat there, across from an undisguised grovix, he knew that it didn't matter what his parents said. He was going to continue on this path and be a Human-Born.

It was a strange thing—deciding to abandon the life he had known. But it was also a little freeing. There was comfort found in it, like he was finally getting in line with the path he was meant to walk along.

The only thing was he had no idea how his parents would react. His father had given him a blessing of sorts, even though it was unspoken. But he had no idea how his mother was going to respond.

As he thought through his own predicament, his mind circled back to the other Human-Borns. Despite the fact that he'd mentioned the First Human-Born several times throughout the day, he hadn't stopped to really think through who they were. What they meant for Tilion. For Earth. For him.

"Hey, Frost?" he asked, slowly looking to his Zaheri.

The grovix was just finishing his food and lifted his gaze to the teen. "Yes?"

"You mentioned that there was a prophecy about us Human-Borns."

"Ah, I did promise that I would go into further detail."

"I don't need to know the whole thing. I don't see the value in that."

Quirking his head to the side, the Zaheri asked, "Then, why have you brought it to the conversation?"

"I just want to know. You said something about me being..." He searched his mind for the word. It was all jumbled with the other information from the day, and he couldn't recall what Frost had said.

"Requisite. Your title."

"Right, well ... what are the others' titles?"

Frost gave him a small smile. "The First has the title of the Raidin. Then the Protector, Warrior, Healer, Shifter, Scholar and, lastly, you, the Requisite."

He squinted at Frost. "What's with the First's title?"

"It is an ancient title, one I am certain has been around for many millennia. Its meaning is 'the Elders Warrior.'"

Alaster's gaze fell to the table, and he fidgeted a little with his fingers. "Is that why you all've placed so much importance on the First Human-Born? Because they have some ancient title?"

The grovix's ears flattened, and he gained a sorrowful look. "Alaster, it does not equate that we do not value you equally."

Shaking his hands to dismiss Frost's concerns, the teen chuckled a bit. "No, it's not that. It ..." He deflated and leaned against the table. "It just seems like a lot, y'know? To place the hope of a nation on one kid's shoulders."

"That could be a fair assessment." His ears perked as he straightened. "However, as I stated previously, you are Seven for a distinct reason."

"Well, on that note"—Alaster sat up and gave Frost a pointed stare—"who gave this prophecy? You mentioned 'Elders.'"

Frost nodded once. "Yes, terribly ancient and powerful dragons. They are three and have provided the law from which Agerius governs."

"So ... a deity?"

Chewing his thoughts for a brief moment, Frost hummed. "Not from a human's perspective."

"What makes them not a deity?"

The grovix raised his brow and gave Alaster a smile. "They are not as your God. We do not pray to them, nor do we seek them out for absolution or salvation from some eternal damnation. The damnation humanity seems to wrap itself in is not something we Agerians suffer. However, we know they have a realm in which they reside. It is our hope that we will find ourselves there upon our deaths."

"Your hope, but ... you have no assurance."

An awkward chuckle escaped Frost. "I cannot explain it. I do not worry of it. I suppose assurance is an appropriate way to describe what I feel when I think on my eventual death. But I cannot take out a scroll and point to some passage or scripture that will provide proof of that assurance."

"So ... these three ancient dragons hold incredible power and, apparently, foresight to be able to prophecy Human-Borns that ... obviously came true," he muttered to himself. "But you don't question why they are, or how they are?"

Frost narrowed his eyes. "You do not question your Creator."

"So, they did create Tilion."

"I cannot say. Though something in my heart says they did not. Perhaps they serve the one who did."

Pursing his lips, Alaster nodded absently. "So, they're sort of like angels."

"Pardon?"

Shaking his head again, Alaster answered, "Nothing. Just trying to get my head around things." He lifted his gaze to look at Frost. "Why do you think there needs to be six other Human-Borns if the first of us is strong enough to stop Cregorous?"

Frost shook his head, his ears flapping slightly. "I do not know. The Elders' prophecy did not state a reason. Perhaps they simply rely on our faith to guide our actions, not absolute knowledge."

"Why? If they know what's going to happen and how things need to happen, why not just tell us all what's going on?"

Frost chuckled. "There must be blind faith sometimes, Alaster. If we were to know everything that were to happen and how it should be accomplished, then how could it ever be that anything of greatness could come to pass? If Cregorous were to have known the path he had taken would lead to this destruction, he would never have turned upon it."

"Exactly. So, why not keep danger from happening?"

A glint filled Frost's eyes as he said, "If you wished for pure devotion from another, would you force them to only know that devotion? Or would you prefer they chose it on their own? Would it not be stronger and that much more pure when it came from their action rather than your own?"

"Someone paid attention when I read *Paradise Lost* to him," Alaster said with a knowing grin. He remembered some talk about a Council and, apparently, Frost was connected to it. He met the grovix's gaze again and said, "Gaeor said something about you being a High Council member?"

With a single nod, Frost answered, "Indeed, I am, and have been for many years."

"So, what made you join the Zeta Team?"

"Well, for one, I was instructed to do so by the Council Leader."

"You didn't choose this."

"My boy, I don't believe any of us chose this. Sometimes, greatness isn't the thing chosen. Sometimes, it does the choosing."

An hour and a brief shower later, Alaster joined the rest of the team in the lounge. The Zaheri all had food stacked on their plates as they ate a hearty meal. It relieved Alaster to see Kedar much more alert and not wincing anymore, though the Team Leader admitted that his ribs felt sore whenever he moved.

An empty mug sat nearby. It smelled of herbs and leaves that Alaster didn't recognize, and it smelled bitter.

As the teen inspected the mug and sniffed at the remaining tea leaves, Kedar gestured to it and said, "It's a blend of Agerian tea and leaves. It helps bolster our healing abilities, but it tastes pretty rancid."

Setting the mug down on the table, Alaster glanced to Taesir. "You thought you might need it here?"

Taesir gestured to Gaeor. "Hey, he smuggled in *guns*."

"Fair play," Alaster said with a small chuckle.

"I am glad to see you well again, Kedar," Frost said.

"I'm glad to be feeling well," the Team Leader answered as he met Frost's gaze. "Gaeor said you three talked about some plan Alaster had while we were resting."

"Only briefly. The discussion needed your ear and must be made by you."

Kedar looked to Alaster. "Well? What're you thinking?"

Shuffling his weight a bit, Alaster said, "I know you were against the idea of all of us running somewhere else because there isn't any-where else for us to go."

His shoulders falling, Kedar let out a sigh. "Alaster, don't dance around the point. What're you thinking?"

"Okay," the teen said a little more assuredly. "We know that there's a high chance Cregorous is targeting this station, and only this station."

"Right," Taesir said with a nod.

"And we've taken care of the remaining fighters from the first wave."

"You're sure?" Kedar asked with a look of uncertainty.

"Yeah," Gaeor said with a nod as he eased back in his seat. "Tae took out the Ferveos that had been hiding, and what we saw was far too few to be anything but stragglers from the first attack."

Scratching his forehead, Kedar asked, "Golden. But, why did they attack if they weren't getting reinforcements?"

Frost sat and answered, "Truthfully, I believe they expected to. The portal activated again just a moment before your shield was attacked."

The Team Leader nodded toward Gaeor. "Yeah, Gaeor told me that there was another massive activation, likely Cregorous sending a second wave. And that something stopped it. But wait—you think the Ferveos could sense the portal's activation?"

"It stands to reason they could. Or perhaps Cregorous sent a telepathic communication. Or perhaps the bratak'ra or werewolves heard the portal. Or perhaps the Caligans felt a tug from the portal as a sign that Cregorous had reconnected our worlds. We cannot be certain. But it appears as though they knew the portal had connected to Earth."

Kedar thought through the situation for a moment before he flicked his eyes to Alaster. "Have you felt anything attacking your shield? Even just a little?"

Shaking his head, the teen answered, "I think it's just the wind from time to time. Feels like when I'm wearing a jacket and it sort of buffers against the fabric."

"Yeah, that's the wind," Kedar said with a few nods. "An attack would feel more deliberate, sharp, and painful."

"Noted," Alaster said with a nod.

"So, assuming that we don't have any enemy fighters out there right now, what are you thinking?"

Looking uneasy, Alaster shrugged. "I'm thinking we should get innocent lives out of here."

"And send them where?" Taesir asked.

"McMurdo. It's about thirty minutes from here by ski-doo. They'll be safe there."

"And we stay here," Kedar said.

Alaster nodded.

Letting out a smooth breath, the Team Leader nodded. "It's not a bad idea. It'll ensure there won't be any casualties whenever we get hit again."

"You think we will?"

"Yeah. Cregorous is maintaining control over the portal. He knows that if he doesn't succeed in striking at you all now, he'll never have it this easy again."

"How do you know that?"

Frost looked to the teen. "Because if, by some miracle, Cregorous was dissuaded from hitting the Human-Borns and left now, we would undoubtedly set up great defenses at the portal. Which would make a future attempt of this magnitude much more difficult for him."

Alaster looked to Kedar. "So, what do you think?"

"Removing the possibility of casualties is the ideal situation. It'll mean we won't have to divide attention, which is invaluable when we're so outnumbered," Kedar said. He looked to his team members. "What about everyone else? Thoughts?"

Taesir, Frost, and Gaeor all shared glances before Frost looked to Kedar. "It is the soundest choice. Our primary focus must be on Alaster's safety. Secondary should be the safety of the humans who have no means of protecting themselves against Caligan incursion."

"It sounds like the safest plan," Gaeor said.

"It does, but ..." Taesir looked to Alaster. "What are you going to tell your parents?"

Ah, the question of the hour.

It was all Alaster could think about throughout the last hour. And still, he hadn't come to a good answer.

Hopefully, he'd be able to find the right words.

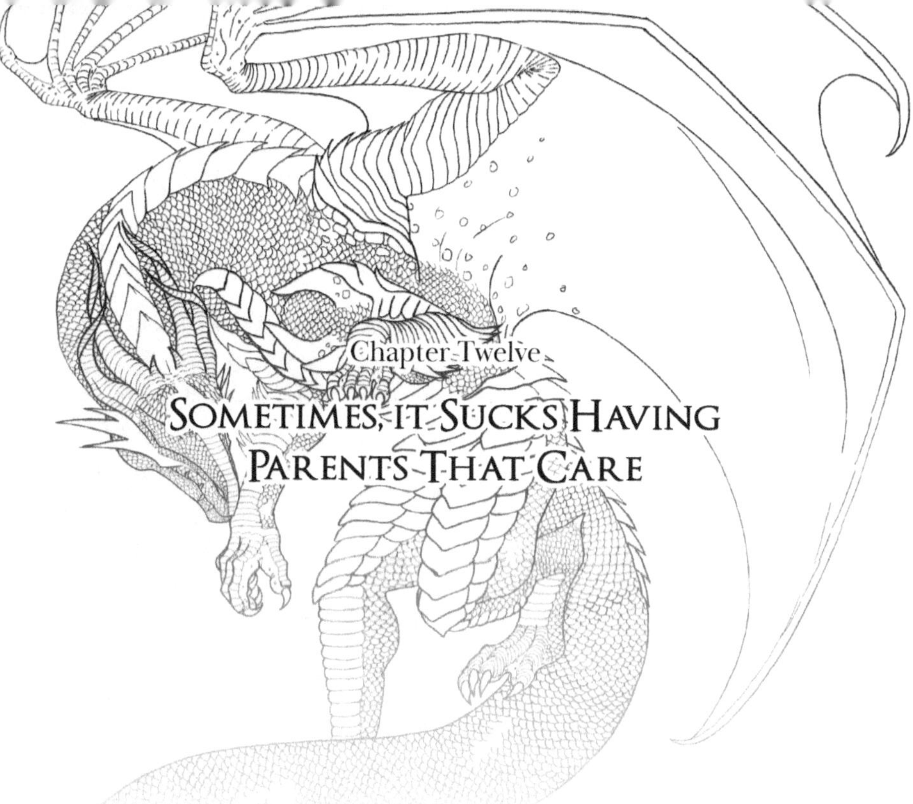

Chapter Twelve

Sometimes, it Sucks Having Parents That Care

As they made their way toward the control tower to find a way to page Dr. Davis and inform him of their intended plans, they saw the man in question step out of one of the labs.

"Dr. Davis!" Kedar called.

The expedition leader turned toward them and walked to meet them down the hall.

"We think it's time to reevaluate our plans."

"I'm all ears," Dr. Davis said with an expectant look on his face.

"We think it would be best for you and the other personnel to leave the station and head to McMurdo until this is over."

Looking warily at Kedar, Dr. Davis said, "I thought you said that was nearly impossible because of your inability to protect us as we traveled."

"It was ... when there were enemy fighters outside. But we've eradicated the opposition, which means the path to McMurdo should be clear."

"Should be."

Shaking his head, Frost answered, "There is no reason the enemy must focus their attention upon any other station on this continent. It is quite obvious that they have targeted this location."

"If we stay, they'll continue to focus here and ignore everything else," Kedar said.

The older man looked doubtful before he moved his attention to Alaster. "Have you told your parents about this, young man?"

With a shake of his head, Alaster said, "No, I was just on my way to do that."

"Then I suggest you wait to see what his parents say." He turned to leave before looking over his shoulder at them and added, "If Doctors O'Brien give Alaster the okay to stay here with you—because that's what I'm assuming you would do—then I will inform the rest of the staff."

The team watched him leave before Gaeor asked the teen, "You want us to go with you?"

Taking a small breath, Alaster said, "No. I need to do this on my own."

Kedar nodded. "Okay. We'll just head back to the lounge then. Come get us when your parents give you an answer."

It was a short walk to his parents' lab, and the whole way was filled with anxiety and tension in Alaster's chest. When he reached the door, he stopped and thought about what he might say. He was, after all, asking them to leave him behind while he fought monsters from another world.

After he had just patched things up with his father, it seemed like he wasn't being fair. He had only just explained things to them, and they probably still didn't understand. He didn't even understand everything fully yet. It wasn't something he could just wrap his head around in a few hours. And that's all it had been—a few hours.

Was this how Cam had felt when he'd left for his deployment?

This was probably so similar to his parents, and yet so different. With Cam, they hadn't been squarely in the middle of the battlefield. And Alaster didn't want them to get hurt.

Because he bounced back where they might not. He knew the punches he'd taken from the Caligan earlier were horribly rough and likely would have torn a human apart. But him?

A few deep gouges, sure, but they'd healed within a half hour.

The dried blood had been his only reminder when he'd grabbed his quick shower earlier.

He'd already lost Cam. He couldn't lose his parents, too. Not when there was something that could be done about it. Not when he could keep them safe. Even if keeping them from harm meant he ran into danger.

It wasn't a scenario he liked. He would have loved nothing more than to not have to go out there and risk getting hurt again. But he had to. If he wanted his family to be safe, if he wanted his Zaheri to survive, he had to take that chance.

Rapping on the door a few times, he pushed it open and walked into the lab.

Dr. McKay was there, excitedly talking about the portal, it seemed. "... It's absolutely amazing. Whatever or whoever is producing this energy is off the charts. And if it is a whoever, they could probably power an entire city, just by themselves!"

His parents turned to him upon his arrival, and his mother again enveloped him into a hug. He returned it and asked, "How're you holding up, Mum?"

She laughed a little against him and pulled back. "I'm grand, Alaster."

"That feels like a lie."

"Now, now, your mum never lies," his father said, slapping his hand on Alaster's shoulder. He gave his son a knowing look. "What is it?"

"Has something happened?" his mother asked.

"Kind of," Alaster admitted with a frown. "We took out the last of the opposition when we went out there earlier, so things are clear. Which means we have an opportunity to do something we couldn't before."

His parents shared a glance before his father said, "Which is?"

"Send all of the scientists and personnel to McMurdo for safety until this whole thing blows over."

"What?" his mother asked.

"It's the only thing we can do to make sure no one else gets hurt."

His father nodded slowly. "All right. So then, when will everyone else be leaving?"

There was a pause as Alaster looked at his parents before he said, "You guys need to leave, too."

Holding his hand out, his father said sternly, "All right, look, I can step aside and let you be who you need to be—I don't like it, but I can do that—but I'm not going to run away with the knowledge that you'll be staying here."

"You can't ask us to leave you. What if something happens and you need help?" his mother asked.

"Okay, on the flip side of that, what if something happens and *you* need help? What if you get hurt? What if you die?" Alaster asked.

His parents looked between one another before his father looked back at him. "We haven't gotten hurt yet."

"*Yet*," Alaster said, trying to do everything in his power to sound confident and sure. "All it would take is one more strike from a Ferveos and *boom!* this wing is gone, too."

"So, you expect us to just leave, knowing full well that you might get hurt?"

"Yes—no—it's just ..." the teenager trailed off and looked toward the ground. "I don't expect anything except your love and understanding." He moved his gaze back to his parents and continued, "I know that this is a lot to ask. I know I'm telling you to do something you don't want to do. I don't want to do it, either. I know that if I were in your situation, I wouldn't want to leave. But I can handle this; you can't."

As his father opened his mouth to say something, Alaster suddenly said, "Remember how you saw that I got hurt last time? The evidence of it, I mean. Because I didn't have any cuts on me anymore?"

Slowly, his parents shrank back and shared uneasy glances.

"I heal so much faster than a normal human. The hits I took..." He grimaced. "I know you don't want to hear this. I know you don't want to imagine it. But ..." Gritting his teeth, he tried again, "The hits I took, I healed from in less than a half hour." He gave his father a grave look. "They would have killed you."

Uttering that knowledge made him want to cry. He felt the pinching of his nose and the stinging of his eyes. Sucking back a steadying breath, Alaster reined in the pain of reality that he had to take hits his parents couldn't. Because if he didn't ... if he wasn't the shield for them, then they would die.

And he couldn't lose them.

His mother stepped forward and said, "Alaster, it's hard for me, as your mother, to just stand here and let you do this."

He deflated a little. "I know, Mum. I do. If I could change this, I would. But I can't. What do you want me to do? I can't do two things at once. I'm not strong enough to keep this shield up and fight off the enemy warriors. One of them needs to give, and I can't let my Zaheri go out there on their own."

His father clenched his jaw before he said, "I understand where you're coming from, Alaster. But ... we can't ..."

"I know, Da," Alaster said. "I know that you can't lose me. And that's why I'm asking you to leave. Because I can't lose *you*. I already lost my brother. I can't lose my parents, too."

Everyone fell into a small quiet for a few seconds. It was then that Doctor McKay cleared his throat. They turned to look at him.

"If I could say something," he said.

Alaster's parents nodded.

"I think your son is right."

"That's just it," his father said, "we know he is."

"We do?" his mother asked, a shocked expression on her face.

Keegan let out a resigned sigh. "We can't expect him to let us stay. After all, we are only human."

Her gaze flicked between her husband and her son. "I don't want to leave him behind."

Alaster offered a small smile and said, "I won't be gone long, Mum. I'll reach you at McMurdo once this is all over. I'll be fine."

"Oh, honey," his mother said as she walked forward and enveloped him into a hug. Her voice was a little watery, and her eyes were holding tears. "You have to promise me you'll be all right."

"I will, Mum," Alaster slightly choked out.

He looked up at his father and saw that his father's eyes held a sheen of tears. It took him a moment before he came over and wrapped both his wife and son in a hug.

If this was how the day would end, Alaster was glad for it. Because after all of the hardships they had endured, at least, in the end of it all, they had come to an understanding.

And for the first time in a long time, he felt that his parents loved and cared for him. There'd never been a doubt of the knowledge that his parents loved him, but he hadn't *felt* their love.

And that was worth more than anything else in the world.

It was strange to walk through the station now that it was empty. All the humans had left ten minutes prior. Alaster had been grateful that, aside from some quick hugs from his parents, they had bravely helped usher others to ski-doos or onto transport vehicles.

It felt like the dead of night during the winter months, when sleeping was far easier to come by with the all-midnight season. When people struggled to stay awake in the cold, dark days. "Nighttime," or rather bedtime, was always oddly quiet. Alaster had liked it plenty, but there was no denying that this quiet was strange and off-putting.

There was a bizarre stillness in the hallway that Alaster wasn't at all used to. With all the people around during the day season, it was always noisy in some regard. But now that they were literally the only five living creatures in the station, there was something incredibly wrong being there in the silence.

They walked down the hall to the galley. Their footfalls were almost soundless but, despite their best efforts, they still echoed. Once there, they all rustled up some tea and snacks. Kedar insisted that keeping their stamina levels up with food was a good idea.

"I'm glad that it worked out this way," Alaster said as they all sat at one of the tables. "I feel a lot better knowing my parents aren't in harm's way anymore." He cradled his mug and looked to Kedar. "What sort of training might I be able to do while we wait?"

"I don't think that's a good idea," Kedar said. "We all need to conserve our strength."

"You think it's going to be that bad?"

Raising his brow a little, Gaeor answered, "If it's true that the First Human-Born stopped Cregorous' second wave from coming, he's probably gonna be rampaging like a blinded Scout. He's liable to throw his whole army at anything Agerian."

"So, we're in for a *really* bad fight," Alaster said as he shrank back.

He was even more grateful they'd gone this route and afforded safety for the humans. "What are battles like? Normally, I mean."

Frost quirked brow. "Battles are few, typically."

"Really?"

"We call them raids. Caligans show up and literally steal things from us," Taesir clarified. "All sorts of different things. Sometimes they make off with cattle; sometimes they make off with people. It's ... ghastly, normally."

"And whenever we push them back out of Agerius, that's when things usually get rough," Kedar said. "Caligans are ruthless. The fights on Tilion were always ones that ended in casualties on both sides."

"That's awful," Alaster said in dismay.

"That's war."

Frost let out a sigh and said, "It is a sad reality. There is only hope that one day it will end."

"Yeah, but as an Elemental, you at least have some idea of what things were like before the war," Gaeor said as he shoved more food into his mouth.

"Why would he know that?" Alaster asked.

"I have faint memories, blurred and murky as they are," Frost said. "After all, two thousand years is quite a passage of time."

Holding out his hand, Alaster said, "Whoa, whoa, wait a second. *Two thousand years?* How old are you guys?"

With a chuckle, Kedar asked, "How old do you think we are?"

"Um ..." Alaster looked around at them. After a few seconds, he answered, "Maybe in your thirties?"

"Oh, Elders," Taesir scoffed. "Do we really look that childish?"

"*Childish?*" Alaster asked. "What do you mean? Being in your thirties is like being a third of the way through your life."

"Maybe for a human," Kedar said.

Furrowing his brow, Alaster asked, "So then, how old are you? I mean, you couldn't possibly be over one hundred."

Kedar grimaced. "I always forget how fragile humans are."

"It's a pity," Gaeor said, "to only live a hundred years."

"Only?" Alaster choked out in a surprised scoff.

Looking at the others, Taesir said, "I'm the youngest. I'm a little over two hundred. Kedar is a little over three hundred, and Gaeor is the oldest."

Throwing Gaeor a shocked look, the teenager asked, "Wait—you're ... you're older than ...?"

"I hit eight hundred last year," Gaeor said begrudgingly.

"He is not the eldest," Frost said.

"Well, of course not, not in comparison to you," Taesir said.

"How old are you, then?" Alaster asked the grovix.

"I remember the dawn of Tilion, which was many thousands of years ago," Frost said.

"So ... how old are you?"

"I am too old to worry over how old I am."

They were quiet for a few seconds before Alaster pointed at Frost. "Do all Council Members speak like this?"

Gaeor snorted while Kedar and Taesir laughed.

Frost glared and snapped his mouth shut.

A flash of red filled Alaster's cheeks, and he quickly said, "I don't mean it like—" He gave Gaeor a cross look. "Don't make me seem like a jerk!"

Waving his hand, Gaeor said, "No, no, it's okay. It's something Frost used to get picked on a lot for."

"By whom?"

"Us," Kedar said as he pointed between himself and Gaeor, wearing a sheepish grin.

"Yes, Taesir is the only one willing to treat me like an intelligent individual and not a common Warrior grovix," Frost said.

"After today, that might change," Taesir said. "Not my respect for you, but you are quite an impressive fighter."

"As I once was meant to be, perhaps," Frost mused. "And to answer your question, yes, most of the Council Members prefer proper speech to common vernacular."

Alaster looked around at them for a few seconds before he said, "I'm going to ask something that might seem insensitive, but I don't mean it that way."

Frost nodded.

"Is it just because you're all older?"

"That is not insensitive," Frost said. "Age is worthy of respect and can provide wisdom. And I could not say for sure on our preference; merely that we do speak in a manner that we deem, I think, reflects our status."

By now, they had all finished their tea and snacks.

Kedar leaned back, stretching a little as he did. "Regardless, it does set them apart from us common Defenders."

A smile came to Frost's face. "It was quite a shock for me when you called me down as one of the members of this team. Although, I do believe I handled it better than Blaze."

"Another grovix?" Alaster asked.

Nodding, Taesir said, "Blaze is the only other grovix Council Member. She's not known for being particularly warm, though."

"I believe she is misunderstood," Frost said.

"She's a member of the Alpha Team," Gaeor said.

His Zaheri began to talk about other things as Alaster sat back and let his thoughts override his hearing.

There was so much about his Zaheri he didn't know. So much he didn't know about their world and their nation. It excited him to know that he was at the beginning of the road that would teach him more. What might the world of Tilion be like? What might be waiting for him there?

His mind spiraled back to the other Human-Borns. A quiet prayer filtered through his thoughts. One that asked for protection and safety for their loved ones. For understanding from their families, as he'd been blessed enough to receive. That their Zaheri would be safe as they worked to protect them. That they wouldn't feel alone.

The last one hit his heart like a dagger.

None of them should feel alone after today. He hoped the other Zaheri had informed the Human-Borns of the fact that there were seven of them. While he hadn't struggled with his singularity, possibly because he was so used to being viewed as the strange boy and had often found it difficult to find friends his own age, he could appreciate that others might have been yearning for connection. For someone to understand them.

Hopefully, they could all meet soon.

The sound of scooting chairs pulled Alaster out of his thoughts as Kedar said, "Let's move to somewhere accessible so we're ready and can move quickly."

Following his Zaheri's lead, Alaster left the galley with them as they headed toward the Destination Zulu entrance.

And now they would wait. Wait for a battle that, by the sounds of it, would be worse than what he'd faced earlier. Because now they were dealing with not just a madman, but a frustrated, tyrannical madman.

He hoped the First Human-Born would be okay. To have to face wrath like that. To have to stare it down and push it away. Defend against it and not quake.

It would take a special kind of person to be able to withstand that kind of attacker.

He hoped that his parents and the other scientists would be all right. That was something he didn't want to dwell on, because if something went wrong, well...

Nothing would go wrong. That was the bottom line.

Still, he prayed.

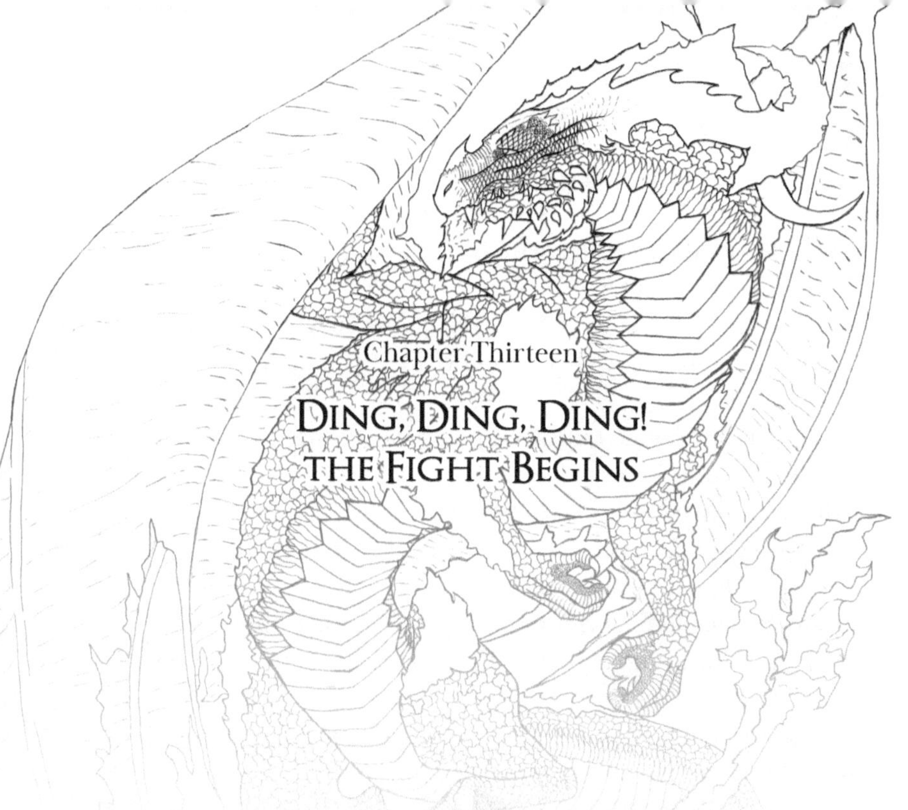

Chapter Thirteen

DING, DING, DING! THE FIGHT BEGINS

It'd been nearly an hour since they'd left the galley, and the lack of activity had all of them fidgeting. Frost paced, lifting his head occasionally to look out the window before his ears would flatten and he'd continue his thumping march.

Taesir wouldn't settle. No matter how much she shifted, it was as though she couldn't allow herself to get comfortable. She'd sit in one position for several moments, then shift to another, then to another, then stand, before starting the process all over again. Meanwhile, Kedar stood resolute but kept cracking his knuckles and playing with his fingers.

Gaeor had disassembled and reassembled his weapon at least five times and was now actively dismantling the rifle used for warding off polar bears. He'd taken off various pieces of the rifle and had used his energy to fuse the parts to his Agerian pistol.

Their unease only served to make Alaster worried.

While they'd had a few small conversations in the time that had passed, the teen hadn't been able to get any long-winded answers from any of them. Everything was curt and short. Which he kind of understood. His Zaheri were on high alert, probably listening. Like he should be doing.

At that moment, stretching his hearing wasn't something he could focus on. He'd tried quite earnestly at first, but then he'd get distracted, thinking about the other Human-Borns again.

He wanted to know if they were okay. Silent prayers kept rattling in his mind, and he tried to recall the map from Doctor McKay's workstation, pinpointing exactly where the other Human-Borns were would prove difficult.

Fishing his phone out of his pocket, he figured he should check. When none of his Zaheri made a comment about his action, he pulled up the web browser and started typing in his search. A moment later, he had hundreds of news reports to sift through. All from varying countries.

Tokyo, Japan. A pillar of light had erupted in the gardens, seen appearing through the cherry trees. Reports that there were dead monsters and dozens of dead bodies strewn throughout the walkways of the garden. Several dead dragons draped across buildings and crumpled in streets.

Oxford, England. Rumor and speculation about the son of a duke. Something about terrorists in custody. Monster bodies found just outside of Oxford. Suspects currently held in Scotland Yard. Not much there. Reports of several women unaccounted for.

Pennsylvania, United States. A high school under attack. Blurry photos of a blue-domed shield over a school complex. Police advising people to stay away. Evacuation orders for the towns. Something about a dragon shot down and killed near the border of New York state.

Sydney, Australia. A nightclub attacked by a terrorist group, possibly. Something about a bomb. A frantic video of the city street awash in golden light as people ran across a gold platform in the air, sounds of fighting amid panicked audio asking what was going on.

"What're you watching?" Gaeor asked, nodding toward Alaster's phone.

Startled, Alaster nearly dropped his phone and shook his head. "Just ... some news reports."

The team members shared a few tense looks.

"You needn't be concerned for the other Human-Borns," Frost said reassuringly.

"Maybe I don't need to be," Alaster sighed as he stood, pocketing his phone, "but I am." He gestured vaguely. "It sounds like things are pretty bad for them right now. How do I not worry about them?"

"Because they have Zaheri, too," Kedar said. "The best Agerian Defenders are out there, doing everything they can to protect the others."

"Just like we are," Taesir said. "They'll be fine. You have to believe they'll be okay."

Alaster scratched his neck and absentmindedly pulled the dog tags out from under his shirt. He started to play with them, pulling them up and down the chain with a zipping noise. "I just feel so helpless."

"Alaster, you don't have to be their protector," Kedar said as he stepped up to the boy.

Maybe he didn't have to be. But something was making him feel awful concerned for their wellbeing.

He continued to play with the dog tags as he looked to Kedar. "You seriously aren't concerned for them?"

"Truthfully?" Kedar asked with a small quirk of his brow. Then he nodded. "Yeah, I'm concerned for them." He scoffed and shrugged. "It's natural to be concerned for the safety of the Human-Borns. Of my friends protecting them. That's normal."

"Then—"

"C'mon, Alaster," the Team Leader said with a knowing grin. "You seriously going to ask me how I can be okay? Are you, of all people, about to question why I have faith that they'll make it through this?"

An awkward smirk came to Alaster's face, and he rolled his eyes. "Okay, fair play."

Kedar laid his hand on Alaster's shoulder. "Hey." He waited for the boy to meet his gaze again. "It's natural to be scared for them. It's natural to be scared given what we're up against."

"Which is ...?"

Blowing air into the barrel of the rifle he had stripped down, Gaeor sat back and said, "A foe with multiple abilities and powers unmatched by none but the First Human-Born."

"But," Kedar said sternly, with a cross stare at Gaeor, "that doesn't mean we have to give in to that fear. We have faith"—he gently knocked the back of his hand against Alaster's chest—"and that's all we need."

Alaster nodded a little. He was about to ask a question when a sharp pain echoed across his temple. Unable to stop himself, he grimaced and let out a small, airy cry.

"Wh—what was that?" Taesir asked, shooting to her feet.

"You okay, kid?" Kedar asked, tightening his hold on Alaster's shoulder.

The pain was gone almost immediately, as if he was just being made aware that it existed somewhere in the world. As if letting him know he wasn't the injured party.

Rubbing his temple in confusion, Alaster carefully met Kedar's worried gaze. "Yeah, I just ... I dunno." Dropping his hand, he shrugged. "This random ..."

For half a second, he could have sworn he heard a frantic voice cry out a garbled string of panic. As if in another language and backward, it shot through his mind and was gone just as quickly as it had arrived. He tried to grope after it, because something about it cried out to him. But it was gone too quickly.

"I dunno," he hushed, his gaze falling to the middle distance.

"Alaster, if—"

Frost shot to attention, making Kedar cut himself off, his ears flying erect and fur bristling across his spine. "Bratak'ra," he growled as his muscles tensed. "I sense their numbers are high."

"The Caligans might not be able to handle the weather," Kedar muttered.

"So there might not be Caligan fighters this time?" Alaster asked.

Gaeor put the barrel onto the Agerian pistol and used his energy to fuse the metals. Gold sparked across the metal, inlaying a swirling pattern that fizzled and popped as Gaeor removed his hand. "The beasts can probably handle the cold better, but we shouldn't discount that Caligans might be forced to come here, no matter their feelings on the temperature."

"Okay," Kedar said as he opened the door. "C'mon; we'll head out to meet them. That oughta make them think the station is still something we're protecting."

"And that'll do what?" Alaster asked he marched down the stairs of the Destination Zulu entrance.

"If any fighters happen to get past us, they might come here, looking for you."

Taesir started to jog once her feet hit the ice, her wings breaking through her shirt as she went. "They probably won't expect us to have you out there with us."

Once they were outside, Taesir took to the sky while Frost tore off into the tundra, taking a swift left. The same direction he and Alaster had ventured earlier that day.

In such a short time, everything had flipped and inverted. The world as Alaster had known it was upside down. And yet, something about it felt so right side up.

That assurance didn't halt the fear in his heart, though.

As they ran into the unassumingly empty frozen world, Alaster felt another strange tug at his thoughts. He pushed it aside, trying to focus his attention on the battle he was running toward.

Even so, something within him fought to seek out whatever tugged at him.

All the scientists had arrived at McMurdo within a half hour. The personnel of the base were surprised at their appearance, especially considering it was nearly the entire expedition team arriving on their proverbial doorstep.

Doctor Davis stepped in immediately and explained the situation. He was met with speculation, which then led to Doctor McKay piping in about the strange energy readings he'd been tracking. Which proved to be their saving grace.

The balding doctor was yanked forward and told to explain things, as the news pertaining to the chaos around the globe had recently reached McMurdo. And there were many questions.

Alaster's parents answered what they could amid the various scientists' jumbled input. After ten minutes or so of haphazard explanations and discussion, Doctor Davis and the general who oversaw McMurdo Base went to speak in private.

Meanwhile, the rest of the expedition team was led to a meeting hall while things were sorted out. It meant that many of the scientists were left to wonder what might become of them. Would they be stuck there? Would they be forced to go back to the Amundsen-Scott Station? What if the monsters came here after all?

Fears were only just beginning to quell about thirty minutes after their arrival at McMurdo when Doctor McKay suddenly hollered, "It's happening again!"

Everyone began to crowd around him, and the O'Briens had to push their way forward a bit to find out what was going on, much to Keegan's annoyance.

Doctor McKay's laptop pinged and dinged various notifications, and the O'Briens took in the map displayed on the screen. Seven points pulsed in time, like homing beacons.

Shaking his head as he tinkered around on the laptop, Doctor McKay said, "Loads of energy is being diverted through each of these points. I think that second wave those reporters were talking about is happening."

"Alaster," Mrs. O'Brien hushed, her eyes glued to the screen. She gripped her husband's hand for support.

The points on the map started lighting up and growing in intensity.

"What's happening?" Keegan asked.

Doctor McKay shook his head again and said, "I don't know. But if what one of those super humans had been saying is right, then this means that either their reinforcements are showing up, or the enemy fighters are coming back. It's different, though. A few of the locations changed."

"What do you mean?"

"Well, look at this." Doctor McKay pulled up a map from earlier. A few of the points had changed location by a few feet in some instances and whole miles in others. Pointing to the screen, he said, "See? The point in Antarctica moved from the center of the continent to closer to Amundsen-Scott."

Looking up at her husband, Alaster's mother said, "We'll just have to trust he knows what he's doing."

With a nod, Keegan replied, "And pray that he makes it back to us all right."

Chapter Fourteen

A CHAMPION AWAKES

They'd only run for five minutes when the opposition came into view. There was a faint brightness in the distance, but Alaster couldn't make out what was causing it. Gauging by the thudding coming from that direction, he guessed it was the portal.

Frost was a good half mile ahead of them when the ice around him picked up, ripping out of the ground in little chunks. The pieces of ice rolled forward, like a monstrous wave. It hit the enemy fighters and rolled around, smashing into them, sending them in every direction.

It appeared as though a number of the bratak'ra had been expecting something like that, as they braced themselves through the wave like you would in the ocean, dipping under the main crest. The monsters' large horns broke through the chunks of ice, allowing them holes to leap through and continue their storming charge.

Caligans and werewolves charged behind them. There had yet to be any Ferveos, though, which Alaster wanted to say was a good thing.

Diving past the oncoming fighters, Frost leaped into the thrall and began attacking as best he could at the wounded fighters. Ice swirled around his form, swiftly taking the shape of arrowheads and slicing through enemies at Frost's back.

Gaeor's modified rifle seemed to work well for him, but every shot made a funny tinning noise as it flew through the barrel. The golden energy along the fused portions would illuminate white as the little blue bullets charged through the interworking of the rifle.

With no Ferveos to keep her airborne, Taesir dove to the ground and began attacking anything nearby, keeping her wings blanketed in gold to rebuff any potential attacks. Werewolves and bratak'ra were met with her protective wings whenever they tried to attack her, letting out grunts and yelps as they collapsed against her golden wings.

Meanwhile, Kedar held his energy as gauntleted storehouses. He sent waves and blasts of gold that sparked in brilliant light. If the brutality of the actions wasn't so deadly, it might have been considered pretty as the golden energy flew across the white landscape.

Alaster did all he could to keep up. Green energy in his left hand and a pistol in his right, he took any opportunity to help protect his Zaheri. Which was proving difficult with how they seemed to bounce around.

Frost was a thundering wave of ice, shards flying one moment and swirls of snow pulling around the grovix's frame the next. The light blue grovix roared, and the ice obeyed. It was a fascinating thing to witness, and Alaster wished he could just watch Frost fight.

Gaeor, for all his griping and considering his Sniper specialty, seemed fluid in the midst of battle. He'd lean back and expertly dodge an attack, land a kick on the opposing Caligan, and then swiftly bring his makeshift rifle back to his mark and take out enemy fighters with deadly accuracy.

Despite her petite stature in comparison to her male teammates, Taesir was a dancing wave of gold. Her covered wings helped her stand out as he would fly through the air and land in the midst of enemy fighters. Kicking and punching with practiced agility, she worked to dodge every hit that tried to land on her.

Kedar certainly seemed to be doing all he could to stay close. The Team Leader kept looking over his shoulder in quick glances to take stock of Alaster's position in the thrall. More than once, he shoved Alaster aside and took a blow intended for the teen.

It hurt Alaster to watch Kedar take so many errant hits. And every time Alaster got swept aside by one of his Zaheri, he noticed a new injury. Their clothing started to become stained with blood. The self-replicating fabric began to fray and tear beyond repair.

A bubbling sensation billowed in Alaster's chest. Something he couldn't explain. Maybe fury over the events of the day? Or maybe frustration that he couldn't do more? He wasn't sure. But there was a definite unknown sensation pulling at his heart, tugging at him and begging him. Begging him to do what? He couldn't say.

He felt as though he was grazing it. Like he could visualize himself grasping some energy core that pulsed and thrummed frantically. But his fingers couldn't actually take hold of it.

And then, just as he felt he might connect with it. Just when he thought he could grasp it and clutch at it, explore whatever it was—

It was gone.

In its absence was silence.

Right about then was when Alaster realized that there had been a subdued thrum in the back of his mind all day. And it was now abruptly gone, as if cut off.

The sensation was so jarring that Alaster faltered in his fighting, stumbled in his footing.

When a fist collided with his face and sent him flying.

His jaw screamed pain as he skittered to his feet and frantically managed to dodge a second blow. Relying on instinct, he deflected blows by slapping the furious movements aside. In desperation, he pushed green energy out from his chest and shoved the Caligan backward.

In that space, Gaeor charged forward and slammed his golden-cloaked fist into the Caligan attacker.

The thrum returned, emanating panic and terror. It was horribly discombobulating, the way this strange something began to scream in his mind. Like a ringing in his ears that wouldn't dull, only intensify. The brightness in the distance disappeared.

He imagined the pulsing energy core again and stretched his hand out toward it. What was it? How did he grasp it? How did he hold it? Would that help him now?

"What are you doing?" Gaeor bellowed in a furious voice.

Alaster snapped his eyes open just before he got shoved backward, landing harshly on the ice. He narrowly avoided a gray attack that flew over his head.

Gaeor let out a grunt of pain, and Alaster whipped his attention to his Zaheri, finding a rough gouge in his Zaheri's arm. But more than that was the man Gaeor leaped into a duel with. Gray and gold flashed and sparked between the two. They were similarly built, but the attacker was the leaner of the two.

With short gray hair, lighter skin, and striking green eyes, the Caligan moved with swiftness that Alaster hadn't seen from the other fighters. His attention seemed laser focused, as though he were well practiced and well trained. And his attire was different than the others. Where the other Caligan fighters had on dull, light gray and roughly worn clothing, this man's outfit was more finely made. Made of darker gray cloth and leather, and bore an emblem stitched onto the back.

Between his appearance and his fighting style, this man stood out starkly against the other Caligans. And it made Alaster momentarily fearful.

But Gaeor was sparring against this man well, which meant it couldn't be Cregorous.

"Get out of here!" Gaeor commanded as he gritted his teeth.

Alaster knew his Zaheri were going to do everything they could to protect him, but he couldn't run. He couldn't abandon them.

He just had to focus. Shove the strange sensation away and stop letting his mind fixate on that phenomenon. It was compromising his ability to fight. It could cause terrible things to happen.

Pushing the fear aside, Alaster stumbled to his feet and quickly looked around, trying to see how he could help.

They weren't near the main thrall. He'd been thrown aside, and there was no telling where Kedar, Taesir, or Frost were. It was just him, Gaeor, and this Caligan.

Which wasn't good.

Gaeor was a Sniper.

And he didn't have his makeshift rifle.

Mustering his courage, Alaster fumblingly took hold of his pistol and pointed it at the Caligan. "Leave us alone!"

"Is that supposed to intimidate me?" the Caligan asked with a crooked grin.

Gaeor moved to land a punch, but the Caligan easily sidestepped him, grasped his wrist, and yanked.

Letting out a cry of pain, Gaeor tried to wrench his arm free.

Gray energy flared so blindingly that all Alaster could do was flinch back and pinch his eyes shut, squinting through the flash. A sickening, ripping noise filled the air, and Alaster felt the oxygen leave his lungs.

In a fluid movement, the Caligan tore through Gaeor's arm, severing it, and threw the Zaheri through the air.

Gaeor landed with a *thud*, his face contorted in pain as he actively worked to not scream in agony. His arm had been taken off just past his shoulder, blood pouring from the missing limb.

The Caligan wore a confident smirk, mindlessly depositing Gaeor's arm as he started toward the wounded Zaheri.

Alaster quickly planted himself between the attacker and his protector. Without knowing why, he pulled green energy into his fists and raised them. His arms trembled. The fact that Gaeor's discarded arm was still in his line of vision sent a wave of nausea in Alaster's stomach.

I'm stronger than my Zaheri. I can do this. I'm stronger than my Zaheri. I can do this, mantraed in Alaster's mind. He had to do this. He had to protect Gaeor in that moment.

He would protect his Zaheri.

Pushing his fears over Gaeor's wellbeing aside, Alaster tried to focus his attention on the enemy in front of him. Gaeor would be fine so long as Alaster didn't get distracted. Distractions caused mistakes. And Alaster had already let enough distract him.

The Caligan stopped a few feet away from them. He wore a bemused expression as he looked at the energy in Alaster's grasp. "Ah, the Human-Born. I assumed as much before, given how stupidly that one was behaving."

Gaeor growled in a shaky way, and Alaster refused to look back at him.

His trembling had quit now that he'd focused himself. And while he wasn't assured, he wasn't terrified of this Caligan. Maybe he should have been, but he wasn't. The fact that he had gray energy meant their attacker wasn't Cregorous. Which meant that Alaster had every right to be able to go toe-to-toe with this guy.

But, at the same time, it might be Cregorous after all, and Alaster might be underestimating the hybrid in front of him.

"I'm the Seventh," Alaster said.

The Caligan nodded. "That isn't news. And, while I'm certain my master would love to dispose of you all himself"—a sick grin filled his features—"he has far better things to do with his time."

Taking a small breath, Alaster was thankful this wasn't Cregorous. But all that meant was the tyrannical monster was attacking another Human-Born. Most likely, the First.

His mind pinged on that, and he nearly screamed at himself to not lose focus. He had to pay attention to the enemy in front of him.

"Who are you?" he asked, trying to buy some time. Maybe Kedar or Taesir would find them soon.

The Caligan scoffed and rolled his eyes. "That doesn't matter, seeing as I'm about to kill you."

It was unnerving that anyone could utter a sentence like that so casually.

"What do we matter to you?" Alaster asked. "We're just a bunch of kids."

With another roll of his eyes, the Caligan said, "If you're upset that your little life is about to end, take that up with the Elders, boy. I did not assign you." Gray energy flew from around his chest and into his grasp. "Enough talking. It's abhorrently cold, and I'm finished with you."

Before Alaster could figure out something to say that might afford more time, the Caligan threw his hands out, and a charging blast of gray surged forward.

With little recourse, Alaster threw his hands up against the storming attack, a green shield appearing in front of him to deflect the attack. Alarm shot through him.

"Wow, that worked," he muttered as the pressure against his shield disappeared.

And then the shield splintered like green glass as the Caligan's fist collided with the protection.

Pain ricocheted through Alaster's body, and he could have sworn all of the bones in his arms had somehow frozen. It was a strange pressure that appeared along his fingers and forearms especially, as if something tightened around his bones.

In a desperate action, Alaster managed to shove an attempted blow aside. But all that did was leave him open to a second punch from the Caligan.

Staggering backward, Alaster did everything he could to not react to the painful hit to his face, even as he felt blood trickle from a gash along his skin.

The Caligan laughed at him. "Is this truly the best they could muster?" He managed to snatch Alaster's hair and send his knee into the boy's face.

Despite the coppery sting of blood in his mouth, Alaster scurried to his feet and hurled an attack at the Caligan. Like a sidearm pitch in baseball, a green orb shot from his fingers and slammed into his attacker.

Though he was thrown back, the Caligan sprang back to his feet fairly easily. Another blast of gray was hurled at Alaster.

Diving aside from the attack, Alaster rolled and pulled a green shield in front of him in time to deflect a blow from the Caligan.

Distance attack followed by close-range melee hits, Alaster thought. This Caligan had a pattern. At least, for right now.

Which meant—

The Caligan leaped back and pulled his arms back to release another attack.

Kicking his shield, Alaster sent the green protection crashing into his attacker. There was a crack that sounded like a bone breaking.

But before Alaster could get his footing, he slammed into the ground as a wave of gray collided with him. At almost the same instant, he felt as though his arm broke and pain radiated across his ribs.

Shakily grasping at the icy terrain, he stumbled to stand, his shoes sliding against the ice that they'd uncovered in the fighting. He managed to spin toward his attacker in time to raise a flickering green shield in front of him. But that didn't stop the Caligan.

Punch after punch landed against his shield. Splintered cracking started to form. That couldn't be good.

In desperation, Alaster begged the shield to do something.

A popping explosion rippled across the shield, and bullet-like shards tore outward. Gray ghosted the Caligan, protecting him against Alaster's counterattack.

The Caligan landed a kick to Alaster's chest, sending the teen skittering backward. They began to trade blows, and Alaster did all he could to not get hit. He failed.

In a flash, the Caligan's hand closed around Alaster's throat. Despite the fact they were nearly the same height, the Caligan lifted Alaster slightly off the ground. Gray charred at Alaster's skin.

Wearing a euphoric look, the Caligan smiled devilishly at the boy fighting his grasp. "This is truly the best the Elders could muster?"

Alaster gagged at the strangle-hold and felt his eyes watering. Green billowed and warbled around his chest and all he could think was, *Attack.*

The Caligan looked to Alaster's green energy and threw his hand up. Gray flashed against the green. The opposing attacks slammed into one another, and an explosion ripped the air.

Landing with a *thud*, Alaster felt the air leave his lungs as his diaphragm spasmed. A choked breath finally coughed its way out of his throat, and he tasted blood.

Everything ached. His broken arm twitched and shook as he rolled onto his stomach. His vision blurred a little, ringed in red. The blows he'd taken to his face must've resulted in a damaged eye. He wasn't sure what to try to heal first.

He coughed again and watched his blood stain the snow beneath him. For a few seconds, it felt like the world slowed down. The ringing hit his mind again, the thrum spiking confusion, and worry, and fear, and a ton of other emotions.

Pinching his eyes shut, he tried to focus. Gaeor. The Caligan. He had to protect his Zaheri.

The ringing wouldn't stop.

When he opened his eyes, he felt his vision skip and fragment. And he could have sworn he saw something.

Gone was his drive to focus on Gaeor. Because the unidentified sensation within him leaped in his chest at what he saw.

A voice filtered through his mind, one he couldn't place and one he didn't understand. It sounded ancient and mighty. Sovereign and just. In that second, Alaster felt his mind blur, as if he were suddenly remembering a dream with events that didn't make sense.

There was a teenage girl curled in the fetal position. And when their eyes met, he felt he knew her. It was like, in that blurry instant, he understood that she was the voice he'd been hearing. The one lost, scared, and unsure. That somehow she was the pulsing energy he kept trying to grasp and understand.

Without thinking, he reached for her. *Do you trust me?* he found himself asking.

The vision skipped and skittered. Flashed a bunch of foreign landscapes and unknown faces.

I do, she responded. Though her mouth didn't move, he knew she'd responded.

Green energy filled his hand as he stretched his fingers out to her. Blue filled her palm as she strained to reach him.

Their fingers grazed, and then they took hold of one another.

Meanwhile, the Caligan sauntered toward him, gray energy billowing around his form. He unleashed an attack at Alaster, intending to end the teen.

A flash of kaleidoscope colors tore through the area, ripped through the gray attack, and made the Caligan stagger backward.

In an instant, Alaster tore forward and collided with the Caligan. They landed with Alaster on top of this attacker. His eyes blazoned with a rainbow of colors, like oil in a stream. Defiance and assurance radiated from his expression as he tightened his grip on the Caligan's throat and glared down at him.

"The Seven united as one," he said. His voice wasn't just his own. A village cried from his mouth, announcing something his conscious mind didn't understand. "The righteous are granted redemption."

The Caligan shoved Alaster off him and started frantically throwing attacks.

Completely undeterred, Alaster swept the attacks aside. Energy flared from him like feathered wings, and he looked wholly terrifying. He marched forward. "The wicked will meet their demise."

"No!" the Caligan screamed in fury, unleashing a violent attack.

Tearing through the gray storm as though it were air, Alaster slammed his palm onto the Caligan's face and stared him dead in the eye. "And all shall fall for one."

Out of desperation, the Caligan threw an attack at Alaster's face just as the teen unleashed a flash of green. The two flew apart in an echoing explosion, and the world went dull in the absence of the radiant colors that had exuded from Alaster a second prior.

The snow hung in the air, creating a foggy mist.

With an airy groan, Alaster felt his vision swim in a never-ending white. Frantic voices called in a muffled way, as if through a wall.

A hand gripped his shoulder.

Where was he? What had happened? How was it everything hurt even more than before? And why couldn't he see anything?

He'd been getting pummeled by the Caligan, and then there had been the faint thrum. That was all he could remember. The faint thrum and the cries of confusion.

"It was Kelek," Kedar's voice filtered through Alaster's slowly returning hearing.

"Gaeor," Alaster managed to croak out. His blurry vision slowly took in Kedar hovering over him.

"It's okay!" the Team Leader said, placing his hand on Alaster's chest to keep the teen down. "You're okay. You chased Kelek away."

"Gaeor, he—"

"We know. Don't move."

"I have frozen the wound until we can get him proper help from a Caretaker. You have several broken bones, Alaster," Frost said from his other side.

A dragon flew overhead. Its scales were golden in color. An Agerian dragon, a Preliator. Reinforcements.

Letting out a labored sigh, Alaster sank against the snow. Though it was cold, there was something refreshing about it against his wounded body.

"Hey, you okay?" Kedar asked. Half of his shirt was soaked in blood. He held his hand to his bloody abdomen.

"I'm fine," Alaster said with a wince.

Kedar gave him a disbelieving look.

With a sigh, Alaster closed his eyes in defeat. "I'm ... Everything hurts."

Hanging his head, Kedar deflated. "Well, you're talking and cognizant." He looked to Frost. "That's a good sign, right?"

"Yes," the grovix said with a nod.

Taesir looked over at Kedar and asked, "Are you all right?"

"I'll be fine once I get a Caretaker to look at me," the Team Leader said as he fell backward with a heavy breath.

Sitting up a little, Alaster let out an airy whine of pain. "Is Gaeor—"

Frost sat behind him, offering support as the teen nearly toppled over.

"He'll be fine," Kedar said. "We just need to get him to Agerius ..."

As if answering the question that formed in Alaster's mind, the Preliator from earlier landed several feet away.

Kedar went to stand, but Taesir held her hand out. "No, you rest. I'll go."

Everything fell into the back of Alaster's mind as he slumped against Frost. He didn't want to think or do anything. His eyes burned, and he felt incredibly weary as his brain pounded against his skull. So long as he didn't look at Gaeor's ripped-off arm, he didn't feel the need to throw up.

A moment later, the flapping of wings alerted them to five smaller dragons—Scouts—flying toward them and beginning their descent.

As the dragons landed, Kedar got to his feet. "Send one of the Scouts to McMurdo base; it's about an hour's walking distance from here in that direction," he said as he pointed behind them.

One of the Scouts stepped forward. The smaller dragons were brightly colored and only stood about three feet taller than a normal human.

"Land before you reach the base or they'll think you're with the Caligans. Call out to them and tell them you're friendly."

"Do I actually say, 'I'm a friend?'" the Scout asked.

Shaking his head, Kedar answered, "No. Tell them you work with Kedar of the Zeta Team and that you bring news of the fight. Also, tell them that the O'Briens' son is safe but has been taken for medical attention."

Staggering to his feet, Alaster said, "I'll go with you."

"You need to be looked over by a Caretaker," Kedar said to the teen.

"I will at McMurdo," Alaster said. "Look, my injuries are ... I have a bunch, but I don't need medical attention. I just need to sleep, I think."

"I shall accompany him," Frost said, rising to stand. "Alaster is correct. You three require more attention than us, and Gaeor should be taken with all swiftness to ensure he recovers well."

"Thanks, Frost," Kedar said with a nod. He grabbed Alaster's arm to steady the teen. "You listen to everything Frost says."

Nodding shakily, the teen answered, "Got it."

Kedar let out a relieved sigh. "I'm glad you're okay, Alaster."

Once he got onto the Scout, Alaster allowed himself to ease and close his eyes. Despite the bitter cold wind that whipped around him, his exhaustion was heavy.

As they flew off and Frost led the way from the ground, Alaster glanced to his other Zaheri. He hoped Gaeor would be all right.

Clenching his jaw, Alaster pinched his eyes shut and rested his head against the Scout's neck. While he was grateful he'd managed to survive, he couldn't deny that this was the hardest day of his life. And it wasn't over yet.

Chapter Fifteen
AFTER THE STORM

Alaster's parents had been less than thrilled when their son had shown up with cuts and bruises, and broken bones. He explained what had happened to Doctor Davis and the general overseeing McMurdo. A team was then sent to check on Amundsen-Scott Station, and to discover the viability of the structure. Despite all the attacks and the destroyed wing, the station was deemed structurally sound. However, with a portion of the station needing severe repairs, it required a winnowing process to determine which scientists would stay assigned to Amundsen-Scott and which ones would move to other facilities until the station could resume full operational procedures.

Amid all of that, Alaster was checked over by a doctor. X-rays were taken, along with an MRI. All of which Alaster begrudgingly agreed to. Shortly after, Doctor Davis found out about the extra tests and demanded that the records be destroyed.

The physician that saw to the tests fought back until Doctor Davis gravely said, "If any information about this young man reaches the wrong people, terrible things could befall him. And I will not stand for a minor being taken advantage of because of negligence."

Before they were destroyed, Alaster took a glance at his torso x-ray and finally got his wish to see how his wing bones fit against his human skeletal structure.

Shortly after his checkup and relative bill of health, Alaster met up with his parents. He was fiercely hugged by them both and reiterated how grateful he was that they had been out of harm's way. His father actually thanked Frost, much to Alaster's surprise.

Once all of that was out of the way, Alaster and Frost were assigned a room, where both of them promptly gave in to their exhaustion. They slept soundly all through the night and woke late the next day.

The day after the attack, Doctor Davis, with the O'Briens and about a third of the personnel and scientists originally stationed there, returned to Amundsen-Scott. The rest were temporarily reassigned.

Kedar and Taesir arrived back at the station late that day. A number of Zaheri had returned to Agerius by nightfall, recounting events similar to their own. They had all been attacked and many of them had barely escaped with their lives. However, everyone was alive and well.

The news of the other Human-Borns being all right sent a wave of relief through Alaster. Especially knowing that one of them had, in fact, faced Cregorous. Eventually, Kedar admitted that the First Human-Born had been the one unfortunate enough to have borne that burden.

"But they're okay?" Alaster asked as they settled in one of the lounges.

Kedar nodded as he closed the door. "Yeah, they're okay."

"And ... Gaeor?"

Sharing a glance with Taesir, Kedar rocked his weight before answering, "He'll be okay. They had to fully remove his arm, and he's angry that he can't fire a rifle one-handed, but he'll be back in action in a few days."

"A few days?" Alaster asked as he raised his brow. "Isn't that a little fast?"

"Not for Gaeor," Taesir said with a smirk.

"He's eager to figure out some way to still use a sniper rifle, despite being one-handed," Kedar added then shrugged a bit. "Something about talking with a tailor and making a belt to ground the butt of the rifle to his chest."

"Sounds ingenious," Alaster said. "I didn't peg Gaeor for an innovator."

Frost narrowed his eyes. "Neither would I."

"Yeah, it wasn't Gaeor's idea," Kedar said with a chuckle. "Asher made an offhand comment, and then Drogar started sketching out designs." He met Frost's gaze. "Ethran apparently had a rough go of it."

Ears flattening, Frost frowned. "That is unfortunate. He will make a full recovery?"

Kedar nodded in response.

"Are these other Zaheri?" Alaster asked, looking between his protectors.

"Yes, they're all fine," Taesir said as she held up her hand to silence Alaster's concerned question. "A few of them just needed some attention from our Caretakers."

Hugging himself slightly, the teen glanced between them. "What does the Council want you guys to do now?"

"Sit tight," Kedar said. "I don't know what they're waiting for, but we only assume that the Council wants to be sure before they make any moves forward."

"What about the other Human-Borns? Should we meet?"

"That isn't for you to worry about. If it would be anyone's job, it'd be the First Human-Born's responsibility to do that."

Alaster slumped a little. "But wouldn't it be better to be proactive?"

"It isn't your job, as the Requisite, to initiate things. If the First Human-Born contacts us, then we'll know what to do," Taesir said.

Silence fell in the room for a moment. Then Alaster asked warily, "So ... what now?"

"Well," Kedar started, glancing to his team members, "I think you're overdue for some training."

A small smile filled Alaster's features as he sat up. "Wait. Seriously?"

"While it's apparent that you held your own against Kelek—"

"He is the Caligan who attacked you," Frost interjected.

"—Gaeor recalled some proof that you're in dire need of training. Especially in hand-to-hand combat and shield techniques."

"Wait—Gaeor was conscious through the fight?" Alaster asked.

"Some of it, yes. He passed out from the blood loss a little bit after you kicked a shield at Kelek."

"Kelek," Alaster muttered, leaning his arms against his thighs. Then he reconnected his gaze with Kedar's. "Who was he?"

"He's one of Cregorous' generals. The ones we told you about yesterday," Taesir said.

Slowly looking between his Zaheri, Alaster said, "He was pretty ruthless."

Nodding a bit, Kedar sighed. "Yeah, that was to be expected."

Alaster opened his mouth to raise his concerns on a few things. One of them being his memory loss. There was a portion of the fight that was just a blurry mess in his mind. He'd gone from being face-down in the snow with a ringing in his ears to lying on his back in a completely different area.

The other thing was the thrum. The weird hum that he had felt tickle the back of his mind. He wanted to bring it up, but he didn't know how to articulate what the sensation was. How could they diagnose something he couldn't even describe?

That strange sensation, coupled with his minor blackout, made him want to tell his Zaheri. But he also knew that would likely only raise their concerns for him. It had been, after all, his first real combat experience.

Maybe that was all it was. Maybe his system had overloaded, and his brain had compensated strangely to offset his abilities as a hybrid.

Whatever it was, he chose to remain silent. For now. He'd bring it up when it felt relevant.

"We need to discuss things with your parents," Kedar said, snapping Alaster out of his wonderings. "They have to give the okay for your training."

"I want to be trained. I *need* to be trained," Alaster emphasized. "I don't want to be caught off guard again."

"Yeah, me neither, but we can't just ignore your parents' wishes. We have to appeal to them."

A knock sounded at the door, and they turned to see Alaster's parents standing in the threshold.

Alaster quickly got to his feet.

His father held up his hand and said, "Don't worry. We came because we wanted to talk to your Zaheri."

Uneasily, Alaster sat back down as his parents entered the room.

His mother spoke first, "We wanted to thank you for keeping our son safe."

"I know he was hurt pretty badly, but he healed up fine. And, to that, we owe you an apology," Alaster's father added.

Kedar looked at the others before he nodded at the O'Briens. "We were actually just talking about that."

"We heard," Alaster's mother said. She labored to continue, "And we agree."

"Although reluctantly," his father added. "But we talked this over last night, and it appears as though, if we had allowed Alaster to train with you, maybe he wouldn't have gotten quite as hurt yesterday."

"Da, it's not your fault," Alaster said.

"Yes, it is," his father answered as he looked at him.

A strange sense of disappointment filled him, even though he wasn't being punished or reprimanded. It was a crummy situation, and he felt awful for putting his parents in the middle of it. Even if none of it was his fault.

His father turned back to Kedar. "From what we heard, there are more kids like Alaster out there, and we can only assume that one day he'll meet them." A smile came to his face as he continued, "I'd hate for my son to be the only one who didn't know how to defend himself properly." He offered his hand to the Team Leader.

Chuckling, Kedar took the offered hand and answered, "We'll do our best, sir."

"We don't doubt that," Alaster's mother said. She turned to Alaster. "We're having dinner at seven."

With a nod, Alaster said, "I'll be there."

His parents looked around at the Zaheri one more time before they left the room.

When they were gone, Kedar let out a disbelieving chuckle. "That went better than I had thought."

Frost looked to Alaster and asked, "How do you feel?"

While the previous day had brought a lot of healing to the family, and had allowed his parents to acknowledge what Alaster was, and who he wanted to be, there was an unspoken question.

Would they allow him to pursue the path ahead of him? Would they really be okay with him being whatever a Human-Born meant?

If he hadn't been so exhausted the night prior, he might have worried over it. But now, here in the lounge with his Zaheri, with the knowledge that Gaeor would be okay, and likely would rejoin them soon. Knowing that the other Human-Borns were okay, and that he would eventually get the chance to meet them ...

The question of whether this was the right path for him never had a clearer answer.

He sighed and let a small smile come to his face before he looked to Frost and said, "For the first time in a long time, I feel like things are going to be okay."

The Zaheri looked between one another before Kedar gave Alaster a smile. "So, where do you want to begin your training?"

It was the best question Alaster could have ever hoped to be asked.

Chapter Sixteen

IT'S A GOOD KIND OF SORE

In the months that followed, Alaster got his wish. Every day was filled with a strict training regimen, resulting in more than a handful of bloody sparring sessions on Alaster's part. Kedar held nothing back and was stern in his resolve to train Alaster effectively. While it was something that Alaster was grateful for, there was no denying that, some days, he wished Kedar would go a little easier on him.

He was lucky that most of the scientists didn't grumble when he took a two-minute-long shower. Every night, he flopped into bed exhausted. His muscles were always sore, but his energy didn't make him twitch anymore. He learned more about shield creation and manip-ulation, aerial combat and utilizing—to his surprise—elbow bone spikes that he realized he had after surveying his x-rays, using his energy in different ways, and even discovering telekinetic abilities.

Gaeor taught him on the makeshift firing range they'd set up outside of the station. Taesir worked with him on learning how to best regulate his body temperature to withstand the bitter cold. Frost created obstacle courses and treacherous terrain for him to spar on. Kedar drilled combat moves into every minute of their time together.

It had paid off. In every regard, Alaster had progressed substantially from his bleak starting point on the day of the attack, not to mention his physique. But that didn't nullify his exhaustion.

Every seven days, he was given his sabbath and would sleep for most of it. With his Bachelor's degree completed, his parents were willing to give him time to figure out what being a Human-Born meant, and train accordingly.

All the while, every now and then, Alaster would get the strange thrum in his mind. Echoed, garbled words that he knew meant something, always linked with a sense of worry, fear, and doubt. But he couldn't grab a hold of it. He couldn't figure out what it was or how to react to it.

The instances were always so brief that he often forgot to bring them up by the time he had the chance to do so. It wasn't that he was actively choosing to not mention the phenomenon to his Zaheri; he simply would become focused on whatever task he had and completely forget about the phantom echoes in his mind until they happened again. Always at the worst times, where he couldn't just quickly ask what they might mean.

He wanted to grab on to them. Whatever those whispers were, the fleeting blips of confusion and terror often linked to them hurt his heart. They felt so scared, and he wanted to offer comfort.

Wincing as he stepped out of his shower for the day, Alaster stretched his sore muscles. It had been arial combat training, and he'd been forced to use his wings a whole lot more powerfully than normal to dodge Taesir's quick movements. Coupled with his rough landing, resulting in a fracture along his leg, he was more than ready for a hot meal and bedtime.

Once he changed in his room, he stepped out into the hall and found Frost waiting. A smile played on the grovix's face.

"I trust your training went well today."

Alaster cracked his neck and rolled his shoulders, feeling his muscles whimper their sore state. "Everything hurts."

"*Tsk*," Frost admonished with a soft scowl. "You begged ceaselessly for this for years. Now that you have obtained it, you regret it?"

"At the moment, yes, I regret ever saying I wanted training."

"You neglected to fix your hair."

"I had higher priorities."

They stepped into the galley to find his parents sitting with the rest of the team. Gaeor still wore the leather belt across his chest that held a slot for the butt of his rifle to snap into. When he wasn't busy helping with Alaster's training, he was undergoing his own refinement.

Gaeor had lost his dominant arm, which meant he now worked to hone his skills firing a rifle one-handed. His aim had been good from the beginning, when he was still working on the adjustments to the straps and snaps for one-armed shooting. But recently, he'd obtained nearly identical accuracy to before.

Alaster had suggested a prosthetic, and the Agerians had looked into the concept. For now, it seemed, Gaeor was content to remain a one-armed warrior.

Gathering food onto a tray for both himself and Frost, Alaster walked over to join the others at their table.

As he sat down and Frost began to gobble his meal, his father said, "Kedar tells me you're slacking a bit."

Throwing Kedar a glare, Alaster answered, "It's been a rough month."

"His form is improving, though," Kedar said as he dabbed his dinner roll into spaghetti sauce. "He's definitely making progress."

Frost sat up a bit. "It appears, however, he regrets requesting training."

"Do you now?" Kedar asked with a tone of enjoyment.

"Maybe we'll just have to work a little harder," Gaeor said with a smirk.

Taesir tsked and shook her head. She looked to the O'Briens. "He's made substantial improvement. You should be very proud of him."

As Kedar and Alaster's father began talking animatedly about the teen's further training, his mother whispered, "Are you okay, dear?"

"I'll be fine, Mum. I'm just … tired," Alaster replied.

A squeal came over the speaker before a voice called, "Agerians to Destination Zulu."

The Agerians in question threw glances to one another in confusion.

"What's that about?" Alaster asked.

"Dunno," Kedar said with a raised brow and a shrug. Then he swiftly made for the hall, the others close behind. Alaster only delayed a second before he followed.

When they reached the Destination Zulu entrance, Kedar asked, "What's going on?"

"That's an excellent question," Doctor Davis said. He gestured toward the door, where a uniformed man stood. His attire was neat and orderly, and he wore a heavy jacket over his uniform.

The stranger nodded to Kedar. "Chief Master Kedar, I've been sent by the High Council."

"For what?" Kedar asked.

"They have requested that your team return to Agerius. Immediately."

"What?" Gaeor snapped.

"Why?" Taesir asked, her face scrunching.

The unknown Agerian let out a small sigh and shook his head. "I cannot say. Only that you've been requested to return."

Hands on his hips, Kedar leaned forward a little and accused, "And leave our charge completely defenseless?"

"No, apologies. You are to remain. The rest of the Eta Team is to return."

Kedar's brow pulled together, and he tapped his foot a few times. He then turned to his team and asked, "Frost?"

The grovix's brow rose in alarm, his eyes wide. "I cannot offer any insight. This is highly irregular."

"Why would they ask most of us to return?" Taesir asked.

"Maybe some sort of check-in?" Gaeor offered, glancing to the others for some other explanation.

Flashing his gaze to Gaeor, Kedar was silent for a second. "Maybe."

Frost looked to the Team Leader before he gained a look of soft reminder. "You must obey."

"Obey a command that doesn't make sense?" Gaeor grumbled.

"You wish to defy your Council?"

"I wish to know what's going on," Kedar said before Gaeor could speak. He glanced at the middle distance for a moment before he straightened. "Frost, I want you to stay here."

The grovix cocked his head as Alaster asked, "Wait—what?"

"But the Council said—"

"I know what the Council said," Kedar gently said as he looked at Taesir. "But ... I'd rather have Frost here. He's the one with the highest advantage in this climate."

Worry filled Alaster's gut. "Are you saying there could be another attack?"

"Alaster, there could be another attack at any moment," Kedar said plainly with a placid expression. "I'm not doing this out of fear; I'm doing it out of what makes the most strategical sense."

"That's fair," Gaeor admitted with a quirk of his brow. "Frost does stand the best chance to offer defense alongside Alaster should something happen in our absence."

Before Alaster could say anything, Kedar held his hand up and said reassuringly, "Don't panic. This is probably nothing. Like Gaeor said, some sort of check-in. Maybe there's been a raid and they need our help, or a Caretaker needs to assess Gaeor's health, or something's gone awry with another Human-Born and they need to relay orders. We don't know what's going on, but we'll go, find out what's up, and come back."

He still didn't like the idea of his Zaheri leaving him.

There was a faint reminder of the fleeting echoes that had whispered in his mind. But just as he thought of it, it was gone. Like when you have a word on the tip of your tongue but can't recall it to save your life.

Alaster nodded in a resigned way and asked, "You promise?"

"Yeah, kid, we'll be back before you know it."

"The Council wouldn't just leave any of the Human-Borns with minimal protection," Taesir offered.

Shrugging, Gaeor gained a laidback stance, which helped calm Alaster's nerves. "Besides, you only had Frost at your side for years. It's not like it's any less than you've had before."

Frost let out a perturbed sigh. "That is a fair point."

Gaeor gave the grovix a cross stare.

Ignoring the other Zaheri's expression, Frost looked to Kedar and said, "You must tell me everything when you return. I am most intrigued to the Council's aim."

"Won't disobeying the Council get you in trouble?" Taesir asked Kedar, wearing a concerned frown.

"I will pardon him and freeze anyone who dares to challenge me," Frost quickly said.

Kedar chuckled. "Wow, Frost, I didn't know you liked me that much."

Gaining a smile, the grovix answered, "You have my utmost respect, Kedar."

The stranger cleared his throat, causing them to turn toward him. "Apologies, Chief Master, but we really must be off."

Nodding a bit, Kedar said, "That's fair. You haven't acclimated to the cold, so we should get going."

"What? Now?" Alaster asked with slight panic.

"Alaster, relax, it's okay," Kedar said as he gently laid a hand on Alaster's shoulder. "Remember, we'll be right back."

Despite the worry in his heart and the warning in his head, Alaster nodded. "Right. Yeah, you're right. It'll be grand."

"Yes, it will," Kedar said with a smile. He looked to Frost. "I'll take notes."

"I expect no less," Frost answered.

As the team left the station, Alaster couldn't stop the frown that filled his face.

Something about this felt really, really wrong.

A day had passed since the rest of the team had left. While it had afforded Alaster the chance to sleep in and spend the day resting and relaxing, his Zaheri's missing presence made him feel terribly off balance. Frost continually reassured him that there was nothing to worry over, but that didn't seem to help Alaster's mind from playing out terrible worst-case scenarios.

None of it made any sense. Not based on what he knew of the

High Council. Not with the whole prophecy and careful protection of the Human-Borns thing that the Council had clearly been all about.

So, what was going on?

Alaster had been sitting in the lounge, attempting to read *The Pilgrim's Progress*. But his eyes kept blurring on the words as his mind would wander.

When, suddenly, there was that thrum again. Louder and more intense. And then...

That voice. The one that cried out in confusion, and pain, and fear. The one he couldn't understand but kept getting phantom-like echoes of.

Alaster hadn't heard it this clearly since the day of the attack. But it was so loud this time. So scared. He could almost hear words with this cry. Still, he couldn't make them out. And there was something attached to it. An emotion he recognized.

It was crippling terror, the type that stole your breath from your lungs and clenched your stomach. Made you feel sick and tremble uncontrollably.

In the last few months, he'd found out a lot about abilities that hybrids could have. What they could possess and do. One of them was telepathy. A "dead ability," as Kedar had called it, because no one in Agerius had the ability anymore. It had sparked a question in Alaster's mind. He stacked what was known about telepathy against what he kept experiencing, and he kept wondering.

Was that what this was? This strange, whispered, shadowy sensation that would randomly hum and pulse against his mind?

He'd carefully been asking questions just in case being outright about his suspicion would cause his Zaheri concern. Because if it was telepathy, why did he have it?

Frost had said the abilities of the Human-Borns were mired in theory and speculation. Some were more carefully assumed than others. But Alaster? His abilities were awash in question marks. Because none of the abilities he'd learned about screamed, *"That belongs to the Requisite."*

But this...

It might've been a mistake, yet something in his soul told him it wasn't.

He imagined reaching toward the voice with a gentle hand. Something to acknowledge it and open up to it. Because every time he'd tried to grasp at it as it had flown past him, like a quickly passing wave, it had retreated too quickly. As if it were too scared of his presence to allow him to come close. So, like it was a scared woodland animal, Alaster gently pushed his mind toward whatever this was.

And all he could think to say was, *"Hang in there."*

There was a jolting sensation, as though whoever he was reaching out to was surprised to hear him.

Great. Now I'm hearing voices, was the response.

His mind short-circuited for a second. Even though he'd been growing suspicious that this was telepathy he was experiencing, a large part of him was positive he was making up some voice in his own head.

Frantically, he thought back, *You mean, you aren't a voice in my head?*

A new wave of startled confusion smacked into him before everything went silent.

Alaster's gaze whipped around the room. Slapping the book shut, he sat up. "Wait, no, come back," he shook out in a quiet plea. But he didn't know where to send the thought. He'd had that one fleeting moment of connection, and it had been tenuous, like he'd only grazed their mind.

He didn't get to tell them it was okay, that whatever they were scared of, they weren't alone.

Assuming he was hearing a Human-Born.

Oh crap, what if he *wasn't* hearing a Human-Born?

What if he just barreled into some poor normal human's mind and now they were terrified that someone was listening in on their thoughts?

Slumping back into the couch, he scrubbed his scalp.

Should he ask Frost what to do?

What if Frost freaked out, thinking that Alaster was connecting with Cregorous? That wasn't possible, was it? It wasn't possible that some monstrous dictator, who had generals as cruel as Kelek, would feel distress to the level that Alaster had felt emanating from the other person.

But ... what if it was?

And if it was...

Did that mean that Cregorous wasn't who they all thought he was?

New confusion danced in his own thoughts. Confusion over what to do next, how to determine who he spoke to, and how to connect with them again.

Chapter Seventeen
SMART BOY, BOUNDLESS FAITH

Everything had been silent. No return of his Zaheri, and no more phantom voice. It was just like all the other times before when he'd had these random thrums against his mind. He went about his day and forgot about it ... mostly.

This time, though ... because he'd actually heard words...

He had so many questions. But he didn't know how to ask Frost about them. Not without causing his Zaheri to react poorly.

One part of him knew he should just say something. Just let Frost know what was happening, what he thought was happening, what he thought it meant, and then move forward. But he was so worried that if he uttered this strange phenomenon, it would somehow cease to happen.

And it was wholly strange and completely illogical, but Alaster wanted to connect with ... whoever it was again.

It was around eight at night, and now that it was an all-dusk season at the station, it was easier to fall asleep during normal sleeping hours. But all of the confusion of the last four days had resulted in Alaster having trouble getting his mind to stop spiraling in questions.

He lay in bed, staring at his ceiling. Frost lay on the floor, drifting in and out of sleep. The lack of activity the last four days had resulted in both of them being a little more lazy than normal. While they'd gone for several long runs to burn off energy, and for Alaster to keep up his stamina, it wasn't enough to bring on exhaustion. So, his mind wandered.

He just wanted to know what was going on. With his other Zaheri, with the random voice in his head, with himself ... It was all so strange. And none of it made sense.

Then, suddenly, just as he was beginning to feel himself settle, a sparking, crippling terror shot through his mind.

This was a different type of terror that the voice felt than before. A terror Alaster knew all too well.

It was the same feeling he'd had when he'd heard Cam was dead. The same feeling he'd had when he'd seen Gaeor lying in the snow, his arm ripped off.

This was the terror of seeing someone you cared about inches away from death, and you didn't know how to stop it.

In that moment, Alaster didn't care if this was Cregorous, or some other Caligan, or a Human-Born. He had to help whoever it was. He had to find out who they were and what was going on.

Gritting his teeth, he felt his mind stampede toward the distressed voice, groping and grappling for it, desperate to take hold of their mind and find out who they were, how he could help.

He felt his vision overlay, as though a movie were suddenly displayed across his mind. And his heart lurched into his throat.

A man with red energy flicking around his frame stood several feet away. His stance was draped in confidence and power, and he was strangling another man who fought against the attacker.

But more than that was the terror felt by the person whose mind he'd connected with. It made Alaster unable to breathe for a moment.

A frantic thought slammed into his mind.

Cregorous was trying to break through Tyron's mind, or he already had. There had to be something she could do. Anything.

It wasn't a thought conveyed so much in words but, somehow, Alaster understood what she was feeling. Whoever she was.

He had to help her.

"Stop it!" she cried, and Alaster felt his heart cripple at how frightened she sounded. "Leave him alone!"

He assumed the man with red energy was Cregorous.

The Caligan grinned, still staring at the man he was torturing. "Why would I do that? Clearly, he's dear to you."

Shoving his thoughts quickly into the girl's mind, Alaster desperately thought, *Don't. You can help him.*

He didn't know how, but he knew that if he didn't stop her from lashing out, she'd do something rash. She'd throw herself at Cregorous. And that wasn't the right answer.

If Cregorous was hurting her Zaheri using his telepathy, she could use his to put up a block. At least, there had to be a way.

It didn't stand to reason that telepathy couldn't be blocked by other Telepaths. Otherwise, how would someone not go crazy? He'd been thinking about it a lot the last four days. There had to be a way to block out others' thoughts so he wasn't always bombarded with them. Not that he was always bombarded with others' thoughts.

Just hers. Whoever she was.

He quickly tried to convey what he was thinking. *Use my telepathy—block his mind.*

Telepathy? she asked in confusion, her mind spiraling in a dance of chaos. Which made sense. Her Zaheri was being threatened by Cregorous, and she clearly felt terror over that. Plus, Alaster was now throwing a huge curveball by telling her what he was thinking.

Because he was almost positive of one thing—the reason he was hearing her wasn't because she was special to him, but because she had telepathy, too. It was the only thing that made sense. Otherwise, wouldn't he hear everyone? Wouldn't he have thoughts randomly filtering into his mind? It had to be that they shared this ability somehow. The hows and whys didn't matter in that moment.

What mattered was saving her Zaheri and helping her.

I think that's what this is, he thought back to her, nodding his head. *I think you can use it.*

Whether she was borrowing his ability or had it herself, or whatever, there had to be a way for her to utilize this random ability to save her Zaheri.

There just had to be.

He felt a swirl in her mind as a memory slammed into him and he winced.

Something about her pushing Cregorous' mind away from hers when they'd first met. On the day of the attack. So, she did have telepathy, too, then.

A new realization clutched Alaster's heart.

This was the First Human-Born. It had to be.

Shut up, idiot! he told himself. *You can worry about who she is later! Focus! Help her!*

He tried to focus on what he could see through her eyes. He didn't know how he was doing it but, somehow, he could at least get glimpses, ideas of where they were. What was going on. What she was seeing.

Tan-colored grass among patches of green. A spindly tree splayed across sunrise. Africa.

He had to show her that he was there for her. That he supported her. That she wasn't alone against Cregorous.

She was saying something, dialoguing with Cregorous, but it was all muffled.

Until, suddenly, it wasn't.

He felt himself standing next to her but couldn't see her, because his gaze was stuck on the man holding a Zaheri hostage.

Cregorous was smirking at her as he finished whatever he'd been saying, "... If you give it to me, I'll let him go." His gaze flicked to Alaster, and his head tilted slightly as his eyes narrowed.

Alaster felt his body tighten at the way Cregorous looked at him. Like he ...

"How interesting," Cregorous whispered.

Oh crap.

Cregorous could see him? How?

That didn't matter. He wasn't leaving.

Especially once he felt a wave of fear crash from the girl at his side.

He wished he could look to her, but his gaze was stuck, fixed ahead. Maybe because she was looking at Cregorous? Could he only see in the direction she saw?

You've gotta get out of here, she said to him.

Yeah, that wasn't happening.

Shaking his head, Alaster thought back defiantly, *I'm not leaving you.*

A second later, he felt a wall smash into his mind, hurtling him away from her, and then he felt his mind slap back into his body.

He gasped and held his suddenly pounding head.

If he wasn't so nauseous, he'd stand up and start running toward the portal to try to figure out how to get to Africa.

"Alaster, what is wrong?" Frost blearily asked, staggering upright and coming to the teen's side.

Gasping in shaky breaths, Alaster sat up and shuddered out, "It's ... nothing." Glancing at Frost, he tried to gather his thoughts. He couldn't ask Frost about it now. He needed more information. Like whom this girl was.

"Sorry, I ..." he said, his breathing returning to normal.

Frost's brow drooped, and his ears flattened. "Another nightmare?"

"Something like that," Alaster muttered.

There was a funny ache in Alaster's temple that spiked randomly for about a half hour. He tried to sleep, but that was impossible. Not with this weird pain in his head. When, suddenly, he felt a thrum in his mind and heard her say, *Oh goody.*

She was okay!

Are you all right? he asked without thinking about whether that was acceptable or not. He'd been so worried about her, wondering what had happened. Had she saved her Zaheri? Had they gotten away from Cregorous? Was she okay?

Annoyance sparked from her, and she thought back, *Oh great. You're back, too. Can I call you back? Now isn't a good time.*

He wasn't sure how to respond to that. His brow pinched as he awkwardly responded, *Um ... sure?*

The thrum disappeared, and her mind cut off from his.

Well...

At least she was okay.

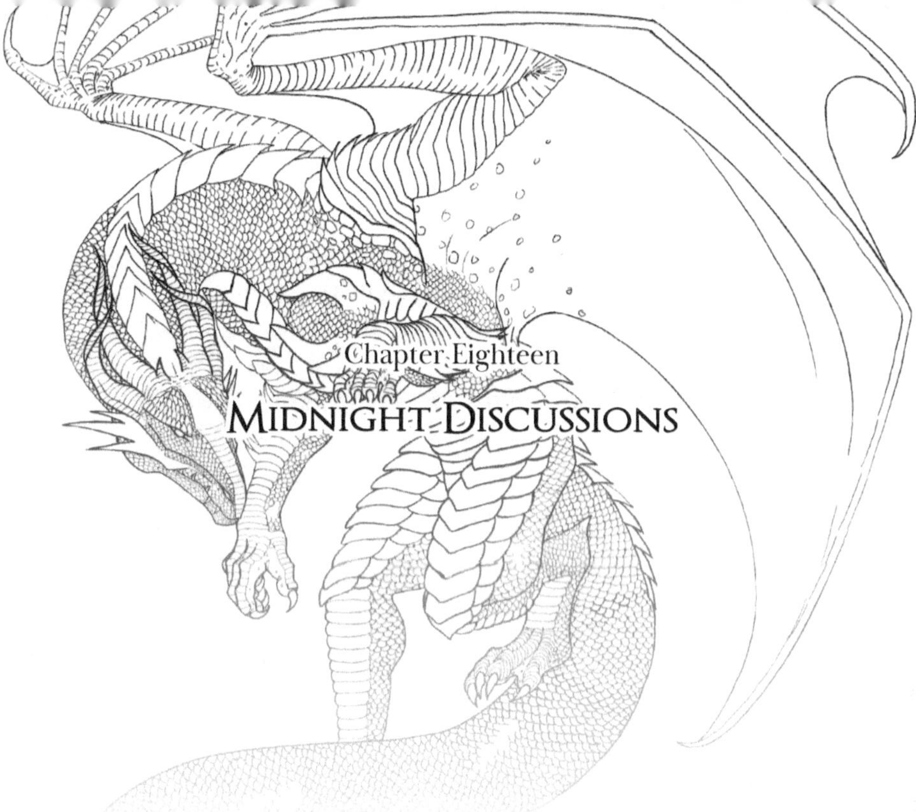

Chapter Eighteen

Midnight Discussions

It was almost midnight.

She hadn't reached back out to him, which had made Alaster run marathons on what could've caused that.

Had Cregorous struck again? Had she actually been okay when he'd briefly talked to her earlier? Or had he just assumed she was when, really, she was imprisoned somewhere, and her annoyance was at the fact that he couldn't help her in her situation? Or *was* she okay and she'd just forgotten about him? Or did she not know how to reach back out to him?

This whole telepathy thing was really weird to stumble into and try to figure out on his own.

And his ceiling wasn't providing any answers to what he should do.

He couldn't sleep. He couldn't stop thinking about her. Wondering what was going on. What had happened. Who she was.

Fidgeting with his blanket, he reached out to the dancing thrum. He'd felt it throughout the day but hadn't wanted to intrude. She'd said she would reach out to him.

But this whole not knowing thing was killing him.

As gently as he could, he asked, *Is now a better time?*

He felt her jerk back, almost as if she'd gasped at his appearance. But then a sense of relief came from her.

His fidgeting stopped at the sensation as he waited for her. She hadn't pushed away or told him to leave her alone. That had to be a good sign, right?

Alaster's gaze flicked across the ceiling as he waited. When he felt the weirdest thing.

Like a tentative hand reaching out for his, gently taking hold of his fingers. As though quietly reaching for comfort.

It was alarmingly gentle.

He flinched a little, anyway. The phantom hand was small in his grasp, and the logic part of his brain wanted to scream that he was crazy. So, he didn't grip it back. Even though his fingers begged to close around the hand reaching out to him.

Yeah, he heard her say quietly.

How did he respond to that?

How did he not stroke his fingers against her gentle grasp?

What the heck was he feeling?

It was such a foreign sensation in his chest that budded and warmed his heart. He felt awkward and confused, and nothing made sense. And he couldn't say it was the telepathy making him think that.

There was a small scoff from her. *Oh, now you go quiet on me.*

Sorry, he said quickly then paused. His fingers twitched. He wanted to tell them to shut up. He wanted to ask if she was okay. If everything was all right. But ... she had shoved him away last time.

He didn't even know her name.

Swallowing back his awkwardness, he said, *I was debating on asking if you were all right.*

There was a *tap, tap, tap* against his finger, and Alaster stiffened. What was that? What was she doing? It felt like she lay next to him, her fingers gently wrapped around his.

Even though she wasn't actually lying next to him, he kept his gaze glued to the ceiling, as if by looking to his right, he might suddenly find her there. The girl with telepathy who was making him feel ... something.

I had a rough day. Are you okay? she finally asked.

A relieved breath escaped him, because the phantom tapping against his fingers had stopped.

His brow pulled together. *Why wouldn't I be?*

You weren't attacked?

He blinked a few times and gently shook his head. *By whom?*

She chuckled, and he felt his face flame. That was probably a stupid question. Who else, idiot?

Whom? she asked, and he swore he could see her smile.

Pushing his nervousness aside, he rolled his eyes. *It is proper terminology.*

It's proper grammar, and it's a little shocking.

He couldn't stop himself from smiling a little at her response. Okay, so she was witty. Maybe she felt just as awkward about this as he did.

Who are you? she asked.

Eyes widening a little, he thought back, *I could be asking you the same question.*

Well, too bad. I asked first.

Touché, he said with a twinge of his brow.

Should he tell her? Was it safe to tell her?

It was definitely a girl he was talking to. American, he thought, based on the way her voice sounded. So it definitely wasn't Cregorous. So it had to be safe to tell her who he was, right?

Throwing caution to the wind, he said, *My name's Alaster.*

He felt her hum, as though mulling over his name. It wasn't that uncommon, was it?

When she didn't respond, he raised his brow and thought, *And you are ...?*

I'm Jen.

Hi, Jen.

Hi, Alaster.

For some reason, he smiled. At least now he knew her name.

He fidgeted a little then awkwardly said, *This might be a stupid question, but ... are you a Human-Born?*

Oh, thank God, she said as he felt a flood of relief from her.

He chuckled, a sense of gratefulness filling him. All things considered, that explained a lot.

I assume the answer is yes? he asked.

I was worried for a little bit.

That the voices in your head were your own?

No. Wait—is that what you were worried about?

Embarrassment crashed into him, and he groaned at how stupid he sounded. He'd really said that? Of course he hadn't thought that!

Okay, so ... maybe he had considered that as an option.

For how smart everyone claimed he was, he felt awfully stupid.

Um ... no comment, he muttered back.

He felt a flash of a vision, of her fighting back a smile.

Blinking away his strange sense of familiarity with her, he thought back to something she'd asked. *You asked if I was attacked.*

Yeah.

Cregorous. Africa.

Is that ...?

His thoughts fell into dread.

She'd been attacked. By Cregorous. Twice.

Alaster? she asked after a moment.

His gaze flitted around the room, and he said, *That was Cregorous, wasn't it?*

The same feelings from earlier hit his chest as he felt her shudder. The gentle grasp on his hand tightened. His instinct was to squeeze her hand back. But ... what might that do?

What the heck was this phantom touch thing? And how was she doing it?

Yeah, she finally answered.

Are you okay? he asked before he could stop himself.

Of course she's okay, idiot, he berated himself. *She wouldn't be talking to you if she wasn't!*

All the same, he felt her calm from his question.

That was a weird response.

Yeah, we all are, she said.

His brow pinched. *All?*

Oh, yeah. Long story short; we're getting the gang together.

The Human-Borns?

Yeah.

A clash of excitement and nervousness erupted in his chest. He was going to meet the other Human-Borns!

But, wait.

Why? And why were they meeting on Earth? He'd always assumed they would all meet up in Agerius.

Blinking away his confusion, he asked, *How many have you met so far?*

Four. So far, we've gone to four different continents. Where are you?

Oh. I'm in Antarctica, he said like that was totally expected.

She paused before saying, *Why in God's name are you in Antarctica?*

That was probably as normal a response as he could have hoped for.

It's ... a long story. I'll tell you later.

Well, the last coordinates make more sense now. I thought we were being lied to.

None of what she'd said answered his wonders.

Why gather all of the Human-Borns? Clearly, something was awry. She'd been attacked by Cregorous—they'd been attacked by Cregorous.

And he'd been stuck here, unable to help them.

They were all okay, but ... what was going on? She hadn't divulged why the Human-Borns were meeting up. Was it right for him to ask?

He had to know.

Am I safe in assuming things aren't okay?

There was a pause for a moment, and he felt her deliberation. That response only coiled worry in his chest.

They want to take the Zaheri away from us, she said.

"What?" Alaster said out loud, snapping Frost awake at his side.

Blearily, the grovix yawned and asked, "Is something wrong?"

Ignoring Frost, Alaster thought back to Jen, *Who is they?*

The High Council.

Sitting upright, Alaster spun to Frost. "Why would the Council take the Zaheri away from us?"

The grovix blinked several times, his brow knitted in confusion. "Alaster, what are you speaking of? The Council would not—"

"Apparently, they would! They're taking the Zaheri away!" He scrubbed his scalp. "Is that why the others haven't come back?"

Rising to stand, Frost said, "Alaster, control yourself. What are you talking about?"

"The Council—your Council—they want to take the Zaheri away from us Human-Borns."

"Where are you getting such nonsense?" Frost asked with a wrinkle of his snout.

Alaster? Jen frantically called to him.

Holding his hand up to silence Frost, Alaster thought back, *Yeah, sorry. Didn't mean to startle you.*

"Alaster, what—"

"In a minute, Frost!" he said a little curtly. He was trying to pay attention to Jen. Her phantom fingers clutched his arm, and fear radiated from her.

Sorry to ask again, but I've got a sense—

I thought something happened, she almost gasped out, distress still emanating from her.

He tried to grasp her, take hold of her hand, figure out how to comfort her.

The attack this morning was so abrupt. I ... What if you're attacked and we can't get there?

"Alaster?" Frost asked, his eyes narrowed as he studied the teen.

"I'm ... talking to one of the Human-Borns," Alaster muttered.

Frost's brow rose, and his ears shot upright in alarm.

He had to reassure her. *Jen, I'll be okay. Nothing's happened. I wasn't attacked today.*

You weren't?

No. I'd know if anything was coming. Right? He'd know. Dr. McKay hadn't said anything about the portal anomaly spiking again. Which meant they were fine.

Alaster could still feel her fear, and he calmly said, *Take a breath. Everything's going to be fine.*

"How are you—"

"Just give me a minute, Frost, okay? Please?" Alaster begged, giving his Zaheri a pleading look.

It was crazy.

But he was more worried about Jen than he was about Frost.

Frost could call him crazy or demand to tell him what was going on, but Alaster would sooner drown Frost out and focus on Jen.

That made no sense. He didn't even know her.

So, why did he want to protect her so badly?

Her fears settled, and he felt the tension in his own body slowly dissipate.

That's good, she said. *We're coming for you, Alaster.*

He couldn't stop himself from smiling a little. *I'm not going anywhere.*

There was a sense of befuddlement from her, and he stilled, trying to gauge what she was thinking.

This was weird. But so strangely right at the same time.

Alaster's mind spun in confusion over how okay he was with what was happening. He was talking to a girl. With telepathy. And he was okay with this?

Maybe he was crazy.

Why were you so adamant about staying with me? Earlier? she asked.

Alaster's shoulders deflated. He didn't know the answer to that. The only answer he had was ... he just couldn't leave her.

I ... I don't know. I just...

He watched Frost sit down, studying Alaster intently but giving the boy the silence he'd asked for.

I couldn't just leave you with him bearing down on you. He swallowed and felt the remembrance from earlier that day. He'd felt compelled to stay at her side because ...

Because she'd been afraid. And he'd wanted to protect her. But how did he convey that without sounding insane? How could he acknowledge that without *feeling* insane?

He didn't even know her.

He shrugged a little uselessly. *I had to do something,* he finally settled on.

He knew you were there.

I know.

And you tried to stay, anyway?

Yeah, that was pretty stupid, huh? Cregorous, the monster he'd been told about, bearing down on him, knowing he was there telepathically, and he wanted to stay? How stupid could he be?

But that was just it.

It was Cregorous, he pressed, trying to convey his understanding of how dangerous her situation had been. *I wasn't about to leave you against him, not if there was something I might be able to do. If I couldn't physically stand with you guys and fight him off…*

He didn't know how to convey what he'd felt in that moment. What he felt now, thinking on it. That, for no good reason, he just wasn't able to let himself flee when he'd known she was in danger.

Gently shaking his head, he added, *I couldn't just leave you.*

He felt her sigh. *I get it.*

A new confusion danced in his mind. *You do?*

Yeah … I mean, if you were in that situation, and I could at least encourage you, give you the strength to keep fighting … Her thoughts trailed off, and he hung on to their connection, waiting for her to continue. After a short pause, she said, *Sometimes that makes all the difference.*

What more might she have to face before they were all together? How could he help her? Stuck on this frozen continent, no way of getting to her physically … there had to be something he could do. Maybe it was as simple as being there for her if she needed him.

It felt awkward to admit that he liked the idea.

With trepidation, he said, *I'm here for you. If you need me …*

I'll call.

Right. Because this was calling someone.

He chuckled a little at the absurdity of what this was between them. This strange communication they could have that shouldn't have been possible, yet here they were.

Think-talking to one another.

Good. I'll be waiting for you, he said.

I promise we'll get there as soon as we can.

The concept of all the Human-Borns rushing to meet up with him, the youngest of them all and, by all accounts, a totally random part of the puzzle, made him want to roll his eyes. *Take your time,* he answered.

There was a strange awkwardness from her before he felt the soft fingers retreat from his hand.

It was stupid. But he'd actually found it comforting.

Slowly, he looked at Frost and found the grovix staring at him unblinkingly.

With a sigh, the Zaheri said, "It appears we have much to discuss."

Frost had been miffed that Alaster hadn't divulged more of the whole telepathy thing, and that he hadn't been more wary. And that he hadn't said something earlier in the evening when he'd obviously begun playing with the telepathy brewing in his mind.

"I yearn to believe that your interaction was indeed with a Human-Born, and that your mind is still your own," Frost said with a small scowl. "However, we have no proof, only the voice's word that—"

"I can't explain it, Frost," Alaster nearly shot out, protectiveness over Jen spiking in his chest. "I—It can't be Cregorous."

"Can it not?" Frost asked with bewilderment, his eyes wide and brow risen. "I would say I am relieved that you are so adept at an ability that has been dormant in Agerius for two millennia, if not for the absurdity of it."

Flabbergasted at Frost's inability to believe that Jen was real, and that Alaster wasn't somehow being manipulated by Cregorous, Alaster searched the wall for an answer, his mouth contorting around a response. "I saw her, Frost! I saw her—"

"You saw Cregorous threatening a man," Frost corrected sternly.

"Fine! Yes! Okay! I ... don't know what she looks like. But Frost, I know what she was feeling! It rippled off of her like waves crashing on the shore, and she was petrified. Do you honestly believe that Cregorous could feel fear? The type of fear I got from her?"

Releasing a slow breath, Frost's shoulders lost their hard edge. "I must admit, imagining Cregorous fearful is not something I can accomplish."

Alaster slumped onto his mattress and rubbed his forehead. "I get it. I really do. This sounds ... insane."

"It sounds dangerous," the grovix amended, his gaze soft. "Telepathy is a vast unknown, and the only one we have certainty of—"

"Is Cregorous, I know. I'm acutely aware that he's the only one hundred percent known Telepath in all of Tilion. You've made the point abundantly clear."

"So you can understand my trepidation."

For a moment, Alaster stewed on the situation. He had to appeal to Frost logically. He wanted to roll his eyes at himself. He had to appeal to *himself* logically. This whole thing was so outside of logical understanding that he was genuinely surprised he was okay with it. It certainly wasn't something he could voice to his parents. They would be unable to grasp it.

Truthfully, he was unable to grasp it. Not fully.

Because so much about this new ability was wrapped up in swelling emotions and strange sensations that Alaster just couldn't understand.

The protectiveness...

Well, the protectiveness made sense, if he thought about it objectively.

Cam. The Zaheri. His parents. People he wanted to keep safe. Some he'd succeeded in protecting. Others ...

He hadn't been able to be there for Cam.

That meant he had to be there to protect those he could. If it was in his power, in his ability, he had to save those he could save.

Maybe Cregorous was that manipulative. Maybe he could understand hidden truths in people's hearts faster than logic would say was possible. Maybe he could totally warp his thought patterns and emotions just to exploit a quiet drive in Alaster's soul.

But there was an undeniable thing. A small voice that prompted him. A faith that pushed him to believe.

Jen was real. She was real, and she was scared, and she'd needed someone to help her.

Taking a calming breath, Alaster met Frost's gaze. "Do I ever get this adamant about something I don't believe in?"

Frost stared at him for a few seconds before he blinked and twitched his brow. "I admit that is a fair assessment."

"I do understand your wariness. It makes sense. I'm not saying you're making totally baseless claims. But ... if Cregorous has abilities that haven't been seen in Agerius for two thousand years, doesn't it stand to reason that maybe part of what makes us Human-Borns so special is the fact that we might possess some of these dormant traits?"

"Of course there is soundness to your claim," the grovix said with a sigh. "But you must understand that it would not be total nonsense to believe Cregorous might appeal to a young teenage boy as a girl to try to sway emotions."

Alaster's gaze clicked about the room for a moment before he focused on Frost. "Why would her being a girl matter?"

A chuckle tumbled from Frost. "Ah, yes, well, I had forgotten that you are not like so many young men, and hormones do not rule your thought process."

Hormones?

Wait, but...

Alaster quickly shoved the brewing question into a black hole in his mind.

Jen was coming with the other Human-Borns. He'd meet her soon enough. Once they were face-to-face, once they could actually see one another, maybe then he'd ask the question.

Right now, he wouldn't even entertain it. Because the basest thought of it felt absolutely stupid.

Attraction via telepathy?

An absurd concept.

Chapter Nineteen

THE BEGINNING

Watching blizzards from the galley was one of Alaster's favorite things to do. He'd always liked seeing snow fall from the comfort and coziness of his home, and the galley's big windows afforded a great view of falling snow.

The worst of the storm had passed from the station, leaving softly falling snow against the dusk-stuck tundra.

In a few days, he'd be shipping back to the States.

He was excited to return to Alaska, because he'd come to miss the cabin they called home there, but he was also a little concerned.

It'd been two days since he'd spoken to Jen last. She'd met four Human-Borns, which meant there was only one more to meet up with before they came for him. But they were running out of time.

He figured that if he didn't hear from her by tonight, he'd try to reach out to her mind and let her know that they'd have to meet up some other way. Because if they all came after he left Antarctica, what chaos might that cause?

The station was in a state of flux. With many of the scientists preparing to leave before the winter season, there were shipping boxes everywhere. Luggage tags were being assigned. Tickets to the States purchased. Plans, deadlines, and orders on where to be when.

Alaster was packed, his books and clothing ready to go. He only had a few clothes left in his drawers, and that was simply to keep things organized.

His parents were a flurry of movement, scrambling to get everything done in time. There'd been attempts to help, only for him to ultimately be in the way.

So, he sat and waited, hoping that the other Human-Borns would arrive soon. He hoped Jen would reach out before they came so that he could go out to the portal's location and meet up with them. Hopefully, she thought ahead about those sorts of things.

Just as he was preparing to go back to his room and find something to read to pass the time, a page came over the station-wide system.

"Alaster O'Brien to Dr. McKay's office. Alaster to Dr. McKay's office."

Quickly depositing his empty mug in the dish room, Alaster ran to Dr. McKay's lab. Frost met him there as they stepped into the cluttered workspace.

The balding doctor looked over his shoulder and said, "Good, you're prompt. We've got something here."

"What's going on?" Alaster asked as he stepped up to the desk. His question was answered as he looked to the monitor and saw the spike of the portal activation displayed. But the readings were different. Lunging forward a bit, Alaster asked, "When did this happen?"

"A minute ago. It's strange, though," Dr. McKay said, shaking his head and squinting. "It's the same thing—the portal. Your portal. Their portal. Whatever. It's clearly in the same location as it was four months ago, but ..."

"The signature's different," Alaster muttered, flicking his gaze across the reading displayed on the screen.

"Yeah, that's not all," McKay said as he cued up another screen. He waggled his finger toward the display. "This has happened a few times in the last couple weeks."

"How'd we miss it?"

"Hello, I've had to move my station at least three times," Dr. McKay said with a twinge of annoyance. "All of this rebuilding of the station, and everyone leaving for the winter—it's been annoying."

"Sorry, you're right," Alaster said, shaking his head. "Have all of the newer readings been this different signature?"

"Yeah. Which, look at this," he brought up a new graph showcasing this activation against the one from the attack, "It's substantially stronger."

Alaster's brow pulled together, and he waved his hand a little toward the screen. "Wait. Where's the activation when the Agerian came?"

Dr. McKay blinked a few times and glanced back at Alaster. "You're right." He turned back to the screen. "That was ... six days ago?"

"Uh, yeah."

The computer beeped, and Dr. McKay shook his head. "This makes no sense. There's no activation displayed here."

"Zoom in."

"Why?"

"Just ... a theory," Alaster muttered as the doctor zoomed in. And zoomed in.

After a few times of zooming in on the graph, the reading popped up. A fraction of the energy was displayed against the spike from moments earlier.

Dr. McKay let out a scoff. "This doesn't make sense. You'd imagine that the energy needed to travel to another world would require a greater input, not a lesser one."

"Perhaps not," Frost mused.

Alaster looked to him as McKay continued to stare at the screen, analyzing the readings.

"The portal was created for travel between worlds. What Cregorous did on the day of the attack required it to act outside of its function."

"So, you're saying—"

"This is highly irregular," Frost said with a look of concern. He flicked his gaze to Alaster's. "If what is happening now shows a greater energy being utilized, it could mean disaster."

Alaster blinked a few times as he turned to face Frost fully. "But maybe it isn't."

Frost cocked his head to the side.

"What if it's Jen?" He gestured to the screen. "What if that's how they're moving across the Earth to gather the Human-Borns?"

The grovix's brow twitched. "I admit, the thought had not occurred to me. If she is the First Human-Born, her power would be greater than Cregorous'."

Out of nowhere, Jen's voice hit his mind as she said, *Alaster?*

He jolted slightly in alarm, and Frost's eyes widened.

"Are you—"

"Sorry, no, I'm fine," Alaster quickly said, holding his hand out to quell any fears. "Jen just startled me."

Jen? he thought back to her.

Oh, thank God. Good. I need your help.

With what?

You're still in Antarctica, right?

It felt like a weird question, but he answered it anyway. *Um... yeah. Haven't gone anywhere.*

Great. We're here.

Wait—that's you? That answered the burning question of the moment.

What's me?

The portal activation.

How are you tracking that?

Long story. Who's we?

He quickly said to Frost, "It's Jen. She used the portal to get here."

"Whoever this Jen is, she's something else," McKay muttered as he hyper-focused on the screen.

Um ... everyone, she answered.

All the Human-Borns?

And Zaheri. Well, not all of the Zaheri. A lot of the Zaheri. Some. Whatever.

Glancing toward the window, Alaster felt a pang of worry. *Jen, this isn't good.*

What isn't?

Your timing! There's a blizzard going on right now!

Yeah, I gathered that. Can you come get us?

He couldn't help but laugh a little at the request. She made it sound so simple, like he just had to go pick her up at the corner store or something.

"Are they all right?" Frost asked.

"Yeah, just ... with the blizzard, I don't know how to get them all here," Alaster said.

Six Human-Borns and at least as many Zaheri. So, at least a dozen people. Maybe more. She made it sound like there were more than six Zaheri. There wasn't a vehicle big enough that could handle the terrain and a blizzard.

Frustration bubbled in his chest that he couldn't find a solution that would work.

I can't. Not everyone, he told her.

So, you could come get me?

Jen, no, he responded quickly, ardently. That was a bad idea. Her alone in this terrain?

I can handle it. Just tell me where to go.

This was a bad idea. On one hand, yes, safer. Guiding one person through a blizzard would be easier. But had she accounted for the frigid temperatures? Her body wouldn't be able to handle that.

Look, I've acclimated to this weather. I can handle it. You can't.

Hey, I just found out I'm a Jumper. I betcha I can handle it.

He almost admired her confidence. If it wasn't so dangerous.

A frown came to his face as he tried to work through it.

Frost's eyes narrowed. "What is wrong?"

"Jen wants to travel in the blizzard on her own, and have me guide her."

"Wait—you can do that?" McKay asked, finally pulling his gaze from the screen. He whipped his gaze around the room and said, "Who's Jen?"

"A girl I'm talking to," Alaster answered dismissively.

"With what?" the doctor asked incredulously.

"She is the First Human-Born, Alaster. It's very likely she could withstand the rigors of the tundra," Frost said.

"But, what if she can't?" Alaster asked then gestured toward the windows. "What if she's from a tropical climate and hasn't ever been in snow before?"

"Does she believe she is capable?"

"Yes, but—"

"Then perhaps you should trust her, as you have asked me to trust her."

Alaster stared back at his Zaheri for a few seconds before a laden sigh escaped him.

Fine. Yes, I can come get you.

Good. Hold please.

His face scrunched in confusion as he muttered, "Hold please?"

"Alaster?"

Shrugging exaggeratingly, he said, "I don't know."

The grovix's gaze drifted. "Perhaps she needs to convey her plan to the others." He refocused on Alaster. "We should prepare ourselves to head to the portal."

Without another word, they left the confused scientist gaping at the interaction. "Wh—how was he talking to someone?" McKay asked no one.

They went to Alaster's room and swiftly got ready. Alaster threw on his snow boots and snatched a mid-weight jacket. He wouldn't need it, but he was almost positive Jen would. Urgency at getting to her as quickly as possible made him forget to change into a self-replicating shirt. Then he scribbled a hasty note and slapped it onto his door, letting his parents know he'd be back as soon as he could.

As they reached the mudroom and started to exit the station, he heard Jen's voice.

Alaster?

Are you on your way? I'll guide you.

Not yet.

He stopped in his tracks, Frost crashing into him and letting out a small yip of surprise. *What are you doing? It's a blizzard in Antarctica! You need to get moving or you'll start to experience loss of feeling in your extremities!*

"Alast—"

"She's not on her way yet! What's she doing? Is she trying to get herself hurt?" He started pacing near the ski-doos.

I will. Soon. Just ... I need to ask you something.

Flailing his arms around, he responded desperately, *Okay, any-thing. What?*

Who are your Zaheri?

Confusion slammed into his mind. *What?*

Your Zaheri. One of mine...

Dread filled his chest.

She hadn't told them? Why?

Oh no.

What if they thought he was Cregorous? What if *she* thought he was Cregorous?

Frost's concern had been valid, but as Alaster had stated: it was clearly a girl he spoke to. He could feel it in his soul that she was who she claimed to be.

But ... he was a guy.

A guy talking to Jen via telepathy. And her Zaheri would land on the same conclusion Frost had—Cregorous was the only known Telepath. So, naturally, they'd fear she'd begun to fall for some trap made by the Caligan.

One of my Zaheri seems to think you might be Cregorous ... trying to trick me. Trick us into a trap, she said.

How could he be so stupid?

Of course her Zaheri wouldn't trust him! Of course they wouldn't let her go wandering into a blizzard, off to meet someone who claimed to be a Human-Born.

He sighed and responded, *Because he has telepathy.*

I need to prove to them you're who you say you are.

But ... he didn't have to prove it to her? Why did that comfort him?

You believe me?

You're not him, she said assuredly.

He let out a small, scoffing chuckle. *How do you know?*

Or could she not articulate their connection, their trust of one another, any better than he could? Was she just as confused at the warm familiarity of their telepathy? That neither of them questioned that they were speaking with a Human-Born and could rely on their word as gold?

It was absurd. But that was how it felt. So natural. So fitting. So...

Strangely pure.

I just ... she started. *You're ... you're calming; he's chaotic. You're sincere; he's deceitful. You're open; he's not.*

Everything she'd said about him made a funny warmth flood his chest. She saw him as calming, sincere, and open? Why did he like that those were the three attributes she'd chosen to describe him?

All his life, the first thing people would say about him was that he was smart. The next thing they might say was that he was handsome.

What Jen had described was the equivalent of rest. Of relaxation. Of sanctuary.

It made him want to figure out how he would describe her.

Shaking his head, he berated himself. He had to answer her. Her Zaheri were probably becoming suspicious of how long it was taking him to provide an answer.

Kedar, Gaeor, Taesir, and Council Member Frost. I can give their specialties, too, he said as swiftly and confidently as possible to remove all doubt for her. To solidify that she could trust him.

Which was stupid. Because it was alarmingly apparent that she already trusted him.

There was silence from her, and he could only assume it was because she now had the battle of convincing her Zaheri that her going alone was the safest bet.

Frost had settled nearby, watching Alaster's manic pacing with a puzzled look on his furry face.

They should start walking toward the portal. Soon enough, Jen would begin her journey, and he wanted to keep her time in the frigid conditions to an absolute minimum.

He turned to Frost and started to march toward the door. "We should get going."

As the grovix rose, he said, "Alaster, this girl ..."

His hand stilled on the handle.

"You trust her?"

More than anyone.

The thought hit him without hesitation and made his breath rattle out in surprise. He swallowed and shook away his confusion over ... everything.

"Yeah, Frost, I trust her."

With a nod, the Zaheri said, "Very well. Let us be off."

A moment later, he heard Jen say, *Alaster, I'm good to go. Which way? I'm already heading your way.*

He felt her smile. Not saw her smile, *felt* her smile. Like it wrapped around his chest as if a blanket warming his soul. He had to force himself to not want to melt into that feeling.

Feelings were stupid.

He'd never understood them.

And now he really wished he could.

Great. But, which way do I go? she asked.

Head into the wind. Right now, it's blowing on my back. Until the storm breaks, we'll have to rely on that to orient you.

Perfect, she scoffed. *So my face is gonna be totally red when we meet.*

He couldn't stop the smile that tore his face, and he chuckled.

Frost threw him a confused look.

Alaster shied away, shoving his sudden embarrassment aside as he responded, *I promise not to take it personally.*

He was about to meet Jen. Face-to-face, he was finally going to meet her.

He wanted to roll his eyes at his absolutely moronic mindset. He'd only met her a few days ago. Was he seriously that excited over meeting her?

Squinting at him, Frost asked, "Alaster, are you all right?"

"What? Yeah, I'm fine," Alaster hastily said.

A doubtful look came to Frost's face. "You are wringing your hands as though they were a drenched towel in need of drying."

Begrudgingly shoving his hands in his pockets, Alaster hunched over a little.

Flicking his gaze between the horizon and the teen at his side, the grovix asked, "Are you worried you were mistaken of Jen's identity?"

"No," Alaster said with a shake of his head. "It's ... I'm ..." A frustrated groan escaped him. "I'm nervous about meeting her."

Frost quirked his brow, his ear twitching a bit. "That is understandable. She is the first Human-Born you will meet. And represents someone who will be capable of relating with you. After all, you are an extraordinary human with unique gifts. Other humans would not be able to grasp one-tenth of what you have experienced in the last several months."

Was that it? Was that the only reason why Alaster felt so anxious about meeting Jen? That made the most sense. And wouldn't require analyzing his emotions.

He'd take that answer.

The storm shifted, and they paused for the third time. In a moment, the blizzard was on top of them.

Groaning in annoyance, Alaster muttered, "Of course this storm is moving in a circle."

He relayed the change to Jen, and then said, *Sorry, I'm almost there.* He glanced toward the snow clouding his vision. At least it wasn't as bad as it had been earlier in the day. It probably would let up soon. *I think,* he added, hoping that they were still headed to the portal.

Oh good. Glad to know your sense of direction is so stellar, she teased.

Hey, you're the one who showed up in a blizzard, he quickly fired back. *It's not like I knew!*

He wanted to jab at her and say she could have called ahead of time, but refrained. He didn't know what she'd been through, so he shouldn't judge her actions.

Heck, she'd been attacked by Cregorous a few days ago. Harrowing events like that weren't easy to bounce back from. He knew that all too well.

Where's the sun right now? For you, I mean, he asked.

If I say, 'the sky,' will you be annoyed?

The playful tone she'd used made him twitch his brow. *Annoyed? No. A little perturbed, yes.*

He could be playful, too.

She scoffed. *Same thing.*

Where is the sun? he asked, trying to redirect his questions to the matter at hand. Even if he got a little turned around, she should keep her bearings.

The sky.

Oh, for heaven's sake. <u>Where is the sun?</u>

In space.

He laughed out loud, startling Frost. Which only spurred him into more chuckling. "Sorry, Frost."

A smile played on the grovix's face. "I can assume you're having a pleasant conversation with Jennifer?"

Ignoring Frost, he responded to Jen, *Maybe you're suffering from delirium. That would explain a lot.*

Hey!

Do you want my faulty sense of direction or not?

I never said it was faulty.

You insinuated it was.

Tomayto-tomato.

Rolling his eyes but still smiling, he asked, *Jen, where is the sun?*

Behind me.

Thank you. Keep the sun behind you.

It'd been about a half hour. Longer than he'd hoped. Which meant she might be having issues with her fingers and toes. But did she realize that?

How're you doing? he asked. *Still able to move your fingers and toes?*

A few seconds passed before she answered, *Yeah, but it's tough.*

Dang. Okay. Hang in there.

What's the worst that'll happen? We are Human-Born. A little frostbite won't kill us.

Wow, he scoffed. *You're taking this so seriously.*

It's not like you've had issues.

I've had three years! And lots of heavy jackets! Gosh, was this why she was so confident that she could handle the tundra? Because he'd been okay? He should've done a better job of conveying how long he'd had to adapt.

Three years? Why in God's name would you stay here for three years?

My parents are scientists.

So, you got to come along?

Well, extenuating circumstances. I'm a rare case.

He hoped she wouldn't ask any probing questions about that. It wasn't that he was afraid to talk about it, but...

He liked that she didn't look at him differently because he was book smart.

Have you talked at all since you started off? he asked.

Um ... no. Why? Do you make a habit of talking to yourself?

Oh stop.

Hey, you're the one who said you were afraid my voice was your own subconscious talking to you.

Crap, really? She really was going to fixate on that one stupid errant comment?

I did not! he defended.

Fine. You insinuated.

Okay, maybe she was really book smart, too. Because she seemed good at recalling random things he'd said. Maybe they had a lot more in common than just being Human-Born.

Returning to why he'd asked if she'd said anything out loud, he said, *I ask because your facial muscles need to flex, too. Make sure your lips haven't frozen shut.*

And, if they have?

Well ... I don't know. Gotta figure that out if that happens.

Scrubbing his scalp, he tried to think through how he could help her if that did happen. A flash of a thought hit his mind and, in flustering horror, he chastised himself, *Tea! You could give her tea, you idiot! Don't be a scumbag!*

Mouth still works, she responded.

There had to be a witty retort to that comment. There just had to be. *No, idiot, be nice.* He settled on replying, *That's good.*

She paused for a moment, and he squinted in confusion.

Were you trying to think through some witty comeback? she asked.

His face contorted in embarrassed pain that she could see through his actions so acutely. To try to appeal to her and make her know he was a gentleman, he quickly said, *Of course not, m'lady.*

M'lady? What are you thinking? his mind hollered. *How stupid could you sound right now? M'lady? M'lady?*

That's a good thing, m'lord, she said, and he let out a surprised chuckle. *For if I were, I might need to hit you when we meet.*

She liked the nickname?

Okay.

Perish the thought, he replied.

And he felt her smile again.

A moment passed, and the snow began to let up, when she suddenly asked, *Alaster? You're sure you haven't had any incidents in the last two days?*

That seemed like a strange thing to ask. Furrowing his brow, he nodded. *I'm pretty sure. There's always the chance that we missed something. Why?*

I think someone's here.

Wait—what?

I don't know.

Someone like who?

Wildly looking to Frost, Alaster said, "Jen thinks someone's near her. You aren't aware of anything that's happened in the last couple days, are you?"

Frost shook his head. "I am not aware of anything."

Alaster, one of Cregorous' generals is here.

What! "What!" echoed in his head and stumbled out of his mouth.

"What is it, Alaster? What is wrong?" Frost asked, his muscles tense.

"One of Cregorous' generals is here!" He frantically started to run. Frost picked up speed at his side.

Don't worry; I've taken him before, Jen said.

That doesn't matter! Where are you? Dang it, you don't know. I'm coming. Jen was woefully unprepared for this encounter.

"What way is the portal?" Alaster hollered, forcing himself faster despite the fresh powder providing a less than ideal grip.

"This way," Frost said, snatching Alaster's sleeve in his teeth and yanking the teen forward. "This is the direction you had been guiding Jennifer."

"You're sure?" the teen asked in a panic.

"As well as I can be."

Wait. Telepathy.

Sliding to a stop, Alaster pushed into Jen's mind. He'd seen through her eyes before; he could do it again. He just needed a clue for her location to verify where he needed to go. If she was where he thought she was, given the time that had elapsed and accounting for the storm and the number of times they'd stopped to reorient themselves, there should be a mountain nearby.

He just had to pray she was standing so he could see it.

The overlay in his vision happened, and he got a flashing glimpse of a man with orange-gold eyes, wearing a leather jacket and a smooth smirk. The mountain range peeked toward her left.

He knew where she was.

"This way!" he screamed, tearing forward, a little more to the left of where Frost had been about to guide them.

Jen said her fingers and toes had been stiff before. That meant her limbs were, too. And the more she used her energy in this cold, her body would probably not be concentrating on keeping her temperature regulated. At least that was how Kedar had described it when he was trying to acclimate to the subzero temperature.

Whoever she was squaring off against didn't seem bothered by the cold, or had already acclimated. Did they get there before she did? When? How did they miss it?

Maybe what Frost had been talking about was true—the portal didn't let off as much radiation when it was opened from Tilion, and vice versa.

Which meant he'd failed.

He'd told Jen there hadn't been any activations. He'd let her saunter into danger unknowingly.

The powder was his nemesis, but he refused to fall or get tripped up. He had to get to Jen and protect her. Because he was the one who could fight in this climate; she couldn't. It wasn't a question of her power, or her abilities, or her strength. It was a simple matter that her body wouldn't work in tandem with her energy like it normally would.

There was the sound of crackling energy, and Alaster surged past Frost, pushing his legs to move faster than normal. Forcing himself to get to her. He'd fly if he thought that would help, but he didn't know what he was getting into. And ripping his shirt and jacket open might only hinder his ability to protect Jen.

He'd never fought with giant holes in his clothing in the bitter cold. He had to be smart about engaging whoever was attacking Jen.

Sparks of blue and gray littered the field ahead. He could see her limbs jerking and shaking, an unresponsiveness likely occurring between her slowly freezing body and her stampeding energy.

A pulse hit the air, and the man attacking Jen disappeared for half a second before reappearing in front of her, slamming her into the ground. His hand closed around her throat, and he started strangling her as he held her down with his weight.

Fierce protectiveness surged through Alaster, and green energy spiraled and sparked around his torso, tearing down his arms and fixing in his hands. It sounded like a storm erupted around him, crackling and crashing in the direness clutching his heart.

He hadn't been able to save Cam.

He hadn't been able to stop the other general from ripping Gae-or's arm off.

He *would not* let this Caligan hurt Jen.

With a yell, Alaster threw his hands out and sent a charging blast of green colliding with the general on top of Jen. Then he leaped over her and planted himself between her and her attacker. His vision felt coated in a green mist, and he fixed a scowl on his face.

Frost landed next to him a second later, his fur bristled and ice shards crackled to form along his fur.

"Leave her alone," Alaster commanded furiously, daring this guy to try even looking at Jen wrong.

In that moment, Alaster was almost positive he'd never felt so resolute. So fixed. So angry.

The general's jaw was tight, and his right arm trembled. Blood pooled in his palm. Good. Alaster had let him know that he wasn't messing around. That he wouldn't let this guy get another finger on Jen.

This monster would have to go through him to get to her. And Alaster was positive he'd sooner tear this guy's arm off than let him touch Jen again.

Glancing between Alaster and Frost, the general spat, "Fine." He straightened and gave Jen a crooked grin. "Till next time, little one." And then he disappeared into gray dust.

He heard Jen let out a heavy sigh, and he spun around, catching her before she fell to the icy terrain. He guided her to rest on her knees and asked, "Are you all right?"

Trembling shivers racked her body.

His grip tightened a little on her shoulders, trying to will his warmth to cover her.

"I will ensure he leaves," Frost said.

Alaster couldn't take his eyes off her. She was so ... normal. There wasn't anything about her that screamed, *"I'm the savior of a world; pay attention to me."* Pale skin, brown hair, hazel eyes.

"Thanks, Frost," he said with a nod.

"Alaster?" Jen asked through chattering teeth.

Leaning back, he started to whip his jacket off, grateful he'd brought it and doubly grateful he hadn't used his wings. She really needed whatever warmth he could offer at that moment.

He'd pull her into his arms and give her his body heat if he wasn't so worried about her slapping him or something.

"That's me. I would assume you're Jen?" he asked with a reassuring smile.

As he took her hand to guide it through his jacket sleeve, there was that sparking reminder of her gentle, telepathic touch on his hand before.

Somehow, in that moment, he could swear his life was never going to be the same again.

SHADE

Glossary

Creatures

ʙRATAK'RA

Four-legged, large creatures, normally around the size of a horse, sometimes smaller, with large horns that adorn their necks and heads. Occasionally, the more powerful bratak'ra have spikes that jut out from their joints. They usually have short ears (think cropped ears on a pitbull), though some have larger ears. Their snouts are typically tall and broad. They have massive paws and always have their claws visible. Many have teeth that jut out of their maw and are visible when they close their mouths. They look naturally horrid, with yellow eyes and small slits for an iris. They have course fur that's rough to touch. Bratak'ra can talk, and their language is limited.

The older a bratak'ra is, the more horns they have. Young ones without horns are called bratak. They earn the 'ra to the end of the name once they gain horns.

Mono-horned gain horns at the crest of their head that sits behind their ears. The horns typically wrap around their skulls and reach past their jaws. Sometimes they don't wrap down and around the skull, sometimes they pull sideways from the head (kind of splay away from the sides of the face).

Dual-horned ones wind up with the equivalent of split horns. The second "set" follow along the cheekbones, while the bottom set sit around the lower jaw.

When a bratak'ra gains a new set of horns, their first set falls off, much like deer. The difference being that bratak'ra horns are very strong and durable, and only fall off when a new set is going to be formed. Bratak'ra gain new horns when the pack needs higher ranked members. It's unknown who or how the bratak'ra choose which ones among them should be given a higher rank. The point behind additional horns is that they provide more opportunities for impalements and ripping of enemies and prey.

Elemental Grovix

All we know is that they are wise grovix that, for some reason, wield and control elements of nature. Blaze summons fire and Frost summons water (ice). Blaze mentioned that she has seven siblings, but we do not yet know who they are, and if each sibling is one of these elemental grovix or not. At the very least, we are aware that Frost and Blaze are both Elementals and Alphas of the grovix of Agerius.

FERVEOS

[Caligan Dragons] They are compatible in height and general size to Preliators of Agerius. Ferveos, however, have darker scale colors. Their main colors are black, gray, and dark brown. These dragons are less intelligent than Preliators and Scouts. They follow blind commands and will not think for themselves while on the battlefield. They will attack anything they deem a threat to them, so they sometimes turn on their own. Ferveos don't normally speak. In fact, it's uncommon for one to know how to speak, let alone be eloquent when they do.

HYBRID

Part-human, part-dragon creatures. We would call them dragonborn. They resemble humans to every extent and can walk among humans undetected. Their wings can reabsorb into their body, the skeletal structure folding into their back. Every hybrid has powers similar to telekinesis and rapid cellular regeneration. Most hybrids, through their telekinetic powers, control raw energy powers that are used as their defense or offense. Each hybrid has varying degrees of strength, and there have been rare cases of hybrids born without the ability to conjure energy. Depending on its use, the energy can take forms of orbs, lightning, shields, or whips, to name a few. Due to their cellular regeneration, they live far longer than humans.

PRELIATOR

[Agerian Dragons] Large dragons. Their size varies between fourteen to fifteen feet tall with their length being as long as twenty-five feet. They are four-legged, have wings, and long whipping tails. They all breathe fire. Their hides are thick; first covered in scales then a fairly substantial thick skin, followed by a thick layer of fat. The colors of Preliators are deep and rustic browns, slight greens, hushed blues, golds, bronzes, etc. A Preliators' cry is low and deep, and when they roar, the sound is like a lion's roar and an inferno as their ability to breathe fire affects how they sound. They don't normally speak, although they do have the ability. They are incredibly intelligent, so don't let their silence fool you.

⚜SCOUT

Small Agerian Dragons. They range from 6 to 9 feet long and 4 to 7 feet tall. Their ability to shoot through the air at quick speeds makes them invaluable to the Agerian Defense. Scout scales are brighter colors and vibrant in nature. They cannot breathe constant streams of fire like their larger counterparts, so their blasts of fire are intense and hotter than their larger counterparts. However, that means they need to rely more heavily on their teeth and claws as they require more time for inhaling and shooting secondary blasts of fire. Additionally, their eyesight and hearing is better than a Preliators'.

Scouts are often raised by hybrids. Since they're substantially smaller as babies than Preliators, it's not uncommon for Scout babies—and even Scout eggs—to sometimes be squashed or brushed aside by Preliators as they navigate the mountains and caves across Tilion. Thus, hybrids stepped in to aid in the rearing of baby Scouts.

After two-thousand-years of hybrids being intricately involved in the raising and breeding of Scouts, it's become apparent that the person raising the Scout has a large impact on the dragon's development and personality. The more time a hybrid spends with their Scout, the more personable a Scout is, and the easier they work alongside Skycaptains.

Warrior Grovix

The more populated build for common grovix. They are built with muscle adorning their bodies and are excellent at combat. They are good for short sprints and leaping on top of enemies, relying mostly on their weight to cause damage before using their claws and teeth. They have strong bones and even stronger jaws. Their crushing strength is immense, and they can easily take down a bratak'ra so long as they avoid the horns. Prone to wearing armor in combat, they are easily distinguishable on a battlefield against werewolves and bratak'ra.

⽊EREWOLF

Little is known of how werewolves came to be, or what the specifics are that make their bites contagious. Werewolves on Tilion don't have the curse merely attack them during the full moon, rather all the time. Once bitten and consumed by the disease, the creatures lose all semblance of themselves and their individuality. There has only ever been one hybrid to survive the bite and retain his sense of self.

Abilities

 Bone Spikes

A fairly rare manifestation amongst hybrids. Spikes that can appear along shoulders, hands, wrists, knuckles, elbows, and occasionally feet. They grow on command, fracturing off of the skeletal structure of the hybrid in question. Hybrids that can manifest bone spikes can make stronger, weaker, and more spikes depending on the amount of calcium they intake. If they have less calcium, they can still produce bone spikes, but they will grow weaker over time.

 Energy

It could be described as a 'magic' of sorts. There is no incanting or spells to perform tasks, however. The bulk of hybrids are capable of raw energy manifestation, pulling strength from within themselves and on occasion, from the world around them. The latter is less common. It can be used as attacks, defense, and can even manifest as semi-corporeal duplicates of the hybrid in question. Hybrids vary in strength, some being substantially stronger than others.

Energy strength cannot be forced to grow. While it can be worked like a muscle, there is a maximum entropy for each wielder based on what is naturally occurring within them. For instance, Cregorous has had enough time to work his energy strength to its maximum entropy. Jen is stronger than him, but as he's had more time to master his power, he could kill her before she reaches the point of training where she can best him in combat.

More powerful hybrids' energy manifestation can allow for telekinetic power. It's very rare, and only the strongest hybrids on the spectrum can perform feats like that. Currently, the known list includes: Cregorous, Jen, and Alaster.

EALING

As the name suggests, these hybrids possess the power to heal ailments, both internal and externally. There's only two known Healers in all of Tilion: Eshe Balewa and Jennifer Monroe. The full extent of healing and what it can accomplish is fairly vague. With no one to guide them, the two girls are left to their devices to determine the totality of the healing ability.

UMPING

Jumpers are Hybrids that, through random circumstance, can "jump" from one dimension to another. We would call it teleporting. Through this ability, they can sneak behind enemy lines and can travel from one point to another faster than walking, running or flying. This is an extremely rare gift. At present, there are a total of six known Jumpers: Krelien, Jen, Lexa, Cregorous, Akeno, and Vorex.

A Jumper must know where they're going and how to get there. If they don't know their 'landing' spot, they can end up inside of walls or in hallways. The more often that a Jumper travels a path, the easier, faster, and less effort that's required by the Jumper. It becomes more instantaneous, as the various Dimensions begin to almost recognize the paths the Jumper takes, making a sort of tunnel for them. But, the Jumper must still know the route to where they're going.

That said, Krelien may appear stupid. But in actuality, he's quite smart. He's retained hundreds if not thousands of routes through dimensions to reach his destinations. He uses it so much, there's tunnels all over the Fifth Dimension specifically designed for him.

ASKS

A unique ability only a handful of Hybrids can accomplish. Requires great concentration and raw strength. The fighter in question creates a duplicate of themselves in their energy that will fight alongside them.

There are only two hybrids known to have this ability. Eccio, of the Delta Team can create up to four Masks when he needs. This is the result of years of long, arduous hours to hone his skills. Takeo is the only other known hybrid with the ability to manifest Masks.

HIELDS

A fairly common ability among hybrids. The strength of a shield varies greatly from one bearer to another. For instance, a common hybrid that can create a shield would fare poorly against opposition. Whereas the Zaheri shield-bearers like Lorn are strong enough to potentially manipulate and merge shields together to strengthen the barrier. Skylar, Jen, and Alaster's shields are vastly superior to any Agerian's shields.

Modifications to shields can vary depending on the bearer: relinquishing control of a shield to someone else, creating multiple shields, having opaque shields, absorbing opposing attacks into the shield, and using shields to heighten eyesight are a few.

TELEPATHY

As the name suggests, telepathy is the ability to read minds. With that, the bearer does hold the potential to invade and force others to do the bearer's bidding. Sometimes it's an outright manipulation and other times it's a subliminal change. Telepathy is very dangerous and exceedingly rare.

Little is known about telepathy, as to date, there's only one known Telepath: Cregorous. Jennifer Monroe seems to have the ability as well, but so far has only outright been able to communicate with Alaster O'Brien. The extent of her telepathy still has yet to be realized. And whether Alaster has telepathy himself still remains to be seen.

VISIONS

Currently, there is evidence that the ability of seeing past or future events resides solely within Sophia, the Scholar. While Jen and Alaster may possess the ability via the "mirror/mimic" like effect they have with their fellow Human-Borns, Sophia is the only hybrid from birth that has possessed the ability. It's unclear whether this is a phenomena solely intended for the Human-Borns, or if it was a more common ability in Ancient Tilion.

WINGS

Wings are a common manifestation for hybrids. Regardless of strength or other abilities, wings can be possible. They're all leather-like, but don't all have talons. The color of a hybrids wings can vary, but almost all of them can harken to the colors of Preliators.

They can fold and be reabsorbed into a hybrid's back. The bones of wings fit along the skeletal frame. As they form, it can appear as though something is ripping out of a hybrid's back, as skin covers the bones as they form into wings.

Places

Tilion

Another world that is linked to Earth specifically. The two worlds share a portal that connects them, but neither place holds links to other worlds aside from the other. So far, all we know is that it's the world where Agerians and Caligans come from. There appears to be ruins of old towns throughout the world.

The portal to Tilion can only be activated by hybrids. As humans cannot manifest raw energy, neither can they produce enough strength to even view the portal in its inactive form.

Agerius

The nation all of the Zaheri come from. It's more so a city than a nation by all appearances. But there's no doubt that the city would require months to explore all the little alleyways and courtyards. Its mountain acts as a natural barrier, and houses the High Council, Infirmary, Guard Quarters, and Archives. They follow the barter system, allowing citizens to haggle for reasonable prices based on what's being traded.

Caliga

The opposing nation of Tilion, where Cregorous and his generals come from. The layout, political system, even the location of Caliga is a complete unknown for Agerius. There's no telling how far away it is, or how it functions. It's assumed that Cregorous runs the nation as a tyrant, but that's just speculation. No one in Ageirus would dare to travel in search of Caliga, as no one would be able to stand up against Cregorous on their own.

Groups

Elders

All we know is that they are ancient, powerful dragons. Agerians appear to show great respect for them, but don't appear to treat them like a deity. Who they are and how they interact with Tilion is still unknown.

High Council

A group of approximately forty members of Agerius' oldest and wisest citizens. Made up of hybrids and grovix alike, they govern laws for the Agerians to follow. They are not the highest level of government in Agerius, merely the most accessible to the people.

They work off majority vote, and have a leader who opens and closes Council sessions.

Agerians can request the Council to hear their problems and solve disputes. Disputes are seldom in Agerius, but they do occur from time to time. In those instances, the High Council acts as an objective voice.

Human-Born

Seven children given the same abilities as hybrids who were born on Earth. They're prophesied to bring about the end of Cregorous' reign. However, the totality of their abilities and how they will end the war is completely unknown.

Zaheri

A grouping of thirty or so of the Agerian army's best fighters, once termed as "The Elite." But, since Jennifer Monroe's birth, they have been known otherwise as the Zaheri. They were charged with the protection and training of the Seven Human-Born hybrids.

The Human-Born Chronicles

Cast of Characters

Listed Alphabetically

AKENO

Cregorous' left hand and nephew. Known by most Agerians as the ruthless general, he has a penchant for torturing his victims and delighting in their pain. Cruel and merciless, those who see him on the battlefield flee for fear of becoming one of his self-described toys. Confident and assured, he breezes into his assignments with all the authority of the one who sent him. He's the first to dismiss any rumors of favoritism and knows full well all the work he put into getting where he is. Even Caligans fear him. Wears mostly leather armor. Sigil burned into his collarbone.

ALASTER KEEGAN O'BRIEN

The Seventh Human-Born. The Requisite. Wields green energy. An optimistic and bright young man. Irish born, he's been brought up around scientists and other brilliant minds. Not one to back down from a challenge, he likes tackling the things other people would say are impossible (or nearly so). He doesn't want recognition or fame—he wants to see what mysteries are still left unsolved because so far, no one's solved them. He doesn't think he's the only one who can, but he won't turn away from trying just because it hasn't been done before.

An Agerian dragon, called a Scout, Ardent stands around 7 feet tall at the crown of her head. Her scales are vibrant blues littered with white speckles. She is wise and careful with her speech, especially among humans, as they are unaccustomed to dragons. However don't mistake that for a timid soul. Ardent fierce in battle, and not shy away from the many Ferveos.

Leader of the Epsilon Team, charged with the protection and training of the Fifth Human-Born, Lexa. With a fiery disposition and feisty spunk, Asher can go toe-to-toe against Lexa's snark and sass. A red-haired beauty, she stands out in Agerius (as red-heads aren't terribly common). Nimble and agile, she can keep pace with even the fastest Runners and Scouts. On the same token, she's strong enough to spar with some of the 'big boys'. A demeanor that makes most men groan because she acts much like everyone's annoying big sister, Asher knows her strengths and acknowledges her weaknesses.

Avemod

One of Cregorous' generals. With softer features and slightly longer hair, he stands out in the lineup. Vorex is the only other of the generals that doesn't immediately look like a warrior. Sinister and seductive, Avemod relishes in ruining others innocence—especially Agerians. A trigger warning walking, he saunters everywhere he goes with sometimes too much confidence (especially when dealing with Akeno, Izel, and Caedex). He's strong enough to be a threat, but relies a lot on his dexterity. Wears leather and metal armor. Sigil on his left gauntlet.

Caedex

The third strongest of the generals, and undeniably the most terrifying by means of power, Caedex is a force to be reckoned with, and is never underestimated by Agerians. When he's seen on the battlefield, you have to be prepared for a long fight. He doesn't go down easily, and can take multiple strong hits before even beginning to show signs of slowing down. Reveling in carnage, he doesn't torture his enemies, instead he's like a tornado that seeks to obliterate anything in his path.

DALIA

Zeta Team Member, assigned to help in the protection of the Sixth Human-Born, Sophia. Raised alongside Scouts, Dalia is at complete comfort among dragons, and seldom fears them. Holding the Skycaptain specialization, she excels in aerial combat, and can fight alongside Preliators and Scouts without issue. She has a bubbly gait, and tends to hop into flight. Her wings and light and nimble. Laughter comes easily to her.

DOVER

Warrior grovix assigned to the Gamma Team to protect the Third Human-Born, Takeo. Though his feet and ears aren't as big, he's one of Archer's brothers and knows the rivalry between his brother and Ryder well. As quick as he is to do things that scare other grovix, he's just as quick to case a ball or go diving into a lake to find that perfect stick. He loves wrestling with Takeo, and has marveled as the boy grew from a toddler into the imposing teenager he is today.

Drogar

Assigned to the Epsilon Team, Drogar and Ar'on are old comrades. Both specializing in sniper rifles and both nearly the same age, the two have similar demeanors and tastes in humor. Despises his nickname from Lexa, simply "D", he's quick to growl at anyone who uses it. There's no such thing as a soft spot for him, as he thinks everyone should be held to the same level of scrutiny. If his wife was a Defender, he would see her the same way. But, as she's a baker, he has quite enough affection for her and only her. He respects Teneo's knowledge but finds the squat man annoying more often than not (but he'll go to the grave with that secret, lest Lexa find out).

Eccio

A member of the Delta Team assigned to protecting the Fourth Human-Born, Eshe, Eccio is the last known Agerian who specializes in creating Masks. Arguably one of the strongest Agerian Defenders, Eccio is quick to be the first at a battle to employ his Masks and keep casualties to a minimum. He's worked tirelessly to refine his skill and he knows full well how rare it is. Lean and limber, Eccio might appear small and defenseless to the untrained eye. In actuality, he would put the greatest martial arts masters to shame. He thinks Eshe is brave and resilient, and greatly admires her steadfast resolve to be a peacemaker and never resort to violence.

Eshe Anan Balewa

The Fourth Human-Born. The Healer. Wields violet energy. An African beauty, Eshe conveys grace and dignity with every step she takes. Her smile is bright and warm, infectious to those around her. Though she is physically strong and quite capable, she has refused to take on any training that would require her to use violence. To this day, she has yet to ever touch a weapon. She respects and has holds warriors in great esteem, but does not feel it is her duty to take up arms in any way. Quick to be barefoot, Eshe dances in rain and runs through open fields. Her long hair is often kept in fine braids and woven atop her head.

Ethran

A ball of chaotic energy and quick dashing smiles, Ethran gets into trouble faster than a toddler learning to walk. Boyish grins and exaggerated shrugs compliment his confident stance. Seldom does he stay upright, as tripping over the flat floor is a talent of his. The only place he's sure of his footing is in the midst of battle, where assured movement could fool anyone into thinking he's light on his feet. The events of the Attacks on Earth left Ethran with very evident battle scars that run the length of his arms and into his shoulders and back. He thinks Asher is really pretty.

ERADOR

Jocular and boisterous, Erador couldn't
be stealthy to save his life. A member of the Beta Team and charged
with protecting Skylar, Erador
stood out among the Team
for his size and skin tone.
Sun-soaked tan skin and dark
dreadlocks accentuate his almost
chaotic fighting style. One of several Elite Zaheri that uses a battle axe,
Erador trained alongside the likes of Neri
and Ethran, and would quickly consider
them some of his best friends. With a deep
voice and a loud laugh, he's easy to pick out in a
crowded room without even seeing him.

FROST

Much like Blaze, Frost was previously a
High Council Member before assigned
to the Eta Team and the protection of
the Seventh Human-Born, Alaster. As the
male Alpha of the grovix in Agerius, he
presides over the conduct and manner of
both Warriors and Runners. Calm in even
the most harrowing instances, he seldom
becomes motivated by emotions. His coat is
light blue, and unlike his sister, he would welcome both admiration and the petting of his fur.
As far as Frost is concerned, he is a grovix, and it
is only natural for humans to wish to pet creatures
they find cute.

Gaeor

A sniper assigned to
the Eta Team and the
protection of the Sev-
enth Human-Born, Alaster.
He is the youngest of the 'old'
Elite Zaheri, who all happen to
be snipers. He trained alongside
Drogar and learned many of his tricks
from Ar'on. Less gruff and stand-offish
than his friends, Gaeor is quicker with a
smile and encouragement than a reprimand.
He admires those charged as Team Leaders, and
does all that he can to assist any of them in their
very difficult task. Though Kedar is much younger
than him, Gaeor doesn't envy the Team Leader, and
is quite grateful to not be in charge of the group, especially with how
many hurdles they had to tackle to get anywhere near Alaster.

Ira

Once an Archivist and student of Agerius'
history, she is now a member of the Beta
Team, tasked with protecting the Second Human-Born, Skylar. Unlike
some of her fellow Elite Zaheri,
Ira is a small and unassuming
woman. With a round face
and softer features, she would
be quick to agree that she prefers
the ambiance of bookshelves than a
battlefield. Skilled in shield creation,
she gained confidence in her secondary
skills under Streya's assured leadership of
the Beta Team.

One of Cregorous' generals. Little is known of Izel. Unlike some of his fellow generals, he speaks very little when attacking or dueling. With a bulk that rivals Caedex, he could be mistaken for the armored general if not for his garb. Wearing a mix of cloth, leather, metal, and chainmail armor adorned with the General's Sigil on his gauntlets, Izel looks much different from Caedex when they both happen to be on the battlefield.

KEDAR

The second youngest of the Team Leaders, he heads up the Eta Team and oversees the protection of the Seventh Human-Born, Alaster. Only a year older than Streya, Kedar might have seemed an unlikely choice for Team Leader at first glance. But much like Tyron—whom he trained alongside of and holds the same specialist title of—Kedar is one of the very best Defenders that specializes in hand-to-hand combat. Add that to his unusually strong shields and you have what makes Kedar a talented Elite Zaheri. He feels blessed by the Elders that Alaster is such a good kid, and has taken to their authority without question.

KELEK

Cregorous' right hand. Aggressive and quick-tempered, Kelek obtained his position by being the second most powerful of the generals, and for his ability to follow orders. Despite the fact that he doesn't hold claim to any notable abilities, his skill and strength solidified his ranking early in Caliga's establishment. His drive to follow Cregorous is seated in a deep devotion to the Caligan leader that borders on worship. Most everything he does is mired in competition against Akeno, whom he despises. The General's Sigil is woven across the back of his shirt.

LEXA TENNILLE ACKART

The Fifth Human-Born and a native born Australian, Lexa has the vocabulary of a sailor and the face of an angel. Stunningly beautiful, she draws attention everywhere she goes and revels in it. Lexa leans more toward apathetic and snarky rather than comforting and reassuring. Holding the title of the Shifter, she is a Jumper, and is furious that Krelien can do things better than her. Wields Orange Energy.

LORN

A member of the Gamma Team, Lorn specializes
in shields. Classified as a Bulwark, he's gained a
reputation for creativity with his shields that
other more seasoned defenders wouldn't
attempt. That flexibility has saved his life,
and the lives of others. So no matter the
danger his out-of-the-box shields may
bring, Lorn doesn't hesitate to use them,
even if they may potentially cause injury to
himself. He frequently will utilize his shields
to heighten his eyesight, sending fragments into
battle and using his ties to the energy in the fragment
to see through the shield.

NERI

A member of the Zeta Team, Neri
is stationed alongside his
wife, Salan. He's laid-back
enough to be able to smile in
tough times but resolved enough
to know when to step into a situation and take action. The time on
Earth has provided him with the chance
to become a sort of "older brother" figure
for Dalia, and he teases her often. On the same
token, he's swift to encourage the younger warrior
to try new things and learn new skills. Holding the
specialist title of Spartan, he wields a deadly scythe as
his weapon.

ROWAN

For how lanky he is, Rowan shouldn't be able to wield the massive weapons he flings about with ease on a battle-field. He's often seen as a "master" to the younger weapon bearers among the Zaheri, and Ethran happily took to calling him "Senpai" once he heard Takeo use the nickname. A member of the Gamma Team, Rowan was always secretly grateful that they didn't have any women on their team to muddy things with emotions. He's a little cold toward those that lead with their heart, which is ironic, considering how fiercely Zelek bases his choices around those he cares most deeply for.

RYDER

A member of the Beta Team, Ryder is one of the three pups assigned as Zaheri grovix. As cuddly as a cactus, Ryder bristles easily, wraps most of what he says in a snarl, and thirsts for fighting. He's a powerful and large War-rior grovix, with a bulk that inspires most pups to cower when he walks by. While he doesn't like Skylar petting him, he will, when necessary, allow the boy to grab hold of him for stability. Though he doesn't outwardly show softness for his teammates, or for Skylar, it's obvious that he takes his role seriously.

The Leader of the Zeta Team. A fierce
warrior and mighty defender, Salan
has proved herself as one of the
strongest of Agerius' Elite, which
awarded her the position of Team
Leader. Her capabilities on the battlefield does not equate a cold demeanor.
She is quick to be loving and kind, swift with
a smile, and first to offer a hug to the hurting.
Bold defiance is her ally on the battlefield, coupled
with practiced assurance. An old friend of Sariel's,
the two have known one another the bulk of their lives,
and would undoubtedly call each other best friends.

SARIEL

The Delta Team Leader, Sariel's
resting expression is soft understanding, a stark contrast to her
husband, Ar'on. Gentle and caring,
she could be classified as "the mom"
of whatever group she's a part of. But all
that gentleness lies within a fiercely strong
woman. Though shields may be her specialty,
she knows how to turn a defensive shield into a
weapon and throw off her enemy, defying expectations. You would be terribly mistaken to assume she
was weak simply because she is kind.

A high-class member of British society, Skylar is not a likely fit for the Second Human-Born at first glance. Tailored clothing, pristine shoes, expensive watches, and proper posture and speech make up first impressions of the young ex-royal. Son to the Duke of Derbyshire, Skylar knows exactly what a gentleman should look like. Recently freed from all responsibility surrounding his royal upbringing, Skylar is learning to lean into the things he cares about, and not the things others force him to do. The Protector, he is actively learning to hone his ability in shield creation. Wields Indigo Energy.

Sophia Angela Gonzalez

The Sixth Human-Born the younger daughter, Sophia is not the loved child in her family. Not a natural beauty like her eldest sister, she has been ostracized within her family since the day she chose a book over a hairbrush. A bibliophile, Sophia devours books of all kinds, and can read both Spanish and English. Though she worries it will be useless, as the Scholar, Sophia possesses the ability to see visions of—she assumes—the past and the future. Wields Yellow Energy.

Specter

An elder Beta grovix, Specter was assigned to the Zeta team to oversee the protection of the Sixth Human-Born, Sophia. Though younger then Warden, she carries herself similarly; with authority and strength in every pawstep. She tends to be tough on pups, and leaves little room for their errors. Her time on Earth has softened her a little, especially upon witnessing the harshness of Sophia's family. Since then, she's taken to allowing the girl to snuggle and pet her. At first, she found it embarrassing, but as time went on, she came to find Sophia's gentle caresses as a sweet way of showing affection.

Streya

The Beta Team Leader, Streya is a spitfire. Crossed arms, confident smirks and popped hips make up what you would see when first meeting her. Spunky and resilient, she's quick on her feet on the battlefield and assured of her strengths. Though she isn't regarded as the best in the specialization, she holds the title of Paragon, someone skilled in hand-to-hand combat. At first blush, you might suggest she's far better at aerial combat, or shields. To which she would flick her hand at you dismissively and say you were wrong. She's been close with Tyron since she was a child, and knows his family well.

TAESIR

Brought up in a family that specialized in Preliator and Scout raising, Taesir is completely comfortable with dragons towering over her. Ferveos don't scare her in the slightest, which makes her a skilled Skycaptain alongside the likes of Dalia and Scouts. Aerial combat is where she excels, and the frigid temperatures of Antarctica don't slow her down one bit. An agile and lean fighter, she knows her strength and can hold her own. A member of the Eta Team, she's comfortable alongside her male teammates, but will be glad when she can spend time with other women when they eventually return to Agerius.

TAKEO RYUU YOSHI

A high strung, energetic Japanese teen, Takeo is the Third Human-Born. Proudly wearing the title of the Warrior, he finds it fitting given all of his training in martial arts. A skilled fighter, Takeo charges into battle with all of the subtlety of a tsunami. Courageous and strong, he holds the very rare ability of making Masks; copies of himself that are made up of his energy. He was orphaned at the age of three, and through unusual circumstances, his Zaheri, Zelek, was able to obtain custody of the boy.

TENEO

Holding the specialist title of Archivist, Teneo
would much prefer a quiet coffee shop and a
good book to a battlefield. Assigned to the Epsilon Team and attempting to train Lexa, he
often wishes someone else had been called
to his station. The knowledge he's acquired
of Agerius' history is his greatest gift, second only to his genuinely powerful ability to
create shields. His wide girth and short stature
would mean intense training if he were to become a
fixture of battle. And at this stage, he's happy to steer
toward his books more than a miles-long run.

VOREX

One of Cregorous' generals. Well recognized by his
apparel, Vorex sports flowing robes, fine linens,
and multiple gemmed piercings in his ears.
While he's the shortest of the generals, and
may appear weak, he's bested many Agerians. Little is known about his fighting
style, because he's an adept Jumper. On
top of that, as Eccio discovers, he's
incredibly skilled at creating gateways
through dimensions, Dimensional
Paths (or Rifts as Caligans call them).

Warden

She could be mistaken for a dusty red lioness, with black speckles adorning her coat, Warden is one of the eldest Beta grovix and was assigned to the Delta Team, protecting Eshe. With a noble brow and regal nature, she conveys a sense of authority no matter where she goes. She's soft with Eshe and fierce with enemies. Over the years on Earth, she's grown quite close with the Scout assigned to the team, Ardent. The two have shared in night-time hunts, and learned to watch out for one another in the African terrain.

Zelek

Noble and steady, Zelek is exactly the kind of person you want standing next to you on a battlefield. Even in the face of a foe he might not be able to beat, he won't waver. He fights hard and unrelentingly for the safety of others, whether he knows them or not. Zelek is Kaldok's brother, and the two of them are very good friends who would fight anyone who dared to demean the other. While Takeo does seem to hold respect for Zelek, there are clear times where a fatherly sternness comes into play.

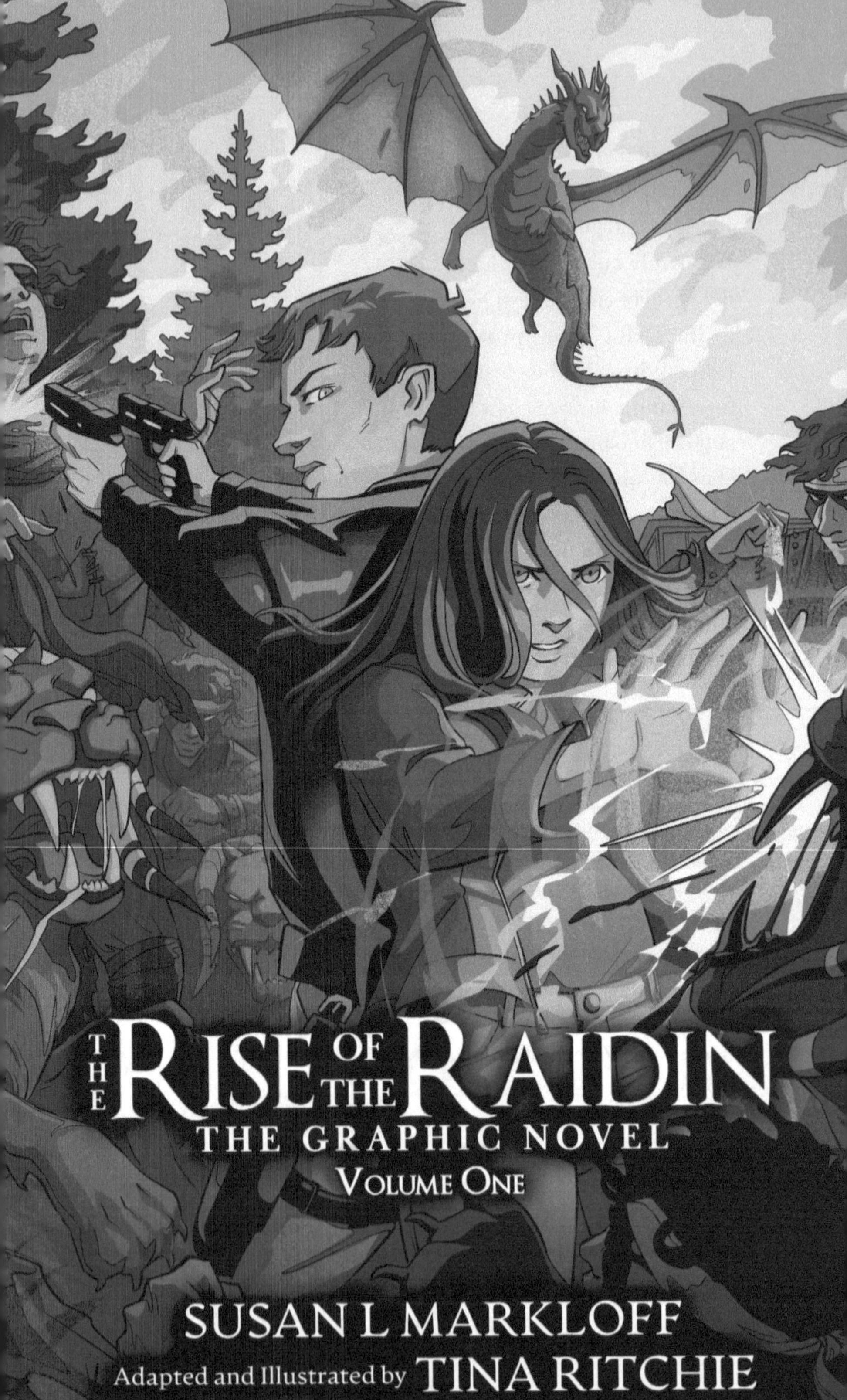

THE RISE OF THE RAIDIN
THE GRAPHIC NOVEL
Volume One
SUSAN L MARKLOFF
Adapted and Illustrated by TINA RITCHIE

Coming Soon as a Graphic Novel

We're endeavoring to adapt *The Rise of the Raidin* into a full-fledged graphic novel, and are raising the funds for the project via Kickstarter. If you want to be part of the process of bringing a graphic novel to life, and want exclusive behind-the-scenes views of the process, as well as your name in the book, check out www.susanlmarkloff.com to learn more about how you can back the next campaign!

While I originally envisioned a hardback omnibus of the HBCs, I've never been a fan of making a hardback book that's identical to the paperback. To me, hardbacks have the chance to provide something special. I ached to have scene illustrations for this book, but alas, I don't have the thousands of dollars necessary for something like that.

If you're someone who already owned the HBCs and bought this anyway, you're the legends. Do you have any idea how much that means to me? You own multiple copies of my books now. You've already dedicated shelf space to my books, and now you've gone and dedicated even more for a duplicate copy.

As a self-published author, that's astronomical. It means more than I can articulate.

Thank you, to the moon, stars, to the galaxies above and back, for all of the support. People like you are the ones that make this whole venture worthwhile.

I would be lost without you.

ABOUT THE AUTHOR

Susan L Markloff is the self-proclaimed "Ambassador for Agerius", and is prone to laughing at her own jokes (or Krelien's), on the regular.

She calls herself a dumb-dumb when she makes mistakes, uses imagery in her day-to-day conversations, and loves to stare at the sky. The radio is her least-favorite thing to listen to, because she doesn't like letting strangers determine what she listens to. Christmas music plays throughout the year, and you cannot stop her from enjoying it when the mood strikes. She can take apart a computer but can't make a pie to save her life. Once upon a time she played string bass, and she can't whistle (she's tried many, many times).

Susan lives on the Eastern side of Pennsylvania (that's the side with Philadelphia, not Pittsburgh). She's six hours away from Pittsburgh, so if you're close to Pittsburgh, no, you are not close to Susan. When she isn't giving herself another story idea or trying to learn yet another new thing, she's madly typing away at her keyboard, frantically trying to get stories onto the page.

www.ingramcontent.com/pod-product-compliance
Lightning Source LLC
Chambersburg PA
CBHW061528190726
48289CB00004B/964